## ALL MY FORTUNES

This time the look he received was blazing, despite the rain.

'Do I look like a child? I am no such thing, I am sixteen! Do you think a schoolchild would offer to take you through the Klukhor Pass? Or offer you the hospitality of Father's roof before obtaining permission? Huh!'

'I'm sorry,' David said meekly, then realised what his companion had just said. 'I say . . . you will take me over the Pass? And it will be all right for me to stay the night? Thanks very much!'

'That's all right.' The remote little face broke into that delightfully wicked smile once again. 'I am too bad . . . how could you know? My name's Pavel; what's yours?'

'Hello, Pavel. I'm David.'

# ALL MY FORTUNES

*Judith Saxton*

ARROW BOOKS

Arrow Books Limited
62–65 Chandos Place, London WC2N 4NW

An imprint of Century Hutchinson Limited

London Melbourne Sydney Auckland
Johannesburg and agencies throughout
the world

First published in Great Britain by Century 1987
Arrow edition 1988

© Judith Saxton 1987

Printed and bound in Great Britain by
Anchor Brendon Limited, Tiptree, Essex

ISBN 0 09 953610 2

For Mike Griffiths,
whose deep knowledge and love
of the Dee estuary inspired me
to write this book.

# ACKNOWLEDGEMENTS

I should like to thank my editor, Nancy Webber, who first introduced me to the Caucasus, Marina Thomas and the rest of the staff of Wrexham Branch Library for their tireless efforts to chase up the most obscure books, and Jack Baines of Anglesey Books, Holyhead, whose knowledge of mountaineering and mountains proved invaluable.

'And all my fortunes at thy foot I'll lay,
And follow thee, my lord, throughout the world.'
*Romeo & Juliet,* Act II, Scene II

# CHAPTER ONE
## 1920

It had been snowing all day, and when night fell a great wind came up and howled through the thin stand of pines behind the village and over the sod walls and roof of the tiny *kosh*, bringing the three little girls within to huddle close to Babushka, as she sat as near as possible to the turf fire, burning sullenly in the fireplace.

Konkordia was nine, old enough to take care of her motherless sisters, so she held Eva, the baby, in her arms and sang to her, though her voice could scarcely be heard above the howling of the wind. Pavel was only five, so she sat between Babushka and her elder sister, pressed against the coarse black of her grandmother's skirt, her eyes half-closed against the smoke. Despite the baby in her arms, Konkordia still felt that she must hug Pavel — had not her mother left her in charge of the little ones? — and she cuddled both her sisters, glad that they were all snug and warm in the *kosh* and not out in the cold, where the sleet rattled against the wooden shutters and the howling might be the wind — or wolves.

Konkordia was afraid of wolves. She had already seen them this winter, just narrowed yellow eyes in the dark when her father had brought her back late one night from cutting peat lower down the mountain. In winter they drove the flock home each night, into the shelter of the stone-walled home field with wolf-fires burning at each corner, or the wolves would carry off a beast at dusk each night until they had no stock left.

Wolves were their enemies. They came right up to the *kosh* when the weather was bad. Babushka had told them hair-raising stories of little girls who ran outside without taking care and were gobbled up on their very doorsteps by wolves made brave by starvation. Of course, if you were a boy, it was different. Boys watched the wolf-fires, huddled up in their

1

little shelters made of rocks piled up one on top of the other, keeping the fuel dry and safe, with their dogs to scare off any wolf which dared approach too near. Boys carried knives, threw stones with force and accuracy, and were altogether superior beings, though Konkordia was always secretly grateful that she was a girl and not expected to stand up to wolves or to go out into the great, howling dark.

Girls worked hard, though, in the *aouls* – the little mountain villages perched high in the Caucasus range. Men might hunt and bargain and herd the sheep and buy and sell horses, but it was the women who cured the skins, dried meat for winter use, beat maize and cooked the thin, crispy biscuits which you ate with goat's cheese, or fish, or pieces of toasted mutton. Girls waited on the men, too, and stood by when they had finished cooking so that the men might take the best of the food. Once they had eaten, of course, the women had their meal, but traditionally the men, the hunters, had the best of what was available.

Last of all, the dogs were fed – which was unfair, really, when you considered how very brave and useful the dogs were. Every *kosh* had two or three of the huge, skinny, snarling creatures sleeping in the doorway at night while two or three more prowled the sheep-fold. Konkordia loved their dogs, Kal and Baru, and tried to save them bits and pieces from her own meals, because she knew that both animals would attack any stranger – wolf or man – who tried to gain entry into the *kosh*. Baru, the bitch, had killed a she-wolf once which was much bigger than she; Petchoren boasted of it still when he was bartering Baru's litters for grain, or sheep, or a new foal.

Konkordia knew that she was too timid, but her mother had understood. She had laughed, and caressed her little girl, and told her that it did not matter; timid girls could give birth to brave men. It was not a woman's place to be brave, only to produce sons and work hard at household chores.

But her mother had died a year ago, and sometimes Konkordia thought that she had been more and more frightened ever since. There were so many things to fear when you were trying to take care of two little sisters. Wolves, giants and gins, the evil goblins who lived in the caves, and the great wild eagles who would carry babies off to their nests and eat them up in a trice. Petchoren said they were just stories, but Babushka talked about them as if they were real, and she was so old that she must know more than her son. Of course she had got a little strange in her poor old head, Petchoren whispered to his daughter sometimes, when Babushka was being particularly difficult, but even so . . . age must bring with it certain knowledge. At any rate, Konkordia was not going to say that giants, gins and goblins did not exist – not while any might have been listening!

It was not only Babushka's stories which frightened her, though. She had not slept well since her mother's death, and lay awake most nights in her bed of sheepskins, listening to the talk around the fire. In their *kosh* there were only two men, Petchoren and Kevi, his brother, but other men from the *aoul* visited them: uncles, cousins, neighbours. Then they spoke of another menace, their voices instinctively lowered, as though the wind itself might overhear. The menace was Russia. Changing ways. The Slavs would come with fire and sword to make all good Caucasians do as they did. From the rich farmers in the narrow, fertile valleys to the herdsmen living in the scattered *aouls*, the Russians would change them all.

Konkordia did not understand change, but she accepted that it was a bad thing because Petchoren, whom she loved, thought so – and all the other men, of course. Even Uncle Kevi.

Even thinking about Uncle Kevi warmed Konkordia and made her less afraid, because Uncle Kevi was a soldier. He had a long rifle, a heavy overcoat made of some strange material, and boots. He was strong as a stallion, clever as ten schoolteachers rolled into one and beautiful as a woman . . . or so Babushka said, and she had been alive for more than a hundred years, so she should know.

Everyone loved Uncle Kevi and was glad when he came home, yet this time it was different. Usually he breezed in on a hired nag, saddlebags laden with presents, stayed for a few weeks and was off, bluff, hearty, glad to be back, glad to be gone. This time he had come quietly, in the dark night, and though he still picked up his nieces and threw them up into the air, teased them and cuddled them as their undemonstrative father never did, he was grave for long hours together. Now and then, though, he jerked out of his abstraction and was the old Uncle Kevi, telling Pavel that since her skin was as white as the eternal snows of Mount Elbruz she must be a fairy princess, begging her not to enchant him, rolling her over on the sheep-skin rug and tickling her tummy. Or he would pick up skinny old Babushka, laughing at her cackle of alarm, and tell her that her maize cakes were better than any food he had tasted in Russia, from the Caspian sea to Moscow city, and he would take bets that she could outcook any woman in the whole continent.

Konkordia did not mind that this time he brought no gifts save for a big sack of coffee, nor that he was sometimes grave, for no man could be for ever laughing, but she knew that there was an atmosphere of tension in the *kosh* because of something Uncle Kevi had done, and she did not like that. Round the fire at night, when she and her sisters and Babushka were supposed to be asleep, the men's voices were lower, their talk more frightening. They spoke of strangers coming, of pursuit, of punishment. Konkordia heard the boys being told to watch out for more than wolves . . . lights in the night, a sound, snow disturbed where it should have been smooth.

So now, with the baby on her lap, Pavel's shoulder in the crook of her arm and her father and Kevi drinking coffee and finishing off the maize cakes and cheese, Konkordia jumped a little when there was a scuffling outside and the heavy wooden door swung outwards. Petchoren and Kevi stiffened, then relaxed as one of the youthful wolf-watchers entered, rubbing his hands and grinning at them.

'Scare you, did I? 'S all right, it's just that we're hungry.' He advanced on the fire, hands held out towards it as the snow on his shoulders and on his sheepskin cap began to melt and trickle down on to the hard earth of the floor. 'It's too wild a night for wolves – or for boys, for that matter. Got any cakes?'

Babushka cackled and shoved Konkordia with her bony knee. 'I baked earlier; get the boy food, girl.'

Konkordia passed the baby to Pavel, who took her almost in her sleep. Pavel, named for an old friend of her father's, was a thin, wispy child, dreamy and obedient, but that, Konkordia thought wisely, as she scrambled over to the cupboard where Babushka kept the food, was how Caucasian men liked their women. Pavel was not beautiful, but she could work hard. Someone would be glad to marry her when her time came; Uncle Kevi was always telling them so.

Putting cakes, cheese and butter into a skin bag, Konkordia

4

reflected that being a boy had its advantages. At night they were all together in the stone shelters, singing songs, keeping each other awake, taking it in turns to go out and tend the fires. Petchoren had already promised her to a family in the village as a wife for one of their sons, and they had said recently that the younger son, who worked by the wolf-fires, might take Pavel as part-payment for his services. Petchoren had only grunted, but Konkordia supposed he would agree, in the end. He had agreed to Dzera having herself, for instance, although she did not like the heavy, surly boy with his thick lips and small eyes, who enjoyed his 'ownership' of her, frequently pinching and squeezing when they were together, so that she dreamed of his early demise with some satisfaction. Childlike, she was sure that someone would rescue her from her fate before she was old enough to be married in earnest.

She carried the food over to the boy, who took it with a grunt which could have been interpreted as thanks were one not used to the ways of boys. Aping the men, they took little notice of girls, having been taught from babyhood that women were put on earth as handmaidens for themselves and nothing more. A pretty girl might get more sly glances than a plain one, but . . . she was only a woman, after all, so what did it matter if she was beautiful? If she could work, spinning, threshing and cooking, she would do well enough.

After the boy had left and the dogs had settled down again against the door, Babushka piled the sheepskins to one side of the hearth and put turf on the embers in such a way that the fire would not break through until morning. Then she and the three girls curled up together, baby Eva in the middle and their shawls and more sheepskins over them. It was a snug nest, and from within it Konkordia heard the wind howling and the sleet lashing the roof with less anxiety. Very soon now, sleep would drag her lids down, cuddle her body close, and she could stop worrying about life until tomorrow morning. She opened an eye, checking that the girls were snug. Babushka's ancient, smelly body was against one wall, her own back, well protected by the piled sheepskins, against another, and Pavel and Eva were curled up in the middle. Soon, very soon, she would sleep.

But the deep murmur of Petchoren's voice would not be stilled; soldiers would come, and agents from the Russians.

Life would never be the same again. Kevi had brought this on them a little earlier, perhaps, than it would have happened left to itself, but they bore him no grudge; this was his place, and he had every right to come back to it when he needed help. Anyway, why should they search for him here? If they used all the logic they were so fond of talking about they would know there was nothing for him here. They would search the big cities, the factories and collectives they were so proud of, not this remote, uncivilised backwater!

I'll go, Kevi said, I won't bring trouble down on you, and Petchoren scoffed gently, beneath his breath, and assured his brother that trouble, when it came, would be less concerned with one man's leaving the army than with the dozen or so in the village who were content with the life they lived and wanted no other.

A cold draught was coming under the door. It was the boy's fault; the snow had been piled up against the wood before the boy had trampled it flat and pulled the door open against it. Now, until it piled up once more, the wicked wolf-wind would howl under the door and chill Konkordia's nose and the tips of her pointed knees where they poked out through a gap in the sheepskins. It would have been a simple matter to turn over and hitch her knees into the warm, but though Eva had not woken Konkordia could tell by Pavel's breathing that the little girl had not yet sunk into slumber. Better lie still and put up with chilly knees for a while, and then, later, she could remedy it.

But now Petchoren's voice was beginning to lull her, its deep tones soothing. Without thinking she turned over and her knees began to warm up. She tucked her chin below the sheepskins and her breath fanned out, warming, soporific. Insensibly, as she began to fall asleep, she began to fight it. She wanted to listen to what Petchoren and Kevi were saying. They had begun to talk more naturally, probably believing that everyone but themselves was asleep. She would just stay awake until they finished talking . . .

'We'd all fight for you, if the Russians try to take you away,' her father was saying. 'We won't let them have you, Kevi. We're only a small village, and scattered, but we'll hang together.'

'There's no sense in that; what about the women and the

6

children? I wouldn't want their lives on my conscience.'

'They'd stay out of sight, in the *koshes*, where they belong, or they could go and hide in the caves,' Petchoren said. 'We wouldn't let them be taken. You'll be all right.'

'I won't have the children suffering. They need you, and . . .'

But Konkordia heard no more; Kevi's voice became one with the howling of the wind as she sank into sleep, blissfully relinquishing her hold on the realities of life and letting her mind rest . . . and dream.

When the dream came, as it did every now and then, Konkordia never recognised it but simply enjoyed being a small child again. It always started the same, always continued in the same way too, until at last she woke.

She was sitting on the flat patch of ground in front of the *kosh*, playing with pebbles and sticks and a carefully mixed ball of mud. Her indulgent mother had gone all the way down to the deep, hurrying river and dipped out a small pot of water and brought it back to her only child, so that Konkordia could make mud pies with soil and water and bake them in her pretend oven, a flat stone in the full sun.

The long afternoon wore away in the game, but the dream-child began to realise that all was not well; there were mutterings from older children that a battle had been raging all day, that the men from their village had got embroiled in a fight with a band of wandering tribesmen over grazing rights, cattle stealing and similar things.

As the sun made its way down the sky, the sound of fighting came closer and closer to the village and even little Konkordia knew that their own men were being driven back. Restlessness prevailed. The wild, beautiful women of the tribe grew tense and afraid. They were like their men: they would die rather than let themselves be taken captive.

The fighting went on all night, and as dawn broke and the sun began to climb the mountains, lending its radiance to each face, each dew-dropped blade of grass, there came a terrible cry from above and the enemy began to pour down the steepness of the crags to enter the *aoul*.

Even in the dream, Konkordia was so afraid that she was unable to move or speak. Her mother seized her in her arms and ran with her towards the cliff-edge. Other women all around were following suit, taking their children and making for the sheer drop into the gorge beneath. The child Konkordia had heard many stories of how the women of her tribe would throw themselves off the cliff and perish on the rocks below rather than be taken captive, but now, in the dream, her gentle, beautiful mother was following the ancient custom.

As her mother ran, bumping her up and down so that the breath caught in her throat, she looked round and saw that if the enemy would only stop, hold back, then everyone could be saved. But the men poured down the rocks into the *aoul*, bloodstained knives waving, faces cruel with victory and lustful for the spoils of war. They began to pursue the women, who, panic-stricken, rushed even more desperately towards the great, echoing drop.

The men ran fast but the women ran faster, corn before the wind. The thin arms round Konkordia were tight, squeezing the breath out of her, bruising her tender ribs. To cry was impossible, but she opened her mouth and a thin, high wail emerged . . . just as her mother reached the edge, hesitated — and leapt.

The wind tore at Konkordia's hair; ice-cold, it speared her cheeks and the soft wetness of her screaming open mouth. Crazily, their bodies turned and spun in the long, fatal drop. Konkordia saw the rocks beneath her in the gorge rushing up, death in their snarling fangs. She wanted to close her eyes but the wind had torn her eyelids wide and would not let them droop. The rocks below had mouths, each one was grinning at the meal about to be crunched up, each was screaming death, *death*, DEATH, and Konkordia felt her body shrink at the pain to come, the crushing, the tearing, the brutal forcing of bone through organs, organs through skin, splatter . . . splinter . . . finish.

She woke. Curled up in the dark beneath the sheepskin she was soaked in sweat, her heart beating nineteen to the dozen, her throat dry and aching from fear and pain. She lay there for ten minutes or so, trying to recover, to remind herself that it was only a dream and over now. But once it had happened, perhaps to a child just like her. She had heard Babushka tell many times of the brave women leaping from the rocks rather than face life as captives of another tribe. And Father, earlier, had been talking of soldiers coming . . . it had sounded threatening, yet it was beyond her understanding why it should be so, for Uncle Kevi was a soldier!

Presently and very quietly, she struggled up, her fair head popping out of the sheepskins; sleep was impossible, so she might as well get up and start seeing to the fire and getting breakfast. But someone was up before her; Babushka slumbered still, and Petchoren was just a hump beneath his *burka*, but Uncle Kevi was pulling the pot over the fire and easing the turves apart with the blackened stick which Babushka used for the purpose. He winked at her, then spoke as she emerged from her nest.

'What's all this? No need for you to get up. Why not snuggle down again and . . .?' Too late, for Konkordia was out of the sheepskins and tugging her skirt into position, putting her trousers right. 'Well, Kon, since you're up, you might as well make yourself useful. Fetch me some food.'

She was taking the black bread from the cupboard when Petchoren spoke behind her, making her jump.

'What are you doing? Kevi, I can read your mind. You think you'll bring us trouble, but you won't get over the Klukhor Pass, not in this weather. Leave it until spring becomes summer . . . wait until you're forgotten, until you've a fine, dark beard and less flesh on you, and then go over the Pass and into Georgia and find yourself a farm and a woman and settle down. Until then, stay here with us.'

'Who says I was making for the Pass? I could have been going back to the plain . . . the steppes for all they're so flat can hide a man, and the Cossacks have a free life.'

Petchoren tossed off his *burka*, yawned, stretched and got to his feet, though no man could stand upright in a *kosh* and even Konkordia, at nine, had to bend her head.

'Ah, Kevi, I *know* you! Stay. If they come, there's always time to get away quietly, either over the Pass or down to the plain. Stay away a day or so and then return. Last night I thought I talked some sense into you. Now I find you stealing out when you think I'm asleep.'

'I'd rather go now, Petchi, than cause trouble for you and yours. The Cossacks . . .'

'Oh, don't go, Uncle Kevi!' Pavel had woken unnoticed and now she flew across the floor and cast herself at her uncle's knees. He smiled and stroked the fine, silky hair, then crouched to chuck her under the chin. Konkordia hurried across for her share of the petting and got her amber curls tugged reprovingly.

'This wicked woman woke, or I might have escaped and no harm done! Your father's right, I suppose, and the storm is too severe to get through the Pass, but when it's over and the glacier's firm and the snow will let a horse cross it, then I must go. I'll drop down into Georgia, Petchi, as you advise, and when these little monkeys are fine grown-up ladies they may come and stay with me and I'll find them a fat Georgian farmer each to take them to wife.'

He squatted down and pulled the children into his lap. Konkordia cuddled closer, basking in his love, but Pavel pulled back and flicked a tail of hair out of her large, almond-shaped eyes.

'Must we wait until we're grown-up ladies, Uncle Kevi? You'll be back to see us, won't you? Won't you come back often, like you did before?'

Uncle Kevi pushed them gently off his lap and made his way over to the fire where the water bubbled in the black iron kettle.

'I dare say I shall,' he said lightly. Too lightly. 'Now who's going to make the coffee and who's going to toast the bread?'

The girls rushed to help, and before Babushka had stirred they had a meal ready for the two men. Konkordia, pouring warm water from a jug over Kevi's hands so that he might wash before he ate, wondered why her uncle had decided to leave them today, right away. Did he have some premonition of danger, or was it just that the *kosh* was crowded and boring when you had to remain in it day and night – for Petchoren had been unwilling for his brother to ride with the herds.

'If you go down to the coast and be a rich farmer, Uncle Kevi, how will you go on being a soldier?' Pavel's words fell into a little silence which grew and grew until it became a great silence, and Konkordia realised that her sister had unwittingly hit the nail on the head; Kevi had loved being a soldier, had boasted and talked and sung of his happiness. Now, abruptly, it seemed it was no longer what he wanted.

'One can grow tired of soldiering . . .' Kevi began, but was abruptly cut short by his brother.

'Pavel, you talk too much. Have you fed the dogs this

10

morning? Or let them out? No?' A heavy hand clipped Pavel's small ear and then caught at her shoulder, swinging her round to face the door. 'Get on with it!'

Pavel stuck out her lower lip but nevertheless went over to the dogs, pushed them aside and began gallantly struggling with the big wooden bolt. Konkordia smiled and went over to help her. The door creaked open, the dogs shot out through the gap and Pavel retreated once more, but Konkordia stood there for a moment, savouring the change in the weather. The wind still howled, to be sure, but there was a difference in the air, a softness, and it was rain which fell now and not sleet. Soon it would be spring and the snow would melt. Soon there would be grass showing and the lambs would be born and the mares would drop their foals. Uncle Kevi could not be bored in the *kosh* when spring came.

Behind her, Babushka was stirring and sitting up, her scraggy hair falling in elf-locks round her thin, grey face, her voice sharp with temper because her sons were up and had not roused her to get their breakfast. Baby Eva, abruptly noticing the absence of warm surrounding bodies, woke and began to whimper and then to wail. Pavel picked her up by the back of her full woollen dress and sat down, sticking her little finger into Eva's open bawling mouth. Eva mumbled on it, realised she had been tricked, pushed her sister's hand aside and began to howl again, louder this time.

Konkordia did not wait to be told what to do, but ran out into the rain in her bare feet and pulled the nanny goat out of the rough byre. Into the *kosh* she brought her, the goat bleating and swinging her heavy udder, and began to milk her into one of the round wooden bowls which were kept in a tottering pile by the fire. Baby Eva, recognising the sounds which heralded the imminent arrival of breakfast, spluttered into a listening silence.

Another day had begun.

A snowball, well aimed and travelling fast, caught David on the chin as he turned out of the stableyard, intending to cross the park and make his way to the lake. He stopped and slid two steps sideways, taking shelter back in the yard once more. Odd! He had left the younger kids where they belonged, in the nursery – Alice had moaned and grumbled a bit, but she had a

11

cold and Nurse would be frantic and furious if she made it worse by going outside, so she had stayed. His elder brother, Ned, had gone off with their mother immediately after lunch, to buy clothes or some such thing. So who on earth was chucking snowballs? And lying in ambush as well, he decided, taking a peep round the edge of the wall and only just jerking his head back in time as another missile grazed his nose.

Still keeping out of sight, he began, in his turn, to gather ammunition, whilst furiously pondering on his attacker. The estate was a large one, but although local children probably did trespass in the grounds it was unlikely that anyone would come this close to the house – why should they, with the woods and meadows and the broad, flat stretches of sand down by the Dee to play on? The servants all lived in the village except for the chauffeur, but Hawke was too old for chucking snowballs and had, to the best of David's knowledge, no children. Ned had a few friends, but they were all much older than David and presumably long past snowballing, and since he had been at boarding school now for nearly five years he had few friends in the vicinity himself – certainly none who would hide just outside the stableyard and bombard him with snowballs!

When he had a good pile of ammunition, David laid his skates down very carefully, picked up the best missile he had manufactured, and tried to peep round the corner without being immediately obvious. He cursed his black curls, though, when they received the full force of yet another direct hit, and dodged back behind the wall, blinking snow out of his eyes. Whoever was out there was an enemy worthy of his steel; he had actually managed to throw without showing himself. David had caught a glimpse of the drive and the oak trees which bordered it – sure as anything his assailant was sheltering behind one of them – but he had not seen any movement before the snowball was literally upon him.

He risked another peep. This time the snowball smote him on the nose . . . Damn my beak, David thought furiously, rubbing the reddened tip and using what his mother would call stable language as he shook snow out of his scarf; Father might say what's wrong with having a large nose but if he'd seen me just now he'd have known. This would never do. Whoever was ambushing him would have to be taught that David Thomas

12

knew a thing or two about war himself. Abandoning his skates and most of his ammunition, David took one good, hard snowball in each hand and crossed the cobbled yard as quickly and quietly as the thick snow allowed. If he went under the arch on to the front drive, then ran like hell all the way round the outside of the stable wall, he would be in the shelter of the shrubbery before he could possibly be spotted. From there, he would be able to dodge from tree to tree until he could see his assailant, whereupon . . . wham . . . wham . . . David told himself, slithering round the side of the house. Whoever it was would get quite a surprise!

It was a good plan, and it worked up to a point. He ran fast, dived into the shelter of the huge old rhododendrons and azaleas which edged the drive and actually managed to find the ambush point. Behind the third oak on the opposite side of the drive, footprints and a conical pile of snowballs showed where the sniper had stood. Standing very still and tracing the prints which he could now clearly see, David could read the story of the attack. The boy – for it must have been a boy – had been wandering aimlessly, as boys will, across the smooth, untrodden snow of the park. He had been trying, though, to reach the stableyard without being seen, for even from here it was clear that he had gone from cover to cover rather than merely meandering. He couldn't have known I was going to appear, because that was just chance, David reasoned, so he was just playing, the way one did.

Having reached this conclusion, David looked around to see what the ambusher had done next. The footprints proceeded from tree to tree in what must have been quick, jinking runs between throws, and ended in a small, trodden patch right by the stable wall, on the other side of which, until a few moments earlier, David himself had crouched. Then they proceeded round and into the stableyard itself.

If I'd stayed there it would have been hand-to-hand fighting, and I'd probably have been whacked because of the surprise, David told himself, awed. Still, I got away in time, so now if I . . .

Wham!

The snowball caught him right behind the ear, almost pitching him on to his face, so great was the force, so considerable the surprise. From behind, as he struggled to free himself from the azalea bush into which he had stumbled, a voice said triumphantly: 'Gotcher!'

David turned. Standing no more than six feet from him, one arm raised, snowball in fist, was an urchin of about his own age. He had a shock of mousy, nibbled hair, a nose as red as a radish, and was wearing a shabby greatcoat, a red and white striped scarf and rubber boots. When David emerged from the bush and turned to grin at him, however, he looked quite as astonished as David had felt moments earlier.

'Hey . . . who are you? I thought you was that girl.'

'Which girl? Do I look like a girl, man? Who are you, anyway? I don't know you, do I?'

'Naw!' The boy's voice expressed scorn at the idea. 'I'm Nibby Hawke, chauffeur's lad.'

'Hawke's son? I didn't know he was married,' David admitted. He held out a leather-gloved hand. 'Hello – I'm David Thomas. Do you live with your father, then, over the stables?'

'Yup.' The shaggy head nodded vigorously. 'Going skating?'

'That's the idea. Got any skates?'

'Yup. Shall I fetch 'em?'

'That 'ud be fine,' David said. 'Any good at it?'

'Not bad. Wait here?'

'I'll walk back to the yard with you and wait there,' David said, falling into step with the other. 'Have you lived here long? I know I'm at school a lot, but I don't see how I could've missed you in the summer, if you were here then.'

'Been here two weeks,' Nibby said, shooting a quick, sideways glance at David under his fringe. 'Mam run off, so Dad said to come to 'im.'

'Oh,' David said, not understanding. He looked thoughtfully at Nibby. About his own age, a bit smaller but strong and wiry . . . just the sort of chap he'd wanted to meet, someone who could mess about with him during the school holidays. Alice was all very well, but you couldn't get away from the fact that she was a girl and did, at times, horribly girlish things, and Ned was a dead loss, thinking of nothing but growing a moustache, drinking beer and chasing females. The others were too young to count, though Michael was a nice little chap in his way. But he was only three . . . fun to tease and play with and so on in the nursery, but useless – worse than useless – for outdoor pursuits.

'They're in the stable . . . my skates. Coming?'

Silently, David followed him to the end stall and up into the loft above. The skates were very old and made of wood. They had been owned by some long-ago Thomas, no doubt, but David saw no reason to point this out. He watched as Nibby got them down from the rafter on which they hung, and they were out of the stable and crossing the yard before he spoke again.

'Those skates . . . have you tried them on? Do they fit?'

'Yup.'

A man of few words, evidently. David nodded and picked up his own skates as they passed under the arch once more. Brightly gleaming, each blade looked as though you could carve a turkey with it. But probably Nibby would turn out to be a marvellous skater – look at him with a snowball!

They reached the lake, sat down on a wooden bench and donned their skates. Presently they clambered on to the ice and began to show off, turning, twisting, speeding, crashing. Nibby was best at crashing. David suspected that his new friend had never skated before, but what did it matter when you saw how quickly he picked it up, how he watched and copied and then did it his own way, even possibly a little better than yours!

When the sun reddened and sank behind the blue hills of Wales they made their way reluctantly back to the house. In the stableyard they said their brief goodbyes.

'Cheers, now. See you tomorrow?'

'Aye. I'm free after me dinner.'

'Grand. Same place?'

'Yup.'

Alice, doomed by her cold to stay indoors, had sat and sulked for five minutes in front of the nursery fire before remembering the attics. It was very cold up there and forbidden territory beside, but what did she care? Her favourite brother home for the Christmas holidays and she must needs catch a vile, horrible head-cold . . . life was too cruel! She might, of course, be punished for going up to the attics, but it would be worth it to get away from the nursery for a bit, and to spy on David. Beast that he was, going skating without her, and she a much better skater than he, able to twirl, pirouette, make a figure eight and go backwards at great speed. She would jolly well go up to the attics, watch him through the little low window, and put a hex on him the way old Maud down in the kitchen said someone had done on her cousin Joan, so that Joan's fellow had jilted her at the altar. And when he fell, or made a fool of himself, she would know she'd done it, and wouldn't she just laugh?

It was, however, extremely cold in the attic and even Alice's feverish cold, which had made her head ache, her nose and eyes run and her skin alternately burn and freeze, did not appreciate the icy chill. However, all round the wide, low-ceilinged room with its sloping walls and low windows there were chests full of last year's rubbish – curtaining, upholstery, bedding, clothing . . . you name it, it was there. So Alice opened up a trunk, abstracted some faded plum velvet curtains and wrapped herself up in them until only her face showed. Then she went and pulled faces at herself in last year's gilded and cherubimed mirror, and hated her swollen red nose and tearful eyes, her pale cheeks and her droopy mouth, hated her limp, dark brown hair and longed for black curls, like David's, or glossy chestnut locks like Lydia's or soft blond fluff, like Michael's.

After that she went over to the window and stared down into the stableyard and waited for David to appear. She adored David! Mrs Beckle, the housekeeper, had once remarked that David's beauty lay in his ugliness, and Alice had known just what she meant, for her brother was like a bulldog pup, ugly yet lovable. David's dark curls were matched by thick dark brows which met over the prow of his commanding nose. His chin was square, cleft and obstinate, his eyes, dark and liquid, could look impenetrably black and wicked when he was cross and his person, like that bulldog pup's, was square, vigorous and without grace.

Alice's small fingers traced, with some dread, the line of her own nose. Ned said it was a beak, like David's. Was it? There was rather a lot of it, she had to admit that, and it had a bump in the middle, too, where she would rather have had it smooth and swooping, or retroussé, like Lydia's pug-snitch. She did not mind about her thick eyebrows, because when she was grown up she would pluck them into nice thin arcs, no matter how it hurt. But there was not a lot one could do about uncompromisingly bumpy noses, or short, stubby eyelashes, or blue-grey eyes, when one would much have preferred brilliant blue (Michael) or deep, dramatic black (David).

Alice was dreaming about the changes in her appearance which must take place some time over the next six years or so, when suddenly she saw a small figure coming across the park, running from tree to tree for all the world like a yacht tacking up the Dee in stormy weather. She had good long-distance sight and knew it was Nibby Hawke within a few seconds of seeing him. She liked Nibby. Listening avidly to the discussions of the servants as they made nursery tea in the upstairs kitchen, she thought Nibby a romantic figure, for Ellen said he was love-begot, which sounded exciting, and Maureen said his mother was no better'n she ougther be, which had a ring of mystery as well – how better should one ougther be, Alice wondered?

However, when Nibby started firing snowballs at David, her attention flew promptly and totally back to the present. How she laughed! How she cheered Nibby's good shots and David's puzzlement, and then how she capered at her window when David decided to outflank the mysterious enemy! Perched in her eyrie, she got an excellent bird's-eye view of the entire proceedings, following most of David's strategy although he was out of sight for several moments. And then, joy of joys, when David reappeared in the shrubbery, and Nibby flung the snowball with such daring accuracy that her brother pitched on to his nose in a bush! Alice, the perfect audience, clapped wildly and jumped up and down and laughed until the tears ran down her cheeks at such a magnificent finish to the snowballing.

And then . . . how typical of beastly boys . . . they went off together, both with skates slung across their shoulders, down to the lake. And Alice was left lonely at her window, because she had forgotten that the ground sloped down towards the Dee estuary and that the lake was halfway between the house and the sands so that she could not see what befell them once they reached it.

After a while, wrapped in her plum velvet curtain, she grew drowsy and tired of straining her eyes into the fading afternoon light in search of them. She sat down on one of the trunks, leaned back against the wall, and fell, surprisingly, asleep.

Leaving his newfound friend in the stableyard, David went in through the side door. In the small, red-tiled cloakroom he kicked his gumboots off and propped his skates against the wall, scattering snow and melting mud without a thought. A housemaid would clean up after him, as always. He slung his scarf down on the floor, because it was muddy and wet, spread his damp overcoat out across three hooks, then scuffed his carpet slippers on to his chilly feet. His hair was always curlier when it was wet; he pulled a face at the sissy stuff and rubbed it roughly with the towel which hung by the little handbasin, then tried to flatten it with vigorous blows from both hands. Failing, he forgot it, crossing the great, marble-tiled hall in a few bounds and going up the wide, shallow stairs two at a time, pausing on the landing to make sure there was still no one about before taking the next flight even faster, for the carpet here was thinner and his feet made a satisfactory thundering sound as he progressed.

This was the children's floor, where they had their schoolroom, nursery, bedrooms and the nursery kitchen. At the top of the stairs he turned into the nursery. They always ate in here rather than in the schoolroom, and he was glad of it, for it was a pleasant room, though it had bars at the windows, a huge brass fireguard usually crowded with underwear neatly laid out to air and an ironing board permanently set up, since the nursery maid spent most of her life pressing the girls' dresses. As he entered the room David put out a proprietorial hand and rocked Hugo, the big rocking horse with his red leather saddle and bridle, his red-rimmed nostrils and big, square white teeth. They all loved Hugo, even Ned who was seventeen, though it was only Michael and Sara and Julia now who rode him into battle or won steeplechases perched on that gleaming, creaking saddle.

Tea, he was glad to see, was already on the table. The blue and white checked tablecloth was almost obscured by bread, cut and ready for Nurse to toast on a long-handled fork before the fire, the wooden rack which would presently be filled with soft-boiled eggs so that the children could help themselves, the plates, knives and spoons and the dishes of yellow butter, sardines, pink home-cured ham and crumbly white and red Cheshire cheeses which were a permanent part of nursery tea.

David's eye noted a big, shallow bowl crammed with water-cress, a tall vase full of celery sticks, a flat dish with frail winter lettuce and of course heaps and heaps of bread and butter. Then there were sugar biscuits with pictures of animals on them, Maud's home-made shortbread, crumbly and rich, and best of all a perfectly enormous dark plum cake. His mouth watered with anticipation at the sight of that cake . . . you had to be ten before you were allowed to eat any, according to Nurse, so the cake would be shared – in theory, at least – between himself, Alice, Lydia and Ned. At seventeen, Ned would not sit at table with the rest of them, because he dined at eight with their parents . . . but you could be sure he would stroll up the stairs presently, smile sweetly at Gill, the nursery maid, put an arm round Nurse . . . and eat his share of that cake!

As David surveyed the table Lydia came in carrying a flat reed basket with the boiled eggs steaming in it. She smiled at him, wrinkling her small nose, then began to put the eggs, one by one, into the wooden rack. Lydia was a pretty thing and knew it. She had bright, bouncing curls, a small, heart-shaped face and very blue eyes. She and David got on quite well if they did not have to see too much of each other; she thought boys uncouth and David thought her conceited and spoilt. Later in the holidays they would rarely be in the same room without swopping opprobrious remarks, but it was early days yet; absence was still making the heart, if not fonder, at least more tolerant.

'Hello, Lyddy. Seen Alice?'

'I thought she'd gone skating with you,' Lydia said, tongue protruding between her little white teeth as she snatched at the hot eggs and transferred them to their rack. 'She's not been in here for ages and ages.'

'Well, she didn't come skating. Nurse said she'd kill her if she tried so I went off by myself. At least . . .' He hesitated. No point in telling Lydia about Nibby; she wouldn't be interested, and might use the information later to get at him. Although only a couple of years younger than himself Lydia was quite different. A howling snob was how David would have de-scribed her. No, he wouldn't mention Nibby.

'At least what? Go and see if she's in the schoolroom, then. The eggs are ready.' Lydia doled out the last one and bustled importantly to the door. 'I'm helping Gill, I can't go and find her.'

David sauntered out of the nursery and into the school-room. Sara and Julia were there, sprawled on the big sofa in front of the roaring fire, watching Nurse, who was mending socks and telling one of her interminable stories about what life had been like when their father had been young.

'. . . so your grandfather went to the dairy, very quiet-like,' she was saying impressively, to her riveted audience, 'and there was your father, Master Alyn, just fishing the cat out of the biggest bowl of cream you've ever seen . . . a black cat, it was . . .'

No Alice. No Michael either, but there were sounds of splashing coming from the bathroom, intermingling with occasional crows of delight and the odd cry of alarm. That probably meant that Gill, a skinny fourteen-year-old, was trying to bath Michael whilst simultaneously helping Ellen or Maureen with the tea. David popped his head round the bathroom door just in case, and received a splash from Michael that missed him but deluged poor Gill; then he looked into the kitchen and very nearly got landed with pushing the trolley through. Finally, he stood in the narrow corridor and wondered where he would have hidden himself had he been stuck indoors with a cold.

The attics were forbidden, so it would be there, of course. And if Alice was still furious about the skating she would probably be perched on some old box, trying to see the lake. David thumped crossly up the stairs. Blow the girl. She had probably had a miserable afternoon whilst he was out en-joying himself. If only he'd thought, he could have waved towards the house now and then so that she would have known herself not forgotten. Which she had been, of course, but still . . .

He got an awful fright when he did find her, though. First, looking into room after room, all of them empty, it had occurred to him that she might have climbed out on to the narrow flat roof to try to see better, and then, what with her feverish cold and the weather, might have fallen off . . . He was in quite a panic when he opened the last door and there she was, her mouth open, her face white, her hair all draggly . . . apparently tied up like a sausage in blood-coloured something-or-other.

20

His gasp woke her. She stirred, tried to clear her throat, coughed thickly, knuckled her eyes, and then looked across at him. He smiled tentatively, wondering whether she was still in a foul mood with him, but something must have happened to cheer her up, for her answering smile was her usual bright beam, though a little marred by what was obviously a gummy feeling to her mouth and the fact that her nose was running.

'Davie! I believe I fell asleep. I saw you with the Hawke boy . . . what's he like? I've tried to meet him, but I had no luck . . . wasn't it grand the way he snowballed you? And then you tracked him and he came up behind you . . . I watched it all through there.' She gestured to the window. 'I say, is he a decent sort of kid?'

'Yes, he . . . Alice, you are ten years old, so don't you forget it!' He frowned at her, but perfunctorily; she ought not to refer to a man of thirteen as a kid, but she was only imitating him, after all, and he was keen to find out a bit more about Nibby. Alice was quiet, but she didn't half take things in! 'What do you know about him? Why's he living here, for a start off?'

'His mother went away and left him, so he came to live with his father; he's love-begot; and his mother's no better'n she oughter be,' Alice chanted, counting her knowledge off on her fingers, one, two, three. 'He's the same age as you and Maud says he's bright's a button. Hawke said the other day in the car, to Daddy, that his son's at the grammar school and doing well there and he wouldn't take him away at fourteen, not for all the tea in China. He's going to get a good education and then he'll go far.'

'Hmm. Come on, then, let's go down for tea – and do take that red thing off, whatever it is. I thought you were dead and in your shroud when I came through that door.'

Nibby had two teas, the first in the kitchen with Maud, Maureen, Robert and Dixon and the second with his father, in their rooms above the stables. The first tea was a good one – masses of bread and butter, smoked haddock, hot apple pie and custard and cheese and biscuits, washed down with cup after cup of scalding tea.

The second tea was better. A big bowl of steaming hot cockles, just boiled, lots and lots of bread and butter, marmalade pudding cooked in a piece of his father's old shirt and, to

21

finish up with, yesterday's cold treacle tart. They washed it down with beer for Hawke and cold milk for Nibby.

'Full, old chap?' John Hawke smiled kindly at his son. 'More milk?'

Nibby knew that Dad thought Mam hadn't fed him properly, which was true; he also knew that Dad had no idea he had been stuffed to the eyebrows in the house before setting foot in the stables and coming up the stairs to their warm and cosy kitchen. But what the eye didn't see . . . and Nibby had no intention of ever being hungry again, if he could help it. He would never forget the three days before his father had rescued him, when his mother had gone off in the middle of the night with some feller, leaving him locked into their two-room flatlet. All that had passed his lips for those three days was water from the tap, because there was nothing else in the house, no one was in the downstairs rooms, and though he supposed he could have got out at a pinch and probably with some injury to himself, for the drop from their window was sheer and the landing on concrete, he had kept hoping that his mother would return, as she had promised, with food for them both.

But now his father was holding out the milk jug, his dark, straight eyebrows raised, the smile still lingering.

'No more milk, thanks, Dad. I say, I went skating this afternoon. With David.'

'Ah, yes. Nice lad. Like him, did you?'

Nibby nodded energetically. 'Aye. He's awright. We're going again tomorrow.'

'Good. He's lonely, that lad. Don't go leading him into mischief, now.'

'No, Dad.' Nibby grinned. 'If I do, I reckon it 'ud be six to one and half a dozen to the other, though.'

'I dare say. But I know who'd get the blame. Shove another log on the fire, there's a good feller.'

# CHAPTER TWO

'Shall I help with the bucket, Kon?' Pavel's shrill little voice cut across the roaring of the river below and Konkordia, lugging the heavy, leaking wooden bucket, smiled gratefully at the younger child. Pavel was always willing to help, though at the moment, burdened by Eva, who was toddling now and apt to cling to any passing leg, she could do little enough.

'It's all right, I can manage. You bring the baby.'

Spring, she reflected, as they made their way back up the steep, zig-zag mountain track, had definitely arrived. The river, swollen by melting snow, was a roaring torrent and up in the village you could hear the ice cracking as it melted and the occasional roar and flurry of an avalanche.

The thaw had started the very day that Uncle Kevi had agreed to stay with them for a while longer, which was just as well, since crossing the pass in weather like this would have meant certain death. As it was, Uncle Kevi's beard was thickening nicely and he had begun to ride out with the herds, though Petchoren was still doubtful as to the wisdom of such an action. However, as the days wore on and no strangers came to the *aoul* he became reconciled to his brother's work with the herds, could even see what a useful thing it was, for his ewes had lambed well, his mares were dropping good strong foals and he needed all the help he could muster to keep his beasts fed.

The other villagers, though, in the other *koshes* sprinkled along the topmost mountain ledges, were made uneasy by Kevi's continued presence. Once, visitors had been constantly in and out of their home and the boys had run up most nights to beg for cakes or milk or cheese-bread to eat during their wolf-vigils. No more. Everyone was polite, but Konkordia could sense that nerves were strained by Kevi's presence. They

23

liked him, but they feared the trouble he might bring.

The bucket was heavy, so when her arm felt that it could bear no more she stood it down in the dust and glanced back to where Pavel and Eva were toiling along behind her. And saw, not just her sisters, but movement below them. A herd of sheep, perhaps, being driven along the river valley to new pastures? Or tribesmen, come to visit? Or . . . She could see that they were all on horseback, and as she concentrated her gaze she could see military cloaks and uniform, the glint of rifles. They were soldiers.

She had carried the water too far to abandon it so she snatched it up and began to run uphill, the bucket clunking against her calves, splashing and spilling. Behind her Pavel shouted and she saw, as she changed direction with the path, that her sister had seized the baby in her arms and was manfully running along in her wake, but she could not stop to explain, indeed, she had no breath to spare for words. Instead she put her head down and ran with all her might, bursting into the *kosh* and dumping the bucket with its reduced contents untidily on the floor. By the fire, Babushka was making a *shurpa* from turnips, mutton bones, water and sour cream. She looked up, her old jaw sagging, her rheumy little eyes rounding with surprise.

'What is it, Konkordia? You've not brought much water, but there's no need for all the rush . . . why, you can hardly breathe . . .'

'Soldiers, Babushka!' The words burst from Konkordia's dry mouth. 'Soldiers, riding along by the river. Coming this way!'

The old woman stiffened and the spoon she had been using to stir the *shurpa* dropped from her fingers and disappeared into the golden-bubbled soup. She put a knotted, veined hand out to her granddaughter, her voice trembling.

'Soldiers? Soldiers? Why should soldiers come? Where is my son?'

'Uncle Kevi? Where *is* he, Babushka? Don't you know? I must find him, warn him.'

'Kevi? He's ridden out on the white mare to see if the pass is clear. Petchoren took two mares and their foals over to the *aoul* in the next valley. They said they might buy . . . it is a fine beast . . . they are both fine beasts.'

Her voice had the mad note which Konkordia had heard creep into it whenever she was badly flustered. But now she must be made to listen, made to understand!

'They've gone, then. What about the boys? Are they near, with the herds?'

'I don't know, dushka. Don't ask me.' Babushka began to whine like a dog, then the whine broke down into whimpers and she squatted heavily back on the floor again and began to stir her *shurpa*. 'Send the soldiers away, Konkordia; I'm too busy for soldiers today.'

There was little help here, then. Konkordia whirled at a sound from the doorway, but it was only Pavel and Eva staggering in, both breathless, Eva already grizzling, a small finger in her mouth, because she had been made to hurry.

'What was the matter, Kon?' Pavel's little face was a shade paler than usual. 'Was it the soldiers? Shall we go and fetch Father?'

'The soldiers won't hurt us; they're all good men,' Konkordia said automatically, but her mind was feverishly examining this new idea. Should they try to go after Petchoren? He, at least, would be able to advise them what best to do. She turned to Babushka, still stirring her soup.

'I think we'll go and find Father, Babushka. Tell the soldiers we've gone to get greens for the pot. Can you remember that?'

'Of course!' Babushka glared at her granddaughter, affronted. 'You've gone to get greens for the pot – don't be late, and don't forget there are bad things abroad in the mountains when dusk falls. Come home before the sun sinks.'

'Yes. Pavel, fill a bag with food.' It had occurred to Konkordia that, though they should be back before dusk, it might be politic for Uncle Kevi to overnight in the open, and he would be glad of any food they might bring. She had told Babushka they were going to look for Petchoren, but she thought, now, that it would be more sensible to go after Kevi. If they could just stop him coming home for a night or two, the soldiers would get tired of waiting and would go away. If, indeed, they were coming to this particular *kosh*, if they were really looking for Uncle Kevi.

'That's right, take food.' Babushka scrambled across to her cupboard and began taking cheese and maize cakes out of it, then added a big new loaf of black bread and some rather wrinkled turnips. 'You must ride; you'll be there quicker if you take the old bay mare. Off with you now, little girls. Yes, Eva too . . . we don't want the baby left here, do we?'

Konkordia scooped Eva up in her arms and Pavel lugged the bulging leather bag of food. Together they hurried out to the fold, where the old bay mare was wandering. Pavel was good with horses, young though she was; very often Uncle Kevi rode with her perched before him on the saddle, and she had been caught several times scrambling on the unbroken foals and risking her life as they charged, squealing and panicky, from side to side in the enclosure. Now, she took the length of rope and called to the mare, who stopped grazing and stood, ears pricked, looking towards the sound. When Pavel reached her she bent her head with the most mannerly gesture and let the child slip the halter round her neck.

'Right. I'll give you a leg up, Pavel, and then I'll climb on the wall and mount from there.' Konkordia took hold of the halter, but Pavel, like the little monkey Uncle Kevi so often called her, had swarmed up the mare's barrel side and was perched aloft, holding her arms out for Eva. Konkordia handed the baby up, led the mare to the stone wall, and climbed aboard herself. She settled them all comfortably, kicked the gate shut behind them, and headed the mare for the mountain top. She risked a glance below, to where the soldiers were riding up the path which only a short time ago had echoed to the sounds of her running feet and clanking bucket. No one was looking up, though, and she knew they would be unlikely to worry about a fat old mare with three little girls on her back, off to the high pastures for a day's fun and green-picking.

They found neither Kevi nor Petchoren, and dusk had fallen long before the little group made its weary way back along the trail to the *aoul*. They passed two or three other *koshes*, all lamplit, the doors closed for the night, and they saw the wolf-fires burning and the shadows of the dogs as they prowled between the stone shelters and the flames. Their home was at the furthest point away from the cluster of the *aoul*, so they reached it last. The door was shut, the windows shuttered. Light showed round the edges of the door and, once, they saw a shadow fall on the shutters. Other than that there was no sign of three missing children: no one paced up and down, waiting for them, no doorway streamed welcoming light. Did it mean that the soldiers had gone and the men were back, or that the men were not back but the soldiers were still there?

The mare slowed and stopped by the byre. She was unshod, so her hooves made no sound on the thick spring turf. Konkordia slid off, put up her arms for Eva, who was asleep once more, and then watched as Pavel sprang lightly down.

It was strange to approach your own door with trepidation; Konkordia was actually stealing towards it, her heart bumping in her mouth, when something else occurred to her. The soldiers had been in a large group, far too large to inhabit the *aoul* and not be seen. She would have noticed strange horses, or tents, or some other form of shelter if the men had remained. She looked round; the moon was full and the stars blazed in the dark indigo sky. In the fold the sheep huddled, and a couple of horses slept on their feet as horses will, two swaying black shadows, heads hung, mouths still for once. She stayed Pavel with her hand whilst her eyes, accustomed to the dark, raked the surrounding countryside. Nothing. Neither strange horse, strange man or strange abode.

Immensely relieved, she pushed at the door of the *kosh*. It was not locked and swung open easily. Kal and Baru rose to their feet, slow and dignified, and came towards her, tails swinging, mouths grinning. Behind them she saw Babushka, squatting by the fire making *shashlik* with lumps of sheepmeat speared on a wooden skewer. Petchoren sat near her, whittling a wooden spoon. Everything was normal!

Konkordia had Eva in her arms and her arms were tired. She swung the child on to her hip and broke into relieved speech.

'Oh, Father, I'm glad you're home! Is Kevi back, or . . .'

She broke off. In the deep shadows at the back of the *kosh* there was a sudden movement and she saw a man turn to face her, saw the glint of steel in his hand, the planes of his high cheekbones, the broad shoulders in a uniform coat. She gasped, stepped back, and trod on Pavel.

The man came forward, crouching to avoid hitting his head on the low roof. He was quite young and rather handsome, and he was smiling at her, but nevertheless Konkordia shrank from him. What had she said? Was this her uncle's enemy, this large young man with the sad eyes? It seemed impossible, but he was a soldier, and Uncle Kevi was afraid of soldiers.

'Where's Kevi, little one? That's what we all want to know.'

There was another man at the back of the *kosh*, another soldier. He had a gun as well. He was lying on his stomach and the gun was pointing at the door. It made Konkordia give a big shudder and she was relieved when, abruptly, Pavel began to cry.

'You trod on me, Kon – it hurt,' she wailed. 'Oh, oh, my foot is hurt!'

The loud noise broke the tension. Unfortunately it also woke Eva, who promptly added her own howls to Pavel's noisy weeping. Babushka clicked her tongue and came forward, offering food and hot milk, saying that she would soon get them cuddled down and comfortable, as little girls should be when dusk has fallen.

'It's a surprise to me you didn't get gobbled up by wolves or carried off by hobgoblins,' she muttered, standing over them as they washed themselves and dabbed ineffectually at Eva's scarlet, shrieking face. 'What a day . . . lost, I suppose?'

'Yes, lost,' Konkordia said dutifully. 'Can I give Eva her milk now? She's terribly tired.'

She was feeding Eva the milk from a mug, with black bread soaked in it, when the soldier who had spoken to her advanced once more, this time on Pavel. He sat down beside her and touched her arm to get her attention. Pavel, spooning her own bread and milk at a great rate, turned and looked seriously at him out of big, shadowed eyes.

'Pavel? Is that really your name? But it's a boy's name and you look like a girl to me. Now why should a little girl get called by a boy's name?'

'I was named for my father's friend,' Pavel said rather thickly, through bread and milk. 'I like to be a girl with a boy's name.'

'And so you should. Now you look like a sensible girl, even if you do sound like a boy! Tell me, Pavelina, little Pavelski, do you know where my friend Kevi is? Did he go out with you this morning, or did he go out earlier, with your father? Or is he visiting friends in the *aoul*?'

Pavel looked at the soldier through her lashes, her head still bent. But she did not reply. She did, however, stop eating bread and milk.

'Well? Cat got your tongue, Pavelinka?' Konkordia saw a

tiny smile begin to curve the corners of her sister's mouth at the old joke. The soldier smiled too, his broad face creasing rather attractively and his mouth opening to show large white teeth.

'She's only a child.' Petchoren spoke dully, as though it did not much matter, but there was a warning in the glance he shot at his middle daughter.

'So she is – and a girl-child, at that!' The soldier put a finger under Pavel's chin and tilted it up. 'A pretty little girl-child – her Uncle Kevi's favourite, I'll be bound.'

'Uncle Kevi's gone, though,' Pavel said, as though at last making up her mind to talk to this large and friendly young man. She smiled at him, a picture of juvenile frankness. 'He's going to be a farmer and marry a big fat lady and live in the sunshine. When we're big we can go and live with him and he'll find us both good husbands . . . probably Eva too, when she's a woman grown.'

'Georgia!' The soldier spoke softly, then turned to the man behind him. 'Looks as though the bird has flown, Levinski. We'll spend the rest of the night here, if these good people don't mind, and then rejoin the others in the morning.' He turned to Babushka. 'I won't trouble you for a meal, but if you could sell us some bread and milk . . .'

'You can eat with us.' The old woman's voice was grudging, but the habit of courtesy to a guest would never leave her whilst she lived. 'We've killed a sheep – I was making *shashlik* when the children returned. Petchoren, cut me another joint of meat.'

Petchoren went over to the door but the soldier Levinski followed him. Kal and Baru, teeth bared, followed them out and returned with them, but they attempted no violence since the men appeared to be guests.

In the bustle that attended the making of *shashlik*, Konkordia caught her father's eye. She went over to him.

'Put yourselves to bed, there's good girls. They'll go as soon as it's light, I dare say. Sleep well.'

Konkordia dared say nothing, other than to murmur obedience. To the sounds of meat frizzling and fat sizzling she fell into a deep but troubled sleep.

She woke once, and eased her head above the skins to look round and see if it had all been a nightmare, if they were just a family sleeping in the *kosh* once more.

It was real. Lying at the back of the *kosh*, furthest from the fire, were the two soldiers. And what was worse, one of them was not sleeping at all; she could see the glint of his eyes in the pale light coming through the cracks in the shutters, and it was not only on his eyes that it glinted, but also on the barrel of his long rifle.

Konkordia awoke because dawn had come and because someone was outside the *kosh*, approaching it on cautious feet. She sensed at once that her father, too, was listening. He seemed just a hump beneath his *burka* but he had propped himself up against a wall and was only feigning sleep. He was as tense and alert as a wolf which scents a lamb.

In front of the door, the dogs had risen to their feet. Long tails stirred but no sound escaped them. It must be Kevi, unless it was one of the boys from the wolf-fires; the dogs would never let a stranger, not even a man from another *kosh*, come within feet of the door without giving tongue.

The door began to open. The wood creaked a little. Konkordia wanted to turn round and see if the soldiers were awake, but she dared not do so in case they were unaware of the intrusion and she alerted them. She watched as Petchoren began, very very slowly, to move towards the door. He had almost reached it when a voice from behind him said warningly, 'Don't move!'

It was the officer, the man who had spoken to Pavel the previous evening. He must have been as wide awake as Petchoren for even as he said the words he was moving like lightning, cutting across the room towards the door.

It all happened so suddenly that Konkordia was totally bewildered. She saw Kevi framed in the doorway for an instant, then he turned and made off into the thick white of the early morning mist. Behind her, the soldier cursed and the officer fired from the hip, the roar of the gun sounding unnaturally loud in the dawn silence.

Petchoren launched himself at the officer, and behind her head Konkordia heard the soldier's gun bark. Petchoren seemed to miss the officer, who ran on out of the *kosh*. Konkordia heard his footsteps stumbling away until the mist swallowed the sound. Her father lay, face down, sprawled on the floor. As Konkordia began to fight her way out of the sheepskins Babushka got shakily to her feet and stared round her. She looked mad, a witch-woman, red-eyed and terrible. The soldier crossed himself and muttered something . . . and then Petchoren rolled over and half sat up.

Konkordia heard her own scream echoed by another. Her father's face! It was dark, blotched and terrible, with a stream of dark blood running from his mouth and soaking into his tunic. He clawed at his throat with his hands and blood spurted, scarlet and bright and living, between his fingers. The soldier made a sickly sort of noise and Babushka screamed again, a higher, fiercer sound than Konkordia's frightened shriek. Behind her, in the sheepskin nest, Pavel woke and began to cry with loud, breathy sobs. Eva woke too and wailed as well. But Petchoren was talking and Konkordia knew it was to her. She struggled forward towards the nightmare figure.

'Take . . . care . . . of them. Babushka, too. She's old and . . . needs you.'

The words bubbled out, were gargled almost, in the blood. Konkordia wept and nodded and tried to say she would look after them all, and then Petchoren fell forward and Babushka grabbed at him, keening, trying to turn him over, imploring him not to die, not to leave his old mother and his little ones.

'He's dead . . .' the soldier had started to say, when a shadow darkened the doorway. Kevi stood there, his handsome, laughing face drained of colour, his arms folded tight across his stomach. Babushka moved forward, beginning to tell Kevi that Petchoren was dead, but Kevi had seen the silent figure on the floor. He put his hands out . . . and blood darkened his shirt and crimsoned his hands. He knelt, or Konkordia thought he knelt, but he might have fallen. Slowly, deliberately it seemed, he sagged forward across Petchoren's body. He gave a little shudder and a little sigh. Then he lay still.

For a moment, shock held them all suspended, speechless. Then, for the third time, Babushka screamed and shambled past the bodies. She lurched out through the doorway, sobbing, wailing, and turned to run uphill, her skinny legs moving with more speed than Konkordia would have thought possible. Konkordia was right behind her, Eva in her arms, Pavel clutching at her skirt. Behind them, the *kosh* was silent, but as Konkordia looked back she saw the soldier emerge into the open air and look round him, heard him shout, in a voice that cracked with fear, for his officer.

'Where are we going, Babushka?' Konkordia croaked, as they came out on the very topmost part of the cliff. 'Why do you run? No one's chasing us . . .'

Babushka might have hesitated, might have listened to reason, but at that very moment, through the milkiness of the mist, they heard the officer call, the soldier answer, and then the clatter of booted feet on the cliff path. They were being pursued.

It galvanised them all, even the unwilling Konkordia, into fresh effort. Babushka made straight for the edge of the precipice, whining and whimpering with reasonless, senile terror. Konkordia, behind her, called her name and Babushka turned, but her eyes did not see them and foam ran down her chin.

'Babushka, don't! It's all right – you mustn't – think of the children!'

She thought, for a moment, that she had reached the old woman, for Babushka turned from the edge of the drop and walked back a dozen or so feet. Then she faced the gorge once again and ran, with all her mad and skinny strength, taking a tremendous leap out into space. As she fell her voice echoed around the chasm, clashing back to her granddaughters in weird cadences of wild sound.

'Come, come, Kon . . . kord . . . eeeeaaaah!'

Konkordia pushed Eva into Pavel's arms. What had Petchoren said? Take care of them. Take care of Babushka. Babushka was calling her; she was awfully old to go on such a journey alone. Her mind was confused, aflame with conflicting thoughts and feelings. She turned to Pavel as the boots continued to crunch and pound up the path.

'Take care of Eva; hide in the little cave – you know the one – until the soldiers have gone. Go! There's something I must do.'

Pavel began to run, Eva's solid, damp body a heavier weight now because she was struggling for release, but Pavel knew better than to disobey her sister, especially as Konkordia was in such distress.

She ran away from the soldiers and the precipice down a little, crooked goat-path, pushing through the swirling mist, her breath coming in short, agonised gasps, a pain in her chest stabbing like a knife.

She was almost at the caves when she heard a sound behind her, from the clifftop. She hesitated as the long, eerie cry of a seagull split the quiet, then died away to nothing. Waiting, she could hear, from far off, that the boots, too, had stopped. She was cold, suddenly, and hugged Eva tightly, glad of the child's warm and human presence.

The boots began to clatter again. It might have been only her imagination but they sounded urgent, somehow. Any moment someone might emerge out of the mist and her chance to hide would be gone. Pavel hurried the last few yards, dropped to her knees, and crawled thankfully into the tiny, child-sized cave. Outside, there was no sound. No voices. No footsteps. Only silence.

# CHAPTER THREE

'Come on, David, they'll be launching in an hour. If you want to come with me you'd better get a move on.' Ned's impatient voice cut across the noise David was making in the bathroom as he splashed water up into his soapy face. 'Hawke's taking the parents, but Dixon says he'll drive you and me down in the Morris – and that Nibby, I suppose.'

'Shan't be a tick,' David bawled, grabbing a towel and attacking his face with it. 'Who's taking the girls?'

'The little ones aren't going, but Alice and Lydia went with the mater, I think. Look, old boy, do get a move on! If you aren't ready in five minutes you can jolly well walk. Peggy Carruthers will be there, and I want a word with her.'

David chucked his towel on to the floor, patted despairingly at his water-flattened hair and rushed into the corridor, to find Ned standing at the ready, holding out his striped blazer.

'Here we are, shove your arms in this. Hello-ello-ello, didn't your nanny ever tell you about hair-combs? Jehosophat, you look like a blinkin' hedgehog! Here, borrow mine.'

David grabbed the proffered comb and dragged it through his hair, then set off, still struggling into the blazer, in his brother's wake. It was odd, he reflected, that Ned, who had never been particularly interested in shipping except as the means to take him to university and then to provide him with a handsome salary, should actually want to be on time for this particular launching. His father's yard, which had been building ships for two hundred years, produced too many vessels for a launching to be an unusual event. But this ship was out of the ordinary – the largest the yard had ever built and probably one of the most important, since it was a new design by a new designer, had been built specially for the trans-Atlantic route, and would, it was hoped, break speed records as well as being a most luxurious way to travel.

And of course there was Peggy Carruthers. Ned was going to start at Cambridge in a few months but right now he was cracked about Peggy. David quite liked her, too; she had lots of thick hair braided into two plaits, a ready laugh and the sort of figure which was just becoming popular – thin with a flat chest and almost no hips. On the other hand, Ned could see Peggy without going to the launch . . . Peggy's family was in shipping too, which meant a good deal of coming and going between the Thomas yard and the Carruthers offices.

Still hurrying, but now neatly buttoned into his blazer, David burst out of the house on Ned's heels and saw the Morris waiting, Dixon already at the wheel and Nibby perched on the back seat. He had put on a grey suit for the occasion and David hardly recognised him, what with that, a white shirt and a red tie, to say nothing of Brylcreemed hair and scrubbed nails.

He said as much as he scrambled into the car, leaving Ned, who wanted to learn to drive, to take the seat next to Dixon. Nibby made a rude noise.

'Posh, am I? No such thing; these are me school clothes! Well, 'cep' for the tie.'

For the short journey to the yard they said little, but once there Ned asked Dixon to return to the car once the ship had gone down the slipway so that he could take them further down the coast to see her actually take to the sea.

'If she's interested, I'll bring Peggy as well,' he said offhandedly to his brother as they parted company on the quayside. 'See you later, then.'

'He's very keen, all of a sudden,' Nibby muttered, as the two of them began to worm their way through the crowds already assembled to a good vantage point. High up, on the launching platform, the family was already grouped, the girls looking self-conscious in their best, Michael in his mother's arms whilst Gill hovered, ready to take him if he began to prove difficult.

'Keen on what? Peggy or ships? If you mean ships, it's probably because he'll be working for the firm during his vacs, to earn himself some pocket money, you know. He'll go into the firm when he leaves, so he says.'

'And you? What'll you do, Dave?'

At thirteen the future stretches ahead of you so rosy bright that you know full well you are born to a brilliant career of some sort. David shrugged, wondering which of his dream-futures to give rein to on this occasion. Explorer, sea-captain, racing driver? He knew his father would have liked him to go into the yard – perhaps in his heart he suspected that he would become a shipbuilder in the fullness of time – but right now it seemed a dull thing to do, to build ships. When he looked out across the Dee estuary, which he loved so much that at times its beauty hurt him, made his eyes water, he could only dream of sailing with the tide, plodding the sands in search of cockles or strange fish in the little pools, lying behind a dune with his binoculars – a recent possession – trained on some rare bird, wintering here in the estuary. Building ships was noisy and nerve-racking, but sailing them . . . ah, that was a very different matter! The wind in the rigging, the roar of the water under the prow as your yacht heeled over to meet the breeze, the crack and slap of the sails . . . if only one could make a living out of sailing a yacht!

'Come on, Dave, what'll you do? Build ships? I'm going to university if I can get there, and then I'll do something with cars . . . don't know what, but it won't be chauffeuring. Dad reckons it's a dying trade; people want to drive themselves, not be driven. Guess I'll make money, then I can do what I like in my spare time.'

David looked at Nibby with respect. That was exactly how he felt, now he had heard it put into words! You were unlikely to get a job which was what you most liked doing, so you looked for one which would make you sufficient money to indulge in your hobbies when you weren't actually working! Looked at that way, the yard was probably as good a way of earning money as any. Besides, it would please his father.

David adored his father. Alyn Thomas was a big man, six foot three inches in his stockinged feet, and his face was best described as rugged – David had inherited his nose and the thick, black eyebrows but not, as yet, the scars which a lifetime of working in all weathers at a job which could be very hazardous had brought. Alyn Thomas had lost a finger from his right hand in an accident with a vice; a stitched scar ran from the left-hand corner of his eye to the centre of his top lip; and a small chip of wood which had flown from a log and embedded itself in his forehead had been ignored and resulted in a poisoned wound which had left a ragged, shiny crease of purply skin just above his right eye.

Yet despite it all, he was as popular with women as he was with his workpeople. He was a hardworking man but a generous employer who made it his business to know all about his work force. His secretary would have laid down more than her life for him, as David had once heard a clerk in the office rudely remarking, and his sisters-in-law thought he was wonderful and never stopped telling Megan, David's mother, what a lucky woman she was.

Now, looking up at his parents from his lowly position on the quayside, David thought them a handsome couple. His father, so tall, so imposing in his dark suit and grey tie, and his mother, the prettiest woman on Deeside, with a face that always seemed to be considering laughter even in repose, the beautiful auburn hair which she had passed on to three of her daughters and the white skin, faintly touched in summer by golden freckles, which would have made her worth a second glance in any company. Mother wore a leaf-green taffeta suit with velvet facings and dear little brown shoes with diamante buckles. She was not wearing a hat and her hair shone in the sunshine. When she put up a hand to touch the deep wave which fell across her forehead, David saw that she was wearing the emeralds . . . a big one on her finger and a necklace with a rough-cut emerald as a pendant around her neck.

David's heart swelled with pride as he looked up at her. No one else had a mother like his — nor a father! Successful, beautiful, yet kind and much-loved. Poor Nibby! But Nibby was watching the Thomases too, and with as much affection as their son felt showing in his unguarded eyes for a moment. It occurred to David that it would be a grand thing to be loved, as his parents were loved, by everyone connected with them, and to deserve it.

'Well? Dammit, Dave, what'll you *do*?' Nibby had returned to his original subject like a terrier to a rathole. 'You must have some idea!'

'Well, I'll go to university, I suppose, and then I may muck about for a bit if I'm let . . . go abroad, see the world . . . but when I've done those things I'll build ships, I expect. I want to come back here. There's no place like the estuary, wouldn't you say?'

Nibby had only lived at Carmel Hall for a few months, but his nod was vigorous. He spent all his spare time out on the sands, or begging rides from the fishermen, or swimming in a quiet pool when the tide race allowed.

'Aye, you're right. And when you get your boat . . .'

David nodded. His boat would be coming in no more than a few weeks. He was so excited about it that he hardly dared let the thought enter his mind, for his impatience was total. He had wanted a boat of his own for ages, but his mother was nervous and his father had not got round to it. Then, during the Easter holidays, he had been very late coming in one night and his father had announced that the boat would be arriving some time over the summer.

'The truth is, lad, that if you've a mind to roam the estuary – and even your mother, bless her, now acknowledges that it's your favourite pastime – then you'd be a good deal safer in a boat than on foot. With a tide that races in faster than a horse can gallop, and quicksands and currents, to say nothing of the way a storm can blow up out of nothing. . . well, once you've got a boat at least we'll know you're afloat and not swimming.

David had agreed eagerly and promised to be as careful when he had a boat as he had always been on foot. He understood his parents' fears well enough, for in the library there was an old manuscript book, written in a crabbed and blotchy hand, which recorded details of all the bodies found in or near the estuary. It made frightening reading on a night when the wind howled outside and the tide was high, and you knew your son was somewhere out there in the windy dark, plodding along in gumboots and oilskins, with a bedraggled pointer at his heels, heading across the sandbanks with a string of fish in one hand, hoping to get home before they sent out a search party.

'It's a good thing it's a fine day; you know how superstitious some of the old fellers can be. Doesn't the ship look grand?'

Nibby's voice jerked David out of his dreaming. He looked up at the ship and acknowledged that she was indeed grand. The biggest thing the yard had ever built, she was poised at the top of the slipway, waiting for the moment when someone – would it be Mother this time, or Lady Ffrith, whose husband had commissioned the ship for their trans-Atlantic line? – would crack the bottle of champagne over the bows, when the band would strike up – it was the Gresford Colliery Band, known far and wide for their stirring music on great occasions – and the ship would have her name cried aloud as she began her ponderous journey down the slipway and into the deep channel of the river Dee.

Up on the platform there was talk, laughter, and moving about as everyone tried to give Lady Ffrith more room, for it was she who was taking the bottle of champagne on its long ribbon and preparing to swing so that it cracked resoundingly against the prow. David held his breath as his father said a few words – and they were very few, for Alyn did not believe in speechifying – and then Lady Ffrith, guided by her husband, launched the bottle. So many things could go wrong at this point. The bottle could miss the prow altogether, or it could simply bounce and refuse to shatter, or it could rebound and knock someone out cold . . . all these things had happened in the past, but today was destined to be different. The bottle flew straight and true, shattered with a magnificent crack, and champagne poured down the ship's glistening paintwork. Lady Ffrith, in time-honoured fashion, gave a feminine flutter of alarm as she was splashed, stepped back into her husband's arm, and waved to the band, who promptly began to play 'Hearts of Oak', whilst everyone cheered and the name *Royal Gold* was on every lip.

'Well, that's that.' David and Nibby turned away as the ship began, very slowly, to move. Men were shouting, releasing ropes, running, but for them the fun would not recommence until the vessel was out in the roads, meeting the waves for the very first time. They would hurry back to Dixon now, get a lift down the coast to a good vantage point, and see her breast the swell!

They were still squiggling through the crowd when someone using a loud-hailer roared, 'David Thomas! Would David Thomas go to the launching platform at once, please,' and David, red about the gills, grabbed Nibby and changed direction.

'Come on! I don't think I've done anything wrong – Dad said I needn't be with the rest of the family – but we'd better make sure.'

They reached the platform and were seized immediately by Alyn Thomas. He grinned down at them.

'Hey, lads . . . want to go downriver with her? The pilot's late; he's being hoisted aboard now. If you'd enjoy a trip I'll send Hawke round to the port for you later on today. You should be ashore again by teatime.'

For a moment they could only goggle at him, but he did not seem to need an answer, for he just said, 'Thought you'd enjoy it,' and then they were being hustled aboard, accompanied by the pilot, who grinned cheerfully at them and then went straight to the bridge, leaving the boys to hang over the rail and wave and shout to those unfortunates left behind on the quayside.

It was not until they were down the slip without accident, and making their way out into midstream with a strange, crabbing motion, that David thought to glance around the deck to see who else was aboard. And almost at once he saw a figure crouched down by the bridge, looking so guilty, so furtive, that his imagination was fired at once. He grabbed Nibby's arm.

'Look – who the hell's that?'

Nibby looked and then a slow grin spread across his face. 'Doncher know? Why, man, it's your sister Alice!'

Strange emotions struggled for a place in David's breast. Alice was a mere girl, and a young one too – why should *she* be aboard? He was thirteen and this was his first trip – was it right that he should share it with a kid of no more than ten? And a girl, at that? On the other hand he was very fond of Alice; she was a spunky kid, and he thought her underrated by both her family and her friends. Everyone expected Alice to be just like Lydia and the other girls, but she was different, a tomboy, always tagging him or imitating him, never content with frilly dresses, dolls and picture books. She was tough and proud of it, could shoot a straight arrow when they got the big, straw-stuffed target out of the loft and bent their bows in competition, could ride her bicycle over the roughest terrain you could think of, could play a fish as well as any boy, though she had to have her hook baited for her on account of a strange fellow-feeling for worms.

But now she was pulling a fast one, he was sure of it. She was a stowaway, no less . . . he really ought to tell on her, get the engineer or one of the officers to let them know, ashore, that she was stealing a ride. On the other hand, if he held his tongue for a bit it would be too late and she could enjoy her rare treat. She would get a fearful wigging, no doubt of that, because their parents would worry, believe her lost. But he knew Alice would consider it worth it to have been aboard the *Royal Gold* on her maiden voyage. And the trip back from Liverpool – for she was bound for that port, to lie alongside the *Royal Purple*, the *Royal Silver* and the *Royal Crimson* at the Ffrith moorings – would be great fun with Alice in the car. He would let it go, just this once.

Strolling with a lordly air across the deck to his sister's side he said as much to Nibby, but Nibby only grinned. Perhaps he realised that Alice was quite capable of hiding herself away in the bowels of the ship until she was too far from land for anyone to do anything about it, but that, he reminded himself, was not his reason for keeping mum. Alice was a good kid. He intended to tell her so.

Alice, having scuttled aboard early in the proceedings when no one seemed to be paying much attention to the ship, had only just come up from below, and the sight of the widening strip of water between the rail and the shore had come as a pleasant shock. She had done it! She was aboard, the only member of the Thomas family ever to stow away! In fact, she told herself, crouching beside the funnel and hoping that she was less conspicuous than she felt, she was the only Thomas aboard, the sole representative of the shipbuilding family whose yard had produced this magnificent ship.

Seeing David and Nibby was a disappointment in one way, but lovely in another. She adored David, even when he was shouting at her for following him when he wanted to be alone. The way his brows came down over his eyes, the way his mouth tightened, even his strong, boy's hands, were all special to her. Of course he would be cross with her for being here at all, but he would admire her, too. She often saw reluctant admiration kindling his dark eyes to warmth over her exploits, even when he was roundly condemning them to her face.

Nibby was another person touched with magic. Alice watched him as a sorcerer's apprentice might watch the wizard to whom he is bound. Nibby made such a good job of being a boy! He was often scruffy, he returned from school muddy, battered and sometimes with torn clothing. His shoes were seldom clean and in any case he sensibly preferred gumboots of a size and stoutness which any girl, doomed to slippers, might have envied. When he had first come to live with Hawke over the stables he had been skinny with short, sparse hair, but now he was filling out, growing strong and muscular, and his hair was proving to be thick and lustrous, a toffee-coloured thatch which daily crept lower towards his eyebrows, hiding him satisfactorily from those who wanted to read his expression.

Like David, he was good at outdoor things. She had watched him rowing one of the creaky old fishing boats whilst its owner reclined at his ease in the stern, dragging out the nets with wiry strength and hitting the fish across the head as he picked them from the weave. She had seen him digging for cockles when it was raining hard and the wind whined round the house like a lost soul and had felt mingled sympathy and envy for his icy fingers and toes, his soaked clothing, his sturdy independence.

She had seldom actually spoken to him, though. He was not, she supposed, the sort of boy who had much time for girls, particularly plain ones who rode their ponies hell for leather rather than prettily trotting, who hung around by the shoreline playing ducks and drakes with pebbles when the day was calm, who slipped, ghostlike, in and out of the stables, round corners, behind trees; lonely, aimless, misunderstood. Boys, she believed, liked the brisk, pretty, feminine girls. The ones with curls, dimples and small noses. She tucked her own nose, and her chin too, as low as she could into the collar of her short wool coat, glad that her tam o' shanter overhung her face. It was not fair that she was cursed with Daddy's nose. Why couldn't she have a dear little straight one, like Mummy's?

'Alice, you are too bad! What do you think Father will say?'

Nibby, she noticed, was grinning sympathetically at her and David's words were belied by the twinkle in his eye. She stopped trying to bury her face in her collar and smiled at them both.

'He won't mind all that much . . . not if you tell him I behaved and didn't get in anyone's way. You'll do that won't you, Davie? Dear, best Davie?'

'I'll tell 'im,' Nibby broke in. 'So'll Dave, of course. Shall we go up front, have a look-see? Or d'you think we might go to the bridge?'

'The bridge!' Alice said, then, 'Oo-oh, but they might send me back, if they know I'm not meant to be here.'

'We'll take care of you,' Nibby said. 'Guess no one knows it was only Dave and me who got put aboard at the last minute. They won't worry about a kid like you if you're with us. Coming?'

The three of them hurried off towards the bridge, Alice gazing up at Nibby with awe. He did not despise her just because she was a girl; he thought she was all right! Her mind began hatching plans: Nibby was at home all through term-time, as Alice herself was, since they both went to day schools. How nice it would be if they could be friends – when Nibby did not have David, of course.

David was talking to a man outside the door of the bridge. Obviously he said the right thing, because the man opened the door, bellowed the name Thomas and some sort of an explanation through it, and then ushered them inside. Alice looked around her. This was paradise! A man's world of instruments and charts and the ship's wheel, a rich turkey carpet underfoot, huge glass windows giving a wonderful view all around – and she, Alice Thomas, was here, with her big brother and his friend . . . their friend.

With shining eyes and a heart so full that it felt as if it were bursting, Alice took her place by the man at the wheel, as he indicated, and watched with all her eyes and listened with all her ears to what he was telling them. Red Letter Day! Not A Boy But Almost!

As it happened, the voyage downriver was far more exciting than anyone had anticipated. Scarcely were they out in mid-stream before the pilot, hurrying to the bows, went head over heels on an untidily stowed length of rope and cracked his head open on a hatch cover.

'We'll manage,' one of the men remarked, as they helped the reeling, cross-eyed man back into the bridge. 'You tell us what to do, like, and we'll do it. No need to move from the chair, is there?'

But the pilot was in no state to tell anyone how to steer the ship, as was made clear when there was an abrupt jolt, a shriek of machinery, and they found themselves wedged into a sandbank. Here was excitement indeed, David thought, as everyone rushed hither and thither and the engineer emerged, oily and scowling, from his underground retreat to ask, in a strong Hibernian accent, 'Wha's gangin' on out here, and whyfore has the telegraph stoppit wairking?'

The pilot, it transpired, was concussed. Following his directions had been worse than using their eyes and their own experience, for the crew was composed of ex-seamen who were ashore now but regularly took vessels up and down between the shipyards and the docks.

Eventually, of course, the ship was backed away from the sandbank, but they had to wait to float her off until the tide had come in and there was deeper water under her keel. Then it was noticed that she was listing to starboard, and men kept coming up to the bridge with reports of damage due to the collision. Nothing much: perhaps a door off its hinges; in the salon a number of dining tables, which had not yet been screwed into position, broken; a heap of china shattered. The bar had fortunately not yet been fitted out completely, but again loose bottles and glasses were smashed and there was a fine smell of sherry trifle and Christmas pudding whenever you passed the doorway.

David, Nibby and Alice were everywhere – they saw to that. What a thrill, on a first voyage, to be near as dammit shipwrecked! They poked about in the kitchen, giving cries of mock dismay over every broken plate but really adoring the drama of it all. They were first down into the hold . . . and first up, too, upon the discovery that the dark and dreadful place was filling with horribly smelly water. They reported each fresh disaster with smiling faces and it said a lot for the even temper of the man in command that he never once shouted at them or tole them to run away but treated each new revelation as of immense importance. He made the day perfect, in short.

Then the ship was for a brief moment really at sea as she rounded the point and actually sailed along the coast – though never, alas, out of sight of land. The list got no worse, but it got no better, either. In fact, by the time she docked, David's euphoria had begun to lessen and reality made itself felt. The collision, or running aground or what would you, had been fun for himself, for Alice and for Nibby, but what about his father? What about the Thomas yard? Would it cost a great deal to put the business right? He consulted the pilot but the pilot's eyes were crossed again and he only smiled mysteriously and then let his head sag back against his chair once more. The man in command was a little more helpful.

'It'll cost a bit, but it'll be covered by the insurance,' he assured David. 'Ship's still your father's responsibility until she's handed over in the dock, which will happen presently. So Ffrith's men will put her right, or should, but being as she's new-built probably they'll send for chaps from the Thomas yard and they'll do the necessary.'

'So Father won't be too upset?'

'He won't be pleased, but worse things happen at sea,' the man said, grinning at his own choice of phrase. 'Now you and the other two had better get ready to go ashore. We'll be putting the lines over in five minutes.'

'Well, Father? Was she all right? The man in command said it was an insurance matter, but he seemed to think we'd come out of it without too much trouble.'

David jumped to his feet. He had been sitting on the window seat in his father's study, waiting for Alyn to come back after a trip to Liverpool to see the ship for himself. Now he looked anxiously at his father's rugged face.

'She's all right. There was some damage to the keel and she was holed below the waterline, but it's nothing that a few days' work can't put straight. No, what's worrying about it is that it highlights the problem we've been trying to ignore up at the yard these past five years. The estuary's silting up and we're too far up it for big ships. I've wanted to get dredgers in but it never seemed worth it; we managed somehow. But now the demand is for bigger ships – liners and so on – and if we're to continue to build 'em then we'll have to dredge the channel and spend money on keeping it clear. Big money.'

'I see. Can we afford it? Ned says we're making money hand over fist and have been ever since the War.'

Alyn perched on his desk and wagged an admonitory finger at his son.

'Don't start running away with the idea that shipbuilding's the way to make big money, because you'd be wrong. It's chancy and risky ... When it goes right and the work is completed in the time-limit, then we can make a pile of money. When it goes wrong, or the men strike or make mistakes and we go over our limit and have to start raking in capital, then we can make a loss on a craft that looked like a winner. But this one's gone well so far, despite the bump. Yes, I'd say we can afford to get some dredging done, especially if one or two of the smaller yards would chip in.'

'Will they? People like the Mathesons and the Cruickshanks, did you mean? What's the alternative?'

'Build small.' Alyn grinned at his son's immediate outcry. 'Well, it's one solution. The other is to move the yard, and that's no small undertaking, but it's been done, in the past. There's land aplenty nearer the mouth of the estuary, though there would be snags . . . it's marshy, and shallow . . . but if we had to, I dare say we could move the yard.'

'Well, so long as it wasn't over to Liverpool or somewhere like that,' David conceded. 'But there's nowhere like here, is there, Father? I never want to live anywhere else, though I wouldn't mind visiting abroad.'

'Aye, you're right, there's nowhere on earth like Carmel Hall, but I can't see us moving from here. There've been Thomases here for two hundred years – it'll take more than a silted-up channel to shift us!' The boom of the gong being struck into a long drone by the butler, Sawyer, made him stand up and head for the door. 'Sorry, old son, but I'm starving and that means dinner in two minutes. Talk some more tomorrow, eh?'

David lingered for a little in the quiet study after his father had left. He looked out of the window and saw the lights of the Wirral begin to prick the dusk. On the water itself, gleaming dull as pewter in what was left of the light, a line of fishing boats returning to port stood out like cut-out silhouettes, the candles in their prows making the masts and bows gleam like gold. Far away, a gull cried, disturbed by some predator perhaps. The peace of the scene, and the beauty of it, filled David with determination. He would never leave this place! He would work like a demon at school and then leave and learn to use a dredger himself, if that was the only way to stay here!

The soldiers found them, of course. Eva's whimpers turned to angry, red-faced screams when no food was forthcoming, and the young officer tracked them down. On all fours, talking gently as to a terrified wild animal, Rudi Lemensk coaxed and persuaded until Pavel, on all fours too and covered in tears and dirt, emerged hesitantly from her tiny refuge. She had let Eva crawl out earlier to empty a bottle of milk, which she had done with great eagerness, tugging at Rudi's hand as she drank and reminding him strongly of a young lamb, butting at the ewe's bag as she sucked with vigorous, innocent lust.

One glance at Pavel, however, was enough to make Rudi realise that the child was in shock, a state of almost catatonic fear and numbness. Rudi was only twenty, younger than a good many of his own men, but he had been soldiering for five years and thought himself hardened enough. Had he not shot Kevi, a man for whom he had felt not merely regard but love? Kevi had taken care of him when he first joined the regiment, had taught him not only how to shoot straight and work when he was dropping and withstand the heat of summer and the bitter chill of winter, but how to treat his fellow soldiers, how to turn away a cruel remark with a laugh.

Then Kevi had deserted, for no reason that Rudi could understand, and, in deserting, had killed a guard, a boy scarcely older than Rudi himself had been when he first joined up. The boy had tagged at Rudi's heels, had been eager to learn, and had died never knowing why or how he had been killed. Kevi could have pushed the boy's rifle up, told him some tale, got past. He had not done so. He had killed him, with the curved knife which all the Caucasians kept somewhere about their persons. And Authority, knowing that the boy had been Rudi's friend, had chosen to send him to fetch Kevi to justice. Dead or alive, they had said, though, and Rudi was glad it was to be dead, because the thought of taking his one-time friend back, bound, as a captive was not something he wished to contemplate. Justice, then, had caught up with Kevi here, and at this very moment, whilst he was still contemplating Pavel's white, dirt-streaked face, his men were digging a grave. A big grave, big enough to hold Kevi, his brother, his old crone of a mother and the child.

He held Pavel between his hands and she was quiet, save for a constant shudder which rippled through her. When he thought of the other little girl, smashed to a pulp on those

47

bloody, bloodstained rocks, he felt sick to his stomach and wanted . . . ah, he wanted to hurt whoever had caused this thing! Not Kevi – Kevi had talked about the little nieces, of how pretty they were, how clever. Nor the old woman, for she must have panicked and jumped. But something had made the child follow . . . what was it? Why had she died, leaving the smaller girls to make their own way in the world? He had watched her in the *kosh* last night, when the children had come in from their day's play, and thought her a lovely little creature, with that swinging bell of amber hair which exactly matched her eyes. So serious she was, so responsible, though she could not be more than eight or nine! He had thought it a pity, he remembered, that she had been born in a place like this, to the life of a Caucasian female, for her beauty would go unnoticed and unremarked and she would be married with or without her consent to some cross-eyed, dirty herdsman who would beat her if she forgot to keep her eyes lowered, mate with her and give her babies – when he was not doing the same with his filthy sheep, Rudi thought vindictively – and probably bury her before she was thirty.

But this was getting him nowhere. He spoke the child's name a couple more times, then stood up and held out his hand to her.

'Come, Pavel.'

She ignored him; he thought she was unaware that he spoke, possibly unaware that he was there, even. He took a few steps away from her, then glanced back. She had not moved. Eva, having finished off the bottle of milk, was sitting in a puddle of her own making, placidly playing with some pebbles. Pavel took no more notice of her than she had of Rudi, yet he had a feeling, quite a strong one, that she was far more conscious of the baby than she appeared. Accordingly, he returned to the pair and picked Eva out of the dust, grimacing as his hands closed round her soggy person. He took three steps along the path . . . and there was Pavel, like an anxious bird-dog, staring up at the child in his arms.

This time, he hunkered down and picked her up, so that he was doubly burdened. Talking reassuringly, though he doubted that she either heard or understood, he continued down the path, skirting the *kosh*; he would not take either girl near the place which had once been home to them. Neither, he decided, would he beg a lodging for them in the *aoul*. He supposed that someone might take them in, but he felt he could do better for them than that. They were Kevi's beloved nieces, after all, and he had loved Kevi once. For the sake of the friendship that had flourished between them, he would see Kevi's little ones as well established as he could manage. If they went to someone else in the *aoul*, it would be a burden which the family might be willing to shed the moment his back was turned – girls were not highly regarded in the Muslim Caucasus – and he did not want more deaths on his conscience. So they would ride on. Somewhere someone wanted them – he knew of one place that was certainly worth a try.

Pavel lay down beneath sheepskins that night in a tent, with her little sister cuddled in her arms and Baru shivering beside them. Outside, the men talked. She listened, but understood none of it.

'You should've left them, that's what I'm saying, sir. These mountain men are like animals. The children would be no worse off left to their own devices than if the parents still lived.'

'You're wrong. Kevi came from the *aoul* we just left and he was no animal – he was as strong and intelligent as any man I ever met. But the other villagers would find two more girls a burden – that's why I've brought them with us.'

'And you'll find them a home where someone really wants 'em? Well, they're a pretty enough pair, but they're two little animals and they've had no training. All they can do is eat and sleep, and with the country in the state it's in two extra mouths to feed are no joke.'

'I know, but . . . remember that couple two days' journey from here, in that wild valley?'

'No, I can't say . . . oh, the Lazarovs! What they need is sons, not a pair of useless daughters.'

'Sons would be best, of course, but since we can't provide boys, we'll see what they say to girls. And now kick that fire out and let's get some sleep.'

The men probably did sleep, but Pavel never closed her eyes once, during the long watches of that first, loneliest, night.

Next morning, Rudi woke his charges, led them to the fire and tried to feed them, though he only succeeded with Eva, who gobbled porridge, guzzled milk and then sat in the stream and let the water gurgle over her fat tummy. Having failed to get a morsel of food into Pavel he left her by the stream, though he watched her carefully whilst appearing to ignore them both. He saw her lean down to the water and drink like the little animal his sergeant had called her, but then she sat back on the bank and let the water dry on her mouth and chin, staring, staring.

All that day he rode with Pavel on the saddle before him and Eva in her arms. She did not speak at all, either to him or the baby, but sometimes he caught her looking. Not at him, never at him, but at the soft curls on the baby's head, or at the view, or even down at the path on which the horse trod, or the grass, the dust, the pine needles.

They stopped at midday and ate coarse bread and white goat's cheese and drank water from a stream. Still Eva prattled and cooed and Pavel remained silent. But she ate a few crumbs of cheese and drank some more water. Picking her up again to put her back on the horse, he fancied she was not quite so stiff and unyielding as she had been earlier. But it might have been wishful thinking. He found that he wanted her to come out of her state of shock, and knew that he felt partly responsible for it, no matter what he might tell himself. He had been responsible for the killing of her uncle and her father before her eyes; because he had pursued them up the steep little mountain path he had as good as killed her babushka and her elder sister. No wonder the poor baby never spoke a word to him!

Looking down at her head as he rode, he noticed how very fine and silky her hair was and wondered idly why it was cut short, like a boy's. She had a boy's name — he remembered Kevi telling him long ago that she was named for Petchoren's dearest friend, who had been killed in an avalanche the year before she was born — but that was no reason, surely, to cut her hair? He decided that she had probably suffered from some illness and they had cropped her hair to strengthen her. He mused over this for some time, but providentially did not think of head lice, or he might not have held her with such comforting closeness.

That night, he wrapped the two children in the sheepskins, and the big dog, which had loped silently at the heels of his horse all day, came up to him and touched his hand with its nose. He smoothed his hand along the great head and fondled the smooth silky ears and saw the dog's tail tremble into a half-response. When the dog lay down beside the children he saw Pavel's little hand come out and curl into the long fur. He felt an enormous, disproportionate satisfaction. She was coming out of it, he was sure she was!

They were within sight of the valley where the Lazarov homestead was situated before he knew he was winning, and even then it was a small thing, so small that he would have missed it had he not been watching Pavel's every movement.

As they rode, leisurely now – for he wanted to arrive at the homestead after their midday meal but before the evening one so that he could talk with the couple before they committed themselves by sharing food – a horsefly landed on his hand, one of the big, brown-bodied, vicious ones whose bite could hurt and turn bad in an hour on a hot day like this. He had the reins looped between his fingers and the other hand was round the child. The horsefly had landed so lightly that he might easily have missed it, but before he could shake his hand or try to rub the fly off a small, stealthy finger and thumb reached out, pinched the horsefly hard, and then, with a quick, airy jerk, flung the twitching corpse down into the dust.

For a moment he was so astonished that he could only stare almost unbelievingly down at Pavel's head. Had she really done it? But he knew she had. Not only was it a movement made completely spontaneously, but it had been a movement designed to save him pain, not to help herself or her baby sister.

'Thank you,' he said, his voice low.

For a moment he thought she would ignore him, but then, for the first time since the tragedy, she spoke.

'Their bites can hurt,' she said matter-of-factly.

'But . . . you seriously mean that no one wants them? They have no mother, no father either, to love them? If you are quite sure . . . there is nothing we want more, nothing we have longed for more than children . . . and two such lovely ones . . . Pavel is a handsome lad and Eva will be a beautiful woman one day!'

51

Nyusha Lazarova clasped her hands and tears filled her large, dark eyes. Despite the fact that she lived in this fertile hollow, she still looked like the hill-women, and this salved Rudi's fear that he might have been wrong to transplant his little hill-flowers down into this valley. However, he hastened to repair an omission.

'I am sorry to have misled you, madam; Pavel is a girl also. She was named for a friend of her father's but she is a girl, nevertheless.'

'Well, that is a shame for my poor Fedor, who needs a boy's help, but it is so nice for me! Two little girls! I can sew very well, you know, and I will teach them to cook . . . oh, they will be happy here, I promise you! When they are older they can go to school . . . what name do they have? Is it permissible that they take the name Fedorovna? It would please Fedor so much . . . and it would please me, too!'

Russian women are called by their father's first name; Nyusha's suggestion meant that Pavel would be Pavel, daughter of Fedor. Rudi hesitated, then nodded quickly. It was very doubtful if Pavel had ever been bothered with a surname, but he rather thought that customs were different in the Caucasus and that Pavel would never have been referred to as Pavel Petchorenovna. This would be a new life for her, and for Eva; let it be really new, with a new name to start off with.

'Yes, that would be better than trying to cling to her old life in any way, I believe. Let them be your children in everything but birth, if that seems possible to you.'

'It seems wonderful,' Nyusha said frankly. 'And the dog? Is he yours?'

'No, he . . . she, I mean . . . belongs to the children. I think you'll have to keep her or shoot her, for she won't come with me and my men; she's made that quite clear already.'

'She's a fine dog. I dare say she'll take care of the little ones?'

'She'll guard them with her life. Now, madam, if I may I'll instruct my men to make camp. I'll stay and speak to your husband, make sure that he's as happy with the situation as you seem to be, and then we must be on our way.'

'Of course, of course . . . but you and your men must eat with us. We have an abundance of food – it's been a good season so far. The oven's lit; I was baking when you first came in. I do hope the cakes aren't burned . . .'

She fluttered about the room, a good-looking young woman probably no more than twenty-seven or eight, with a gentle expression and a plump and shapely figure. Rudi, watching her, thought — hoped — believed — that she would make his charges a better mother than most.

But since they arrived Pavel had gone back to being her little wooden self once again. Not a word, not a glance, not a sign that she was alive, or, indeed, that they were. She simply sat.

As the day wore on and life came and went in the big, comfortable kitchen, Rudi found himself watching Pavel more and more eagerly. Surely *this* would stir some reaction from her — or that — or the other? But nothing did.

When at last he got up to leave he hoped, stupidly, that she would run to him, make some sign. But there was nothing. She just sat, staring in front of her, eyes vacant, mouth at half-cock.

As a matter of form, almost, he went over to her, took her cold little hand in his and said goodbye and be a good girl, but her fingers lay like little dead things in his grasp and he turned away quickly, telling himself that it would do nothing but harm if she came out of her trance now and begged him not to go, when he had to go, could not stay. As he left he glanced at her, white-faced and staring at nothing, and felt his heart contract sharply at the horrid thought that she might just continue to sit there until she dropped dead from exhaustion and lack of food. But there was Eva; she would not desert her little sister. He scooped the baby up from the floor — she was dry and sweet-smelling now, her hair shining from its recent wash, her flesh pink and healthy.

'Goodbye, little Eva. Be a good girl, now.'

Then he was striding away from the homestead, towards his troops, and he felt young again, and in command. They would be all right, Kevi's little ones. At least he had done his best to ensure their wellbeing.

Pavel had struggled out of the nightmare which her life had become twice since the Man had brought her away, but now, once again, she was suspended in a cold nothingness, a daze in which she merely existed. Unfortunately, though, the nothingness had no power to stop her re-living the past. Over and over again she saw, clearly and horribly, her Uncle Kevi and her father die. Over and over she saw Babushka take her wild leap from the cliff, heard her voice calling to Konkordia echoing into silence. Over and over Pavel crawled into the little cave, propelling baby Eva before her, and heard that seagull shriek its last lament.

The first time the nothingness had lifted for a little she had been in her sheepskin nest, and she had recognised, with some surprise, Baru, whom she had assumed lost, gone into the void with everyone else she loved. It had been a comfort to know Baru was here, to touch her soft fur, to feel the rough warmth of the dog's wet tongue caressing her hand.

The second time, the Man had almost been bitten by a horrible horsefly; Pavel knew well how a horsefly bite could hurt, how it could swell and turn purple and scarlet and ooze yellow stuff and be a burden to one. So she had nipped it dead, and for a moment had been right back in the real world, feeling the sunshine, smelling the nice scent of hot horse, knowing that she was hungry and would like to eat.

But then the cold nothingness had returned, and it had not lifted again until this moment, when it suddenly did so and she found herself in totally strange surroundings. Curiosity made her look around her, though she managed to do so without moving her head. She was in a *kosh,* of a sort, though where was the roof? You had to look up – up – up, and there it was, nearly as far away as the sky, and what sort of a roof was that? The fire was there, but it was in a sort of pot, tamed, meekly burning, and the floor had the strangest skins she had ever seen laid out on it – coloured, striped and checked . . . no, not skins at all, but stuff, the stuff they made *burkas* out of, only *burkas* were black.

There was a table made of wood, but it had long legs so that you wondered why anyone should want a table like that indoors – at home, the tall table was outside, so that the women could stand before it pouring the maize or churning the butter. There were stools here too, but apart from one or two they were long-legged things, and they had backs . . . very odd. The windows had stuff in them so that the wind couldn't blow through, and lengths of material hung at either side, similar to the curtain made of matted sheepskins which hung above their door and was let down in very severe weather.

Pavel's eyes could slide no further, but she had the distinct

54

impression that she and Eva were not alone in this strange place. There had been a woman . . . she turned her head and saw the woman bending over a hole in the wall from which came warmth and a delicious smell. Pavel's nose twitched. The woman was lifting out a tray with cakes on it – they smelt so good! And then she turned and put the cakes down on the table, and there was a big jug with milk in it, and it was fresh milk and smelt almost as good as the cakes.

The woman glanced quickly at Pavel and then continued with her tasks. She was a very young woman – or at least she seemed so after Babushka. She wore no turban over her dark hair, though, and she had bare earlobes, bare wrists! Was she *very* poor? She was plump and her clothing was the finest Pavel had ever seen, yet she must be poor if her man could not afford even one bangle . . . Pavel's fingers touched her own small ears; from each of them hung a tiny crescent of gold, and on each wrist thin silver bangles tinkled. Even baby Eva had gold crescents in her ears, though she only had one bangle on each wrist.

The woman was pouring milk now, into two mugs, and putting cakes on to two plates. Water rushed into Pavel's mouth and she swallowed convulsively. She was hungry! She could not remember eating for ages . . . she tried to remember whether she had eaten that last morning in the *kosh*, when . . . but her mind had decided to forget all about that last morning. The door through which the sad and frightening memories had streamed seemed to have slammed shut, and she was glad of it. Something told her that she was here to live, and that was better than . . . well, better than whatever it was she could not quite remember.

Presently the woman fetched a big jug of warm water and a bowl and put the bowl down in front of the tamed fire. Then she picked Eva up and began to wash her, and Eva laughed and slapped her fat fingers in the water and splashed Pavel. It seemed natural to go and stand by the bowl, though she still said nothing. And then, when Eva was bare and clean as a new pin, the door opened and a man walked in. Pavel actually looked round and she very nearly smiled, because she thought it was the Man, but it was not, it was another. Taller, grey-haired, older. Not frightening or terrible – he smiled at her and at the woman and at Eva, and he said, 'Now who's enjoying

55

that most, I wonder?' and his voice was soft and indulgent. But it was not the Man and suddenly, piercingly, Pavel knew that the Man had gone and would not return.

The kind woman stood up and handed Eva to the new man, and then she knelt down and began to wash Pavel's filthy little face. And then a strange thing happened. Quite without meaning to, Pavel began to cry. Tears ran down her cheeks and sobs tumbled over each other in their eagerness to be out, and she choked and her chest heaved and she wept and wept.

The woman dropped the flannel back into the water and pulled Pavel into her warm and cuddly arms, close to her warm and cuddly bosom, and hugged her tight, and she murmured love-words into Pavel's ear, and she rocked her and kissed her wet cheeks and made much of her.

And Pavel cried and cried and felt all the coldness dripping away with the tears and all the shock and uncertainty following it. She nestled close to the woman's lovely, sweet-smelling body and when they offered her milk and cakes she ate and drank and then, quite without meaning to again, she slid down further on the woman's cushiony lap and fell fast asleep.

# CHAPTER FOUR

'If you ask me, there's a storm brewing, Dave.' Nibby, in the bows of David's beloved boat, cast a knowing look at the piled-up clouds on the horizon. 'D'you think we ought to leave it for today? We could go tomorrow, or the day after. You don't leave until Tuesday, do you?'

'No, but we'd better go today,' David said, eyeing the clouds calculatingly. 'Tomorrow I'm taking Alice over to the Mount-joys', or rather I'm going with her, because I promised I would. She's not at all bad for a little kid, but I didn't want her coming along with us today and there was only one way out of it that I could see. Then Sunday it'll be church in the morning, tea with Grandma in the afternoon, and dinner at night with the parents as a treat, because of going back to school next week. Monday I've got to pick up my new uniform blazer, my overcoat and two pairs of longs in the morning, and in the afternoon Father said he wanted me to pop down to the yard. So it's now or never, because you know what seals are — once they're full-grown they're shy of people.'

The previous day, when he had been pottering about alone in his boat with a whole long, sunny day in front of him, he had sailed out to Point of Ayr because he had some crab pots down and wanted to see if he had caught anything. As it chanced, on his way home again at low tide he had come across a group of seals, hauled out on a sandbank. Enchanting creatures, they had blinked curiously at him as he sailed past, big, mild eyes following his progress with lazy interest. And then two of the youngsters had slid leisurely into the water and followed him, bobbing along in his wake, and when he had shortened sail and brought her head round to have a better look the seals had come really close, their delightful muzzles with their slit nostrils snorting anxiously yet at the same time their necks at

57

full stretch to see him better, gentle, friendly curiosity in every movement of their streamlined bodies.

David's imagination had been fired. Not only did he want Nibby to see the colony, he wanted to have someone with him to take care of the boat whilst he slipped into the water and swam with the animals. Last night he had daydreamed, in the way boys will, of an experience which would end up with him forming a deep and lasting friendship with at least one member of the group. He would swim with the seals and one of them would become attached to him, would remember him, would come whenever he whistled. The dream grew wilder and more satisfactory: the seal would follow him up to the house when he moored his boat; he would teach it to give three barks outside his window when it wanted to play. Eventually, of course, it would follow the ship on which he embarked to sail to . . . to America, and the ship would be wrecked and his seal would rescue him, carry him to a desert island, fish for him and sniff out a source of fresh water in the deep jungly undergrowth. Eventually it would sight and bring to his aid a ship which would take both of them home to Carmel Hall and, naturally, fame and fortune.

So now, looking at the dark clouds and listening to the wind shrilling in the rigging of the *Delight*, David was loth to abandon both his plan and one of the most satisfying fantasies he had had for ages. After all, they would be safe enough, since they would not sail out of the estuary or even as far as Point of Ayr. The seal colony was well inside the area of Mostyn Bank, and as the tide was at the half they would be within easy reach of land throughout their little voyage.

'I think we might as well go,' he urged, when Nibby still looked doubtful. 'The storm probably won't strike for an hour, and by then we can have reached the Bank and be home, if we want to. And anyway, we haven't got to go all the way back home if the weather turns nasty; we can moor in any sheltered inlet.'

'Yes, all right, if it's your last chance,' Nibby agreed, and came over to help him hoist the sail and, as soon as it caught the wind, to turn the *Delight*'s head out to sea.

They soon saw, however, that they had underestimated the speed with which the storm would strike. The wind suddenly began to increase and the *Delight*, speeding along with the sail taut and full as a balloon, began to cover the distance to Mostyn Bank incredibly quickly.

'We'll be there sooner than I thought,' David yelled presently above the roar of the wind in the sail and the louder roar of the water against the hull. 'What are we doing, do you reckon? Ten knots?'

'A hundred miles an hour, I shouldn't wonder,' Nibby bawled, far less nautically minded than his friend. 'We'll be past before we know it; shall we put a reef in the sail?'

'Yes, perhaps we should,' David shouted back. 'I say, look at that sky!'

The clouds gathering on the horizon had looked dark, but now they were overhead, and black, with yellowy-grey edges. Ominous. David had been at the tiller, but now he got up and began to edge his way nearer the mains'l whilst still keeping the tiller more or less in the right position with one knee.

It was not a good moment to try to reef the sail, but in the event it proved unnecessary. Nibby suddenly gasped and pointed ahead, raising his voice to a shriek.

'Look what's coming!'

Many times David had seen a squall hit the water, but this was different. The water had been rough before, but now it looked as if it had been stirred by a giant and invisible hand. And with the squall came the rain. They saw it before it reached them, sheeting down and almost horizontal. As the rain hit them, the wind wrenched viciously at the puffed sail and for a second, perhaps, it strained fatter-cheeked than ever. Then it tore with a crack like a pistol shot and one half flung itself crazily round the mast whilst the other, borne on the gale, flapped off into the darkness like some nightmare seabird. Both boys were soaked to the skin in seconds and David's hands, covered in rope burns, clutched helplessly at his friend, dragging him down into the comparative quiet of the well.

'We're going as fast as ever, even without the sail,' he shouted, when they were crouched side by side in the stern. 'I think the rudder's gone, or the tiller's broken . . . it just waggles, there's no resistance.'

'Can't we get her head round, turn her for the bank, and throw ourselves ashore?' Nibby shouted back. 'We're being carried straight out to sea, Dave . . . I don't like the look of it.'

'Chuck out the anchor . . .' David began, and then his words were cut off by a clap of thunder so enormous that it dwarfed even the roar of wind and water. A flash of lightning followed so close on its heels that they knew the storm was right overhead. It illumined everything for the briefest of seconds – the sandbanks raging past, the angry white-tipped waves, the smallness of their cockleshell craft.

Nibby heaved the anchor overboard but it made not the slightest difference to their onward rush. But when he grabbed the tiller he felt a tug and knew that whatever had rendered it useless did so no longer – there was a chance, if they could only get her head round!

Together they fought the tiller, fought for control, no longer caring whether they veered to left or right so long as they did veer, did slow and stop with their nose buried in a sandbank somewhere. The walk ashore might be a long one and their punishment for losing the boat and putting themselves in such danger terrible, but it was preferable to a watery grave. It occurred to neither of them that the tide was on the turn and that, in conditions like these, even had they been able to get out of the channel and on to one of the sandbanks they would have been unlikely to have struggled safely ashore before the returning tide roared up over them.

Crouching as far below the level of the hull as they could, the boys almost stopped thinking rationally. All they could do was hang on to the tiller and pray for deliverance. David had not given the seals a thought since the storm hit them – certainly he never considered a seal-rescue. All he longed for was a spit of sand longer than the rest upon which the *Delight* could capsize, thus, as he thought, saving their lives.

Overhead the thunder bellowed, splitting the skies apart with a sound like the knell of doom. Lightning illumined the scene again, just as, for the first time, the children felt the lift of a big wave. They were at the mouth of the estuary, with nothing between them and the open sea, and on a night like this they would soon be truly lost. Once they got into the Liverpool roads there would be no land to be cast up on until they reached Ireland!

David turned to scream this information to Nibby just as Nibby began to tell him the same thing, but at that moment the *Delight* began to climb another big wave and David looked down and saw, directly beneath him as the boat heeled, the black, foam-speckled wickedness of that storm-racked sea. For the first time in his thirteen years he found himself looking directly into the throat of death, for in that sea neither he nor Nibby would stand a chance. They would be sucked down and smothered, crushed by the sheer weight of water before they could even begin to use their swimming skills.

And then it seemed to David that they were not travelling quite so fast nor so furiously and that the *Delight*, left to her own devices, was climbing the waves merrily and plunging lightheartedly down the smooth slippery combers into the troughs. The tide had turned! If they kept their heads all might not be lost!

'Nibs . . . leave the tiller; let her have her head. The tide's turned – if we're lucky it'll carry us back! Ah, she's a good little boat, isn't she?'

Even through the dark, David saw Nibby nod and knew his friend was as conscious as he of the *Delight*'s marvellous performance as she curtsied, bounded, and turned. With delightful insouciance, she seemed to decide to ignore the roaring wind and the storm and she followed her head round until they were pretty sure they were actually heading back up the estuary once more.

David was gabbling two prayers simultaneously in his mind – one a prayer for deliverance and the other a paean of thankfulness for safety-so-far – when he heard another noise . . . or perhaps not so much another noise as a change in the existing tumult. Surf! He lifted his head to gaze over the side of the boat and a great, curling sea took him full in the face, making him gasp and splutter and grasp Nibby's bony arm. But even then, with the stinging, streaming water in his eyes and the bitterness of it rasping his throat, he saw what he was looking for.

The shore! God knew where it was or how they had come to be heading for it, but there was land no more than ten or a dozen yards away and the *Delight* was bearing down on it like a steam train heading for a tunnel.

They were more hurled than cast ashore, but when the boat ploughed into the beach and they found themselves flying through the air the last thought in either mind was that they would strike hard sand – and when they did so, not all the bruises and abrasions of the impact could lessen their incredulous joy. Safe! Wet, battered and exhausted, but alive! Together they crept further up the beach and watched as the poor *Delight* was first dragged back by a wave and then hurled ashore once more, until David got up sufficient courage to totter down to the water's edge, grab a trailing rope and, with Nibby's help, haul her up as far as their combined strength would take her.

And then for a moment they just sank down on the hard sand and panted, until Nibby turned to David and spoke, his voice oddly hoarse and croaking.

'Reckon I know where we are.'

'Where?'

'Hilbury island. Stands to reason.' A brilliant flash of lightning lit up the scene and he nudged David's shoulder. 'Look behind you!'

In the next flash of lightning, David looked, and saw that Nibby was right. They were not, as he had supposed, on a sandbank, for no sandbank bears a church on its crest as this one did. He scrambled to his feet, then nearly sank down again, so loudly and painfully did his protesting knee-joints crack.

'By George, you're right! If it was low tide we could get right ashore at West Kirby but even now we're safer than I thought – we can shelter in the church!'

'What about the boat?' Nibby said, regarding their prized possession with fondness for all the trouble she had led them into. 'The tide's only just turned – is she high enough?'

'Probably . . . but we'll drag her a bit further if you think we ought.'

They dragged her further and it nearly killed them; then they staggered and limped and tottered up to the church. The wooden doors were swollen and stiff, but they managed to force them open and went inside. They could not shut the doors again, but even so the quiet after the storm seemed magical to them both. A wooden pew each made the softest, most comfortable bed in the world. Within two minutes of forcing open the doors and collapsing on to the pews, both boys were asleep.

Outside the storm roared still, reaching a climax unguessed at by either boy, since the stout stone walls kept out all but the whine of the wind and the rumble of thunder. Even when hailstones bounced off the slates and cracked against the windows, neither David nor Nibby moved a muscle, except to creep nearer one another for warmth. They simply slept and slept.

They awoke because dawn was breaking, because they were hungry and cold, and because they had slept heavily and in one position for more than twelve hours. They awoke cross.

'Damn you, Nibs, get your bloody great feet off my shins,' David muttered, trying to curl round and go back to sleep once more.

'Damn you, too,' Nibs said, aggrieved. 'If my feet are on your shins, where do you suppose your feet are?'

'Round my neck, by the way I feel.' David knuckled his eyes and sat up grudgingly. 'Corks, the door's still open. I suppose we forgot to shut it. Give it a shove, there's a good fellow – it was the cold that woke me, I suppose.'

'Give it a shove yourself. Anyway it won't shut; it wouldn't last night – or can't you remember last night?'

'I'm trying very hard not to remember it. Go on, shove it, you're nearer than I am. Who got us into this mess, anyhow?'

Nibby laughed bitterly but did not move nearer the door. 'You did; who else?'

'Me? Why, if it wasn't for me you'd have gone on tugging at that tiller and keeping her head to the waves and we'd be fathoms deep by now, us and the *Delight*.'

'Oh, balls! I wanted to go home when I saw the storm coming – it was you who insisted that we try to see the seals. Still, no point in quarrelling; I wonder what time it is?'

'Don't know, my watch has stopped.' David sighed and began to stretch, then hastily lowered his arms to his sides, wincing. 'Dear God, I hurt all over. I say, I'm starving! I wonder what state the tide's at? If it's gone down far enough we could walk over to West Kirby and beg some breakfast.'

'It's still the middle of the night,' Nibby said, trying to curl back on to the pew again. 'If we can sleep for another hour or two it'll be morning proper. Come on, lie down; we might as well get warm again.'

'It's no use, I can't settle,' David announced. He got stiffly to his feet, groaning and waving his arms feebly to restore the circulation, then stomped off towards the open door. He gave it a peevish kick but then he looked outside and saw that day had actually come, in a weird, yellowy light, but that the storm was still raging. It was clear that only an idiot would attempt to reach West Kirby in these conditions. He turned his head to inform Nibby of these salient points, then looked out to sea.

'It is daytime – it's just very overcast, and . . . I say, come here! Look at that!'

Out to sea, just at the mouth of the estuary, was a large ship. She must have been seeking the shelter of the land, David supposed, for otherwise why would she come so close inshore? There was a lighthouse at Point of Ayr, another at Hoylake, so she could not, surely, have missed the fact that land was near?

He was still wondering when Nibby joined him, boots in one hand, the other clutching the small of his back. He looked aggrieved, but perked up when he saw the ship.

'I say, what's she doing there? Looks as though she's drifting!'

She was; apparently unable to help herself, she was simply being carried, by tide, current and wind, closer and closer to the treacherous shallow waters which surrounded the coast, closer to the sandbanks and shoals which are a hazard at all river mouths. Even as they watched they saw her strike, saw the shudder which ran from stem to stern as her onward momentum was abruptly terminated. Both boys gasped. Though they could do nothing, though they were too far away for any but an onlooker's role, they burst out of the church porch and ran as fast as they could to the shore. The ship was plainly hard hit, yet she was only on the edge of the bank, with deep water all but under her keel . . . David found himself shouting 'Back off, back off!' as though the captain of the stricken vessel would not have tried that for himself, had it been possible.

The storm was clearly abating as day drew on, but even so the waves were so high that at times the two boys lost sight of the ship altogether. Then a trough would show her, still stranded but lower than ever in the water, the angle at which she lay more acute. It was in one of these troughs that David recognised her.

'Nibs, it's the *Royal Gold*! One of ours – the one we sailed to Liverpool on!'

'It can't be — you can't recognise her in this,' Nibby protested. 'Though now you've said it, I believe you're right,' he
added after a long, frowning look. 'I hope you're wrong, but if
you're not . . .'

He stopped short. Some freak of the wind had brought
sounds to them for the first time: the deep, grinding crunch as
the doomed vessel was driven further on to the sand; then the
drag and shriek as she was dragged off again; and above it all,
faint as seagulls' cries, the screams of those aboard as she
suddenly broke free from the bank and was driven by the wind
out into the deep once more.

'She'll be all right! They shouted because of the shock of the
jerk, I expect,' David said, turning thankfully to his friend.
'She'll put out a sea anchor now and ride the rest of the
storm . . .'

'No. Look.'

At Nibby's words David turned and peered once more out
to sea. And saw the last throes of his father's ship as she sank
with incredible suddenness into the raging, storm-tossed ocean.


'There's to be an investigation.' Alyn Thomas put his paper
down on the breakfast table, took off his reading glasses and
laid them beside his plate. He sighed, then pushed his cup
towards his wife. 'Any more coffee in the pot?'

'An investigation?' Megan poured coffee into the cup, picked
up the milk jug and added hot milk, and pushed the cup back
towards her husband. 'Is that a good thing or a bad one? And
what will they investigate, anyway? Apart from David and
Hawke's lad, no one saw the ship go down, there were hardly
any survivors . . . and they were all passengers except for a
couple of ratings . . . so who will they question? I don't see the
point, because who can say whose fault it was, now? You built
a wonderful ship, which broke the record for the Liverpool to
New York crossing on her maiden voyage, and that means she
had a good captain and crew. Surely one can't investigate a
storm, and it was clearly the storm which caused the tragedy. I
asked David and he said the lights were flashing away at Point
of Ayr and Hoylake, so the ship could hardly have been
ignorant of her position.'

'I said an investigation, Meggie, not a fault-finding exercise.
It's always necessary for a tribunal to do its best to discover the

cause of a new ship's going down, especially one with such a record as the *Royal Gold* had made in her short existence. And let's not forget those illustrious passengers who lost their lives. I could wish that kinema stars and members of parliament had not wished to travel aboard our ship, but at the time no one had any hesitation in recommending her. She was a beautiful creature, the *Royal Gold*, and her ending was all the more tragic because of it.'

'The film star was a pretty young thing,' Megan said, refilling her own coffee cup. 'I cried when I heard she was amongst the missing, though I never met her. And John Jackson was an honest man, which you can't say of all politicians. I suppose you're right – I suppose they must do their best to find out why she went down. But it was the storm . . . why, we nearly lost our Davie that night, and he and Nibby were in the estuary, not out at sea!'

'It didn't do the *Delight* much good, either,' Alyn remarked, sipping coffee. 'I was going to have her repaired anyway, but now I think I'll have an engine fitted as well. Just think, Meggie, if they'd had even a small engine aboard they could probably have got themselves out of trouble as soon as they realised a storm was blowing up.'

Megan groaned, shaking her head indulgently at her husband.

'You're going to have it repaired, when I felt for weeks that all I wanted was to see it cut up for firewood? I'm sure I'd feel safer knowing our Davie was on dry land. Why does he fret after a boat so? Ned never had one, and never wanted one, either.'

'I've told you before, sweetheart, and I'll tell you again; the boy's safer in a boat than he would be trekking across the sands, with the tide liable to come roaring in when he's far out of reach of dry land, peering at a seabird's eggs or digging for bait or some such thing.'

'Yes, I suppose. Or when there's mist and you can't tell which way you've turned. I always used to worry that he might turn out to sea and think he was making for the shore,' Megan admitted. 'Like in the Kingsley poem, you know: *The rolling mist came down and hid the land: and never home came she.*'

'Yes, that's right,' Alyn said shortly. No man born and bred on Deeside had not had the Kingsley poem dinned into him from the age of five onward. 'I wonder if they'll want the boys to appear before the tribunal? If so, we'll have to get Davie home from school for a few days.'

'Oh, I shouldn't think so. After all, what could they see from Hilbury? They're only quite little boys, after all.'

'I think she was drifting when she struck, sir – the way she hit the bank was all wrong for a ship under way. She drove on to the bank almost sideways, and then the waves were so violent and the wind so strong that she was just lifted off again. I . . . I thought she'd be all right once she got deep water under her. I turned to Ni – to my friend John Hawke and said as much, and he said to look again, so I did. And she was going down. As quick as that! It happened in seconds . . . no one could have done a thing, even if they'd been nearer than we were.'

David, telling the story for the umpteenth time, this time to the tribunal, remembered that moment, as he would remember it for the rest of his life. The screams . . . the way he and Nibby had charged into the sea, knowing it was pointless yet unable to hear those cries without some response . . . the bodies they had seen, briefly, bobbing in the immense waves. Telling his story he could feel again the harshness of the wind on his cheek, the way the surf had crashed and surged around him, scalding his skin with its burden of stirred-up sand, so that he and Nibby had looked like burn-victims for days afterwards. He remembered the woman who had been washed up on Hilbury, long pale hair floating on the surface of the water, white limbs, the rags of her dress, and when they turned her over . . . His mind shuddered away from the recollection of that drowned face.

'So you think the ship had already struck when you first caught sight of her? Is that it?'

The stern, elderly face above his was trying, David thought, to be fair. But he, in his turn, had to be honest, tell what he believed to be the truth.

'I don't really know, sir. I didn't think of that. I could see she wasn't answering to her helm, but I didn't wonder why . . . there wasn't time. It all happened very quickly and I'd never seen a ship in trouble before, far less one which was about to go down. I suppose she could have been perfectly all right, and her master may have brought her head round for some reason that wasn't clear to us . . . but it looked as though she was drifting. I've wondered, since, whether she misread the signals from Point of Ayr and Hoylake and believed herself to be somewhere else, because the waves were so high and the night so dark.'

The tribunal made no comment this time, or at least not to David. Elderly mouths got closer to elderly ears and there was a refined buzz of whispering, but at the end of it they said nothing, only dismissed him and called John Hawke.

Nibby was nervous, showing the whites of his eyes as he answered in a voice which creaked and squeaked. In addition, his accent got thicker and thicker until by the time the tribunal had heard half his story it was almost impossible to understand him.

'And did you think the ship was drifting when she struck?'

A thin old man, white-haired, refined, with pince-nez glasses and eyes that blinked a lot.

'Yessir! If David says . . .'

'No, my boy, we're not interested in what your friend said any more; we want to hear your side of the story.'

But Nibby could tell them very little. He had seen the ship, watched as she was driven on to the sand, had been watching when she suddenly sank. But as to *why* . . . It was clear he had not previously asked himself why the accident had occurred because to him the answer had seemed so obvious. The storm. No vessel could stand against such a storm. But these old men with their clever faces and fancy voices seemed to want more of him than he could give, and it frightened and confused him. By the time he had given his evidence he was as white as a sheet and looking as guilty as though he had personally engineered the destruction of the *Royal Gold*. Leaving the assembly rooms where the tribunal had been held, Nibby was sick into a bed of daffodils. Not all the reassurance in the world would be enough to convince him that he had been believed and had behaved just as he ought.

When the Thomas family heard who was also giving evidence they had been puzzled, at first, by one particular name. Blydden Evans. He must have been watching when the ship went down, Alyn hazarded, because he was not on the list of those saved, but this proved not to be the case. Blydden, it transpired, had been employed for a short time as a carpenter by the Thomas yard. When the *Royal Gold* was completed his employment had been terminated, not with any ill-feeling on either side but simply because the intricate work for which he had become known was only needed occasionally in a ship-yard. When he took the stand it was seen that he was a big, reliable-looking man with a sad, jowly face and shoulders so broad and muscular that they made the rest of his body look puny by comparison.

'There was a lot against her, when she was abuilding,' he said in answer to a question about the ship's construction. 'Too big for the yard, some reckoned, and the water that high up the estuary too shallow to take her draught. As all know, she went aground within two miles of the yard on her voyage round to the docks . . . top-'eavy, some reckoned. She was damaged, of course.'

After that there was a lot more in similar vein and not just from Blydden Evans. The men who had sailed her down the channel and out to sea on the occasion of the accident, people in the crowd, men who had been employed by the Thomas yard ten, a dozen years earlier, all pressed forward to give their opinion. And they were listened to as gravely and courteously as though what they said had some bearing on the case.

'The hull was built to a new design . . . keel an' all,' one of the men said. 'It was that caused trouble on her maiden voyage, more than the pilot falling sick.'

'I allus thought there were something strange about her screw,' another muttered darkly. 'Not the usual position, and when it was in motion it had an odd turn to it. I allus thought that were strange.'

The Thomases' own shipwrights, however, were behind their boss and his yard and his ship to a man. They said that the *Royal Gold*, though of a newer and more practical design, had nevertheless been not only absolutely safe but absolutely seaworthy and as fast and reliable as could be – had she not broken all the records on her maiden voyage? Her initial grounding in shoal water was nothing out of the ordinary, now that the channel was so rapidly silting up, but the damage had been slight and speedily repaired. The ship had most certainly not been top-heavy; she had been as near perfect as made no difference; her loss had been a tragic accident and the elements alone were to blame.

When at last the tribunal's verdict was delivered it exonerated the Thomas family, the captain and crew and the owners completely. It was a freak accident, a tragedy which could have happened to any craft caught in the Liverpool roads on that particular night.

Leaving the assembly rooms after the verdict, hurrying along with Nibby at his side, David rejoiced that justice had prevailed.

'It's all over and now everyone knows the ship was a good one, built by good men, and our yard will go on and produce even better vessels,' he said happily to his attentive friend. 'What's more, I'm going to help design 'em. Dad says I can go to university to learn how, and to do research on marine engines. I wasn't sure what I wanted to do, but one thing I *do* know – I want to show all those mean-spirited people who tried to make things look black for our yard that we can build a better ship yet!'

'We'll be rich men, you and me,' Nibby said, poking David in the ribs with a sharp elbow. 'I'll take a berth on your luxury liners and you can ride in my Rolls-Royce – only since I'll invent it and build it it'll be called a something Hawke instead, I suppose, or a Hawke something.'

'It's a date! I say, Dad's having the *Delight* mended, but I'm not to keep her, because he's getting me a bigger one, with a cabin fit for two or even three people. He says if we work hard at it, we can sail over to Ireland next summer – are you on?'

'With your dad? That would be great! Count me in!'

'OK, I will. Coming up to the yard now? Dad's having a celebration – everyone's coming, even the men. There'll be champagne – we can have a sip or two, since we're nearly men – and those little biscuity things with scraps perched on 'em, and no end of stuff they've been making up at the house. Oh, and a huge cake with lots of candles and writing on it. Maud's doing it – she said she'd write "Without a stain", or something like that, to show the yard was completely exonerated. Gosh, I'm relieved!'

The boys went happily on their way, for they had not yet read the newspapers.

*

'When are you going back to school, Davie? I suppose you'll have to go, even though it means leaving us all alone? Mother's wonderful, but she's so . . . so *stricken* that she isn't much help to us, and all the girls do is cry and hang on each other's shoulders. You know what girls can be like.'

Alice and David were sitting on the low stone coping which surrounded the terrace, looking, David thought, like a couple of young crows in their black clothing. It was two days since their father's funeral and two years since the wreck of the *Royal Gold* which had, indirectly, brought about Alyn Thomas's death.

'I wish I *could* stay . . . well, I wish I could in a way, but Mother said it was Dad's most earnest wish that I should go on with my education,' David said, and felt a prig for saying it. 'The men have been marvellous, Mother says, but Ned told me, privately you know, when Mother was out of earshot, that things are in a bad state down there. No orders, men being laid off, and of course the channel silting up like billyo and no one willing to lend us money to hire dredging equipment.'

'Ever since Father's first stroke things have been awful,' Alice said mournfully. She pushed her hair back behind her ears in a familiar gesture and then, remembering, pulled it forward again. It was easier to hide red eyes and tearstained cheeks by letting your hair swing down across your face, David realised, looking at her with affection. She was a darling, trying so hard to help everyone, but there was very little anyone could do.

'Yes. At first, you know, in spite of everything, I thought we'd win through. Father's reputation was so terrific – everyone admired him and knew he was quite capable of picking the yard up by its bootlaces, so to speak, and making things hum again. But the heart seemed to go out of him when he realised what had happened, and then he had the stroke . . . Ned's a fine bloke but not half the man Dad was.'

'I still don't really understand what went wrong,' Alice admitted, biting at a lock of hair she had twined around her mouth. 'The tribunal said it was just the weather; they cleared the yard and the master and the owners of any comp – com – oh, of any blame. Why, we had the party, do you remember? It was so lovely, and we had champagne and wore our best dresses. And then just in a moment it had all changed, and Father was grim and Mother cried . . . and I didn't understand and I still don't.'

'My dear idiot, it wasn't the tribunal, it was the others – trial by journalist, Father called it, when he read the papers next day. He thought it would all blow over, though – that it was just one paper which had got hold of the wrong end of the stick. When he realised it was most of them – and that it was deliberate, what's more – it did change him. I think he stopped liking people, or trusting them.'

'I know everyone said it was the newspapers, but I read them, Davie, and I couldn't see what was so awful. They reported all the lies and the rumours, I'll grant you. But they reported other things too, and they never said Father or the yard was responsible for the *Royal Gold*'s going down – they even said it was a good ship! In fact the thing they said most often was only that the channel was silting up, which we all knew was true, and that the same thing would happen again if the channel wasn't cleared, which was true too.'

'Yes, of course it was true; but you can tell the truth in such a way that it's worse than the worst sort of lies,' David said, exasperated by his sister's guileless view of what had been a smear campaign by unscrupulous sensationmongers. He did not know who had been behind it – he supposed he would never know – but you'd have had to be awfully stupid not to notice how well the two yards nearest them were doing, or how very quiet the owners of those yards had kept over the past couple of years. 'Newspapers are quite canny about the law of libel; it was the *way* the message was put over that did for the yard. Lots of space for people like Bleddyn Evans, about two lines for old Hughes, who'd been with our yard for the best part of half a century. And then every time they drew attention to the channel's silting up they said it was impossible for a yard, no matter how excellent, to build ships where there was no draught to launch them . . . that damage done under such conditions can never be properly assessed . . . see?'

'Yes, I suppose so. Only I don't see why they tried to harm Father – he never hurt anyone, did he, Davie?'

David had to turn away and gaze out over the estuary to hide the sudden rush of tears to his eyes. He got by most of the time because he simply could not believe that his father was not still around. When he was at the yard, his father was up at the house; when he was at the house, his father was at work in the yard. On the shore he was in the gardens, in the gardens, on the shore. His presence was still everywhere, his height, his grin, his accent with its touch of Wales and the slight Scouse overtones acquired from working constantly amongst Liverpudlians. David, seeing the sands suddenly blur, had to remind himself very fiercely indeed that fellows of over fifteen did not cry before he could blink the tears back where they belonged and face his sister once more.

'No, old girl, Father never did hurt anyone. He had lots of friends who loved him, and they'll stand by us, you see. Mother's hard hit now – it's worse for her than any of us – but she'll come round. Before you know it, things will be back to normal . . . or as normal as they can be without Dad.'

As normal as they could be without normality, that meant. As normal as an abnormal world, because Carmel Hall without Dad was an empty shell and every time he reminded himself that Dad really was gone, and for good, David felt like the snail that had once been in that shell – naked, cold, infinitely vulnerable.

'But Davie, I heard Mother talking to Ned, and they were saying they'd have to sell the Hall. If they sell Carmel, where will we go? I couldn't live anywhere else!'

'Sell Carmel? Oh, no, Alice, they wouldn't do that! Dad used to say that Thomases had lived at Carmel for two hundred years. We couldn't possibly sell up! Mark my words, they'll find a way out which will let us stay here. Mark my words!'

Nibby was going fishing. Since it seemed as though the entire world was about to collapse round his ears he had made himself some bread and cheese, put his bait tin and a bottle of ginger beer into a knapsack, picked up his rod and headed for the estuary.

It would have been a perfect spring day, he told himself gloomily, if he had been able to appreciate the warm sunshine, the blue sky, and the birds singing overhead. The young green of the leaves spoke of the summer to come and despite his misery Nibby's step was light as he moved quietly down through the budding woodlands towards the distant streak of sand and sea. What a day, and David not here to share it! He tried to push out of his mind the suspicion that he and David might never share things again, but it was there, the spectre at the feast, spoiling the walk through the trees as it would presently, no doubt, ruin the fishing.

Because he was thinking instead of watching where he trod he very nearly stepped on Alice. She, silly female, just went on staring up at the blue sky and the dappling leaves overhead, instead of cursing him and moving, the way any sensible girl would have done.

'Oh! Sorry. I didn't see you lying there,' he began gruffly, and then he saw that Alice had been crying – in fact was still crying. Tears were making snail-tracks down her face, which was very dirty, and her mouth was pulled so far down at the corners that she looked quite comical. He poked her with one foot, embarrassed and annoyed because he felt silly.

'What's the matter? People who want to lie and howl usually find somewhere private, not right in the middle of a wood.'

Alice sniffed and said stiffly, 'The wood *is* private – or it was until *you* came along,' and the tartness in her tone cheered him up a bit. It sounded as though she had finished crying, even if her eyes were still at it.

'You're on the footpath; that isn't private. And you shouldn't lie on your back to cry, you should lie on your front. Then, if someone comes by, they can pretend not to know you're howling and you can pretend you've not seen them.'

Alice sat up. She scrubbed fiercely at her eyes and then glared at Nibby.

'Don't be so *stupid*! Everyone who knows about us must know we're all crying, every one of us, from little Michael to Mother. Wouldn't *you* cry, if you were losing your home?'

Nibby scuffed his boots in last year's beech mast. Women! Logic was unknown to them.

'I am, aren't I? And I'm not crying . . . lads don't.'

At once Alice was on her feet, her dirty little face anxious, her red-rimmed eyes remorseful.

'Oh, Nibs, I am a fool . . . and wicked! I never thought – of course if we leave you'll have to go as well. Oh, I am sorry! I try very hard not to be selfish, and to think of others, but in my heart I can't believe that anyone else loves Carmel as I do.'

'For me it's more than Carmel,' Nibby reminded her. 'It's Dave. And the rest of you. Oh, and the estuary, the boat, everything.'

'Oh, *poor* Nibby! What'll you and Mr Hawke do, then? Where will you go?'

'Well, Dad doesn't reckon he'll get another job chauffeuring; says there was only one place like this and this was it. He reckons we'll go to Manchester or Birmingham, to the car factories.'

'Gosh, that really is dreadful. Mother won't move far from here, she says. It's cheaper living in the country, thank goodness, and Ned will be the one who lives in a city and makes some money. Actually, I believe there are things called annuities and shares and certificates which let you do things like school . . . they pay the fees, I suppose . . . and college and so on – it's just that they can't run huge houses like Carmel, and feed a great tribe like us.'

'I expect your mother will get a lot of money for the Hall, with the grounds and all,' Nibby said. 'I dare say you'll go somewhere nice . . . a farmhouse, perhaps. It'll be better than a flat in Birmingham, at any rate. Look, it's a grand day – do you want to come fishing? If you'd like it, we could use the boat. Dave said I could, only I don't much like going out alone in it.'

Alice's face lit up and she smiled for the first time since he had found her.

'I would like to fish; thanks very much, Nibby. But I don't have a rod or bait or anything.'

'That's all right, you can borrow my stuff,' Nibby said grandly. 'You can have a bit of my bread and cheese, too, and a pull at my beer.'

'You're kind,' Alice decided, skipping along beside him as Nibby continued his descent through the woodland. 'When I write to David I'll tell him how kind you've been. Tell you what, leave me your new address and I'll write to you as well.'

'Will you?' Nibby had never set much store by letters but now he found himself absurdly pleased that she had made the offer. 'That 'ud be grand. I wouldn't feel so far away if you wrote.'

'Well, you'd have to write as well, or I'd get bored and not keep it up,' Alice said seriously. 'Don't forget, if you get your new address first you write first, but if we go first, I'll write to you here.'

'Or I could always get you care of the yard, I suppose?' Nibby said with some delicacy. The two looked solemnly at each other.

'For a bit; I don't know how long, though,' Alice admitted. 'Do you know, I'm ever so glad I'm only twelve. I think I'd die if I was grown up and had to deal with all these things.'

'You couldn't speak a truer word,' Nibby vowed fervently. Never had the spectre of adulthood raised an uglier head. 'Come on then, let's see who can reach the jetty first!'

It was not a farmhouse, but neither was it a flat – nor a tiny terraced house, which threat had made Lydia, now a young lady of thirteen with bobbed hair and a shrill voice, afraid, she said, to face her friends. It was a neat, semi-detached Victorian villa, set in a row of similar villas, each with its own small, well kept garden with gravelled path, a view of the estuary – two miles distant – and net curtains at every window so that passers-by could not leer at the Dresden china on the mantel or the daughter of the house as she sewed a fine seam.

Not, Alice reflected, sitting in the small drawing-room and irritably stabbing her darning needle into the heel of a practically footless stocking, that this could be described as sewing finely – far from it. It was a loathsome task performed with reluctance and with absolutely no skill whatsoever. She regarded her index finger, the bloodied proof of her incompetence, sourly for a moment. Why could she not darn? Why had she never been taught something so essential to female life? Once, Nurse or Gill had darned stockings, though more often than not when a stocking sprang a huge hole like this one it had been abandoned to the bin. Now she must do it – and not only for herself but for Julia, Sara and Michael too, though Michael did wear socks and not stockings.

When Mother had first broached the prospect of being poor Alice knew she had not been the only one to think it rather romantic, to imagine that they would eat shrimps with thick slices of bread and butter rather than trout hollandaise, that they would wear blue serge coats and felt hats for school instead of maroon wool and straw. They had envisaged the entire family holding out their chilly fingers to warm at a driftwood fire, instead of being cosy before brightly burning coal. They had not imagined this down-to-earth business of mending your own stockings, making your own beds and having to put up with an endless succession of meals cooked by a fifteen-year-old half-wit, who boiled cabbage slugs and all and made bread-and-butter pudding every day for a week because she had not the ingenuity – or the skill – to produce anything different.

By the end of the first month any romantic glow that might have existed had worn off. Mother was pale and exhausted, apt to fall into a chair with her bright hair dangling in rats' tails instead of in its usual sunny cluster of curls and announce that she had done all she could for one day and would one of them kindly see to Michael?

Lydia was not good in adversity. She sulked and pouted and shut herself in her bedroom – which was also Alice's – and only ate the nicer food, which meant that she lost weight and worried Mother. Julia and Sara were much better, possibly because, at seven and eight, their lives were really lived mainly in their imaginations still. They giggled a lot, and played weird games and liked making toffee in the kitchen with Gladys on rainy days and walking, arms round each other's waists, in the dusty little municipal park when it was sunny. They did not even complain much about the food, because they had transferred their affection from Gill to Gladys without a qualm, faithless pair; but Alice was astute enough to realise that their affection for servants was a shallow thing, easily given, and was grateful for Gladys's sake because Gladys needed affection. She was an orphan, plain but agreeable, and if only she had been able to cook Alice would probably have got on very well with her; but the trouble was that Gladys had been told she could cook and she believed it. So when Megan Thomas tried, very kindly and tactfully, to show her how to make a gooseberry tart with soft gooseberries in it and not marbles, she resented the implied criticism and said 'Yes, ma'am, yes ma'am' and kept her mind tightly sealed against the unwanted advice and produced gooseberry tart for the third Sunday running which only the truly uncritical – and those with iron digestions – could even contemplate devouring.

'Alice, why don't you make our tea today?'

Michael's hopeful little voice made his sister put her

stocking down and actually smile at his sunny face as it peered round the drawing-room door. She was really trying to learn to cook, and Mother quite enjoyed teaching her when she had time . . . but oh, the misery of having Gladys tell her that she was doing it all wrong, when Gladys made the heaviest pastry known to man and could burn boiled eggs, curdle custard and actually produced rock cakes which could be mistaken for the real thing.

'I would, Mikey darling, but I don't want to upset Gladys.'

An upset Gladys broke china, left saucepans congealing in a two-day layer of mouldy food and, Alice suspected, kicked the cat.

'Gladys went to take a message for Mummy,' Michael said artlessly. 'Mummy said she'd do tea, but she's got a headache.'

Alice got to her feet, happily abandoning stocking, needle and her stiff, over-upholstered chair.

'Rightio then, Mikey, I'll do it. Want to help? What's Gladys got in the pantry, do you know?'

Summer came, and the Thomases found the little house more irksome than they had dreamed; but almost without realising it they were growing accustomed. Alice had longed for David's return, yet when he wrote and announced that he had been invited to visit a schoolfriend she was glad for his sake. New people had bought Carmel and they had a daughter of Lydia's age. Lydia was visiting their old home and bringing home stories . . . Alice tried to shut her ears to the list of 'improvements', but it was difficult. They were not interested in boating and they talked of removing the jetty because Mr Raft said 'people used it', which, surely, was no crime? They did not keep horses either and were planning to convert the stables into housing units, whatever that might mean. Alice disliked Maria Raft and suspected that the family had bought the Hall for some nefarious purpose, as yet unrevealed, and she knew that David, so much braver than she, would probably have trespassed in the grounds to see just what was going on, so it was as well that he was safely out of the way in Scotland, sailing a three-man-and-one-skivvy (his description, it appeared, of his friend's sister) craft round the Scottish islands.

At Christmas time he would be back . . . and then another letter arrived – wasn't Mother an angel? The school was taking a party skiing in Switzerland – he had not even mentioned it, knowing how difficult things were – yet Mother had booked him in for it. Imagine, Alice, Christmas in one of those picture-book wooden chalets with the snow lying thick outside and weighing down the branches of the pine trees, and inside firelight, steins of beer and masses of nice food, and all the gaiety of the *après-ski*, which some friends at school actually preferred to the thrill of racing down a long snow-slope at goodness knows what speed, with the wind tugging at your clothing and goggles protecting your eyes from the glare . . . by Jove, he was looking forward to it! She would receive a postcard every day, as well as so many letters that she would grow bored with them.

He was as good as his word and Alice, admiring the postcards, enjoying the letters and manfully struggling with their own somewhat truncated holiday treats, told herself that she did not grudge him one hour of his fun – and hoped she was speaking the truth.

Easter . . . he would not come home just for three weeks, because he had exams as soon as he got back to school, quite important ones. He was not going to a crammer, precisely, but Mother had arranged for him to stay with a fellow who tutored people in languages. Languages were the coming thing and an old boy of the school, who was working abroad as an engineer, had told them all that if they wanted a head start the way to get it was to work abroad, in a less developed country than their own, for a few years. Engineering projects in Britain, it appeared, were slowing down because of the depression; but some countries, Russia in particular, were doing all sorts of exciting things that needed qualified men and chose, obviously, those who had some smattering of the language first. So Alice would have to make do with letters once again, until the long summer vac., when they would catch up on all their doings face to face.

Alice soldiered on; she wrote regularly to David and almost as regularly to Nibby, but she was conscious that her letters must be dull. It came home to her most sharply when, in answer to one of hers, David asked innocently who Gladys was and why Alice seemed so glad that she had left. For a moment, Alice just stared dumbly at the sheet. How could David not have known who Gladys was, if he had been reading as well as receiving her letters? Gladys's incompetence, stubbornness and sulks when put out had filled her mind and almost overcome her on occasion for two whole years! More . . . nearly three! First she had struggled to help Gladys, then to teach her the rudiments of cookery and housewifery which Megan was slowly passing on to her daughter. Finally she had told her mother that Gladys must either leave them or stick to housework and let the family do the marketing and cooking. Megan, notoriously soft-hearted, had said she would do her best to find a way out of the imbroglio without hurting Gladys, and had at last done so. She had found her a respectable place with a family of small children who wanted not a cook but a nanny.

'She'll be far better off there,' Megan told her daughters optimistically. 'Mrs Twdor-Evans is an excellent cook and housewife, but she simply doesn't have time to give the children much attention when she's helping her husband with the farm and dairy work, so Gladys will feel needed.'

'She'll probably poison the kids, or give them nervous twitches,' Lydia said with a grin. 'Rather them than us, that's all I can say! Frederick says . . .'

Lydia had used that phrase a lot lately. Frederick's sayings were bruited abroad in the Thomas family to an almost unbearable extent. Though Lydia was only sixteen, she had fallen heavily in love with a neighbour's son, a twenty-two-year-old auctioneer who had joined an old-established firm and risen speedily to the top, owing partly to his efficiency and far more, Alice thought, to his charm and good looks. Fortunately, Frederick had also fallen in love with Lydia, admiring her prettiness, to be sure, but undoubtedly succumbing to her liveliness. Alice told herself she would be glad when Frederick carried off his love and married her, but she did hope, by then, that they would have replaced Gladys. So far, her mother had not attempted to do so and they had managed well enough, but one day it will be me who wants some sort of social life, Alice told herself sometimes, when she was particularly tired. One day I'll want to go to dances and parties, and then who will there be to keep an eye on Julia and Sara, and see that Michael gets his tea on time and doesn't disappear with his friends for hours on end and reappear covered in what looks suspiciously like Dee mud?

Then something rather pleasant happened. Alice had woken up to find a brilliant sun shining in through her bedroom window. She had got up, put on her vest and knickers, washed briskly in cold water from the jug on her washstand, and pulled the curtains wide.

It was the most glorious day, and suddenly she decided that she would not hang about the house today, doing everyone's bidding. Lydia could take a share for once.

It did not take long to dress, to steal downstairs through the sleeping house, grab a loaf of bread, a bag of tomatoes and some of the rosy Beauty of Bath apples which grew on the tree closest to the house, and stuff them into a paper bag. Out of consideration for the family she left a note propped up against the marmalade pot – *Gone out for the day, back by teatime*, it read – and then she was off, running down the path, feeling fifteen instead of fifty-five for once and guiltily conscious of being downright selfish.

She headed for the estuary. It was very early indeed, not even six o'clock, but if she took the risk of going through the grounds of Carmel Hall she was sure to be spotted by someone. Instead, she trespassed across several summery meadows, where the grazing heifers followed close at her heels, scattering every time she turned to face them but then pursuing once more, pushing, shoving and chewing for all the world like a group of nosy schoolchildren. At this point, where the meadows ended the sea marshes began. It was possible to cross them dry-shod after so many weeks without more than the odd shower of rain, but Alice took her sandals off anyway, and ran across the quaking bog and the firmer tussocks without coming to grief.

It was ages . . . years . . . since she had come right down to the estuary. In the old days, when they had lived at the Hall, she had been down here most days in spring and summer, probably once or twice a week even in the depths of winter. Now it smiled back at her, unchanged, not reproaching her for her desertion, glad to see her back.

I've been a fool not to have come before, Alice told herself, making her way down to the hard sand. It cost her a pang to step on to it, though, with its reminder of happier days, but even so the feel of the ridged beach beneath her feet and the sight of the little waves, curling gently towards her as the tide

81

meandered in, was refreshing and delightful, worth all the reproaches she would probably receive for her temporary desertion when she returned.

A lifetime of living cheek by jowl with the estuary, however, had bred in her an inbuilt caution about the tide, and though she paddled happily for a while she turned inland soon enough, to where tussocky, sheep-cropped grass came right down to the sands. She strolled along looking for rabbits, wandered further inland to pick wild raspberries, then made her way back again to the sand, idly rubbing wormcasts flat with her toes and wishing she had brought a bucket and spade for cockles – cockles for tea were popular and Lydia never minded boiling them, though Alice could not bear the squeaks.

Someone else was down here, too. A small figure, black against the azure water, was digging for bait. Alice wondered who it was, whether it was someone she knew – a school-fellow, or an ex-employee of the Thomas yard. If so, he must have fallen on hard times, or possibly retired, for it was a weekday, and most men would be at work – and, as she got nearer, she could see that it was a man.

Within hailing distance she was sure the figure was no one she knew. But her natural friendliness would not let her turn away now; the man had seen her. He straightened, a hand to the small of his back, and waited for her to reach him.

'Good morning,' Alice said politely, when they were separated by a mere ten feet or so. 'Is it cockles you're after, or bait? I've just been wishing I'd brought my spade and bucket with me. I could have dug a few before the tide came right up.'

He was quite a young man, probably not yet twenty, and three or four inches taller than she, even barefoot. He had a thick thatch of toffee-coloured hair, a blue shirt open at the neck and tucked into grey flannels, and light blue eyes with a darker line around the iris which looked somehow familiar, as though she had known someone with eyes like his once.

'Good morning. I'm digging for bait *and* cockles actually; cockles for my tea and bait for my rod. I take it you've forgotten me, Alice?'

He grinned, and it was Nibby Hawke – a Nibby a foot taller and several stones heavier than the boy who had once taken her fishing, and who had written to her for over a year. But the letters had gradually dwindled, and Alice had not tried to revitalise the correspondence; there seemed no point in it once she left Carmel and never even had titbits about David to pass on.

'Nibby! Gosh, what a coincidence! Do you know, this is the first time I've come down to the estuary since we sold the Hall? There hasn't been time, and anyway I was afraid it would make my homesickness worse, so I stayed away. I wish I hadn't; it's even lovelier than I remembered. But what on earth are *you* doing here? You're in Birmingham, making cars!'

'Not now I'm not – I'm on holiday. In fact, I shan't be making cars any more for a year or two. I've got a scholarship I'm going to university to try for a degree in engineering, like Dave!'

'You haven't! Nibby, how wonderful!' Alice bounced across the space that separated them and took Nibby's hands in both of hers. 'Oh, many congratulations! I'm sure you'll get your degree and turn out to be a really good engineer. Do you remember when we were young, how you and Davie used to talk? He was going to build the best ships in the world and you were going to make cars . . . I don't suppose Davie will ever build ships now, but it's so good to know you may still end up making cars.'

'And what were you going to do, Alice? You dreamed too – and not just of marriage and babies, like most girls.'

'I was going to be a teacher . . . a headmistress, actually . . . once,' Alice recalled, not without difficulty. 'And for a long time I thought I'd be a mountaineer. Then . . . do you remember? . . . I decided I wanted to drive a bus and if they wouldn't let me do that I'd be a conductor. And for a while I thought I'd make rather a good farmer because Mrs Blakewell let me milk the cow until I got quite expert at it. But I expect I'll learn shorthand and typing and work in an office. That's what Lydia's doing now – learning shorthand and typing, I mean. Though she's also getting married when she's seventeen, to a young man called Frederick who lives near us.'

'Little Lydia getting married? Not that I remember her all that clearly, because I must confess I don't. She was always very feminine, not like . . .' He stopped short, belatedly aware that he was about to put his foot in it.

Alice, however, was a realist.

'Not like me,' she finished for him, twinkling. 'And I'm

worse now, Nibby, because I've had a taste of domesticity and being a grown-up woman and I don't like it a bit.'

Nibby raised his eyebrows. 'Oh, really? And how am I meant to take that?'

'The way I said it, I suppose,' unsophisticated Alice assured him, with some slight surprise that he should have any doubts on the matter. 'Ever since we moved into town I've been cooking meals, cleaning rooms, darning stockings and looking after the little ones, and I don't find it to my taste at all. In fact, I shall probably rather enjoy office work, just because it doesn't take place in the same stuffy house you eat and sleep in.'

'Goodness, you do sound fed up,' Nibby said lightly, but there was affection in his eyes as they met hers. 'Well, since it's a fine day and I've dug quite enough cockles for now, how about coming for a tramp with me? I'm going to walk right round the coast, to Point of Ayr, then strike inland to a fisherman's cottage I know. Actually, it's owned by the widow of a fisherman and she does the best shrimp teas ever. Care to join me?'

'Yes, please, if you'll share my dinner. It's only bread, tomatoes and apples, but it'll keep the wolf from the door until we reach your fisherman's cottage.'

'That's fine.' Nibby carried his bucket over to the bank and cached it and the spade beneath a bush, then retrieved his gumboots from that same bush and took Alice's hand. There was sand on his fingers and he was a bit damp still, so it was odd how a thrill of pure delight ran through Alice; she wondered if he, too, liked the friendly feel of a hand in his, and hoped that he did. 'Now, my girl; are you fit?'

'Yes!' Alice hastily scuffed her sandals on to her wet and sandy feet. Nibby let go of her hand whilst she collected herself, then took the food from her, shoved it into one of his trouser pockets, and took her hand again. He held it warmly, confidently. Alice liked it more.

'Right. Let's start walking, then.'

They walked most of the day, and talked constantly. They visited the fisherman's cottage and devoured the best tea Alice had had for ages. Shrimps, bread and butter, a dish of salad, a plate of cockles, a whole loaf of *bara brith*, half a fruitcake, a helping of trifle and two sticky buns went down the hatch, as Nibby put it, before either paused for breath. And then there was tea in thick white cups and a bowl of raspberries and cream, after which, as Alice said, they were so full that walking was out of the question and even talking called for more concentration than they possessed.

After paying an absurdly small sum they strolled out of the cottage, through the tiny but blossomy front garden, and into the dusty lane. Close by was common land, where the turf was short and sweet and starred all over at this time of year with the tiny purple flowers of wild thyme. Nibby led her over to the very edge of the turf, where they could look down at the great expanse of sea, and first sat and then lay, crushing the scented thyme so that its heady perfume would remind them, for ever, of this moment.

'A little snooze, I think, is called for,' Nibby remarked. He lay stretched out on his back, looking up into the blue sky. 'Wake me before sunset!'

Alice, lying beside him, said drowsily, 'The last time I lay down like this was in the wood, when I knew Carmel was being sold – you found me there; do you remember?'

Nibby put out a hand and stroked her cheek. It was a light touch, but Alice smiled blissfully and turned her face towards him.

'Of course I remember,' Nibby said. 'You were crying, poor little kid, and I didn't know how to comfort you, so I took you fishing. We had fun, too, didn't we!'

'Yes, we did. I always have fun with you,' Alice said honestly. 'We mustn't laze about here for too long, though, Nibby, or we won't get back before dark.'

'No, I know. Just ten minutes, then.'

They stopped talking. The sun was very warm and the scent of the wild thyme soporific. Presently, they slept.

It was late when they woke. The sun was setting in streamered brilliance over a sea of molten gold, but Alice was too panicky to notice.

'Nibby! Wake up! It'll be dark long before we get back . . . Oh, *do* wake up. We'll have to run all the way at this rate!'

Nibby opened his eyes and stared up at her for a moment, plainly still more asleep than awake. Then he reached up, caught hold of her neck, and pulled her gently down on top of him. Their lips met in a kiss of great sweetness and tenderness. Alice, who had held back, startled, relaxed on to his chest and he rolled sideways so that they were lying face to face, breast to breast. He put his arms right round her and began nuzzling into her neck, against her ear, and then his hands started caressing her and Alice forgot that they would have to walk home, or possibly run, and simply enjoyed her very first taste of being petted and cuddled.

Left to herself, she did not know when she could have called a halt, but fortunately Nibby was more practical than she. He gave her one last kiss, smoothed his hand the full length of her back right down to the curve where her hips started, and then held her gently away from him.

'There, that's stopped you worrying about getting home! But you're right, of course; we'd never make it before it began to get dusk and your mother would worry. So we'll walk into Gwespyr and hire a car – or a pony-cart, if there's nothing else – and get home in fine style!'

'But can you afford it? What'll it cost? You've already bought me a super tea . . .'

'I can afford it.' He got to his feet and pulled her up with him. 'Come along, Miss Worry, we'll be home before you know it.'

He was right; long before dusk they had clip-clopped into town. Alice asked him to come in and say hello to the rest of the family, but Nibby declined on the grounds that she was not the only one who was a bit later than expected.

'I've got a train to catch,' he reminded her. 'I'm staying with an aunt in Chester. But I'll see you again, if the weather holds and I'm able to get down here for the odd day.'

Alice waved him off, and then, her paper bag now full of the cockles he had insisted on sharing with her, she made her way indoors. What a day it had been! What an absolutely tremendous day! Naturally, she was in love.

Nibby just missed the train he had intended to catch, but it did not much matter; there was another in about thirty minutes. He bought a paper and a bar of chocolate and sat on a rather hard wooden seat, reading the first and nibbling at the second. He did not know when he had last enjoyed a day so much.

That little Alice, Dave's sister, was going to be quite a girl one of these days. Although he congratulated himself on his forbearance when cuddling her on the downs, he had noticed that beneath her childish cotton frock there lurked a budding figure – breasts like little lemons, unripe as yet but with a promise of things to come, a small, pliant waist and hips which were just beginning to curve into womanliness.

However, he never should have kissed her – never would have kissed her, had not he woken up under a misapprehension. He had seen a female face above his own, heard a female voice – and leapt to the conclusion, half asleep as he was, that it was Carrie. Having so leapt, he had acted accordingly. And kissed, not Carrie, but dear little fifteen-year-old Alice. But there was no harm done, after all. Because of their long friendship Carrie allowed him certain liberties he would not have dreamed of taking with Alice, but there was no doubt about it: kissing a girl made a fellow think rather longingly of certain liberties! He had been away from Carrie now for a whole week, and it felt like a month. Perhaps he would cut his holiday short and return to Birmingham, although if he did that he would find himself with an awful lot of time on his hands. His first term did not start until October and he had left his job a fortnight since, so he had no work to go back to.

The train came in with a great deal of fuss and steam and Nibby got leisurely to his feet. He found a window seat, sat down and unfurled his paper once more. It had been a lovely day, one of the best; probably it would be wiser to return to Birmingham now, when he could hold today like a jewel in his mind. If he stayed on he might come down to this place again and find no joy in it, for it would not do to keep trailing young Alice round with him – it might give her ideas.

He had all but made up his mind to return to Birmingham when he remembered something Alice had said about David coming home in a couple of weeks. If Dave really was coming back, then he would definitely stay on. He had made a few good friends since leaving Deeside but none of the new relationships had quite the depth and strength of that early attachment. What was more, it would enable him to keep a brotherly eye on Alice. He did not want her himself, having no taste, he told himself, for infants still wet behind the ears, but he would not like to see some oaf taking advantage of all that innocent friendliness.

Having made up his mind, he spread the newspaper over his face and slept until the train reached Chester.

# CHAPTER FIVE
## Russia 1932

David was laboriously peeling potatoes at the small kitchen sink in the flat when the doorbell rang. Cursing under his breath, for it was probably only a neighbour wanting to borrow something, he threw the blunt little knife and the half-peeled potato down on the draining board and crossed the room in two strides, the hallway in a stride and a half, and opened the front door.

A waft of warm and stuffy air blew in, and so did a young woman in a dowdy brown cotton dress, with peasant-type sandals on her large feet and a smile on her broad face.

'David, darling, it's me! Not unwelcome, I hope?' She beamed at him, wiping away a trickle of perspiration with one rather dirty hand. 'Phew, it's hot today! And why haven't you clasped me to your manly bosom and given me a big kiss?'

'Hello, Natasha,' David said rather guardedly. 'Since you're sleeping with my flatmate, who might return from shopping any minute, I don't think kissing's in order, do you?'

'Oh, pooh, how old-fashioned you English are, how narrow and hidebound,' Natasha said airily, standing on tiptoe and grabbing David round the neck in order to kiss his mouth in a manner both forthright and frank. There was a short silence whilst they wrestled fairly amicably, Natasha attempting to prise David's mouth open and David trying to escape. Right from the start he had suspected Natasha of wanting to try an English lover, and he had been truly thankful when she started sleeping with Yuri Obreimov. It was not that free love did not appeal to him, he told himself defensively, keeping the girl at arm's length — with some difficulty, for she was sturdy and muscular despite her plumpness and flaunted femininity — it was just that self-opinionated women engineers left him cold.

Not that it would ever do to let Natasha suspect it or she might consider him a challenge. David went cold all over at the thought.

'And how is the delightful Galya? Back in Moscow, I suppose? Well, well, if you will take a ballet girl for your mistress what can you expect? By now she'll have found a richer patron than an engineer . . . perhaps a Party member will take pity on her and send her flowers and chocolates.'

David turned and walked back into the kitchen. His bestowing of a huge box of English chocolates on Galya Strenikovna had aroused Natasha's wildest envy, for she was passionately fond of sweets. Not that he cared what Natasha thought; she was Yuri's problem, not his, thank God!

'Where are you going? Aha, you peel the potato, I see. I shall stay and lunch with you,' Natasha said, perching heavily on the edge of the wooden table. 'Will Yuri be long? I particularly want to see him on an urgent matter. Did you say he was shopping? Where? At the market? Not at the co-operative, surely? I thought you'd spent all your vouchers for this month. Or can he be going around the kiosks?'

'If you'd like to finish peeling the potatoes, I'll go and look for him,' David said hopefully, but he was not so easily to escape Natasha's company.

'Peel them yourself; I'm a liberated woman, not a serf,' Natasha said crossly, but her bark was worse than her bite, and having watched his clumsy manoeuvres for a few moments she exclaimed impatiently and snatched the knife, finishing off the rest of the task with a speed and dexterity which led David to assume that she had peeled a lot more spuds than he for all her boasts of liberation.

'There you are, all done. Now we can both go and find Yuri,' she said triumphantly, collecting the peelings up with both hands and flinging them through the open window with total disregard for whoever might be passing below. David had never got used to what he thought of as the inconsistencies of the Russian character. They talked constantly about progress and modern methods, about equality and brotherhood. They preached propaganda about the high ideals and good works of the Party and the horrors of capitalist systems. They revered education and paid their scientists and leading community lights far more than they paid others. And they threw potato peelings out of fourth-floor windows on to the unsuspecting heads of passers-by as airily as they would relieve themselves in a quiet corridor or a lift shaft, should the need arise.

'I do have other things I should be getting on with,' David said, putting the peeled potatoes into a pan and setting it on the tiny stove. 'You go, Natasha. You'll enjoy being with Yuri, and anyway you know what shopping's like. He could be gone ages.'

The availability of food varied wildly with the season, but shopping always took a long time, thanks to the odd method of buying goods. One went into a shop, selected with the eye alone the objects one intended to purchase, and added up the sum one would be spending. Then one queued to buy tickets for the correct sum from an invariably surly shop assistant. Finally, armed with the tickets, one queued once more to hand the tickets to yet another shop assistant in exchange . . . at last! . . . for goods. It was a cumbersome and time-consuming business, but no one in Russia, it appeared, could be trusted to buy goods for cash in the ordinary fashion. And that was doubtless why the markets and kiosks, though often privately owned, did such a roaring trade despite high prices.

'I would appreciate your company, David,' Natasha said; suddenly, he sensed, very serious. David in his turn became grave. Had she discovered that Yuri was also sleeping with a dark-haired and vivacious student from the university, or that his frequent weekend trips into the country were not, as he claimed, to examine the work in progress at various sub-stations and prospective sites, but to continue his relationship with a golden-haired peasant girl who supplied him not only with oodles of fun but also with fresh eggs and, occasionally, a side of pork?

David had been working in various parts of the Soviet Union ever since he had got his degree in engineering. The time he had spent with the language tutor had paid off, for he spoke Russian as easily, now, as he spoke English, and the experience he was gaining was, he hoped, valuable. Certainly it was not experience that he could have got in Britain, where the last thing on their minds was building enormous power stations across the length and breadth of the country or dragging the peasants, albeit kicking and screaming, into the twentieth century.

'Very well, then, we'll go together,' David said now, accepting defeat. It was far too hot for coats or hats, so they both left the flat exactly as they were, Natasha in her dowdy brown cotton and David in worn grey flannels and the blue, open-necked shirt.

The flat was in one of the newer parts of Leningrad, but on leaving it one immediately entered an area so run-down that the word 'slum' could fairly be used to describe it. Huge old houses had been partitioned off into tiny sections into which vast numbers of Soviet citizens crammed themselves, their children and even occasionally their animals. The authorities were getting round to clearing and repairing and rebuilding, but they had not yet reached this neighbourhood. The wood-block pavements were rotting and holes gaped where people had rooted up the wood for their fires during the winter cold; the unmade streets were thick with dust and treacherous with pits and humps; and because of the extremes of temperature, as David well knew, the bridges that were mended one year had swollen and burst apart in the cold six months later.

But it was being put right. David, glumly walking along the dusty thoroughfare with Natasha hanging on to his arm, thought that Leningrad might never attain the grandeur of the tsars' St Petersburg, but it was a good deal handsomer than it had been now that the New Economic Policy was getting to work. New sewers were under construction; the streets were lit by electricity instead of the old gas, which had broken down under the dreadful conditions in the winter of '24; new shops and some quite good restaurants were opening every day; and engineers and university students kept the city lively and ensured that it was second only to Moscow for entertainment and importance.

Soon, though, he would probably be moved on. His work with the Volchovstroi hydro-electric power station was coming to an end; he wondered where he would be sent next. He would have liked Moscow, except that they said foreigners were constantly spied on there, and that it was not easy to make Russian friends because any Russian who fraternised was either forced by the State to become an informer or was suspect himself. David knew his movements were carefully watched even here in Leningrad, but it was further from the spiritual home of the Ogs, as the English had taken to calling the dreaded OGPU, the secret police – whose spiritual home, according to Moss Richards, David's boss, was the Kremlin – so things were a little more relaxed. Certainly one could make good friends of Russians without anyone wondering about it – witness himself and Yuri.

They turned down a wide street and headed for the shops, though David steered Natasha away from the co-operatives. She was right, of course; they always seemed to use up their vouchers too soon, so Yuri would either be in a private emporium, using the kiosks, or indulging in barter at the market – David suspected the latter, and led her there as fast as he could persuade her stocky legs to go.

'Is it being personal to ask why you want to see Yuri?' David asked presently, as they approached the street which held the enormous, open-air market. It was already thronged with people; it would not be easy to pick Yuri out from that crowd but he supposed, gloomily, that they had better try or he would be landed with the girl for hours.

'Yes, but I don't mind. David, we work together, we've been good friends for two years . . . David, I need to share your flat just for a little while. I mentioned it to Yuri and he said it was *your* flat and he had no say in the matter, but he did say he'd ask you; has he done so? I am desperate!'

'There isn't room for a mouse in the flat as well as Yuri and me,' David said, feeling his heart sink like a stone at the prospect. He did not think Natasha washed very often; glancing sideways at her now he could see a tideline around the base of her neck, and the skin below it was greyish. Ugh! 'What's wrong with your own flat, anyway?'

Natasha's mouth tightened and her eyes seemed to crawl closer together. 'Sanya's invited another girl in . . . a Ukrainian peasant . . . a Jew, for all I know. She's hateful . . . ugly . . . skinny . . . I don't know what Sanya sees in her, but I can't go on . . .'

David realised, with horror, that Natasha was crying. He shook her arm in a brotherly fashion and patted her fat, tanned little hand. He hoped it was tanned.

'Now come on, old girl, if there's room for another . . .'

'There isn't!' wailed Natasha. 'She's sleeping in our bed . . . imagine, three of us! It would be all right if we all liked one another, but I can't stand her, she's horrible. David, if you

93

don't say I can come I'll camp on your doorstep and tell everyone at the station you and Yuri are perverts! I'm desperate, desperate!'

'Perverts?' David sniggered. 'Well, so we are . . . oh, you mean with each other! Who on earth would believe that, what with you and . . . well, and Galya, and so on?'

'In Russia, people believe what they want to believe,' Natasha said with a certain amount of truth. 'You're a foreigner, and if I say you're a pervert there are people who'll believe it – people in high places, what's more. And it's not impossible for a man to like women *and* other men, you know.'

'Well, I've never heard of it,' David said, but he spoke thoughtfully. It would make far more sense of Natasha's outburst, of course, if she had an interest in Sanya herself – which, when you realised that they slept in the same bed in the normal course of things . . . he would have to think about this!

'David? Will you have me to stay in your place for a few days? Just until I get something sorted out? I'd cook your meals and keep the place clean . . .'

'Hey, there's Yuri,' David said with relief, steering Natasha over to where his flatmate, basket on arm like all the other peasants, was haggling over a number of large green gherkins and some scarlet peppers. 'Look, I'll talk to him about it and let you know. Will that do?'

'Oh, but when? I wanted to know *now*. I wanted to be able to go back to Sanya and tell her she could do what she liked with that fleapit because I'd be staying with friends.'

'Tell you what,' David said, visited by inspiration. 'You go off now – have a word with Yuri if you like, but then pretend you've got to leave – and come back at about two o'clock. We'll have had a chance to talk properly, and we'll give you our answer then.'

'Oh. But I thought it would be nicer if we all three talked it over.' Natasha looked hopefully up at him but David did not allow himself the weakness of a smile. He looked straight back at her, solemnly. 'Oh well, all right, if that'll make it easier.'

They reached the stall just as Yuri had concluded his bargaining and was pushing the fruit higgledypiggledy into his basket. He grinned at them, put a casual arm round Natasha's firm waist, and said, 'Hello, why the deputation?'

'Natasha's just leaving,' David said quickly. 'Have you finished the shopping? If so, we'll go straight home.'

'Yes, I am leaving,' Natasha said, scowling. 'But when you are talking, David, just remember I don't say what I don't mean. If you hurt me . . . it is only for a few days, remember . . . then before you know it they'll all be whispering behind their hands and you'll be on the Ogs' visiting list.'

'What did she mean?' Yuri asked apprehensively, as Natasha's stout figure disappeared into the crowd. 'Sometimes I wish I'd never taken up with that woman.' He scratched his thick fair hair and frowned down at David, for he was two or three inches the taller. 'I can't imagine what possessed me!'

'Lust?' David suggested mildly as they made their way back towards the flat. 'After all, when you decided to make her the happiest woman on earth you hadn't met many girls out here.'

'True. It was impatience, though, rather than lust, old man.' Yuri gave David the benefit of his charming, lopsided smile. He practised his smile whilst he shaved, David remembered, and smiled back with a good deal of cynicism.

'And what do you suggest we do about her threats?'

'Threats? What threats?'

'She says she'll tell people we won't let her share the flat because we're perverts, too keen to get at each other to worry about a woman,' David muttered. 'I suppose it's a pretty hollow threat, really . . .'

'Hollow? No, Davidski, it isn't hollow at all; she's a spiteful bitch, that one, and she might easily put rumours about.' Yuri clutched his hair and groaned. 'Oh, my God . . . why didn't I leave her alone that night in the wine cellar, when I knew very well she was a lesbian!'

'A lesbian?' The speedy confirmation of David's fears still came as a shock. 'You mean, knowing that . . .'

'It was quite titillating, I suppose,' Yuri said mournfully. 'I'd heard about them, of course, but she was my first. Probably she was a challenge – yes, that's it, that's why I started the affair. And having started it, I don't seem to have got round to stopping.'

'You stand there quite calmly telling me you've been getting into a lesbian when you must have *known* it was risky, that you might be letting yourself in for all sorts of trouble, knowing you were sharing a flat with a foreigner . . .' Rage almost left David speechless. Yuri was really too bad! But Yuri, however, did not see it like that.

'Risky? Healthwise, you mean? Oh no, I don't think Natasha's like that, I think it was just . . .'

'You moron! It's risky because the State says there are no sexual deviants in the Soviet Union! She's a blot on their landscape and you could easily find yourself mopped up with her! And now, if she does start spreading rumours . . .'

By this time they had reached the apartment block and were mounting the stairs. Yuri shook his head and made signs for quiet.

'Not now. Wait till we're behind closed doors.'

Once in the flat, however, he lit the flame beneath the pan, emptied various vegetables on to the table and began cutting them into rough chunks.

'You're right, of course. I was a bit of an idiot, and we don't want to take any chances with the Ogs. On the other hand, we don't want Natasha moving in here . . . don't believe any of that crap about a few days. Once she got in she'd stay.' He gave a scornful sniff and put a tiny knob of lard into the pan, pushed the potatoes to one side whilst he sizzled it, then began dropping handfuls of vegetables into the fat. 'Some girls would be quite fun, but not Natasha.'

'Some girls wouldn't be fun at all – they'd just make it into a slum,' David assured him. 'It's too bloody small for the two of us, if we're honest; add another soul and we're overcrowded to such an extent that neither of us would get any drawings or paperwork done at all.'

'That's right. Then what do we do?'

'Tell her to jump in the Volga? Or threaten her with telling the authorities about her own activities?'

'We could do that, all right, but whether it would make us more or less suspect I wouldn't like to say. No, I've had a *much* better plan! You're due for time off, aren't you, the same as me?'

'Yes, that's right. Only I was going to save mine and take it all next summer, so that I could get home. Why?'

'Well, we could go down to Odessa or somewhere warm . . . I know it's hot now, but it's city-hot, not sunbathing-hot . . . and laze around for a few weeks. Natasha could borrow the flat whilst we were gone, on the strict understanding that she was out of it when we got back.'

'Run away? And anyway, Yuri, how can we get her out if she's still here when we return?'

'My dear David, how trusting you are! She will be living in our flat, right?' At David's nod, he continued, 'And we shall be enjoying our holiday somewhere. She will know we shan't be back, so what do you suppose she'll do once she's got the place to herself?'

'I don't know — unless you mean she'll ask some fellow to share with her?'

'Precisely! Accommodation is hard to find, and this is a decent little flat, for all your British sneerings. Of course, she might ask a girl to share, but in any event we come home early ... not much, just a day or two ... and send them both packing. Because not the most perverted person in the world could conceive of four people in this flat!'

'And Natasha, furious because we've turned her out of her love-nest, tells lies to the authorities about us.'

'My dear David, how wrongly you read our little friend's character! She might tell lies *now*, because she's miserable and rejected, and because she needs a roof over her head. But she'll shack up with this ... this person, and she'll be happy. She's a reasonable girl, and she'll know very well, having lived here, that it won't hold four. So she'll start looking out for a place for the two of them, whoever they are. See?'

'It sounds quite logical,' David said, after a pause for thought. 'But what if she doesn't bring someone else in? What if she lives here by herself all the time we're away?'

'Ha! Well, in that unlikely event, we'll have to think again. Now, where shall we go, and when?'

'To the mountains,' David said at once, looking at the window reflecting the remorseless, sticky heat from apartment blocks and pavements. 'If we go to the Caucasus we might find snow!'

'And if we went right over the mountains, we'd find Georgia,' Yuri said dreamily. 'Waving palm trees, warm seas, tropical fruit ... and the women, I believe, are just like the Greek legends ... ah, yes, we'll go to the Caucasus.'

'Won't it cost rather a lot?'

'No. We'll go by rail to the foothills and then we'll hire

97

horses and camp out. We've camped out before – remember that week we spent on the steppes? That was fun, wasn't it?'

David nodded. It had been fun, and it occurred to him now that he had not had a lot of fun these past two or three years. Earning money to send home to help Alice and the family, saving up all his leave like a miser in order to be able to get home the following year, had all led to a degree of sameness in his life which a Russian might think natural but which any Briton – particularly a Celt – would consider unnecessarily boring for a man of his age.

'Well, then? Are you on?'

David glanced round the tiny, cluttered little kitchen; at the piles of vegetables, the bag of coarse flour, the remains of the lard. At the wooden chairs and the wooden table and the ugly curtains at the window. Through in the other room . . . the only other room . . . were two narrow beds with straw-stuffed mattresses, a washstand with a tin bowl and jug on it, and a home-made hanging cupboard which contained all their few clothes. Soap was almost unobtainable, razorblades could be sold for several roubles since they were also in short supply, fruit and vegetables were plentiful in summer but other food was expensive and rationed, too.

Train travel in Russia was overcrowded, no food was sold on the trains themselves and they could be anything from three hours to three days late. In the mountains, far from civilisation, food would probably be even more difficult to obtain and they would have horses to feed as well as themselves – though grass, presumably, would be plentiful and free.

But at least, in the mountains, there would be cool air to breathe and no one except themselves for miles and miles. Water from streams and rivers would not be turned off every other day whilst repairs were carried out to the system. And they would be free from all the pettifogging restrictions which irked a foreigner wherever he went in the cities; from the fear, unacknowledged as yet but, David thought, growing, that by even speaking to a foreigner one might in some way be offending against some unwritten Soviet law.

'Yes, I'm on. And heaven help you, Yuri, if we get back here and find her safely ensconced!'

When he and Yuri had first envisaged the trip it had seemed a simple enough matter, but nothing in the Soviet Union, David recalled as he joined yet another queue, was ever simple. The monarchy might be dead but Beaurocracy reigned in its stead. It took them a full week to book their tickets to the small town which was to be their jumping off point, and meant countless trips to the station, enquiries, cash payments, and eventually turning up on the platform complete with camping gear only to find that the porter had been unable to book them 'soft' class but hoped that they would be content with the equivalent of 'standing room only'. They were not, and they stormed and raged and went home, and next time they sallied forth they did indeed have 'soft' accommodation – with bunks at opposite ends of the train, which was, naturally, a non-corridor one.

David was on the point of turning back and slinking off the station once more when, before his eyes, Yuri turned into a tyrant, a veritable Russian autocrat. He roared at the porter, he roared at a higher and nastier official who came to see what all the fuss was about, he roared at a couple of clerks who were ill-advised enough to run out of the booking office to see the fun. And he got precisely what they wanted. 'Soft' accommodation for two persons sharing a four-berth compartment. A thing which first the booking clerks, then the porter and finally the high official had said was impossible . . . out of the question . . . beyond anyone's power to arrange.

As they climbed aboard with all their luggage, knapsacks, bedrolls and food, David could not help smiling to himself at the lengths to which one could be driven by a woman, for he had no doubt that it was Natasha who had caused Yuri to act in such an out-of-character fashion. She had moved in with them.

'Once I thought that musky, animal perfume attractive, God help me,' Yuri moaned to David after two days. 'Now I find it merely means she never washes. And isn't she a bad cook? She *ruined* that spaghetti – when shall we get real spaghetti like that again?'

'And who else could burn spaghetti?' David agreed. He had paid for the pasta at black market prices, because there was a glut of tomatoes and onions were cheap. It had pained him very much to see it, a seething mass of pulp, being turned on to a plate and presented to him as a meal. It had been still more painful to taste the burn which Natasha had discarded but which had flavoured the entire saucepanful.

'It was bad for you, but worse for me,' argued Yuri. 'I'd never tasted spaghetti Napolitano . . . I thought for one awful moment that you had depraved tastes, and that it was *meant* to taste like that!'

'Well, never mind. When we light our camp-fire on our first night under the stars, I'll cook you ratatouille . . . I bet you've never tasted that, either.'

And here they were at last, actually on board the train which would take them to the foothills of the Caucasus! It was impossible not to be excited, even when David confronted the bunk on which he would spend the next three nights – a wooden shelf which let down to serve as seat or bed and could be tucked out of the way whilst you were dressing, shaving and so on. Closer examination showed that there were thin mattresses too, though, and the slatted blinds at the window could be pulled down to keep out the early morning light if you wanted a lie-in.

'I wonder what the other people in here will be like?' David said idly, as he and Yuri began to stow their luggage away under their bunks.

'Oh, all right, I expect. So long as they aren't garlic-chewing peasants who want to lie in bed all day – that can be awkward, because it means that the top bunk stays down and there's not much room, and if they try to keep the blinds down as well you can nearly go mad. But I dare say they'll be all right.'

'Look, Yuri, melons! Shall I or will you?'

The question was rhetorical since David, dressed and ready, was sitting on the lower bunk whilst Yuri, in trousers and nothing else, was standing in front of a propped-up fragment of looking-glass, trying to shave with the aid of a cup of warm water, a stick of shaving soap and a very blunt razor. On the opposite side of the compartment their travelling companions were coaxing the samovar to make them all tea – they were Jev and Nina, he a bespectacled young Communist, she also a Communist but a good deal prettier. They were living together but had no immediate intention of marrying, and already all four were good friends. It might have been difficult for a girl to live with three young men for three days and nights, but Nina was both good-natured and easy-going and tended to mother the men, though her grasp of Communist doctrine was very good and her ideals shone like good deeds in a naughty world. If all she believed was true . . . if all she expected happened . . . Russia would indeed be the best and happiest country in the world.

'Would you get them, Davidski? And whilst you're on the platform, could you buy some corn-cobs, if there are any for sale? We need some more hot water, but Jev will queue for that whilst you get the food, if you would be so good.'·

'Corn-cobs and melons. Right, I'll get them.' David opened the door and jumped down on to the small country station. It was crowded, as were all the stations they had passed. Perhaps it was the cheapness of rail travel, perhaps it was that Russians simply loved moving from one part of their vast country to another, but for whatever reason anyone travelling far by train could be forgiven for concluding that the entire populace was on the move. Every seat was always taken, some seemed to be permanently double-booked, and the patient peasants were quite prepared to stand for hours, at stations or in the train itself, in order to get from one place to another.

David fought his way through the people, some no doubt would-be passengers, others like himself from the train, still others selling their wares. He reached the melon-seller and picked up two of the largest and most succulent melons, demanding to know the price. The woman told him, he took up a third melon and a fourth, put down the first two . . . but at the end of a minute or so he had parted with his kopeks and was fighting his way out of the scrum, the richer by half a dozen golden fruit and poorer by a tiny sum of money.

He had taken a bag with him, into which he crammed the melons before he found a seller of corn-cobs and bought half a dozen of them as well. Further on he snapped up four pancakes stuffed with soft cheese, a shiny plaited loaf of sweet bread flavoured with almond, and a container of fresh goat's milk. Laden with his booty he returned to the train, just as, in the annoying manner of Russian trains, it decided to leave the station without so much as a toot on a whistle to inform its passengers of the fact. Laden, he sprinted alongside, found his own carriage, threw his bag in ahead of him and then hurled himself up on to the floor. Jev and the hot water were back, the samovar was purring like a fat contented cat, and Nina had put her loose hair into a bun at the back of her head and was setting out cups for the tea. She looked round and laughed at his precipitate entry, then unpacked the food from the bag and began to prepare the first meal of the day.

'It's only goat's milk, but it's better than nothing,' David said, as Nina sloshed some into a cup for Jev. He liked milk, but she would have made him drink it anyway, as she said he needed building up for the winter ahead. Last winter, apparently, he had been very ill, though to look at him now it was difficult to credit, so sturdy and tanned did he appear.

'Goat's milk is more healthy,' Nina observed, watching Jev lovingly as he drank. 'When the Five Year Plan has made the whole country secure and everyone has money to spare, I shall not have to buy goat's milk for Jev; people in cities as well as in the country will take cow's milk for granted as part of their diet.'

David and Yuri smiled and continued to prepare breakfast. Soon all four of them were eating pancakes, laughing at each other as the cream cheese spurted messily down cheeks and chins, but David was unable to resist asking a question or two.

'Do you really think the Five Year Plan will make the whole country rich? Peasants and all?'

'Not rich, equal,' Jev corrected, between bites of pancake. 'That is all the Party promises – equality.'

'Yet I get paid more than the woman who cleans the streets, so I can afford milk now and she can't.'

'We are not yet equal; the Five Year Plan is still working for us.'

'What about the fishermen who brought back record catches of fish last autumn and the plant to process them wasn't ready, so the Party told them to go away and come back in a few weeks?'

'Ah, that's just a little knot in the smooth thread of progress,' Jev said indulgently, but Nina looked troubled.

'Yes . . . but it was a foolish thing to say to men who had worked hard, who could not possibly keep their fish fresh for a few days, let alone a few weeks. Sometimes the Party tries to do too much and then someone has to be let down; I just wish it was not the very poor, like the fishermen.'

'So when the Five Year Plan has finished working,' Yuri said through a mouthful of almond bread, 'you mean that the woman who cleans the streets will earn as much money as an engineer? Come on, Jev; that would never work. You'd get people with brilliant brains working in the fields because they preferred manual work, and you'd get thick-headed peasants sitting in offices biting their pens because they were too lazy to till the fields.'

'No, no, you've got it all wrong! The engineer will be paid *more*, I grant you, but the woman in the street will be paid sufficiently well to buy all the things she needs . . . good food, decent clothing, somewhere to live . . .'

'Utopia,' David said, unable to keep a trace of the sarcasm he felt from showing in his voice. 'And if the street-cleaner decides she wants more than good food – that she wants excellent food . . .?'

'Then she will have to learn to be an engineer; more tea, David?'

David, laughing, held out his cup and the subject was changed, but he found both Jev and Nina rather touching. Such starry-eyed belief was bound to end in a rude awakening, but, until then, surely even the holding of such high ideals must do a person good? Unless, of course, the person became embittered when the ideals failed to materialise. He did not think, though, that Jev and Nina were likely to become embittered, for they were, essentially, innocents. The very strength of their belief was a safeguard against the glibness, the parroting of Party slogans, which characterised many of the young Communists David had met. He liked both Jev and his girl and he wished that they could have accompanied him and Yuri on their great adventure across the Caucasus. But this, their first trip to a sanatorium, was something breathlessly anticipated. They were getting as much enjoyment out of the fact that they had been deemed worthy, David believed, as they would from the holiday itself, for in Russia a sanatorium was a pleasure-palace where the righteous (card-carrying Communists) went to enjoy their leisure and take their ease.

The train, jerking as it crossed some points, caused tea to spill, Yuri to bite his tongue, and Nina, who was standing, to fall back on the bottom bunk, giggling. Since breakfast was nearly finished, they washed up the cups in what was left of the water Jev had brought at the last stop, put away the remaining food, and settled back in their seats to admire the countryside.

Beyond the windows, Russia fled past. They were crossing the steppes now; Cossack country. Yuri told David that Cossack villages had been founded around the *sotnias*, groups of a hundred horsemen, but that now they were just farming communities. Thatched, whitewashed cottages, wattle fencing, cherry orchards straight out of Chekhov, they passed them all, along with market places black with people, horses and cattle.

As the day wore on, it began to seem as though the steppes were endless. The sky remained blue, the sun shone, and the sea of grey-green grass, glistening with dew at sunrise, darkening to shades of slate and purple as dusk crept down, continued seemingly eternally, stretching from horizon to horizon. The four inmates of the compartment slept, played cards, slept again. Jev and Nina held hands, told stories about their families and friends back in Leningrad, and speculated on the future of their adored Mother Russia. David did some talking too, but when he talked about his beloved Wales and the banks of the Dee he sometimes felt that there was a disbelieving silence coming from Jev and Nina rather than a listening silence. They could not believe that a capitalist system – if the British system could go by such a name – cared at all about the people. It was clear they felt that the peasants who had worked in the Thomas yard had been exploited, and no amount of assurance could convince them that this was totally untrue, so inundated by propaganda had they been.

Day followed night followed day followed night, and David found himself, for the first time, physically aware of the immenseness of Russia and not just mentally conscious of it. The four of them enjoyed one another's company but it was natural that they should spend long periods reading, writing letters, chatting in twosomes or simply staring out of the window, and it was during his quiet periods that David began, for the first time, to consciously consider the enigma that was Russia.

He had not travelled about much, but he had seen vast tracts of forest, huge rivers, great plains, the steppes. He had known terrible cold and extreme heat. He knew personally cultured and intelligent men and men who, until these last two or three years, had not known a wheeled vehicle and could not imagine how such a thing would function. At home in Britain he had heard people talking about the enigma that was Russia, about its paradoxes, and he had thought, *What rot, it's just a place like any other filled with people like any other*, but now he knew this was not true. The tsars had tried to stretch themselves to rule over their vast and complex empire, and they had failed. Now the Party was trying to do the same – would it fail, in its turn? But it was not one man, or one family, or one dynasty, even; it was a multi-tentacled monstrosity which sprawled out across the land, spying, decreeing, imprisoning, rewarding. And, in a way, he began to see that it had to be the way it was, if it was ever to succeed in disciplining its vast family of very different children into one great unit which thought and acted as a flock of birds or a shoal of fish acts – simultaneously, as though one mind controlled a thousand bodies.

Because, as they travelled, he came to realise more than ever how very diverse the people of Russia were. Not all Slavs, not by a long chalk, nor all Europeans nor all Chinese, Muslim, peasants, princes. They jostled and pushed on the platforms at every station; yellow faces, black ones, copper ones, white ones, pink ones, tanned ones. As they neared the mountains they began to see Caucasians, and they were very different from their brothers of the lowlands. Cossacks were different from Ukrainians, Georgians were unlike either. People from the Scandinavian borders had yellow hair and blue eyes; Cossacks tended to be dark-haired and dark-eyed; those living near the Mongolian border had flat, Mongoloid faces and the narrow eyes and ivory skin one associated with Asiatics.

David felt quite dizzy, contemplating the size and diversity of the country and the wide range of different nationalities which came together under the banner of the Soviet Republic. Party members could make a tremendous impact if they talked of the difficulties of moulding all those different backgrounds, different types, into one – why did they not boast about the differentness of this great country, instead of trying to convince the people that they were all alike really, and that they all wanted the same thing – the iron hand in the iron glove, the Victorian father figure . . . the Party?

Perhaps one day they will see it more clearly, though, David dreamed, gazing out through the window as the train steamed towards the foothills of the great Caucasian range. Perhaps one day they will acknowledge that you can't force a great, diverse people into the same narrow mould, any more than you can turn a sturdily independent farmer into someone willing to work for a small wage at an uninspiring job like building tractors – even if you tell him that he will, in the end, benefit the State. The State, when you look hard at it, just blurs and dissolves into people, after all!

Some of this he tried, hesitantly, to express to Jev and Nina, and because train travel takes people out of themselves, puts them into a different world and allows them, for a short time, to say things they would never dream of saying aloud at any other time or in any other place, they listened to him, and agreed with quite half the things he said, and warmed to this foreigner who was trying so very hard to see the good in their beloved Party.

They all agreed, though, on a national characteristic – at any rate in the big cities – which distressed everyone who came in contact with it, peasant, foreigner or merely an out-of-town Russian, disorientated by the bustle of Moscow, Leningrad or Gorki. This was quite simply a rudeness and nastiness which was turned totally without cause or reason on anyone who crossed the path of any person in authority. And such a little authority! Porters, shop girls, cash-till operators, hotel clerks . . . they were not only nasty to their customers, they were nasty to each other, and their rudeness and indifference to anyone already flustered had to be seen to be believed.

'Yet a dozen peasants, in a queue, will hear someone say I'm a foreigner and promptly push me to the front,' David said, honestly puzzled. 'And when I get to the front, the girl on the till is so rude and unpleasant . . . well, it's unbelievable.'

'Yes, I know. And in Leningrad I've seen a blind man knocked down in the rush for a bus, and no one even tried to help him up, let alone apologise for the accident,' Nina contributed. 'It's as if people put on nastiness like a veil as soon as they step outside their own homes, and don't take it off again until they get indoors.'

'Perhaps,' David said slowly, after some thought, 'it's a defence. To keep a bit of themselves different, individual. Perhaps that's all it is.'

And so they talked, as the train rushed towards Kislovodsk, where they would all leave the railway for their different destinations.

'You'll write? You really will? Promise, now.'

Nina, bright-eyed with anticipation, had already written neatly in her small notebook all the details she had asked for. Names, addresses, work places and, in David's case, his English home, had all been filed away for future reference.

'She'll write to you both,' Jev promised them, his friendly little eyes twinkling behind the lenses of his thick glasses. 'She's a great girl for writing letters, is Nina. And think what a lot she'll have to tell you – all about the sanatorium, and who else stayed there, and how many lovers she took . . .'

Nina batted him over the head with her notebook at that point and ended the discussion, but not before David had committed their address in Moscow to paper.

'We have been working in Leningrad,' Jev had explained. 'But we are both Muscovites, and after our time at the sanatorium we shall return to the capital.'

'A nice couple,' David observed, as he and Yuri waved them off and set forth, on foot, to find somewhere to stay for the night and then a couple of horses to hire for the next stage of their journey.

'Sure, very nice. Just remember, my lad, that "once a Party member always a Party member" ought to be constantly in your mind when dealing with Russians. They can't help it, but the Party comes first and if it meant throwing you to the wolves they'd do it with a clean conscience and without blinking.'

'Oh, cynical, aren't you?' David, weighed down by his impedimenta, groaned and waved hopefully at a man in a *droshky*. The man pulled his horse to a halt, grinned at them, and got down.

'Yes, comrades? Do you want a hand with all that baggage? Somewhere to sleep for a night or so? Advice? A hot meal? Somewhere to erect a tent? If so, Jorg is the man to help you!'

'We'll have a hotel or a guest house first, I think,' Yuri said decisively. 'Tomorrow's another day . . . right now we need a meal, a good sit down in a chair that neither rocks nor sways and a comfortable bed.'

'I'm your man,' Jorg assured them, hefting their luggage into his vehicle. 'I know just the place!'

They found a couple of rather weary-looking nags to hire the first day, but agreed to take them only thirty miles or so and then to leave them with the owner's brother-in-law, in a village further into the hills.

'I won't deny they'd have a job if you took them much further,' their owner admitted, patting his possessions' scraggy necks. 'Never mind. Once you get to Khassaut you'll find proper mountain ponies; they'll suit you far better.'

After the days and nights on the train, it was good to be in the open air and on horseback. David rode ahead, being the more experienced rider of the two, but that, he reflected, was not saying much. Sticking on Alice's pony whilst it turned and jinked around the home pasture was one thing; riding an elderly nag along mountain paths covered in sharp flints in the dusk, quite another. But the moon was rising, a silver disc against the blue, and the scent of new grass and pines was deliciously refreshing after all the weeks and months spent in cities and on the sites of power stations. David rode along, dreaming, and Yuri rode behind, grumbling.

'Ah . . . oh . . . ah . . . damn it, my bloody animal slid *again* . . . why doesn't yours slide, David?'

No answer from David, enjoying the night sounds and keeping his eyes on the track ahead.

'David . . . is it much further? I don't like this business of riding on after dark because . . . aah . . . that's a ravine! Oh, my God, my God, suppose this evil-eyed stinking donkey falls over?' A sound of little stones tap-tapping their way into the gorge below. 'Oh, my God, did you hear that? This son of Satan wants me to die of fright – he just kicked a great slab of rock down that sheer drop. David? David, are you deaf?'

When they came to a slanting meadow slope with soft grass and a tiny, bubbling spring of water David took pity on his friend and they made camp. As they crawled into the shelter of their small tent David was thinking, Why didn't I do this months and months ago? Why didn't I give myself a break, like this, to learn to love the country? And Yuri, pulling himself crossly into his sleeping bag, was remarking bitterly that he must be mad ever to have agreed to come at all.

# CHAPTER SIX

'It never occurred to me that we'd get weather like this; why didn't anyone tell us it rains four days out of five in mountainous country?' Yuri, astride his tough mountain pony, moaned and tried to shrug himself even deeper into his waterproof, and then gurgled in exasperation as the stiff folds around his neck repositioned themselves, sending a waterfall straight down the front of his chest.

'I don't know why it didn't occur to me, considering that the Welsh mountains are often in cloud or belting rain when it's quite fine down on Deeside,' David remembered, tugging his own waterproof closer. It had seemed a sensible garment in Leningrad, but he had not been on horseback there, nor out in all the worst of the weather for nine or ten hours at a stretch. 'Tell you what, I'm going to take a lesson from the locals; the next time we reach a town I'm going to buy one of those lambskin caps they all wear, and that kind of cloak thing. And I vote we forget the tent for a night or two, and get someone to give us lodgings.'

It had only rained for forty-eight hours, but when you are sleeping in a very small tent forty-eight hours can seem remarkably like eternity. Deep into the mountains now, with villages few and far between and those that they came across wild and somewhat uncivilised, it had seemed sensible to camp out most nights. But last night the rain had turned into a storm, they had pitched their tent right in the path of a tiny stream which had turned into a very big stream indeed once the deluge started, and they were running short of food.

'I thought you bought enough apples to last a fortnight in Kislovodsk,' Yuri groaned, when his demand for sustenance had brought forth only a very small, very stale, piece of cheese. 'You said your saddlebag was groaning with the things.'

'It was. We've eaten them,' David said shortly. 'We'll buy some food at the next village.'

'Villagers don't like foreigners,' Yuri said dolefully. A rain-drop hung for a moment on the end of his nose, getting larger and larger, then descended with a plop on to the back of his chilly blue hand. 'I've got some gloves in one of my knapsacks; do you suppose we could stop for a moment so I could put them on?'

David pulled his pony to a stop and turned in the saddle. Poor Yuri, he looked so totally depressed! But never mind — when they found a village and got themselves under a roof for a night or two he'd soon be his cheerful self once more. He had thoroughly enjoyed their first few days in the mountains, singing, telling jokes, stretching out on the grass of a wild meadow or by a stream to eat his food and taking off his shirt so that his back could feel the benefit of the sunshine. It was only since the rain had started that his enthusiasm had dwindled away.

'Sorry, old boy, I didn't realise you'd not put gloves on. You carry on — I'll wait.'

Whilst he waited, he looked down at the tiny goat-path they were following. It was alive with snails — big ones, little ones, medium-sized ones, all going somewhere at as lively a pace as a snail can manage. He counted two dozen without effort, then turned to inform Yuri of their companions.

'Look, Yuri, dozens of snails! I suppose the rain brings them out — but why, I wonder? Do they go courting in the rain?'

'Only if they're mad! I say, there are a lot — there's one with a cream and brown striped shell and another with pink and maroon bands round it. Hey!'

'Why hey? I thought you were ready — that's why I kicked my horse on,' David exclaimed. 'Still not got the gloves on?'

'My fingers are numb,' Yuri muttered. 'I thought horses ate grass?'

'So they do; mine's at it.' David glanced round. 'Why?'

'Well, look at mine!'

Yuri's horse, with every appearance of satisfaction, was sniffing for and then crunching up the snails nearest his nose. David laughed but Yuri announced that his horse was an unnatural beast and that he would like to change mounts.

'No!' David said forcibly, kicking his pony's sides and

110

setting off at a determined trot. 'Just sit on yours and shut up and we'll soon be there.'

'Where?'

'There. That herdsman said the village was only half a day's ride along this track.'

'Or did he say a day?' But Yuri gave his mount the office to start and presently, as the track widened, he rode up beside David so that they could converse more easily.

'I hear a river, I think,' David said at length, as they approached a bluff. 'It's good weather for fishing . . . do you think we ought to get our rods out and have a go for some trout?'

But Yuri was saved the trouble of a reply, for as they rounded the bluff they both saw below them in the valley not merely the river, but a good-sized village, and from their vantage point high on the hill above it they could also see that it was market day.

'They're kicking up quite a din,' Yuri remarked, in a lively tone very different from his previous lugubrious notes. 'I wonder we didn't hear them miles back.'

'What, against the din the rain's kicking up, to say nothing of your moans?' David reined his horse in as they began the steep descent. 'At least we shan't have any difficulty in buying food, by the look of it. It's a big market – they must have come from miles around, I should think.'

'There's lots of fruit,' Yuri said, as they got nearer. 'Lots of girls, too.'

'Oh, sure, but the girls won't be for sale, old boy!' David grinned to himself at his friend's typical preoccupation. Poor Yuri had missed girls dreadfully; probably even Natasha, had she suddenly appeared, would have been welcomed with open arms.

'That's where you're wrong,' Yuri said, as the horses, hooves clattering, arrived in a meandering lane which led straight into the market square. 'This is Muslim country; the Caucasians probably sell their women a lot more happily than they part with their horses . . . they think women of little or no account, I'm told. You watch them – only don't let the men see you're watching them or you'll get your throat slit.'

'First they'll sell me a girl without a quibble, then they'll slit my throat if I so much as eye one,' David protested. He pushed

111

his hands through his soaking curls, getting them out of his eyes. 'I say, hats! I bet someone's selling those cloak things, too.'

'If not, offer to buy one off one of the horsemen,' Yuri suggested. It was not as silly as it might sound, either, David reflected as they rode into the vivid throng. There were men on horseback everywhere, lithe, dark-haired Caucasian men who had ridden horses since before they could walk and were seldom seen without an animal either between their knees or following close at hand.

But it was not necessary to try to buy a man's cloak from him, for almost the first thing that met their eyes, as they dismounted and led their horses to a tethering-post, was a stall laden with the very lambskin caps that David had desired, and a little further on was stall after stall of skins – sheepskins, wolfskins, mountain bear skins – and it was here, after only the most cursory glance round, that they saw a number of the square-shouldered 'cloak things', spread out on the ground and protected from the rain by a piece of ragged awning.

David went over and hefted one. It was heavy but beautifully made, the fastenings silver with leather thongs, the thick felt brushed like a bearskin outside and smoothly warm within. David liked the feel of it and was sure it must do its job, since none of the men in the market was wearing a waterproof of any description; each one had only his *burka* to keep him warm and dry, covering not only himself but most of his horse into the bargain.

David asked the price, haggled briefly, and purchased the garment of his choice and a black astrakhan hat to go with it. As soon as he had paid he shed his waterproof and donned his new acquisitions, and Yuri, after one envious glance at the jaunty angle of the hat and the undoubted warmth and weatherproofing of the *burka*, bought a similar garment and then a similar hat.

'I say, if I look as good as you I sure look good,' David exclaimed. 'They make you look twice the man you are.'

Yuri grinned. 'It's the shoulders,' he admitted. 'They're padded, so you look broad-shouldered whether you are or not. But I tell you, Davidski, if you think I look good you should see yourself! With all that dark curly hair and the beard you're sprouting you look like some mountain brigand out of an opera.'

112

'I feel like one. I'm going to get one of those great silver daggers, even if it's only as a souvenir,' David told him. 'And the boots . . . aren't they splendid?'

However, their attention was diverted at that point by a display of hot food at a little stall which made their mouths water – and not only the food, David realised, seeing Yuri ogling the girl acting as saleswoman. She was a lovely thing, with dusky hair, perfect features and the secret, three-cornered smile of her race. She was wearing a high-waisted floral print dress with baggy trousers drawn in tight at the ankles under it, and her arms carried a good weight of fine silver bangles which tinkled as she moved. Yuri tried to engage her in conversation as he bought pancakes and *shashlik*, hot on its wooden skewer, but as soon as she raised her eyes the owner of the vegetable stall next door strolled over with such a menacing air that Yuri decided, hurriedly, that he needed some fresh fruit and the two young men moved on.

When they had exhausted the possibilities of the market – which took a long time as David wanted to buy small presents for his sisters and his mother – Yuri suggested that they might ask someone where they could stay for the night. Although the village was a large one for the area, it was clear that an inn or hotel was unheard of. It would have to be a room in a private house . . . though a glance at the houses told David quite conclusively that they would be sharing the room with the rest of the household – this was a very primitive community, though they built their houses well enough, with stone walls and wooden shutters.

'Ask the horsemen,' Yuri advised in a low voice. 'No use approaching any of the women, and the men on the stalls seem to be mainly from outside the village since they're packing up.'

It was true; the stallholders, most with considerably depleted stocks, were beginning to pack their wares into baskets, boxes and bags in order to load ponies or donkeys or little carts and go on their way. David approached what appeared to be a group of local men and asked them where he and Yuri might spend the night.

The rain was still falling, though the pair had almost ceased to notice it in their new warm clothing and with their new surroundings to take their minds off it. The men looked round, puzzled, and one began to say, haltingly, that there was nowhere suitable when another interrupted.

'Anyone in the village would be honoured to have strangers spending the night under his roof,' he said politely. 'But the schoolhouse is newly built – of brick, too, mark you – and is both warm and commodious. Perhaps it would be best if you approached the schoolmaster first, since he and his wife have no children and you would only have to share the accommodation with the two of them.'

'The schoolteacher is here, buying food,' the first man said, his face clearing. 'See . . . the little man with light-coloured hair.'

They could scarcely have missed him, so different was he from the mountain men. As spherical as a ball, with gold pince-nez, a faded dark suit and an oilskin whose original bright yellow was overlaid with what looked like generations of mud, he stood out like a sore thumb amidst the black *burkas* and lean, swaggering figures of the Caucasians.

'Do we approach him here or go to the schoolhouse?' David wondered, but Yuri had no such doubts.

'Good afternoon! I believe you teach the children here?' he called as the small man slipped and slithered past them, his arms full of fruit and vegetables. 'My friend and I are searching for somewhere to stay the night and these gentlemen suggested that you might be able to find a corner for us.'

'Stay the night?' The round face beamed as Yuri's words sank in. 'My dear chap, I couldn't be more delighted. The locals are the best of good fellows, but they can't read, they treat their women like slaves, and their conversation is limited to the abilities of their horses and the size of their herds.'

'What about our horses?' David asked, as the two of them fell into step with their host. 'They're tethered over there' – he jerked a thumb – 'at the moment but we can't leave them without fodder. Do you have somewhere suitable?'

'Of course, of course. Some of the children come to school on horseback, so we've a shed and a piece of fenced-off grass. Untie your steeds, gentlemen, and you can take their tack off and leave them to graze whilst we eat.' He waited with them as they untied the horses, then bustled ahead, talking to them over his shoulder. 'My wife is an excellent cook, and I bought sheepmeat this morning and all this stuff this afternoon, so I

114

can promise you a good meal tonight and a hot breakfast tomorrow. Will you be staying for a few days, perhaps?'

'I don't think so,' David said rather apologetically. 'We're crossing the Caucasus via the Klukhor Pass and going down to Georgia. We thought we'd sail along the coast of the Black Sea to Novorossiysk, then strike inland to Armavir and pick up the railway to go back to Leningrad by train.'

'I see; then you've no time to lose. Pity, pity.' The little man shook his head sadly but seemed to accept their reasoning. 'Nice to hear that adventure isn't dead . . . ah, but the Black Sea coast . . . the palm trees, the little cafés, the women . . . delicious, quite delicious.'

He led them to a tiny, shaky stable where they hung up their bridles and slipped rope headcollars on to the ponies before releasing them into the field. The grass was good and the ponies began to eat at once. David was glad of it, because they had not been able to hire ponies once they got into real mountain country and could not say with much certainty where or how far they would travel. Understandably no one wanted to part with a good horse and then never see it again. Instead, they had bought these two outright, and would sell them – probably at a profit, the optimistic Yuri said hopefully – when they reached the Georgian coast.

Having shown them the shed and pointed out quite unnecessarily the door of the schoolhouse through which they should enter – it was the only door – the little schoolteacher, whose name was Alexander Yenuki, left them to take his shopping in to his wife. He had spent the walk back from the market explaining that though his mother had been a German citizen his father was pure Cossack, so that he felt himself to be a true Don Cossack and was only sorry that the local people could not accept him as such.

'It's odd how people see themselves, isn't it?' Yuri said presently, as they strolled across to the schoolhouse, their saddles across their arms and saddlebags, knapsacks and bedrolls all over their persons. 'That fat little beggar sees himself as a fearless rider of the open steppes, whereas we see him simply as a schoolteacher who fits perfectly into the role. I wonder how his wife sees him?'

'To a plump little German *Hausfrau* he probably seems quite big and Russian,' David said, backing into the door and opening it with his hip. 'I wonder where he found a German wife out here?'

'He mentioned studying in Moscow,' Yuri said, following him into a small and rather smelly vestibule. 'And it was his mother who was German, not his wife – or I thought that was what he said.'

'Did you? I thought . . . oh!'

The schoolroom door opened and Alexander beamed at them. By his side was his wife.

'Ah, here you are! Come in, come in. Tanya is already cooking the meal . . . she wishes to welcome you both . . . come along, bring your luggage and put it down in the corner by the stove.'

His wife was a mountain girl, slim, dark-eyed, very young. She did not look directly at the two young men but came over to them, eyes lowered, long lashes brushing ivory cheeks, and stood a basin of water on the wooden table. She had set soap and a towel out ready, and when they had soaped their hands she poured warm water over the suds, rinsing them off into the basin. Then, still with her eyes fixed on the floor, or the table, or something at their feet, she picked up the towel and handed it over. She said nothing as she performed what was obviously a ritual greeting, but David thought the sloe eyes followed him – and probably Yuri – rather wistfully as they moved around the schoolroom making themselves at home.

The meal, when it came, was excellent. Oatcakes with thick cheese inside them so that when they were cooked the cheese melted and ran out on to the iron hob to be toasted to a crackly brown lace frill round each cake. Then roast lamb garnished with lemon juice and potatoes cooked in sour cream, with a tomato and gherkin salad. Afterwards they had honey and almond cakes – Tanya's speciality, her husband assured them proudly. They had flat beer with the meal, and after they had eaten David and Yuri made coffee which they drank from the bakelite mugs David had brought with him all the way from Deeside.

When the meal was finished the table was pushed back against the wall and the three men gathered round the fire to talk. The schoolteacher was almost pathetically glad to talk to 'educated men', as he put it, but in fact most of the questions he asked were still unanswerable: was the Five Year Plan working? Would the Russians do as they threatened and collectivise the Cossack farms on the steppes, and come into the mountains to change things here too? Were conditions better than they had been in the cities for the very poor? They were, in the main, self-supporting here, so they had little idea of how the wonderful plans were working out in practice – though every now and then Communist advisers paid them a short visit.

'But they tell us only what *will* happen, and exhort us to save our money or spend it in State shops because the State needs every kopek it can get to make the Plan work . . . we don't have a State shop,' he added, in case there should be any misunderstanding, 'but there is a wireless set in the next village . . . we listen to that, sometimes.'

David had never grown accustomed to the stream of propaganda which emanated from Soviet-run radio, but he supposed that, to people so cut off, it must be more interesting than the more usual exchange of local gossip. When, later in the evening, a large crowd appeared in the schoolroom to talk to the strangers and he ventured this opinion, he was surprised at the response.

'Ha!' a white-bearded old patriarch jeered, slapping his beer mug down on the floor by his side. 'Before, they had to take a long journey and look us in the eye when they wanted to lie to us. Now they can do it through a box without moving a mile from Moscow!'

It was a point of view which would be safer held here than in the lowlands, David thought, grinning at Yuri, who grinned back. The schoolteacher, though, for all his boasted Cossack blood, was not prepared to be quite so bold.

'Now, Achinitz, you're being over-critical; who knows? All the wonderful things they tell us about may be happening – not perhaps in Leningrad, where our guests hail from, but possibly in Moscow.'

'Ha! If they come here and tell me how to raise cattle and when to move my herds they'll get a boot up the arse for their trouble,' the irrepressible Achinitz replied. 'Let them save their schemes and false talk for plainsmen and peasants – *we* are men!'

The company grinned and agreed, and after more talk and a good deal of laughter the schoolteacher, his wife, Yuri and

David were left to make their preparations for bed.

'You can put your bedrolls here,' Alexander told them, fussing over the exact spot and straightening the saddles, which both men used as a combination of pillow and draught excluder, with mathematical precision. 'Tanya and I sleep to the right of the stove, so if you sleep to the left we shall all be warm and comfortable.'

The schoolhouse, it appeared, was just that. There was a little lean-to where food and bits and pieces were stored, the tiny vestibule, and the schoolroom itself with its hot stove on which Tanya cooked and by which pupils and teacher warmed themselves. It was clear that the schoolmaster thought there was nothing strange in eating, sleeping and teaching in one room, still less in entertaining two guests there.

David and Yuri fussed over their bedding, which looked miserably inadequate compared to the pile of multi-coloured quilts the schoolteacher's wife had spread out on the floor. However, although the rain still poured down outside, inside it was very warm and as dry as the most critical person could wish. David was taking off his outer clothing when he glimpsed a movement out of the corner of his eye, and glancing across to the pile of quilts he saw, with some consternation, that the schoolteacher's wife was just removing her last garment, a sort of long underskirt, and that beneath it she was completely naked. David hastily looked away, and it was not until he began to get into his own sleeping bag that he glanced across again, to find that host and hostess were now but a couple of mounds beneath their quilts.

'Are we ready for sleep?' Alexander asked presently. 'If so, I shall douse the lantern.' He reached out and turned the kerosene lamp off, then disappeared into the quilts once more. Moonlight came through the window shutters in pale stripes and fell on the room, transforming it into a symphony in black and white. David settled down but Yuri shuffled his bedding a bit closer and leaned out.

'Well, what about that?' he whispered in English, which they had already ascertained that the schoolteacher did not speak. 'A pretty little thing like her tied to a man twice her age and with a belly on him like a melon! When she undressed I saw her . . .'

'Shut up! Don't be crude.'

118

'My God, David, are you made of stone? Didn't you see her br . . .'

'Yes, I did. I couldn't help it. Now do shut up, there's a good chap. I'm trying to get warm and it's uphill work; there's a hellish draught coming under the door. I wonder why they don't have platforms to sleep on, like the Chinese?'

'I'm not cold, I got all hot when I saw that lovely, rosy . . .'

'Shut *up*!'

David curled up in his bag with his knees close to his chin so that he could rub his icy feet warm, but presently he was nudged in the ribs by a hearty elbow.

'What's that rustling? Don't say Fatty's going to start something, with us no more than six feet away!'

Horribly embarrassed by his friend, who had lapsed back into Russian, David tried to fake a snore. He hoped that it would simultaneously allow the schoolteacher to do whatever he wanted to do, believing himself to be the only male in the room still awake, and drown any further rustlings. Yuri, however, had no such inhibitions. David, in mid-snore, heard a nearer rustling than that emanating from the quilts and opened his eyes to see Yuri lying on his stomach, staring avidly at the pile of quilts. David looked too. The quilts were heaving. Rhythmically? No. Not rhythmically, quite randomly. In his turn, David nudged Yuri with his knee.

'Stop staring, idiot. They are married, you know, it's up to them what they do.'

'Ah, that's true. But it isn't anything. He's just heaving about, though for a moment I thought . . .'

'I don't care what you thought and you've no right to think things like that anyway. For heaven's sake go to sleep!'

For ten minutes they lay there in silence. David began to get a little warmer but he was still too cold to sleep. Then, very softly, he heard tiny snores beginning to come from the pile of quilts. Thank heaven, the other two were sleeping; if he moved very carefully indeed, he could hook his *burka* off the table and scuttle back to bed with it, and then perhaps he would be able to sleep. The thought of the extra warmth was so delightful that presently David actually left his sleeping bag, scuttled across the floor, snatched the *burkas* from where they lay and tiptoed back to his bed. He flung Yuri's *burka* across to him just as his friend rolled on to his back. Yuri grunted.

'Hey, mind my . . . I say, that's an idea! We'll be warm as toast under these.'

They were. In fact, had it not been for the positive volley of snores, grunts and wheezes coming from the schoolteacher, David would undoubtedly have slept, for he was very tired. As it was, fascinated despite himself by the noise, he was actually staring across at the quilts when the schoolteacher gave a particularly loud snore accompanied by a particularly violent heave and his young wife, naked as the day she was born, was ejected from the pile of quilts, to lie for a stunned moment on the chilly bare boards of the schoolroom floor. Her husband, obviously not realising what he had done, was now pressed lovingly against the stove, his arms wrapped round a big pile of bedding whilst his rosy face, innocent now of spectacles or expression, proceeded to trumpet forth snore after snore.

David was just wondering what a gentleman should do in the circumstances when the puzzle was solved in an unexpected manner. Yuri leaned up on his elbow, made a long arm, and caught hold of the schoolteacher's wife. He heaved himself towards her and rolled her towards him and, whilst David's eyebrows were still on their way up to his hairline, the girl slithered neatly into Yuri's sleeping bag, Yuri heaved the *burka* up as far as it would go, and the two of them disappeared from view.

David hissed Yuri's name and sat up like a jack-in-the-box just as the snoring faltered. He promptly lay flat again, his heart thumping. Alexander had boasted earlier that he was a true Don Cossack; how would a Cossack revenge himself on someone who took his woman, even if he had only taken her in the nicest possible sense of the word? But David, eyeing the stealthy movements which were causing Yuri's *burka* to rise and fall gently, decided he was being too generous to his friend; what Yuri appeared to be doing could scarcely be termed nice in any language, or at least not from the schoolteacher's viewpoint.

Fortunately for David's peace of mind the snores started up louder than ever and the schoolteacher slumbered on. Beneath the *burka*, which was heaving like a storm-tossed sea, no one could possibly have slept. No one rested, either. Torn between amusement, indignation and envy David lay awake, half expecting a slap to ring out like a pistol shot, or a scream to split the night, but nothing of the sort occurred. The gentle, sloe-eyed maiden appeared to be enjoying the activity beneath the *burka* just as much as Yuri.

Presently, however, the warmth conferred by his own additional covering began to make sleeping seem possible at last. Toes unfroze, kneecaps no longer ached with the cold and gradually, as warmth seeped through him, David became very drowsy indeed. For a while he clung to consciousness, convinced that the schoolteacher would wake or his wife would suddenly come to her senses and cry out, but as he grew sleepier it seemed to matter less and less and at last he slept, telling himself that he would wake the moment the girl tried to leave Yuri's bed. And wouldn't he have a word or two to say to Yuri in the morning!

David only woke once in the course of the night, when he peered across at the quilts and then at his friend's bedding, but in the moonlight it was impossible to tell which bed held two people and which one, so when a hissing of Yuri's name failed to elicit any response David simply snuggled down again and went back to sleep. He had meant to be wakeful and alert but he was far too tired, so if Yuri woke to find his throat had been cut it would be just too bad.

He was finally woken, in broad daylight, by the schoolteacher's wife, bearing a glass of tea. She smiled at him without catching his eye, put the tea down beside him and glided out of the room again. David sat up. Yuri had gone, taking his sleeping bag with him as well as all his clothing and his *burka*, though the saddle was still in the centre of the floor. Of Alexander Yenuki, too, there was no sign.

David struggled out of his bag and drank his tea, then padded across to the basin which he and Yuri had used to wash in the previous evening. It was filled with fresh water now, and the soap and towel beside it were also clean and new-looking. David washed, dressed, and headed for the outside world. Would he find a duel in progress in the sunshine? What had happened whilst he, insensitive clod that he was, had slumbered? In short, with whom had the schoolteacher's wife been sleeping when dawn broke?

Stepping outside, David took a deep breath of the clean mountain air. It was a glorious morning. After the rain of the previous few days the mountains shone, new-washed, and the clouds which sped briskly across the blue sky looked as white as newborn lambs. Even the leaves on the trees which surrounded the market square looked as though someone had just painted them a glossy, invigorating green.

To one side of the schoolhouse there was a yard, roughly cobbled, and it was here that Yuri and the schoolteacher sat with a small, wobbly deal table between them. The schoolteacher's wife was standing, pouring something from a jug into two familiar-looking bakelite mugs. David sniffed. Freshly brewed coffee! And there were plump white bread rolls and creamy butter and a jar with jam in it. Breakfast was to be alfresco this morning, it seemed. Obviously, the schoolteacher's wife had woken up where she belonged — or perhaps it would be more accurate to say the schoolteacher had woken up to find his wife where she belonged! David crossed the cobblestones and took the third chair.

'Good morning. How nice to see the sun.'

'Good morning, good morning . . . sit, dear sir . . . eat!' The schoolteacher's smile stretched from ear to ear. 'Your travelling companion has given my wife . . .' Help, thought David involuntarily, but the schoolteacher had hesitated only to search for the correct word, '. . . coffee beans, and has shown her how to crush them, so now she has made this delicious beverage which you were kind enough to share with us last night. You must enjoy it too . . . and the white bread, another rare treat.'

'Will your wife not join us?' David said, as the girl stood back, hands folded, watching the table and never raising her eyes. 'After all, it is she we have to thank for this delicious breakfast.'

The schoolteacher rubbed his hands together, his glasses glinting in the sunshine. He looked pleased and proud, not at all like a man who suspected he had been cuckolded by one of his guests during the night.

'Ah, my wife . . . I appreciate your thoughtfulness, but she's a local girl, you see, and she would not put herself forward. She would think it unbecoming to sit down with men, or to eat with them. She will eat when we have finished, as is her custom.'

David flashed a quick glance at Yuri after this artless speech, but his friend's face reflected nothing but enjoyment of the food and pleasure in the bright morning. David took a roll, split it open and buttered it. It was as soft and fresh as any bread he had ever tasted, totally different from the heavy, unleavened stuff they were usually offered. He said as much to Alexander Yenuki, who nodded wisely.

'Ah, yes, for you see though my father was a Cossack warrior my mother worked for a pastrycook in Moscow before the revolution. She taught me to bake and I taught my wife. Of course, it is not always possible to get the correct ingredients, but from time to time fate smiles on us and we enjoy white bread.'

After they had broken their fast the two friends went to pack their belongings and to tack up the horses, and David had a chance to ask Yuri the questions that were burning in his mind.

'Just what were you up to last night, old man, as if I didn't know?'

'Up to?' Yuri looked surprised. 'Whatever do you mean? I slept . . . what else should I have done?'

'Oh, I dare say you did sleep, afterwards. What time did you kick her out? I take it she got back into bed with her husband before he woke, or he might not have been quite so complaisant this morning. Really, Yuri, it was too bad; you were a guest in the schoolhouse . . .'

Yuri interrupted him.

'My dear chap, what on earth are you talking about? I slept pretty soundly, once I dropped off. I didn't even stir until the girl woke me with a glass of tea.'

'*My dear chap*,' David mimicked savagely, 'I'm telling you I was awake, I saw it all! The girl slid out of the quilts, you pulled her in with you . . . don't try to fool *me*, Yuri – I saw you!'

'I pulled the girl in with *me*?' Yuri's face was bewildered, his voice rising. David shushed him with a quick gesture.

'Yes . . . no need to tell the whole village, though. I saw the whole thing.'

'You were dreaming,' Yuri said positively. 'Wish I had dreams like that! You don't mean to tell me you thought I actually had my way with the fellow's wife, with you lying six inches away and he no more than six feet off? By Jupiter, you must think me the devil of a fellow!'

123

'I think you've got the devil's own cheek,' David growled. 'Well, if you say I was dreaming we'd better forget it. Only I could have sworn I saw you . . .'

'Perhaps it was you,' Yuri said, grinning. 'Perhaps you crawled over there and fished her out of her bed and carried her back to your sleeping bag! And now you're trying to blame me to clear your own conscience.'

'Ha! Well, that's my horse ready to move on. Ought we to pay for our night's lodging, do you suppose?'

'A gift would probably be more tactful than money,' Yuri said after a moment's thought. 'There are still some stalls left in the market, so we could buy them something down there. There isn't much furniture in that schoolroom when you think about it.'

'Yes, all right,' David said, and the two of them set off for the market square, David still not at all sure in his own mind that he *had* imagined the goings-on of the previous night.

Once in the market they separated, David to buy some fruit for their journey and Yuri a thick slab of the honey and almond cake they had seen and tasted several times already. When they met, they agreed on two magnificent cushions, a blue one and an emerald green one, the satin covers so thoroughly stuffed that they looked like two little brightly coloured pigs. The schoolteacher and his wife were delighted and almost over-come. Alexander Yenuki thanked them profusely – he was tired of sitting on the floor all the time, it would be a real pleasure and a luxury to use these fine cushions, every time he sat on them he would remember his friends David and Yuri from faraway Leningrad. When they rode away he was urging his pupils to admire the cushions, and doing it so loudly that most of the village had wandered over to stare and marvel.

The last David saw of the schoolteacher's wife was a little vignette which stayed with him for a long time. She was standing in the tiny cobbled yard in front of the table, staring into space. With her left hand she was pushing the bangles on her right wrist up and down, up and down, and they gleamed silver and gold against her ivory flesh. As David and Yuri crossed her line of vision she smiled very sweetly and the fingers which had been playing with the bangles left them for a moment, fluttered briefly, and then returned to their former task.

Was she waving farewell? On whom had those dark eyes rested, as they rode away? And was it his imagination that he had seen gold as well as silver on her delicate wrist? Last night he had noticed particularly that she wore only silver bangles. Was there a new, gold, bangle amongst the silver?

For the rest of the morning he puzzled over the incident. Had he really imagined the entire business the previous night? Was Yuri as innocent as he pretended? David had half expected excuses or prevarication when the time had come to leave, but Yuri had packed up amicably enough and had not even suggested a longer stay.

I must have imagined it, David decided at last, as the ponies began to pick their way up the steep ascent on the further side of the valley. What with the moonlight and the schoolteacher's snores and the fact that I was absolutely worn out . . . yes, I either imagined it or dreamed it.

So busy was he with his own thoughts that he quite failed to notice the warm, reminiscent smile which curved his friend's lips, or his unusual silence.

'You mean you've gone far enough? But why, Yuri? You were as keen as I to see Georgia — keener! The weather's getting warmer and pleasanter every day, we've still got lots of food left and we can buy more in the *aouls* and *koshes*. People here are the most hospitable I've ever encountered . . . you must feel it too. You don't really want to go off back to Leningrad before you've got to, do you?'

'I'm holding you back, you know I am,' Yuri said flatly. The two of them were sitting on a fallen pine tree, in the shade of a belt of evergreens, looking out over one of those incredible views to which not even the most jaded of travellers ever becomes accustomed. Below them sloped a deep valley, green now, but scattered with great rocks, and ahead stretched peak after peak, grim, rocky, snow-capped, the mighty mountains still to be conquered.

'Holding me back? Scarcely, my dear chap! I wouldn't pretend you were the world's finest horseman, and I know you aren't keen on heights, but what's the hurry, anyway? I'm enjoying our leisurely pace.'

It was not quite true, but it was better than admitting that Yuri's steady stream of grumbling whenever they had to traverse a tiny track high in the mountains with a deep drop on one side of them and a sheer rock wall on the other *was* beginning to get him down. And it did not help that Yuri had suddenly decided that he would be a good deal safer – and happier – on foot. They used his pony to carry all their belongings, but it naturally meant that the small expedition had to go at a slow walking pace instead of whatever the horses could manage.

'Even if that were true, which I know it isn't, how much of Georgia do you think we'll see if we continue at this "leisurely pace"? Precious little! And Davidski, it's going to get worse, not better. As we go higher I feel sick with apprehension that that damned donkey is going to tip me over the edge, and you know I've never climbed in my life . . . we don't do much mountain climbing in the Ukraine . . . and I think I'm just too old to start now. It was a great idea and I've enjoyed it, but now's the time to quit.'

'Well, if you really feel so strongly, we'd better turn back first thing tomorrow morning,' David said with real regret. He had known and loved the country and solitude for so many years, and it was only since recapturing it here in the Caucasus that he realised how much he had missed it and how he was valuing it. He dreaded the return to Leningrad, but he must be fair. If Yuri really was hating every minute, then they must give the trip up. But Yuri, it appeared, had no such intention – or not for David, at any rate.

'You turn back? David, you must be mad! As if I'd ask you to abandon your adventure! No, no, you must go on! As for turning back, I shan't go right back to Leningrad and into the dread arms of Natasha – no fear! What I thought I'd do was go back to that decent little hotel in Kislovodsk and stay there until our holiday is finished. And then last night, when the herdsman told you how difficult it was to get over the Klukhor Pass at this time of year, I had another plan. You go ahead and try to get through to Georgia, but if you can't you can pick me up in Kislovodsk on your way back. How does that appeal to you?'

'Well . . . I do want to have a go at the Pass, and I'd certainly go insane hanging round Kislovodsk for days at a time,' David said slowly. 'If you're absolutely sure, I reckon I could still do the whole trip in the time I've got left. Only . . . it makes me feel such a selfish blighter.'

'Rubbish! I tell you, if you insisted and made me come along I should think you selfish, but if you go on alone I shall know you're a hero. There, I can't say fairer than that, can I?'

David sighed and got to his feet. He began to collect pine cones and dry twigs to make a fire.

'I suppose not. Very well, if you're sure . . . you and I will part company. But don't think I'm letting you traverse all those hair-raising mountain paths alone, because I'm not going to do that. I'll come back with you to that *aoul* we passed yesterday and we'll get a fellow to ride back to the foothills with you. And then you can pay him by giving him either the pony or the rest of your food or whatever you feel is appropriate.'

'Not the pony — I intend to live on that pony while you're gone,' Yuri said, and laughed at David's expression. 'I shan't *eat* it, you fool. I shall sell it for a good price and use the money to pay for my food. If you're sure you don't mind spending a day coming back to that *aoul* with me, I would be most grateful.'

'Goodbye, old fellow . . . give my regards to Georgia . . . the Black Sea . . . Sebastopol . . . Tell them I'll get there one day, but it won't be on horseback!'

Yuri turned in his saddle and shouted his message back whilst his companion, a cheerful, red-faced herdsman who had needed no bribery to take him down to the foothills with the young foreigner since he was betrothed to a girl there, waved on his own account to the friends who had gathered to see him off.

'Be good, Yuri . . . don't go messing with the local ladies . . . and if you run out of money just take the train home,' David roared. 'Take care of yourself.'

'And you.'

Yuri's voice was small already, and a lot more cheerful. Poor fellow, David reflected, as he turned his own mount towards the great peaks once more, he was not cut out for roughing it or scrambling on horseback; probably he would have hated the climbing almost as much as he imagined he would.

As he left the *aoul* behind him, a new lightness came over him, and a new freedom brought a song to his lips. Fond though he was of Yuri, there was absolutely nothing quite so good as being alone, with your bed and your food on your back, heading for the hills! For a moment he imagined Nibby's reproachful look if he knew how David's thoughts were running and, hastily, he placated his old friend. The only thing better than being alone in mountain country was being alone with Nibby in mountain country.

It was a sunny day but the wind was strong, a buffeting, friendly wind which seemed sportive and playful, bending the grass now one way, now another. David sang into the wind, songs of home, songs of his youth, and he took off his astrakhan hat and kicked his pony into a wild canter and then a gallop over the sloping sandy bank of a river, pulling the little creature up when the terrain became rocky and treacherous once more.

This time yesterday he had been plodding up this valley with Yuri muttering behind him, complaining about the strangest things: the number of trees, the dearth of trees. The warmth of the sun, the coldness of the wind at dusk. The sour taste of the cheese, the too-sweet flavour of honey cake.

Today I can please myself, David thought exultantly, turning his pony up a narrow track which would lead them out of this valley, over the next mountain ridge, and down into another valley. What could be nicer than that?

Not much further to the Klukhor Pass, and then I can find myself a guide and tackle it with his assistance, David told himself five days later. He rode through the deepening dusk, hoping that he would soon come to a *kosh* or a homestead where he might shelter for the night. It had been a wild and windy day and the rain, which had started late in the afternoon, had come suddenly and soaked him before he could unstrap his *burka* from its place on his horse's back or get out his astrakhan hat. Accordingly, he was dripping wet, and though he was quite capable of erecting his tent, lighting a fire and getting himself comfortable he did think that on such a night a roof – a solid roof – over his head might not be a bad thing. Furthermore, he was running rather short on food; fresh milk and meat would be welcome and most of the mountain men were only too willing to sell him enough for his simple needs.

He was at the head of the valley when he looked down it and was surprised but happy to see a farm of some size nestling below him. It was a big place, considerably larger than the *koshes* he had been passing for some days now, and it had fenced fields or pastures, unusual in a country where the inhabitants had never really settled down from their nomadic ways and still took their herds great distances to graze.

Screwing up his eyes to see better against the rain, which was now coming down in torrents, David decided he'd ride down that way and hope the farmer was hospitable. So far, his experiences had been happy indeed, with the lonely *kosh*-dwellers delighted to see him and eager to entertain a foreigner in their homes, particularly when they found he was not a Russian but from a tiny island called Britain, far away from their mighty homeland. But this man was no herdsman, he was a person of property. Still, there could be no harm in approaching the place.

His pony clearly approved of the idea when he turned its head towards the lush valley below; it was a game little beast and scrambled cheerfully down a path so steep that David would have hesitated to descend it on foot in the miserable grey light which was all the rainclouds afforded them. At the foot of it, he could no longer see the homestead; the valley was long and wide, far larger than he had realised when seeing it from his bird's-eye view on the mountain above, but since it was still raining he might as well make his way towards the farm. If it got much darker he would be forced to bivouac wherever he happened to be, or risk being benighted in strange country.

Halfway to the farm it occurred to him that he would have to run the gamut of the dogs. Every *kosh* in the high mountains kept a number of huge and vicious dogs, apparently eager to see if they could take a thigh-bone or two from each passer-by. Reining in his horse, he looked hopefully around him. If he could find a herdsman . . .

He spotted a herd higher up the slopes which appeared to be coming towards him and was about to turn his horse in that direction when the very creature he had intended to guard against found him. A huge dog, the largest he had seen, which was saying something, came charging down the slope heading straight for him. Fortunately it was white, which meant that David saw it earlier than he might have done. With the instinctive caution of one who had encountered Caucasian dogs before, he slid his feet free of the stirrups and prepared to repel boarders. Not that he had ever been attacked or even menaced when on horseback, but there was always a first time and this looked horribly like it.

'Baru! Stay!'

The words were roared out from a distance, but even so they were sufficient to bring the big dog screaming to a halt, all four legs braced, its head turning at once to the source of the shout. Through the driving rain David followed the direction of the dog's gaze and saw the herdsman. He was on horseback and *burka*-clad, of course, with the inevitable sheepskin cap keeping the rain off his head. He rode closer, a little wary as all the mountain men were with strangers.

'Yes? You are wishing to see Fedor, or are you just passing through?'

It was a gruff young voice and David saw that the herdsman was a lad of probably no more than fourteen or fifteen. He grinned at him.

'Phew, your dog gave me a turn! I'm on my way up to the Klukhor Pass. I'm hoping to go across into Georgia, but I shall need a guide and I was wondering if there's room in the farmhouse . . .' he gestured vaguely in the direction of the homestead he had seen from his former position, '. . . room in the farmhouse for me to spend the night? I've got a tent and all my equipment but it's raining pretty hard and it looks as though it's set in for the night now.'

The boy flicked a quick glance at the sky, then a longer, more curious look at David.

'Baru is a good guard dog; one needs her, out here. She would not let harm come to me but sometimes she's a little . . . over-zealous.' The boy's rather serious face was split, suddenly, by an attractively wicked grin. 'If you had ridden off at speed she'd have had you off your horse at a word from me – I've trained her to do it without actually shedding blood.'

'What about breaking legs, or doesn't it worry you if she cracks a few shins?' But David grinned back. 'I'm glad, in that case, that I stood my ground. Is Fedor your father?'

Mountain manners, he remembered a little late, demanded that one never said outright that one was looking for lodgings. The dog's sudden arrival had flustered him into making the unforgivable request . . . oh damn, and it had to happen in a cloudburst, when he really didn't fancy wet canvas and cold food.

The lad nodded.

'That's right. He knows the Klukhor Pass well, as indeed I do myself.'

'It seems I've come to the right place for a guide, then – if you or your father could spare the time? I would like to set out within the next three or four days, though, if that's possible.'

'We can ask him.' The two of them were riding abreast, heading for the low, creeper-hung house which was just in view now despite the grey curtain of the rain. 'You are from Moscow?'

'Not really. I'm living in Leningrad at the moment, working on a government scheme, but actually I'm British.'

'British? Ah, English!'

David smiled. 'Do I call you Russian? In fact I'm Welsh, which is like you saying . . .'

'I am Caucasian; I see.' The boy turned and grinned again, the rain running down his face making him blink as drops clung to his lashes. 'That is a good thing to remember; British is all of them, English is one of them, Welsh is another. Are there more?'

'Yes, the Irish and the Scots are British but not English.'

'I see. Yet I *am* Russian, I suppose. Though if I said that before my father he would not be pleased. He calls them plainsmen, Slavs, all sorts, but rarely Russian. It's strange, isn't it, that though he is quite a young man he still remembers that the Caucasus has only been a part of the Soviet Union for sixty-odd years? He let my sister and me go to school though he knew we would be taught by Party members, but we were warned every morning before we rode off that one accepts the whole fruit but selects what is worth eating and what is better thrown away! They taught us to read and write so that they could get us used to the idea of collectivism, but Fedor said education was like an orange – you threw away the thick old peel and the bitter pips and ate the good flesh only.'

131

'Quite a philosopher,' David said. 'You've left school? Or is today a holiday?'

This time the look he received was blazing, despite the rain.

'Do I look like a child? I am no such thing, I am sixteen! Do you think a schoolchild would offer to take you through the Klukhor Pass? Or offer you the hospitality of Father's roof before obtaining permission? Huh!'

'I'm sorry,' David said meekly, then realised what his companion had just said. 'I say . . . you will take me over the Pass? And it will be all right for me to stay the night? Thanks very much!'

'That's all right.' The remote little face broke into that delightfully wicked smile once again. 'I am too bad . . . how could you know? My name's Pavel; what's yours?'

'Hello, Pavel. I'm David. Are you a large family? I have four sisters and two brothers.'

He said it only to forestall the inevitable questions, for those who live in lonely places are always curious about the few strangers they meet and usually as eager to tell of themselves, but Pavel, it seemed, was an exception.

'I have one sister. Baru, to heel.'

Baru, who had been sniffing curiously at David's bedroll, trotted back to pace majestically along in Pavel's horse's footsteps. Ahead of them, an open gate in a fenced-off corral was obviously a known and accepted destination for the herd of small black cattle, for they streamed inside and Pavel leaned over and shut the gate, then looped a piece of rope round it.

'There, safe for the night. You are sure you would not prefer to erect your tent?'

He was grinning again, and David smiled too, shaking his head.

'I think I can resist the lure of the open, if you're sure your father won't mind an uninvited guest?'

'You've been invited,' the boy snapped back at once. 'Fedor would not insult my judgement by refusing to honour my invitation.'

Stiff-necked young idiot, David thought; how careful you had to be not to hurt the dignity of these wild young men, who could ride a horse as if they were a part of it, climb mountains better than the local goats, shoot straight, kill a man with the two-foot dagger that hung at every belt . . . yet, because they

132

were young and untried by wars, needed constant reassurance that there was a place for them in this new world which their fathers denied but which their own common sense must tell them would come even to the mountain country one day.

Since David said nothing, Pavel obviously considered there was no more to be said and they rode in silence until they were within twenty yards or so of the homestead, when two great dogs shot out like arrows from a bow and stood either side of David's horse. They had excellent teeth, David noticed without approval.

'Baru, tell them this is a friend,' the boy said briefly over his shoulder, swinging his horse to the right so that they passed in front of the house itself and made for what was obviously an outbuilding, built in an L-shape on one end of the house. To David, he added, 'We'll deal with the horses first, then I'll take you in. The dogs won't interfere with you now . . . unless you act in a way which seems to them strange or threatening.'

'I wouldn't want to upset them,' David assured his new acquaintance, swinging down from his horse and beginning to unpack his belongings. It was good to be under the shelter of a roof again, though it was rather dark in the stable and quite stuffy. 'Tell me what they dislike and I won't do it.'

This time the boy's grin was reluctant. 'Just forget them; whilst a member of the family's with you you're safe enough.'

'Do they tear many visitors limb from limb?' David asked, as the two of them worked on the horses. 'When you were at school, suppose a teacher or a fellow pupil came by, what would happen then?'

'They never did. Too far. But when men from the *aoul* want to consult Fedor over something, they make their presence known from afar – the dogs won't leave the immediate vicinity of the house unless they're told to do so. Nyusha hears the men hallooing and comes out to get the dogs indoors. So you see when men come . . if they did, I mean . . . to steal our sheep or cattle, the dogs warn us by barking first and then, if we tell them to do so, they charge out and deal with the thieves.'

'And do thieves often come?' David asked, as they made their way across the hard dirt yard. 'You're so remote!'

'No, only wolves and, once, a bear,' Pavel said calmly. 'The wolves usually come in winter . . . then we have wolf-fires and we pay a boy from the *aoul* to tend them . . . and the bears come to the river after fish. Sometimes they come for the crops, but hardly ever. I've only ever seen one. No, the usual thing is that a wandering tribe from a distant village settles down with its beasts on our grazing, and then Father and I and all the dogs but one go up and deal with them.'

'Not violently, I trust?'

Pavel laughed. 'Not so far; it hasn't been necessary. But if they refused to move on we would use violence. Naturally; who would not?'

They reached the door and Pavel flung it open, calling, 'Nyusha?' as he stepped into the room beyond. David, following, was pleasantly surprised by the lightness and brightness of the place and also by its resemblance to a farmhouse kitchen back in his native Wales. The small windows had wooden shutters, but also checked curtains, and the floor, though only hard-packed earth, was scattered with bright woven rugs and a sheepskin or two. There was a dresser with thick white china displayed on it, a wooden table whitened by much scrubbing, and a number of obviously home-made chairs and stools, all complete with brightly coloured cushions and embroidered cloths over their backs. There were pictures on two of the walls, and an open door to one side of the entrance through which Pavel had ushered David showed a well stocked storeroom with onions dangling in strings from the ceiling, a ham, some long, dark purple sausage and various bags and boxes which could have held anything as well as immediately identifiable heaps of cabbages, swedes and carrots piled up against one wall.

There was also a small girl, standing on a stool, kneading dough in a large wooden bowl. She was a pretty child with bright curls which at the moment were falling forward over her flushed face. She wore a very large apron which all but obscured her pink cotton dress and she looked up as they entered, pushing her hair behind her ears as she did so.

'Pavel, you're dripping all over my . . . oh!'

'A guest . . . David,' Pavel said gruffly. 'Where's Nyusha?'

'Fetching more flour; I made the dough too wet so now we've got to use more flour before I can roll it out. It's all right though, don't you think?' She tipped the bowl towards the two newcomers. 'See? One day my bread will be as good as hers, just you see!'

'Huh! You shouldn't jump up and down on dough with all your weight like that. You should treat it gently, with respect.'

'A fat lot you know! When did you last make bread, clever clogs?' The small sister glared up at the slim young man, his *burka* dripping all over the floor and darkening the rug on which he stood. 'Oh, I know you've *tried*, but I don't think Nyusha ought to let you; you have all the fun of herding. Housework is for me!'

'Fun? Not in the winter it's not, when your fingers freeze to the reins and the wolves come far too close,' Pavel said with considerable relish. 'I'd like to see you throw a burning faggot at a wolf that got too near . . . and it's raining rivers out there right now, but who gets the flour? Not little Eva!'

'I would've, but you know what it's like when your fists are covered in dough and Mother said she'd just as soon . . . Pavel, if you don't stop smirking I'll not let you have even a taste of my bread,' the small girl said wrathfully. 'You are a pig!'

'And you, little madam, are . . .'

'Don't fight, you two! For goodness sake, Pavel, the moment you come in lately you seem to fall out.' A plump, pretty woman emerged from the store-room clutching a sack. 'Here, pour some of this out on the table and stop baiting your sister. Oh!'

She, too, had noticed David, standing a little behind Pavel.

'I've brought a guest, Mother, David, an Eng . . . I mean he's British,' Pavel said hastily. 'He wants to go over the Klukhor Pass and asked if Fedor or I could guide him. It's a foul evening and I've offered him the hospitality of our home. And a meal, of course.'

'Of course.' She smiled at David, a comfortable, placid smile which immediately put him at his ease and made him feel like a desired guest and not an outsider. 'I'm afraid we'll have to ask you to sleep in here, as we've only two bedrooms, but you'll be very welcome indeed. I have blankets and pillows in plenty and of course we grow most of our own food, so you're welcome to stay as many nights as you wish.'

'It's good of you,' David said. He was in a slight dilemma, not knowing whether to offer to shake hands or not, but Nyusha solved it for him by taking his hand in both of hers and and formally kissing his cheek. As she stepped back, he

135

finished, 'If the weather clears, I'd like to try the Pass tomorrow, so I shan't impose upon you for very long.'

'We like having a guest. But this valley is deep and sheltered, you know; the nearer you get to the Pass the harsher the climate. Today, probably, whilst we've had rain, it's snowed up there – conditions can be dangerous there when all seems set fair here.'

'Dangerous? I know I'll be climbing in snow . . .'

Pavel interrupted him. 'It isn't the snow that's the problem, it's avalanches, and there's a glacier one has to cross. Nyusha's trying to say that the Pass can be almost more dangerous now than at any other time of year. It's beginning to thaw, you see, and the snow and ice are beginning to slither and slide. In three, four weeks you would get through with no trouble, but now everything depends on the weather at the moment you decide to go through. Do you see?'

'I'm beginning to,' David said ruefully. 'That's what ignorance does, you see – or perhaps I should say a bit of knowledge. I've climbed in our Welsh mountains at home many times, even in deep winter, but our conditions are different – not as violent, I imagine. Well, I don't think our mountains are quite as high, come to think of it! This means, I suppose, that I shall have to change my plans.'

'Not at all,' Pavel said briskly. 'Don't give up too soon. Tomorrow, if the weather's reasonable, or the day after that, we'll go up to the Pass and you can see for yourself what conditions are like. We won't attempt to go through, of course, until it's safe to do so.'

'It's very good of you,' David said gratefully. 'I can always erect my tent if I have to stay a night or two longer.'

'Nonsense, David, it makes us very happy to have you as our guest. Fedor will be delighted; he says there are too many females in this house for his good! Pavel, my dear, go and get changed . . . take some water to your room. David can clean up in here whilst Eva and I see to the milking.'

Eva, looking rather startled, began to protest, and David, wanting to be helpful, said: 'If Pavel doesn't mind, may I share his room for a moment and change out of my wet things?'

He was surprised by the family's reaction to this. Pavel, pouring water from a big iron kettle steaming on top of the stove, went very red and muttered something. Eva giggled and then clapped her hand over her mouth. Only Nyusha seemed unperturbed.

'Pavel wears breeches and the *burka* when she herds the cattle, David, but actually she was named for a friend of her father's. She's a girl.'

'A girl?' David goggled at Pavel's slim back in its black tunic, for she had turned her shoulder on the room as soon as her mother started to speak. 'I'm so sorry, I had no idea – I hope I didn't say anything I shouldn't have said?'

'It doesn't matter,' Pavel said gruffly. She snatched off her sheepskin hat and her hair tumbled over her shoulders, fawn overlaid with gold from the summer sun. 'I wish I *was* a boy . . . but I'm as good as, Fedor says.'

'We don't try to deceive anyone into believing that Pavel's a boy,' Nyusha said gently, patting her daughter's slim shoulder. 'We love her just as she is. But we have no sons and Pavel rides better than most lads, so when we decided she should be allowed to herd the cattle with Fedor we thought it would be wiser to let her wear the breeches and *burka*. Sometimes she's far from home with only Baru and her horse . . . there are wandering tribes . . . even people on walking tours . . . we felt it was safer.'

'Yes,' David said weakly. He was still searching his memory for some unwise thing he might have said, but concluded that he had behaved quite well, having thought that the 'lad' was both young and inexperienced. He smiled at Pavel. 'You're not cross? You had me completely fooled. You even quarrelled with your sister just as a brother would!'

That won a smile from her and David chided himself for having thought, even for a moment, that she could have been a youth; so sweet, so wickedly feminine was her smile that he decided her parents had indeed been wise to dress her in the *burka*. God knew what might have happened to her otherwise, amongst the wild tribesmen who lived in the *aouls* and considered a woman to be a convenient form of slave!

'Well, since I can't share your room, Pavel, could I perhaps share that water? Just a drop, to get the travel mud off me?'

'No, certainly not. You will have a whole kettleful,' Nyusha interposed. 'Have you made the dough into loaves, Eva? Good girl. Now we'll stand them down here, by the stove, to prove. Then presently, when David's finished changing,

137

we'll pop them into the oven. Off with you, Pavel! Come along, Eva, let's get the cow milked.'

The three women bustled out, leaving David alone with the kettle of water, the stove, and the pleasant, warm kitchen.

Later that evening, when the meal was almost ready and the two girls – Pavel now looking very feminine in a grey stuff frock with a white apron round it – were setting the table, the door opened and Fedor Lazarov walked in. He showed no surprise at the sight of David sitting in a chair by the stove but came straight across, a hand held out, a smile on his face. He was a tall, thickset man with a bushy moustache and dark hair going grey. One glance at his countenance, David thought, was enough to see why this place was so different from the *koshes* and *aouls* he had previously visited. This was a very intelligent man who had worked hard for success and enjoyed it now it had come his way.

'I saw your horse,' he said briefly as the two shook hands and David ventured to ask how he had guessed the family was entertaining a visitor. 'Knew at once it wasn't one of ours, nor a neighbour's.' He cocked an eye at David. 'Foreigner?' he hazarded.

'That's right. Can you guess where from?'

After a glance which took in his clothing, his person and probably a good deal more beside, Fedor nodded. 'Estonia?'

David was gratified that, though obviously not a Caucasian, he had still sounded like a Russian – his grasp of the language, after two years, was good enough to fool most people.

'No, Britain. What made you guess Estonia?'

'Near enough to Finland to get some perks, like modern clothing, I guessed. Fair skin . . . mind you, the dark hair made me consider Georgia, for a moment.'

'And I suppose you don't meet many Estonians . . . it's a world away, isn't it?'

'True. But I knew one years ago, when I was at university in Leningrad.'

'In Leningrad! Tell me, how did you end up here?'

Fedor laughed and indicated the table and the girls, waiting for the food.

'It's an old story . . . after we've eaten we'll go for a walk and I'll tell you all about it whilst the girls wash up and clear away.'

'I ought to come with you, Fedor,' Pavel said, setting down a large bowl of floury boiled potatoes on the table. 'After all, as the son of the house . . .'

Eva shouted, Fedor laughed, and David wondered once again how he could have been so completely taken in, for she looked very feminine now, going about her work. Yet in breeches, with her hair tucked out of sight under the cap, she had been the complete, swaggering, rather touchy youth.

'You may be my daughter for tonight. Tomorrow you will be Pavel Lazarov once more.'

The rain had stopped, though the cloud cover was complete, and in the dusky light Fedor led David out past the corrals where the beasts stood, humped and dark, chewing the cud or sleeping or just waiting for morning.

'In the winter we have fires at each corner, because of wolves,' he said conversationally as they walked. 'I never thought, years ago, that I'd end up guarding flocks! But it's not such a bad life — better than a mass grave in Siberia, or a chain-gang somewhere.'

'As bad as that, eh? Did you flee from justice? Is that why you ended up in the Caucasus?'

Fedor chuckled. He pulled a pipe out of his pocket and they stood for a moment as he packed and lighted it before resuming his quiet stroll.

'Not exactly. I was on the wrong side in the civil war . . . the revolution . . . call it what you will. I was at university studying chemistry at the time, and naturally I joined the forces of the tsar; my father was commanding a battalion . . . I had no choice. Not that I'm apologising for what I did; I'm simply saying that it was not my desire to grind the faces of the poor in the dirt or any such nonsense. I fought where I was told to fight, I saw terrible things done by both sides . . . and when it was over, and the Soviet was triumphant, I saw that I could never go home — not that there was any home to go to, by then. My parents were dead, our estate divided . . . no point.'

'So what did you do?' David asked curiously. 'Chemists must have been needed, surely? You were very young . . .'

'Ah, youth was no excuse for being on the wrong side! I had been wounded, though, and I was looked after by peasants in the Ukraine — they were small farmers, really. When I was strong enough they advised me for my own sake to forget the young man I had been, and to become someone else. In the confusion I would be believed dead and the New Me, if you'll excuse a somewhat flamboyant expression, could simply start to live.'

'And that is what you did? But why here, why the Caucasus?'

'Accident, my boy, accident! I made my way slowly and with great difficulty across Russia, heading for Georgia. My family had come from there. I reached the foothills, came to a small village and stopped there hoping someone would employ me for a few days – it was the time of the harvest, you see – so that I could eat and perhaps save some food for the trek through the mountains. And I met . . . Nyusha.'

'Your wife. I see!'

'Yes, you see. She was not only the most beautiful girl I had ever seen, she was . . . oh, sympathetic, tender. I cannot describe how I felt about her, virtually from our first meeting – I cannot even describe the way I felt when she told me she felt the same about me. But I no longer wanted to live as a peasant farmer in Georgia – it no longer appealed to me. I wanted to make good – every young man in love wants to make good – and show Nyusha that I was worthy of her affection. So I worked hard, for a year, and then I told Nyusha's father that I wanted to marry his youngest daughter, and showed him the money I'd saved.

'I said we would buy a cow, a pig and a sheep with the money, and go up into the mountains with my old *burka* and the nag he'd lent me, and in a year I would have a farm of my own.

'He laughed at me, but she was his youngest daughter – youngest of fifteen children, ten of them female – and he said he'd let me scrub out his beast-houses if I crawled back, starving, after six months. We married and set off with our little herd – Nyusha brought two sheep of her own and three piglets. Later, passing through an *aoul*, we swopped a fine wool shawl which Nyusha's mother had given her for a couple of scrawny hens.'

'And you came here? And built this?' David's gesture encompassed the homestead, the corrals, the stabling.

'Well, no, not at once. We were poor for a year . . . probably nearly two, but all the time we were together, which was what mattered, and our tiny herd was thriving. One day we came across this valley, and built a rough shelter of fallen boughs with its back against the woodland and the river nearby. In twelve months we had built a log cabin, in twenty-four we had planted potatoes, in three years we'd seen our stock double . . . more than double . . . and everything we'd planted come to fruition. We knew, then, that we'd win.'

'And you had your little daughters, and your father-in-law was astonished,' David finished for him. 'That's a marvellous story, Fedor. The girls must be proud of you – and of your wife.'

'They work hard too.'

'Why did you call the eldest Pavel, though?' David asked presently, as they strolled beneath the boughs of a big oak. 'Did you not hope for a son to call after your friend?'

'Ah, I see Nyusha did not explain all. Pavel came to us with her little sister when she was four or five and Eva perhaps eighteen months. They have a story of their own, I dare say, but unfortunately we don't really know it. We only know that they were brought here by soldiers because their parents and relatives were dead and the village they came from was too poor to undertake the upbringing of two small orphans without undue hardship. The young officer had visited the farm on his way into the mountains and knew we were childless. He brought Pavel and Eva here – and Baru, the big white bitch who never strays far from Pavel's side.'

'And do they know what happened to their people? Was it sickness? Tribal warfare?'

Fedor drew on his pipe, tilted back his head, and blew the smoke in a steady stream towards the branches overhead.

'We don't know. Pavel was in a state of shock when she arrived; we were far too worried to dare to question her then, and when we decided we could risk a casual remark or two she appeared to have forgotten everything. We even had to tell her we were not her natural parents.'

'And what future do you have in mind for them?' David asked as they turned back towards the homestead. 'You are thirty miles from the nearest village, though I dare say there are *aouls* and the odd *kosh* nearer. Pavel seems bright – when did her schooling finish?'

'When the commissars from Moscow came and found that we owned more than the odd cow or two,' Fedor said in a low voice. 'She was doing so well at school that we wanted her to go to a university and become a teacher, perhaps even go in for one of the sciences. Her teacher was a good man, eager to see his prize pupil do well. But when the commissars decided we were capitalists we were forced to take both girls away from school; we were told that education – free education, that is – was for the people and not for such as us. I went to the school – the commissars knew full well that the only educational establishments for hundreds of miles were the State schools – and offered money, which they refused. They assured us that Pavel could not, in any case, go to university until collectivisation had made us all equal, and then we feared it would be too late.'

'It's beaurocracy gone berserk,' David said gloomily. 'Probably the wiser elements of the Party would be horrified by the loss of a good brain to the State and would say it couldn't happen. It can, of course, when you give power to small men with small minds. So what will you do with them, your girls?'

'I don't want them to marry mountain Muslims,' Fedor said decidedly. 'Perhaps it's wrong of me, because they were almost certainly of Muslim birth, but they're neither of them going to do that if I can prevent it. The men of the hill tribes treat their women as possessions, nothing more. No, one of these days when Pavel's a bit older I'm going to take her down to the lowlands and see if I can get her decent work in a place where she'll meet decent young men. Men who'll value her for her mind as well as for the number of sacks of potatoes she can carry. I was down in Khassaut once, taking some cattle to the market, when I heard two men talking about a mare one was selling to the other. You know how men boast when they're bargaining. Well, the seller said she could carry a full load uphill for five miles without flagging and the buyer said that was nothing, he had one which could take a load eight miles uphill and then turn round and cart full buckets from the river to his *kosh* all morning. It was only when the buyer said, triumphantly, after more similar boasts, that his had done her feat for the first time before she had come to her full strength and, furthermore, when she was far gone with child, that I realised I was listening to bride-bartering and not horse-dealing. It decided me that my girls would be spared that, at all costs!'

'I should hope so!' David found the thought of those two girls crawling in and out of a *kosh* repugnant enough without adding the physical harshness of a Muslim woman's lot. 'But forgive me . . . does Nyusha not come from the Caucasian peoples?'

'Ah yes, but from the lowlands. She was never of Muslim stock. Her parents' home had the holy icons and she was taught to worship Christ. If it were not for the girls, I dare say we should have our icons on the wall in our living-room instead of tucked away in our bedrooms. But there you are — one does not invite trouble.'

'Is it that bad? I should have thought you were remote enough out here to be spared most Party visitors.'

'True. But they are thorough, so they will come here again one day, in the fullness of time. Now let's see if they've finished the clearing up yet and got the kettle on the go again!'

# CHAPTER SEVEN

David was woken early next morning by Eva, tiptoeing barefoot across the kitchen and into the store-room. She put her finger to her lips and shushed him when he rolled over and sat up.

'It's all right, it's only me, going out to milk the goats and the cow. The others aren't up yet, so go back to sleep or Nyusha will chide me for being noisy and waking you.'

'You weren't noisy. I've been awake for a while,' David said, kindly but untruthfully, since Eva had gasped so loudly when her warm feet had touched the cold stone slab which floored the store-room that he had got quite a fright. 'Do you milk every morning?'

Eva picked up a galvanised bucket and a piece of sacking and came back into the kitchen. He thought her about eleven or twelve, but already she was more woman than child, which came, he supposed, of having left school and being her mother's chief assistant. He had tasted the bread she had baked and the butter she had made and realised that she was being groomed to be a farmer's wife – and very well groomed, too.

'Not every morning, no. Nyusha and I usually take it in turns, but sometimes Pavel will milk, and sometimes Fedor.' She put the bucket down on the floor and went over to the table. 'Since you're awake, I'm going to have some bread and jam; I don't know why, but I'm always starving first thing in the morning.'

David watched her as she sliced bread and spread it with jam. She was not terribly like Pavel, who had the almost boyish features of a young Greek deity, but she was going to be lovely one day. The rich blonde curls framed a neat little face with very large blue-grey eyes. She had a dimply smile and pink cheeks and David concluded that if Pavel were to marry and

144

move away no one, no matter how carefully she was disguised, would take Eva for anything but a female. Her figure, though unformed, was plumper and her limbs were more rounded than her sister's slimmer and more athletic physique.

'Want a bit of bread? There's honey somewhere, if you'd rather have that than jam.'

David realised his stare had been misinterpreted, and accepted bread and jam, though a glance at his watch told him that it was still horribly early. Dawn might have broken — the streaks of light showing through the shutters were pale grey, or so he thought — but the sun had not yet risen.

'There.' Eva finished her bread and jam and then, with a sigh, picked up the big iron kettle and staggered over to the stove with it. She opened the front, jiggled around with a poker until it began to roar, then took the hob plate off the top and slid the kettle over the hole. 'Now I'll go and get on with the milking. By the time I get back the kettle should have boiled, so you can have tea as an early treat!'

'I thought you advised me to go back to sleep,' David said, curling down in his sleeping bag once more. 'I could do with a nap.'

'Why not? You'll wake when Nyusha comes in and starts breakfast, I expect. Come to think of it, when Pavel gets up you can go into our room and dress there.'

'Right,' David said drowsily. 'Wake me when it's time.'

He did not really expect to be able to sleep again, but somehow he dropped off and was woken for the second time that morning by his hostess opening the shutters. She turned to him, smiling, as he yawned and stretched.

'Good morning, young man! Eva said you were sleeping like the dead and I thought you'd rather be woken before everyone troops in for breakfast. Pavel's up and outside, getting the horses in and brushing them down for the day's work, so if you want to use the girls' room you're very welcome. You can take some hot water through with you.'

David, accepting the suggestion eagerly, thought how different this was from the tent . . . he would have crept out of his sleeping bag, gone down to the river for a freezing cold splash or possibly even a dip, and then returned to face lighting a fire, cooking something hot, striking camp as soon as the last mouthful was eaten . . . this was definitely luxury!

The girls' room was small, neat and very basic. An icon on the wall, some books in a little wooden bookcase, two plain beds with straw mattresses – he sat on one for a moment just to make sure – and plenty of hand-woven blankets. There was also – rare luxury – a little washstand with soap in a wooden dish, a couple of flannels and two towels in addition to the thick new one Nyusha had given him when she had handed over the jug of hot water.

He washed and shaved, put on his shirt and trousers – he had slept in his underpants since pyjamas were an unnecessary luxury when travelling rough – and returned to the kitchen. A good deal had gone on since he had left it twenty minutes earlier. The table was set for five people, Fedor was already seated with a large cup of tea in front of him, Pavel was spooning porridge into five bowls and Eva was pouring the tea. Nyusha was wielding the big frying pan; bacon sizzled and eggs spat impatiently.

'How marvellous to have English breakfast,' David said, taking his place at the table. 'Do you always have it, or is this a treat for us all?'

'I had an English friend at university,' Fedor said, beginning to eat porridge and then stopping to pour goat's milk on to it. 'He taught me to enjoy English breakfast, but we don't have it as a rule – just this morning, in your honour. We have porridge, usually . . . black pudding and eggs sometimes . . . and always tea, of course, and always bread . . . lots of bread. But not bacon and eggs.'

'The porridge is very good,' David said, spooning it in. 'You eat well, Fedor – better than the majority of Russians, I believe.'

'We are self-supporting, that's why,' Fedor said complacently. 'Except for tea, coffee which we rarely have, and a few things like sugar and salt. We make our own soap, rear our own pigs, and have a mill so we can grind our own flour, though we do buy a sack of white flour if it's available when I'm down at the market. Yes, we do quite well one way and another.'

'Razorblades?' David touched his own chin, still a little sore from the attention of blunted blades. 'How do you manage for them? You're clean-shaven, I see.'

'An old cut-throat, which I sharpen myself on a whetstone.'

Fedor finished his porridge and helped himself from the dish of bacon and eggs which Nyusha had put down in the middle of the table. Pavel, David noticed, was in breeches and a shirt this morning, with her hair tied back. She was almost a lad again; you could see how easily the transformation would be made as soon as she went out to work.

'Well now, having boasted of our self-sufficiency, Fedor, will you outline your plans for the day to David, so that he knows what's what?' Nyusha turned to Pavel, starting energetically on the bacon. 'Has Father told you that he'll go down to the market alone?'

Fedor banged a hand down on the table and scowled at his wife. 'Woman, either I tell David or you do, but not the pair of us!' He turned to the younger man. 'It's not too bad today. The sun's up and the sky's clear enough, though there's a bad feel to the wind . . . it'll blow up rough later on, or perhaps tomorrow – some time in the next twenty-four hours, anyway, unless I'm much mistaken. So I want you and Pavel to go up to the Pass and take a look at it, study the terrain. If it's fairly clear and safe, then she can take you halfway, maybe even more, but you must return tonight, because it's a tricky time of year. You might get all the way through and Pavel might get stranded coming back, you see? So, if it's clear, we'll both accompany you tomorrow – or perhaps I'll come myself, leaving Pavel to watch the herds.'

'What about Pavel setting me on the path and then returning home?' David suggested. 'If we got over halfway, might it not be possible for me to continue alone?'

Fedor shrugged but looked uneasy.

'It might be possible, but I don't like it. We know that pass like the backs of our hands; we go through a lot in August and September, when it's clear and safe, because we can get food easily in Georgia. You, on the other hand, could easily get into trouble . . . No, I'd feel happier if you just took a look at conditions today.'

'That's fine by me,' David said rather mendaciously. In fact he thought it would be best if he let them think he meant to return, but persuaded Pavel to let him do the last half of the Pass on his own. He knew that it was foolish to go alone, but he also knew that he had no time to spare. Either he went through the Pass in the next four or five days or he did not go at all. It was far easier and quicker to get back to Leningrad the way he had come than it would be to cross through the Klukhor, take ship at the nearest Black Sea port and go right along the coast to meet up with the railway again some hundreds of miles further on.

'Very well. We are agreed. Pavel, pack some food. David, would it be best to rest your mount and borrow one of ours? Then, if all's clear, you can take your own horse tomorrow, knowing it's rested and eager to go.'

'Oh! Yes, I suppose it's a good idea ... but it seems unfair that I should take your horse. I'll take mine, and then if it's clear we can leave a day in between and the horse will be rested again anyway.'

Fedor looked at him shrewdly. 'I see how the land lies; it's urgent for you to get through in the next few days, eh?'

'Well, it is, really,' David said apologetically. 'You see I've only got leave from my job for a certain time, and though the journey back is more interesting if I go via the Pass and down through Georgia it's also a good deal longer, and probably slower as well.'

'And you think that if the Pass is clear you can do the second leg alone?' Fedor shook his head. 'Do you want to be found next spring, iced in, just another corpse to prove that the Caucasians are not like other mountains? Let Pavel take you all the way, then, and take care of her for me until I can get through. Then we will return together. Will that satisfy you?'

'I feel so ungrateful, after all your hospitality and kindness,' David said shamefacedly. 'But it really is important that I'm not late back; my bosses would not be pleased.'

'Of course. We understand. In that case I shall keep your horse here, rest it well today, and ride it through the Pass tomorrow. You will be resting my horse in Georgia, in the foothills below the Pass, and we will simply exchange beasts. How will that suit you?'

'It will suit me admirably. But ... does Pavel have a tent, sleeping bag, food ... if she is to come right through with me and remain with me until you arrive?'

'Hmm.' Fedor frowned massively, and then his brow cleared. 'What an idiot I am. I can't go with you today – I have to take beasts to the market – but if I take you tomorrow, then you will get safely through. There is no need for Pavel to take you today at all.'

'Yes, but the whole point of my going today,' Pavel broke in, 'is to see if it's fit for tomorrow. I don't see why we can't stick to the original plan. I think David's being silly.'

'You're right, Pavel,' David said, over a roar from Fedor commanding her to apologise and a scandalised reproof from Nyusha. 'I was being silly. I thought I could get across today and save a day. Of course one or two days don't matter, though more would.'

'Then you simply misunderstand the situation,' Pavel said impatiently. 'If the Pass is clear today it will be clear tomorrow, unless of course a freak storm blew up, and even then it would probably clear again very quickly. But if, as I know Fedor suspects, we're still too early, then we won't be able to get you through safely, no matter how hard we try, until about three weeks have gone by. It's the glacier and the state of the snow that matter, not just whether it rains or shines.'

'Oh,' David said, feeling rather silly. 'Then if we get up there and it's plain sailing, it will be plain sailing tomorrow as well?'

'That's right, more or less.' Fedor was looking relieved. 'I didn't realise you thought the Pass might be clear one day and blocked the next! No, the girl's right; if you can get through tomorrow you'll be able to get through every day until mid to late September.'

'Then we'd better be off – and on your horse, and thank you very much for the loan,' David said, finishing off his breakfast with a thick slice of bread and jam. 'How long will it take us to get ready, Pavel? I won't bother with my gear – we'll just go as we are, shall we?'

But this no one would allow; the Pass could be tricky and it would take them most of the day in any case just to go halfway along it and back again. When David went out to the stable his borrowed horse was already loaded with all his equipment, right down to the primus stove, the tent and the bedroll.

'One should always guard against every eventuality, especially in the high mountains,' Pavel said primly, when he queried the necessity on what would, after all, only be a day's excursion from her home. She was very much the boy now, and he realised she would resent any attempt on his part to make her feel feminine, so he let her behave exactly as she would have done had he not known her secret — she had already saddled and bridled the horses but she led them into the yard, checked that her *burka* was safely strapped to one side of her saddle and her parcel of food to the other, cast a critical eye over David, his horse and his impedimenta, and then gave the word to leave.

'We'll ride for four hours, then eat and take a rest, then ride on for another hour or so to gain the Pass,' she said as they set off, and even her voice was different; huskier, more sure of itself. 'Once we're above the snowline it won't be very pleasant stopping for a meal, so we'll do that before we're too high. I know a good place. If we had time, we could have tried out your rod on the local trout.'

'We? You cheeky little blighter — no one but me uses my trout rod!'

Pavel pulled a face at him.

'Oh, indeed? I've probably caught more trout than you've had hot dinners. But we haven't got time, so there's no point in talking about it.'

'True. Tell me about yourself, and what you want to do with your life.'

'Nothing to tell. Did Fedor tell you I can't remember anything before I came to him and Nyusha? I don't even know how old I am . . . isn't it a strange thing not to know how old you are? The children at school thought I was quite mad.'

'Yes, it is weird, I suppose. Birthdays are important events in Britain — we get presents and a special tea and a cake all in our honour . . . cards, too, wishing us a happy birthday. Even older people won't let their birthdays go by without some acknowledgement.'

'Yes . . . we celebrate Eva's birthday and mine on the same day. The day we first came to the Lazarov homestead. As for what I want . . . I keep telling Fedor I *have* what I want! A free life, plenty of horse-riding, tending the beasts, being out in the air. We live well, eat well . . . I have the best of both worlds, wouldn't you think?'

She was referring, of course, to being Pavel the boy during her working hours and Pavel the girl in the evenings. Or was she? David glanced across at her. The line of her hair was hidden by her sheepskin cap, and although she wore no *burka* because of the warmth of the sun she had a tunic, loosely buttoned and far too big for her, over her shirt which effectively hid any sign of her shape.

'The best of both worlds? It depends what you mean by that.'

'Well, I had a little learning, at school – enough to mean that I love to read and write. I have books, but better than that I have some fat exercise books that the schoolteacher gave me when we left. They were to teach Eva with, but she is a quick little girl and she had learned all she needed to know within twelve months of leaving school, so I had the books for myself. I write in them . . . stories, poems, a diary of how we live . . . and one day, when I'm old, I shall get it published. So that's one world – the world of the mind as I think of it. The other world is the world of action, which I've already told you about. So you see, I want nothing more.'

'That's all very well for now, but one day . . . surely you'll want a husband . . . a home of your own? Children?'

'I have a home of my own already, and when Fedor and Nyusha die the farm will belong to Eva and me. I expect Eva will marry, though, so I'll probably have the homestead all to myself one day.'

'Yes, but . . . won't you be lonely?'

Pavel glanced sideways at him and grinned.

'You mean I ought to marry myself a little wife so that there's someone to bake for me and clean my house when Eva goes? Well, I might do that, if I got truly lonely. As for babies . . . I can't say I yearn for them, exactly.'

David laughed. 'You're not much more than a baby yourself. What about more books? You must have read the ones in your room a dozen times or more.'

'A dozen? More like a hundred. Yes, books are a problem, but whenever Fedor goes on a long journey to sell cattle or buy seed or something else we need he brings me back as many books as he can manage. One day, I'll go with him, and choose my own reading matter.'

'I see. How fortunate you are, to want no more than you have.'

There was a short pause and then Pavel said suspiciously, 'That makes me sound smug; did you mean to do that?'

'No, I didn't. But I can't help wondering if you're telling me the whole truth. You see, Fedor said that you'd hoped to continue with your education and perhaps go to university one day, as he did. Surely you must regret that? He said you were almost certain of a place and then it was snatched from you. Don't you ever wonder about the other child, the child who *did* continue with his or her education, who had the chance that you were denied?'

She sighed, a long, soft sound, and then nodded slowly, her expression rueful.

'How clever you are! Yes, of course I have wondered – I'm only human, after all. But they explained, the teacher and the man from Moscow, that it was not fair that I should have a good home and loving parents and all the food I needed, and go to university too. They said that a child from the *aouls* who had nothing but kicks and hard work deserved the place in a way I could not. It was fair, I could see that. What I could *not* understand was how the child from the *aoul* would use the education and the knowledge that she acquired for the State's betterment – I would have! But it's no use even thinking about it because my chance has gone. And what I have is so good!' She raised her face to the sun as she spoke and closed her eyes, and for a moment David knew the ecstasy she felt in her wild, outdoor life and unfettered existence, but then it was gone and he could see once more that Fedor was right to worry.

'And what of the collectivisation that your father speaks of? If that comes . . .'

'Oh, if!' She gave a scornful sniff and slanted her big, greeny-grey eyes at him in a look both feminine and enticing, though he was very sure that she had no idea of being either. 'Well, I've tried to explain to Fedor that if they do it it's only because we have too much, and it would be fairer to share the land out amongst people who otherwise would have nothing.'

'Oh? Then you would invite the people of the nearest *aoul*, the one no more than five miles away, to share your farm?'

'No, of course not – why should we? They could have done as Fedor did, worked, saved, ploughed the land, traded their lambs for better stock . . . but they couldn't be bothered; all they think about is their horses and who has the most lambs, never the finest or the strongest. Why should we share with such lazy, feckless ones?'

'But the people the State may send here might be even more lazy and feckless. They may be plainsmen who know nothing

152

about hill farming. They may know nothing about stock . . . they may fear wolves and refuse to light wolf-fires . . . they may . . .'

'I hate you, David Thomas!' Pavel's cheeks were pink, her eyes very bright. 'The State would not do such a thing. They want more food for the people in our country who are hungry, not less, so they would send experienced men who knew how to make animals thrive, or . . . or folk who wanted to learn. How can you try to frighten me with such nonsense?'

'Because, my dear child, it's plain to me that you admire the theory behind collectivisation, but don't want to face up to the facts! If men are already experienced farmers, then why should the State move them? If they are ignorant, bigoted peasants who've been unable to scrape a living from their own soil, why should they do better on yours?'

'You talk like Fedor. You talk like my nightmares. Why don't you just stop talking and concentrate on riding a bit faster?' Pavel dug her heels hard into her mount's round sides and cantered ahead of him, casting a malicious glance over her shoulder as she did so. Little imp, David thought, kicking his own horse into a reluctant jog-trot; she knew very well that he could not ride as she could. Ahead of him, she gave a yodel and swung out of the saddle, sideways, bending down, almost causing his heart to stop – if she fell!

But she did not; she snatched at a handful of the bright alpine flowers which grew in the grass at this height and then rode on, bending over every now and then to pluck another blossom, all at the same mad speed and without parting company with her pony once.

Reluctantly, he gave her best; she was a magnificent horse-woman, even if she was a wild, untamed brat who refused to look further than her own nose and was content to believe everything the Party liked to tell her. A pity that her beautiful, lively intelligence would probably become numbed and ne-gated by the life she would lead once the long arm of authority reached her valley home. But this was an immense country and she was no more than a single blade of grass on the steppes – there were so many similar blades, and one could not feel for all of them as the scythe swung round.

\*

153

'What's that, up there?'

David and Pavel had stopped for their meal just where she had said they would. A wild and bubbling mountain stream came tumbling down from the heights and cascaded in a series of tiny waterfalls down its rocky bed, and at the point where it slowed to cross a meadow lush with grass and flowers Pavel had chosen to light their fire.

'Here we have fuel . . . those birch trees, which also provide us with shade – or would if we felt the need for it,' she said instructively as they dismounted. 'The horses can graze at will – they won't go any higher because the grass gets sparser from now on, and they won't go lower, or not much, because the escarpments are too steep. So we can eat, they can eat, and neither of us will worry about losing the other.'

'I didn't know horses worried about losing their riders,' David said, raising a lazy brow at her, but Pavel just shook her head pityingly at him.

'You don't know lots of things, Davidski! My horse . . . Romany . . . is my good friend and feels a lot safer with me than without. He comes when I whistle – I won't show you now, because it wouldn't be fair to him, but later, when we want to move on, I'll demonstrate. Now, I've pine cones in my saddlebag, if you'll gather birch twigs . . .'

The fire burned brightly and cheered their meal by giving them a hot drink to go with it, and David found he was glad of it, for as they climbed so the air had grown colder. He said as much to Pavel, who nodded and spoke through a mouthful of bread and cheese.

'Yes, that's true, but the reason you're colder now is probably because the weather's changing – Fedor said it would.'

'It doesn't look much different,' David objected, sipping hot coffee. 'The sun's still shining.'

'Yes, but there's a cold wind, and look at the clouds . . .'

David looked and was forced to acknowledge that she was right. There were quite a lot of clouds, whereas earlier in the day the sky had been clear.

'Never mind. We'll be home before it breaks, I dare say,' Pavel said, when David voiced his disquiet over the size and colour of the clouds. 'It isn't far to the Pass now, only about an hour's riding. And it's still early; we've made quite good time.' She leaned over and plucked David's bakelite mug from his hand, took a swig and handed it back, wiping her mouth with the back of her sleeve, that enchanting smile teasing him again. 'Well now, Davidski, what about *you*? Do you intend to spend the rest of your life in another man's country, building his power stations, or will you go home? And if you do, what do you want of life in Eng . . . in Britain, I mean?'

'I'll go home, of course. I don't suppose I'll get what I want, but I'd like my home back . . . I'm as fond of my home as you are of yours, because it's been in my family for two hundred years.'

'Oh, like that, was it? You're a *pomeishik*, David! No wonder you don't hold much brief for collectivisation, or the State!'

'No more a rich landowner than Fedor, my child! But anyway, that was before the wreck. After the wreck we had to sell our home . . . my father died, my mother moved the family into a much smaller house, and things became very difficult. Now my sisters and little brother are squeezed into this place and they don't enjoy life as once we did. My favourite sister, Alice, isn't married and she works very hard to help the younger children make some sort of life for themselves, and she tries to keep my mother cheerful and to see that everyone is fed and clothed . . . I'll help her, when I go home.'

'Why don't you go at once, David? Why stay here, far from your own place?'

'That's an easy one, Pavelinka! I'm an engineer, as you know, but there's a depression on in Britain, a fact which may have escaped you. There are huge numbers of people unemployed and if I had to go home tomorrow I wouldn't be as much help to my family as I have been by staying away, because the Soviet pays me well for my work, and I'm getting experience which would have been impossible in Britain. We aren't building many great dams and power stations at the moment, and those that we do build are employing experienced older men and not young untried engineers.'

'I see. Tell me about your home.'

David began, but it was uphill work, telling this child of the wild Caucasus about Deeside when she had never seen a brick building, never heard the sound of the waves on the shore, could only shake her head in wonder at his description of the din and clamour of a shipyard in full production.

He enjoyed watching Pavel as he spoke. She fixed her big eyes on the horizon and he could tell she was seeing – or trying to see – a picture of what he was telling her. And because of her fascinated attention, and perhaps a little because she pulled off her sheepskin cap and let her shining hair cascade down past her tender neck, breaking into surf as it touched her shoulders, David enjoyed her breathless interest, and told her more than he had ever told anyone about his feelings for his home and the dumb despair which had gripped him when he first heard that the yard and the Hall were to be sold.

When he had finished his recital she nodded and lay back on the grass, closing her eyes against the sun's brightness.

'That is a sad story. Your father's ship was a good ship, yet propaganda ruined him as thoroughly as a bad ship would have done. So what will you do when you go home again? Obviously you will want to prove your father's innocence – how will you go about it? Building ships yourself would not do it, even if your family still owned the yard. Could you not dive down to the wreck and find the reason for the sinking?'

David was totally taken aback, so that for a few moments he was literally speechless. Propaganda? And reasons? Had the girl listened? Probably she had not understood, he had not made it clear.

'I doubt that one could find the reason for the sinking. Nibby and I both saw the ship go down – the conditions were fearful; no ship could have survived.'

'Oh? But when you were telling me the story just now you said that when she was lifted off the sandbank you turned away because you were sure she would be all right.'

'Did I? Yes, you're right, I did. But I was very young, only a child really, and hadn't fully realised . . . she must have broken her back when she drove on to the sandbank.'

'Why did she drive on to the sandbank, then? Was it her captain's carelessness, or some fault in the ship? Could a severe storm simply drive a ship to do what neither she nor her captain wanted? I don't understand very well, but that seems strange.'

It seemed strange to David, now that she put it into words. He had been lying back as well, but now he sat up, picked a handful of little pink flowers, and then flung them, one by one, on to Pavel's calm face. Her mouth curved but she did not open her eyes, merely asking, 'Well? The answer to my ignorant question, if you please.'

'You horrid child, I don't know the answer! I suppose that was what the board of enquiry wanted to get at, the reason for the original collision. The captain might have misread the light from Point of Ayr and believed himself safe to go nearer the shore at that point. There were survivors, though none of them were able to explain what had happened with any clarity. The passengers were all below, but they were all fairly sure that the engines were running right up to the moment of impact. It all happened extremely quickly, you see.'

'And no divers went down to her? I know such a thing is possible now. I've read that it is done.'

'No divers went down. It's very deep and tricky there, with treacherous currents. There seemed no point, because after all the tribunal had judged the accident to be the result of an Act of God – the storm. Later, when Father realised that he was being ruined by . . . by propaganda, as you call it, I don't think it occurred to him to try to *disprove* what was being hinted at, and anyway we needed all the money we could get just to keep the yard going.'

'Well, then, your duty is clear. You'll go home when your job here is over, and dive down to the ship and tell everyone why she sank. Then, even if you cannot get your yard back, or your home, you will know that there is no slur on your father's good name and good ships.'

David thought about it, stirred and excited by being given, all in a moment, a Cause. It would not bring back the yard nor the Hall, but she was right: there would be enormous personal satisfaction in proving his father right and those other scandal-mongers wrong. His mind began to play with ideas. He could not dive himself, but there were others . . . and he could, of course, learn to dive! Why should he not do that? It might be a costly business, but once the family was off his hands . . . As if she had divined his thoughts Pavel spoke again.

'What was she carrying beside passengers, this ship?'

'In addition to my father's reputation, you mean? To be honest, I don't know, but some of the passengers were very rich . . . some of the bodies washed ashore were wearing quite a lot of jewellery . . . does it matter?'

'Yes. It will cost money to dive down and see the ship.' Pavel sat up and clasped her hands, her eyes dancing. 'Oh, Davidski, what a wonderful thing it would be to dive through the green water and find the ship and discover jewels and gold! I wish . . . I *wish* she had sunk in Soviet waters, off the Black Sea, for instance. Then I could have come with you, through the Pass and along the Military Road to the sea, and we could have gone down and searched for treasure together!'

'Can you swim, then?'

'Of course! Next month, when the sun is stronger, the glacier will melt and form a lake. Eva and I will swim and dive and play in the water, though it's so cold that it makes your bones ache. And we swim in the river, too, because it's cool when the sun is hot.'

'Hmm. Tell you what, you save up your roubles and come to Britain and we'll dive for the wreck together! How's that?'

'Oh, ha! Which roubles, Davidski? Kopeks, even, rarely come my way.'

It had not occurred to him before, but now he looked across at her and asked the difficult question.

'Doesn't Fedor pay you for your work?'

'Of course not! But I eat, and am clothed. What would I spend money on?'

'Personal things. Books.'

'Ah . . . personal things. No, I don't get paid. Sometimes it seems a bit unfair, but for the most part I don't mind at all. I want for nothing.'

'Then in that case, I'll have to dive for my wreck myself. If I decide to take your advice, Babushka!'

She giggled, then jumped to her feet and began packing the remaining food back into its bag, scattering the fire by stamping on it, and generally preparing to depart.

'Dedushka, you mean! Remember my breeches! Come on, let's get going. We've had a good rest; now for the worst part of the work.'

David soon discovered that Pavel had not exaggerated. As they gained height the way grew steeper and stonier and the snow thicker, until in places they were struggling through a foot or more of the slushy stuff.

Presently, when they seemed to be on top of the world, with only the topmost peaks higher than they, David glanced ahead and then, after a long stare, turned to Pavel.

'What's that? That shining thing?'

'It's the glacier. It's quite frightening, I always think. We have to go round it at this time of year, because it wouldn't be safe to go across, but in winter one can traverse it, with care.'

As they drew nearer, David was better able to appreciate both its menace and its beauty. A great lake of ice, the waterfalls that fed it were a mass of icicles save for the central stream, which leapt and bounced still, and then fell sheer on to the ice, to form ice itself almost as soon as it landed. Because it was sunny the ice reflected a million tiny rainbows, and the very rocks that sloped up and away from it were touched with their colours.

'It's beautiful . . . amazing,' David breathed, drawing his horse to a halt the better to absorb the picture before him. 'I've never seen anything like it in my life.'

'Yes.' Pavel's smile was the smile of proud ownership. 'We'll have to dismount here and lead the horses . . . it gets tricky. If it gets too difficult we'll turn back.'

Tricky, David thought as they edged onward, was an understatement. First his borrowed horse fell into a snow-covered hollow and had to be extricated with great labour and considerable ingenuity. Then, barely fifty feet further on, when they could actually feel the spray from the waterfall on their cheeks, Pavel's horse disappeared. When they had laboriously heaved and persuaded it clear of the slushy morass which had all but swallowed it up, Pavel unbuckled the saddlebags and slung them across her shoulders, then clapped her mount on the rump and watched it disappear down the path once more.

'Do the same with yours, Davidski,' she advised briskly, beginning to unbuckle his gear. 'You'll not get a horse through, it's far too dangerous. We'll go a bit further and take a look, and then tomorrow or the day after you and Fedor can come up here on foot and perhaps try to get across. If you ask me, it won't be possible with horses for at least a month.'

David's mount disappeared with alacrity in the direction its companion had taken. Pavel slung the saddlebags on David's shoulders and then, after a moment's hesitation, balanced tent, bedroll and camping gear on a flat-topped rock.

'We won't bother to lug that lot over the glacier,' she said. 'We would only be held back if we tried. If we were doing the climb in earnest we would have to go over twice, once with half the stuff and the second time with the rest. Are you ready?'

'Yes, I think so,' David said doubtfully. 'Why must we take anything? Why can't we just climb with our hands free, since we're only looking?'

'Because if the worst happened and we were stranded on the far side of the glacier – say we were cut off by an avalanche or a rockfall – then at least we would have some food, some dry clothing and a bit of wood to start a fire with.' She did up the top fastening of her *burka*, squared her shoulders, and began to trudge up one side of the glacier. 'This way, I think.'

It was one of the hardest climbs David had ever undertaken. They scrambled and slid and scrambled again up and over the first frozen waterfall, clinging in places to what looked at first glance like sheer rock faces, and then had to do the same over the second. All the time, below them, the comparative flatness of the glacier beckoned, seeming to promise a much easier route, but Pavel was adamant.

'We wouldn't get more than a few yards before we started the whole thing moving,' she said, when he suggested descending and trying the seemingly easier path. 'We've not got much further to go, and then you'll be able to see what lies ahead.'

She was right, for all too soon they finished the rock climb and were looking into the valley which led through into Georgia. They stood and stared at it as at the Promised Land.

'Well?' Pavel asked at length. 'What do you think?'

'I think you're right: it would be foolish and incredibly dangerous to attempt it,' David said, keeping his voice low and steady. Not for the world would he have raised it in this atmosphere of brooding and incipient avalanches with everywhere you looked great folds and swathes of dripping snow waiting an opportunity to plummet into the valley below. 'How long will it take to thaw completely?'

Pavel shrugged. 'It should be clear in a month – though by clear I don't mean clear of ice and snow, just clear of slides and avalanches. It will be no better than this tomorrow or the day after – possibly it will be worse.'

'Well, since I've not got four weeks to wait, we might as well turn back and I'll go home via Kislovodsk, as I came,' David said ruefully. 'Tell you what, I'll make a date with you – we'll come back in two days and if it still isn't clear to cross I'll come back in twelve months' time, giving myself a longer holiday, and go through then. How about it?'

'Silly, it may be no better in twelve months! Come in August and be sure. Now shall we turn back? We could go very carefully over the tops as far as the next ridge, if you want. If we went very slowly and watched the snow for the first sign of movement . . .'

'No, we won't bother. We'll turn back.'

It was as well that they did, for halfway back across the rocks that edged the glacier, inching along a narrow ledge with their backs pressed to the sheer rock wall behind them, they heard the rumbling roar of falling snow and, turning, saw the beginnings of the avalanche. Slowly at first, but rapidly building up speed as it travelled, the great mass of snow on the western side of the Pass began to thunder down into the valley, taking with it boulders the size of houses. David, freed for the first time of the need to keep his voice low, turned and grabbed Pavel's arm and shouted above the roar: 'God almighty! We might have been caught in that lot!'

They were above the waterfall and the ledge was slippery with wet ice. Pavel gasped, a foot slid outward, she began to speak, and then they were both falling, still clutching each other, heading for the glacier below.

Fortunately, it was not a long fall, and they would not have far to struggle to reach the glacier's edge once more, but it was a very wet landing. Struggling to their feet with the waterfall jetting icily all over them, clutching one another, slipping, gasping for air between inadvertent mouthfuls of water, they somehow managed to fall and fight their way out of the stinging, icy wetness and reach the disgusting slush that was the bank.

'Ge-get t-to the t-t-t-tent,' Pavel commanded between chattering teeth, pushing David ahead of her so that he floundered and fell in the snow. 'L-l-light the p-p-primus . . . we m-must have sh-shelter.'

David knew she was right. They were both soaked to the skin, the sun was sinking fast and soon dusk would be upon them, but he was too cold and shocked to move quickly. He began to unbuckle the first saddlebag and she thrust him aside, tearing at the straps with small, quick fingers, getting it undone, heaving out the canvas, forcing herself to move quickly, he saw, because numbness must be spreading through her as it was through him.

'Rocks . . . get it to the rocks . . .' He snatched the material away from her. He knew he could never erect the tent with iced-up fingers; they would have to drape it across two rocks and do the best they could within its chancy shelter.

She acknowledged what he was doing with a nod, and began tearing the other bags open. She wrenched out the tiny primus and began to pump it; presently it flowered with blue flame and by then David had indeed managed to rig up a presentable shelter and was dragging their things into it. The wind was getting up and even as he glanced at it the sun slid out of sight behind the shoulder of the mountain, and he imagined he could actually sense the increased chill.

Pavel crawled over and made adjustments to David's shelter, then put the primus stove right in the gap at the front and tugged David in behind it.

'There, that's the best we can do for a minute. Get your dry things out.'

'But won't they get wet? There's snow underfoot . . .'

'Shove them at the back, in the rock crevice.'

David did so, and saw that she was right; the snow had not penetrated to the back of their shelter, for he had chosen a V-shaped rock formation, almost a cave, and now that he thought about it he realised they were actually out of the wind. Even the hissing primus was sheltered, for the little flames burned steadily.

'Done it? Right. Get your things off.'

It made sense, but he hesitated.

'What about you? Do you have dry things?'

'No . . . I don't usually fall into water! I'll wear some of yours.'

'Well, all right, but' – he remembered even as he reached to the back of the crevice for his dry things – 'Nyusha took most of my spare stuff to wash it so that I'd start out with clean underwear! All I've got is a shirt, a jersey, some socks and my corduroys.'

'I'll have the shirt,' Pavel said briefly. 'Get a move on, David, or these wet things will start to freeze on us.'

Driven by the sense of what she had said, David suddenly thought of his sleeping bag. He could wear that! He pushed the clothing over to where Pavel was already out of her *burka* and peeling off her boots and breeches and made the suggestion.

'Well done,' she said at once, her teeth still chattering as briskly as a gypsy dancer's castanets. 'Once we get our things out on the rocks they'll dry quickly enough. Pass me the shirt, would you?'

She had turned her back on him to pull off her tunic but now she half-turned, holding out a hand. He saw a glimpse of a rounded, pink-tipped breast with a curl of wet hair across it, and then she was struggling into his shirt and he was too busy stripping off his own wet things and crawling clammily into the sleeping bag to have prurient thoughts about the body he had so briefly glimpsed.

'There, that's better.' She faced him, clad warmly if baggily in his shirt and jumper. Since they reached to her knees she plainly felt the trousers to be an unnecessary addition and David, in the sleeping bag, grabbed them, shoved them down to the bottom of the bag and began to pull them on. Already, in only ten minutes or so, their shelter was cosy, the wet clothing steaming merrily, a good heat radiating from the primus.

'This is marvellous,' he said, kicking off the sleeping bag and kneeling in his respectable trousers to ferret around in the nearest saddlebag. 'I've got a little pan here somewhere. We can melt some snow and make ourselves a hot drink, and there's food left over from our luncheon, I'm sure.'

'There certainly is. Nyusha packed enough for a meal on the way home as well.' Pavel knelt beside him, going through the other bag, and began to produce parcels of food. 'David, I'm awfully sorry.'

'Sorry? For what? For rescuing us from the consequences of my stupid action? It's I who should be sorry.'

'Yes, but I was your guide; I should have taken better care of you. I should have guessed that the avalanche would startle you, I should have stepped away from you, not nearer. And now I've benighted you in the snow, without a proper fire or anything.'

'Are we benighted?' David asked with interest. 'But the sun only went down a few minutes ago – it can't be dark yet. Surely, as soon as our clothes are dry, we shall be able to leave here?'

'Not unless you can see in the dark, and are prepared for a

long walk. We let the horses go, which would have been fine had we been able to walk down to the lower pastures before dark, but as it is they'll make for their stables. They're sensible animals, and will realise that they must get into shelter.' She looked across at him in the primus's glow, and her wicked smile touched her lips for a moment. 'I don't think you'd get far out there wrapped in a sleeping bag, and you'd freeze in a second in nothing but those trousers!'

'Well, you wouldn't stay warm for long in my shirt!' He was laughing at her, but he realised suddenly that she was not laughing back; her face drooped and her lower lip was trembling. 'What's the matter, Pavelina?'

'Fedor will be angry with me, and justifiably. He'll say no son of his would have behaved so irresponsibly. And look at our *burkas*. They're so thick they'll take ages and ages to dry!'

'To hell with it,' David said bracingly. 'The fault, if it's anyone's, is mine. Come here, little elf!'

The little elf, red-nosed and wet-haired, crawled across the small space between them and found herself firmly and reassuringly hugged.

'There! I'll protect you from Fedor's wrath – not that he'll be cross with you, little idiot. You've done marvellously well. Left to myself I'd have frozen like a board long ago. Now look, if we're here for the night we must be sensible. We'll make a hot drink and have some food and then we'll both squiggle into the sleeping bag, cuddle down, and turn the primus off until morning. But first I'm going to rearrange the tent so that we're completely enclosed, and then I reckon body-heat will be sufficient. I don't want to leave the primus burning in case it runs out of fuel.'

In his embrace, Pavel actually snuggled closer for a moment before pulling herself free and crawling over to the entrance to scoop snow into the little tin pan, for the snow inside had long since melted or been pushed out in their struggles to make themselves a warm shelter.

'Right. Sorry I whined, David. You rearrange the tent if you can do it without bringing the whole lot down on top of us. I know I couldn't; I'm not tall enough. I'll get us food and that drink you spoke of.'

David had to bend his head when he stood up, but he managed to bring the tent fully around them so that they were enclosed in a warm and cosy cave, half rock, half tent, from which not so much as a star of the outside world could be seen. Sitting down rather breathlessly on the sleeping bag, which had been pushed to the very back of their shelter so that it rested on dry rock, he announced that he was ready to be fed.

'Coffee first,' Pavel said, pouring hot water from the pan on to some coffee grounds which she had tipped into two of David's mugs. 'No milk, but plenty of sugar. Then I shall toast some bread and put butter on it, and then we might as well eat the rest of the bread and those sardines you said were so nice.'

'Gorgeous,' David said presently, with his mouth full. 'Sardines have never tasted better. How about an apple to finish off with? There are at least four in my saddlebags somewhere.'

They found the apples and crunched for a moment in companionable silence, but when they had eaten even the cores – waste not want not, Pavel had reproached him, when he tried to throw the core under the tent flap – David poured them a second drink and settled down on top of the sleeping bag, with Pavel beside him.

'You may entertain me with talk of your previous expeditions,' he said loftily to his small companion, 'since you referred to yourself earlier as my guide. Guides always tell tales round the camp-fire, you know.'

'I don't mind. You told me a very good tale earlier,' Pavel said placidly, sitting close beside him and pulling up her knees so that she could wrap her arms round them and gaze into the blue flames of the primus. 'Shall I tell you about before I came to Fedor's place?'

'Certainly,' David said, remembering that she had assured him she remembered nothing of that earlier period in her life. 'Only I thought . . .'

'Oh, I don't *know* what happened, but it's what I imagine. I think that Fedor was wrong when he said we – Eva and I – came from a mountain *aoul*. After all, he was only guessing. I think the soldier probably told him that because he knew we would not be welcome under our true identity. I think we're the children of some prince who was discredited during the revolution and came to the mountains to hide away. I think the Red Army found him and killed him and his wife and all his servants, but could not bring themselves to let two innocent children die. So they took us to Fedor, and he, not knowing any better, brought us up as his own. Though I'm sure not even the prince and princess could be a better mother and father than Fedor and Nyusha have been,' she added hastily, blending fiction and truth rather neatly, David thought.

'That's very romantic, and it would account for your brains, if not for your beauty,' David said cautiously after a moment. 'Would you like to believe it, little one? Because birth is just an accident, you know – it's what one makes of life that matters.'

'If not for my beauty? What do you mean?'

'Well, the Caucasus has always been famed for its beautiful women. Long ago, the men of the Caucasus used to sell their daughters into slavery in the Arabian harems because no one else was beautiful enough for the kings and princes of that country. Didn't you know that?'

'No, they never told us that at school. What else do you know about us? Tell me about those beautiful Caucasian slaves.'

'Well, I don't know much about them . . . but did you know that it used to be thought that the old Greek gods lived hereabouts? Mount Elbruz may have been the home of those gods, and these mountains were certainly the home of the Amazons – have you heard of them?'

'No.' She was staring at him, her eyes very big and shining, her attention riveted. 'Tell me!'

'Well, the Amazons were a tribe of beautiful and very fierce women. They kept a few men around, no doubt, for the usual purpose, but it was the women who mattered, who ruled. They lived in these mountains and men went mad for them but they would only give themselves where they loved. It's a legend . . . I should have thought you'd have heard it!'

Pavel shuffled a little nearer to him. 'How wonderful! What did they look like? Eva will be beautiful one day, Nyusha says; will she be like the Amazon women?'

David leaned over and cupped her face in his hands. She was just a child; let her have her illusions of high birth if it pleased her, and certainly she was lovely, with a face and figure sufficiently different from most to stand out in any company.

'They were fair-skinned, with very large, greeny-grey eyes,' he said solemnly, trying not to let his mouth reveal his amusement. 'They had long smooth hair and mostly it was a light beigy-brown, overlaid with gold in the summer time, rather as yours is. They had tiny little gold freckles across their little straight noses, and their mouths . . .'

She was staring at him, her mouth a little open, her eyes wide, the lashes curling up so that they almost touched the delicate line of her brows. It seemed natural to bring his face closer and closer as he talked, to brush her mouth with his lips, and then, when she did not draw back, to return to her lips with a light and casual kiss.

Her face cupped in his hands, he felt a little shiver run through her as his mouth touched hers and he drew back quickly, a little confused, a little ashamed of his own behaviour. Why on earth had he kissed her? She was a funny little thing with her talk of princes and princesses, but she was very self-confident and indeed quite bossy as a rule. She was the nearest thing to a son Fedor had, and she was quite determined to take the dominant role in their relationship of guide and traveller – or had been. This unexpected and unwelcome adventure had taken her off guard and turned her, for a moment at any rate, back into an uncertain sixteen-year-old girl. Fedor, he realised, would never have let him go off unaccompanied with Pavelina, but it was Pavel who had left the homestead with him that morning and it would have been Pavel who returned with him that evening had he not caused the accident. So . . . no nonsense, just because she was suddenly uncertain.

'Were they really like me? The Amazons?' He could see the dream forming even as he began, laughingly, to tell her that no one knew what the Amazons looked like or even if they existed at all, and desisted. Who was he to put her dreams to flight? And he had an uneasy feeling that she would need all her dreams one of these days.

'So I might have been the child of one who, long ago . . . David, what did you mean when you said the Amazons kept a few men for the usual purpose?'

Now it was David's turn to lose his calm; she was a farmer's daughter, she must know why a woman needed a man! But it was clear after one glance at her that what she accepted as normal between cows and sheep was plainly inconceivable between men and women!

'David? Why did they need men?'

'To beget children,' David said briefly. He leaned over and

167

felt the clothing nearest him. It was definitely drier, and after a few more hours in front of the stove would no doubt be fit to wear. But for now he thought they had done quite enough talking. Sleep, and the primus heat saved for the morning, should be next on their agenda.

'We'll both get into the sleeping bag,' he instructed his companion, having told her that the primus must be doused. 'We'll be very snug.'

'Oh . . . but must we have the primus out? Couldn't we leave it turned down very low?'

'It would be a bit risky. If it went out for lack of fuel we wouldn't be able to start off warm tomorrow, and we ought to have some of that porridge before we leave here. Why? You're not frightened, are you?'

He meant not frightened of him, but she shook her head, her eyes so wide and large that he felt compelled to hug her again, squeezing her narrow shoulders, holding her close.

'Well, if you aren't frightened of me . . . as if I'd hurt you! . . . then what are you scared of? Why don't you want the primus turned out?'

'The dark. I – I'm scared of complete dark, I always have been,' Pavel said in a very small voice. 'It's no good telling me I'm silly, it's the way I am.'

'I wouldn't dream of telling you you're silly,' David said bracingly. He moved off the sleeping bag, opened it, crawled inside, and then held it invitingly apart. 'Come on, in here with me; I won't let you be frightened, not even of the dark.'

She heaved a deep sigh, and then crawled across to him. She pushed her feet into the bag first, then wriggled lower until she was wedged in beside him. David put his arm round her shoulders and squeezed again. The breath hissed out of her and he laughed and apologised.

'Sorry, did I hurt? Here we are, snug as two bugs in a rug. You won't be frightened of the dark now, will you? I couldn't be much closer if I tried.'

He would not have admitted it, but because of the tremble he could feel still shaking her body, and the size and darkness of her eyes as they stared, hypnotised, towards the light, he was suddenly aware of a desire which had nothing, he told himself, to do with her. It was simply the proximity of one body to another in a very confined space, and for some reason which he could not explain the fact that the other body was afraid simply increased his desire not merely to comfort her but to impose on her body the strength and dominance of his own.

'All right? Now I'll have to get out of here and turn the bloody primus off . . . what an idiot I am!'

He made to unfasten the bag but she was quicker than he. She slithered out like a trout escaping from a cupped hand and padded over to the primus. She bent over it and David's shirt rose so that he saw the smooth curve of her bottom for one brief, tantalising second before the light went out and they were in darkness.

Cursing the natural anatomical result of that short glimpse, David moved on to his back as she climbed into the bag again, chilled in even that short trip. She snuggled against him and for the first time he realised that her fear of the dark was a very real thing, changing her from the independent young creature who had laughed with him earlier into a clinging child who shuts out fear with physical closeness.

'All right? It isn't too bad, is it?' He put his arms round her and drew her close, feeling the thumpety-thump of her heart against his own calmer thud-thud. She shivered and because he knew her fear was genuine he murmured love-words to her, calling her his little elf, his golden crumb, his little cabbage.

'Don't be afraid,' he said against her hair. 'I'm here and you're safe with me and will be safe the whole night through.' She muttered that she was all right, she knew she was safe with him, but he was not to leave her, and at the demand, which came out more like a soft entreaty, all his desire for dominance returned and he turned her easily in his arms so that they lay breast to breast and kissed her mouth, gently at first and then harder, sliding his hands up her back so that she was pressed hard against him. Comfort her, because she's afraid of the dark, poor, pretty little boy-girl, little Amazon with your strong, slim limbs and your soft mouth which will open when I demand entry and your silky hair that falls across my naked chest and your body with its boy's strength and suppleness and its glorious feminine softnesses and firmnesses.

He pushed a hand up her neck, fingers tangling with that silky hair, and opened her mouth with his. He tasted her delicately, then greedily, clipping her hard against him when she struggled, seemed to want to cry out. But then he moved his mouth from hers, down to her neck, the soft spot beneath her ear, across her cheek, down to the delicate hollows of her collar bones, and between touching her with his mouth he talked comfortingly, gentling her with speech and with touch, telling her that she was still afraid, that her heart was beating far too quickly . . . a hand cupping her breast, speeding up her heartbeat . . . that she must relax . . . fingers gliding across her taut stomach muscles, his knee pushing against her legs . . . and all the while knowing, in an ashamed and buried part of his mind, that he was using her fear of the dark for his own selfish ends.

The trouble was that the more he touched the more he wanted, until desire was so strong, so overwhelming, that it drowned out the last little sigh of conscience. He turned her easily on to her back and tore off his trousers, then knelt between her thighs, feeling her shaking and shuddering beneath him and not caring as he squeezed and mouthed her, lifting her shoulders, and finally moving into position for what he told himself was seduction but which he knew, in his heart, would have been rape.

Would have been. Because, even as he moved over her, his mouth to her breast, she reared up and he felt her hands close round his head. For the first time, caressing. For the first time, accepting what he did as natural, if not of her own choosing. The frightened whimpers which he had ignored as his lust grew had died away and now, as his hot mouth sought her small nipple, she gave only murmurs of purring content.

It was like a gift, for she was giving him herself, and with horrid, cold-water realisation he knew that it was a gift he must not accept. What he would have stolen from her he could not let her give, when she was so young, so innocent of men and their works. Perhaps, he thought ruefully, as he slid down beside her and began, lovingly, to cuddle and gentle her, he would not have taken her when it came to the point. He hoped he would have come to his senses of his own accord, as her sweet acceptance had brought him.

Once he had made up his mind, it was no longer impossible to keep his hands quietly on her back, to lie still. He did both, murmuring soothingly, and suddenly realised, to his secret chagrin, that she had gone gently to sleep whilst he fought and conquered his lust.

Had she not wanted him, then, even when he had done his best to rouse her? He knew that she had not; all she had wanted had been reassurance and cuddling. Sighing, he kissed the soft and silky hair on top of her head and she stirred and muttered something.

'Sleep now, dushka,' David murmured softly. 'I'm still here; sleep well and dream sweetly.'

She sighed and murmured his name and then her breathing deepened and he knew that she slept once more.

He had been half hoping that she would hurl herself at him with an inarticulate cry, giving him, in deeds if not in words, the right to continue with his lovemaking, but she did no such thing. She sighed, curled up as much as she could in the restricted space, and continued to sleep.

David lay there for what seemed like hours, burning. He dared not move in case he reawakened the lust which he now admitted he had barely managed to banish. He thought he would never sleep yet, insensibly, drowsiness overcame him. He was actually telling himself, bitterly, that it was only right and proper that a near-rogue such as himself should lie awake and suffer the pangs of unrequited sexual ardour when his thoughts slowed and slumbered, as he did.

# CHAPTER EIGHT

During the night the wind rose and Pavel woke David twice by clutching him and muttering that there were wolves . . . did he not hear them? . . . but he managed to reassure her that it was only the wind and that, even if wolves did come, he would frighten them off before they could do any harm, and on both occasions she fell asleep quite quickly, comforted.

In fact, possibly because of her disturbed night, she slept later than usual and only woke when an incautious movement brought her arm out of the sleeping bag and after about thirty seconds, the icy cold made the bone ache so that sleep became impossible.

Her first thought was to slide her arm back into the warm, and then she lay there, staring up at the oddly coloured ceiling above her head, wondering where she was. In front of her nose was a small mound of unfamiliar clothing: a dark blue shirt, a light grey pullover, and beyond them a pair of dark grey trousers. And then, even as she recognised David's spare clothes, he moved against her. She felt his body, warm and close as though he and she were all one person, and recollection flooded her. That was it – she had let him tip them both off a ledge into the waterfall, they had been benighted on the mountain, and they had made a shelter and crawled into his sleeping bag whilst the primus dried their clothing.

She frowned, trying to remember the evening and night in more detail. She had admitted to her fear of the dark and he had been very good to her, very kind and understanding. Later, waking, she had thought there were wolves, and he had been kind then, too, sleepily kind. And now? Light came filtering through the canvas; it was full morning. She really should light the primus so that their clothes and footwear could dry out.

Very cautiously she reached out and tugged the mound of clothes into the sleeping bag with her; they were horribly cold but soon warmed, clutched to her naked stomach. Then she pulled on the shirt, kicked the rest of the stuff down to the bottom of the bag, wriggled out, lit the primus, regulated it and shot back down the bed, shuddering. No point in remaining outside until the temperature rose a bit!

She fancied that David would wake with her abrupt descent into the sleeping bag once more, and indeed his thick lashes did flicker, but apparently he thought better of it and continued to sleep, giving her an opportunity to take a good look at his face whilst he knew nothing about it. She liked his looks, she decided. His hair was thick and dark and fell untidily across his broad brow, and his nose was big, with a bump in it. His mouth was *very* nice; it was the sort of mouth that has made its mind up and doesn't intend to change it in a hurry, and his chin had a cleft in it and would be quite difficult to shave, she imagined. At the moment it was shaded with blue – he needed a shave, but she liked it; it made his skin interestingly rough. She put out a finger and tested, very carefully, and she was right: it was just like stroking the sandpaper that Fedor used when he was smoothing off a bit of wood. However, she had no opportunity to test it further, since he suddenly turned his head to one side and grabbed her cautious finger in his mouth, going 'grrrrr' and pretending to bite it whilst she gave a shriek that was only half in fun and leapt back, nearly splitting the bag down its whole length.

'Don't, oh, don't,' she gasped, when she could speak through her giggles. 'I nearly died of fright. I thought you were still asleep.'

He let go her finger and she rubbed it ruefully, but it was not that which made her heart beat so fast and the colour stain her cheeks. It was some mystery that had happened when he had grabbed and growled, a peculiar response to his touch and the tone of his voice. She was not at all sure she liked it, but it certainly caused her stomach to churn in an exciting sort of way.

'Well? How's the drying going on? You got out earlier and lit the primus, I suppose, since it's gloriously warm now.' He stretched and his arms shot out of the bag and reached up, muscles rippling. He yawned widely and she saw his red

tongue and his white even teeth. Her stomach gave a big clutch
and she climbed quickly out of the bag before she had any
more peculiar physical reactions.

'Yes, I lit the stove. I'll boil the pan of water, shall I, then we
can have coffee? There's bread . . . I'll toast it presently. My
own shirt's dry . . . I'll put it on . . . and my tunic's very nearly
ready to wear.' She was gabbling, but better gabble than an
unnatural silence. 'Oh, the rest of your clothes are in the
bottom of the sleeping bag. I pulled them in to warm them up.
And I'll give you your shirt back, too.'

He was lying on his back with his hands behind his head,
smiling lazily at her. Now he said, very softly, 'It suits you
better than it does me.'

She looked down at it doubtfully. It was a lovely shirt,
but . . .

'It's a bit big! Mine's dry . . .' She turned her back on him
and pulled it over her head, reached for her own and put it on,
then turned back to him, but he had disappeared. From the
violent movements inside the bag she guessed that he was
dressing down there. She heard a muffled curse or two before
his head popped out again and he began to struggle out of
the bag. He was wearing his corduroy trousers and some
socks.

'Right, here I am, all ready to help get breakfast – you've put
the water on to boil, I see . . . what shall I do?'

'Make the coffee whilst I toast the bread,' Pavel said practically. She had pulled on her breeches whilst he was struggling
with his corduroys and now she spiked a slice of bread on a
pointed stick and held it out to the primus. As soon as it was
brown on one side she smeared it with butter and handed it to
David.

'There you are; the quicker we eat up the sooner we can start
walking!'


'There he is! I told you Fedor would guess what had happened
when the horses went home and would come for us! Now we
shan't have quite so far to walk.'

Fedor, smiling, was riding towards them as they rounded
the corner of the bluff. Already, the snow was thinning;
another turn or two of the path, another few feet lower, and
the snow would have disappeared. Warm, dry and on horse-

back, the journey back to the homestead would be positively pleasant in the sunshine!

Pavel greeted her foster-father with a shout and was greeted herself, as soon as they were close enough, with a bear-hug.

'I was sure you'd be all right, but we heard an avalanche just as the light was fading last evening and Nyusha was worried that David might have persuaded you to get as far as the valley beyond the glacier, but I said I'd back your good sense against David's urgency any time,' he told her. He reached out from his horse and clapped David's shoulder. 'Too late crossing the glacier, eh? Got benighted? Happens to all of us at some time or another.'

Pavel had actually opened her mouth to tell him that it was nothing so simple that had held them up when she saw David shoot a quick, frowning glance at her. Before she could speak he had cut across her, agreeing easily that they had decided to remain where they were rather than risk a night-time descent of the mountain without horses.

It seemed a strange thing to do, to suppress the story of their ridiculous little accident, but Pavel began to strap their equipment on to the saddles once more and presently they set off, David and Fedor in the lead, talking animatedly about mountaineering in general and the Caucasus in particular. Having leisure to think, Pavel found herself wondering why David had removed his shirt from her person during the long watches of that cuddlesome night, and why he had taken off his own corduroy trousers? And then there was the odd business of not telling Fedor about their involuntary dip in the waterfall. She believed David to be far too strong a person to worry that Fedor might blame *him* for the mishap, and he could not have feared that her foster-father would think it was her fault. So why? She knew very little about young men – they were mysterious creatures – but it puzzled her that his actions, otherwise so sensible and understandable, should, in those two regards, have been both unnecessary and inconsistent.

It suddenly occurred to her that David's action in removing their clothing had probably been akin to Nyusha's snatching her *burka* from her if she let it remain on her shoulders for too long within doors.

'You won't feel the benefit when you go out,' she was wont to exclaim.

That must be it! Of course, David was older and more sensible than she, even if he did not understand the mountains so well. He must have realised that, clad in his shirt and pullover and cuddled down in the sleeping bag all night, she would have been loth indeed to get out of their cosy nest and set off, with only the addition of breeches and the possibly damp *burka*, into the outdoors once more.

It was a weight, albeit a slight one, off her mind, for she had already rationalised all the kissings, cuddlings, squeezings and fuss as nothing more than a kindly and sensible attempt to keep her circulation moving briskly and her mind off wolves and the dark. It had succeeded, admirably; indeed, she remembered being rather sorry when he had decided she was warm enough and settled down to sleep.

Comforted by the thought that David had done everything only for her good, she rode along behind the two men, memorising David's back view, which was a particularly nice one. She liked him so much. It was probably because she met so few people, she supposed, but she knew she would miss him terribly when he went back to Leningrad. He had said he would return the following year, but at the thought of the twelve long months which would have to pass before he came again she felt an unfamiliar and unwelcome sinking of the heart. It would be a weary wait for her, and suppose he did not even do that? Suppose he just went away and forgot both herself and his resolve to go through the Klukhor Pass?

Presently, however, they reached the pastures where Fedor had left his beasts grazing, and with a wave he cantered smoothly off and Pavel was able to nudge her horse alongside David's until they were so close that every time the horses swayed their knees touched. She looked sideways at him. He felt her eyes and turned his head and immediately he smiled with tenderness and understanding, and you forgot his thick dark brows and the sternness of his mouth in repose and thought only that this was David, who liked you.

'Well, little one? You must think it strange that I let your father believe we were just benighted, when we both know very well that I dunked the pair of us in the waterfall, but I had my reasons.'

'You did?' Pavel cocked an intelligent eye at him. 'What were they, please?'

176

This, for some reason, seemed to make him uncomfortable. He flushed, then grinned, then leaned over and took her hand, not an easy thing to do whilst riding along a rough and downward-sloping mountain track.

'I was afraid, Pavelina, that your father might disapprove of you and me spending the night in one sleeping bag. He's a good man, and he knows the value of a good daughter. He wants you to marry one day and he might feel that . . . that it wasn't right to spend the night in such a manner with someone who is, after all, no more than a chance traveller.'

'Well, he must have known we spent the night in the tent together,' Pavel said, her brow creasing into a scowl. 'So what's the difference?'

'Oh, dear! It was having to take off our wet things and get into the same sleeping bag which made the difference. If we'd not got soaked then we could have slept separately, under our own *burkas*.'

'Oh, could we? Well, I'm glad we got wet, then – you were very kind to me, David, and stopped me being afraid of the dark or the wolves, and I'm grateful. I'm sure Fedor would thank you, too, if he knew.'

'Yes, well . . . I shouldn't have done it,' David said in a rush. His eyes met Pavel's squarely, then slid guiltily away. 'It was wrong of me to . . . to cuddle you the way I did, and I'm sorry for it. You needn't worry, though, it was quite all right – there was no harm in it and no harm can come of it.'

'Harm?' Pavel's large and limpidly enquiring eyes met David's in a look so bewildered that he had to laugh and, in laughing, he leaned over and took her hand, carried it to his lips and kissed the small, work-roughened palm.

'Pavelina, did they teach you *nothing* in school? About men and women, I mean? Or about babies and how they are made?'

'I can't remember anything like that,' Pavel confessed, after some thought. 'They taught us how to add and subtract and also how to multiply . . .'

'There you are, then,' David broke in irrepressibly, increasing Pavel's bewilderment threefold. 'Oh, *dushinka*, I'm making a joke, and in very poor taste. Don't worry, it means nothing. Tell me what else you learned in school.'

But Pavel would not. She stuck out her lower lip, dug her heels into her horse, and was already in the farm kitchen, spreading her clothing out before the fire, when David came clattering across the yard.

'Why can't I go to the market with you and David, Pavelinka? You wouldn't take me out herding the stock – which I can understand, because it does need good riders – and you wouldn't take me when you went to have another look at the Pass, although David's spent too much time here now and couldn't go that way even if it was clear as clear, but the market in the big town would be such fun! I don't have much fun, do I, dushka? And you could make me so happy, you and David, just by saying you'd let me go with you tomorrow. You could at least ask him!'

The two girls were lying side by side on their straw mattresses, their blankets pushed down round their waists, for it was a warm night. Summer was well established, and had David had more time at his disposal he could easily have gone through the Pass and down into Georgia, but he had been with the Lazarovs for two weeks now, and would have to return as he had come.

A mosquito hummed viciously past and Pavel swiped at it in the dark, considering her sister's request. It was fair enough, really, except that neither she nor David would want any company but their own, for it was only when they were alone that they could talk freely, walk hand in hand and gaze, in Pavel's case at least with undisguised longing, into each other's eyes.

However, fair was fair and Eva had been very good, never whining or grumbling that her sister's attention was so suddenly and completely switched away from herself and her small affairs to this stranger from a far country.

'Don't see why you shouldn't come, my love,' she said at last, after some thought. 'David won't mind, and we can take it slowly in both directions so you won't have to ride fast. I'll talk to him in the morning, but I'm sure he'll say yes.'

'Oh, Pavel, I love you! David's nice, too, don't you think? I like his teasy smile.'

Pavel muttered something and turned over. Soon enough Eva's breathing steadied and she slept, but Pavel just lay in the quiet dark, reliving her time with David.

There had been the day when they lay in the high pastures on the soft grass with tiny flowers scattered all over it, and she had studied his face as he slept. At first, it had been enough just to look, to take note of the black brows, the thick lashes, the nose with its flared nostrils and the mouth which conveyed humour to Pavel even in repose. She had put a finger on his mouth, knowing it would wake him, and he had pretended to bite it as he had done on the morning they had woken on the mountain in their small shelter, only this time, when she jumped and shrieked, he had not meekly let her go but had sat up and pulled her into his arms.

They kissed briefly, and then David had held her back from him, resting her in the crook of his arm, and had said flatly, 'I can't bear to leave you. I dread the thought of going back to Leningrad,' and then he had grabbed her very tightly, so tightly that afterwards she found blue bruises on her upper arms, and had kissed her hard, thoroughly and so intoxicatingly that he awoke strange feelings in her which clawed at her stomach and demanded instant gratification – only she did not know what it was they wanted so badly.

Presently they moved apart again, hearts pounding, bodies unsatisfied, and Pavel cried a little and hoped he would comfort her, but he just stared off into the distance as though he could see something on the far horizon, and it occurred to Pavel that he could have continued to kiss and hug her had he wanted to do so, and perhaps he did not want to because she was not a pretty, feminine girl but just a wild mountain boy-girl, and in any case who could love someone who did not even know who her father or mother were? And then she thought that perhaps David had a real woman of his own back in Leningrad, and perhaps it was guilt which drew him from her own arms before he had done any of the more interesting things which she suspected he knew all about, even if she did not.

The thought hurt like the stab of a sharp stitch in the side when you're tired of running yet cannot stop, and the pain made her angry with David, its innocent cause, and gave her courage. If he has a woman in Leningrad he should not kiss me, even if I *am* of no account, she told herself. She sat up and grabbed his hard, broad shoulders and shook him.

'David! What's wrong with me? Why do you kiss me and then turn away? Why don't you continue to love me, as you did before? I am not a child, you know, I'm a woman, and I want what you want.'

He looked at her. His lids drooped over his eyes and his mouth was a little open. His lower lip looked heavy and there was something in his face which was strange to her and rather frightening, but that only made her courage rear higher, more defiant. Deliberately she put her mouth against his, and when he did not respond she flickered her tongue against his lips. He drew back a little and she cast herself on his breast and announced peevishly, 'If you don't tell me what's wrong I'll bite!'

'There's nothing wrong with you – that's the trouble! Pavelinka, you're a little girl of sixteen and I'm . . .'

'I'm *not* a little girl! Eva's a little girl – I'm a woman! All right, be mysterious, don't love me, see if I care! Go back to Leningrad right now and don't ever come to my mountains again!'

By the end of the speech, though, her voice was ragged with tears, and more were spilling down her cheeks. It was dreadful to hear herself telling him to go when she wanted him to stay so much! But it did the trick; all the harshness and the strangeness left his face and he began to laugh, and to smooth her cheeks and the side of her neck with his thumbs, whilst his fingers framed her face.

'Stupiditcha! Dushka, don't you understand, I love you? When a man loves a girl he doesn't want to do something which they would both be sorry for later. I can't cuddle and kiss you with impunity, not now that I know I love you, because kisses and cuddles will go on and become something much more serious. I can't behave irresponsibly towards you – you're much too important to me.'

'Well . . . but we kissed and cuddled in our little *dacha* that night on the mountain and no harm came. I felt so safe, so – so loved!'

'And so you were, sweetheart, but then I did not value you as deeply as I do now. Look, I'm nearly ten years older than you – and a foreigner, to make things worse. How do you feel about me?'

'I love you much . . . very much,' Pavel said fiercely. She took his hand and kissed and bit all along the knuckles. 'All I want is to be with you, to stay with you; all!'

'I feel the same. But you are so young, you see, and you've met very few men . . . but if you're quite, quite sure, there's no problem. When I go back to Leningrad in three or four days, I shall ask your father if I may marry you and take you back with me. That way you will be mine and I yours and we shall be together for ever, and take care of each other. When my time in Russia is finished I'll take you home to Britain – you'll love my home and my family – and we'll live by the seaside and build boats or fish for herring or put out pots for crabs and lobsters . . . I'll think of something. And we'll live happily ever after, as they do in story books.'

'Marry me?' Pavel sighed blissfully. 'And we shall go to Leningrad together, and then to Britain? But will Fedor and Nyusha agree? I work very hard and am useful to them. I really don't know how they'd manage without me.'

But already in her heart she had left them, said goodbye to her valley home and her little sister, for she wanted to be with David more than anything else.

'I know how hard you work, but I've thought about it, and, you know, Fedor could get a couple of lads from the *aouls* to help out. I'm not saying they'd be as good as you've been . . . stands to reason they wouldn't . . . but they'd keep him going until they were into his ways. I'm sure it would work.'

'Then when shall we tell Fedor?'

'Ask him, you mean, dushka. In a day or two, when it's nearly time for me to leave. I don't want him saying it's an infatuation, just something that might die away if we were parted for a while, I want him to see it's the real thing.'

Now, lying in her hot bed, Pavel thought how easy it would be to slip out of the bed and out of the room and go to David, probably lying equally hot and equally wakeful in the kitchen next door. But she would not do it, because it would be foolish to take risks. They had to have Nyusha and Fedor on their side, show them they were responsible people who wanted to live together always.

With a sigh, she turned over and tried, once more, to sleep.

David took both sisters to the market and they had a good day despite Eva's presence, for she was a nice little girl, only too keen for her sister to be happy. She thought nothing of their habit of walking hand in hand, or of David's arm being around

Pavel's waist; indeed, she merely attached herself to any hand or arm at present unoccupied and in that fashion swung along beside them, chattering or silent, enjoying her day wholeheartedly.

The market was a good one, and David took pleasure in buying a few gifts for the sisters and for Nyusha, though all he could think of for Fedor was pipe tobacco. Pavel had silver bangles, Eva had some too, and deep in David's pocket nestled a gold ring which he thought would fit his beloved. He liked being with both girls and reflected that if Pavel was at that strange stage of development, a child emerging from the tunnel of adolescence into the full light of womanhood, then Eva was just about to enter the tunnel from which her sister had escaped. He thought Pavel lovely, his young Amazon woman, slim and strong yet pliant and tender, and he could see that one day Eva, too, would be beautiful – perhaps more conventionally beautiful than her sister, for she had curls, blue eyes and the rounded limbs which Pavel lacked. But he did not repine; no one could hold a candle to Pavel in David's eyes. The more he saw of her the more he adored her. She was brave, she was beautiful, she had not once cried out the day she had cut her foot almost to the bone on a flint in the river, yet she was terrified by complete darkness and had a strong dislike of wolves.

That she never let her fear of wolves and the dark stop her from tending the wolf-fires he thought admirable, wonderful. How Fedor would miss her! But he would make it up to the older man – besides, her foster-father had said he wanted more for his girls than the mountain Muslims who were the only men they were likely to meet.

The three of them rode home from the market in late afternoon, when the sun was low and golden in the sky and they were sated with the pleasure of looking at strange and wonderful things, eating new and different foods and buying the small tokens they could afford. They reached home when Fedor was just back from a day's herding and they all went in together. Tired but happy, the girls chattered all evening, but just before they made their way to bed David managed to have a word with Fedor.

'You're taking the beasts back to the high pasture tomorrow? May I come with you? Eva and Pavel are going to make cheese, and you might be glad of another pair of hands.'

Fedor agreed and went unsuspectingly to bed.

'I can't believe my ears, Fedor! I thought you'd be pleased – glad that Pavel would have the chance of a normal life. I love her, she loves me, and we want to marry; what's so unthinkable about that?'

David had broached the question of marriage as soon as he and Fedor had sat down to eat their midday snack, and he had been thunderstruck by Fedor's calm refusal to even consider such a thing.

'My dear lad,' Fedor had said, between mouthfuls of bread and cheese, 'she is far too young, far too inexperienced, for such a step. You would not only be taking her far away from the only people she knows, you would be introducing her to a totally new life – city life. I think you would both realise your mistake very quickly, but that would not save my Pavel. Remember, she has played at being a boy for six years now, and that alone means she has known more freedom than that ever enjoyed even by a mountain girl, let alone a city one. How do you think she'd cope with being in a house all day? How would she manage to cook, to housekeep? Let her learn to be a woman before she learns to be a wife.'

David pointed out that he lived not in a house but in a small flat, and that since at the moment he did all his own shopping, cooking and housework it would be no great hardship to continue to do so if Pavel could not or would not learn. He assured Fedor that they had discussed the lack of horses and herds in central Leningrad and Pavel did not mind a bit; rather she was looking forward to the challenge of being able to discuss various subjects with other young people. He hoped she might take a course of some description, if not an actual university degree, because wives of foreigners were sometimes given opportunities denied to the Russian people themselves.

Having made these points he looked hopefully at Fedor. Fedor looked hunted but continued with his *niet, niet, niet* every time David paused for breath.

'Very well, you think Pavel would be unhappy in a city. But how long will we remain there? A year, perhaps two, and then I shall be sent back to Britain and my home there is in deep country, where there are mountains galore and the sea . . . a wild, outdoor sort of existence is what I should enjoy most, with Pavel by my side.'

It was all useless. Pavel was too young, too innocent, too boyish, to fit in with any life David was able to offer. She would miss her sister terribly, she would pine for the Lazarovs and for the mountains, she . . .

'She's too useful,' David said bluntly, when he saw that all his good arguments were simply being ignored. 'You think of her as a son and you'd never let a son go – no farmer would.'

Fedor's eyes flickered and David realised guiltily that his host could not acknowledge, even to himself, that this might well be the truth. Instead, he began to make promises, to sweeten his *niet* with hope of a sort.

'Look, David, I don't want to seem unreasonable, so come back next year, as you'd planned, when we've had a chance to prepare her a little, and she will have had time to teach a boy from the *aoul* her tasks. This idea of whisking her off to Leningrad is daft, a whirlwind romance which you'd probably both regret in twelve weeks. Come again in twelve months, Davidski, and if you and the girl are still of the same mind you shall have her, with my blessing. Is that unfair? Is it not what most fathers would say after a mere three-week acquaintance?'

The devil of it was that he was right, given the average father of the average sixteen-year-old daughter. But Pavel was not average, and Fedor was not her father. She was living an unnatural life for a young girl, she needed what he could provide – company, conversation and some normal, healthy admiration. He discounted, for the moment, the physical side of marriage.

'Fedor, I agree with a good many things you've said, and if it's marriage you disapprove of then yes, I agree perhaps it's all a bit sudden, a bit whirlwind – though I certainly shan't change my mind in a few decades, let alone a few weeks. However, I respect your feelings. Let me take Pavel back to Leningrad with me, to share a flat with an intelligent young woman who works as an engineer at the power station. She's a good girl, and she'll take great care of Pavel . . . you can visit your daughter, see that nothing's going on that shouldn't be going on. She . . . my friend Natasha . . . can teach Pavel not only how to be a young woman but how to be a young city woman, if that's what you want. And another bonus is that she'll meet lots of young men without being tied to me in any way. Would that suit you?'

It was a facer, but Fedor rose above it. He shook his head in massive, regretful, refusal. *Niet, niet, niet!*

'Alas, I could not send her away, I would not like to have it on my conscience. That another female should see how little she is prepared to meet the world . . . no, Davidski, I could not agree. After all, I trust you, I like you, I think you would make Pavel an excellent husband. In a year, come again, and we will all dance at your wedding.'

'What if she decides to come anyway?' David said, greatly daring. 'She has a mind of her own, my little Pavel. She might simply say she'll come with me and that will be that.'

Fedor's heavy head shook again. More firmly than ever.

'No, she will do no such thing. She is under age, she has a precarious position in the Soviet anyway . . . she would get you into trouble by such an attitude, and I should certainly have to tell her that. And you know, David, she's fond of Nyusha and of me, and she adores Eva. I don't think she'd just abandon Eva, no matter how she might long to be with you.' He finished his bread and cheese and took out his pipe. 'You must learn patience, my boy, and so must Pavel. It won't harm either of you to wait for a year.'

They parted with a pretence of friendship, for David's liking and admiration for the older man had worn very thin indeed during the interview. It was easy to see the grasping peasant attitude which he held towards Pavel, though he would probably have indignantly denied it had he been openly accused. She was a son-substitute, though, there could be no doubt of that, and her going would put a good deal of extra work on Fedor, even if he took David's advice and employed lads from the *aoul* to herd for him.

And I am not fooled for one moment by promises of giving her to me willingly in twelve months, David told himself grimly as he wriggled into his sleeping bag that night. When next year comes the story will be a little different but the *niets* just as firm. Eva will need her guidance or the lads from the *aoul* will have proved useless or Pavel will have taken to a local fellow and won't be free to see me. Oh no, I shan't be put off for a whole year, just to be put off again!

He was almost asleep on the straw-filled mattress which Nyusha had laid on the kitchen floor so that he would be quite comfortable in his sleeping bag, when a shadow slipped into the streaks of moonlight coming in through the shutters. It was Pavel. She came over to him, noiseless as a cat on her bare feet. Wordlessly he held open his sleeping bag and she slid into it, her cold feet bringing gooseflesh in their wake as they touched his warm skin.

Cuddled down, there was still no relaxation in her, so he guessed Fedor had spoken to his daughter, and her first words confirmed it.

'I'm not allowed,' she whispered. 'When he told me I thought I would come anyway, but he says if I do he'll see we both regret it. He'll inform on us to the authorities even if it means he has to go to Leningrad or Moscow to do it; he says if he tells them you ran away with his daughter, who's under age, they'll send you back to Britain and never let you come to Russia again. He says they will know I'm a disobedient, bad girl and they'll send me to a Siberian labour camp where it's always cold and there's little food and no decent clothing. He says women there live like animals and that I deserve no better when you consider I was taken in out of charity. But if we wait willingly for a year, everything will be good. We shall have a big wedding, lots of gifts . . . Eva will be allowed to come and stay with us even if we are in Eng . . . Britain, I mean. So I suppose we must be patient.'

'Oh, my dearest, my little darling one, what can the authorities do if we love one another? Aren't they always preaching about freedom to love? I'm sure they don't send girls to Siberia for loving foreigners, and equally sure they don't send foreigners home for having the good taste to love beautiful Russian girls. I don't want you to disobey Fedor, but I'm deathly afraid that when the year is up he'll find some other excuse to keep us apart.'

'Yes, I too was afraid, but . . . it's true, isn't it, that I'm not yet old enough to marry as I wish?'

He knew it was true, and a part of his mind even acknowledged that Fedor was right to say they should wait. Three weeks was not a long time to know one another. To be sure, their physical attraction was strong, but suppose when they were married they found that it was not enough? Yet even whilst acknowledging that this was true, he knew that Fedor's reasoning was wrong. It was as if Pavel was caged and he her one chance of escape, and Fedor was playing the heavy father and denying her the right to leave for his own ends. He was certain that if a boy turned up tomorrow capable of doing Pavel's work and agreed to do it for nothing, all Fedor's objections to their marriage would disappear like snow in a thaw. On the other hand, to an outsider the logic of his own case was suspect, if not downright unarguable. She was only sixteen, he was a great deal older, and her father could undoubtedly make things difficult for them both if he chose to do so.

'David? Why don't you answer?'

'Oh . . . because you're right, and it's true, you aren't old enough to marry as you wish, not yet. And you're being very sensible and I can't be nearly as wise. I can't believe I've got to leave you and not see you at all for a whole year.' He put his arms round her and pulled her close. 'It will seem an eternity.'

'Yes. It will be worse for me, because I only have Eva, who doesn't want me to go, and Nyusha, who wants it probably less, and Fedor, who is cross with me for falling in love before he was ready for it and making him act unkindly. But a year will pass . . . we will make it pass quicker, perhaps, if we write many letters and think about each other all the time.'

'You're right. We'll write long, long letters, and post them every two or three days . . . can you write long letters? What about stamps? Where will you buy them? I could send them, I suppose, when I write . . . but I don't recall seeing a post-box round here.'

She giggled, a delicious purr of sound hastily stifled against his neck. It sent a frisson of desire arrowing through him but he repressed it firmly.

'Oh, David, you are quite mad – I've never bought stamps in my life. But I dare say I'll find a way. You aren't cross with me for giving in and agreeing to the wait?'

'Of course not. I'm annoyed with Fedor, because I think he withheld his permission for all the wrong reasons, but it's true that you're very young, so we'll wait the year.'

Their leave-taking, when it came, was very nearly David's undoing. In front of her parents and sister she was restrained, sensible, offering him her hand and then her cheek, speaking in a low voice. She was Pavel, her father's son, David realised. The Lazarovs would not have recognised *his* Pavel, he thought, as he shook hands with Fedor, kissed Nyusha on both cheeks, and teased Eva about the letters she was going to write him. Their Pavel was quiet and efficient about the house, a boy out of doors. They had never met the clinging, affectionate creature, teasing, laughing, wild, whom he had grown to know so well – and to love so much.

After all the farewells he managed a quiet whisper as their fingers met in a cool handshake. 'Come down to the valley, to the broken pine, in an hour,' he muttered.

She gave no sign that she had heard and, thanking her parents in all sincerity for their hospitality and kindness, he did wonder whether she would be able to get away. They would surely suspect a rendezvous if Pavel wandered off too soon after his departure.

Despite his doubts, he waited at the broken pine because the doubts were lip-service. Come hell or high water, righteously indignant father or locked doors, his Pavel would keep her word, even though it had not been spoken. She would come.

And come she did, though she was very late and when she appeared it was clear she had run all the way; she was breathless, cheeks flying scarlet banners, a hand to her side. For a moment she could not even speak but merely clung to him, her chest heaving as she fought to get her breathing under control. But then, when she was calmer, she did not seem to want to talk. Shivering, she simply clung to him like a burr, with her face in his shirt-front, her fingers digging into his arms, sliding up to his shoulders, across his collarbones and up his neck, as if she was trying to memorise the way it felt to be in his arms.

Presently, he realised she was trying to memorise all of him. Closing her eyes she touched his face, running her fingers over his lips, eyes, cheeks and chin as though she were blind and could only know him by touch. Then she pulled his face close and explored it with her lips, not kissing, not exactly tasting, more an intimate and delicate touching which presently included his hair, his neck and the brown V of skin at the front of his shirt.

'You have such a good smell,' she said at last, in a small

voice, nestling once more in his arms. 'Two . . . no, three good smells. There's your hair, your body and your hands – they all smell good, but quite different. My fingers will remember the way your skin is and how your hair grows, even if my eyes should forget. It is good to remember someone you love with all your senses, not just sight.'

'You're right; I must remember you that way, too.' He shut his eyes and traced the lines of her with his fingers; down the short nose, across the dip and curve of her lips, down to the small, rounded chin, the length of her throat, until he understood just what she meant. He would never forget how she looked, nor the special smell of her skin and hair, but the strangeness of learning her by touch was an experience he had had with no one else; it evoked a perfect memory, a picture in the mind's eye, in the nostrils and in the fingertips.

They sat down on the broken pine tree and walked a little and dreaded the eventual parting, yet when it came it was quick: a clean break.

'I must go, dear David.' Pavel stood up; she was wearing her tunic and breeches and her soft Caucasian shoes. 'Goodbye, my love. I shall see you at this very spot in a year.'

'I swear it.' David had got to his feet as she did, but on the words he took a couple of steps towards her even as she turned and strode away, resolutely facing towards the homestead. He longed to have one last embrace, one last word even, to remind her to write . . . to think about him, to love him for ever, but she did not look back even when he called her name and there was something in the set of her narrow shoulders and the way she held her head which told him she was near breaking point. A year, for him, would soon go, for he had such a full and busy life, so many friends and acquaintances, such an assortment of things to do. But for her? Ah, he must let her go now, to begin her vigil; he must not make it harder for her.

So, as the sun sank, he made his way down out of the shadow of the high peaks and into the foothills. In a day or so he would be crossing the steppes, the great Russian plain, heading for civilisation . . . and for loneliness.

The train arrived in Leningrad five hours late. Cross, dirty and exhausted, David got off and, burdened with his knapsacks, his bedroll and a variety of cheap paper bags containing dirty linen, made his way slowly across the city to the flat.

He had been away nine weeks, yet his heart did not lift at the sight of this place that he had called home for so long; quite the opposite. It lurched into his boots at the familiar smells, the box-like lobby, the impersonal, scruffy stairway. He reached his front door and rapped on it, not wanting to have to ferret through his knapsack for the key; Yuri would be home by now and could let him in.

No one came for a moment, and then, just as he was piling his belongings wearily on to the floor preparatory to beginning the search for the key, he heard light shuffling feet slap-slapping on the tiles and someone fidgeted with the door. It opened six inches and a nose and an eye could be seen through the aperture, peering at him.

'Who that?'

'It's me, David Thomas. Who the devil are *you*? This is my flat!'

The door opened fully. To David's embarrassment he saw a face he recognised without actually being able to say how he knew the owner or when he had seen her last, far less put a name to it. It was an oval face with slanting dark eyes and dark hair flowing, in regular waves, down past the sloping shoulders. It was . . . oh, dammit to hell, who on earth was she?

'Hello! You wan' Yuri?'

It came to him then like a thunderclap: it was Tanya Yenuki, the schoolteacher's wife!

For a moment, David could not have said a word for a million roubles. So Yuri had lied to him, had pretended he was saddlesore and a burden, had even made out he was going to wait at Kislovodsk, when all the time he had been itching to rush back to Leningrad with his inamorata.

Naturally enough, however, David said none of these things; he simply gaped, jaw dropped, eyes no doubt out on stalks with disbelief. But the girl had no inhibitions about their last meeting, evidently. She put her hands together and bowed her head in the traditional greeting, then stood aside so that he might enter the flat.

'Yuri!'

David roared his friend's name, wondering just what glib explanation Yuri would trot out to explain away the fact that he was living with another man's wife. It would be nice to see

Yuri embarrassed and at a loss for once. But it was not to be; Yuri had, after all, had a month to decide what line he was going to take. At David's shout he emerged from the kitchen, clad in nothing but a towel, wet-haired and with water running down the sides of his face. In addition to the towel, he wore a broad grin.

'David! You're back! It's good to see you, you old blighter!'

'Yes, I'm back,' David said briefly, pushing past his friend and slinging his baggage down on the kitchen floor. 'You lying old bugger . . . what's *she* doing here?'

'She? Oh, you mean Tanya. She's living here for a while, old boy; just until we can find somewhere else — you were away, after all. I didn't think you'd mind, in the circumstances, but of course I'll get her somewhere else today . . . or tomorrow at the latest.'

'Today,' David said firmly. 'Look, old boy, this is *my* flat which *I* share with *you*, if you remember. I won't share with two, regardless of whether it's you and Natasha or you and this . . .'

'Tanya.'

'All right, you and this Tanya. Damn it, Yuri, she's another man's wife! For all I know he's hot on her trail and will turn up here swearing vengeance and not knowing which of us seduced her.'

'Seduced her? I like that . . .'

'Yes, I'm sure you did . . . and do, no doubt . . . but that doesn't change the facts. I don't necessarily mean sexually seduced, either — I mean seduced her away from her home and husband. When he arrives on our doorstep . . .'

'My dear chap, what sort of idiot do you take me for? He doesn't know she's come to me, he simply knows she's left him. Probably searching the bazaars for some smelly cameldriver or other for all I know.'

'So you acknowledge she has a taste for smelly cameldrivers? Well, it takes one to know one. And just how did you get hold of her without her husband finding out? If you went back to the village for her . . .'

'I didn't, so calm down! When we left I told her to be on the bridge outside the town in eight days' time, at sunset. She was. I'd already sold the horse, so I bought her a ticket and a couple more bangles and we left by rail the same night.'

'I see, pre-arranged,' nodded David. 'And I dreamed all that business about you dragging her into your sleeping bag . . . *what* an imagination I've got, haven't I, Yuri? But for sheer, bold-faced lying, you're definitely the master; I don't know anyone to equal you.'

'Oh, come on, Davidski, it wasn't lying, it was just prevaricating,' Yuri said defensively. 'Look, old chap, I don't know that I can find her anywhere today, but I swear that tomorrow I'll really put myself out, find her something . . . and in the meantime we shan't be any trouble to you. We can sleep in the kitchen – curl up under the table or somewhere – though I'm sure we wouldn't kick up a row in the bedroom . . . we've been sleeping together ever since we arrived back here nearly three weeks ago.'

'I think you'd better both leave,' David said. He poured himself a cup of tea from the quietly simmering samovar and slumped into a chair. 'God, what a homecoming!'

'You're worn out,' Yuri said at once, all concern. 'Why not go straight to bed – things won't seem so black in the morning. For one thing, Tanya's a superb cook – much better than you or I – and she's a marvellous one for bargaining, really she is. She doesn't speak ordinary Russian, and she's got a very thick accent . . . I think she speaks some wild Tartar language or other . . . and she pretends not to understand until the price drops, and then she just picks up her purchases, flings down the kopeks, and walks away.'

'Charming! We'll have commissars and policemen falling over themselves to get us into court for fraud,' David muttered sulkily. It was too bad, really it was. Yuri lied to him, turned up with a woman and installed her in David's flat, talked gaily about the advantages of what amounted to a *ménage à trois*, and plainly believed that he only had to smile and exchange a few words with David for all to be forgiven and probably forgotten as well.

'Don't be silly, Davidski. She doesn't cheat the peasants – you couldn't, they're too busy cheating us – she just gets the best price possible. Now, you've had some letters whilst you were away. Do you want to read them now? Tanya's making her very own mutton stew – it has to be tasted to be believed.'

Wearily, David agreed that he might as well read his letters, and presently, without at all meaning to do so, he found himself sitting at the table eating a big bowl full of excellent stew with freshly baked bread to accompany it, reading the five or six family letters which had piled up in his absence.

As he ate – with Yuri for company, since Tanya refused to eat with the men – he thought that life without Yuri would be pretty dull, really, and it was clear that his friend could scarcely turn Tanya out. She would not survive long without someone to look after her. And she was a very good cook. If they looked on her as a sort of housekeeper . . . if they could find her a folding bed, so she could sleep in the kitchen . . .

Long after he had succumbed to his exhaustion and gone off to bed, David woke. In the other bed, on the other side of the room, a faint rustling sound had dragged him out of the depths of sleep. He listened; in a vague mumble, interspersed with sobs, Tanya was explaining to Yuri that she was cold in the kitchen, and afraid, and if only he would let her get into his bed she would be very good, very quiet!

Yuri was obviously too sleepy to take advantage of this offer, for after some initial rustling, as Tanya bedded herself down on the narrow little mattress, Yuri's rumbling snores once more made the night hideous. David could not help grinning to himself as he remembered the last night he had spent with this particular couple. Familiarity, in this case at any rate, plainly bred contempt, and he was glad of it!

# CHAPTER NINE

Winter came, and Pavel settled down, with what patience she could muster, to a regime of short days and long nights. Once the snow was thick and the storms raged every few days, it was not easy to get out at all and pointless to move the herds, since there was no grass to be got in the high mountains.

Thanks to their careful farming policy throughout the summer, the lofts were full of hay and a good supply of root crops was clamped against the weather with a thick covering of soil in the home pasture, and it was these which allowed them to keep their herds and flocks more or less intact instead of having to kill off large numbers against the hungry days of winter.

Pavel worked through her days as she always had; she read, she learned to cook, to sew, to knit, and she wrote long letters to David, though she had to write very small because the letters could only be sent off about once a month and then they tended to be more like parcels than letters — untidy stacks of loose paper with string round them.

In the end, of course, having given the matter careful thought, Pavel decided that it was pointless sending David these masses and masses of words, so she wrote a day-to-day diary and then précised it for her monthly letter. Even so she needed a good deal of paper to get it done.

After some lengthy discussions between Fedor and Nyusha which she was not privileged to hear, it was decided that Pavel should not watch the wolf-fires every other night, as she had done the previous winter and for a good five or six years before that. Instead, they got two lads from the *aouls* to watch as well, and this meant that Pavel and Fedor first had company and then, when the lads were capable of managing alone, had two or three nights' sleep in their own beds instead of sitting up wrapped in their *burkas*, patiently feeding the flames and now and then walking round the field edges with a flaming branch to discourage any wolf which might be bolder than its fellows and have come after the sheep.

David's letters to her could only be collected when they went into the village for marketing, but to Pavel they were more precious than gold. She read them through from beginning to end at least once every day and sometimes twice. She quoted his opinions and doings until even the patient Eva was known to pull a face and disappear when her sister started a sentence with 'David says . . .' or 'David thinks . . .'. And she drew herself a calendar and marked off the days with a thick black pencil . . . one fewer day to wait before he came again.

It was pleasant, though, to find herself treated in a rather more special way by her parents. Nyusha approved of David and had actually had the temerity to tell Fedor – naturally when she believed both the girls to be well out of earshot – that he had been wrong to keep Pavel and David apart for a whole year.

'She's a good girl, a hard-working girl, and we have so little future to offer her,' she said distractedly, as she and Fedor unpacked the waggon which they had just brought back from the village and Pavel, writing her diary in the hayloft, listened avidly. 'I think you should have consulted me; I would have advised you to let her go with him. After all, suppose he doesn't return? She'll be heartbroken, poor child.'

So they do intend to let me go with David when he comes back next summer, Pavel realised thankfully. And her next letter to David was a paeon of praise for Nyusha and a complete retelling of the overheard conversation.

'Spring will be arriving in Leningrad,' Pavel said, one March day when the snow in the Caucasus showed no signs of lifting. 'There will be little spring flowers and warm breezes and David will be starting to get together his camping equipment for the summer. He writes that he has given Yuri . . . Yuri shares the flat . . . notice to quit from August, when he will bring me back with him.'

'I'll miss you more than anything,' Eva said mournfully. The two girls were sitting up at the kitchen table, making themselves new woollen skirts for the spring. Earlier in the winter they had spun the raw hanks of washed sheep's wool into thread, helped Nyusha to dye it, and toiled over the weaving of the cloth – all the biggest knots are mine, Pavel reminded Eva triumphantly – and now they were making it into their spring skirts.

'I'll miss you as well,' Pavel assured her. 'But not for long. David says you must come and stay with us before he leaves Russia, and of course when we live in Britain you must come there, too. We will buy you a ticket, I expect . . . if one has tickets on boats?'

'What do you suppose David is doing now?' Eva asked; a favourite game when a letter had just arrived. Pavel considered, her needle poised. The snag was that letters were usually a month or more out of date, so that when David talked of Christmas, or the pleasure of skating on the frozen river, it was a pleasure long past and probably all but forgotten.

'Let me see . . . he was going to the ballet, but he'll have been there by now. If spring is on its way perhaps he will be strolling down the Nevski Prospect in the sunshine, on his way to have a meal in that special restaurant he mentioned in his last letter. Or of course he might be at work, balanced on some great piece of machinery showing the men how to fit the next bit on. Or he might be sitting in the park admiring the green grass and planning his next letter to me.'

'Green grass?' Eva spared a quick look out of the window, at the yard where the snow was churned to brown slush and the roofs from which foot-long icicles still hung. 'They can't have green grass yet, surely?'

'Can't they? It's mid-March. But probably you're right. Tell you what, Fedor said he was going to market in ten days . . . if we've finished these skirts we could go with him and see if we can buy a bit of silky stuff for shawls.'

'We might . . . he's going to take some tiny lambs, isn't he?'

'Yes, so he says.'

Eva ran out of cotton, tied the ends neatly and began to thread another length. She was a neat and careful seamstress; her skirt would be more efficiently made than Pavel's. 'You think he'd take us?'

'He might. He'll need me, of course, in breeches, to help with the flock.' Pavel was quite ashamed of her own liking for boy's attire, but there was no doubt about it, a boy had much more liberty than a girl, and one could ride on horseback without either sharing a mount – a particularly disgraceful thing to one who could ride – or being put on the back of a tiny pony to tittup along subserviently in the rear, never asked for one's opinion, never allowed to give it.

'And I suppose you think there might be a letter,' Eva guessed, smiling. 'Have you got one ready for sending?'

'As it happens . . . but the last one came five weeks ago and you know what the post's like. Still, I do rather hope . . .'

'Summer's getting nearer,' Eva said comfortingly. 'Only another five months and it will be August again.'

'Less. I get terribly excited when I think about it. David was asking his boss if he could book his leave now, so that we don't have to wait a moment longer than necessary. I told him in my last letter that I was learning more housekeeping than I ever had before; I expect he'll be pleased.'

'Not if you keep forgetting all the tips I've given you about bread,' Eva said severely, starting to stitch once more. 'First, you must have nice cold hands. Oh, no – that's for pastry. Start again. First . . .'

The door burst open and Fedor stood there.

'Pavel . . . oh, God, you're in a skirt. Get changed, dear, and come straight out to the home pasture. There's a calf coming feet first; if I'm to deliver it alive without harming the mother I need help . . . tell Nyusha! Eva, bring a bucket of the hottest water you can get out to me, would you? I would have got her into cover but she'd started before I noticed.'

He dashed out again. Snowflakes blew in as he slammed the door. Pavel, running to her room and hurling off her girl-clothes, tugging on breeches and shirt, wondered if David ever wondered about her as she did so often about him. He would not guess in a thousand years that she was about to help Fedor deliver a breech calf in the teeth of a snowstorm!

'There's a telegram, Dave. It came an hour ago but you weren't here, so I took it in. I've not read it.'

David had only just entered the flat, kicking snow off his boots, for even in March the snow was still thick enough to obstruct the streets. He took the telegram in one gloved hand, thanked Yuri through his muffler, and preceded him into the kitchen where Tanya was busily cooking their meal.

'Hope it's not bad news.' He shed gloves, thick scarf and top-coat, then ripped open the small envelope. He scanned the brief message, then swore. 'Oh, damn! I've spent three hours in the post office getting a letter sent to Pavel, and now it looks as though I'll have to go back. Look,' and he thrust the telegram under Yuri's nose. MOTHER SERIOUSLY ILL STOP COME AT ONCE STOP ALICE

'It says come at once,' Yuri observed, having read it and translated the message into his own language for Tanya's benefit. Her Russian was getting quite good and she had no difficulty, now, in understanding their conversation.

'Well, yes, I know, but it can't be that urgent, not really. Mother's very healthy, and quite young, as well. I suppose Alice is panicking because Mother's got 'flu or something.'

'Does Alice panic? When you've spoken of her she has not sounded the sort to panic for nothing.'

'No, she's very level-headed . . .' David, who had cast the telegram down on to the table, picked it up and re-read it as though this second perusal would cast a light on something he had missed. 'You're right. Mother must be really ill. I'll have to go home!'

'See Mr Powell,' Yuri advised, wandering over to the stove and picking a succulent curl of vegetable out of the concoction simmering there. Tanya tutted and slapped his wrist with her long-handled spoon. 'You don't want to take any leave, because of going back to the mountains in July or August. Tell him you'll take time off without pay.'

'Yes, I could do that. I just wish there was some way of getting in touch quicker . . . Yuri, I'm worried. I'm going along to the British consulate to see if they can get any more information.'

'You could try,' Yuri said doubtfully as David put back the outer clothing he had just taken off. 'There'll be some method of getting in touch, I suppose. But if I were you, I'd start trying to arrange the travelling — tickets and so on. You know how long that can take.'

'Yes, you're probably right. But I'll go to the British consulate first and get them to make some enquiries,' David said, heading for the door. 'It can't be too bad . . . can it? I mean, I had a letter only ten days ago and everything was all right then.'

'Good luck!' Yuri shouted, then turned back to Tanya, placidly laying the table. 'Better make it just for two. You know how long these officials take to get things done.'

But he was thinking of Russian officials, not British ones, and the British consulate, compared with its Russian equivalent, could move like greased lightning. Within a week, David was on a ship sailing from Archangel to Liverpool, homeward bound.

'She's dying, Davie. But she wants to see you – I'm so glad you arrived in time.'

Alice had met her favourite brother off the train and brought him back to the house. She had not seen him for almost three years and was amazed at how he had changed; he had always been tall, but when he had last been home he had still had remnants of that adolescent stringiness which shows that a youth has not yet reached his full strength. Now he was sturdy, strong, with heavy shoulders and a determined look to his jaw which was mirrored in his dark, rather heavily lidded eyes.

When he had got off the train and was standing on the platform collecting his gear he had looked distressingly unlike her own dear David; it was only after her tentative approach, that first smile, when he had suddenly smiled back, that she had known for certain it was he. To her initial distress he also spoke differently – more slowly, with less crisp incisiveness – but that was quickly explained.

'You try speaking Russian all day and every day for three years at a stretch; you'd find, as I'm finding, that when you talk English it doesn't come at all easily to your tongue,' he assured her, as they got into the cab she had hired. 'Now, I gathered from the British consul in Leningrad that Mother's illness was only sudden in that she had kept the symptoms from everyone until she could hide them no longer.'

'That's right. Once she told us, though, she seemed to go downhill very fast. You . . .' She hesitated, hating to have to say the words, '. . . you may not immediately recognise her . . . she's very thin . . .'

And now David stood in his mother's bedroom and tried to hide the shattering blow that her appearance had dealt him.

She was not just thin, she was a living skeleton; her hair, abundant and gleaming, as brightly coloured as he remembered it, looked like a wig, springing as it did from her tiny, shrunken face, all eye sockets and thin, ridged nose. She was not sleeping but seemed to be in some sort of daze, for she simply lay there, against the snowy pillows – but they were no whiter than she – looking blankly out at the bare branches of the sycamore outside her window.

'Mother?' David's voice trembled a little, but the gaunt head on the pillow turned at once towards him and the thin, bloodless lips twitched into the travesty of a smile.

'David! My dear boy . . . you've come home at last!'

'That's right, Mother. I've come home to see you, and to give Alice a hand.'

He had been pretty shaken by Alice's appearance as well, he would be the first to admit. She was very thin, all the pretty shape he remembered seeming to have turned into straight lines, and there was a rigidity about her which he knew very well must be the result of anxiety over his mother's illness and managing the younger ones.

'Yes, dear, Alice could do with some help. So good she's been! Never a word of complaint, though having to give up her job was hard on her. And I keep telling her she doesn't get out enough – or eat enough, either; that's why she's gone so thin.'

'You're a good one to talk,' David said rallyingly. 'You can't eat enough to keep a sparrow alive.'

'Oh, me . . . I *can't* eat, that's why I've gone to skin and bone,' his mother said indifferently. 'It's time you came home, David. Time you married, like Ned.'

Ned had been married for several years and had a hopeful young family of his own. He was practising law in Liverpool and was very happy, Alice had said in her letters, but reading between the lines David had gathered that Ned did not have time to share her responsibility for their younger brother and sisters or for their mother, though he paid his financial whack willingly enough.

'Time enough for that, Mother. Is there anything I can do for you? Anything you want?'

His mother closed her eyes. The lids were such a pale, frail blue that David got the impression they must be paper thin and almost transparent. He shifted uneasily.

'Yes, David, I do want something. But I'm very tired, now. Could you come back tomorrow morning, when I'm a little fresher? I'll tell you all about it then.'

Dismissed, David and his sister left the room. David said nothing until they were downstairs again and then, in the small, dark square of the hall, he turned to Alice.

'Allie, you poor little creature, how have you borne to see her wasting so? Does she suffer much? Who takes care of her at night? I'll do anything I can, you know that. I'm sure the company will give me compassionate leave until . . . well, until there's no more I can do.'

'I usually sleep on a truckle bed down by hers,' Alice said, in answer to his last question. 'She's marvellous – she hardly ever calls out or needs anything in the night – or if she does, she keeps it to herself. But we do have a nurse who comes in morning and evening, just to make sure we don't do anything wrong. I hate to rush you, Davie, but if you wouldn't mind having a meal now and then getting to bed . . . Mother wakes early, and for the first hour, as she says, she's capable of quite long sustained conversation. I really think it would be best if you could see her then. You must have guessed . . . you must realise . . . it won't be long, Davie.'

'What time shall I come to her? You tell me and I'll be there.'

'Well, about seven would be best. I'll wake you with a cup of tea at about six thirty and you can dress and come through. The nurse arrives around eight o'clock, usually, and gives Mother something which eases her pain but tends to make her drowsy and unlike herself. So if it isn't too much to ask, we'll say seven o'clock.'

'My dear Alice, after all you've had to put up with, I'd think myself a pretty rotten chap if I couldn't get up early for once! Anyway, I have to be at work for eight in Russia, so it's no particular hardship.' David turned and opened the door of the sitting-room, ushering Alice inside. They had the house to themselves at this hour of the afternoon, so it seemed a good moment to catch up on the news. 'Do you have time to sit and chat? I want to know everything that's happened lately . . . what about Mother, though? Ought we to sit with her?'

'No, she'll sleep now for an hour or two. I pop in from time to time to see she's all right, but I don't stay with her when she's sleepy like this.' Alice sat down in a chair on one side of the hearth and motioned her brother to the other. 'Well, fire ahead! What do you want to know?'

'Ned's in Liverpool with his wife and family, Lydia's married with a little son of ten months or so, Julia is engaged to a gentleman farmer. What about Sara? And Michael? And most important, Allie, what about you?'

'Sara is a bluestocking,' Alice said with mock severity. 'How we ever came to have such a clever sister, you and I, I shall never know. She matriculated without effort a year before she should have done and now she's sitting for her higher and everyone says she'll waltz away with it and get a place at Cambridge. She wants to be a doctor, if you please!'

'That's marvellous, but can we afford it? Her going to Cambridge, I mean? You know I send what I can, but Ned and I only got through university because of that educational trust Father set up. Does it cover girls as well as boys?'

'Honestly, David, what a thing to say! Yes, it does . . . or rather it didn't specify, so Mr Jenkins says that Sara will be covered.'

'That's good. And Michael?'

'He's another bright boy, just like you, David. He insists he'll be an engineer like you and not a lawyer like Ned, and I expect he will be. He works hard at the things he likes and not at all at the things he doesn't like . . .'

'Also like me,' David said before Alice could get it out. 'And now, Allie, what about you? Don't think I'm being rude, my dear girl, but you look thin – too thin – and tired. You look as though you're so busy keeping a stiff upper lip that you've forgotten how to relax. Mother said something about you giving up your job . . . you never mentioned it to me when you wrote.'

'Didn't I? It didn't seem important. Yes, I gave my job up when Mother fell ill. It wasn't a marvellous job, but it was interesting and it meant we could employ a maid to give a hand in the house and a woman to do the rough work, as well as a chap to help in the garden and grow us some vegetables. But I was needed at home, so I told my employer I'd have to leave and he was very nice about it. Said if I needed a job again, later, to get in touch with him and he'd see what he could do.'

'A job! Alice, why aren't you engaged, like Julia? Or thinking about going to university, like Sara?'

'Because I'm not pretty like Julia and not clever like Sara,' Alice said tartly. 'Do talk sense, David! Now, tell me what's been happening to you.'

'You are pretty! You used to be very pretty indeed, but now you've gone thin and worried . . . but you're still pretty! And you're a clever girl – not brilliant, perhaps, like Sara, but very clever. Why didn't you do anything with your brains? You were a clerical worker in a shipyard, weren't you?'

Alice pulled a face at him and for the first time since arriving home David saw the ghost of those dimples which Alice had once sported every time she smiled.

'Oh, Davie, could you be prejudiced?' She sighed and leaned forward to balance another log on the small and fitfully burning fire. 'It's so nice of you to say those things and I *do* think I was quite passable, once. But you know I never had time . . . it was all rush, what with the younger children and Mother not being terribly good with the staff – and to be honest all I wanted was to earn some money so that things would be a bit easier. And there was a fellow . . . he went away . . . so here I am, sweet twenty-one and never been kissed, apart from the odd peck on the cheek at parties.'

'Are the young men on Deeside mad, or blind? I shall take you back to Russia with me when . . . when I go, and you'll be married within six months, I guarantee it!'

'Ha! Easy to say, Davie bach. Incidentally, I've been meaning to ask you when I wrote, but haven't got round to it. Did you ever meet Nibby Hawke over there? He's in Moscow.'

'Nibby Hawke? Well, I'm damned! What's he doing? Engineering of some sort, I suppose? The rotten old devil not to get in touch – or didn't he know I was there as well?'

'I really can't say,' Alice said, holding out her thin hands to the fire. 'We wrote quite regularly at one time – me more than him, though, I must admit – but when he heard he was going to Russia he was over the moon, terribly excited, and somehow he never got round to answering my letters or perhaps he left before he received them, I can't be sure. But anyway, I've not heard from him for a couple of years.'

'He wrote to me for a bit, but he was a rotten correspondent,' David admitted. 'I was every bit as busy as he, we were both at university, and the letters just lapsed, I suppose. I did write and tell him I was off to Russia . . . or I seem to remember doing so, but I may just have told him I'd put in for a job out there. Yes, come to think of it I'm sure that's what I did, and since I'd put in for work in Germany and Sweden and the United States he may not have realised where I went. What a thing! Do you have an address for him in Moscow? I'll look him up when I get back.'

'No, I don't,' Alice said regretfully. 'He never said where he was going apart from Moscow. Is there any way of finding out?'

'Oh, yes, easiest thing in the world now I know he's in the country,' David assured her cheerfully. 'We're quite a close-knit community in Leningrad, and I bet they're the same in Moscow. Ask any Englishman where I am if he knows David Thomas and he'd scarcely have to think about it. Tell me, did you see much of Nibby whilst he was in Britain?'

'Yes, I suppose I did, quite a bit. He came over to Chester to stay with an aunt or something one summer and we had a marvellous day out together. After that I hoped he'd come back but didn't really believe he would, and perhaps he wouldn't have bothered, but there was the boat, and fishing, and we talked a lot about you . . . I suppose we met four or five times a year until he went to Russia. And wrote.'

'Was it Nibby you meant when you said there had been a chap in your life but he went away? Because if he's been playing fast and loose with you I'll tear his head from his shoulders next time I see him,' David said, scowling. 'Not that you'd fall for Nibby . . . unless he's changed a helluva lot.'

'He has,' Alice said simply. 'He's taller, of course, and broader, but his hair's grown up rather nicely – remember how it always used to look as though rats had been nibbling it?'

'Could I ever forget? I suppose his da went at it with shears every time it got too long.'

'Shears? A blunt penknife, I'd have said.'

'Or a tyre lever.'

They laughed without malice; they both loved Nibby in their different ways.

'Yes, well, whatever, now he's older it's smoother, all one length, and his face isn't so . . . so sharp, somehow. I think his expression was adult before he was, so he's grown to fit it. Does that make sense?'

'To me it does. So you fell for Nibby's manly charms. Hmm. I wonder whether it would have worked out. Our Nibby burned with ambition as a kid, you know. It was all how he'd succeed and make money – I don't think it mattered whether he enjoyed what he did so long as he did well at it.'

'He's still a bit like that – or was, a couple of years ago,' Alice admitted. 'But he was great fun. I liked being with him better than I've liked being with anyone since you went away.'

'And he never kissed you? He's a poor fish, then, for all you think he's improved,' David said cunningly. 'How long was he coming over here for? A couple of years? And he never even kissed you? Booby!'

Alice, however, was not to be drawn. 'He came over to see me because you weren't here, and he wouldn't have kissed you! He was just a very good friend. The fact that I felt fonder of him than just a friend . . . if I did; I'm not sure . . . obviously didn't affect his attitude to me.'

'Hmm. Did he have a girl wherever he was?'

'Oh, David, don't try to make Nibby out to be a philanderer or something, because he was no such thing. He did have a girl at first, but then I think he stopped seeing her, but I don't really know, because we didn't talk much about his social life, just his work and here. Oh, and his father remarried so he told me a bit about his stepmother; she sounded nice.'

'Well, I think it might be a good idea . . .'

David's sentence was cut of short by the tumultuous entrance into the room of Michael and Sara. They were fighting and Michael was getting the better of his sister despite being three years her junior. Sara was trying to hold him off, laughing, shouting and generally seeming a good deal younger than her seventeen years. She saw David, tried to silence her brother with a hand over his mouth, got bitten, shrieked, and finally sat down with a thump on the hard little sofa and appealed to the world in general to save her.

'Help, someone! Michael, remember my dignity . . . my seniority . . . my sex!'

'She's got my catapult,' Michael shouted, hurling himself at his unfortunate sister once more. 'It's in her blazer, in the inside pocket . . . I'll get it, Sassy, if I have to kill you for it!'

'Oh, charming! Allie won't let you kill me, so . . . aaargh!'

David, watching Alice quell the riot, remove the offending catapult and put it on the mantelpiece behind the clock, soothe Michael with promises of its return subject to good behaviour and Sara with comforting assurances that it would only be used on defunct tin cans and similar unfeeling objects, marvelled at his sister. She was only twenty-two yet she had the tact, humour and patience of a woman who has been a mother to a large family for twenty years.

He also wondered at Alice's description of Sara as a blue-stocking. Clever she might be, but in no other way did she fit the description. She was small and slim with what promised to be a very good figure and a head of most beautiful coppery curls, tight as a lamb's fleece, which clung close to a small and shapely head. She was also very pretty, and very like Megan Thomas as a girl, David imagined, with the small, slightly upturned nose, white skin and large hazel-green eyes which had once charmed Alyn Thomas into marrying far too young and without the faintest notion of caring for a wife or fathering children.

'There we are, then. Peace for a bit?'

Michael was still golden-fair, still cherubic – to look at, anyway. The coppery curls and the fair nodded enthusiastically and Michael said hopefully: 'If it's peace, my merry men, how about some tea?'

'Belly on legs,' Sara growled in an unladylike way, but Alice just shook her head reprovingly and started out of the room.

'All right. It would have been ready by now, but what with David arriving and one thing and another I'm afraid it's not. Never mind, it won't take long to prepare.'

'Hello, David,' Sara said, giving her brother a bewitching smile. 'I thought it was you . . . but I wasn't sure. Not that Alice is in the habit of entertaining young men in here, but you might have been the insurance man or something.'

'Don't listen to *her*, bo,' Michael said scornfully before David could reply. 'Insurance men aren't tough . . . all Thomases are tough. Well, all the men, anyway. Have you seen Mum? She's not so well, is she?'

'Yes, I've seen her. She's obviously very ill,' David said cautiously, not sure how much his younger brother and sister knew. 'I'm to see her again tomorrow morning, early. She says she'll feel more like talking then.'

'Yes, she's much better early,' Michael said. 'It's hateful now she's ill. Allie has to stay here all day and the woman who used to come in and cook our dinners and teas had to leave because we didn't have enough money to pay her.'

'Mother doesn't even come downstairs any more,' Sara supplied. 'Julia sits with her sometimes and reads to her, but she's a rotten cook, so Allie gets landed with all the meals. Good thing Julia's marrying someone with oodles of money, because he'd starve pretty quick if he didn't employ a cook!'

'And what do you two do?' David asked. 'Why don't you go through and help Alice now, if you can see she's got too much to do? She's awfully thin and tired – that was the first thing I noticed when I got off the train.'

'I'm rotten at things like that,' Sara said immediately, showing the whites of her eyes. 'Anyway, I've got masses of prep., and Alice is ever so keen to see me get to Cambridge, like you. She wouldn't want me under her feet.'

'And you, Michael? What's *your* excuse?'

'Men don't cook,' Michael said at once. 'Particularly not if they're going to be engineers. Well, you don't cook, do you!'

'Yes, regularly, or I wouldn't eat much,' David assured him. 'Once you move away from home, old boy, you'd be surprised how useful it is to be able to get yourself a hot meal, particularly in Russia, where the winters are so bitterly cold and food is rationed and hard to come by.'

'Rationed? Hard to come by? Tell us.' Sara sat forward, eyes sparkling. 'What was it like when you left?'

'Cold,' David said briefly. 'Come on, both of you. Show me the way to the kitchen and I'll show you how an engineer who's worth his salt can turn his hand to anything!'

'Here I am, Mother.' It was not quite seven o'clock, but David had eaten porridge, toast and a boiled egg and drunk quantities of coffee, so when Alice had agreed he might go in he had slid cautiously into his mother's bedroom. She was sitting up this morning, her eyes on the door, plainly expecting him, for she smiled with a trace of her old gaiety and patted the bed.

'Sit down, dear. What are your plans?'

'Plans? I said I'd stay here, Mother, until you were . . .'

'Now don't say better, my dear, because Alice and I both

know that isn't going to happen. Until I don't need you any more seems practical.'

'Yes. Right. Until then. After that I'll go back to Russia and finish the work on the power station and then I'll see. I might get more work over there, and if I do I shall have to take it, because the money's awfully good and the experience is unrivalled. But in a couple of years I think I'll be coming back to Britain.'

'I see. And do you have any . . . any more personal plans, dear?'

A picture of Pavel's face as he had last seen it, steeled against his going, popped into his mind. He nodded.

'Yes, Mother, I do. I've met a girl . . . she's Russian, of course; a farmer's daughter from the high Caucasus . . . we'd like to marry.'

'I see. I wondered if something like this might happen. Is she a good girl, dear?'

For a moment David wondered what on earth his mother was talking about, and then he remembered, with some amusement, articles he had been told about in the British press. The thought of free love, which had been one of the things most talked about in connection with Communism, had obviously filled his mother with deep foreboding.

'She's a very good girl, Mother. She comes from a backward community, perhaps, where purity is highly valued, but even if she lived in the heart of Leningrad she'd be a good girl.'

'Ah.' There could be no mistaking the satisfaction in that sigh. 'And does she want to marry you? Do her parents want her to marry you?'

'Yes to both questions. She's very young.' David crossed his fingers behind his back; he did not intend to burden a mortally sick woman with a truth that would only worry her. 'She isn't yet twenty. That's why I didn't marry her last summer, when we first met. Her parents wanted her to wait, so I'm going back in August and we'll marry and she'll come back to Leningrad with me for a while, and then we'll both come home together.'

'Good. I would have liked you to marry a local girl, but if you love this Russian child you'll be happy with her. What's her name?'

'Pavel Fedorovna.'

'And what does she look like?'

208

David tried to explain; the soft fawny-coloured hair lightened to gold by the sun, the wide, grey-green eyes, the classical line of her profile and the boyish, graceful figure. He made, he thought, a poor job of it, but perhaps his mother was reading between the lines rather than the actual words, for she nodded her approval.

'Good, good. There are two things I want to ask of you, David. One is that you'll look after Alice and the younger ones to the best of your ability after I've gone. The second is . . . different. Harder to explain.'

'Try,' David said encouragingly, as the silence stretched. 'I'll do my best to understand.'

'It seems silly. All these years, dear, ever since your father died, I've meant to try to find out who was at the root of that newspaper campaign. Your father would never believe ill of anyone unless it was a proven fact, and I could never get him to see that it was not just stupidity and sensationalism which made the papers twist the truth the way they did. If you could try to find out for me? My curiosity won't be satisfied, but if you knew who did it and why, then there might be some way . . .' Her voice trailed into silence and she put a transparent hand up to her head. 'Oh, it sounds foolish, melodramatic . . . but your father loved the Hall and wanted it to stay in the family. Ned says he'll save all his money and buy it back, but that won't work – he'll never manage it. Anyway, perhaps it isn't the Hall that matters to me so much as *proving* your father built a good ship. If you could find some way to prove it, Davie, I believe things would get better for you all. We still own the design of the *Royal Gold*, you know, and though there were one or two enquiries I would never sell. I wanted a ship to be built to the same design, you see, but I knew very well that no one would dare – not until it was proved without a shadow of a doubt that she went down through no fault in the design.'

It exhausted her. She lay back and David saw that a blue line had appeared round her mouth and her eyes seemed sunk into black pits of weariness, but he could see she was pleased with herself as well. Her mouth had a sweet lift to it, as though she would have smiled had she the strength.

'Well?' It was a whisper, but he gripped her hand hard and grinned too, with all the gaiety and optimism he could muster.

209

'It's a wonderful idea . . . and a strange one, because when I first told Pavelinka about the *Royal Gold* she said at once that I must hire divers to go down and find out exactly what made her sink. Ever since then it's been in the back of my mind that I would do it, once I'm home for good. Pavel asked whether any of her cargo was valuable, too, and I said it was possible since she was carrying rich passengers, and Pavel pointed out that any valuables we found would help to pay for the divers and so on. It seemed a crazy idea, but you're right, of course. If we still own the copyright on the plans and can prove she sank through no fault in the design . . . well, it could go a long way to mending the family fortunes.'

'Oh, Davie!' His mother's thin face was wreathed in smiles, and her eyes actually had a sparkle in their depths. 'Oh, Davie, you don't know what it means to me to know you'll carry on the fight as your father would have done! Now I don't mind' – her hand waved feebly, encompassing her wasted body, the bed, the bottles of medicine on the dressing-table – 'all this so much. You've made me happy for the first time for years.'

David got up, bent over the bed, and kissed her gently on the cheek. 'That's marvellous. And if you think I'll be fighting alone, you don't know my Pavel – she can't wait to get here so that she can mastermind the great adventure.'

'Good girl . . . good girl. Wait until she gets here . . . dear Davie, I knew if any of them cared it would be you. Not that I'm saying . . . but the girls can't do much and Ned's got his family, and Martha's a good wife to him but a home-body. Oh, Davie . . .'

Alice put her head round the door. Her gaze flicked quickly from her mother to David and back again. Then she smiled.

'Nurse has arrived, Mother, and I've faithfully promised that David should walk Michael to school – show the fellows that it isn't all petticoat government up here! So if you've had your little chat . . .'

'Yes, he can go now. Give her a big kiss from me, Davie, when you go back.'

There was no need for more. David pressed his mother's hand again and then left the room. Passing Alice, on her way into the room, he squeezed her shoulder but did not speak; time enough for talk later.

He enjoyed his walk to school with Michael and Sara,

though Sara's place of education lay further on and he felt obliged, for the sake of masculine solidarity, to remain with Michael and two or three of his brother's friends until the bell went at eight forty-five.

Walking home alone, he pondered the conversation with his mother. She had a bee in her bonnet right enough, but he had done the best thing, he was positive. At that moment he would have made any promises to bring his mother peace of mind, and that was precisely what he had done, although the more he thought about it the slimmer seemed his chances of getting down to the *Royal Gold* and finding any evidence which would prove why she had sunk. A dozen years would have done their work well, and what proof could there be now – or indeed twelve years ago? He would scarcely find a sign attached to her superstructure saying *Went down due to captain's error* or *Sank when rock pierced her bows*, useful though such a sign would be!

It was interesting that they still held the copyright on the design; he remembered the hours his father had laboured over the plans, getting them exactly right so that she would have speed and stability yet would not cost too much . . . it did seem a crime that no one was prepared to build another ship to the same design . . . that would be proof, wouldn't it? If he could build the same ship . . . but he was air-dreaming. There was absolutely no chance of anyone's letting him have the money for such a project . . . unless there really was a fortune of some description in the sunken wreck.

It was a pity that he had had to lie to his mother, though, even with the best of intentions, for he had no desire now to find out who had made mischief for them through the newspapers. He still thought it just the natural if nasty digging up of scandal stories, and saw little or no point in pursuing it further. And he had very little expectation of actually *doing* anything about the ship, either. In theory, one could certainly get divers to investigate a wreck; in practice, too, if one had plenty of money. But the more David thought about it the more foolish it seemed to worry about something which had happened so long ago. No, better put it all behind him, work hard, save up what he could, and when the children were all off Alice's hands try to buy a house with a bit of land down by the Dee, so that they could boat, and dig for cockles, and generally enjoy themselves, even if they could never again own Carmel Hall.

He slipped in through the front door and met Alice coming down the stairs. She had been crying. He held out his arms to her without a word and she flew into them.

'Oh, Davie, I'm so glad you came home in time,' she sobbed against his shirt. 'She died five minutes ago.'

# CHAPTER TEN

After the funeral Ned gave luncheon to the mourners, but not at the house, which could not have held half of them. Instead, he arranged for the use of his father-in-law's big, old-fashioned house which was no more than ten minutes' walk from the church, and it was here that David met Maria Raft for the first time. She had accompanied her parents to Megan Thomas's funeral partly because they were friendly with Lydia and partly, so fat, coarse-faced Mrs Raft ingenuously explained, because they knew all the best people would come to pay their respects to one so well loved.

Maria was not particularly like either of her parents. She was a tall, raw-boned girl with dark hair crimped into a permanent wave and a broad, red-cheeked face.

'She looks more like a farmer's favourite mare than a rich man's only child,' David muttered to Alice, and was rewarded by a stifled giggle closely followed by a reproving frown – Alice was a kind creature and had schooled herself out of disliking Maria because she lived in Carmel Hall into pitying her for her unprepossessing appearance.

'Actually, she's quite nice,' she murmured, taking a sausage roll and a helping of salad from the dishes on the buffet table. 'Lydia and she were rather thick at one time – Lyddy wanted to get to know the Rafts because they were living at the Hall, of course – and she used to bring her to tea occasionally. Maria always ate anything you offered, she wasn't a bit fussy, and she laughed at all the jokes and played Monopoly or Snap with Michael. She's not terribly bright but her heart's in the right place.'

'Oh, well, so long as her heart's in the right place I shouldn't grumble because her wig's crooked and her bust seems to have slipped a yard or so,' David said nastily. He knew the girl could not help it that her father had bought Carmel Hall, yet he could not help blaming her, wishing her anywhere but at his mother's funeral, though it was clear that the Rafts were anxious to show respect and hoped, by so doing, to shuffle themselves a little further into what David imagined they thought of as 'society'.

'That's cruel,' Alice said reproachfully. 'It's only that permanent wave, so set and ridged. And the – the other thing you said isn't true either; it's just a bit unfortunate that she's wearing the high waist. It doesn't suit everyone.'

'Purple doesn't suit everyone either,' David said crossly. 'She's a fright, Allie, so stop denying it.'

It was at this inauspicious moment that Ned's mother-in-law, Mrs Maud Twdor-Evans, chose to come up to the two Thomases, her hand tucked possessively into the crook of Maria Raft's elbow.

'Ah, David, I just want to introduce you to Miss Raft . . . her father bought Carmel Hall years ago – do you remember meeting him then? You know Alice quite well, I believe, Maria? Very well then, let me get my introductions right . . . Miss Raft, may I present David Thomas, Alice's big brother? David, let me introduce you to Maria Raft.'

Maria's high complexion deepened and she held out a hand big as a cockle spade to take David's.

'How d'you do, David? You don't mind if I call you David? Your sisters were always talking about their brother David years ago, when I was a regular visitor at your mother's house.'

'How d'you do,' muttered David ungraciously. 'Nice to meet you. I don't think I came in contact with your father at all when he was buying our house.'

Her handshake had nearly dislocated his wrist – he had not expected the brief, hard downward jerk which was probably the result of uncertainty and a degree of embarrassment. He jammed his hands into his pockets, then withdrew them on seeing Alice's reproachful gaze fixed on them. Oh, damn the Raft, why didn't she float off?

'No, you were only a lad then, I suppose.' She giggled, then caught her full lower lip with large white teeth. 'Oh, sorry, I forgot.'

'It's all right.' His upbringing rescued him from being really rude and just walking away. He turned to Alice. 'Look, I'll

214

leave you and . . . and Maria to have a chat. I want to have a word with Michael.'

'Oh, there's no need . . . I'll go and find my mother,' Maria said hastily. 'I'm sorry, this is a difficult time for you . . . I didn't mean to intrude.'

'It isn't that,' David said gruffly. 'It's just that the girls will be riding home in a cab but I've a fancy to get some fresh air, and I thought Michael might enjoy a walk as well.'

'Yes, of course,' Maria said in a subdued tone. 'Alice, do come and visit us some time . . . your brother would be very welcome too. We haven't made too many changes, or so we tell ourselves, and those that we've made are all . . .' She saw David's frosty eyes on her and stuttered to a distressed halt. You could actually see her trying to change the ending of the sentence from 'improvements' to something a little less critical to the Thomas family, David thought.

'It's very kind of you, Maria, but we're awfully busy just now,' Alice said in her most mollifying tone. 'You can imagine how busy when I tell you we're putting the house on the market. But we'd be very pleased to see you any time, if you'd care to call on us.'

David judged that it was now politic to move away. As he did so, as unobtrusively as possible, he saw, out of the corner of his eye, Maria lean closer to Alice, her face now beet-red. Poor girl, he thought a little guiltily as he searched for Michael, so plain and not a grain of tact to make up for it!

'Oh, Alice, I do hope your brother doesn't think me awful!' Maria whispered. 'The thing is, I saw him . . . I was with Mrs Feathers and frightfully bored . . . and I wanted *so* much to meet him . . . well, he's terribly good-looking, isn't he? . . . so I collared your aunt or whatever she is and said would she introduce us. She gave me the most awful, withering up-and-down look, and then she sort of thawed and brought me over, I can't imagine why.'

I can, Alice thought grimly, whilst murmuring some conventional answer. Martha's mother has been terrified of seeing her dear little daughter landed with the task of rearing assorted young Thomases, and no doubt she looked at Maria, recognised the heiress, and decided to try her hand at a bit of matchmaking. Well, she might as well have saved herself the trouble, for if there was one thing she did know about David it was that he would never marry for money; there would have to be love as well. As for poor Maria . . . but poor Maria was talking again, so she had better listen.

'He isn't precisely handsome, I suppose,' she was saying, her head so close to Alice's that a strand of her over-permanent wave tickled the younger girl's cheek, 'but he looks so strong and dominant . . . I'm sure girls must be forever falling at his feet.'

'Oh, I doubt it,' Alice said rather tartly. 'He's been in Russia working on an engineering project for the last three years. I imagine from what I've read that girls over there don't lie around at blokes' feet, they do something practical about it.'

'Oh, Alice!' breathed Maria. She put a hand to her throat. 'Do you mean he's a *rake*?'

'I don't *think* I do,' said the literal Alice. 'What I mean is, men are opportunists; if women persisted in falling at their feet I suppose they'd take advantage of it, that's all. Particularly in Russia – all that free love,' she added as an afterthought, in case Maria did not bother much with newspapers.

'Oh. Yes, I do see.' Maria's bafflement was plain, however. 'Well, if you think it's all right, I will come round and see you. Is David going back to Russia? Though I dare say he won't be able to, from what Father was saying at breakfast,' she added.

'He'll be going back in two or three months, when we've sorted ourselves out a bit,' Alice said. 'Whatever makes your father think he won't be able to do so?'

'Well, I'm not sure,' Maria said, frowning. 'Something about a put-up job . . . apparently there are some engineers in Moscow in prison, accused of spying . . . and they'd probably only accused them as an excuse not to have any more Englishmen in their precious country.'

Alice felt a pang of real alarm shoot through her. Of course it was probably only tittle-tattle, and Maria would be sure to have got hold of the wrong end of the stick, but . . . Nibby was in Moscow! She just hoped he had not got himself into any sort of trouble, though when David went back he could sort it out, perhaps. Still, she thought she ought to try to catch up with David and tell him what Maria had said, even if it was all back to front and topsy-turvy, as so much of Maria's information always was.

'I do understand . . . kind of . . . that things have changed,' Michael was saying gruffly as he and David strode down the pavement in the direction of their home, 'but I'm not sure about *why* they've changed. Why should Mother dying mean we have to sell the house, for instance?'

'We don't have to sell it; we could stay there,' David said patiently, catching a glimpse of some daffodils in full bloom in someone's garden and hearing the springtime shouts of birds no longer desperate for every morsel and too busy searching for food to waste time in song. It seems my fate to explain to the youngsters why things change after a death, he thought rather morbidly, remembering the scene on the terrace when he had told Alice about the newspapers' smear campaign. 'I'd better start at the beginning, young Mike, and explain from there. You ready to pin back your ears and listen like anything?'

Michael nodded, grinning.

'Oh, I'll listen like billyo, but I can't guarantee I'll understand unless you talk a lot clearer than that solicitor-johnny did.'

'I shall. Now, until Mother died she had money from a trust which Father had arranged for her; all right? That means there was a lump sum in the bank and she got a bit of it each month. Well, when she died that arrangement came to an end but the money – what was left of it – was willed to the family, evenly shared.

'Now we older ones . . . Ned, Lydia and myself . . . don't want it, because we're already earning. Julia's getting married and will have a sum towards her wedding dress and so on, but doesn't want the bulk of her share. That leaves only you, Mike, and Sara and Alice. Alice said she didn't want her share either as she'd start work again as soon as she could get another job, but since she has to take care of you younger ones we told her to put all the money into a trust . . . a sort of trust, not a regular one like Mother had . . . and draw out what she needed until you two were able to fend for yourselves.'

'I see. Is there lots of money? If so, why are we selling the house?'

'Mainly because it's too big for you and costs too much to run. With just you, Alice and Sara at home – and Sara won't be at home during termtime when she's at Cambridge – you don't need a house with five bedrooms. Alice says she and Sara can share a room, you can have one to yourself, and she'd like a spare for visitors, so quite a small place would do. It would be so much easier, you see, for Alice to keep clean.'

'I get it. And will it mean that I can stay on at school and Sara can go to Cambridge?'

'Yes, it'll mean all that. If the house sells well, and Alice doesn't have many fears on that score, then we hope to get a decent little cottage with a bit of land so that when I come home from Russia I can grow some vegetables and put in a few fruit trees and so on. At the moment I feel terribly cramped and useless.'

'Gosh, you aren't useless,' Michael said fervently. 'It's been jolly fine to have another fellow about the house, I can tell you. And Alice won't know which way to turn when you leave, honest injun. She cried at the funeral, I know – well, I did too – but apart from that she's hardly cried at all since you came back.'

'It's good of you to say so, Mike,' David was beginning solemnly, when a car screeched noisily to a halt beside them. They both turned their heads and a violent waving from within made David cringe. 'Oh, lor, Mike, it's that Raft woman . . . don't forget, we need the exercise, we don't want a lift!'

But this, it transpired, was the last thing on Miss Raft's mind. Alice was sitting beside her and she wound down the window and leaned out.

'Davie, something rather important's come up. At least, I don't know how important it is, but Maria told me that there's been some trouble in Russia which might affect your going back. She came with me and we went and got a copy of the newspaper she'd been reading earlier today. Here, can you read it?' She thrust the newspaper through the window of the cab and then said over her shoulder, 'Thanks very much for the lift, Maria, but I think I'll walk the rest of the way home with David and Mike. I think we may have quite a lot of talking to do.'

After the taxi had driven off, with Maria Raft waving lustily through the back window, she shook out her crushed black wool coat, straightened her lavender straw hat, and turned to her elder brother.

'See? Right there on the front page. I don't know whether it means anything to you, but Mr Raft told Maria it would mean trouble and he can't have got as rich as he is without knowing a thing or two.'

David shook his head and shushed her, still reading, but at the end of the article he sighed and tapped the page with his forefinger.

'Mr Raft was right, I think. They've arrested a score or so of engineers – British ones, I mean – and accused them of being spies for the British government. They say they've been working against the Soviet, sabotaging plant, setting fire to warehouses and breaking machinery. It's all because their wretched Five Year Plan failed – and no wonder, when you think of the huge scale of their inefficiency!'

'But what will they do to them? Do you think Nibby's been arrested? Oh, David, what will they do to *you* if you try to go back?'

'Try? My dear girl, this may mean . . . look, I've got to find out what's happening! I feel dreadful about it, but I'll have to zip up to London and see what they can tell me up there. Don't worry, I shan't desert you. I can go up in the morning and come home later the same day. Curse Stalin. He would have to start a witch-hunt right now!'

Michael, a silent but avid listener to all this, caught Alice's arm.

'I'll help you, Allie, particularly if you're going to look at houses; I love looking at houses. And David'll only be gone a day, so don't look so down in the mouth!'

'Oh, it isn't that I mind Davie going off for a day or two,' Alice said. 'It's just that I'm wondering whether Nibby's mixed up in it.' She turned to David. 'You know what he can be like – he can be awfully aggressive when people fling accusations. You don't think . . .'

'I doubt it, love! I think they'll be after bigger fish than Nibby! But I'll find out for sure tomorrow. I'll catch the express from Chester to London and talk to our people.'

It was quiet in the Lubianka prison. Nibby had been incarcerated for only about ten hours – he could not be more precise since his wristwatch had been taken from him, along with such items as his braces, his tie and his shoe laces – but he had hardly heard a sound since, unless you counted the shutter across the judas in the door which was raised every few minutes so that prison guards could check that he had not somehow managed to spirit himself away. Since he was not gifted with the ability to pass through stone walls which were probably several feet thick, or to disappear up his own orifice as certain mythical birds were reputed to do, he felt the constant staring in of the guards to be a trifle unnecessary, but he knew the reputation of the OGPU – and of course of the Lubianka – too well to try shouting out. A solitary confinement prison where even the guards were only allowed to converse in whispers . . . a shout would not have made him popular with those in charge!

He had been sitting on his bed, but now, for a change of scene, he stared round his cell. It was a largish room, about twelve feet by nine, he guessed, with colour-washed walls, a central heating radiator which actually worked – a miracle in itself, he thought sourly, considering the usual level of efficiency in hotels and suchlike – a barred window with a shield in front of it so that you could not see out, a rickety table, an iron bedstead and a thin straw mattress. He had been brought in in the middle of the night, hair standing on end, eyes still gummy with sleep, so he had not been as resentful of the one thin blanket which was all his bedding consisted of as he might have been. And that was it. No chair, no floor covering – no shadows, even, for the brilliant electric light in the middle of the room could only reflect a black shadow beneath the rickety table and another under Nibby himself, sitting sullenly on the bed.

Still, it was an experience, even if he would rather have passed it by. Not many Englishmen could boast of having been incarcerated in the infamous Lubianka, even if only for a few hours and by accident at that. Because obviously it was all a mistake; how could anyone believe that he had deliberately broken machines which he had spent weeks installing and testing? It was absurd . . . but it would make a good after-dinner story when he got home . . .

The shutter over the judas rose again with a clicking clatter, there was a pause, and then came the obvious sounds of the cell door being unlocked. A warder looked round the door, started to whisper something, then changed his mind and just beckoned. Out? At last – just let them wait until he got to someone in authority, he would make them smart!

He strode out, arms swinging, beside the warder, looking forward to getting his belongings back and smelling fresh air untainted with disinfectant. But his hopes were dashed on reaching their destination, which turned out to be an exceedingly white and chilly washroom, with cubicled lavatories at one end. It was empty save for himself and his silent companion. Nibby raised his eyebrows at the man.

'Well? Where's my towel, my soap, my scented talc?'

He said it in Russian and in normal tones. The man blinked and winced as if he'd been hit.

'Quietly, prisoner,' he hissed. 'Use the latrines, then wash. There is towel.'

'No soap?'

'No soap.'

Things were obviously no better here as far as shortages were concerned. Nibby relieved himself, pushing the little half-door across and avoiding the warder's eyes as best he could, then wandered nonchalantly out and washed. The water was cold; it did not encourage much splashing about, though Nibby pretended to be invigorated and managed to send water all over the place. He hoped, nastily, that his warder would be reprimanded for the mess.

He was taken straight back to his cell afterwards; no chat of any kind might be indulged in, apparently. He was in the middle of asking the warder when he might see a representative from the British embassy when the warder locked the door in his face. Nibby swore; but in English, just in case.

Hours seemed to pass before the door opened again, but it was probably no more than fifteen minutes. This time his visitor was a woman in a white coat with five slices of black bread; no butter, of course. After another short wait, during which Nibby and the black bread eyed one another with loathing, the cell door was unlocked again and a soldier entered with a large kettle from which he proceeded to pour a stream of what looked like weak tea into a tin mug.

'Is it tea?' Nibby said inquisitively. The soldier winced just as the warder had done at the uninhibited normality of his prisoner's tone, but nodded, then turned and left the cell.

'Breakfast,' Nibby mused to no one in particular. There was the bread – no plate, no butter, but the bread – and there was the tin mug full of weak tea. This was it, then?

It was.

The morning dragged on. Nibby began to wonder just how long it would take the embassy to discover that he was incarcerated. He shared a flat with two other Englishmen and worked with half a dozen more. They would realise he needed help, surely, and get in touch with the embassy? It took him an hour to reach the conclusion that if he was worth putting in prison, then James and Freddy were probably equally worthy. Were probably in the cells on either side of him, in fact. Upon which he kicked his rickety table and shouted in English . . . and, with a mixture of dread and pleasure, heard, faint and far off, someone singing 'God Save the King' in his native tongue.

When the next interruption came, he hoped it was lunch — and something a good deal more interesting than black bread and tea. It was certainly more interesting, though it was equally certainly not lunch. It was a black-browed, baby-faced warder who shushed him with a finger like a fat pork sausage and bade him, in a squeaky, feminine little voice, to 'Follow me; an officer of the OGPU wishes to ask you some questions'.

What an idiot I am, Nibby told himself as he followed the warder. Why should my stomach sink and churn and my knees feel weak at the thought of answering a few questions? No one could be more innocent than I, and they won't dare treat a foreigner the way they treat their own, so why should I feel so uneasy? Unless, of course, it's because I've not yet eaten today.

The thought cheered him and put an added spring into his step; that was it, naturally! Hunger could make you feel very low — he would demand food as soon as he got to wherever they were going!

He did. He walked into a small room with white walls and polished linoleum flooring, nodded briefly to the man behind the desk and announced: 'When am I going to get some decent food?'

The man was obviously taken aback. He jerked his head and blinked, and then his reptilian countenance hardened and the lids drooped over the snakelike brilliance of his light eyes.

'You are hungry? You may send out for food when you return to your cell,' he said indifferently. 'Sit down, Mr Hawke.'

Nibby did not sit. 'Then we must make this interview a short one, if you please. I've not yet eaten today.'

The man rocked forward on his hands, back, then forward again. He really was rather like a snake trying to hypnotise a bird, Nibby thought.

'You have not eaten? That is very wrong . . . we are not trying to break your spirit by leaving you without food. You should have had breakfast at least two hours ago.'

'Someone brought what looked like widdle in a kettle and some slices of black bread earlier; I didn't eat it,' Nibby said, trying to sound bored and a little annoyed and not at all afraid. 'I didn't care for it.'

'Then you weren't very hungry,' the man said sharply. 'Sit down.'

'I wasn't hungry then; I am hungry now,' Nibby pointed out, taking a seat. He leaned forward on the desk exactly as his interlocutor was leaning. He also smiled, which was more than the Russian did. 'Well? How can I help you?'

'I am Bergenoski.'

The name rang some unpleasantly familiar bells in Nibby's memory, but he kept his face carefully blank.

'Really?' He held out a hand. 'John Hawke . . . but you already know my name, of course.'

They shook hands and this time Nibby really did have a job to keep his countenance, for Bergenoski's hand was as cold as a codfish and very nearly as clammy. But he was buoyed up by the fact that the other man had looked extremely surprised by the proffered hand – and not at all pleased. Probably murderers and torturers rarely find themselves shaking hands in an interrogation room, Nibby thought. Ah well, he would soon find out whether the course he had decided to take was the right one.

'Now, Mr Hawke. You know why you're here, of course?'

'No.'

'Oh, come! I'm very sure my men, when they arrested you, told you what you had been accused of!'

'Well, they said something about sabotaging the machines at my place of work, but since I've spent all my waking hours for the past year trying to get the machines to work perfectly I realised they must have got hold of the wrong end of the stick somehow. In fact, I suppose the whole thing is an error on someone's part.' Here Nibby leaned forward again and treated Bergenoski to his most sugary and insincere smile. 'Perhaps you can put me straight, Mr . . . er . . . er . . . on my reason for being here?'

Nibby felt he had done well up to this point, but the question seemed to put new – and unpleasant – life into the other man. His mouth opened and a stream of ridiculous accusations poured out, mainly concerned with sabotaging the machinery at the factory but with offshoots such as spying on a new military establishment, writing seditious anti-Soviet literature and corrupting innocent comrades of the regime.

'Writing seditious material? Which? When? Where?'

'I ask the questions,' Bergenoski snapped. 'You know very well what I mean.'

There was a clock on the wall in here. Nibby was able to watch lunchtime move by without lunch and teatime without tea. His only solace was the fact that no matter how well Bergenoski had breakfasted, he, too, must be feeling the pinch by now. At length, at what Nibby decided was dinnertime, Bergenoski snapped to his feet and paced quickly across the room to the door.

'I shall leave you for a few moments,' he snarled over his shoulder. 'Stay there.'

'No. I'll return to my cell, if you please,' Nibby said with the utmost politeness, following the other man to the door. 'After all, if you've no further questions – and really, comrade, you've spent most of your time repeating the same questions over and over – then I might as well go back and send out for that food you mentioned.'

There was a rather dangerous pause, during which Bergenoski wrestled with what Nibby imagined was a desire to cleave his prisoner in two with the nearest solid object, and then he heaved a deep sigh and beckoned to an armed soldier further down the corridor.

'Send out for two decent meals,' he snapped. 'This man and I will eat in my room.'

Whilst they waited, Nibby entertained Bergenoski with stories of his life at university. Rather to his surprise, Bergenoski replied in kind, though his sense of humour and Nibby's were somewhat different. When the food arrived they both ate with a good appetite, and when the interrogation was resumed

Nibby got the feeling that his opponent was as tired of it as he was himself. However, protocol had to be observed, and it was a very weary young man who returned to his cell at three a.m. in the morning and sank into a deep, exhausted and very troubled sleep.

'Well, from what I can discover, it's all a blind to try to convince the workers that it wasn't the Five Year Plan which failed, it was all a capitalist trick. They've got a number of our chaps clapped up in the Lubianka, but it's only a ploy. They say the whole thing will be cleared up in three or four days and I can go back. Not that I will, until you're settled.'

Alice and David had just met at the station, Alice pale and weary after a long day of clearing out her mother's things, David scarcely less so. They had decided to walk rather than take a cab, so Alice's hand rested in the crook of David's arm and they both stepped out quickly, enjoying the spring scents still coming from the flowers even though dusk was falling.

David was content to look nostalgically down on the Dee estuary, on the gleaming water and the stretches of dark gold sand, then switch his gaze to where the blue mountains of Wales beckoned, but Alice still had something on her mind.

'But did you ask about Nibby?'

'Of course I did. He's all right, I'm sure he is . . .' David hesitated. Impossible to keep her in the dark, and Alice was no fool; she would find out for herself if he did not tell her. 'The fact is, love, he's in the Lubianka with the rest, but they'll be out before you can say Jack Robinson!'

'In *prison*?' Alice did not sound at all convinced that this was just a passing whim on the part of the Soviet government. 'What have they accused him of? Did he do it? Can we help him? Davie, you must go back if it will make a difference . . . can you do more there than you can here?'

'For starters, old girl, I keep telling you I can't go back – they won't have me, not while all this is going on. Next, there's been a blanket accusation from what I can make out – they say that the British engineers have been sabotaging their own machinery. Quite mad, but impossible to deny with conviction when there's no proof either way. Allie, my dear, all we *can* do is wait, but I do suggest you write to him. And we'll get in touch with his father and persuade him to write as well, and make as much fuss as the embassy thinks will do good rather than bad. But apart from that we're all equally helpless.'

'I can't believe we can't help at all . . . but if you say so, I suppose you know best. I went and put an advertisement in the paper, as you said, saying that the house was for sale, but I don't think we'll have much trouble selling. Mr Rutherford's brother-in-law's been looking for somewhere near . . . Mr Rutherford lives about four doors down from us . . . and he's coming over to take a look at the weekend. And there's a farm cottage for sale, awfully cheap . . . I could cycle to work and Mike could do the same to get in to school . . . shall we do out there tomorrow and take a look?'

'Yes, fine. How far is it from town?'

'Not more than five miles, I don't think. There's probably a bus, or I suppose we could get a cab, though it's awfully extravagant.'

'So it is. Tell you what, Allie, if it's just you and me, let's cycle. I'm not proud – I'll use Sara's machine if you can persuade her to lend it to me.'

Alice was laughing at the thought of David's long legs somehow fitting Sara's bicycle when a car drew up beside them. A head popped out of the driver's window.

'Hello! What a coincidence! Can I give you chaps a lift anywhere?'

It was Maria.


'The woman's haunting me.' David, following Alice into the kitchen, sounded plaintive, but Alice only laughed and shook her head at him.

'Don't complain because you're so devastatingly attractive; you're proud of it! As for haunting you, why not? You're unattached and a member of the class her parents long to join . . . and she's awfully rich! Tell you what, Davie, why bother to make your fortune? Why not just marry Carmel Hall, because that's what it would amount to! She's old haddock-head's only child, the light of his life, and she'll inherit the lot when they go. All you need do is pop the question.'

'Ha! Who said I was unattached, anyway? Not me!'

'Oh, Davie, do you have a lady friend? Who, who?'

'She's a Russian.' David shook his head reproachfully at his sister. 'Don't look so disappointed – you'll love her when you

226

meet her. She's a sweetheart, and she loves country living . . . at least, it's all she knows, if I'm honest, but I'm sure she'll love it here.'

'Hmm. Russian. I always imagine a sturdy peasant woman with a broad face and little eyes and lots and lots of guile.'

'You aren't far wrong if you're looking at the great Russian plain,' David admitted. 'There are quite a lot of peasants just like that. But my Pavel comes from the Caucasus mountains . . .'

'Pavel? That's rather a pretty name.'

'Yes, Pavel Fedorovna, which means Pavel daughter of Fedor. Actually, Pavel's usually a boy's name, in Russia, but her father named her for his dearest friend. The family call her Pavelina and Pavelinka and suchlike, little love-names.'

'And what do you call her?'

'Dushka . . . that means darling, in case you wonder.'

'Well, I suppose she's a darling all right, if she saves you from Maria. Not that there's any harm in the girl, and she *is* rich, but somehow I don't see her as my sister-in-law.'

'You won't, unless Michael falls for her,' David assured his sister. 'What about wanting to drive us to the cottage, though? My mind simply stopped working; I could only boggle at her and pray you'd think of something.'

'And so I did.' Alice seized a loaf from the pantry, carried it to the table, and began to slice it into rather chunky pieces. 'Butter this lot, would you, Davie? When the children come home they do rather expect tea to be on the table.'

'Ye-es. But saying a friend had already offered was a bit risky, wasn't it? I mean, she may see us pedalling off tomorrow and be awfully hurt.'

'Oh, David, as if I'd tell a huge lie like that! A friend *has* offered, as I'd have told you if you hadn't started on about cycling.'

'You said we could get a bus or hire a cab . . .' began David, but Alice cut him short.

'Yes, and I was about to add or we could accept Lydia's husband's offer, only you went off at a tangent about bicycles.'

'Lydia's husband? That really is good of him – giving up his morning to watch you and me poke penknives into old oak beams and rattle hinges.'

'He isn't . . . he's offered to lend you his car,' Alice explained patiently, slicing away. 'You can drive, can't you? Well then.'

'It's marvellous of him to lend the car,' David said, butter knife poised, butter slowly dropping from its tip. 'I only hope I'll be all right. I've not driven for three years, you know.'

'Oh, you'll manage. He's bringing it round tomorrow morning, and he wants you to run him into Chester before we set off for the cottage. That way we should be safe enough from Maria.'

'We'll be even safer,' David said with gleaming eyes, 'if you go and see her this evening and tell her about Pavel.'

But this Alice thought too cruel. Let her have her moment of being a bit in love, she said, as they laid the table for tea. Don't snatch it all away from her at one go. After all, when you go back to Russia . . .

So David weakly consented to keep quiet about Pavel for a while, and took two pieces of Alice's best butter shortbread for his kindness and good behaviour, and then the door burst open and Michael and Sara came rushing into the kitchen and Maria was forgotten, for the moment.

'It isn't everyone's idea of a decent home,' David said slowly, as he and Alice stood on the brick path before the cottage and tried to view it dispassionately after they had viewed it very literally, doing all the poking and prying and testing which he had envisaged the day before. 'But it's got a good atmosphere, it's dry – or seems to be – it doesn't seem to have dry rot or wet rot or deathwatch beetle . . . and the garden's really fine.'

It was. Not merely a garden, either, but a long strip of pasture which led almost down to the Dee and a little orchard full of bearded and lichened old apple, pear and plum trees. And a wood which might not belong to them but did not seem to belong to anyone else either.

'I like it,' Alice said decidedly. 'It's quite small, and it's in a bit of a state . . . birds' nests in the bedroom, quite possibly rats in the kitchen and of course no bathroom and a jolly odd smell in the outhouse . . . but you expect that with somewhere old. Shall we?'

'I vote we bring the kids out here at the weekend,' David said, after a moment. 'After all, Allie, you and I go along with it, but I'm going back to Russia for another year and possibly two and you're probably going to get married once I'm back, so it could easily be more important to Mike and Sassy than anyone else.'

'Sara won't hang around at home; she'll go to Cambridge and marry a marvellous old professor with white whiskers who'll adore her and treat her like a queen,' Alice said ruefully. 'I love all my sisters and all my brothers but Sassy is rather a favourite of mine. Lydia's terribly beautiful but very detached, and Julia's the same, but Sassy likes to cuddle and be loved and purrs like a dear little ginger kitten when you're nice to her.'

'Don't let her hear you call her that,' David said, grinning. 'I hope the professors at Cambridge like cats! We'll put it to the kids when they come in for their tea that they come and vet the cottage on Saturday or Sunday.'

'And we'll see if Norman can spare the car again,' Alice said optimistically. 'Otherwise it'll be bikes – or Shanks's pony.'

It really seemed as though they were going to have to walk to the cottage at the weekend, or hire a cab, but then Sara came dancing in on Friday evening and slung her satchel across the kitchen, grabbing a piece of Alice's fruit cake in one hand and fending off Michael's attempts to share it with the other.

'Everyone can thank *me* when they hear what a clever thing I've done,' she announced through a mouthful of cake. 'I've got us a car for Sunday!'

'Who's a clever kitten, then?' David was getting quite domesticated; just now he was sitting in front of the fire peeling potatoes. 'Tell big brother how you did it. I suppose you went and made up to Norman?'

'Nope. Try again.'

'Not Julia's Harmer? Not that he's got a car, but I suppose his father runs one.'

'No. Actually, it wasn't a relative at all. It was Mr Raft. He stopped when he saw us coming home and offered us a lift, but it wasn't worth it, not for that short distance. And then he said he'd let Michael steer for a bit and whilst I was still refusing – but very politely, mind – Mike had jolly well hopped into the front passenger seat, darned cheek, where of course Mr Raft thought I would go, so anyway I got in the back and he said he supposed we must miss car rides so naturally Mike said we didn't and in fact David had borrowed Norman's car earlier in the week to take Alice cottage-viewing, and had said us younger ones could go as well this Sunday if he could borrow the car again. And then there was a sort of quiet moment whilst Mr Raft changed gears or whatever it is they do, and I said idly, just idly, honestly, that he'd got a beautiful car hadn't he . . . and he offered!'

'It was jolly generous, but we can't possibly accept, Sassy,' David said wistfully. 'It would be fine to drive that big car, but suppose I mucked it up? No, you'll have to telephone him and say we've made other arrangements.'

'It's all right,' Sara said airily, 'I thought of that. And Mr Raft must have done, too, because he's lent us a driver, as well – imagine the luxury!'

'A driver? His chauffeur, you mean?'

'Well, I suppose so. Wasn't it nice of him? He isn't really such a beast as he looks.'

There was a short pause whilst Sara stuffed fruit cake into her mouth, Michael raided the biscuit box, and Alice looked thoughtfully at her brother. He was frowning, as if something teased at the edge of his mind but would not be brought into the open. Alice decided to give it a hand.

'Who doesn't have a chauffeur, Davie-boy?'

David uttered a yelp and buried his head in his hands. Alice grinned. So he had remembered!

'That's right, it's the good old Raft family. But they can all drive, except for old Mrs Raft. Mr Raft and Maria can both drive. Guess who'll be chauffeuring us to the cottage on Sunday, my irresistible brother!'

It was Nibby's fifth day in prison, and any hopes he had had that this was merely a mistake and would soon be put right were long gone. All that remained now were fear, boredom, and fury, roughly in that order. When he was not being interrogated in a biased and spiteful fashion, when he was not refusing to sign statements purporting to have been made by him, he was sitting on his bed, in his very clean cell, being extremely bored. Or he was lying on his bed planning revenge on the entire population of Soviet Russia. Or he was asleep.

For his first two days in captivity he let his thoughts go round and round in the pointless and futile way that thoughts will when the thinker is trapped in a situation not of his own making. How to get out, how to avoid the consequences of consistently telling the truth and refusing to lie as the authorities obviously wished him to do, how to get in touch with friends . . . all these things buzzed round in his brain. On the third day he began to channel his thoughts a little more deliberately, telling himself to forget all this and to think, instead, of better times and pleasanter things. He thought about a particularly fetching little girl who was studying chemistry at Moscow University; she spoke hardly any English, but it did not much matter since he spoke quite good Russian, and she had been his mistress for the best part of a year. They had had good times together and he found himself thinking wistfully of the way she kissed, the provocative manner in which she wriggled into bed beside him, even the ribbon – pale blue cotton – which she used to tie back her hair before bedtime.

On the fourth day he was taken to the interrogation room and sat down opposite the ubiquitous Bergenoski, who suddenly excused himself in the middle of a particularly boring routine of question and answer, left the room for perhaps two minutes and came back pushing before him Nibby's chemistry student. She was white and shaking, her eyes huge and dark in her small face, and for the first time Nibby felt crawling horror towards the Lubianka and his interrogator.

'What the hell have you done to her? Why is she here? For God's sake, man . . . she's a girl of nineteen, she knows no state secrets, has no access to anything important . . .'

'It's all right, Mr Hawke, she's confessed everything. As you say, she's a good Soviet citizen; she has no reason to keep your secrets for you. Tell Mr Hawke, Svetalia, what you have told us.'

'I – I stayed in Mr Hawke's apartment, s-several times,' stammered the unfortunate girl. 'H-he was kind to me . . . I didn't know it was wrong, that the State would p-punish me . . .'

Abruptly, Nibby changed his tune. He smiled reassuringly at Svetalia. 'It's all right, love; you've done nothing wrong and neither have I. You tell them everything you know – it won't be much. Tell them everything you and I have ever done; there was no harm in any of it. But don't let them persuade you into lies, because they may think, and they may try to make you think, that lies will help your country. Well, they won't, Svetalia, they'll just make fools of you all.'

'Talk like that won't get you out of here, Mr Hawke,' Bergenoski said menacingly. 'This girl has told us things about you . . . things you've said to her . . . which have made it clear all our accusations are true. She has proof . . .'

'Oh, comrade, all I told you was of our times together!' Svetalia exclaimed. 'Nibby, I keep telling them that if I knew evil of you, or even good, I'd tell them. But I don't!'

Bergenoski gave an exclamation of impatience and fury and dragged Svetalia out of the room, leaving Nibby to sink back on to his chair, his knees shaking and a feeling of sick dread pervading him. How could they drag that child in here and try to make her lie about him? How dared they!

That was the morning of the fourth day. After the unsuccessful confrontation with Svetalia they left him alone, presumably to ponder on his sins. Instead, he decided he had had enough of the whole filthy business. He lay back on his bed, arms behind his head, and directed his thoughts both long ago and far away. To his childhood. To Deeside. And thence to Alice.

'There hasn't been a letter for ages and ages, and now this big fat one!' Pavel held up the envelope, grinning from ear to ear. 'Oh, Evalinka, I don't know how to wait, but I really should open it when we get home . . . it's such a damp sort of day down here.'

She was right. The little market town was full of people steaming gently as the rain continued to fall. It was still not warm – the wind was bitter – but in the shelter of the stalls and with the sheep warm and wet at their knees the two girls felt positively stuffy after the cold of their own much higher valley.

'Open it now, Pavel, dushka,' Eva urged, hopping up and down. 'It has a very odd stamp on it.'

'Well, all right then, if you think I should.' Pavel slitted the envelope and spread out the first sheet. She began to read, then gasped and stared at her sister. 'Eva, he's in Britain! His mother is very ill and he's had to go home! This letter was written on board the ship and posted somewhere on the way – that's why the stamp is strange! Oh, Eva!'

The day's greyness had been inexplicably brightened by the letter; now, with the knowledge that David was no longer in the same country as she, the sky inexplicably darkened.

'He may be back by now,' Eva said after a moment's thought. 'When is it dated?'

Pavel examined the top of the letter and her brow cleared a little. 'Yes, you're right, it was written a long time ago . . . the middle of March, that's nearly six weeks. I wonder how long it took him to get back there? And how long he'll stay? And when he'll come here again?'

'Oh, Pavel, he'll come as soon as he can,' Eva assured her. 'Read the rest of the letter . . . here, we'll go and get some tea from that stall, then we can sit down and drink it and you can read under the canvas shelter so the ink won't run with the rain. And do cheer up. If Nyusha was ill you'd fly back to her, wouldn't you?'

'Yes, of course I would. Come on, then. You fetch the tea whilst I read the letter, and then I'll read you all the bits that aren't very, very private.'

'All right. And as soon as we get home you write another letter, addressed to his home in Britain this time. Then at least you'll be keeping in touch, even if he's away for ages.'

'Will it get sent, though? Over all those miles and miles of sea?'

'Oh, Pavel, you know very well he'll get it! Now sit down and start reading, because I'll be back in two shakes of a lamb's tail!'

'You're free to go, but you must not leave Moscow. This matter will be brought to court and you must appear when you are called. Is that clear?'

The stony-faced official handed Nibby his wristwatch, tie and shoe laces and stood aside as Nibby walked through the doorway. Neither spoke, and Nibby would not have broken that silence for the world. Suppose the fellow was just playing a trick on him? He had heard often enough of how one's spirit was broken by just such tricks; a man so bitterly disappointed is suddenly willing to sign papers which he would not even read through before.

Together, they went along the narrow grey corridors. They reached the lift and were carried down to ground-floor level.

The doors were there – the ordinary doors, not prison doors – and his companion moved forward and pushed them open.

'The commandant has ordered you a taxi-cab. You can pay the driver when you reach your apartment block.'

Nibby inclined his head and went with measured tread through the doorway. Outside it was cold, but the clean air smelt so good that he forgot the desire to get as far away as possible from the Lubianka and Lubianski Square and stood quite still, inhaling deeply. Freedom! So this was what the much used and little understood word really meant! A giddying sensation of power, a lifting of the heart and a lightening of the spirit. And clean air! He took a couple more breaths, realised he was extremely cold and that the cab driver was staring at him rather strangely, and bounded over to the vehicle.

Once inside, he looked back at the prison. No one was staring out of the numerous windows. No one was following him. The square was empty of all save a couple of small figures in the distance. But . . . what would he find when he reached the apartment? Bergenoski, eager to see his face when he was re-arrested? Or just the secret police? He leaned forward and tapped the driver on the shoulder.

'Take me to the British embassy, if you please.'

'The embassy?' The man had revved his engine and started the taxi, but now he slowed to a crawl. 'Why the embassy? They told me to take you to the foreigners' apartment block in Minorski Street.'

It was to be a trap, then! But it would not do to panic, to leap out of the taxi and start running; what he must do was to keep cool and pretend he did not see the cage closing on him.

'Start driving, please,' Nibby said crisply. The driver obediently swung the cab round and they left the square; when they were well clear of it and driving through the quiet early morning streets the driver said conversationally, 'Why did you want the British embassy, comrade?'

'Because I thought you'd like to be paid; I have no money in the apartment,' Nibby said casually. 'Naturally I want to go back to my place – to have a shave, for a start.'

The driver chuckled but took the next left-hand turn.

'Why didn't you say so at first? The embassy it shall be, then. How long were you . . . you know?'

'Ten days . . . perhaps a fortnight.' Shaming to admit you'd lost track of the days despite your determination to keep a record. 'Can't you tell by my beard?'

Although they had allowed him to wash, shaving was apparently out of the question. Razors, even safety razors, might, Nibby supposed, be used to open a vein so that their prisoners escaped them by bleeding to death, but he thought it was more probably another sign of the shortages that beset the country; no soap, no razor blades, so don't hand them over to mere prisoners, even if they do happen to be foreign nationals illegally held.

'Ah, the beard! Well, you know what it's like, comrade, particularly in winter. What with the cold, and blades so hard to get, many a fellow grows a beard.' He swung round, nevertheless, and subjected Nibby's chin-fungus to a hard scrutiny. 'Hmm, that's a fortnight's worth of beard unless I'm losing my touch. Of course I shouldn't be talking to you like this, they'd have my guts for garters if they knew, but a lot of us reckon it's just a cover-up. They don't want criticism from the workers because of the bread shortage and so on, but they realise that someone will have to take the blame, so why not a bunch of foreigners?'

'I think you're right, but you shouldn't go around saying it,' Nibby warned the older man. 'What's the point? You wanted the Party – now you'll have to either accept it, warts and all, or find some way of voting in an alternative.'

'Voting? What's that?' The man guffawed and drew the car to a halt beside the kerb. 'I'm from Georgia; we're realists, like Stalin was before . . .' He stopped speaking and got out to open the cab door. 'Here we are, comrade; if you'll just nip in and get my fare I'll be off.'

As soon as Nibby entered the hallway of the embassy, he realised he had been expected. The place was thronged with engineers, all of them bearded and a trifle haggard. He began to explain that he had a cab outside waiting to be paid but one of the secretaries shushed him with a flap of the hand, took some money out of a drawer and hurried out, to return presently and take him by the arm.

'All accounted for, then. Did you come straight here, Hawke? Most of the others were dropped off at the apartment blocks and had to make their way here privately.'

'I came straight from the Lubianka,' Nibby said, running a hand across his beard, which was less bristly and more like a real beard than it had been at first. 'My driver was a decent fellow and succumbed to the thought of being paid here and unpaid at the apartment. Thanks for the money, by the way. I spent all mine on meals, and then damn me if they didn't feed me anyway, once they were sure all my cash had gone.'

'They'll probably send you a bill, Nibs,' a dark-haired engineer named Peter who lived in the same apartment block as Nibby said gloomily. He fingered his light reddish beard, which accorded strangely with his hair colouring. 'The ambassador's trying to straighten things out right now – we've all been told we mustn't leave Moscow and he wants to make sure we'll be safe from re-arrest in the flats, otherwise we'll all have to stay here.'

'If it's all right to go home, then I'm having a hot bath, a shave and a huge meal, in that order,' Nibby assured his fellow sufferer. 'Is it really going to go to trial? I didn't admit to any of the lies they fancied pinning on me and I'm pretty sure everyone else will have done the same, so what evidence will they have?'

Peter grinned sourly.

'Oh, they'll cook something up, never fear. But if the ambassador's right they won't want trouble with our respective countries so they'll just announce we're guilty as hell and send us home. That's another reason for this stupid business; we've pretty well finished our work here, all of us. Their own people can finish what we haven't done, so why pay good money to foreigners when the country needs every kopek it can lay its hands on?'

'I suppose that's possible,' Nibby said gloomily. 'If they imprison us they'll have to pay for our food, which would go against the grain. No, it's a trumped-up charge and they can't make it stick. Not a man amongst us would give evidence . . . we're not their own nationals with families and friends to be threatened.'

The secretary, a thin, white-haired man who had been in Moscow many years, shook his head at Nibby.

'Don't you know that all the accused aren't yet out of the Lubianka, John? There must be thirty or forty still imprisoned.'

'No! When I came in you said all accounted for, so I thought I was the last. Who's still there?'

'Oh, you were the last of the English. It's the Russians. Engineers who worked with you, typists, mechanics . . . they've all been hauled off to make statements. Some of them will probably bear the brunt of this whole miserable business.'

'Oh, but their own people . . . and as innocent as us . . . they wouldn't do that!'

'No?' The secretary's smile was the smile of one who has long grown accustomed to man's inhumanity to man. 'Shall I quote your own words to you, John? *We're not their own nationals with families and friends to be threatened.* Remember?'

And Nibby, remembering, began to fear for the future.

# CHAPTER ELEVEN

'Wasn't it strange? Just as though talking about Nibby had made him think of us after all this time. He's out of prison and wanted us to know he's all right. Shall I write back at once, Davie, telling him that you'll be back in Russia in a few weeks?'

'I don't think I'll be going back.' David walked over to where Alice sat perched on the edge of the kitchen table and put a hand on her shoulder. 'Haven't you heard? The papers are full of it. The engineers were found guilty on various minor charges and told to leave the country within seventy-two hours. There won't be a job for me . . . Nibby himself will be out of work. Whatever we do, Allie, it won't be engineering in Russia.'

'Oh, David, how awful for you! What will you do? Are you sure they won't change their minds and have you back? I mean, you weren't involved, you were out of the country!'

'They won't want any Brits back, you can be sure of that. We know too much about their methods and their inefficiencies – remember, it's their own people they're trying to fool . . . not as easy as you might think, because they've got plenty of highly intelligent men in their factories and offices who must know they've been duped. They won't want the British around to rub their noses in it.'

'Well, I can't say I'm sorry in a way, because it's been marvellous having you here – someone else to talk things over with, someone to lean on. But what about your girl . . . Pavel? What will you do about her?'

'I'll go over as an ordinary citizen . . . but after what's happened will they let us marry? They can be so strange . . . though surely they won't refuse to let her come here, if I marry her?'

'I don't see why they should; why not let two people go and be happy rather than keep one unhappy person to breed discontent?'

'Yes, that's true. It's awfully hard, but I think I'll have to keep quiet about it until the fuss over the trial has blown over. I'll write to Pavel immediately.'

'And I'll write to Nibby, care of the embassy.' Alice jumped off the table and gave her brother a hug. 'Don't look so miserable, Davie; it'll be all right, you'll see. They won't stop you marrying Pavel, they wouldn't be so cruel, and it does mean you'll be able to help us move into the cottage.'

It was true, David reflected as he walked through into the living-room to write his letter, that Alice needed him – or someone like him, at any rate. She was blossoming visibly, her cheeks pinker, her hair shinier, her figure softer, less rigidly upright. And her laugh more often heard. If he had not been at home all the worry and responsibility for the move would have been hers, and she would not have been able to contemplate looking for a job again, as she was beginning to do.

I wonder if I ought to start job-hunting myself? David mused, getting out writing paper, pen and blotter. After all, if I'm here until the Russians decide to let me go back, then I'm here for ever, so I really should do something about it. But he knew he would not, not until he had made his bid to get Pavel here.

He had been up and down to London and the Foreign Office a dozen or more times since the trouble had blown up in Moscow, but he had never actually confided to anyone that he was in love with a Russian citizen. He guessed that they would feel sorry for him but would only advise him to wait, and waiting without any sort of knowledge was hardest of all.

Sitting at the desk, he began his letter. Usually it was one of his nicest tasks, because as soon as he started to write Pavel was before his eyes, her face as clear as if they really shared the same room, but today it was different. She seemed very far away, his mental image of her misty, and he was aware after only a few sentences that his writing was stilted, miserable, as he strove to tell her that things would sort themselves out, that he would come back for her as he had promised, that the delay might be a little longer than they had hoped, but they must be patient.

239

Presently he brought the letter to a close, signed it, sealed it, and went through to the kitchen. Alice was writing in pencil in an old exercise book, her tongue stuck out with effort. On the stove a kettle steamed, disregarded. David smiled. It was clear that Alice had completely forgotten her surroundings in her eagerness to tell Nibby how glad they all were that he was safe.

'I'm taking my letter down to the post office; want to come? Or do you want me to drop yours off for you at the same time? Odd, when you think about it, that we should both be writing letters bound for Russia.'

'Yes, very odd,' Alice murmured absently. 'I'll be a while yet, David. You go. I'll post this tomorrow.'

'Rightyho.' David went into the hall to fetch his Burberry, for it was still too cool to go without a coat though it was nearly the end of April. He came back to pop his head round the kitchen door. 'Want anything from the shops?'

'No thanks; unless you could buy me some icing sugar? I've gone and run out.'

'What do you want icing sugar for? Yes, all right, I'll get some. How much do you want? A pound? Two?'

'A couple of pounds, I think. As for why I want it, I'm going to bake a big fruitcake and ice it for when Nibby comes home.'

'Oh, Allie, what makes you think he'll come here?' David said jokingly, and then regretted it; it had been a cruel thing to say. But his sister took the remark at its face value.

'I know he will. I've told him you're home. He'd come anyway, because he's so fond of you, but the fact that you've been in Russia too is bound to fetch him. Cut off, old boy, and get my icing sugar.'

The old boy obeyed, but despite the flowers dancing in the gardens and the joyous surge of the white-tipped waves in the estuary, he could not summon up much enthusiasm for his walk. After all their hopes, he would not be going back to the Caucasus this summer, to carry Pavel triumphantly home as his wife. The autumn, perhaps? He did not think so; memories were longer than that in Russia. But perhaps next spring . . . next summer? He refused to let the miserable prospect of putting their wedding off daunt him.

Coming back from town, laden with icing sugar and a bag of wrinkled apples for Sara and Michael to keep them quiet until tea was ready, it occurred to David that it might be possible for

Pavel to come to him. Why not? She was a lively and intelligent girl, why should she not get on a ship and travel to England on it? He knew of course that the Party was not keen on Russian nationals leaving the country unless there was some strong tie to bring them home, but if they could somehow give Pavel a legitimate excuse for leaving – what a pity she was not a ballet dancer allowed to dance abroad – all she would have to do would be not to return! Only . . . she was fond of Nyusha and Fedor, and she adored Eva. What *would* they do? Oh, if only the Five Year Plan had worked, if only it had never occurred to the Powers that Be to try to blame it all on the engineers!

'Hello there, David! That looks like a lot of shopping; can I give you a lift?'

Sometimes, David thought grimly as he climbed into the passenger seat of the Rafts' big Rolls, sometimes I think she spends all her days and a good part of her nights simply hovering outside our house, waiting for me to emerge. I wish there was a polite way to send her packing! She can't possibly care two hoots for me as a person, because she doesn't know me. It's a crush, or a pash, or whatever young girls call these puppy-love things – only she's no puppy, she's a full-grown . . . er . . . girl.

'Thanks very much, Maria,' he said as he settled himself and his shopping. 'It's awfully good of you – what are you doing driving along here at this time in the afternoon?'

There was a perceptible hesitation before she answered; she *does* hover in the hopes, David told himself bitterly. Why couldn't he attract some stunning little blonde if he had to attract anyone? Why did it have to be the gawky Miss Maria Raft?

Maria saw him ahead of her down the road and immediately her heart began to beat faster and she felt the hot blood rise to her cheeks. He was so special that his tall figure wore, for her, a glow which was sufficiently bright to pick him out in any crowd. She loved him! Everything about him was right, from the way his dark hair grew and flopped across his brow to his thick, angry-looking eyebrows and the square shape of his hands.

He was so polite, as well. He never gave her sideways looks, as his sisters occasionally did, as though they thought she would not notice their rather strained kindness. He smiled when she made a little joke, he saw her through doorways first, he had touched her twice ... every bone in her body had melted when his fingers had closed around her wrist, she told herself dramatically; positively melted!

On the other hand, she was not at all sure that he had ever really noticed her, or thought about her, except as an acquaintance of his sisters. She spent a lot of time watching the house, drifting up and down the road in the car, driving around town when she knew he was there, shopping with Alice. Sometimes she was lucky, sometimes not. She had given the whole family a lift to see the little cottage they had bought; it had been a marvellous treat, a whole afternoon completely surrounded by Thomases, with her favourite Thomas – David, of course – full of good humour, talking about how he would do the garden, replant the orchard, stock the vegetable plot with good things. She had trailed along behind him wherever he went, agreeing with everything he said, because someone so perfect must be right, and he had not seemed too annoyed by her constant presence, though she had heard him puff out a great breath of relief when she had dropped them outside their gate once more. But she had soon persuaded herself that it was not relief at her leaving but rather relief at getting home after a long day. So that was all right.

She followed him for a while in the car, rehearsing her speeches, and then she drove alongside and offered him a lift and he accepted at once, climbing into the passenger seat and asking her where she had been going with perfect good humour. Once or twice he had said, almost curtly, that he was walking for exercise thank you very much and had refused to ride with her, but he could scarcely say that now, laden with parcels as he was.

'Where've you been, David?' she said presently, when she had stumbled out some suitable-sounding lie as to her own reasons for being where she was.

'Me? Oh, to post a letter. To my young lady.'

The bottom dropped out of her world. She had heard that it happened but had never experienced it before. She felt ill, her stomach thudded into her shoes and her heart began to bump unevenly. She slowed the car because just for a moment she could not see where she was going, and she peered through the windscreen as if through thick fog. But her voice was worth ten of the rest of her; it said, quite flatly, 'Oh? I shouldn't have thought you'd been home long enough to get one of them.'

'She's not in Britain,' he said calmly, obviously unaware of the shattering effect his words had had on her. 'She's in Russia. Her name's Pavel Fedorovna and we're getting married when I go back.'

'Really? You're engaged, then?'

'No. Her father wouldn't allow it last year, he thought she was too young, but we're going to get married this summer, with his consent.'

'Really?' She drew the car to a halt outside his house. It was on a higher level than the pavement; he would have to climb up quite a steep little concrete path to reach his front door. Normally she would have looked forward to watching him, knowing he was too busy getting his parcels into the house to notice that she had not immediately driven off. But today she would leave at once and go and nurse the hurt he had dealt her. A young lady! She felt deceived, yet knew that the only person to deceive her had been herself. He was so beautiful that naturally he would have a young lady. How could she have been so blind as to think he would be heart-whole, and him quite twenty-five?

'Thanks, Maria.' He got out of the car and hesitated on the pavement, one hand resting on the top of the door. She loved the way his nails grew! 'Look, we're just going to have tea. Would you like to come in and have a cup and a biscuit or something? Alice would . . .'

'No. I've got to go.' It was an invitation she would have leapt at like a trout at a fly an hour . . . half an hour . . . earlier. Now all she wanted was to get away. But of course he could not know that.

'Oh, all right then, some other time,' he said easily. 'Cheerio, Maria, and thanks again for the lift.'

He turned and started to climb up the narrow little path between the neat, conventional flower borders. Maria watched him although she knew it was a stupid thing to do, but he did not turn round or look back. He opened the front door, slid inside, and shut it.

Maria sat.

*

'Hello, David. Did you get my icing sugar?'

Alice had taken his place at the desk, facing out across the front garden with its view of the distant estuary. She smiled hopefully at him.

'Yes, of course, I put it on the kitchen table. Maria gave me a lift home. I asked her in for a cup of tea but she said she couldn't, which was a good job because we'll want to talk. I've brought the brats some apples to eat whilst we get something cooked.'

'I've finished my letter.' Alice folded the sheets and put them into a blue envelope. 'Later on I'll walk down to the post with this . . . how much did yours cost to send?'

David told her and Alice fished the correct number of stamps out of her worn purse.

'Right; that shall go later, then.' A thump and a clatter announced another arrival. 'Ah, the children are back. I'll go and put the kettle on.'

David turned and opened the door, peering into the hall where the back views of his brother and sister could be seen as they dropped satchels, blazers and books uncaringly on to the floor and headed for the kitchen.

'Pick those things up!' David ordered without ceremony. If he did not make them, Alice would do it for them and Sara and Michael were quite spoilt enough as it was without making them worse.

However, they were thoughtless rather than wicked; they both turned back and grabbed their belongings with unimpaired cheerfulness, hanging blazers and satchels on the appropriate hooks and putting the books on the hall table.

'Guess what we saw as we came in the gate,' Sara said, turning towards the kitchen once again. 'That girl . . . Maria Raft . . . sitting in her car out in the road, all bent up over the steering wheel.'

'She gave David a lift home; I hope she's all right,' Alice said anxiously. 'David, was she all right? Did she say she wasn't feeling well? Come to think of it, she wouldn't come in for a cup of tea when you asked her, would she?'

'Oh, she was all right.' David rubbed the tip of his nose with his thumb, a trick he'd had since he was small. 'Probably waiting for me to emerge again so she can take Allie's letter to the post as well.'

244

'Do you have a letter to post, Allie?' Sara said at once, all brightness and good cheer. 'I wouldn't mind taking it down, after tea. I could cycle.'

'She wasn't all right,' Michael said. He picked up an apple and waved it at David. 'Can I? Oh, thanks very much.' He took a huge bite, wiped a hand across his mouth, and then added, 'She was crying.'

'Who? What on earth are you on about, Mike?'

'That girl ... Maria, the one who took us over to the cottage. She was crying, I tell you – heaps of tears and lots of heavings and shufflings and bawlings. She didn't take the slightest notice of us though we both said good afternoon very politely.'

'Crying? Oh, Davie dear, did you upset her? What did you say to her?'

'Nothing! Well, nothing to make her cry. I just said I'd been posting a letter to my young lady, that's all.'

'All!' For a moment Alice's eyes sparkled and she looked extremely cross, then she sighed and relaxed. 'Oh well, I suppose it isn't fair to expect you to put up with hero-worship all the time, and this way perhaps she won't be too badly hurt.'

'Hurt? Her? Look, I never asked her to come round here in her huge great car offering me lifts and making me very uncomfortable! She's got no right to sit outside my garden gate bawling her eyes out and making me look a worse fool than she's done already! It's bad enough that it doesn't look as though Pavel and I will be able to meet and marry in the summer after all without her making it worse.'

'All right, all right, don't lose your rag. At least you've told her now and she'll have no more excuse for following you around. Now let's have a cup of tea and I'll put the steak pie in the oven – David's peeled the potatoes, haven't you, Davie? – and then we can eat. Will that suit everyone?'

Nibby was met off the ship not only by the drum-beating, flag-waving populace but also by his father. Reg Hawke was grey now, but otherwise he had not changed much from the smart, upright figure in the chauffeur's uniform whom David and Alice remembered. They saw him approach the small group of men coming down the gangplank and Alice actually realised that it was Mr Hawke before she recognised Nibby.

'There he is . . . see, his father's shaking hands with him . . . now he's giving him a big hug . . . *much* better!' Alice was jumping up and down, longing to rush over and join father and son yet feeling that it would not be right to interrupt their first meeting for so long. 'I say, fancy Nibs growing himself a beard – it looks beautifully silky, not a bit like his hair used to be . . . if that's Moscow tailoring give me Liverpool every time . . . ah, they're heading this way!'

They passed within a couple of feet of the brother and sister and would probably have continued by without noticing them, but Alice was having none of that.

'Nibby . . . Mr Hawke!' she called. 'It's David and me – we've come to say how glad we are that you're back safe and sound!'

Mr Hawke spotted them and lifted a hand, a smile spreading across his face, but Nibby dived through the people that separated them, shook Alice's hand, gave David a hug, then hugged Alice and shook David's hand, all the while grinning away, pleased as punch, just like the boy David had known so well years ago.

'What a pair you are! Fancy you being in Russia too, Dave – you don't know what a horrid time you've missed! Two of our chaps are back in prison, and they handed out sentences to their own nationals as if they were bouquets! Mr Moorhouse called it a frame-up – that was the polite way of putting it. But we can't talk here . . . Dad, where can we get a cup of tea and have a chat?'

'There's a little place I know of . . . here, Mr David, Miss Alice, you come along with me. My car's parked handy, and we'll all be sitting down to a good tea in a brace of shakes.'

Alice was impressed with Mr Hawke's car; it was a Morris Ten, very black and shiny and obviously the apple of Mr Hawke's eye. He ushered them into its gleaming interior and, as he had said, in a very short space of time they were sitting in a tiny corner café, eating an assortment of very good cakes and drinking tea from a huge, family-sized pot.

'That's better!' Nibby said at last, leaning back in his chair and grinning round at the company. 'I know Russians think nothing can touch their tea, but I like a good old-fashioned cup of English char! Now let's catch up with each other's news. The only consolation for being clapped up in the Lubianka was that it got my name in the English papers so good old Alice wrote to me. It's been an uncommonly nasty couple of months and I never thought I'd be so relieved to be expelled from a country, but that's water under the bridge now. Dave, what are you going to do? Britain's not like Russia, with a new scheme waiting for engineers round every corner.'

'Don't I know it! I haven't got a clue, old fellow. What about you?'

Nibby shrugged and sipped tea.

'I've had enough of foreigners to last me a lifetime, frankly. I'd like to settle down here somewhere, if I could find a job. But Dad tells me there's even been unemployment in the car industry.'

'There's unemployment in the shipping industry,' David said. 'You should walk down where the yards are . . . or perhaps I should say were. Silence. Never heard anything like it down there – the noise used to hit you as you got near the river, and now it's just quiet, with seabirds crying. Makes you want to do the same . . . sit down and blub. And the young men are in mischief because there's no work for 'em.'

'Hmm, not good. You tried for work yet?'

'No, not yet. It took me a while to realise that I wouldn't be going back – to Russia, I mean. I'd been saving, and fortunately I'd had all my money sent home, but that won't last for ever.'

'You want to set up on your own, or rather together, just the two of you,' Mr Hawke remarked, as the silence lengthened. 'It's not impossible to make a go of it these days, starting small.'

'What, us? Go into partnership?' David goggled at Nibby. 'Gosh, wouldn't it be grand? But what could we do, and where?'

'The garden at the cottage slopes down to the Dee,' Alice said brightly. 'And I suppose you could build a shed or something. Would that do, just for a start?'

'A cottage? Last time I came round your way you had a semi, out on the coast road. Very posh!'

'No, not posh, expensive,' David said, grinning. 'With a tiny garden and too many rooms to keep clean. So in two weeks we're moving into this cottage Allie mentioned. It isn't very big . . . could we start something there, do you reckon?'

'I could get a room in the nearest village,' Nibby said. 'What say we have a go? Perhaps we could build ourselves a fishing boat and go out after the mackerel.'

'You could share David's room,' Alice said, quick as lightning. 'It would save you a bit of money, and a bit of time as well with both of you under one roof.'

'My great-great-something or other probably started by building himself a fishing boat,' David remarked. 'And look where his descendant has ended up – fishing boat to fishing boat via the biggest shipyard in the north-west in eight generations!'

'It 'ud be a laugh,' Mr Hawke said thoughtfully, 'but to my mind it 'ud be more than that. It 'ud make the pair of you, very like. Doesn't matter what you make – cars, boats, or just cupboards for the rich to keep their money in – provided you make 'em well and sell 'em for a fair sum. Aye, with jobs so hard to come by it's not a bad idea, setting up for yourselves.'

'We've got a spare bed; I was going to sell it but we'll keep it for you, Nibby,' Alice planned busily. 'We've got absolutely lashings of furniture, more than enough, and carpets and curtains, so we shan't have to spend money on things like that. But I want a decent sink put in . . . oh, and there isn't a bathroom and there's only one toilet, outside – do you think we ought to do something about that?'

'No!' David and Nibby said in chorus, then they both laughed and David explained, 'They don't run to very good plumbing in the Soviet Union; we're both used to pretty rough conditions so far as that goes. You leave the toilet where it is and we'll show our engineering skill by putting your sink and taps and things in ourselves first off, won't we, Nibby?'

'Sure will. You move in a fortnight? Well, had I better come over tomorrow, take a look at the place, and then go and buy the equipment we'll need to put the sink in? Time's quite important, really, when we'll want to be settled in quickly so we can start to work. What I'd suggest is . . .' The two heads, one dark and one taffy-coloured, were close together, the two voices chimed in one on top of the other just as they had as boys. Alice smiled across at Mr Hawke.

'Well, it was your idea, Mr Hawke, and it certainly didn't fall on stony ground! Do you really think it'll work?'

Mr Hawke got out a pipe and began tamping tobacco into it. He frowned down at the bowl, fished out a box of matches, and then raised an interrogative brow. 'D'you mind?'

'No, carry on,' Alice said readily. 'I'm waiting so eagerly for a reply that I wouldn't notice if you set alight.'

Mr Hawke chuckled. 'Like that, is it? Well, just you think back, young Alice . . . Nibby told me David said to drop the Mr and Miss, which don't come natural to me now, not after years in a car factory . . . just you think back to the old days, when those two boys were thick as thieves together and getting up to all sorts. Remember the night they got cast ashore in that little cockleshell of a boat? They did all right that night, I can tell you. Most others would've drowned and well your father knew it . . . proud as punch he was and I felt similar. They're resourceful, that's what your father said, and daring . . . lots of guts . . . and whenever they undertook to do something, as lads, that something got well and truly done, whether it was a bit of good work or some wicked mischief.'

'So you think they can make a go of . . . of whatever they start?'

'I do. What the one can't manage the other can, and that's a good thing for partners. And they're both hard workers, always was. And I wouldn't call either of 'em moody or temperamental. Another good thing when you're in partnership.'

'Then I just hope you're right,' Alice said, pouring herself another cup of tea and taking the last cake, unheeded by the two eager planners.

'I hope so too. Tell you what, young Alice. This would've pleased your father more than anything. He wouldn't care if it were ships or cars or moving picture shows, so long as they were doing it for themselves. He loved ships, but he loved men and work more, I do believe. He'd be chuckling away if he could see our sons now!'

'That's a good thought,' Alice said softly. Her memories of her father, even after all the years between, could still bring great warmth to her heart. 'But what about Nibby's social life? Didn't he have friends and so on in Birmingham? He mentioned a girl once . . .'

'Did he! There were half a dozen before he went to Russia, but none since that I've heard tell of. Carrie . . . fast little piece . . . married a foreman at my mate Fred's shop, and the other one who springs to mind, Ethel her name was, ran away with a band-leader and got herself in the family way a good six months before he did the decent thing by her.'

'Gosh! Didn't any of them write to him, then?' Alice asked innocently but with a thumping heart.

'Write? Them lot? No, I'm sure they didn't. Only one who ever wrote to him was you, young Alice! Loved getting your letters, he did, though answering them was a terrible chore. Always better with figures than letters, our Nibby. Not that I ought to call him that when he was John to me for many a year, but it's a nickname that's stuck and now I think of him as Nibby more than I do as John.'

'Why *is* he called Nibby? I've often wondered.'

'It came about after his mother had left me, so I don't know the ins and outs, but apparently when he first started school he thought himself a cut above the other kids in the board-school kindergarten – which I'm bound to say he would've been, because she took him to a right slum when she ran off. Anyway, some of the kids took umbrage and began to call him His Nibs; then as they got to know him better and like him better, too, they changed it to Nibs, or Nibby. And it stuck.'

'That's fascinating – the last thing I thought of.' Alice glanced at the little gold watch her mother had given her just before she died. 'I don't want to break the party up, Mr Hawke, but what time does your wife expect you home? It's getting on for five o'clock and we've got a train and bus to catch, and then we've got a bit of a walk.'

'No you haven't, my dear, because Nibby and I want you to come back to Chester with us and meet the wife and my sister, the one Nibby used to stay with when he was in Chester for his vacations. We'll have some tea and then I'll run you right home in the car.'

'It's awfully good of you, but it's a long way, and then there's Nibby's luggage . . . David, did you hear that? Mr Hawke's asked us home to tea with his wife and sister and says he'll run us back home afterwards. What do you . . . oh, David! *David*!'

'No use, love, violence is called for,' Mr Hawke said,

smiling. He caught Nibby by his collar, David by his, and heaved them physically apart. 'Now come along. Call yourselves gentlemen, and a lady addresses you and not a word do you say in answer! Will you and your sister come back to tea with us, David? We'll run you home in the car later.'

'Oh yes, thanks very much, Mr Hawke, that would be lovely. If we wanted to try the very newest thing, of course, Nibs, we'd need a good deal of . . .'

'Heaven preserve us, they're as good as dead to the rest of the world bar each other,' Mr Hawke remarked. 'Come along, Alice. If we get up and go perhaps they'll follow.'

They did, still talking nineteen to the dozen, but Alice and Mr Hawke had each other's company and they let the two young men sit in the back of the car and wrangle amicably all the way from Liverpool to Chester, and then, when they'd had their tea and met Lily Purvis and the charming Mrs Anne Hawke, they wrangled all the way from Chester to the Thomases' home.

'We'll be at Aunt Lily's tonight, but I'll come over first thing,' Nibby promised, as he got out of the back seat and into the front. 'Thanks for coming to meet the ship, by the way – it was greatly appreciated, wasn't it, Dad?'

'Oh, aye. If Alice hadn't been there I dare say I'd have faded away and you'd not have noticed! Goodnight, both; see you early in the morning, because I'll run the lad over as soon as he's downed his breakfast.'

Alice and David waved them off and then went tiredly indoors. Lydia had undertaken to have Michael and Sara for the night so the house was quiet and dark, but David was still so on fire with excitement that he did not seem to notice. He hurried ahead of Alice, lighting up, and in the kitchen, with its stove down to a tiny glow in the grate and their tea – a piece of steak each and a pile of cold boiled potatoes waiting to be fried – sitting, sullen and neglected, in the middle of the kitchen table, he turned excitedly to her.

'I say, won't it be prime? The three of us, in it together! And Mr Hawke was quite right when he said Dad would have been thrilled to bits!'

'Pass us the bucket, Mike! And keep your feet clear of the third board along; Nibby says it needs some attention.'

Alice, balancing on a board stretched between two shaky stepladders, was whitewashing the living-room ceiling in the cottage. In the next room, the kitchen, David and Nibby were laboriously running a supply of piped water in from the well to the sink which they had bought but not yet fitted. Sara, singing at the top of her voice, was papering the bedroom that would one day be hers and Alice's, and outside, Mr Hawke was supervising the building of an extension – they would do everything themselves but the outer walls, David had said – which would one day be a neat little bathroom, an indoor lavatory and a fourth bedroom.

'You can make do and mend for so long and then it becomes an additional burden,' Mr Hawke said severely, when Alice had objected to an extra room or two on the grounds of cost. 'These young men plan to make money from this venture, young Alice, and they'll do it, too. But not at the cost of your sweet temperament. To be blunt, they'll drive you insane in a year if you try to keep them cooped up, and it's not right for a young woman to have to keep abandoning her kitchen whilst her menfolk take a bath. Making things, my dear, is dirty work.'

So now Mr Hawke and two friends of his who just happened to be bricklayers and were out of work – or had been – were constructing their new rooms. As soon as all the work was finished and they could move in, the men intended to start on a large, airy shed in which David and Nibby could make whatever it was they intended to build, for it was still not quite settled. However, since the estuary was so close they would start with the fishing boat that Nibby had first suggested, built to their own design, with David doing the hull and Nibby making the engine – for she was to be a motorboat and not merely a sailboat.

'When Mr Hawke goes home tonight he's taking me in to the solicitor's office,' David had said casually earlier that morning. 'I've made an appointment. I want to take a look at all the old paperwork connected with the Thomas yard. There may be designs that would be useful to us . . . not that we're planning to build ships, of course, but Father didn't just build ships, he built all sorts in the early days – trawlers, drifters, the odd pleasure yacht – and Mother told me he kept all his designs. Why, my old boat, the *Delight*, was made in the yard, from one of Father's drawings.'

Did it worry him, Alice wondered, as she sloshed whitewash happily on to the ceiling above her head and dodged the occasional drip, did it worry him that he had never done anything about their mother's last wish? He did not know she knew about it, of course – certainly David himself had never breathed a word of it – but Megan Thomas had told her daughter long before she was sure that David would be able to return in time.

'If I die before he arrives you won't forget to tell him what I'd like him to do?' she had pleaded, her eyes huge and luminous with the strength of her desire. 'It means so much to me, Allie dear, and it could mean so much to the boys . . . you and the other girls won't bear the name of Thomas for very much longer, but David and Michael will be Thomases for the rest of their lives. It was a proud name and should be so still.'

David had thrown himself into the venture with Nibby with great enthusiasm, though; was it partly because he knew how much it would have pleased both his parents? She hoped and believed this was the case.


'Can you shove a bit more pipe through, Nibby? Oh, curse the thing, it just won't reach!'

David, filthy dirty, on hands and knees, was tugging delicately at a great length of lead piping which, if he could just get another six inches or so fed through the hole they had bored in the cottage's thick outer wall, would marry up very neatly with the downpipe he had already fixed.

'What?' Nibby's voice reached him faintly from the yard outside where he, too, laboured with the pipe.

'Deaf adder!' bawled David. 'More *pipe*!'

'What?'

'More . . . aargh!' The pipe shot through the wall, a good foot of it, nearly impaling David as it came. He sighed, and lumbered over to the back door. Nibby was standing by the wall, wiping his hands down his filthy flannels. The machinery which would pump up the water for them was a good deal cleaner than either of its neophytes. Nibby looked across at him and raised his brows.

'Sorry, did you say more pipe?'

'Well, I did, yes. Only I wanted about six inches and you shoved through a good foot. Do you think you could possibly pull some of it out again? Very slowly, and stop the moment you hear me shout?'

'Sure. Tell you what, I'll measure six inches before I start pulling back, then at least I'll have a rough idea.'

'That's grand. Off we go, then.'

Back in the kitchen with just the right length of pipe, David lit his soldering torch and began to fix the lengths together. He was very happy, and what was even better, he knew it. He was loving the work, loving being with his friend again after their long separation and loving the cottage with an increasing fondness. It was so good to be within spitting distance of the sea once more, so good to have a home which they could manage easily without outside help. He knew how Alice had hated giving orders to reluctant or lazy maidservants; he even guessed how much she must have grown to dislike the gloomy Victorian house with its overtones of their mother's deep unhappiness and the feeling of failure which had seemed a part of it. But here she was thoroughly happy, even enjoying – or seeming to enjoy – her hated household chores. Mind you, he told himself, there hasn't been much to do, because you can't count decorating and scrubbing and renewing the woodwork round the windows as housework, exactly. The difference would be that this cottage was theirs, the Thomas children's, in a way that the gloomy old semi-detached suburban villa was not. They would all have worked very hard indeed with their own hands to turn this cottage into the sort of home they wanted, and that, he was convinced, would make it more precious to each one of them.

Working away, it occurred to him that he had not thought of Pavel more than two or three times since they had started work on the cottage. It was a stunning realisation and for a moment or two he felt truly guilty. Then he reminded himself that it was not much use repining; he would not get back to Russia this summer. He must keep busy and do his best to get their little business – whatever it was – established before hurrying off to fetch his bride. Tonight, if I'm not too tired, I'll write to her, explain the situation as it now stands, he told himself. A nice long letter so she won't think I've forgotten her. Which I most certainly have not. Not by a long chalk.

But he was well on the way to being reconciled to her absence.

'Oh, good, you're back.' Eva raised a flushed face from her butter-churning as Pavel slipped into the kitchen. 'Nyusha's been worried . . . even in the village there has been talk . . . did you sell the wool well? And the lambs?'

'Yes, we sold everything, and for fair prices.' Pavel shrugged off her *burka* and threw it across a chair. Autumn was upon them now; the long-awaited summer had passed in fading hope, increasing bitterness, for David had not come. If his letters had come to explain his non-arrival it would have been easier, but it had been late August before she had received the one he had written in April and by then her hopes had been raised and dashed so often that the reason for his absence seemed trivial compared to the pains she had suffered in the waiting.

'Oh, good. Did Fedor buy the things he needed as well? The seed and the new bull and a horse to replace poor Netchevi?'

'Yes, I think so. The new horse . . . it's a mare, actually . . . is in foal. Her owner said he was selling because by the time she dropped her foal he would have been sent to a timber camp in the far north, so he was getting his money together while he could. I don't know what he planned, if anything.'

'Was he a *kulak*, then? Living on the earnings and hard work of others?'

'No, of course not, he was just a better farmer than most. Eva . . . it was very selfish of me, but when the rumours first started, in the summer, I believed what Stalin said on the radio, despite what Fedor kept telling us. I thought the peasants being sent to the timber camps really were men who exploited their fellows, indulged in money-lending at exorbitant rates . . . all the things we were told, in fact. But now that it's sweeping across the country and getting nearer and nearer home, I can see that it's all lies, like the rest. Anyone who has worked hard and succeeded in making a decent living for themselves is an enemy of the people! It's mad and frightening and I want to run, I want all of us to run, but where should we run to? If they find us here they'll find us wherever we go.'

'I don't think we can run; we've just got to wait and see what happens,' Eva said, starting to churn again. 'Why did you say it was selfish of you to believe the rumours?'

'Oh, well, I suppose because I felt I'd be gone anyway before things got difficult here, so I didn't try terribly hard to discover whether we were in danger or not. Don't think of me as wicked, but I was stupid; I thought David could save us all, somehow. Only now, when he does come . . . if he comes . . . it will be too late. We'll be gone from here.'

'Gone?' The churning stopped and Eva's face, pink from exertion, paled. 'What do you mean? Oh, Pavel, you've had a letter!'

'Yes. Eva, it's been opened.'

'By *them*? Why would they want to open a letter from a boy to a girl?'

'Because of the foreign stamp, I dare say. Usually the envelopes of my letters show signs of the distance they've travelled; this one shows little on the envelope but the paper inside must have been through a score of hands.' Pavel felt her own fingers begin to tremble; it was as though her love for David and his for her had been violated by those prying, uninvited fingers and the eyes which had read every word.

'Well, that's horrid, but what does David *say*? When is he coming?'

'He still doesn't know, but he does say he'll have to wait until the authorities forget he was ever an engineer. He's been to somewhere in London called the Foreign Office and they've advised him to wait until next summer . . . nearly a year . . . before even aplying for a passport to enter the country as a tourist. Imagine, a whole year!'

'It won't be a whole year, dearest, more like nine months,' Eva said, gesturing to the window. Outside, the trees were clinging precariously to their last few red-gold leaves and soon – too soon – the winter would start to grip. 'Possibly even less . . . you could hope for seven months.'

'But Eva, they've read the letter! Do you suppose they'll give him a passport now? And that isn't all; he makes a suggestion . . . oh, dear God, I'm so frightened! If there is trouble, then it may well be David's letter which brings it down on us.'

'Look, you're talking in riddles.' Eva abandoned the churning and walked her sister to the back door and out into the still sunny yard. 'Come along, take a deep breath and collect your thoughts, and then we'll go into the woods; it's easier to think there, sometimes, and we won't run the risk of Fedor or Nyusha coming in suddenly. I take it you didn't say anything to him?'

'No. I dare not . . . and besides, I wanted to talk it over with you first. You're a sensible thing, Eva, even if you are my sister!'

Together, they walked out across the cobbled yard and into the trees. It was pleasant in the wood with the piles of leaves underfoot rustling with each step, but the sisters were too intent on the contents of the letter in Pavel's hand to ponder overmuch on their surroundings. Pavel, looking quickly up through the thinning leaves at the pale blue of the sky, only wondered how many more times she would walk here knowing the trees to belong, through Fedor and Nyusha of course, to herself and Eva.

'Well? Do you want me to read it for myself?'

Pavel shook her head and unfolded the pages, going through the sheets until she found the appropriate one.

'No need, I'll read it to you. It's quite short. *In view of the uncertainty surrounding my return to Russia, I am wondering if we might try another plan? Would it be possible for you, my love, to come to me? I could send you money, though not roubles, but if you could somehow cross the mountains and then go through Georgia to the coast, I dare say it would be possible to bribe a fisherman to take you to sea and land you in Turkey. You could pay him there, dushka, in local currency which I can send you. If you agree, then write to me as soon as possible telling me when you hope to reach say Trabzon, and I'll make all the arrangements from there.*' She stopped reading and turned to Eva. 'You see? They've read the letter, they know I'm in love with an Englishman — and one of the engineers, furthermore, who have already turned world opinion against the Soviet. They'll never let him come back into the country again, of course . . . but they will also want to stop me joining him. See how dirty the letter is, how creased and crumpled the pages are! I can only suppose I've been allowed to receive it as evidence that we've all been plotting against the State.'

'Oh, Pavel . . . let's burn it at once!' Eva cried urgently, tugging at her sister's arm. 'You must tell Fedor and Nyusha right away and then we must all run. We'll go over the mountains to Georgia and into Turkey, and dear, kind David will rescue all of us, not just you. I'm so afraid of the timber camps, and being torn from you and my home and my parents. Let's all go to David!'

'We'll tell Fedor and Nyusha this evening,' Pavel said heavily. 'I'll show them the letter – they might as well read it, since apparently the whole of Moscow, certainly most of the OGPU, have seen it already. But how much time have we left? Fedor will need money and we've been buying stock, not saving – it seemed such an opportunity, with farming people in the lowlands and on the plain selling up as fast as they could. I suppose they felt that if they were fortunate and got sent to the collectives they would have a hoard of personal money to see them through the worst of the early years, and if they were unfortunate and sent to the timber camps it might help them to buy their freedom. Or possibly keep their wives and children for a few years. Though wives go with their husbands, don't they?'

'I think so . . . I don't know, I'm confused by the whole business,' Eva muttered, a hand to her head. 'When was the letter written, Pavelinka?'

'Umm . . . not sure. It's been almost rubbed off by all the handling, but from other things he says it was early summer. Why?'

'Because he'll be expecting a reply. Should you write immediately, tonight, and then go down to the village and drop it in at the post office? Otherwise David won't know when we're arriving at that place . . . Trez something . . . so he won't be able to arrange to meet us there.'

'The letter would take too long to get through.' Pavel turned and hugged Eva fiercely. 'What have we done, between us? Fedor and Nyusha, this was their life, this place! They took us in . . . oh, it was nothing to do with you, dearest . . . but they took us in and I go and bring the State down on them. I didn't mean it; I never thought . . .'

'Come back indoors and have a glass of tea,' Eva said bracingly, returning the hug. 'As if you are to blame, dushka! If only Fedor had let you go when you wanted to you would have been in a position to help us now, instead of being in a mess with us! And you know very well that we've been whistling into the wind . . . the State was bound to catch up with us and Fedor was bound to suffer for the sin of being a good and successful farmer. It's wrong and wicked that it should be so, but it is so and no amount of weeping will change it — not yet, at any rate. So we'll all go, shall we? We'll tell Fedor and Nyusha as soon as the food's on the table and we're all sitting down, and then we'll make our plans to leave.'

'Here's Fedor. Sit down, now, girls, and do take those solemn expressions off your faces, the pair of you. Anyone would think the world was about to come to an end.' Nyusha bustled about the table, putting out dishes of vegetables before bringing on the roast lamb. 'Now then, let's eat. After that Fedor can tell us what he got for our lambs, what he paid for that fine black bull out in the pasture, and what name we should give that beautiful mare which I know very well must have been a bargain, since she's in foal and we have good brood mares of our own. Fedor would only have bought her if she was going cheap.'

'Before Fedor tells us anything, I want you both to read a letter I received today,' Pavel said stiffly. 'Read it carefully — as others have done before you.'

Fedor looked up sharply, but Nyusha continued to pass round the vegetables.

'You're not actually letting little Eva see your letters? Well, if it's good news . . .' She looked again at Pavel's face. 'Oh, my dear, has he hurt you? But there are as good fish in the sea as ever came out of it, it's just that we don't see many like David up here.'

'Read the letter,' Eva advised. 'Pavel, you could carve the lamb, couldn't you?'

'Yes.' Pavel took the knife and slid the dish out from under Fedor's nose, passing him the letter with the relevant page on top. 'I think you'd better read that page first, and then if you want to continue to read the rest you may do so.'

She began to carve and Fedor to read. After only a moment he exclaimed sharply, and shot a look at Pavel and another at Eva. Then he read the page before him again and without a word handed it on to Nyusha.

There was silence whilst she, slower than her husband, read it too. She finished it at last and looked from face to face, puzzled, fear dawning but not, as yet, the knowledge of why she was afraid; it was simply a reaction to the tension she felt all around her.

'It's very sad that David can't come back, perhaps not even next summer,' she said slowly. 'But why should you have to go to Turkey? Ships go to Britain from Archangel – I remember you telling me that's how David went – wouldn't it be easier to go that way?'

'The Party doesn't like people leaving the country,' Fedor explained slowly. 'Don't you ever listen to the wireless set? They speak of it as treason.'

'No, I don't listen to the wireless much; it's all talk about tractors and collectivisation and boring things like that,' Nyusha confessed. 'I like a bit of music . . . but then the voices come on so I turn it off.' She looked hopefully up at her husband. 'So? I think Pavel should go to Turkey if she still wants to marry David, and I'm sure she does.'

'Nyusha, when the letter arrived it had been opened.' Pavel leaned across the table and pointed to the sheet. 'See how dirty it is, and how crumpled? Yet I only opened it three or four hours ago. It has been read by others . . . in Moscow.'

'Well, that is very bad . . .' Nyusha began doubtfully, but her words were cut short by Fedor.

'It is worse than bad, sweetheart, it could well be disastrous. Those who read the letter now know that Pavelinka has a young man, an engineer, who wants to marry her. They know that he is biding his time before applying for permission to re-enter the country. Possibly they guess that he does not intend to tell anyone he is going to marry Pavel until it is an established fact, but they may not have got that far. What is certain is that they are now in possession of the plan David has dreamed up – that Pavel should travel over the mountains to Georgia and cross the frontier illegally, probably by boat, to be with him.'

'Yes, but she's only a girl; what good would she be to them?' Nyusha asked practically. 'They wouldn't let her use her brains for their benefit, if you remember; they denied her even the schooling they allow the most illiterate peasants. Why shouldn't she go where she'll be appreciated?'

'No reason, but the State doesn't reason. Why should it steal the land from a simple man who has worked hard and wrested a living from the country he farms? And then give it to a poor fool from the plains who had the same opportunity – exactly the same – to make good and lost it through laziness and inefficiency? None of this makes sense. You must not expect sense from this regime, only a sort of remote spitefulness. Well, Pavelinka, what do you want to do?'

'I want to go, but all of us, not just me,' Pavel said simply. 'No one should stay here.'

'I agree. It isn't as if there's a chance, really, of being allowed to stay once they get round to it. We might have another month or two; they might even leave us until after the spring planting, but why should we work for them?' Fedor grinned round at them, his expression livelier than it had been for a long while. 'We've started with nothing before, haven't we, Nyusha? Why shouldn't we do it again? At least we'll have our lives and each other. And our freedom. I've never been fooled by what they say on the wireless about the timber camps – they're slave labour camps, that's all, somewhere to die slowly and in pain, not somewhere to live! We'll sell up and go.'

'Sell up?' Nyusha echoed doubtfully. 'But won't that take time and perhaps cause comment? Why can't we just go . . . tonight . . . with some of the herd and the dogs and the strongest horses? If we wait much longer we won't get animals over the Klukhor Pass.'

'That's why we'll sell up, because we can't take animals with us, it would lead to being caught,' Fedor explained patiently. 'Write a letter to David, Pavel my dear, but don't send it to his English address; do you remember that fellow he talked about, the one he shared a flat with? Yuri something-or-other?'

'Yuri Obreimov. Yes, I remember him.'

'Well, put the letter to David in an envelope, then get another envelope, a bigger one, and put the first envelope into it. Address the big envelope to Yuri at the address David used to have, and enclose a note asking him to send your letter on to David. That way the chances of their opening it are much smaller . . . wait, I've a better plan. Ask him to send it to David's address, but is there some other name we could use, so they don't put two and two together?'

'His second name is Alyn, after his father,' Pavel said, having given the matter some thought. 'Would that do?'

'Yes, that would be perfect. Do that tonight and then tomorrow you can take the letter down to the village . . . no, it might be better to go right into the town . . . and send it off from the post office. Whilst you're there you can sell the mare in foal – she should fetch a good price. You can lead her without trouble; she's slow with the foal and sweet-natured.'

'Right. Shall Eva come with me?'

'No, we'll need her here. I don't want to delay too long, now that we know they're on to us. She and Nyusha can pack our things whilst I sell off all the beasts that I can. Then at the first word of strangers we can go, just simply slip out of the door and melt into the woods. We shall need all our wits about us at the other end of the Klukhor Pass, for they have spies every-where. It may be necessary for us to part company for a while and go our separate ways, but we'll make arrangements later, when we see what we're up against.' He smiled round at them all, then squared his elbows and began to eat. 'Come on, this is good food, and we may not get many such meals for a while; tuck in!'

That night, when they were safely in bed, Pavel and Eva discussed the future. It was exciting to know that they were leaving their home, but sad, too.

'But there are other beautiful places,' Eva said hopefully. 'There will be a valley just like ours somewhere else. Or perhaps it will be better, Pavelinka, for remember I had very little schooling, less than you. Oh, I can read and write and figure, but I never saw that globe of the world you talked about, because that was for older pupils, and I would like so much to have more lessons and learn more about life and the way other people live.'

'I'm looking forward to seeing David most,' Pavel said, ticking her anticipations off on her fingers, 'and Georgia next, I think, and Turkey next and Britain . . . well, really Britain should come right next to David. And there's the sea – I've dreamed of the sea and it's always a wonderful thing – and boats and ships . . . oh, an endless procession! I wonder what Baru will think of Britain?'

'You can't take Baru!' Eva exclaimed. 'You heard what Fedor said, we can't take the animals.'

'Baru isn't an animal, she's all we have left of before,' Pavel said rather obscurely. 'I couldn't leave her – I'd sooner stay myself and get carried off to a timber camp.'

'Oh, but Pavelinka, she's so *big*; will they have her on the sea?'

'Of course. She's old enough to behave herself . . . let me see, if you're nearly thirteen then she's going on for twelve.'

'That's old, for a dog,' Eva admitted. 'When will we leave, do you think? And what's Georgia like?'

'I don't know when we'll leave, probably in a week or two. As for Georgia, I know no more than you. Except once, long ago . . .' She hesitated and then spoke soft and deep, as though she were repeating a lesson, well learned. 'When these little monkeys are fine grown-up ladies, they may come and stay with me and I'll find them a fat Georgian farmer each to take them to wife.'

'Who said that? Was it Fedor? I don't remember him saying that.'

'I can't imagine; perhaps I read it,' Pavel said lightly, but the words had come into her head together with a picture – a man, tall and fair-skinned, with curly black hair and loving eyes, crouching on the ground, pulling two girl-children into his lap. One was herself, but the other . . .? She did not know the other, did not want to know, did not want to remember. She stirred restlessly in her bed and the straw mattress rustled as though mice were skittling and scuttling in its depths. 'Georgia's got a warm climate. Palm trees grow there, and probably exotic fruits, and there's the sea, of course. It's very beautiful. If we think about that perhaps we'll go to sleep quicker and dream nice dreams.'

She closed her eyes determinedly, and though Eva tried to persuade her to talk again she would not and soon Eva slept. But Pavel could not sleep. The words that she had spoken teased and worried at her mind. Someone had said them once, someone she loved very much, someone who meant a lot to her. Had it been in the time *before*, as she always put it to herself? Was the beautiful man with the loving eyes her long-dead father? If so, who was the other little girl? She wished she had not remembered that other little girl because she knew by the way her mind had shrunk away from the picture it had made that she would do better not to remember and not even to try.

But once memory wakes from its long and inexplicable sleep it won't simply go away for the asking. Far into the night the small, fair face of the other child haunted her and filled her with a terrible sadness and sense of loss.

When she finally slept, however, it was deeply and apparently dreamlessly; at any rate Eva did not hear her moving or calling out. But when Eva woke and ran over to shake Pavel awake also, the first thing she noticed were the tears shining on her sister's cheeks.

# CHAPTER TWELVE

It was a clear autumn day, with colours brighter, perhaps, than they would ever seem again as Pavel rode away from the homestead. She left behind her a scene of such bustle and activity that you could have been forgiven for thinking that the family was preparing for a wedding instead of merely abandoning the home which had taken them a lifetime to create to go out into the mountains with a future as uncertain as the wind that now gusted, now died, now breathed soft on Pavel's cheek.

Riding Katya up the narrow path and out of the valley, Pavel glanced back. She had been very happy there, but leaving it was not as hard for her as it would be for Nyusha and Fedor – particularly Fedor – because she had been planning to go for more than a year. Eva, too, had accepted that she would also leave in the fullness of time, though whether to England to her sister or merely to a city to find a husband had not been fully thought out.

From the height she had already attained Pavel could see the homestead and the outbuildings clearly. A small figure moved around the pasture, a large dog loping at his heel. That was Fedor and one of the hounds, it was too far away to see which. They would be cutting out the best of the cattle so that they could be driven to the nearest market on the next market day, and presently they would do the same with the sheep. If she stared very hard at the kitchen window she could almost imagine she could see Nyusha there, baking busily. Hard biscuits, she had suggested that morning, would be best to carry, and oatcakes, maize bread, a good deal of hard cheese and just a small pot of soft . . . there were apples in the loft and some of the big, hard pears from Fedor's new little tree. And they must take some clothing, so Eva must wash and press all their best things . . . they would travel in old working clothes but take their decent stuff for when they arrived wherever they were going.

That morning, over breakfast, Fedor had told them they would not take the path their enemies would expect – the Klukhor Pass.

'We shall have to follow it through the most impenetrable part of the mountain,' he said regretfully, 'but as soon as we're through there's a path I know of . . . you've been that way with me, Pavelinka . . . which goes off to the right. It's a long way round, but safer, if you're being followed, or expected the other end.'

'If I'm to take my best things, what shall Pavel take?' Eva had interrupted to ask plaintively. 'Boy's breeches or dresses?'

'She can ride out as a boy and take her dresses to change into when she gets over the border into Turkey,' Fedor had decided. 'Now come along, little empty-headed one, go and fetch water for all this washing and freshening, then we can start packing in good earnest.'

Excitement, Pavel decided as she reached the lip of the valley and began to trot Katya down the narrow path which led into the next gorge, was keeping them going, not letting them spend time grieving over what they were about to lose. Eva was young enough not to regret the losing of material possessions, Fedor perhaps old enough to realise truly that freedom was more important than the efficient and much-loved farm he had built up. Only Nyusha would linger when at last they left, needing the comfort of material possessions to make up for the loss of the home she had made. Pavel smiled as she thought of her foster-mother staggering out with the butter churn in her arms, the wash-tub balanced on her head, and her heart yearning over every rag rug, every gleaming spoon, left behind. But even so, Nyusha was a sensible and intelligent woman; she accepted the need to go and would continue to do so – and would start home-making again as soon as they settled anywhere, no matter how briefly.

Presently she whistled Baru to heel – for she was ranging around as she liked to do, sniffing at every clump of grass they passed – unfastened her *burka* to let the sun warm her arms, and thought about the letter, warm against her thigh in her breeches pocket. It was going such a long way and by such a circuitous route, yet it would probably be with David before she was! She had no doubt that they would reach Georgia easily enough and probably would have little difficulty in arriving eventually in Turkey, but she was equally certain that it would take very much longer than they expected. It would be months and not weeks before she saw David, yet that she could happily accept. It was the thought of never seeing him again that had struck such miserable unhappiness into her heart, and at least this way she would be actively doing something, actively trying to reach him and not sitting passively back, waiting for him to reach her!

It was a good twenty miles to town, but it was mostly downhill and she made good progress. On reflection, Fedor had decided that selling the mare would not make up for the time it would take the creature to reach the town, so instead he had given Pavel a satchel crammed with cheese and her panniers were laden with butter whilst four chickens, plucked and drawn, hung by their feet from the pommel. She was to sell them for as much as she could get, post her letter and then return, having first ascertained that there would indeed be a market in a neighbouring town the family seldom visited the following day.

Pavel was well known at the post office and she entered it today with some trepidation, in case the hard-faced woman behind the counter had been told to look out for her, but everything was as usual. She bought stamps, fortunately re-membering in time that she would not need as many as usual, posted the letter, and then went and sold her dairy products and poultry to the fat old woman squeezed behind the counter in the local shop. She was pleased with the price she got and left with a light step, chuckling to herself at the woman's last words.

'Thank 'ee, thank 'ee,' she had said, beaming at Pavel over a mountain range of fat pink chins. 'You're growing up, my lad . . . you'll be making some woman happy one of these days!'

It was odd, really, because the woman in the shop had seen Pavel both as herself, in print frocks and sandals, and as Fedor's son who was so useful at the herding, yet she obviously thought them two different people and had never questioned their similarity, assuming them to be brother and sister.

It was rather pleasant to mount Katya again with money in

her pocket and a sense of achievement bringing a smile to her face whenever she thought about it. She had sent the letter – with that she seemed to have launched herself on a course, though whether a good or a bad one remained to be seen – and she had bargained briskly enough with their fat friend to believe herself not the loser, at any rate. Now she would ride home in the golden afternoon and help with the preparations for what would, when all was said and done, be the greatest adventure of her life so far.

But it was a long ride home, and Pavel soon found that climbing steep hills, even on horseback, was not as easy as descending them. She sighed for company, for she rarely rode so far alone, and she found herself fervently hoping that the sun would not sink in the west before she arrived back at the valley. Baru was with her, to be sure, so wolves held little or no real danger, but she was frightened of the thought of them . . . suppose they set on her dog and she could not save her? And the thought of riding in the dark was not too pleasant, either. On the only occasion when she had been benighted she had had David's loving company . . . even thinking of that night sent a pleasant tingle up her spine . . . but she did not wish to repeat the experience on her own.

However, the sun was still descending in the sky as she reached the valley and began to take the long downward path which would lead, through thick forest and then beside the river and across meadowland, to home. From the cliff at the top of the valley she had one brief glimpse of the homestead, but apart from noticing that Fedor was still moving the cattle between the home pasture and the outer ones she saw nothing unusual.

It was not until she rode out of the shelter of the trees and into the approach to the farm that she realised something was happening. There were strange horses tethered in the yard and through the open back door leading into the kitchen she could see a great commotion of some sort. Frowning, she ordered Baru to stay where she was, kicked her mount into a trot and then a canter and was still cantering when a dark figure stepped out of a clump of pines and ordered her harshly to stop or it would be the worse for her.

Katya reared and Pavel was too busy clinging for a moment to wonder just what was going on, but as the man leaned forward and grabbed irritably at her horse's mouth she saw that he had a rifle in one hand and wore a scruffy, military-type uniform, grey and dusty but still obviously soldiers' garb.

'You! Name? Where are you going?'

'I'm . . . Ryazanov.'

'And what are you doing here, eh? Visiting?'

Pavel glanced towards the farm. She did not know why she had lied except that it seemed a sensible thing to do when faced with an armed and antagonistic man in uniform.

'Yes . . . to buy. I'm told the chap's selling some of his stock before winter.'

'Hmm. See anyone as you rode up the valley? A girl, perhaps? Know the girl, do you? Sweet on her?'

'A girl? I know a few.' Pavel had dropped her voice several degrees; if he thought her a boy well and good, and since she was riding astride and wearing her breeches and *burka* there was no reason why he should think her anything else. 'How old would this one be – the one you're after?'

'Oh, seventeen, eighteen . . . a young lady, perhaps you'd prefer me to call her. Name of Pavelinka Fedorovna. Farmer's daughter.' He jerked a thumb behind him, to the homestead.

'I know her. Why? What do you want from her?'

'None of your business, mate.' The man jerked at Katya's mouth and Katya tried to rear away from him but was held by an iron hand. 'Have you seen her? She's gone missing from home. My officer wants to ask her a few questions.'

'Nope.' Pavel moved her body so that Katya, expecting to be kicked into a trot again, would fidget and tug. Katya did as she had hoped and Pavel added in a meek boy's growl, 'Can I go now? Up to the house? My business is with the farmer, not his daughter.'

'He won't be doing business with you or anyone else for a long time to come.' Pavel's heart sank into her stomach at the gloating cruelty in the man's voice. 'Better go up there, though. My officer will have a word.'

Pavel dug her heels gently into Katya's sides as the man's grimy hand fell from the bridle. Her whole body was trembling with reaction from the brief encounter and with fear of what was to come, but she knew she must go through with it. She would approach the farmhouse and hope the officer, whoever he might be, would accept her story and let her go on her way.

She could hide in the woods overnight and then return to the farm when the men had left. Not even to herself could she voice the worst fear, that when they left they would leave nothing – or rather no one – behind.

She rode into the yard. To her surprise someone ran forward and took Katya's bridle from her as she swung herself out of the saddle. It was a small, squat boy of perhaps nine or ten with Mongoloid features and a shaved bullet head. He was dressed in a tattered cotton shirt and dark trousers several sizes too large for him.

'Thank you,' Pavel said automatically, and he smiled, a strange, sly movement of thick lips which bubbled when he opened his mouth a little.

'Go in. It's good in there.'

His voice was rasping and he spoke with a very odd accent indeed, but Pavel was not interested in him. She strode quickly into the house.

Fedor was huddled against the kitchen table. She knew it was he because she recognised his *tcherkasska* and his riding breeches. She would not have recognised his face, bruised, battered and bloodied as it was. One arm was held at an odd angle and his feet were bare, the toes crushed and blackened where someone with boots ... she swallowed and looked away, afraid she would faint or start to scream.

Eva and Nyusha were sitting by the table on the hard wooden chairs with the hand-made cushions on the seats and the woven back-rests. They were staring straight at Pavel. They looked like a pair of poor, bright little birds, stunned and hypnotised into immobility by some huge snake. Neither spoke or moved; Pavel could see that they dared not. Eva's cheek had a bruise on it and she was nursing a wrist which was so red it might have been burned. Nyusha's normally rosy face was grey and terror had darkened her eyes to burning black pits. Her hands were clasped in her lap but all the while Pavel watched her the fingers moved, restless, jittery, poking and pleating and tucking and smoothing at her skirt.

'What's all this?' She spoke with a boy's gruffness but even so her voice wavered. There were other people in the kitchen, she realised, as someone moved. Two soldiers, brutal-faced, crop-headed men in dingy uniforms, and a big woman with a white headsquare round her thinning hair; a man, tall and knobbly, with tufty dark hair and round blue frightened eyes, and another man, short and bent, white-haired, white-bearded, inscrutable.

'These are *kulaks*, rich people who take the food from the mouths of the peasants,' one of the soldiers said in a dull monotone; you could hear that he had learned it by heart and said it a thousand times before.

'*Kulaks*? This man is a farmer. He has no workers under him to exploit; he employs no peasants.'

The soldier's eyes, which had been half-shut, snapped wide. 'You know them well? Where, then, is the girl, Pavelinka?'

Eva moved. It was the tiniest of movements but Pavel caught it out of the corner of her eye. She glanced across and one of Eva's eyelids fluttered for a moment in a brief wink. Say nothing, the wink said, and we may yet come out of this imbroglio with whole skins.

'The girl?' Pavel shrugged, hand on hip. 'I've already told a fellow outside I haven't a clue. Dead, for all I know. What does she matter, anyhow?'

'Treasonable activities against the State,' the soldier said, enjoying each word, mumbling them through his puffy lips. 'Been here before?'

'Yup. Only a few days ago. She wasn't here then, the older girl.'

'Hmm.' The soldier jerked a thumb at Fedor's heavily breathing but motionless figure. 'Told us the same; wonder if it's true?' He turned to his companion. 'This lad's no part of it and he says the girl's been gone a couple or more days. What do you think?'

'Gone, gone.' Pavel looked round, startled, to find the source of the sound and it was Fedor, muttering the words through his damaged lips. When he spoke blood trickled from the corner of his mouth.

'All right, comrade, if you say so she's gone.' The soldier, oddly enough, did not seem to bear any antipathy towards Fedor, having either beaten him or seen him beaten by another. 'Right; our orders are to take the whole family, but if one's already left she's already left.' He moved round to where Eva and Nyusha sat, numb and still. 'Get up, the pair of you. We've a long way to go before dawn.'

The other soldier moved across and pulled Fedor away from

the table. He swayed for a moment, then groaned and collapsed. Nyusha rushed forward and was cuffed back; Eva clung to her.

'It's all right, we'll put him across one of the horses. Here, you boy, give us a hand.' He beckoned Pavel who went forward with assumed reluctance but her mind was working quickly; if only she could get Eva alone just for a moment, she might find out where they were bound!

They carried Fedor outside and draped him over a horse. Katya stood still. She had got very warm cantering down the valley and her flanks steamed; she trembled when she smelt the blood which dappled Fedor's shirt and still ran down the side of his mouth, dripping slowly off his chin. The horse who received the man's recumbent body did not tremble, it merely squared its stance. It's used to carrying mutilated burdens Pavel thought and felt her gorge rise; she was going to be sick, she had to be sick!

'The girl will ride before me, the woman before you,' a voice from the shadows announced. A tall man, fair-haired, squint-eyed, strode out of the stable leading a big horse; its bridle clinked. The man had an apple in his hand. From our apple loft, Pavel thought without surprise or anger. She knew it was no longer their apple loft. The peasants in the kitchen – and others to follow, no doubt – were being given their home, their land. Fedor and Nyusha were being taken away, as was Eva. She must find out where they were going, and when she had done that she would ride away and think . . . think!

Pavel stood in the cobbled yard and watched them go. There was nothing she could do and she dared not speak even when her sister brushed past her. She watched them ride off into the deepening dusk. Behind her, the peasants talked in low tones one to another; they were enormously impressed with everything, she could tell, and they were discovering newer and nicer things with every moment that passed. The child who had enjoyed the spectacle of Fedor being beaten passed her, heading for the kitchen. Little monster, she thought, without any real feeling. Well, let them have it all; it's only a farm, and the house and its contents only things. They will make as much use of it as that mountain child made of my place at university, no doubt . . . let them. The State, when it came down to it, only got what it deserved.

Presently, because there was nothing else to do, she mounted Katya and rode her slowly past the stable block. A whiff of clean horses, straw and hay and the apples above caressed her nostrils; a pang shot through her. This she did mind, leaving the animals, who had done no harm, to these ignorant peasants. A thought occurred to her. She slid off Katya's back and led her over to the back door, which was still open. Inside, the woman was lighting a lamp; her face was neither beautiful nor intelligent but just for a moment it was transformed. A kind of wondering pride lit it, as though she had seen a miracle performed by someone she loved.

Pavel stepped inside and was immediately aware that she had committed a solecism; one did not step, unasked, over someone else's threshold.

'Excuse me,' she stammered, 'I . . . I live not too far away . . . the dusk is deepening every minute and I wondered if you knew about the wolf-fires?'

There was a silence for a moment, whether of suspicion or simply ignorance she could not tell. Then the short man spoke.

'Wolf-fires? What do you want wolf-fires for? Surely they would not attack the house?'

'Oh, no. The wolf-fires are lit each night around the home pasture . . . the big meadow near the house, d'you see it? There are little stone shelters too . . . usually one or two men stay in the shelters overnight to feed the fires and patrol the fencing. Then your stock is safe, you see.'

The woman giggled. Her face had lost its rapt expression and now showed merely greed.

'Our herds . . . our stock . . . dear me, I still can't believe it!'

'If you don't light the wolf-fires you won't have much to believe,' Pavel said as kindly as she could. 'Do go out and light the fires! The wolves will take all the yearling lambs if you don't, and then where will you be?'

The short man shrugged.

'We know nothing of it. They did not say we had to stay up all night to tend fires! Perhaps, when the others come, we will make them do it.' He turned away from Pavel, towards the woman. 'Where's my dinner? I'm hungry and there's food in that cupboard-room there.'

At the mention of food eyes lit, but Pavel remained stubbornly where she was, ignoring the impatient looks cast in her direction.

'I'm going home when I find out where the family have gone,' she said loudly. 'Can you tell me, please?'

'Which family?' the woman said. She was stroking Nyusha's newly baked fruit cake as though it were a dog or a cat.

'The family who lived here . . . the people who've just been taken away by the soldiers.'

'Oh, them. The *kulaks*, you mean. They might have gone to a collective or they might have gone to a timber camp; probably to a camp, since the man fought like a tiger to try to stop them killing the dogs, and . . .'

'Killing the dogs?' Pavel's heart gave a great thump. Thank God she had ordered Baru to stay on the far side of the clearing! 'Why did they kill the dogs?'

'Well, the dogs wouldn't let us in, you see,' the tall man said almost apologetically. 'The soldiers shot them . . . one was badly bitten first, though.'

'I see. Well, thank you.' Pavel turned and walked out. Behind her the woman suggested, in a voice that trembled slightly, that the young man might like to stay and share their meal. Pavel walked on; so Fedor had fought and would probably go to a timber camp . . . what was it he had said about them? Better to have freedom and each other than to die slowly. And now, because of her, he would do just that; die in pain and shut away, caged like a canary, unable to sing.

Presently, her feet scuffled through leaves and she realised that she had walked right away from the homestead, leading Katya, and was rapidly nearing the spot where she had left Baru. She peered into the darkness ahead and felt her heart lift as she saw the dog's great white body. She was lying on the pine needles, well off the main track, out of sight unless you were looking for her. Pavel whistled softly, under her breath, and Baru came bounding towards her, her long tail swishing gently from side to side, her mouth opening in a pleased grin.

'I'm back, girl,' Pavel bent and kissed the top of her head, then mounted her horse. 'Heel, Baru.'

She began to ride through the dark trees. It no longer frightened her and she no longer feared wolves. Why should she, when the world had turned topsy-turvy, when her life had been shattered?

By the time she emerged from the valley, she was calmer, thinking a little less confusedly. She should go through the Klukhor Pass immediately, before it occurred to them that she might even now be traversing its narrow passageway. But she could not do that, not with those she loved bound for a timber camp in the cruel north.

Of course, she loved David even more than she loved Eva and Fedor and Nyusha . . . or anyway, just as much. She could not split herself in two, so she must either go to David – and freedom – in Turkey or follow her family. And she remembered that someone had said they did not take children to those camps, because they would only get in the way and prevent the adults from working properly. So Eva, sooner or later, would leave Fedor and Nyusha and be alone. As she, Pavel, was.

Then there was Baru. She was not the sort of dog you forgot; if Pavel managed to trace Fedor and follow him, then sooner or later someone would notice the young lad with the huge white dog and then she would be taken in and questioned and she had no papers, no means of identification, indeed she did not wish to be identified, for if they knew she was Pavel Fedorovna then she, too, would be imprisoned.

She was riding along in the dark and the moon was coming up over the top of Mount Elbruz when she seemed to hear Fedor's voice in her ear; it was kindly now, perhaps even a little contrite.

'Sleep on it,' he was saying, 'and when morning comes you will know where your duty lies. Your mother and I are capable people, but Eva is only a child. Take care of your little sister.'

It was Fedor's voice, yet even as she nodded to herself over the good sense of his words it occurred to her that what she heard was an echo of something similar said to her long, long ago. In the time *before*? It was possible. She was out on the mountain top now, though, silvered by the moon. She had ridden without much purpose, but now she remembered the shepherd's hut they used sometimes in lambing time. She turned Katya's head in that direction and was soon taking off the horse's tack. Katya was a good little mare; she whinnied softly as she felt herself freed of the burden of saddle and bridle, then trotted off to roll in the still sweet grass and drink from a tiny mountain stream which ran nearby before beginning to graze.

Baru went straight to the shepherd's hut and investigated it, then returned to Pavel, wagging her plumy tail. She was saying in her own fashion that the hut was empty and there was nothing to be afraid of.

Pavel went into the hut and spread out the dried grass and bracken that was formed into a rough bed at one side. She lay down and wrapped herself in her *burka*. Outside, far off, she heard a wolf howl on one long, pensive note. It reminded her of something which niggled at her mind for a full minute before she was overcome by sleep.

Pavel awoke next morning to driving rain and a chilly wind, but neither was colder than her mood. She would find Eva, or she would have a very good try, and if she did not succeed then she would go to David. She would cross the Klukhor, drop down into Georgia and find a way, somehow, to get from there to Turkey. Common sense told her that to go at once would in any case not help her much. David could not possibly get her letter for at least a month, and then he would take a month, if not more, to arrive in Turkey himself. Russia was a big country, but Pavel was no fool; she would not simply launch herself indiscriminately into a search for her sister. She would follow Eva's trail and find her that way. If she could catch up with her in six or seven weeks well and good, she would somehow manage to spirit the pair of them to Turkey, but if not she reckoned the trail would be cold anyway and further search useless. Only then would she set out alone on the journey.

She eyed Baru with love and exasperation as they set off, however. She must sell Katya and journey by train, for she knew from talk in the market that most of the so-called *kulaks* were transported to their various destinations by rail, so whatever they had in store for Eva she imagined she would go there by train as well. But she could no more have sold Baru than she would have put a price on her own head. Also, of course, she was a marvellous guard dog and had frequently tracked, by smell alone, a lost animal. Perhaps she could sniff Eva out? Pavel wished she had had the foresight to go into the homestead and get some piece of Eva's clothing, but it did not really matter; a bit of cloth would lose its scent in time.

She would have to get Baru a collar though, and a piece of rope to lead her by, for though the dog would stick close to Pavel she might become panic-stricken on a train and try to jump off or bite someone.

It was then that Pavel remembered, for the first time, the huge amount of money on her person. That was marvellous – she could afford a ticket on the train right away, so she would not have to wait and beg or earn enough to follow her sister. She would ride Katya down to the market in the neighbouring town and she would sell her dear mare for as much as she could possibly get, and then she would go down to the railway station and ask some questions – discreetly, of course. And if anyone tried to molest her they would have Baru to deal with!

It rained steadily as horse, Pavel and dog made their way down the steep and soon slippery mountain paths, but Pavel spread her *burka* wide and Baru kept as close to Katya as she could get and probably none of them worried much about the weather – Pavel certainly did not; she must be hot on Eva's trail, for her sister had come this way barely twelve hours before her.

It took them all day, though, to reach their destination, and they arrived there too late to do much, a soaked lad, a soaked horse, a soaked dog.

Stabling and lodging cost money, which Pavel had but did not wish to spend too soon, so she let her horse loose in a field full of other horses and curled up under the hedge with Baru's body curled round her protectively. In the morning she would do so many things . . . in the morning she would find Eva and rescue her, sell Katya, catch a train to Turkey, befriend a dragon, rescue a knight in full armour, ride on a pink camel through the streets of Moscow first and London second . . . despite the rain and the burrs in the hedge, Pavel slept soundly and dreamed wildly all the long night through.

'It's a first-rate little boat; the chap's ever so pleased with it.'

Nibby spoke with his mouth full of toast and marmalade, and Alice, acting as mother to her family, leaned across the table and tapped his knuckles with her buttery knife.

'John Hawke, where are your manners?'

'Yes please, Allie, I'd love another cup of coffee.' Nibby

grinned at her spontaneous spurt of laughter. 'Sorry, but I was excited. So would you be if you sold the very first thing you made as quick as that.'

'I think we asked too little for her,' David observed, finishing his mouthful before he spoke, however; something told him that Alice's knife would have descended a lot harder had the fault been his! 'We were daft – we should have asked around a bit.'

'Oh, I don't know. We added up the wood and so on, put on something for our time, added a bit for luck and bob's your uncle!' Nibby took his refilled cup from Alice and cocked an eye at Michael, eating porridge with the fierce concentration of one who had arrived at the table a good twenty minutes after everyone else. 'Hi, old boy, don't choke yourself! It's downhill all the way, you can make it!'

'What's downhill? The road the porridge must take to hit the jackpot, in other words Mike's stomach? Ha!'

'Oh, David, you know very well Nibby means school.' Sara, demurely crunching toast, finished the last bite, wiped her mouth on her napkin, dusted her hands together and then addressed Alice. 'Please may I get down?'

'Yes, of course, love. Are you bicycling today?'

'No, I'm catching the bus, but I don't have to be in until nearly ten o'clock.' She pulled a face at Michael, still shovelling porridge. 'One of the very few privileges of being in the sixth form. And I'll be cycling home tonight, groan groan.'

'Why? Oh, of course, you left your cycle at school yesterday because you got a lift home. The only thing I worry about is wintertime, when they may not get through on their cycles,' Alice confessed as Sara rushed from the room in her normal breakneck fashion. 'Michael's getting taller and stronger every day, aren't you, duckie? but Sara's a little'un and I doubt she'll grow even an inch bigger.'

'She's tough enough, Sara is,' Michael said gloomily, scraping his porridge bowl with horrible squeaking noises of metal on china. 'If you think she's weak you want to get into the bathroom before her and forget to lock the door, that's all.'

'Why? Did she march in and drag you naked from the tub?' Nibby enquired. Alice frowned at him; she was not sure he ought to use words like naked in front of a young boy, and

Michael was rude enough without encouragement. However, Michael merely shook his head and grabbed a slice of rather cold toast.

'No, of course not. I mean in the morning – I don't have a bath in the morning. Well actually, I was washing . . . she said cat's lick and a promise but it was pretty vile washing really, the sort where you even take your jumper off and roll back your shirt collar . . . you know, real washing.'

'It's been known to take Mikey two weeks to reach the point,' David interrupted impatiently. 'I don't want to cramp your style, Mike old boy, but I do want a word with Nibs about the next boat and I find . . .'

'So there I was, really washing,' Michael went on, unperturbed by his elder brother's strictures, 'and in she comes, all red-faced and furious, grabs me by the hair, the short bits at the back actually, and runs me out into the corridor. I was wet . . . my collar was, I mean . . . and I still had the soap in one paw, and I couldn't see for water in my eyes and all I get for an apology is shrieks about a science class and needing sustenance and having to bicycle swear-word swear-word number of miles.'

'What? Bicycle swear-word swear-word? Mikey, have you gone off your chump at last?'

'Oh, do you want chapter and verse?' Michael opened his mouth, glanced at Alice, and thought better of it. 'Well, she said she needed sustenance because she was having to bicycle a darned blinking long way to school.'

'Sara never swore! Mikey, it's wrong and wicked of you to pretend she would.' Alice tried to look scandalised and failed miserably. The trouble was she was barely five years older than Sara herself and found it trying, to put it no stronger, being a mother to such a live-wire. As for Michael, she supposed he needed a father, but she pitied anyone who tried to curb his endless fund of breathy anecdotes or endeavoured to keep his physical energy from fizzing over every hour or so.

They were having breakfast in the kitchen as they usually did, but it was a far cry from the tiny room in which David had knelt on the sloping quarry tiles trying to solder water pipes together. The extension had somehow grown to include a nice large bit added to the kitchen, a separate pantry out to the side, and a neat little bedroom which Nibby inhabited quite cheerfully, and this had enabled them to turn one of the upstairs bedrooms into a bathroom.

'Post!' Sara announced, shooting the door open abruptly. She took aim and shied the letters into the middle of the table, where one knocked over the salt cellar and another landed upright in the butter. 'Sorry, chaps! Tennis is my game really, not cricket. Can I take a shilling out of the vase on the mantelpiece for my lunch, or will you make me some sandwiches, Allie?'

'A *shilling*? Good God, girl, school dinners are about three-pence, aren't they?' David reached over and rescued the letter still sticking out of the butter like a hatchet. 'Aha, for me.'

'Dinners may be threepence but stockings aren't, and I won't face the world with ladders all up and down my incredibly beautiful legs,' Sara told him. 'Tell you what, Allie, if you make me some butties I'll only take sixpence; I should be able to get some cheap stockings for that.'

'We can't dish out sixpences like water,' Alice protested. 'I'll make your sandwiches, dearest, but you'll have to darn the stockings. Why can't you wear socks, anyway? It's still quite warm even if it is October.'

'Allie, a sixth-former, wear socks? Look, I'd paint my legs black if it would help the family coffers . . .'

'It would,' Nibby said bluntly. 'Don't be so selfish, Sara. Alice is doing her best to manage on a shoestring until Dave and I make all our fortunes. Couldn't you ease off a bit?'

Sara promptly turned from a charming ginger kitten into a small but defiant cat. Her eyes sparkled and her mouth tightened, both dangerous signs. At first she had been charming to Nibby all the time, but lately she had started treating him not as a stranger to be impressed but as a brother. She hugged him boisterously when things went right and snarled and spat at him when they did not. Now he was daring to criticise, and it was clear to Alice that a dose of sisterly comment was about to be hurled at his unhardened only-child head.

'Oh, shut up, Nibby – if you bothered about family fortunes you wouldn't be here at all. You eat our breakfasts and dinners and then have the nerve to lecture me about being selfish!'

'Nibby pays for his keep, Sara,' Alice said warningly. 'Just be careful or you'll say something you'll be sorry for afterwards.'

Sara promptly rounded on her.

'Oh, shall I? You think he's marvellous, don't you, Alice? Dear Nibby, helping us to build our extension, making the engine for David's precious fishing boat, giving me a hand with my maths and showing Mike how the internal combustion engine works. Well, he's not family, whatever he might think, so why doesn't he keep his mouth shut?'

'I'll put you over my knee in a moment and give you the leathering you richly deserve,' Nibby said without heat. 'You're a spoilt brat, Sara Thomas, and the sooner you realise it and stop treating your sister like a slave and your brothers like dirt the better.'

'Me? Me? I adore Alice and the only person I treat badly at all, even a tiny bit, is Mike, and he understands, being a blood relation. Just mind your own business, Nibby Hawke, and leave me to mind mine!'

'Temper temper,' Nibby said insultingly, eyeing Sara from beneath his pale brown thatch. 'Redheads are all the same, fly off the handle the moment someone criticises, even . . . or perhaps I should say especially . . . if it's the truth they're hearing.'

Alice saw the slap coming; she winced for Nibby, but too soon. Used to fighting with David and wrestling with his university chums, Nibby simply grabbed both Sara's wrists, held them down, and then, whilst she was still raging, pinned them with one hand and smacked her bottom hard half a dozen times with the other.

When he let her go Sara stepped back and eyed him broodingly, her mouth trembling. Alice, who knew her sister very well indeed, guessed that she was poised between giggling and bursting into tears of frustration. Fortunately, giggles won.

'You cheeky blighter,' she said, but her eyes were shining. 'Nibby Hawke, how dare you, and me a young lady too! Why, anyone would think you were my brother, and brothers have died for less, let me tell you.'

'Going to say sorry to Alice and go off to school now, without any lunch unless you make it yourself? And definitely without money for yet more stockings?'

'Well, I'll think about it. Tell you what, you come and make me just a little teensy weensy packed lunch, Allie, and I'll somehow manage with these rotten old stockings for a week or two longer. In fact I'll go and see David's treasure tonight, on my way back from school, and see if she's got a moment free to darn them for me.'

The family had been referring to Maria Raft as David's treasure for several weeks, ever since David had coolly rung Maria up in an emergency and asked for the loan of her car.

'If she's fool enough to have a hopeless pash on someone who obviously doesn't return her interest, then she might as well be useful,' he told his sisters, when they reproached him for his heartlessness. 'Besides, we needed transport and hers was the free sort; much better than a cab.'

'Next you'll ask her to darn your socks for you,' the irrepressible Sara had exclaimed . . . and now it appeared she intended to do just that herself. David, who had kept diplomatically silent whilst the battle raged, thought it time to step in.

'If you go taking advantage of Maria you'll answer to me, young lady, and I shan't stop at a smacked bottom! Don't you have any of your allowance left?'

'No, I spent it all ages ago . . . why don't I borrow some from the vase on the mantelpiece until the next lot's due?' Sarah smiled brightly round the table, then whisked neatly to the door. 'That's that, then. Alice, my love, if you'll just get a move on with my packed lunch . . .'

'She's incorrigible,' David sighed as the door slammed behind his younger sister. 'Nibby's right, Alice, you shouldn't let the kids turn you into a sort of part mother, part housekeeper, part slave the way you do. I know you're trying to make up because they don't have any mother at all, but from what I can recall Mother never did what you do for them, she made them stand on their own feet a lot more.'

'I know; but have you ever been in the kitchen when Sara's making herself a snack? It's a lot easier for me to make it for her, really it is. And she's at the stage where appearance is terribly important, though Nibby's right about the stockings; she keeps asking for money for them and for other little things and it all mounts up and she really must learn to keep to a budget. When she's married she'll be grateful that she was taught economy at home . . . only I don't have the heart!'

The last few words came out as a wail. Both David and Nibby laughed, though David leaned over the table and squeezed her fingers.

'Poor Allie, all that and us and a job as well! Do you realise, you're the only breadwinner in this family at the moment? We are trying, we really are.'

'I know you are, very trying,' Alice said, smiling at them both. 'As for being the only wage-earner, what about that boat? How clever you were, selling it to the very first chap who came round to look! Now you must build another, and charge more for it this time.' She looked curiously at the buttery envelope in David's hand. 'Why don't you read that letter? Who's it from?'

'Yuri Obreimov, it says on the back – you know, that fellow who shared my flat in Leningrad; I wonder what he wants?' David stared at the envelope for a minute before wiping it with his napkin and slipping it into his pocket. 'I'll read it later, in our coffee break. Right now we've got to get down to the woodyard and pick ourselves out some decent timber for the next boat.'

'What about that letter then, Dave?'

The two men were sitting in the kitchen, both reprehensibly smoking, since Alice disapproved and would not let a cigarette or a pipe be lit up indoors when she was home to stop it. But the windows were open, the coffee was almost ready for drinking and Nibby liked to smoke at every opportunity, though David was too keen on his own physical fitness to have more than the occasional drag.

'Yes . . . I almost forgot.' But David, fishing the letter out of his pocket, knew he lied. He had not forgotten, he was just . . . wary. He did not really want to open it, find himself involved. Yuri was a good bloke in his way but it all seemed a long time ago – it was almost two years, when you thought about it – and it was best forgotten. They had parted friends, though if he'd realised he was going for good . . . but then he had done his best by Yuri, sending him parcels of soap, razorblades, insect powder and coffee beans whenever he could afford it.

'Go on, open it, don't just stare at it! Pretend it's from Pavel!'

'I wish it was; she hasn't written for months. I worry about what might be happening to her.' He opened the letter and there was a note from Yuri and an envelope addressed to David Alyn in her handwriting.

Just for a moment his heart plummeted, though a second later he would have indignantly denied it had done any such thing. It was excitement, perhaps a little worry over why she should have written to him via Yuri . . . he ripped open the second envelope but did not unfold the sheets therein; instead, he read Yuri's note.

*David – sorry your little girl seems to be in trouble, but after that business I suppose it was to be expected. I've sent her letter on unopened, of course, but she enclosed a note to me, as well. If I can help in any way let me know. Your friend, Yuri.*

What business? Surely not the trial of the engineers? To his knowledge his name had not been mentioned in connection with the alleged sabotage. He pushed the note across to Nibby, who read it and shook his head.

'I'm sorry, old boy. For God's sake, open her letter and read it. It may not be too bad.'

'I will, presently. But Nibs, Yuri wrote over three weeks ago – anything might have happened by now.'

'Read it!'

David smoothed out the sheets. There were only two of them and the writing was big, not at all like Pavel's usual neat hand, but as he read he realised why. Presently he laid the sheets down and turned to Nibby.

'She's going to leave the farm . . . they all are. Things were getting hot anyway, the State was obviously moving in, people in the lowlands had been losing their farms . . . Then the letter from me arrived, the one I told you about, suggesting that since I didn't seem able to get permission to travel to her she might come to me. Through the Klukhor Pass and then into Turkey. It had been opened, she said, and well scrutinised. I gather from this that she realised it was now or never . . . then or never, I mean . . . and the family planned to move out soon after she posted this. It's undated, which means she may be arriving in Turkey any day! My God, I'll have to go up to London, see if I can get some money to her at Trabzon . . . that was the plan I suggested. Do you mind if I desert you for a couple of days, old boy?'

'A couple of *days*? But you won't get to Turkey in a couple of days — it'll be more like a month, and then you'll have to wait for her; you said yourself it might take them longer to get across than one would imagine.'

'Well, I can't actually go *myself*,' David said, staring at his friend. 'I couldn't just go off . . . what about the business? And then there's the expense, and as you said the time . . . no, I'll have to see what the Foreign Office advises.'

He got up abruptly and left the room, calling over his shoulder as he did so, 'Just going to get my train timetable.'

Nibby stubbed out his cigarette and picked up his cup of coffee. He sipped but it had gone cold so he got up, poured the remainder down the sink, and made himself fresh. Brooding over the drink, he looked at the upside-down letter with its scrawling, panic-stricken script. It was in Russian, so David was safe enough; no one but David and Nibby himself in this household would be able to read a word. Poor little blighter, though . . . only a scrap of a girl, barely seventeen, yet David talked quite calmly of her making her way through some of the most hostile mountain country in the world, traversing another part of that same country which would be swarming with people who just conceivably might be her enemies, then illegally crossing a border . . . and all, so far as he could see, without a penny piece to bless herself with until after she had completed her journey.

David was expecting a lot of his girl . . . she must be quite a character. And then not even to meet her in Turkey, but to expect her to get herself on board a ship bound for Britain, to travel across a country whose language was as foreign to her as Russian would be to Sara, and to make her way to him. Unless he planned to meet her ship . . . not that he would be able to do so, since it was very unlikely that she would be able to tell him which ship it was and when she would be landing until too late.

Nibby sipped coffee and frowned at the letter upside down. David dushka . . . darling David. Without feeling at all guilty he began to read, though for some obscure reason he allowed the pages to remain upside down; it was less sinful that way, less like reading someone else's correspondence and more like doing a jigsaw puzzle.

David had told him most of what was in the letter, but naturally enough he had not managed to convey the fear, the disillusion, the pain of leaving her home and the worse pain because he would not be with her, which was all there for a discerning eye to read. She loved her little sister and worried about taking her on such a journey and then having to abandon her in a strange country, but was a little comforted because at least Eva would be with their parents, Fedor and Nyusha. She was taking Baru . . . that would be the dog David had mentioned, the one the girl had prevented from tearing him limb from limb on their first meeting. Well, that should mean that Pavel kept clear of the more obvious troubles . . . but then her father, or foster-father rather, would scarcely stand by and see her molested.

The second page was covered by the first but having gone so far . . . Nibby shifted the first page over so that he could finish reading. She was *not* afraid, she would come to him, he need not fear for her and she was, as ever, his loving Pavelinka.

Nibby shifted the first page back into position and drank the rest of his coffee. Inside him, a good deal of feeling against David was growing. It was not like his friend to let a girl go through hell and high water for him. Why was David apparently content to let her do it? Absence was supposed to make the heart grow fonder . . . or was it a case of out of sight out of mind? Was it possible that David had fallen imperceptibly out of love with Pavel? Because if Alice was in a fix like that I wouldn't send her money and write cheerful letters advising her how to cope, I'd go right there, even if it meant spending every penny I had, borrowing more and losing my little business, Nibby thought. And I'm not even in love with her! It was only as he said the words in his mind that Nibby knew, suddenly, that Alice meant something to him. He *liked* the girl, dammit, had liked her ever since that long-ago day when he'd found her howling her eyes out in the wood and taken her fishing. She was a sport, and something more: she was kind and courageous. She wasn't much more than a kid herself, yet she had tackled bringing up her younger brother and sisters with zest and was looking after himself and David with a good deal of skill, holding down a job as a shorthand typist with a firm of solicitors in Chester, coping with Sara's teenage depressions and elations equally well and never complaining that they expected too much, that she needed more help than was ever offered.

If it was Alice, Nibby dreamed, as the sun crept round and touched the letter with gold, if it was Alice I'd not hesitate, I'd leave everything and go off to Antarctica if need be to help her on her way. He could see it all so plainly, the frozen wastes, Alice in furs crouching on the peak of an iceberg being carried away from all she knew and loved. Cold, starving, terrified, he would find her, comfort her and put her on his reindeer sleigh, and before she knew it she would be tucked up snugly in a nice warm igloo which Nibby had built with his own fur-mittened hands, drinking hot seal-blubber soup and eating polar bear steaks and in between bites looking at him adoringly and saying, 'Oh, Nibby . . . you saved my life! I'll love you for ever!'

It was only as he reached this satisfactory conclusion and was leaning forward to take his just reward that it hit him like a blinding light, like a bolt from the blue, that he loved Alice. Damn David's waverings, blow his feelings for the little Russian girl, Nibby Hawke was in love – and it had taken his friend's lukewarm attitude to show Nibby's heart to Nibby's thick head!

When David came bouncing into the room two minutes later, waving his railway timetable, Nibby was sitting at the table staring into space with a particularly soppy look on his face. David frowned; had Nibby been reading his letter? Was he about to make some fatuous remark about Pavel's way of expressing herself? But Nibby said nothing, just continued to gaze in front of him as though he could see something marvellous – and slightly comic – there.

'I've got the timetable. I can catch the eight o five tomorrow morning and be in London by eleven. Why don't we dash down to the timber yard straight away and get the timber and any bits and bobs we need, and then come back here and get on with the early stages? After all, if we're going to follow the same procedure for this boat as we did with the last we'll work quite separately at first, until I've got the hull marked out and you've got the engine more or less together.' He waited for a reply, but Nibby continued to stare and smile. 'Nibby! I'm talking! What on earth's the matter with you? You look as mad as a hatter!'

'I was, but I'm not any more. I'm as sane as you. No, I'm a good deal saner than you.' Nibby came out of his abstraction and stared accusingly at his friend. 'Do you love Pavel or don't you?'

David was so surprised that for a moment he could only stare, mouth open, eyes round, but then he snapped out of it.

'Love her? Well, what do you think? Writing letters for months and months, trying to get permission to go to Russia again, travelling up and down to London when I could have been working, and now planning to get her out through Turkey so that we can get married. If that isn't love I don't know what is!'

'Love would be getting a move on and going to Turkey just on the off-chance of being able to help her,' Nibby said positively. 'Love would be hiring a fishing boat and lying offshore near the port you advised her to embark from. Love would be doing it yourself, not expecting someone else to do it for you.'

'You're mad!' David scowled. 'As if you've got a notion what love is! Oh, you've had scores of girls, I don't doubt it for one moment, but I do doubt that you've ever felt anything for them other than the usual urges and a mild affection. I *would* like to go to Pavel, of course I would, but it simply isn't practical, can't you see that?'

'Yes, I can see it isn't practical, but I can also see that if a girl's worth anything to you she's worth a bit of madness now and then. As for not having a notion what love is, you couldn't be more wrong; I've been in love for weeks . . . no, months . . . no, dammit, *years* . . . I was just too bloody thick to realise it. And now that I have I'm going to do something about it. Not right this minute because . . . but that's my affair. Take my advice, Dave, and be very sure of yourself before you send for Pavel, because as I see it she's one hell of a girl and she'll probably reach you somehow. And if you don't love her . . . tell her now, before it's too late!'

He saw David's face flush, saw his fist draw back, and then lights exploded before his eyes, there was blackness, and then pain was spreading from his nose to the rest of his face, and he and David were fighting in earnest for the first time in their lives. Punches, kicks, grabbings at hair, knees in groins, feet in faces, they rolled round the kitchen floor using language which would have turned Alice's hair white had she heard, until they were too exhausted to put any power behind their blows.

At last they stopped, each probably convinced that he had put the other to rout. David, breathing heavily, said: 'Well? Did you like that? You'll get more of it if you talk to me like that again.'

'More of what? You may have started it, my friend, but I fancy it wasn't you who finished it! Nose hurts, does it? And I reckon I loosened a tooth or two with that last punch.'

'That? It didn't shake one hair of my head; you're no boxer, Hawke. If you'd care to apologise . . .'

'Apologise? For what, may I ask?'

'For your hellish cheek in daring to doubt my love for Pavel.'

'Do you know, I'd quite forgotten what started it,' Nibby admitted. He touched his nose with a tentative finger; it hurt and the finger came away red. 'Perhaps I shouldn't have said it, but you shouldn't have said I didn't know what love was – not when I'd just that minute realised I'd been in love without knowing it for donkey's years.'

'Oh, is *that* why you had such a daft expression on your face?' David grinned. 'I thought you'd been reading my letter and found it amusing that she's so loving to me.'

'There's nothing amusing about . . .' Nibby began to bristle, then subsided, grinning. 'I say, I ache in every limb; how about you?'

'Snap! Still, we've got rid of most of our excess energy; now I shan't find sitting in the train all the way to London nearly so trying.'

'Glad I've done some good in the world.' The two eyed one another measuringly. 'We're too evenly matched, that's the trouble. It isn't a contest when we fight, it's who gets sick of the stupidity of it first.' Nibby looked round the kitchen; they had knocked the table askew, broken a chair and covered the floor with an assortment of coffee cups – smashed – coffee – spilt and biscuits – powdered beneath heaving bodies. 'We'd better clear up the mess. Alice is not going to be pleased.'

'Right. You take a cloth and do the wet bits, and I'll pick up the broken china.' David stood the chair upright and it fell sideways again. 'Oh hell, the stupid leg's gone! Never mind, we'll buy another bit from the timber merchant when we go down presently . . . shall we take a taxi? I don't know why, but I don't really fancy getting on the bus . . . look at your face!'

'Look at your own,' Nibby retorted, peering at his reflection in the window pane. 'Gosh, I do look a bit grim. All right, I'll ring for a taxi.' A telephone, fortunately, was essential to both their work and Alice's arrangements.

'OK. And whilst you're doing that I'll write to Yuri, telling him that I'd like to keep in touch. I won't say anything about Pavel – it might be too dangerous.'

But it was not until they were in the taxi and on their way to the timber merchant's that David said what was on his mind.

'Nibs . . . I wouldn't want you to think that your stupid talk had got to me, or that I cared a pin for your opinion or that I didn't thoroughly enjoy bashing you up . . . well, all right, I enjoyed being bashed too . . . but I think I may go to Turkey after all – I probably would have anyway, when it came down to it. But you made me think . . . no, you didn't make me think . . . I've simply decided that, in the circumstances . . .'

'Say no more,' Nibby said, grinning. 'I'll make two engines whilst you're gone and you can work damned hard when you get back and make two hulls. You wouldn't hit me in a taxi, would you?'

'I wouldn't bank on it. Why?'

'Well, I'd just like to say good for you.'

David grinned back. 'Feel free.'

'Good for you, then. Don't you want to ask me who I'm in love with, by the way?'

Now it was David's turn to do a bit of gloating. He raised his eyebrows. 'Me, ask you? When I've known for ages and ages? Go teach your grandmother to suck eggs!'

The taxi driver, no doubt listening avidly to a conversation he could not possibly understand, drew up at that point, shot open his little window, and addressed his customers.

'You've arrived, gentlemen; next round, please!'

Even taxi drivers, it seemed, could leap to correct conclusions sometimes.

# CHAPTER THIRTEEN

Pavel and Baru sat as inconspicuously as possible at one side of the big station platform, sharing a loaf of black bread. Pavel was nearer despair than she had ever been. They had followed Eva on that September morning a month ago, but somewhere along the line someone had thought they remembered her and been mistaken, or had mentioned the wrong train, or perhaps it was just that she had gone further and faster than they. At any rate, Pavel thought, it was time she admitted that they had lost her, and moved back into the country where Baru would not stand out quite so much and where she might find work.

At first, she had told herself that Russia was a huge country and she would disappear into its vastness like a drop of water into a lake, but she had not taken into account the Russian love of bureaucracy. Food was rationed – where was her ration card? In order to get a train ticket she must show some means of identification – what did she have to identify her? But she had got by, because she was young, willing to work, and in her black *burka* and walnut-brown *tcherkasska* clearly came from the Caucasus – a country cousin for whom the people of the plains had considerable respect.

But I'm lamentably dirty, Pavel told herself now, looking at the tan on her hands which was less than half the result of the sun; the rest was due to grime. She washed when she could, but opportunities were few once the countryside was left behind, and now that winter was stretching its chilly fingers across the land only an idiot would bathe in a stream when there were no means of getting either dry or warm again afterwards.

She and Baru were also hungry, hence the rapid disappearance of the loaf. It had not been so bad as she crossed the steppes and nipped off the train from time to time to buy food from the peasants who thronged the platforms of every small station, but here in Moscow it was different. She had obtained the loaf of bread illegally, she was pretty sure, but what did it matter? The boy in the baker's shop had offered it for a silver bangle and it had seemed cheap at the price . . . not that the bangle was a thin, poor one, for it was not. But when your stomach is flapping against your backbone, Pavel told herself severely, bangles don't matter all that much. Anyway, she was not supposed to be wearing bangles — lads did not — but she had pushed them right up her arm above her elbow and forgotten about them and this morning one of them had slid into view, probably because she had lost so much weight, and the baker's boy had seen it, so the bargain was struck . . . and she and Baru were eating their first square meal since the previous day.

One good thing about being in Moscow was that there were so many people that she could not possibly be noticed. David had lived here once and his friend Yuri lived here now, in the same block, she sincerely hoped, that he had moved to soon after the Moscow trials. At least, David had given her the address only about six months previously and mentioned it was not a good district; he knew because during his own time in the city he had also lived in that area.

She pondered on the advisability of going to see him, but decided against it. To be sure he could contact David for her, but what could he tell him? And could she trust him? She had no idea whether her original letter telling David that they were leaving and would go to Turkey had reached its destination.

Meanwhile, here she was at the centre of the Russian world, with all the things she had heard about at school available to her seeking eyes, and she was not at all sure she cared to go looking. She was very cold, very hungry despite the black bread, and very frightened. What good would it do her to see Red Square for herself, admire the Kremlin, feast her eyes on the minarets and spires, the domes and arches, of St Basil's? David, teasingly, had called it the Big Village, a colloquial saying which the people of Leningrad were fond of using, but to Pavel's awed eyes it was very far from the truth. Huge modern apartment blocks, asphalt streets and pavements, electric street lighting, all made Pavel feel thoroughly uneasy. Baru was stared at, too, in the streets, and she was glad to take her by her collar and hurry her back to the big railway station. But where next? She still had some money left, but dared she buy a ticket from here for herself and her dog? She had come to Moscow in a peasant's ox-cart full of cabbages because someone had told her about the wild children, the *bez prizorney*, who came into the cities when winter turned the country into a howling wasteland of snow and gales. In the cities at least they could find shelter in abandoned churches, and people would feed them from time to time, in return for carrying parcels, perhaps, or just because they were sorry for these young ones whose parents had been sent to the timber camps or killed during some trouble.

She had seen a tribe of the *bez prizorney*, but Eva had not been amongst them, so she might as well leave. The sheer size of Moscow frightened her, and her own position was so illegal, so fraught with terror, that she nearly fainted every time someone addressed her — she was not even the sex she was pretending to be, let alone the person!

The trouble was, even in this huge city it would be hard to get a rail ticket, especially, she imagined, for Kislovodsk, which was the station nearest to her erstwhile home. She could not go back there, of course, but she could return to the village and perhaps get a few days' work before striking up through the Klukhor Pass. On the other hand, with the worsening weather she would not get very far on foot, so the station it would have to be. Tonight? she asked herself dolefully, having come to her decision. Must I really buy a ticket by tonight? And her inner conscience told her that it would be advisable, for once on the train at least no one would take much notice of her, and she could eat whilst her money lasted.

She thought about telling Baru to stay, but it seemed rather risky; she was as little used to great concourses of people as Pavel herself and quite a lot more scared. She was trembling now; it would be too bad to desert her, to walk off to the booking office and leave her here surrounded by strangers and with the prospect of presently seeing another of the roaring dragons which was how Pavel imagined the dog thought of the trains. Instead, she looped her fingers through her collar and drew Baru with her to the clerk who sold the cheapest tickets of all, standing room only, packed into the trucks to sit or lie or squat on straw and sawdust, whilst the heat generated by one's fellow passengers at least ensured that no one died of cold during the journey.

A ticket to Kislovodsk was not expensive, but it took an awful lot of Pavel's remaining roubles and kopeks. Worse, though was the clerk's laconic explanation that the next train she could catch did not leave for two days. Two days! She and Baru could not spend two whole days and two nights as well on the crowded station! Yet what to do? She could not fritter her money away on a lodging, and anyway people in Moscow were frightened of Baru and steered clear of the dog's leanness and her excellent teeth.

But during her very brief walk through the city Pavel had noticed what appeared to be large areas of park; she and Baru could find somewhere to curl up there, and with her *burka* to cover them they would be safe enough if it would just forbear to rain or snow.

And then, as she began to move towards the station exit, she saw something which brought her heart leaping hopefully into a wild, staccato rhythm. A lean man, with a sheepskin cap on his dark head, wearing a *burka* which swirled round his calves much as Pavel's swirled round hers!

Pavel rushed forward and grabbed at the man's sleeve.

'Please . . . I see you are from my country . . . could you help me? I'm a long way from home and I've nowhere to stay . . . could you advise me?'

The man looked down at her. He had a dark, heavy face and rather thick lips, but he did not seem unfriendly.

'Yes? How do you need help, boy? What are you doing in Moscow in that rig?'

'Searching for my little sister,' Pavel said eagerly. 'They took our parents . . . I thought I might find her amongst the *bez prizorney*, but I've looked, and though they tell me more children will make their way here as the weather worsens she is not with those already in the city.'

'The *bez prizorney*!' The man made a gesture cut off short; Pavel saw that he had been about to cross himself and had suddenly remembered the State's views on religion. 'If your little sister is with them you'd do better not to find her. They're diseased, they say, suffering from all sorts of filthy ailments . . . tuberculosis, syphilis . . . if she's with them you'd better forget her, for she's as good as dead.'

'Oh, but she wouldn't have been with them very long,' Pavel said eagerly, still clutching the man's *burka*. 'They seized our farm about four or five weeks ago, no more. If I could find her now it might not be too late.'

'True. Do you want to stay in Moscow? Wait until the cold forces the *prizorney* within the walls to seek shelter? If so, I know a place where you and the animal could sleep for a few kopeks – not officially, you understand . . .' he winked at her, 'but on the quiet. And you can eat at a communal dining-room nearby. Would that suit you?'

'It would be wonderful,' Pavel said earnestly. 'Can you show me to this place?'

'Come with me and I'll point it out. My sister-in-law lives on the Street of the Red Candles. She's just divorced her husband and there are no children; she'll let you stay with her for a few days, I dare say. How old are you? Fourteen? Fifteen?' He tutted. 'It's a wonder you didn't run with the *prizorney* yourself, but boys of your age can be sensible enough when troubles strike.'

The man, who said his name was Caball, took her all the way to his sister-in-law's flat in the end and it was as well that he did, for Pavel would never have found it left to her own devices. It was on a mean and narrow street but it was quite a modern building, and it was strange to glance from cobbles set in sawdust and about as even as a stormy sea to the straight and ugly lines of pale brick.

'Sixth floor,' Caball said briefly. 'No lift; we'll have to use the stairs.'

Pavel saw that others had used the stairs, very literally, and stepped round the piles of human excrement on every bend with distaste. People behaved a good deal better than that in the country: you went on the muck-heap, where at least your contribution offended no one and could be used to enrich the soil!

The apartment, when they reached it, was one room, with, her hostess informed her, the use of a communal kitchen. She made a fuss of Baru, saying that she reminded her of her childhood, when dogs very similar to this great white beast had slept in the doorway at night and guarded the *kosh* by day, and it warmed Pavel's heart to hear the mountain word so far from home.

'Just to have company is good,' the woman said, when Caball had left them. 'My brother-in-law says you search for your little sister – you think she may have joined the *bez prizorney*?'

'It's possible. They took her away when they took our parents. I had been at market, selling our dairy produce, and when I came back I heard from neighbours that they had gone. I followed, but though I was not far behind I never caught a glimpse of them. So now I've come to Moscow just in case Eva should be here.'

The woman shook her head doubtfully. 'It's a big city, and the *prizorney* are shy, like wild animals. You may see one or two, but that merely means there are dozens more hiding under cover. It's like fleas; if you find one on a cat's back that means a hundred live in the thick of the fur.'

'Yes, but if I ask them . . .'

'Ask them? Well, I suppose you might get one to stand still long enough to ask, you being only a lad yourself. But right now you and that great long hound of yours need a meal and then some sleep. Will you go down to the communal dining-room? You can come with me . . . I'll say you're my nephew come to stay.'

'Will they let me? That would solve a lot of problems. And now how much do you want me to pay for my bed?'

The woman protested that she was glad of the company, but finally accepted a very small amount in kopeks and showed Pavel where she should sleep. She had laid a straw mattress on the floor in one corner of the room and it looked extremely inviting to one who had slept on the hard earth for more nights than she cared to remember.

'But first, food,' the woman said, bustling over to pick up a capacious handbag. 'Down we go . . . it isn't far but I'll pop my coat round my shoulders.'

She had a leather coat, dark and oily with age, but it looked warm – though nothing, Pavel thought, thankfully huddling into her own, compared with the *burka* for warmth and weatherproofing.

The communal dining-room was large and full of people, steam and food. Pavel and her new friend queued for plates of *bortsch* and drank it down with hunks of black bread. It was poor stuff, the beetroot thin and earthy, the sour cream non-existent, but to Pavel's starved stomach it was manna straight from heaven and she cleared her bowl. The trouble came, however, when she went for her main course.

'A nephew, eh? Then she'll be handing in your ration card with her own, I suppose. How long are you staying?'

Ration cards! Of course, she might have guessed she should have a ration card for this place. With food so scarce and winter coming on there would have to be some arrangement. But the man who had questioned her, a surly fellow so fat that his skin was stretched and shiny, proceeded to give her the answer to his question.

'Well, hers is due in another four days, so I s'pose I'll get yours then.' He sighed and picked a piece of potato off a plate, popping it into his mouth almost absently and swallowing it with scarcely a chew. 'Well, well, just like 'Tasha; very irregular, but I suppose it'll be all right.'

The main course was a good quantity of plain boiled potatoes and a very small piece of cheese. Afterwards there were glasses of tea and tiny, wrinkled apples. It might have seemed unimpressive to some but to Pavel it was all delicious, perhaps better for being virtually stolen from the State. She voiced the thought to her hostess, whose name, Natasha, seemed oddly unsuited to such a plain, frumpish woman. But when they returned to their room Natasha shed the heavy coat, sat down before a small piece of looking-glass, and proceeded to make up her face. She did it quite well and when at last she combed out her heavy brown hair and licked her finger to smooth it along her dark, nicely shaped brows, Pavel would scarcely have recognised her.

'You do look nice,' she said sincerely. 'Where are you going? Somewhere special?'

Natasha giggled.

'Special? Not particularly. I'm a single woman again now, remember. I thought I'd go out and see if I can meet a friend. I shan't be long. You can settle down to sleep if you want; I shan't disturb you coming in. I've got my key.'

Next morning, when Pavel woke, her first thought was that Natasha would undoubtedly turn her out today and no wonder! She had returned in the middle of the night, when Pavel had been sound asleep for several hours, with a friend, and

Baru had taken an instant — and dangerous — dislike to the friend, to whom she had not been introduced. Her thunderous growls woke Pavel, but before she could sort out her muddled, sleepy wits Baru had launched herself almost silently across the small room and seized Natasha's friend by the elbow.

The noise and fuss had come solely from Natasha's friend, and that had been of short duration because Baru had made it perfectly plain that she had no objection whatsoever to the friend provided he did not attempt to set foot in the room which Baru now regarded as her home.

'It's all right, love, you go back to bed. I'll be in presently,' was all Natasha had said last night, and sure enough after about twenty minutes Pavel had heard, even through her dreams, the older woman slip quietly in, lock the door behind her and creak into bed.

Now, sitting up in her rustling straw, Pavel peered cautiously across the room. It was pretty bare, just boards with a rag rug in front of the stove, a table and three wooden chairs. Natasha's clothes hung behind a curtain in the corner, her food was in a little wooden cupboard, and her personal possessions were few and kept either on the chairs or under her bed. The small square window, however, let in a lot of light, bright sunshine, and that plus Natasha's choice of tablecloth and rug — both blue and red — gave the plain room a cheery look. Pavel sighed for Baru, happily slumbering at the foot of the straw mattress, but did not blame her. She had been brought up to protect her own; you could not expect her to change overnight.

There was also a samovar, Pavel now saw, standing on top of the food cupboard. She slipped out of bed. Baru woke and wagged her tail slightly, then went back to sleep. She was no longer young, and had had a disturbed night. Pavel lit the charcoal in the base of the samovar and made the tea, and when it was simmering well and a good, clear brown, she poured a glass for herself and another for Natasha. Rather timidly she went over to her companion, who was just stirring.

'Natasha . . . I'm awfully sorry about Baru chasing your friend . . . I've made you a glass of tea.'

'Oh, my head!' Natasha sat up, clasped her brow for a moment, and then reached out a trembling hand for the tea. 'May that teach me not to drink neat vodka with a Cossack!

What a good lad you are. Fancy me getting my tea brought to me in bed . . . Franz would never believe it.'

'Was Franz your husband?' Pavel asked, sitting down on one of the wooden chairs. 'It's a German name, isn't it?'

'It is and he was . . . my husband, I mean. He came from German stock, may he rot.' Natasha sipped tea and the pained frown lifted from her forehead. 'Ah, that's better. I can think straight now. It's the tea; wonderful stuff, I try never to be without it. Where were we?'

'Where? Oh, I see! I'd just apologised for Baru's chasing your friend.'

'That's all right – I should have remembered what our dogs were like when I was small. He was an odd chap, too, probably best dealt with outside.' She grinned suddenly, looking younger and a good deal nicer sitting up in bed with no make-up on and her hair shining in the morning sun. She was not as old as Pavel had thought last night, either. 'Well, what do you want to do today?'

'Look for Eva,' Pavel said promptly. 'I think I should tell you, though, that I don't have a ration card. So I shan't be able to come down to the dining-room with you again.'

'Not come down? Why ever not? Oh, you're afraid you'll be clapped into the Lubianka for not having a card!' She chuckled richly and sipped her tea. 'No you won't, my dear, not whilst you're staying with me. I've done too many favours for fat Nik and the others, and anyway, it's simple enough to fool 'em. They're on for three or four days and then they have two days off. So you just say you gave your card in the day before, or you'll give it in when it's due, the day after tomorrow, and they'll be so busy with their own lives that they won't give it another thought.' She finished her tea and flung her legs out of bed, then appeared to think better of it. 'Shall I get up when you leave? I've got to clean up a bit.'

'No, why . . . oh, I see!' Pavel made a quick decision. 'I should tell you, Natasha, since you've been so good already – I'm a girl, not a boy. I'm wearing boy's gear because, as you must remember, mountain girls aren't usually allowed to do things like sell produce at market and so on. Well, they can sit behind a stall and sell, but not stride round the auction rings with cattle and poke at sheep with a long staff and then ride back with the herd.'

299

'A *girl*?' Natasha giggled, then threw back the bedclothes again and put her feet down on the floor. 'Well, that would make Caball think! I know very well why he brought you here, apart from wanting to give you a helping hand, like. He thought if I had a young lad about the place, especially a young lad with a great dog like Baru, I wouldn't go bringing fellers back.'

'He was right,' Pavel pointed out, grinning. 'Though you did try! What's wrong with bringing fellers back?'

'The State doesn't approve, and for once the church would agree with it, if it counted any more, which it doesn't. But Caball is still very religious and disapproves of a girl making up for marrying a wet-mouthed, pussy-footing lump of lard like Franz by taking another chap in now and again.'

'You took me in,' Pavel observed, drinking her own tea carefully, for it was still hot. Natasha, she thought, must have leather lips. 'In fact it was Caball who brought me here, so why should he disapprove of other men?'

'Other men! For one thing you're a lass, and for another even when you were pretending to be a lad you were a helluva baby one! I like men, really like 'em. Besides, I make a few kopeks here and there, or they bring me tea, or fancy biscuits or silk stockings . . . whatever they can manage; I'm not greedy. See what I mean?'

'Er . . . yes, I see what you mean,' Pavel echoed hollowly. She had heard of what Fedor had called wicked women, women of darkness, sisters in sin; had she now met one – nay, spent the night with one! But Natasha had round and innocent eyes and a gay smile and her body was comfortable, neither lean nor fat but a pleasant, bulging sort of shape. Motherly. That was it: motherly.

'Well, there's no harm in it. Now you make more tea, luv, and I'll have a good think whilst I dress. Caball knows I feed the *bez prizorney*, same as I would birds, when the winter sets in. Mind, that doesn't mean to say I *know* them, but like birds they get to trust you. I dare say I might ask them a question or two in a few weeks, when the snow's really thick and they need all the food they can get hold of. What's your sister's name again? Eva. Hmm. Well, I can ask. And what's your name, chick, if it isn't Pavel?'

'It is; I was named for a friend of my father's.' Pavel busied herself with the samovar and watched Natasha's ablutions with approval. Might she, too, presently wash with equal fervour? It was a good job she was a girl in truth, for Natasha had simply tossed aside her stained petticoat and there was nothing beneath it except Natasha's satiny pink flesh. But Natasha, scrubbing briskly, was still thinking about her new friend's problem.

'A little girl, eh? You're sure she didn't go with your parents? If so, they might have ended up on a collective. Are you sure they were sent north, to the camps?'

'Yes, pretty sure.' Briefly, Pavel sketched her meeting with the peasants and her last view of her family as they were carried off. Natasha listened gravely, nodding from time to time.

'I agree,' she said when the story was finished. 'They'll have gone to the camps; your father was too hard-working to escape that, and your mother by the sound of her. But the child . . . who can tell? They did take her? They didn't leave her in the village?'

'No. I asked. She was put on the train with the others.'

'Was she very young? Or was she a capable child, strong and good with her hands?'

'She was nearly thirteen and very domesticated. She could do most of the things that Nyusha . . . our mother . . . could do. She was strong, too, for her age, though I was very much stronger because of having to be Fedor's son most of the time.'

'I wonder? She might have gone to a collective, you see, in which case you needn't worry about her. She'll work hard but she'll be fairly treated and will probably marry well. Pretty, was she?'

'Oh yes, much prettier than me! Curls, blue eyes . . . that sort of thing.'

'You're very pretty,' Natasha assured her. She put her petticoat down on the bed and picked up another one, much washed but clean, slipped into it, and added a brown woollen skirt and a natural wool cardigan. She had talked of silk stockings but slid her bare feet into heavy walking shoes without even a cotton pair on. 'Now, I'm off to work as soon as we've eaten – will scrambled eggs on toast suit you? Good. I work at the tram depot. Today I'm eight thirty until four o'clock, so can you take care of yourself whilst I'm gone? We'll eat in the dining-room tonight, but if I were you I'd keep the wolves at bay with a handful of nuts or a hot corncob from one of the kiosks rather than risk the dining-room without me. And in the meantime you can wander round Moscow and see the sights and ask for that little sister of yours.'

'That's fine by me,' Pavel assured her. 'Is there anything I can do for you, though? Any shopping? Or housework?'

'No, not really. I'll make up the stove before I go, though one of these days I'm going to get myself a gas fire – they're so much less work. You spend today getting to know the city and searching out the haunts of the *bez prizorney*. Later on, if you'd like it, I'll see if I can get you a job, but not yet. Do your learning of the city first.'

They gobbled scrambled eggs on toast in companionable silence, drank another glass of tea apiece, and then Natasha jumped to her feet as outside a clock chimed the hour.

'Heavens, I must dash; they hate it if I'm late, it puts all the shifts out,' she said, inexplicably to Pavel. 'See you later, chick!'

Left to herself Pavel washed up, wiped up, put away, tidied, dusted . . . and then remembered that Baru had been indoors since the previous night. So she slung her *burka* over one shoulder – it was a fine and sunny day, but there was a nip in the air – and started down the stairs, not forgetting to lock the door behind her with Natasha's spare key which she had lent for the purpose.

'Come on, Baru, let's take a look at the place,' she said to the dog as the two of them descended the smelly staircase. 'It'll be quite fun now we've got somewhere to lay our heads.'

'Wake up. Wake *up*, will you? We'll have the entire Red Army down on us if you go on making that noise!'

Eva woke; she was trembling and sweat streamed from her. When the dream came it had to be endured, but she was grateful to Kevi for waking her and she sat up, rubbed her eyes and looked about her, seeing the familiar shape of the ruined church gratefully, even smelling the dirty, animal-like smell of the *bez prizorney* with something like pleasure.

'You all right? Were you dreaming about the day they came?'

Eva nodded, relaxing now against the wooden pew which

was the nearest thing to a home she had just at present. She never knew quite what the worst part of the dream was, whether it was seeing the soldier beating Fedor's face to a pulp, or whether it was what happened afterwards, on the train.

She had not told even Kevi about what happened on the train, though she sometimes wondered if he knew; he was a very knowing boy, though only a couple of years older than she. But he had been on the loose much longer, as long as he could remember, almost, though he did sometimes talk of another life, long ago, when he had had a mother of his own and she had spoken of his father, a soldier with that same Red Army who were his sworn enemies.

'Why did you leave them? Why did you join the *prizorney*?' she had asked him, but he was vague about it, as so many of them were. His father had left one day and never returned, his mother had found a man to take care of them both, but he was a cruel man, a beater of small boys who were not of his own getting . . . he had run, hidden . . . when he had returned, cold, starved and without hope, they had gone. Other people lived in his step-father's small log cabin, tilled his mean acres. When he asked, he was told that his stepfather had had too much money and too high a position, and had been taken away by Them.

Them, in this instance, meant the authorities, which probably meant the Red Army. So Kevi had been truly homeless and not just a runaway, and he had begun to steal, to run very fast, to hate.

Most of the *bez prizorney* hated, and with reason. Every man's hand seemed to be against them, yet it was no fault of theirs that they were cast on the land to live as best they might. They had all had parents once, and good homes . . . the better the homes, it seemed to Eva, the harder they had fallen from grace, as though being punished for the hard work of their parents by becoming homeless, hungry and scorned.

Her own case was really no different. Her parents had been taken to the camps in the north and she had jumped from the train, so whether or not they had intended to house her on a collective with good people to take care of her (and that was their avowed intent) she had no means of knowing. She had not taken the chance; she had jumped train, had hidden, had starved . . . and had been rescued by Kevi.

He was her saviour and therefore her God. He was tall for his calling, for the *prizorney* tended to be stunted through disease and lack of food, and he was handsome, too, by their standards, with his tangled dark curls, his broad forehead, high cheekbones and dark, dark eyes. He was thin, that went without saying, but he was very strong, and he had a desire to be clean which again was unusual in the company he kept and had a strong sense of compassion for those less able, which made him a natural leader.

He had found Eva trying to sleep under a bench in a park in some town which was, to her, nameless. He had picked her up as another might have picked up an abandoned puppy, fussed her, fed her, and told her to follow, and like the puppy Eva had adored and obeyed.

He led his tribe well, with a good deal more flair and finesse than most, so Eva was assured by other children. Igor was next in age and importance to Kevi and he had run with other tribes, but this was the only regime, as he put it, under which he had grown fatter and happier. Kevi wanted to lead for the good of all and not just for himself. Eva, Igor said impressively, was a very fortunate girl to have come first under the wing of such as Kevi.

But meanwhile, Eva was awake and hungry and rapidly forgetting her dream as the chilly autumn air, with winter on its breath, whistled through the dilapidated wooden door hanging off its hinges and in at the gaping, glassless windows. However, it was a better shelter than most; at least you had a roof over your head, and when the snow came it would only come into the building during gales and storms, when it would drive through the gaps and no one, not even Kevi, could block up so many and such various apertures.

Everyone was either awake now or stirring. There were a dozen of them, their ages varying from Kevi's fifteen or so to Katinka's eight or nine. Kevi had an old blanket which he had fashioned into a crude cloak; he slept in it and only removed it when the weather was warm enough to wash, briefly, in street fountains, or in rivers and streams when the tribe was in the country. But now he was unfastening the strings round his neck and having an almost ritualistic dabble in the great stone font which had collected rainwater as it blew in from outside.

'There . . . have a wash, of sorts,' he invited his merry men, all of whom knew better than to disobey, though Igor had assured Eva that no other tribe of the *prizorney* would ever dream of using water for such a strange purpose. Katinka, last as usual, whined and tried to escape, but Kevi would have none of that; if you were with him then you did as he said. He grabbed Katinka's little grey neck in one strong paw and dunked her hands, rubbed her face briefly and then took a remnant of rag from under his particular pew and allowed her to dry herself as best she could.

'It's getting bloody cold for washing,' Igor said mildly, as they began to file towards the church door. 'When the snow comes we don't, though he makes us rub snow into our hands and faces before we eat, and if we find clothes we're supposed to change whenever we can.' He had taken it upon himself to instruct Eva in the way Kevi ran their daily lives, though since Kevi was always dropping bits of information her way it was scarcely necessary. Eva knew the one golden rule – obey Kevi or go. She would not have disobeyed him for the world, even if he had told her to go and jump off a high cliff, because she knew his commands made sense. The first time she had stolen for the tribe he had gone with her and when she had bungled it, as he must have guessed she would, he had created a diversion so masterly that she had escaped at a jog-trot. Now, of course, she was as efficient a thief as he could wish because he had taught her himself. Most tribes relied upon snatch and run, but Kevi's people had perfected the art of stealing slowly, without even being suspected half the time, let alone caught. You had to look respectable for a start, which was one good reason for washing, and you had to have a few kopeks, which was why he would never let them spend until they were sure of another few kopeks to fish out of a grubby pocket and thus attain instant respectability. *Bez prizorney* did not own money; they did not earn money, either. But Kevi's people did. A reasonably clean child might be asked to carry home a parcel, brush snow off a pathway, hold a horse or a dog whilst its owner went into a shop, but a filthy, starving ragamuffin would not even get the time of day from a passer-by.

With money thus earned a child would be sent to a baker's shop, where he or she would purchase quite legally a bag of buns. But with quick and gentle cunning that same child, whilst waiting in a queue or leaning over a display to point out the particular bun he or she had set its heart on, would sweep into its dilapidated old carrier bag any number of desired items.

Respectability was retained by stealing clothes put out to dry, by using an ancient piece of comb and of course by the washing Kevi thought so essential. Also, he very sensibly tried to catch his tribe members as soon as they went on to the streets; not for Kevi the sly, quick-fingered pickpocket who had been on the loose for years, or the filthy guttersnipe begging on street corners. He would sooner have an illiterate, untrained peasant of six or seven, with a background of cleanliness, honesty and hard work, even if the child then had to unlearn most of his upbringing.

'Where are we going?' Eva asked softly, as they clustered just inside the church door. Another rule was never to leave a building all together. Once They knew a tribe of *bez prizorney* were gathered in one spot, They would not rest until They had either run them out of town, thrown them into prison, or exterminated them.

'To get maize,' Kevi said briefly. 'Not all of us, just . . .' his eyes slid over them, 'just Ivan, Eva and me. It's early still, so it won't be difficult.' His eyes travelled over them again. 'You . . . you . . . the two of you can get some milk. The rest light a *very* small fire in the place at the end, using the dry wood. Clear?'

Nods from everyone, no arguing.

'Right. Ivan, d'you want to go first?'

No one really wanted to go first, because if They were waiting for you . . . it was like being the first mouse out of the hole in the morning, or the first sparrow down on the ground. But it was a test of strength and they recognised it as good for them. Ivan nodded bravely. He was a fair lad of twelve or so with pointed, prominent ears that went red when he felt embarrassed; they went red now, and looked like two roses on either side of his thin face.

'Eva; next?'

Eva nodded too; she loved being second out. Nice and safe in the middle, with Kevi, strong and wonderful and brave, to keep your back warm.

'Right. Then Fedya and Katinka for the milk. You can go together, but not out of the front door, out of the window round the back. Off you go, Ivan.'

Ivan went to the door and pushed it open a crack; he looked through the crack, into the grey morning. Then he slid round the wood. Eva allowed him the regulation hundred steady, normal breaths and then slid through the same gap in the same manner, but the moment you were out in the open you began to act. You weren't going anywhere in particular, you were just wandering . . . you were thinking about visiting the child next door, who sometimes asked you to breakfast . . . you were on your way to school and not too keen to get there . . . you were shopping for your mother but the bag was heavy and you hated shopping . . . it must all be there, in your attitude, in the angle at which you held your head, the way your feet slopped through puddles or shushed through fallen leaves or slurred through thick snow.

The maize was kept piled high in sacks in a warehouse. Sooner or later the warehousemen would think they had a rat . . . the hole in the sack was nibbled-looking, genuine. They would blame their three fat cats and the sharp, cocky little terrier dog who patrolled the building; Eva was sorry for that, sorry that the animals would be blamed, but better that than to be found, to be seized, to be punished for all the bad things – the stealing, the deception, the trespass. And, for her, the thing that had happened on the train.

She did not know what the punishment was for her own particular, hard-kept secret. She did not want to know. She just wanted to avoid it and to stay with Kevi and the tribe, so she scuffed and idled her way to the warehouse, slid down the side of it, and, with the two boys, made her way in through the little door which the men used, silent as a shadow, quick as a flicker, using their knowledge, built up over days, of how the place was run. A nightwatchman grew weary towards grey dawn and dreamed and dozed in his chair. No one knew the *bez prizorney* were in town, so no one took precautions against them. Slip in through the little door, go down on all fours and crawl quietly and quickly into the shelter of the first sacks, reach the holed one, bring out your stealing bag made of soft linen and sewn up with nice clean string and begin to scoop out the golden maize until your bag is comfortably full.

There was string round her waist under her full skirt. She attached the bag to the string, leaving her hands free, and, at a signal from Kevi, retraced her steps, going through exactly the same routine in reverse. Outside once more, with three full bags of maize, they separated, also as before. One child was less suspicious than three, could spot a pursuer more easily, and would then have two others to call on for a diversion, for the other two would not be far away.

Back at the church the fire was burning steadily and the milk was being poured into a pan. Eva was a good cook, and Kevi had been heard to boast that he had *known* she was a good cook as soon as he set eyes on her. Now, she sat down, untied her bag of maize, and went and fetched the stuff which they had crushed yesterday. She mixed it with milk, some butter and a very tiny bit of sugar and then flattened it into thin rounds on a piece of tin. It was not ideal, but baked it was more than palatable, it was good. She made up sufficient cakes for them all and Katinka squatted on her heels on the far side of the fire and heated the milk. When it was ready they had hot bread and milk followed by the maize cakes. It filled them, satisfied them really, for the long day ahead.

When everyone had eaten – Katinka was very slow – Kevi doled out their tasks for the day. Two would pound the maize acquired that morning, two would try to get a corner of the church fairly protected against the weather so that they could lie dry even when it snowed, two would do their best to make a very large stolen shirt fit Igor. The rest would go to the market and wander around nice and slowly, with a kopek or two in their pockets for cover, seeing what they could pick up and if they could get a job, payable either in cash or in kind. It was schooltime, so he did not want the little ones in the market, but the others were safe enough. Even Ivan, who looked far younger than he was, could easily have left school.

'Can I come with you?' Eva asked, as they tidied away all traces of their breakfast. No one ever came into the church, but if they did it would not do for them to see traces of occupation. Kevi considered, then nodded.

'Don't see why not. We do rather well together, don't we?' It was true; they were an attractive couple, and Eva's clothes still fitted her, which meant that she was not forced to wear unsuitable garments. Kevi, as leader, naturally had his pick of whatever was available, so he usually managed to keep fairly neat. 'I want some vegetables – a cabbage or two would be nice

308

-- and apples if there are any -- we'll try working for them first, though.'

They would try to work for them first not because of any objection to stealing but because one could not steal fruit and vegetables and then continue to stroll around and look for work -- if a cabbage fell out of a girl's knickers she would be unlikely to be trusted near a stall which sold them!

The market was full. Peasants sold, townspeople bought, there were children both buying and selling. Presently, Kevi quickened his pace and got ahead of Eva and right up against a stall full of cabbages. Someone jostled, someone shoved . . . and one of the legs of the stall unaccountably folded in, or under. At any rate, the cabbages tipped on to the ground, a bouncing, rolling river of them, whilst the stallholder roared and tried to prevent a pile of carrots and parsnips from following suit.

Kevi was quick and helpful. He shouted to the man to grab the table, bent down and straightened the erring leg -- which he had just kicked out with his own clever foot, as Eva had seen -- and then began to pick up the cabbages, shouting to his little sister to do the same.

Eva collected cabbages in her skirt and carried them to Kevi, who piled them back so neatly and beautifully, in such symmetrical pyramids, that the stallholder was moved to observe that the stall looked all the better for the accident -- and to present Kevi with five kopeks and Eva with her pick of the cabbages.

The morning's work had got off to a good start. Eva, with dawning delight -- all feigned, naturally -- picked the cabbage she had had her eye on and had meant to acquire by fair means or foul, Kevi thanked the stallholder profusely and offered to come by when he'd done his mother's marketing and help the man to clear up, and the two of them strolled on their way, well satisfied. Possibly it crossed Eva's mind that they could have got away with half a dozen carrots and a parsnip or two if they had merely grabbed and run, but that would have been the last thing they would have had from the market that day. This way -- Kevi's way -- the pickings might well continue to come thick and fast for three or four hours.

'It's not too bad, is it, young 'un, whilst the weather holds,' Kevi observed as they walked. 'It gets tough when the snow starts, though. But we'll get through, you wait and see.'

If he was talking to calm doubts, they were his own and not Eva's. She had faith in her God.

'Do you know, I was going to leave Moscow? If your brother-in-law hadn't come along I'd have waited on the station for two days and gone back to the mountains. But now that I've met you and got somewhere to stay, I'm more determined than ever to search the city properly. And there's another thing . . . if I was respectable and in a job, might it not be possible for someone to tell me where Eva was sent? If it was a collective I might visit her legitimately, might I not? And you say they wouldn't send her to a timber camp, but that she might have been turned off the train anywhere if they didn't have plans for her.'

'That's right. If the State did what it said it would do and let all the children of so-called *kulaks* go on to the collectives there would be no *bez prizorney*, so it's clear that most of the children simply escape the net because the soldiers know that there's nowhere for them to go, not really. The peasants on the collectives don't want kids everywhere, and discontented kids, furthermore, with sizeable chips on their shoulders – kids who know a good deal better than the peasants how to run big farms. But you say she's efficient and pretty, so she might easily have been sent to a collective, found useful and kept. It's my belief that the children who are dumped on the collectives by the State don't run away at all, they're turned out. After all, they must be a drain on the community.'

Pavel and Natasha were sitting in the Park of Culture and Rest, eating hot pancakes which dribbled thin fruit jam on to their fingers. It was a chilly day with a lot of high cloud and a brisk wind, but Natasha had been shut in her stuffy office at the tram terminal for six long days and this was her day off, so she had suggested a visit to the Park.

'You can go into the stadium or the planetarium if you feel like watching athletes practising or want to see how the stars move in their courses,' Natasha had remarked. 'For my part I simply need to breathe some fresh air, eat something more amusing than the stuff served in the communal dining-room, and watch the passers-by.'

Despite her feelings, though, she had consented to stroll

310

round the various pavilions, chattering like a starling all the while, so that Pavel could see the wonders of science and contemplate the miracles which would presently be done by the Communist Party for the good of the people.

Having stimulated their minds and fed their faces – Natasha's choice of phrase – they drank weak lemonade and took shelter from the now much stronger wind in a kiosk erected for the purpose. Here they laughed together over the faces and figures of every well set up young man who passed them, and Natasha tried to persuade Pavel to put on a skirt and high-heeled shoes and try her hand at catching a fellow, as she put it. Pavel, however, was firm. She was safer in her breeches and *burka*, Eva would instantly recognise the garment as being from her own country, and besides, she did not want a young man.

'I have David, who is going to marry me,' she explained rather proudly. 'One day we shall be together.'

'Well, don't keep him waiting too long,' said the practical Natasha, 'or you may wake up one morning and find he's someone else's husband. Does he know where you are now?'

'Well, no. But he – he's a long way away himself, so he won't worry for a bit.'

'No? Well, if I were you I'd get in touch.'

'I would, but letters take weeks and weeks and they get opened.'

Natasha laughed. 'Opened? My dear girl, you're imagining it! Why on earth should anyone want to open a love-letter?'

'He's not Russian,' Pavel said briefly. 'His letters to me were opened and mine to him.'

'Ah, I see. A foreigner, eh? All right, all right, don't tell me if you don't think I'm trustworthy.'

'It isn't that! As if I could doubt you after all you've done for me! But it could be dangerous for you to know too much, really it could.'

'Oh, come on! Just to know his nationality? I don't get it.'

'All right, then. He's English. He's an engineer.'

'My God!' Natasha looked at her young friend with new respect. 'One of the traitors, you mean?'

'No! I don't suppose any of them were traitors, but he'd left the country months before the trial. His mother was taken very ill, so he had to go home, and of course they won't let him

311

back. We – we were to be married last summer.'

'You were? And of course you couldn't . . . oh, poor Pavel-inka! Never mind, you'll marry your engineer some day, perhaps.'

'I will. If he were here I dare say he'd be able to find out what's happened to Eva for me. Oh! Now I wonder . . . at least I could get word to him not to . . . Natasha, I *do* know someone in Moscow who might be able to help me.'

'You do? Who?'

'David's friend, Yuri Obreimov. I've got his address and everything. He might even get a message to David!'

'Well, why didn't you say so at first! What's his address? We could go there now.'

'I don't know it by heart, but it's written down in my room, in the little book I keep by my bed. I'll think about it before I go, though. You see, he was David's friend a year or two ago, but I don't know whether they've kept in touch. He might not want to be involved.'

'Well, think about it. And now . . .' Natasha stretched and yawned, showing her very white and even teeth and the scarlet of her tongue. 'Now I think we ought to go home, so that I can make myself beautiful for this evening.'

Baru had enjoyed the walk to the Park and had behaved beautifully, and when they got home Pavel fed her and settled her on her piece of old blanket in the corner before lying down on her own bed. She wanted to think. She had not been speaking the truth when she told Natasha she did not know Yuri's address by heart: it had been on her mind ever since she arrived in Moscow. She was half afraid to go there, though, in case he no longer lived in the apartment or had not received her letter to David. However, she had spoken no more than the truth when she told Natasha that he might be able to help her – he really might. He could get in touch with David, for a start, and explain that Pavel could not possibly just abandon Eva and leave the country. He could say that Pavel would go to Turkey as soon as she could, but now it would not be until next spring, or possibly even next summer. Someone, once, had bidden her to take care of Eva, but though she had tried she had not succeeded in keeping her little sister safe. It worried her that sometimes she had dreams which always broke off before they got to the point; she would be in a poor sort of place, in the dark, men would talk, women would cry out, there would be sharp noises and a brilliant flash of light . . . and then she would wake up, with tears on her cheeks, unable to remember what her dream had been about or why she should have been crying. All she did know was that the dreams were in some way connected with Eva, that they had something to do with the person who had bade her take care of her little sister.

So now, with a train ticket to the mountains hidden away beneath her straw mattress, she could not just turn tail and run to David. She simply must try to find Eva, even if it took her months. And one way to find her could well be to contact Yuri. He was in some sort of government service; he could easily find out whether a child named Eva Fedorovna was living on a collective farm somewhere in Russia.

The more she knew of Natasha though, the more she liked her and the more she realised that the older woman wished her nothing but good. Yet she could also see that Natasha was by nature open and easy-going. If someone asked her something about Pavel the chances were that she would genuinely forget her guest wanted secrecy, and might easily blurt out a truth which would endanger them both – Natasha for hiding her and deceiving the communal dining-room about her so-called nephew, and Pavel for being here, without papers of any sort, when she should by rights have been in a timber camp, working herself to a slow death.

So she would contact Yuri, but she would do so whilst Natasha was working at the tram terminus and she would not let her friend know what she had done. For once she would leave Baru in the flat, which she would hate, but she simply dare not risk taking her to Yuri's apartment; she was too noticeable. If David's friend did not answer the door she would simply say she was a relative of a friend; if Yuri himself asked her in then she would still pretend to be merely a relative of Pavel Fedorovna's, until she was quite sure that Yuri would not inform on her to the State.

Just how she was to make sure she had no idea, but at least her mind was now made up. Comforted, she got out of bed, undressed down to her shirt, got under the covers and fell asleep quickly.

Perhaps because she had made her mind up to consult Yuri, or perhaps because she had got very tired walking all round the Park of Culture and Rest, she slept at once.

She did not dream.

It was in an unexpectedly shabby and neglected area of the city when at last she found it, but Yuri's apartment block was very respectable, its brickwork clean and unscored by the weather, its small foyer spotless and gleaming. There was a lift, but Pavel did not fancy being shut into it so she took the stairs, counting flights until she emerged at last on to the right floor and walked along the shiny corridor, now counting door numbers until she came to E57. She knocked.

She did not have long to wait; the door opened and a woman's face appeared round it. She looked enquiringly at Pavel. She did not smile.

'Yes?'

'Umm . . . is Yuri Obreimov at home, please? I'm related to a friend of his, and I'd like to see him for a few minutes, if I may.'

The woman did not answer yes or no, she simply shut the door, but it was a modern, flimsy door and Pavel was able to hear quite distinctly the one-sided conversation which followed.

'Yuri? There's a young fellow outside, says he's a friend of yours, wants to see you.'

Short pause for mumbles, then: 'I didn't ask. Shall I?'

More mumbles, then the door opened about six inches.

'What's your name, please?'

'He doesn't know *me*, it's my friend he knows . . . oh, tell him it's Pavel.'

It was a very common name, God knew, and a fellow's name to boot, so it would mean nothing to Yuri. And she was right, it meant nothing. There was more talk through the door and then it was opened fully and a man stood there. He was tall and thin, with thick, light brown hair and a pair of ugly little glasses perched on his nose. He was wearing a blue open-necked shirt and flannels and his feet were bare.

'I'm awfully sorry, old chap, but my woman's got a bit muddled . . . said you were a friend of mine but I've never seen you in my life before, so it's obviously a mistake. You were looking for me, were you? Yuri Obreimov?'

'Yes . . . I'm a friend of a friend,' Pavel was beginning, when she heard the whine of the lift ascending. It meant nothing to her, but suddenly she found herself grabbed by the *burka* and hauled into the flat. Yuri slammed the door behind her and blew out his cheeks with a relieved whistle.

'Phew! I suddenly realised . . . you're wearing that cloak thing we saw all over the Caucasus . . . do you come from . . . you can't be . . . and the lift was coming up – if it was the fellow who manages these flats you wouldn't want to be seen coming here and I wouldn't want you to be seen here either. Did you meet anyone in the foyer or in the lift?'

'No. I came up the stairs. What's the matter? Who do you think I am?' Pavel was beginning to feel scared.

'Come into the kitchen, will you? The walls here are so thin . . .' Yuri led her to the kitchen, saw her in and then shut the door firmly. The woman who had answered the door had disappeared.

'Sit down; you are Pavel Fedorovna, aren't you? You wrote to me a while back . . . thanks very much for the letter, by the way, I sent the enclosure on to David as you asked . . . and David talked so much about you that I feel I know you quite well already.'

'Oh!' Pavel's carefully prepared lies were abandoned. He knew who she was and she rather liked the look of him anyway. 'Yes, I'm that Pavel. I'm in trouble.'

'Yes, I rather thought so. You said you were all leaving – I suppose they accused your father of making too much money?'

'Something like that. I could not tell you, but David asked me to go through the Klukhor and into Turkey. In the letter you sent, I said I would. But as you see, things did not happen quite as we expected, and I am not in Turkey.'

'No. Do you want money? Help to get back to the mountains? Do you want me to warn David that you'll be late arriving?'

'I don't want money, thanks all the same, and I've got a train ticket, though it's probably out of date now, if tickets go out of date. But could you get a message through to David, please?'

'Yes, I think so. It can't go direct, or ostensibly from me, because I've had trouble with snoopers . . . OGPU, of course.

They've put a man to watch me lately, I don't know why. I don't suppose it's got anything to do with you – at least, I'm sure your letter wasn't opened, and I don't think for one moment mine to David was tampered with. He's changed his address, you know . . . moved . . . and so there was nothing on the envelope to connect him with the David Thomas Moscow knows and loves – I used the name David Alyn as you did.'

'How will you do it? I want you to tell him I can't possibly be at our meeting place now until spring or perhaps even summer. You see . . .'

She told him the story as briefly as she could and saw his face soften as she reached the terrible moment when the family had broken up.

'You poor kid! And that poor little sister of yours. In a collective, eh? It's possible . . . I should be able to find out, I've got friends working in various departments . . . look, how long will you be in Moscow?'

'Until I hear word that Eva's safe, or find her,' Pavel said with as much determination as she could muster. 'I can't just go . . . she's only thirteen.'

'Hmm, quite. Well look, don't for God's sake come here again – it isn't a good idea, not whilst I've got a tail. And don't tell me where you're living, either; the less I know the less I might let slip. We'll meet somewhere neutral . . . give me a moment and I'll think of somewhere suitable.'

'The kiosk where they sell drinks just as you come of the planetarium in the Park of Culture and Rest? Seven days from now?'

Yuri looked at Pavel with considerable respect.

'Why not? And seven days should give me a chance to see whether I can find out anything at all. Now, how am I going to get you out unnoticed?'

'Does it matter? After all, once I'm on the stairs I could have been visiting anyone's place.'

'Perhaps I'm being paranoid, but I'd feel happier . . . I know!' He called, and the woman who had opened the door to Pavel slid into the room. 'Tanya, I don't want the caretaker to see this young . . . young person when he leaves. What do you suggest?'

'Shall I get stuck in the lift? Or if Berengia's in we could go and get him to look at her sink.' She shot a quick glance at

Pavel and smiled with the air of one who is quite pleased with her initiative. 'Always she's pouring fat and other rubbish down it; he would not bother to come up for others, but he finds Berengia very attractive.'

Yuri pulled a face. 'Poor Berengia! That would be easier, love, if you don't mind. That lift trick might easily go wrong.'

'Very well; give me ten minutes.'

She disappeared as silently as she had come and Pavel, to make the ten minutes pass more quickly, said: 'You must have done this before, judging by the way your wife reacted.'

'Yes. More times than I care to think. Even innocent people who could have no possible worries about being seen here prefer to come and go unnoticed by the caretaker, or the OGPU man who follows me. Suspicion breeds suspicion, I suppose, and we are, at the moment, a people who take nothing and nobody on trust.'

'That doesn't apply to you, though,' Pavel pointed out. 'You trusted me.'

'Ah, but you're David's girl and David's an old friend. I think it will be safe for you to make your way down and out of the block in a couple of minutes. Did you hear the lift go past?'

'No, but I wasn't really listening. How can you tell it was the caretaker in the lift, though?'

'I can't, but knowing Tanya and Berengia I'd take a bet that it was! I'll see you in seven days' time, in the kiosk nearest to the planetarium.'

# CHAPTER FOURTEEN

It took a good deal of arranging, in the end, a trip to Turkey which just might include a highly illegal rush over the border into Georgia. Left to himself David would not have mentioned the possibility of going into Russia if Pavel did not turn up at the rendezvous, but when he went to the Foreign Office he met a schoolfriend, Roy Masters, who had apparently followed his career in Russia with some interest.

'I know you've applied to go back and they've warned you off,' he said casually, as the two of them sipped coffee in his nondescript and obviously non-executive office. 'We've been wondering for a while whether you'd manage to get the girl out . . . you must realise that with the restrictions placed on travellers, and the security web in which our diplomats and journalists are enmeshed, we know surprisingly little about feelings in the country at large.'

'I don't know that Pavel will be much wiser,' David admitted. 'She's living on a farm, or she was, a long way from civilisation, and the Caucasus really are difficult of access, even with modern means of communication – to say nothing of the fact that Caucasians themselves are fanatical about freedom and hate the Russians of the plains.'

'Yes, we realised that, old boy. At one time we rather hoped you'd marry her and stay there for a few years . . . you could have been a useful contact. As it is, should you need to actually go in and fetch her out, keep your eyes and ears open. Feeling, opinion, the general trend of thought about the way the State acts and thinks compared with the way it *says* it acts and thinks . . . feathers in the wind, you know.'

'If I had to go in, would you support me?' David asked incredulously, and was not much surprised by his friend's

318

raised brows and slight, supercilious smile.

'Support a national acting illegally? Quite impossible, old fruit. But unofficially, with contacts, places, the odd spot of advice . . . by all means.'

'Well look, I'll put it like this . . . I don't want to go in, because Party memories are long and they missed me out when they were pillorying other British engineers . . . they'd nail me as a spy and I'd be stuck in the Lubianka for ever and a day. But if I *have* to go in, I'd appreciate anything you can tell me which will help me find out what's happened to my girl. And her sister and people too, if that's possible. But quite honestly they're a resourceful family, the Lazarovs. Fedor's hard as nails and knows his way about, and Nyusha adores her girls, even though they aren't actually the children of her body – they're fostered. It may take time . . . I shan't be there myself for quite a while, what with the voyage and papers and so on . . but I'm sure they'll make it, in the end.'

'If so, bully for them; if not, then you'll need our advice. We've a fellow in Trabzon; I'll tell you how to contact him, then if you want help you can go through him. Fair enough?'

'Sounds it. Hey, hang on, does he speak English, or Russian? I can cope with them, but not with Turkish or Armenian or whatever.'

Roy chuckled. 'You won't need anything other than English; he comes from Istanbul, where they're an extremely cosmopolitan lot. Incidentally, your girl may well have slipped over the border somewhere, but she hasn't yet turned up in Trabzon.'

'Now how on earth would you know that?'

'Well, I'm being a bit positive, but let's say it's unlikely she's there yet. A girl on her own might have got through, of course, but a family of four Russians . . . they would be noticed, and our chap's very good about reporting back. As I said, we don't know enough about the Soviet and need to know more; refugees are often helpful.'

'Right. Well, I can't promise anything except that I've my berth booked and should leave in about ten days.'


The Bosphorus should have been dark blue, the waves tipped with silver. Istanbul should have held up its golden domes, its lapis lazuli arches, its alabaster columns to a sunset aflame with scarlet and gold. A turquoise sky should have glowed above the mosques and minarets.

When David disembarked, however, it was raining. Huge, angry drops made miniature bomb-bursts all over the quay and the sea heaved and surged, gunmetal grey and uninviting. Burdened with his suitcase and attacked by the downpour, David slid and slopped along the quay to the first vehicle he saw, a horse and cart, the horse sagging wearily between the shafts. It was wearing a straw hat with poppies round the brim; probably in sunshine the hat and possibly even the horse would have looked perky. Now, with the rain flattening the poppies to a dingy maroon mess, they both looked worn out and fit only for the scrap heap.

However, beggars can't be choosers. David stepped up to the driver and asked, in uncompromising English, to be taken to a decent hotel.

It was obviously as good as a tonic; the hunched, dripping figure holding the reins straightened, brightened, and answered in a torrent of splintered but perfectly understandable English that he knew the very place: it was owned and run by a relative and he could both guarantee David a warm welcome and promise reasonable rates.

Since David was booked in on another ship in the morning, to sail up the coast to Trabzon, he was not as interested in the hotel's excellence or reputation as in its situation – however, that was immaterial, his driver explained over his shoulder as he whipped up his nag, since he would personally call for David at whatever hour he was required and drive him straight to the ship, making sure that his client was aboard in good time for his voyage.

David grunted. He had less than twenty-four hours in a city famed for its exoticism, beauty, mystery and wickedness, and what did it do? It rained like Wales!

'The Galata Bridge,' his driver informed him. David peered round the edge of the inefficient hood-like object which was supposed to protect him from the weather and saw that the rain almost hid a large, dark object.

'Taksim Square.'

David dutifully peered again. More rain, but a sense of space, perhaps.

'Mosque of Suleiman the Magnificent.'

Something very large loomed behind the curtain of slanting, silver drops. David drew his head back in like a bad-tempered turtle and addressed his driver's back.

'Where's this bloody hotel? I can't sleep in a mosque.'

After that the driver kept his information to himself and in a very short time drew up opposite a canopied entrance with a hovering liveried person who rushed out, snatched David's case from his hand and bundled him out of the rain.

'Have you fifty kurus? That will be plenty, plenty,' the liveried one announced, holding out a large, square hand. 'I will pay him for you; tomorrow he will return, he says, and drive you round Istanbul and then to the harbour.'

'I have no Turkish money,' David admitted. He stuck a hand in his pocket and drew out some coins. 'Can he change any of this?'

The other sorted out two shillings and a sixpence, considerably more in value than the kurus, but David let it go. He was longing to have a hot bath and get out of his wet clothing; for now, that would be quite sufficient paradise.

He went over to the desk and a girl as beautiful as any long-ago seraglio inhabitant smiled at him and gave him a key, whilst a boy of about twelve, uniformed in chocolate brown with gold braid like the commissionaire now paying off the *fayton* driver, seized his case.

'Follow me, sir,' he said chirpily. 'Eating in, sir?'

'When I've had a bath,' David said, still grumpy. 'Is there a bathroom near my room?'

'Next door, sir; shared with one other gentleman, sir, only he's been out all day so you've got it to yourself. You'll be very comfortable here, sir.'

'You speak very good English,' David said, fishing about for a tip as they entered a pleasant if rather ornate bedroom. 'How did you come to learn it so well?'

'Went to the English school, sir,' the boy said immediately. 'My father owns this hotel.'

They're an odd lot, the Turks, David decided as he opened the second door in his room and discovered his shared bathroom. A son at English school yet he employs him as a bell-boy when he's no more than twelve or so. On the other hand, the kid spoke excellent English and was no doubt very useful in a big hotel like this.

It was good to run a hot bath, to relax in it, and then to climb out and dry himself on a very large warmed bath-sheet. He had very little luggage but he changed into a dry shirt and slacks, put on a sports jacket and brogues and made his way downstairs once more. The dining-room was large, carpeted naturally with a turkey rug, and perhaps a trifle ostentatious with gilded pillars, satin wallpaper and tables elaborately set with cloths of ivory damask and what looked like silver cutlery, but after wondering briefly what his bill would be like next morning David settled down to enjoy a touch of class. He had come over on a cargo boat, not an exhilarating experience, and would join a coastal vessel tomorrow which would hop from port to port to Trabzon, collecting and delivering all the way. Both voyages were cheap, so he might as well splash out a bit tonight.

It was an excellent dinner, and after it, as he crossed the hall, the commissionaire came up to him.

'You would like to explore Istanbul this evening, sir? I can get you a taxi . . . or a *fayton* if you would prefer . . . to take you to see all the sights. The bazaars . . .'

'No thanks, I'm going to have an early night,' David said rather regretfully. He was extremely tired and this would be his only night on dry land for at least a week, so he ought to make the most of it. He was still unsure of how he would contact Pavel when he reached Trabzon; his plan to meet there had been too sketchy and vague when he had first suggested it to do more than pick out the name on the map. But first he must get there; then he could set about searching the place.

In the morning the sun was shining and already the air was shimmering with the promise of heat to come. Behind him, Istanbul seemed to stir and stretch, the skyline of domes, minarets and towers reaching with rose, amber, ivory fingers into the deepening blue. David leaned on the rail as the ship left the harbour and watched, through the clear green water, a cloud of jellyfish drift by, every detail of their variegated beauty plain although they were probably a fathom or two down in the transparent depths.

He already knew that it would be several days before they made their landfall at Trabzon, so he should make the most of the voyage. It was no longer early autumn, so if Pavel had not arrived it might easily mean that she would be tackling the Klukhor Pass at a time when deep snow, the glacier and appalling storms would make her crossing difficult. But if all had gone well she would be accompanied by Fedor, a man who knew the Pass and the tricks the mountains could play as well as David himself knew the Dee estuary. They would get through; it was just a matter of how long it would take them.

Relaxing on a slow sea voyage, however, when you long for your arrival, is not easy. David played poker until he began to lose rather too many lira, then he let one of the ship's officers, a garrulous fellow who spoke passable English, begin to teach him Turkish. He ate very large meals, and quantities of *loukoum*, the sickly, sticky pink and white stuff which is quite different from its English equivalent. When they made a landfall he mooched around the little towns wondering how Nibby was managing without him, whether any more orders had followed his departure, and how Alice was coping. Bathing was good, it washed off the dust and sweat of the deck and made him forget the inadequacies of his tiny, cramped cabin and narrow straw-filled mattress, but even bathing could not take his mind off his problems for long. What would he do when they reached Trabzon if the Lazarovs were not there? Who would he contact? How would he set about discovering just what had happened in Russia?

But the day came at last when it was Trabzon which came over the horizon and gradually grew clearer as they approached.

It looked a pleasant enough place, this last real port between Turkey and Russia; white minarets, houses roofed with round, rust-red tiles, cobbled streets and walled gardens rich with flowers and fruit. David disembarked, said a jubilant farewell to the poker school and a regretful one to his part-time teacher, and set off with his suitcase. It was quite a large town – it had a British consul hidden away somewhere and several hotels fronting on to the dark beach – but David could see after only a very short walk through the principal streets that the Lazarovs would stand out here as he did.

It was very Turkish; men wore the curly-toed shoes out of the Arabian Nights, and fezes, of course. Women dressed, Muslim-fashion, in dresses and bloomers, and most of them tucked a corner of their headcloths into their mouths, semi-veiling themselves. In such a throng, two Russian males (or seeming males, rather) in *burkas*, breeches and lambskin hats accompanied by two unveiled females, one with curly, light-coloured hair, would do more than turn heads, they would stop the traffic. He understood Roy Masters's boast a good deal better now that he was on the spot.

He thought about searching for his contact at once, but it was foolish, really, when you considered that he still had nowhere to lay his head and was the cynosure of all eyes. First he must behave like a tourist, look around him, buy a few bits and pieces in the local bazaar, possibly even visit the consul for a few words. He could keep his eyes open, of course, for any trace of the Lazarovs, but it would be unwise to go further than that at this stage.

So David humped his suitcase into the foyer of the nearest small hotel, booked himself in with a desk-clerk cursed by a villainous squint, and went to his room. He had told the clerk that he would be here for a few days since he could not guess when the Lazarovs might appear, and in any event he did not yet know whether the hotel was possible; he did not intend to eat here, but even sleeping might be out of the question if the bedlinen was dirty or the staff dishonest. The room was not very big but it was clean enough and had a large, old-fashioned sash window with white net curtains very reminiscent of home, and the bedlinen was fresh, though faded.

It would do, David decided, beginning to unpack.


'Any letters?'

Nibby was eating toast and spoke rather thickly through a mouthful. Alice, sipping coffee, shook her head and then nodded it instead.

'No . . . well, not for you or me. There's one for David, though. It must be from that friend of his since it's addressed to Alyn and not Thomas. I suppose we could try to forward it to David, but it could take weeks – do you think we're justified in opening it?'

Nibby's answer was to slit open the envelope, causing Alice to gasp; although she was sure he was right the inborn taboo against opening another's post was strong in her. In Nibby, however, it appeared to be non-existent. He spread out the thin paper and read, frowning.

'You are awful! But since you've done it, what does he say?'

Nibby shook his head and shushed her; read the letter through to the finish and then went back to the first page and read it again.

'Oh come on, Nibs – it was addressed to my brother, after all!'

'True. But my Russian isn't as good as Dave's, I have to read a thing a couple of times to get the full meaning. Yuri says Pavel's in Moscow. She visited him at the flat and told him that the family's been split up. Her parents were sent to a timber camp and the little girl, Eva, was destined for a children's home somewhere in the Ukraine. But he doesn't think she ever got there, though he won't be sure for a bit. It's such a huge country and the name Lazarov isn't all that rare . . . and the girls' bearing the patronymic confuses the issue still further, of course.'

'Patro-what?'

'A Russian girl-child becomes . . . oh well, take Pavel. She's Pavel Fedorovna; in English we'd say daughter of Fedor. So we're talking about Fedor Lazarov, Nyusha Lazarova – wife of Lazarov – and the daughters, Pavel and Eva Fedorovna.'

'Oh, yes, I see. It used to be like that in Wales, a bit. Son of was more well known, though – that's why you get people called Rhys ap Owen, or even Rhys ap Rhys . . . Rhys son of Rhys. I remember someone telling me once that it's even worse when you're trying to do a family tree and going back through the generations, because the Welsh didn't allow themselves to be bound by custom or tradition. A family might be known as the ap Owens, and then they would change the last name, dig out a Jones connection or something, so that finding the direct line, the link, would be just about impossible.' Alice smiled at Nibby's expression. 'Sorry, I'm rambling. Go on.'

'You are, a bit. Where was I? Oh, well, the letter just says that Pavel feels she's got to stay in Moscow for a bit, until Yuri gets a line of some sort on the little sister. If the parents are in a timber camp I don't suppose they'll escape alive, but Eva, the sister, could easily be roaming the country. The trouble is Yuri can't find out where she was bound, which might be a start, without the risk of drawing too much attention.' He leaned back in his chair and whistled at the ceiling. 'Phew, here's a pretty state of affairs! Now how on earth do we get a message to Dave so that he doesn't hang around in Turkey waiting for her?'

'I don't know — letters take such ages. But when David wanted to get in touch with people quickly he went to the Foreign Office, didn't he? You must know people there, Nibby. Couldn't you go up to London and see what they can do?'

'I could, I suppose,' Nibby agreed. 'What about that fellow he was at school with? Roy something or other.'

'Roy Masters, wasn't it? Yes, he's Foreign Office; you could try him.'

'I could telephone; that would be better in a way. I don't fancy going off and leaving you to the tender mercies of Sassy and Mike.'

'Oh, go on, you'd only be gone a day. David used to go for the day, didn't he? Another thing is . . . well, I've never been to London. Suppose I came up too? We could be back here before the kids go to bed and Sassy's seventeen, after all. Quite old enough to have some responsibility thrust on her for once.'

'You're right,' Nibby agreed with alacrity. 'Is it a date, then? We'll both go to the Foreign Office and then we could take a look at London, if you'd like that.'

'I'd like it very much.' Alice smiled at Nibby. Although David had been gone a month she had not drawn closer to Nibby now that they were the only two adults in the house; quite the opposite. Nibby seemed to take great care to be out of the way as much as possible: he seldom came home early enough for an evening together, he worked at weekends, he was barely in the house for longer than it took to snatch a sandwich and a cup of coffee at lunchtimes.

However, the weather was getting finer every day, and Alice clung to the hope that Nibby would suggest an expedition of some sort for the two of them, in the course of which he might feel impelled to Speak.

Alice knew very well how she felt about him — how she had felt for years, indeed — and she caught him looking at her sometimes with a look that she could not interpret . . . a look which sent exciting little shivers down her spine and made her stomach clench and knot and tangle in a highly peculiar fashion.

Now was no time to be thinking such thoughts, however,

not with a whole day in London alone with Nibby in prospect. Alice jumped to her feet and began to clear the breakfast table. At first she had fantasised that she would feel hands at her waist, a warm mouth nuzzling in her neck, but she had become accustomed to the realisation that this would not happen. Nibby was too honourable to play around with a girl he had known since they were both kids, and he was obviously not as sure of his own feelings as she. So Alice began to do her quick rush round the house, which was the only sort of housekeeping she could manage during the week, and Nibby grabbed the last piece of toast, buttered it, folded it and made for the back door.

'Cheerio, Alice,' he called back as he opened it. 'See you this evening.'

'Oh . . . all right. Shall I arrange for a day off, then? And what about the tickets?'

'Oh, I'll see to everything, except your day off, of course. The trouble is I'll have to agree to go whenever this bloke . . . Masters . . . can see me. Do you suppose that will be all right with your boss?'

'It'll have to be.' Alice snatched the kettle off the top of the stove, checked with an expert sweep of the eyes that all was as it should be, and headed for the back door, a light jacket over her arm. Nibby would be in at lunchtime for his sandwich and coffee, but otherwise the house would remain undisturbed until the evening, when she and the young ones returned to the house more or less together. She heard Nibby crossing the back yard and caught a glimpse of his dark blue jersey, and then he was round the corner and out of sight, heading for the riverside and his latest precious boat.

'See you tonight then, Nibs,' Alice sang out at the top of her voice, unlatching the gate and slipping through it. She would have to run or she'd miss the bus . . . but even so she lingered for a second or two by the gate, hoping to hear Nibby's voice raised in answer.

There was no sound, though; he was probably too far away to have heard her call. Alice made for the lower main road at a determined trot.

When the perfect moment comes, *how* I'll sweep her off her feet, Nibby dreamed, working a plank of wood into velvet smoothness with long sweeps of his plane. The moment was bound to come – he'd been expecting it for a whole month now – but as yet it had not presented itself. Mike and Sassy were there too much of the time, or Alice was working, or it was a dull day when she would certainly tell him to go about his business, or she looked tired or she didn't look tired . . . it was never the perfect moment.

However, now he had arranged a day out for them, a day in London. Surely, in the course of that day, the perfect moment would manifest itself? He could, of course, help it on a little . . . a bunch of flowers, a meal at an expensive restaurant. Then they might get a carriage to themselves on the return journey . . . exciting pictures darted through Nibby's mind. Moonlight, darkness, a train disaster – nothing too bad, mind – in the course of which he would be forced to seize Alice in his arms . . . oh, the possibilities of a day in London were endless.

Working away, whistling quietly under his breath, Nibby began to think back over the past month. Could he truly put his hand on his heart and say that there had been no opportunities to tell Alice how he felt, no chances to ask her whether she had grown a little fond of him? There had been dozens, possibly even hundreds, and he had pushed all of them aside. Why, in heaven's name? Did he not think himself good enough for her? That was rubbish, he was extremely eligible, he reminded himself crossly. Then was he not sure of his feelings? More rubbish – he was considerably experienced, and his one-time mistress in Russia, Svetalia, had been adorable, much admired, endlessly envied by others. There had been girls in Britain too, even since he had returned home. He blushed to confess that he had made a special friend down near the docks for those long evenings when he had missed the attentions of his little student. But none of the feelings he had nurtured for any of these damsels came anywhere near the feeling he had for Alice. He admired her, he adored her and he both revered and desired her, two emotions which he had previously thought diametrically opposed. For the first time in his happily irresponsible life he wanted to look after someone else, thought of her happiness before his own, and wanted what was good for her, even, perhaps, at his own cost. And marriage, that state which had seemed to the old Nibby to be the final clanging shut of the cage door, was now a necessity for his happiness. Without it he had no authority, no real right to interfere when he saw Alice being badly treated or taken for granted.

Then why, he asked himself, tackling his plank now with a piece of fine sandpaper, why won't you ask her to marry you? And the answer was because, if she refused, he would feel that his existence was meaningless, and, worse, that he could no longer continue to live in the house which was hers and David's. If he moved out, as he would have to, countless complications would follow, perhaps even the end of the partnership he and David had formed, simply because he had changed their comfortable relationship.

No wonder I'm scared to chance my luck, Nibby thought, sandpapering so vigorously that the wood began to smoke; there's a lot at stake. But nevertheless he made a vow. He would not return from the day trip to London without having at least done his best to discover how Alice felt.

'No, none of those is quite what I'm looking for. Don't you have others . . . perhaps with silver thread?'

David had thought the carefully learned sentence stupid, in London. Why on earth should he say such a thing to make contact with Masters's fellow? But here in the small, narrow alley in the bazaar, before the stall over which hung the sign of the grasshopper, it did not seem so strange. The stallholder sold materials, not just rolls or bolts of cloth, but material already exquisitely embroidered, probably at the expense of the eyesight of dozens of poor young women, David thought, admiring the deep reds, purples and golds with their wonderfully artistic designs.

'Silver thread, your honour?' The man was fat and sleek, his skin shining with oil or perspiration, it was difficult to guess which. He was sitting on a camel-stool amidst his wares, but at David's words he hoisted himself to his feet and turned away from the alley towards the interior of the shop. 'If you'll come with me . . . there are many, many more designs . . .'

David followed, not without difficulty, for the shop itself was crammed with unlikely items all placed, it seemed, where they might best trip – or trap – the unwary. However, he reached the small door at the back of the shop and was gestured through by his guide.

'There, your honour; see? Silver thread, gold thread, emerald . . . would you like to browse, your honour? Choose at your leisure?'

He shoved David through the little door and closed it behind him with a finality which, to David, suggested that a key had probably been turned. His heart gave a ridiculous thump and skip, and then he saw that at least he was not alone. Another man sat in one corner of the dark little room, almost hidden by the piles of embroidery. He was thin, dark-skinned and dark-haired, yet David did not think him Turkish, perhaps because he was wearing a light grey suit over a white shirt. He looked up as David entered and raised his brows, and as David approached him he stood up and held out a hand. His feet, incongruously, were bare.

'Morning, m'dear fellow. You'll be David Thomas?'

'Er, yes. I'm afraid I don't know your name, but Roy Ma . . .'

'Quite, quite. No names no pack-drill, eh? You can call me Selim.'

'Oh? You are Turkish?' David's rather obvious incredulity appeared to delight the man, for a broad smile spread across his thin face, creasing his cheeks and bringing light to the dark eyes. They shook hands and then Selim gestured to a chair.

'In fact I am a Turk, though I spent all my formative years in your country . . . at Eton, in fact. I'm completely bilingual, though, and I speak French and Russian too, which has come in useful one way and another. Now, let's get down to business. Have you heard from the young lady?'

'No. Well, I couldn't very well, there hasn't been time. But no word came before I left England. She's not crossed the border to your knowledge?'

The other man shook his head.

'No, I think not, neither alone nor accompanied. I'm afraid people tend to disappear over there and we've virtually no contacts to give us even a clue as to what's going on. We have people in consuls and embassies, but they're watched and followed and spied on all the time, so that it's more or less impossible for them to find out anything. As for reporters, they often maintain that they get more news from reading *Pravda* and foreign newspapers than they are given by the authorities, let alone than they can obtain from other sources. If they do happen on a nice story the chances are it'll be cut by the Russian censors — not because it's dangerous to the State, but because the Party prefers outsiders to know nothing whatsoever about Soviet society, good or bad.'

'When you say people disappear . . .'

'My dear fellow, I didn't mean to worry you! They do, of course, but that wasn't what I meant — after all, your young lady hasn't fallen foul of the Party so far as we know. No, what I meant was that it's such a vast country that one person — or even four — can simply disappear into it and until they choose to let the outside world know what's happened to them there's no possible way of finding out.'

'No way?'

Selim smiled. It was a smile at once world-weary and rather ingenuous. David discovered that he rather liked the man, and what was more he believed that Selim would do his best to help, even if he was doing it more in the hope of getting information out of Russia than simply to rescue Pavel.

'Yes, of course there is a way, but I would not blame you if you felt it was not much to be commended. One can go in and take a look around.'

'One?'

Selim's smile broadened.

'You like things to be clear, don't you, not devious! How very English! Yes, I meant that you could go in and take a look around. My place is here, but I also cross the border and can go with fair impunity as far as the steppes. I look Caucasian, wouldn't you say? But then you see I don't know your little lady; if I were to walk up to her in a shop I would go right on by, whereas you . . . you wouldn't need to question or doubt, you would know her at once.'

'But . . . if she's not here, surely she'll still be at home? If they haven't left the farm I know exactly where to find them, but if they have . . .'

'You may be right or you may be wrong, but the principle still applies. You can go to the farm and recognise the occupants at a glance. You can say *there's Fedor, there's Pavel*, whereas I can only say *there's a farmer and his child*; do you understand?'

'No, I don't. Surely if you see a farmer there you'll know it's Fedor, and . . .'

'Ah no, my dear fellow, you are so wrong! If the State has moved peasants into the farm to run it as a collective they most certainly will not have left Fedor or his wife there, though it may be possible that they would leave the youngsters, I suppose. But far likelier they would move the entire family on.'

'It doesn't make sense,' David began, then remembered that to the State Fedor was a *kulak* and therefore automatically guilty. He would be lucky to get some poor position on a third-rate collective on the plain – they would never allow him to remain on what had once been his own acres. 'Yes, of course, I was forgetting. Then you think I should go over? How does one enter Georgia without anyone knowing?'

'I can cook you up a false identity easily enough; sufficiently good to get you by for a few weeks. As for entry, that can be done as you had planned for Pavel; a fishing boat, a dark, moonless night, and somewhere to lie up until midday when there is nothing unusual in a stranger walking into town. But wait a few days, just in case refugees come across or news reaches us.'

'Very well. A few days.'

'And now, Mr Thomas, which of these pieces of material will you buy? You cannot walk out of here after all this time with nothing, or suspicions would be aroused.'

'Oh, any . . . not that I want a piece of embroidery,' David said impatiently. 'That bit . . . the one with peacocks all over it.'

'That one? It's pricy, but if that's your choice . . .'

'I don't really have to buy it, surely!' David exclaimed, his Welsh soul cringing at the thought of spending his hard-earned money on what he considered unnecessarily gaudy embroidery. 'What'll I do with it? I'm certainly not crossing the border with that under one arm! And I can't afford much . . . which is the cheapest?'

Selim laughed.

'It is the rent for our meeting-place which Abdul expects and, indeed, earns, therefore the firm will pay. Go on, my dear chap, choose what your young lady would like! I will give you the money to hand over to Abdul for your purchase.'

'Well, I don't know . . .' David began doubtfully, but Selim forestalled him.

'The young lady has been a boy for so long that you don't

332

know what she would like, eh? But most tourists buy this embroidery not for a dress but for their homes. Do you own a house? In your living-room, is there not a sofa or couch which could have cushions in this . . .? Or this? That cream-coloured one with the red and gold stitchery? Peacocks? Panthers? Sturgeon?'

That was different. Reassured, David chose with care, a wonderful silk in a deep, peacock blue, embroidered all over with a lavishness and brilliance which, he acknowledged, would fill Alice's housewifely heart with pride should it bedeck her furniture and not her person.

'You choose well.' Selim measured, dug in his pocket and pressed lira into David's hand. 'Come again in three days; by then all will be arranged, unless either you or myself hear from London or Moscow before then.'

'Very well. Do I say the same thing again? To Abdul, I mean?'

'Yes, I think so. To those who sell in a bazaar, one foreigner is very like another and they all say foolish things.' He held out a hand. 'Goodbye, Mr Thomas, until Friday.'

'Goodbye, Selim. And thank you.'

The door was not locked. David passed through the doorway, closing the door carefully behind him, the silk over one arm. Abdul rolled a black eye enquiringly, heaved himself to his feet, measured the silk, extolled it, wrapped it, and named a price at least twice the value of the money David held in his hand. With an indignant exclamation all but on his lips David suddenly realised that he was meant to bargain and did so enthusiastically, almost driving Abdul below the sum of money he had been given in the heat of the moment. But the cash changed hands, there were mutual compliments, David admired a very fine pattern on a creamy-gold material and said he would doubtless return before he left Trabzon, and then he emerged into the filtered and dusty sunshine of the streets once more. He carried his silk carefully; it was, after all, his passport and his payment for the dubious pleasure of trespassing into Russian territory. As he walked, though, he found it increasingly difficult to believe that such an act of sheer foolhardiness would be required of him. They would hear from Pavel, surely, saying that she was coming through on such and such a day, and then he would simply have to wait.

Of course, if there was no alternative, he would go ahead with the plan, but it would obviously be a good deal better for everyone concerned if Pavel came to him.

He reached his hotel room, spread his silk out on the carpet the better to admire it, and then flopped on to his bed. He would rest for a bit since this was the hottest part of the day, then he would have a light meal, then he would have a swim. In three days, if nothing had happened, he would return to the bazaar, but in the meantime he might as well enjoy himself.

The trip to London was arranged, and Alice, wide-eyed and eager in a green plaid skirt and pale grey pullover, grey court shoes, and a little green hat pulled down over one eye, set off beside Nibby in a state of subdued excitement only partly caused by the thought of seeing London for the first time.

She had planned everything carefully: Sassy and Mike had money for tea in town and then a trip to the cinema. This would induce a mood of friendship and mellowness in them both, Alice hoped, and it would also mean that they would not spend the whole evening sparring, or possibly downright fighting.

The film unfortunately did not finish in time for the last bus, but Sara and Michael both had sturdy bicycles with good strong lights front and rear, so Alice had to trust them to cycle back from town, and she hoped that what with having a meal out, seeing an exciting film-show and then riding home, the two of them would simply fall into their beds and not wake until the next morning, when she and Nibby would have returned from their jaunt.

Unfortunately, they had chosen a popular train for their trip, so popular that Alice sat one side of the carriage and Nibby the other, but when they arrived at Euston station Nibby took Alice's arm and tucked her hand into his elbow in a manner both proprietorial and fond, she told herself.

'We'll go by underground,' he said. 'You'll enjoy that.'

Actually, Alice found it nerve-racking, but it was undoubtedly an experience so she did not repine. And then, at last, they were walking down the street, into the hallway and up the stairs to Roy Masters's office.

He was a surprise to them both; younger than Nibby had imagined, handsomer than Alice had expected. And he was friendly, too, and forthcoming, which David had certainly never mentioned.

'Morning, Mr Hawke, Miss Thomas,' he said, getting to his feet and shaking first Alice and then Nibby warmly by the hand. 'Up for the day, eh? Well, business first . . . and then how about a spot of lunch?'

The business did not take long. Nibby simply handed Yuri's letter over with the appropriate sentences underlined and asked if it was possible to pass the news on to David. Roy Masters whipped a pair of gold-rimmed half-moon spectacles out of his top pocket, read the message, grunted, nodded thoughtfully, and handed the letter back to Nibby.

'Yes . . . that does alter things. I wonder how David will feel? He may be more determined than ever to go into Russia, or it may change his whole attitude. Leave it with me; I'll make sure he gets it as soon as possible.'

'Thanks very much.' Nibby returned the letter to his pocket and smiled at Alice. 'That makes us feel a good deal better, doesn't it, Alice?' He turned back to Masters after her murmured affirmative. 'By the way, how soon will you know if David's gone over?'

'Oh . . . hard to tell. Within the week, probably. Though I'm afraid I shan't be able to tell you much . . . it's pretty confidential, you know.'

'No, that's all right. But you see he's my business partner as well as my friend, so I'd be most grateful if you could let me know, even if you only dropped me a line . . . nothing specific, and no names, of course. If you could just say "unobtainable", then I'd get the gist.'

'I don't see why not,' Masters said after a moment's thought. 'Now just let me get my coat and we'll go and find a suitable restaurant.'

The day was not going as planned, Nibby reflected gloomily, making a poor third in the animated little group which took their places at the table in the elegant, cosily lit restaurant where Masters . . . call me Roy; after all, David and I were at school together . . . had decided they should eat. Not only was Masters no older than he – despite the fact that he and David had been at school together, Nibby had allowed a mental picture to form of a man far older than either of them – but he had a smooth cap of shining dark blond hair, tanned skin and even features. He was also, Nibby realised at once, that despicable thing, a ladies' man. He directed all his attention at Alice, made her laugh, smiled at all her jokes, reminded her of exploits either carried out or witnessed by David when they were kids, and generally put himself out to entertain her.

Together, Roy and Alice laughed over the menu, chose dishes, derided each other's choice, chose again, laughed some more. Wine was tasted and said to sparkle like Alice's eyes. Nibby curled a lip and asked if there was no beer available. Roy began to talk of foreign countries, of the women he had met, the men he had mixed with. They were not the boastful tales of a Don Juan but the amusing stories of a born raconteur. Nibby hated him more every time Alice's dimples sprang to life, and when, at the end of a long and delicious lunch, he asked what Alice would most like to see and Alice said with regrettable promptitude the Tower of London, Westminster Abbey and the zoo before Nibby could think of a polite way to say 'your back', Nibby could willingly have strangled the other man.

Alice, however, had no such feelings. Joyously she sprang into the taxi he hailed, wide-eyed she explored the Tower . . . there were lots and lots of towers, Nibby discovered, far from delighted by the revelation . . . and then Westminster Abbey, down to the last tomb, and finally she hung on to Roy's arm with her left hand and Nibby's with her right and they slogged round the zoo, an unhappy trio though a happy duo, if such a remark could make any sort of sense.

'No, no, my dear fellow, as if I'd let you go off by underground when the firm can pay for a taxi,' Roy said, when the despairing Nibby faintly suggested that it was time they left. 'You'll want to catch the six o five, I dare say? Right . . . a cup of tea and a cream cake or two will keep the wolf from the door until you get back to Holywell Junction, so that's how we'll spend the next half hour.'

They did. Then he and his taxi took them to Euston, where he bought a handful of expensive magazines, a box of chocolates and a bunch of violets for Alice before waving the train off, with Alice leaning so far out and waving back with such enthusiasm that Nibby felt obliged to put an arm round her shoulders just in case.

'Well, isn't he *nice*?' Alice said as soon as they were back in their seats once more. 'A real gentleman; no wonder David trusts him the way he does. I would myself. Have a chocolate . . . gosh, I remember Mother having these on anniversaries from Father, when I was very small. Go on, Nibby . . . the ones with crystallised violets on top are delicious. Do try one.'

'No thanks,' Nibby said coldly. 'I don't know how you can either, after all that tea.'

'That was hours ago,' Alice protested, carefully selecting a large, rich-looking chocolate and popping it into her mouth. She looked round the carriage, which was full, then offered the box to the only child present, a boy of eight or nine, who took one with alacrity.

Nibby could have wept; of course, Alice being Alice, the box continued its round of the carriage and under the influence of such chocolates – and such generosity – friendliness and chat became general. For three solid hours Nibby muttered sulkily when directly addressed and Alice and her new friends chattered like starlings.

When they reached Chester and changed on to their branch line, Nibby stomped ahead whilst Alice waved and exchanged addresses with the little boy and his mother, the only other passengers who had not either left the train earlier or continued on with it. The local train was crowded too, but by dint of being pushful and quite unpleasant Nibby managed to find himself and Alice two adjacent seats. He sank morosely into his whilst Alice disposed of the empty chocolate box, said ruefully that what Michael and Sara had never seen they would never miss, and then sat down beside him.

'Soon be home,' she remarked, glancing sideways at him. 'It's been a lovely day, hasn't it, Nibby? Thank you *so* much for letting me come along.'

Nibby opened his mouth to make some tired, automatic response – and said nothing, because he had just been hit squarely amidships by a stunning and rather unpleasant idea. He had told himself he had not spoken about his feelings for Alice in case she turned him down, thus making both their lives appreciably more difficult. He had lied. He had, in his heart, up to that very moment, thought that Alice would be not only delighted by his proposal but honoured! He had been afraid, not that she might refuse and make things uncomfortable, but that by accepting she might make him realise that he did not, after all, want to be tied to one woman no matter how special.

He had, in other words, accepted her at her own valuation; as being a girl neither as pretty nor as charming as her sisters and one, moreover, with a big nose, doomed to spinsterhood.

Nibby turned in his seat and stared at Alice as though he had never seen her before, trying to see her through that confounded bounder's eyes. How had Roy Masters seen her? As an ordinary girl in ordinary clothes, with a big nose, a pale face and straggly brown hair? A raving beauty? A sweet character? His face got nearer and nearer to Alice's as he strove to see what Masters had seen. Pale skin, and dark brown hair with a shine on it which brought out coppery tones. Grey-blue eyes with softly curling, dusky lashes. A mouth which trembled on a smile and then, as he got nearer, stopped smiling. Ordinary? Beautiful? Plain? None of those things. She was Alice.

He put both his arms round her and dragged her into his embrace and then, because her mouth was so near, he kissed her. And went on kissing her, whilst all around them the carriageful of people buzzed and whispered.

And Alice neither struggled nor tried to push him away; she simply kissed him back.

# CHAPTER FIFTEEN

Winter was with them now, and no amount of extra clothing could keep Eva warm. The old church had been dealt with as best they could but it was no use, they could not sleep for the cold, so Kevi had decided they must make a move. He spent the whole of one day simply stalking round the church, dark-browed, wrapped in his thoughts, but then all of a sudden he rounded on his followers.

'That's it, of course! Over here, fellows!'

There was a little room at the back of the church where, once, the priest and his acolytes had robed themselves for the ceremonies which they presided over in the body of the church, before the altar. In one wall was a small and narrow door. It was locked, and the *bez prizorney* had never bothered to open it because Kevi said they would save the hymnals and missals it undoubtedly contained for when they had no alternative fuel, but now he got a brick and broke the lock.

Steps. Leading down into darkness, and a dreadful smell, composed of must and airlessness and rotting vegetation of some sort. Kevi took a broken candle and lit it, then began to descend the stone stairs. Igor was close behind and Ivan and Fedya followed, but the girls, with one accord, held back. Even Eva, who wanted to be with Kevi more than anything else in her life, could not bring herself to walk down into that unknown, evil-smelling dark.

'Are you all right?' Marushka's voice echoed thinly round the damp stone walls. A reassuring shout came back, and then Ivan's fair little face appeared round the corner at the foot of the stairs. He was grinning.

'Come down . . . Kevi says.'

Then it must be all right, Eva told herself, going first with Katinka clinging to her skirt. Kevi would not order them to

339

follow him into danger. But once at the foot of the stairs, staring round in the candlelight, she almost changed her mind and made for the church above.

It was, she supposed, a family vault. All round the walls were niches in the brick, some glassed in, some not. The ones which were not glassed in contained what she supposed were stone coffins but the others . . . it was difficult to see because of the reflected candlelight. She moved forward and nearly fainted. Bones! No, skeletons! Rags which were crumbling into dust lay amongst the bones; one skull faced outwards, seeming to look directly at her with its hollow eye sockets. It had a grin . . . she backed, trod on Katinka and gave a high whimper.

'Shut it!' Kevi's voice was brusque. He must have been pretty shocked himself but he did not want anyone becoming hysterical, Eva guessed. 'It's all right, they've been dead a long time, they aren't going to hurt anyone. If you girls don't like it we'll break the glass and get rid of them, but we've got to use this place. Don't you see, being underground there won't be any draughts and no snow will blow in.'

'Oh, but Kevi, it's graves . . . dead people.' Ania's voice quivered. 'I don't want to live with dead people!'

'But you want to live, Ania. If we stay in the church the cold'll kill us – not all of us, but the weaker ones.' Kevi did not say that Ania was weak; he did not have to, she knew it. Her cough was worse, not better, her limbs more frail. Kevi had whispered to Eva once that he doubted Ania would be with them by the spring. 'You'd rather be snug down here than freezing upstairs, wouldn't you?'

Ania's doubtful expression said that never had being snug seemed less attractive, but Kevi continued as though he had not noticed.

'We'll bring wood down here and spread our bedding out in the corners, where the walls will protect us from cold once we've stacked all the old papers we can find between us and the stone. We'll keep our food here, too, where we can keep an eye on it – it's going to be a very hard winter, so they're saying in the market.'

'Do you want us to start work on this place now?'

Kevi nodded briskly at Igor's quavering question.

'Yes, right away. Umm . . . girls, what do you think about the bones?'

'They're only worn-out people,' Eva said at once, not because she believed it but because she knew that they were the words Kevi wanted to hear. 'They won't hurt us, and the glass looks pretty tough; let them stay. But if anyone finds some bits of material big enough we could hang sort of curtains.'

'So we could. Well done, Eva.' Kevi smiled approvingly and Eva's heart lightened. If she was afraid, sick at heart at the mere idea of living down here with the skeletal dead, that was her problem and one she must conquer. The others would take their lead from Kevi and to an extent from her, because she was his favourite. She owed it to her position, therefore, to be braver than the other girls. 'Look, work hard, all of you. I want the place converted into our new headquarters before tonight.'

'What about smoke?' Igor said, as they began carrying stuff down the steep stone steps. 'If we light a fire down here, where'll the smoke go?'

'If we leave the door open a crack and use the third step from the bottom as a fireplace, then the smoke should go up,' Kevi told him. Eva waited for someone to remark that this would cut off their only retreat as well as drawing immediate attention to the door, but no one did. And once the fire was laid and lit she saw that she was wrong. The stairs were wide and quite deep, the fire small because they had to hoard their fuel for the long months ahead. For safety's sake they lit it in the corner, against the wall, which meant that they could still go up and down the stairs, provided that, when the fire was burning well, they kept right to the outside of the steps and took a double step down and up, avoiding the fireplace altogether.

'We'll have maize cakes and the last of the cabbage,' Kevi announced that night, when the fire was going well and they were all in the vault, the door above them wedged open an inch to let the smoke escape. He looked round approvingly. The skeletons were hidden in a masterly fashion — someone had stolen a tin of thick old paint and the glass was now painted over, more or less, so that the grisly remains were completely hidden unless you really peered. Every scrap of paper the gang had collected carpeted the corners and went a foot or so up the walls where their bedding lay bunched. Piles of rags, more paper, anything into which one could burrow had been used. Food was becoming more and more scarce but what there was had been gathered into a soggy cardboard box which stood in one corner, and fuel, in the shape of wattle dragged out from the ruins of a nearby building, was stacked beside it. 'Well, that's the best we can do for now – what do you think?'

Admiring murmurs made him smile slightly; he must have known, Eva thought, how the little ones could not completely forget their silent companions behind the smeared glass, but he was far too shrewd to admit it.

'There you are, then, our winter palace! Pity we haven't more food and so on, but at least it's a start. Eva, put the pan on.'

'So you got a message through?'

Pavel met Yuri quite often now, though always out of doors, and in such a casual manner that they might have been two strangers passing by with no more than a word, until they were quite certain that no one was following either of them. Only then would they speak. Now, in the small café, both gripping a glass of hot tea with ice-cold fingers, they sat at separate tables and conversed without looking directly at each other, though they were the only customers in this particular part of the café.

Yuri nodded at Pavel's words.

'Yes. I told David that you were in Moscow and would be unable to join him yet, but I've had no luck with the others. There are so many, you see – the State needs cheap labour – and children seem to disappear, to slip through its fingers like a drop of mercury. I've made what enquiries I can, but the children's homes are open, not prisons, and half the time the authorities don't know who's in them and who isn't. Children in school are a little easier to trace, but Eva hasn't turned up in any of the systems that I've managed to check, though God knows there are plenty I've no idea about.'

'I see. It's pretty hopeless, I suppose, but I can't bring myself to abandon her. She's all I've got and I'm all she's got. They made such a point of asking me to take care of her, you see.'

'They? Oh, your parents.'

'Well, yes, but I wasn't thinking of them. Earlier, long ago. Before we went to Fedor's they told me to take care of her.'

There was a pause whilst Yuri sipped his tea and stared straight before him. Pavel followed his eyes. Outside, in the thick snow which covered the Park of Culture and Rest – and indeed the entire city of Moscow – some children were playing. Warmly wrapped, their faces rosy with effort, they were snowballing each other.

'Pavel, I hate to ask, but has it ever crossed your mind that Eva might be dead?'

Before Pavel's eyes a picture flashed: a stony mountain path, the swirl of mist, a small child's hand in hers as they hurried along. They had just turned away from someone . . . something . . . but she could not recall who or what it was. Somewhere in the mist, however, there were men and danger, so she and the child hurried . . . whilst behind them there was a clatter, followed by a faint gull's cry.

'Dead? Oh no, why should she be dead? She's done nothing, there's no reason for her to die.'

'My dear girl, children die all the time, especially in conditions like these. A night in the open . . . but no, you're probably right, she'll still be around somewhere.'

'Yes, I believe so. Look, thanks very much, Yuri . . . can you meet me again in a week or so, when you've had a chance to make more enquiries? If there's still nothing I'll have to make my way back . . . I owe it to David.'

Sipping their tea, they made arrangements to meet in twelve days' time, when Yuri had another day off, and then he got up and left. Pavel sat on for a good twenty minutes before she, too, made her way out of the café. She turned in the opposite direction to that Yuri had taken, and walked slowly but purposefully. She would go into a big shop and see if she could buy some food, though little remained unrationed. She would go into a shop anyway, though; it muddled the trail should anyone be following her, though she was pretty sure she was clean. She stuck her hands into the wide sleeves of her *burka* and crossed the road. Poor Baru had been left behind, a rare occurrence, but Pavel never took her with her when she met Yuri; the dog was far too recognisable.

Presently she reached the shop doorway and went inside. A great many Muscovites were arguing and jostling over the few articles for sale, so she joined them. She kept a careful eye on the doorway for a few minutes but no one else came in, and when at last she emerged again no one lingered in the street and no one slid out of the shop to follow her.

She was only a matter of yards from the shop, indeed, when it began to snow, thick, whirling flakes which cut visibility down to a matter of feet in as few moments. Glad of the cover, though not of the stinging cold on her face, Pavel headed straight for home.

Yuri noticed that his tail had picked him up again when he left his head office. One of these days, of course, the man was not going to be so easily fooled, but for now it seemed that to dive into the office block, get into the lift, get off at the wrong floor and escape through the back door was too intellectual an exercise for his follower to envisage. At the moment the man who hung around the flats obviously thought following Yuri was routine, the result of a vague feeling on the part of someone higher up in the Party that since Yuri was an engineer and had actually shared a flat with an Englishman it might not be a bad idea to keep an eye on him.

And then his living with Tanya would not exactly please them. Caucasians were a wild, proud people who did not bend easily to the State's demands. Probably the Party thought her a subversive influence – but one glance at her dark beauty, her generous curves, would surely convince them that she was the old-fashioned sort of woman who did not bother her head with politics – or, indeed, with much else – but simply took care of her man.

In any event, the tail had once more been fooled. After his rendezvous with Pavel, Yuri had entered the office building as he had left it, through the back door, and now he had left by the front as though he had spent all day either slaving over paperwork or chatting to his secretary.

As he was making his way home the snowstorm hit and he paused in a doorway, wondering whether to wait for one of the horribly overcrowded trams or whether to continue on foot. He also wondered how long he could go on making enquiries about a non-existent cousin who had disappeared from her home before someone began to ask questions. It was not as if he had a snowball's chance in hell of discovering the truth, either, he told himself, slogging grimly along the pavement, head down against the giddying spiral of the flakes. All he was doing was risking his neck, possibly Tanya's, definitely Pavel's, if she ever got caught.

He turned into the foyer of the block of flats at last, glancing behind him as he always did. He could see no one, but continued to stand there, kicking snow off his boots and shaking his hat and shoulders clear of it, whilst idly scanning what he could see of the road outside.

No one. Plainly, his tail had decided that in such fearful conditions he might as well go home himself rather than hang about when only an idiot would venture forth again. Perversely, Yuri thought that he might just slip to Stanis's place later. Stanis worked in the education department. Just one more try, for David's girl and thus for David, Yuri promised himself as he headed for the lift. Just one more try and then I'll give up.

'He's boring . . . not worth the bother, particularly in this weather.' Yuri's follower was a small, skinny, ordinary little man with protruding ears which he hid under his hat and a rasping voice which his victims seldom heard. Now, sprawling at his ease in a chair at OGPU headquarters, he was perilously close to whining. What an assignment! Weeks and weeks of following a minor engineering worker who apparently led the most blameless – and boring – of lives, only to be told that he must persevere for a few more weeks.

'Look, comrade,' the man behind the desk said impressively, 'he writes letters, we know that much, and we know nothing's gone to the fellow we're interested in, neither to his address nor to his name. But that doesn't mean they aren't in correspondence. You've been in the flat?'

'Of course!' The other was indignant, his ears crimsoning against the implied slur, though in fact it happened to be justified; he had never set foot in Yuri's flat. Two attempts to do so had both failed because of the woman who lived there. She claimed to speak almost no Russian and when he demanded admittance to check that she had no unauthorised gas appliances she had just trotted out two short sentences which said that she spoke very little Russian, she did not understand what he had just said, and that her man, who was the tenant, would be home at such and such a time. Since no one tailing a suspect wishes to meet his quarry face to face, he had on both occasions chosen to mutter that he would be back and to ignore the chance of a second visit.

'Yes, of course, I'm sorry. It wasn't that I doubted you . . . and what did you see? No papers, no interesting letters? Nothing that would help us?'

'Nothing. It is a small flat, bare and dull, like its owner. However, if you think it worthwhile I'll continue with the surveillance.' He stood up, rubbed his face vigorously with both hands and turned to the door. 'What next? He has very few visitors, nearly all colleagues or friends of the woman's from other flats in the block. You've had all their names.'

'Hmm. Sometimes I wonder if he's genuine and this whole business is a mistake. At other times I wonder if he's so fly no one knows what he's up to!' The older man laughed as the tail stopped in the doorway, the giveaway ears slowly reddening once more. 'Sorry, Yakov, I'm sure it's the former! Come and see me in a week, ten days, and probably you'll be moved on to another case.'

'Very well, comrade.'

The door opened and closed behind him and his footsteps died away into silence.


'There's a message.'

Across the small, dark room with its stacked material, David's eyes gleamed with excitement as they met Selim's. At last, contact had been established!

'Marvellous! Is she coming? When?'

'No, she's not. It seems she got separated from her sister and she's been trying to find her. Pavel's been in touch with Yuri, which is how we know what's going on. She's travelled to Moscow, hoping to discover where the little one has gone.'

'Separated? In Russia? Christ, what chance does she think she's got of finding Eva in all that lot? Or did they arrange to meet in Moscow? Where are Fedor and Nyusha? Are they with Eva or with Pavel? She's not in trouble, is she?'

The questions tumbled off his tongue so that he stammered in his haste to get an answer, but Selim could only shake his head.

'We don't know, my dear fellow, we can only tell you what we ourselves have been told. Yuri wrote to your friend, and your friend took the letter up to Masters in London. It said that the Lazarovs had been taken to a timber camp in the north, but that the girl and her sister had got separated and that Pavel was trying to trace Eva through Moscow. Reading between the lines, if the parents are in a timber camp whatever Pavel does will be against the law . . . she's old enough to be with them, you see.'

'With them? But why, for God's sake? No one can call a sixteen-year-old girl a *kulak*.'

'No, but a girl of that age can work . . . anyway, she's seventeen now, isn't she?'

'Yes, I suppose . . . then she's in danger!'

'Undoubtedly.'

'And . . . you still want me to go in?'

'If you go, we'll give you all the help we can. Money, papers . . . the best we can manage. A false identity isn't easy because you could find yourself in trouble if we used the identity of a refugee or someone who had recently died . . . the State can seize the papers of the totally innocent person for no particular cause, you see, and then you would be exposed.'

'But if I go in as an ordinary peasant, with an invented name, wouldn't that do?'

Selim laughed.

'My dear fellow, how long is it since you visited Russia? You tell me you lived there for years, yet you can, in all seriousness, make that suggestion? You are far too well nourished for a peasant, you show no signs of manual labour, your face is the wrong shape . . . I don't think you could expect to last more than thirty minutes if you go into Moscow looking as you do now and telling folk you're a peasant.'

'What, then? A clerk? A minor Party official?'

'Yes, that would do. It's probably easier to pretend to be a minor official because there are so many of them and they are all so tyrannous, in their small way. You are very dark, so you could be a Caucasian. There will be men of the Caucasus in high places, there's no doubt of that; the regime takes a man here, a man there, and makes them its own. Look, come to my place and we'll work hard for a few days and see what we can make of you.'

'Your place? Then you do have something a bit more official than the back of a cloth-merchant's shop?'

'A bit more. Be ready in your hotel foyer at two this afternoon and a driver will come for you.'

'The trouble is, Yuri, that I can't stay here indefinitely. I'll have to go simply because my money will run out. Natasha's

347

awfully good; she won't take money for letting me stay in her flat and for the food that Baru and I get through, but things are getting more and more difficult. Rationing is almost a joke when there's so little in the shops, and the dining-room is enough to make you cry. The bortsch is pale pink because they use so much water and so few beetroot to make it, and the slices of bread get thinner and thinner, the bread coarser and coarser.'

Yuri and Pavel were sitting in yet another café, an even smaller and dirtier one than the kiosk at the Park of Culture. The tea here was straw-coloured but at least it was hot, and because the place was so tiny and so empty and tucked away they sat side by side at a counter, on flimsy, badly made wooden stools, able to talk without fear of interruption or surveillance.

'I can let you have a little more money,' Yuri offered. 'It's nothing compared to what David sent me, you know that. And when you're with him you can always send parcels which would more than make up for a loan.'

'It's awfully good of you, you've been marvellous,' Pavel told him, 'but I think I'm wasting my time. I've done my best to get to know the *bez prizorney* who've come into the city, but they don't know Eva and I'm as sure as anyone can be that she isn't here. I'll never find her the way things are and she'll never find me, so I might as well cut my losses and get back to the mountains, even if I can't actually join David until next summer. Surely I can get work somewhere . . . I'm a good herdsman, you know, and I'm good with sheep and cattle – I can deliver a breech calf without harm to the baby or its dam. Surely I can find work to keep myself until next summer, when I can cross the mountains safely?'

'You should get across *now*,' Yuri said urgently. 'I've written to David telling him that you won't be in Trabzon as you'd planned but that you're coming later. Now, the road may be hard, but it won't be as dangerous as it will be in spring, when the glaciers are moving and avalanches start. At this time of year, with skill and care, you should be able to cross by the Georgian Military Highway . . . but buy a good horse, I'll lend you money for that . . . and before you know it you'll be in Tbilisi and on your way.'

'It will take months,' Pavel said gloomily. 'I'll have to stop

348

and work on the way. Oh, Yuri, why can life never be simple? I know the very moment I start off I shall regret not trying harder to find Eva. How *can* I leave the country without her?'

'Because you love David, and if you don't get out soon you'll never see him again. Look at it this way, girl; if Eva's happy, if she's living with good people who care for her, you'll never find her, and if you did she might not want to throw everything up and set off to face the unknown again. She's a pretty girl, you said?'

'She is, very pretty.'

'And she must be fourteen or so now?'

'Yes, about that.'

'Then does it not occur to you that she may have found some young man to take care of her? After all, you did just that, and you had far fewer opportunities for meeting men than Eva will be getting.'

'I suppose it's possible, but Eva's such a child! I feel she needs me . . . only of course she might have met a family who are good to her . . . she is pretty and very sweet. Capable, too. Oh dear, Yuri, what *am* I to do?'

'Leave, and take Baru,' Yuri told her. 'I'll write again to David and tell him you're on your way. Do you promise you'll go?'

Pavel looked long and steadily across at him. He was sensible, was Yuri. Not as wise as David, but despite his frizzy pale hair, his glasses and his funny ways, she trusted him to know what was best for her.

'You think I should, don't you? Very well, then, I promise.'

Yuri leaned across and took her hand, pressing her fingers slightly; he was looking at her ruefully, with an expression which reminded Pavel that David had stigmatised his friend as a considerable womaniser, but then he shook her hand lightly and let it drop into her lap.

'Sensible little Pavelinka! In a week I shall come and put you on a train which will take you back to your mountains. You will have to make your way over them as best you can, into Georgia, and from there either down to the coast so that you can get a fishing boat to Turkey or perhaps over the border if you can find an ill-guarded spot.'

'Why wait a week?' Having made up her mind, Pavel felt that she should set off at once, but Yuri shook his head at her.

'No, no, wait a week in case an answer comes to my letter, either in the form of a reply or perhaps as a message, one can never tell. And then you'll need money – don't shake your head at me, young lady – and you'll want to settle things up all round. After all, Natasha has to explain what's happened to you if you suddenly disappear from the communal dining-room, and you don't want questions asked.'

'Very well.' It was Pavel's turn to leave the place first. She gave him a quick, downward glance and a smile, then slid off her stool and walked to the door, fastening her *burka* as she did so. She did not look back but made her way swiftly through the narrow streets of this particular part of the city, walking rapidly and purposefully until she gained the more populated shopping centre, whereupon she slowed to a casual stroll. Presently she spotted a suitably crowded shop and went inside.

She never looked back, but she had taken at least half a dozen opportunities afforded by shop windows and reflective objects to see if she was being followed, yet she missed the small, skinny man in the bulky dark coat with the hat jammed well down over prominent ears.

It was bitterly cold even in the vault, once the fire had been allowed to die down. There was only one thing to do at such a time, and that was to burrow as deeply into the mounds of rags and paper as one could and try to sleep.

Eva was promoted now to the same corner as Kevi. They slept away from the others because they were the leaders, or at least Kevi was the leader and she his acknowledged favourite. It was good to curl up in the rags with Kevi, who was warmer and stronger than anyone else, sometimes to talk a little in low voices, sometimes just to get as close as they could to share their warmth, and sleep.

Food was never easy but now it was becoming impossible ever to feel satisfied; hunger gnawed, day and night, un-assuaged by the bits of bread, the tiny maize cakes, the chunks of dried-up, indigestible beet or carrot snatched from the gutter in the market.

Stealing was only possible when someone had something to steal, and though there was food in the market it was scarce and poor quality and closely guarded by those who were trying to sell. Bread queues were long; black-clad women waited hour after hour in the cold, inching forward slowly until they disappeared into the temporary warmth of the shop. Sometimes the bread ran out before your turn and then you had to leave unsatisfied and return home, to huddle beneath your thin blankets and pray for morning and a shorter bread queue. Of course the *bez prizorney* could not queue for bread where it was cheapest and best, in the co-operative shops, but they could join in the scrum for other food when it was available. Only you had to have money, and money was increasingly hard to come by.

But just now Eva felt almost comfortable, because Kevi and Igor had found a turnip clamp and had managed to dig their way in at one end like a couple of terriers after a rat. Their good fortune would not last, the farmer would discover the hole and set a guard on it, but they had done the best they could in the time at their disposal; they had carried a good number to a spot a few fields away and had, with enormous labour, dug a shallow pit into which they had put their ill-gotten gains. The rest — as many as they could manage — they had brought back over the miles to the town and their winter palace where Eva had cooked them and everyone had filled themselves as full as they could hold.

So now Eva's tummy felt round and full and Kevi, lying with his arms round her, felt fatter than usual, as though the turnip had already made its way all over him, increasing his size and warmth and fitness.

'You asleep?'

Eva had thought Kevi had dropped off, so she jumped a bit and heard their bedding rustling as though it were amused. Kevi chuckled too; but he gave her a squeeze to show that he was laughing with rather than at her.

'It's all right, I just wondered because usually when you fall asleep your breathing changes. I say, Eva.'

'What?'

'Ordinary people are getting hungry; not just us, people with ration cards. Have you noticed?'

'I never think about them, not any more,' Eva said truthfully.

'Don't you think about your parents at all now, then? Or that sister of yours you used to talk about?'

'Not often. Fedor and Nyusha are in prison and Pavel was going to her chap, her English fellow. I expect she's far away by now.'

'Mm. Then you're on your own.'

'I'm not!' Eva's voice was indignant and Kevi shifted and squeezed her again, chuckling as the breath hissed out of her.

'Why, have you suddenly remembered a cousin or an uncle? For all you know they could be dead, or in a timber camp.'

'No, that's not what I meant. I meant I wasn't alone because I've got you.'

'Ah. That's what I was coming to. You've got me and I've got you, and I don't want it any different.'

'Nor me,' Eva said. Her voice was growing drowsy but Kevi nudged her again and she jerked herself awake; plainly she was not meant to sleep whilst her lord and master was talking to her.

'Don't go to sleep, girl! If we live through this winter and things are better in the spring, what'll you do?'

'Do? Whatever you do, I suppose.'

'You won't leave? Try to get back to your old home, or try to find your sister, or that old couple you talk about?'

'No. Course not. It would be nice to have lots of food and a proper home and clothes again, but I'd rather have you than all the rest.'

Kevi was quiet for a moment. Eva could hear his even breathing, feel the warmth of that breath stir her hair. When he spoke it was so low and quiet that she had to strain to hear.

'You'll have both one day; I swear it on my life. You'll have lots of food and a proper home and all the clothes you want . . . and me. For ever. I swear it on my life.'

Eva wriggled round to face him, despite the inrush of cold air that such a violent movement caused. She kissed him, a sissyish gesture which he would have clouted her for had they not been safe behind the curtaining dark. As it was, he suffered her mouth on his cheek, chin and neck and then, with a suddenness that almost made her cry out, he squeezed her to him, squeezed so hard that she felt her ribs were on the verge of cracking.

'Eva, I love you. They wouldn't understand, They'd part us if they could. I'll never leave you; swear you'll never leave me.'

The thought was absurd, so absurd that she laughed softly

and kissed his hand, then curled round like a puppy in his embrace, butting her head into the warmth of his chest.

'As if I would! Dear Kevi, I'll never *never* leave you!'

Presently, they both slept.

Eva dreamed. She did not know, of course, whether she dreamed because of her talk with Kevi or because of the heavy meal of boiled turnips; she simply found herself in the frightful toils of the dream.

Not that the dream was frightful at first; to begin with it was comforting, familiar, it was only later that it reached nightmare proportions. It was a recurring dream yet it never varied in the slightest degree and she always woke before the dreaded climax.

On this occasion Kevi woke her, shaking her roughly and then kissing the softness of her neck just below her ear. Eva stared up into the dark as the fear slowly receded and Kevi's breathing slowed and deepened once more. Why did she have to suffer the dream, when there was so much suffering in this new life? What was more, it stirred old memories, memories that she wished might remain buried for ever. The terrible day when the men had come to the farm, the soldier beating Fedor, the blood, Nyusha's tears, the way she and her father had been hit and what had happened in the train. She hated trains. She hated Them, or was beginning to do so, though it still seemed like treachery, for once she had loved ordinary people with ordinary ways and had believed theft and lies to be very wrong.

Yet those ordinary people had turned against her, as they had turned against all the *bez prizorney*. If you tried to feed yourself by grabbing a bit of bread they pursued you and shouted thief and called for the militia to drag you off to prison and beat you. Sometimes they would not even let you help them a little, for a few crumbs of food, because they were afraid you would rob them. And besides, they wanted whatever food there was for themselves.

At first, Eva had spent a lot of time wondering what the State really wanted of all the children it had deliberately deprived of homes and parents. The little ones, like Katinka and their newest recruit, a seven-year-old boy called Josef. Poor Josef had been in a children's home, but they had starved him and beaten him and once, when a rich gentleman had asked him how he came by his bruises and his skinny, starving frame, Josef had answered truthfully that he had been beaten and underfed in the home.

'The man's face went dark and angry,' Josef had told them, his lip trembling. 'And he took me into a room by myself and he beat me until I couldn't stand and he shouted that no children of the State were deprived of food or ill-used, I was a liar, a wicked, sinful liar! And then he fell down on the floor, with his dreadful purple face all wet and white foam running out of his mouth. And he snored, like this . . . grrrrooomph, grrrroomph. And I ran away, because when They saw him lying on the floor I knew They would say it was somehow my fault.'

'It shall be a lesson to all of us,' Kevi said to them, when Josef had finished his story. 'I've told you before that we're something They would rather not see; that must be our lesson to remain unseen. If They catch a glimpse of us we're as good as dead.'

'But people don't kill children,' Fedya said. 'It's wicked. Only Herod killed children and look what happened to him!'

'What?' Katinka said eagerly, probably hoping for horror stories, but Fedya had merely looked rather embarrassed and replied that they might be sure he got his just deserts.

'They would kill us rather than admit there was anything wrong with their old State,' Kevi said, after giving the matter some thought. 'I've heard bigger boys say the same . . . that They made us what we are yet They hate us for it. We . . . we threaten Them.'

'Us? Threaten *Them*? You've got it wrong, Kevi,' someone objected, looking round their small and shabby band. 'We couldn't hurt a fly.'

'I know what you mean, but I'm right, just you wait and see,' Kevi had said. 'And in the meantime, don't forget; lie low. Haven't They done us harm enough?'

So now Eva was growing used to the thought of the world's hand being against her, for that was what it amounted to. The *bez prizorney* helped each other as far as they were able, they shared their last crust, they defended the little ones from the dreaded children's homes, they saw to it that even a child of seven got a fair share of what was available. But other children felt no such solidarity. You could see them in the street, telling a parent if they saw one of the ragged ones near so that the parent could hit out, snatch back, deprive the *prizorney* of whatever they had taken. In fact, now that food was so scarce and poor, even a scrap of food rightfully bought with real money would have been taken from them by anyone stronger than they.

It was Eva's first winter amongst the *prizorney*, and it was a bad one. Already they had seen dreadful things. Other gangs of children had come in from the countryside to take shelter amongst the ruined buildings of the cities now that winter had closed down on them. Eva had seen a boy of ten lose a finger, slashed off by a farmer's knife, when the boy had slid his thieving hand into the farmer's pocket. The boy had bled to death, too weak to go to the hospital and risk capture, too undernourished to withstand the shock and the blood loss.

It was odd and rather awful when she thought about it, how quickly a child who had been loved and well fed all its life could turn into a sly, snatching, starving little thing who behaved like a cornered rat when an adult approached. One no longer looked at an adult's face, one simply reacted – fast – to the size and the probable intent.

But Eva had thought herself far away from the dream and the past and now at last she could let sleep return as a friend and not as an enemy to be fought against and denied. She allowed her thoughts to drift, idle as a summer breeze, into the bright future, for one day she, Kevi and the others would be grown up, and then how different things would be! Food would be available to everyone, she and Kevi would have a dear little house in the country with pigs, horses and lots of sheep and cattle, and the sun would shine all day long.

I'm past fourteen already, was Eva's last thought before she slept. I'm on the way; no one can stop me growing up! Unless they kill me before I get there, of course.

'Sassy, was it true? *Did* they get married whilst they were in London?'

Michael had scarcely waited to reach the gate before the words burst from his lips. He and his sister had come out of the cinema to find Nibby and Alice waiting for them in a taxi, all smiles, Nibby with his arm round their sister's shoulders.

'Come on,' he had shouted to them. 'We've had a good day but we're absolutely exhausted; can't wait to get home, can we, darling?'

'Darling?' Sassy had climbed into the taxi ahead of Michael, who simply stood on the pavement and stared at a man fool enough to use a silly endearment like *darling* to dull old Alice. 'What are you up to, Nibby, trying to get round Alice like that?'

'Oh, sorry, did I call you darling, darling?' Nibby waggled his head reprovingly and looked foolish. Michael wondered if the fellow had been drinking. 'Alice and I have had a most enjoyable day, but, as I said, we're confoundedly tired and want to get home, so get a move on, spud!'

'I didn't think you enjoyed yourself all that much, Nibby,' Alice said as Michael and Sassy seated themselves on the little tip-up seats taxis unfold for extra passengers. The two older ones were occupying most of the large, creaking leather seat and made no attempt to squeeze up. 'In fact, at one point, I felt quite sorry for you; you seemed to be having a wretched time.'

'Oh, then.' The two of them gazed into each other's eyes and then both started giggling. I was right, Michael concluded triumphantly, the stupid things have been drinking, they're tight as owls . . . or Nibby is, Alice is just being a woman, I suppose. 'Ye-es,' Nibby continued, laying a casual hand around Alice's shoulders, 'ye-es, I suppose you may have noticed a certain dissatisfaction on my part. But it all disappeared as soon as we got into the local train. Yes sirree, disappeared!'

They both laughed again, and Nibby leaned forward until his forehead was resting on Alice's and their noses were only a fraction apart. He said, in a particularly sloppy and indulgent voice, 'Who's a pretty girl, then?' and Alice fluttered her eyelashes and said, 'Well, really, Mr Hawke!' in the very tones of a maid they had once had.

Things continued in this distressing vein until they got out of the taxi and went indoors. Then there was some slight unpleasantness over the state of the kitchen which in fact was exactly as Michael and Sara had left it that morning. Reluctant apologies were extracted from Sara for leaving it thus and from Michael for not helping his sister and then the pair of them were shushed off to bed like little kids, as Michael put it later, when Sassy came into his room to compare notes.

'They're drunk,' had been Michael's answer to everything, but Sara was not so sure.

'They're still downstairs,' she announced, having crept on bare toes quite halfway down the flight. 'They're in the front room . . . and the door's shut.'

'So what? They're drunk, I tell you; or at least Nibby is. And why shouldn't the door be shut; they're probably lying on the floor tipping the last of David's boat-sherry down their throats.' David had bought sherry when they sold their first fishing craft.

Sara giggled at the picture her brother painted, but continued to assure him that neither Nibby nor Alice was drunk.

'They're just up in the air . . . high-flown . . . frightfully pleased with themselves,' she said. 'I can't think what could have happened in London to make them . . . oh shush . . . they're coming!'

She took a flying leap on to Michael's bed and then slid off it, to lie on the floor the other side. Michael, taking his cue from her, lay flat and closed his eyes, but neither need have bothered for no one came in, and presently they heard water running, murmured conversation, and then the closing of a bedroom door.

'Safe!' Sara scrambled to her feet, then sank down on her brother's bed again. 'Wait a moment, though. Who's in the bathroom now?'

'Nibby; he let Alice have first go, like a gent,' Michael said. 'Can't you hear him whistling? Selfish swine, isn't he, never giving a thought to us kids trying to sleep.'

'Really, Mikey, watch your language! Well, now we shan't find out what went on until morning,' Sara was saying when the bathroom door opened and they heard Nibby's cautious step on the landing. They heard him go along, open the bedroom door, close it . . . and then the creak of bed-springs.

'Good, he's settled, now I can go to bed myself,' Sara said, heading for the door whilst Michael, who was really very tired after his long day, snuggled down. But within moments she was back, wide-eyed, shaking him so hard that he hit out at her before sleepily sitting up.

'What's bitten you?' he asked angrily, staring at her face in the moonlight coming through the window. 'Can't you sleep, or what?'

'No . . . yes . . . oh, Mike, you are stupid . . . well, so was I. Nibby's room is downstairs!'

'So what? Oh, didn't he go down? Then I expect he's using David's for tonight.'

'If he is, so's Alice. Mike, she isn't in her bed in our room! Do you know what I think happened when they were in London? I think they got married!'

But that was last night; now, out on the garden path struggling with the gate latch, all the conjecture of last night seemed wild fantasy, though Nibby and Alice had been very nice to each other over the toast and coffee.

Sara had hung back a little and followed Alice into the outhouse when she went through to check that the back door was locked, and Michael had known at once, by her determined expression, that she would ask Alice outright what had gone on in London. After all, the two of them had spent a good thirty minutes shut up in David's bedroom before Alice had gone sneaking back into her own bed.

So now he looked expectantly at his sister, all agog. If they had got married it was a good thing, because they couldn't expect a fellow to be a page, or whatever, in a velvet suit with breeches . . . not that he *would*, not if they went down on their knees!

'So? Did they or didn't they?'

'She says they didn't,' Sara said darkly, shoving the gate open and wheeling her machine out so carelessly that a pedal caught in the hedge. 'Damn, look what you made me do!' She abstracted her machine and began to hop along beside it in the way females so often do, not being in the habit of flinging an airy leg over the saddle as we men can, Michael thought pityingly.

'I didn't make you do anything. Sassy, if they aren't married, why did they go into David's room last night?'

'She *said* because they still had a lot to talk about,' his sister answered, at last succeeding in mounting her fiery steed and wobbling off down the road. 'Nibby slept there and she said she just went in for a moment to ask about shopping for dinner tonight. But she was in her nightgown . . . well, I don't mind telling you, Mikey, I thought it was a jolly silly way to go on. Especially with David away.'

'Marrying's silly as well,' Michael remarked, zooming up alongside at such a speed and braking so suddenly that he nearly sent his sister into the ditch. 'Why didn't they talk downstairs?'

'That's what I said! And Alice went rather red and muttered that they'd finished talking downstairs, only when they got upstairs and she popped in to say goodnight to Nibby, he remembered something else and so she stayed for a bit.'

'That does happen, sometimes,' Michael admitted, pedalling slowly abreast of his sister as they reached the long hill. 'It's like when you're almost asleep and a thought comes into your head like a bolt from the blue and after that you keep thinking and getting livelier and livelier, and you don't go to sleep for absolutely centuries.'

'Fancy you knowing that; I thought little boys slept like little pigs, the same as they eat,' Sara said insultingly. Michael leaned over and clocked her ear, then pedalled his fastest, leaving her wails of wrath far behind, no more than an echo on the wind.

'Hey, Mike, wait for me!'

Michael did not need to turn to know that Topper had come out of his drive, neither did he slow his speed, and sure enough in two minutes Topper, breathing heavily, had drawn alongside.

'What's the rush? Police found out at last?'

'No, it's Sassy. Not that she can do much, girls are hopeless on two wheels, but you know how she can scream and let a fellow down! What's our first lesson?'

'Maths; why?'

Michael groaned. 'Alice and Nibby were in London yesterday so they gave us money to go to the flicks, and some for tea, as well. Alice told us to go to the teashop in Mount Street because it's quiet and there's plenty of room at the tables, she said we could do our prep. there without anyone trying to rush us. Only we went to Bennetts, it's more fun, and I've not done any work at all.'

'Right. You can copy mine if you make it snappy. I'll slide you my book before we go into hall and you can hide in the cloakroom and get it done before class starts.'

'You're a real pal,' Michael said gratefully. 'I'll do the same for you one day.'

Together, they slowed and turned in unison into the school yard.

As the door closed behind the children, Alice caught Nibby's eye across the kitchen and smiled guiltily. They heard the latch of the gate go, and then Nibby put a hand out across the table and stroked Alice's cheek.

'My love! Did Sassy give you a hard time?'

The ready blush fired Alice's face, but she shook her head, laughing at him.

'No, not really. Little devil, she wanted to know why I went into David's room with you and shut the door! If I'd known she was awake I'd never have been so foolish – what an example to set to a featherbrained, hot-blooded little thing like Sara!'

'If the pair of 'em had walked in they wouldn't have seen a thing they shouldn't,' Nibby said a trifle gloomily. 'Just a bit of kissing and cuddling, horizontal instead of vertical.'

'If they'd walked in they'd have seen me dead of shock,' Alice said. 'Nice girls don't go into men's bedrooms when the men are in them, let alone lie all over their beds and kiss them.'

'Ah, but no one said you were a nice girl! I don't want to marry a nice girl, I want to marry naughty, exciting, arousing Alice Thomas.'

Alice got up, went round the table, and sat on Nibby's lap. Then she put both her arms round him and squeezed. Then she kissed his mouth, and for a few moments there was silence in the room except for some rather heavy breathing. When they broke apart she touched his lips with her forefinger.

'You're a clever bloke, Nibby – you've no idea how I've hated being a nice girl for the past few years! Nice Alice, respectable Alice, *thoughtful* Alice! The sort of steady girl no one minded their sons taking out, the type women suggest their husbands dance with, because, poor thing, she doesn't have much of a time. Now I want to be really wicked!'

'Right.' Nibby stood up with her in his arms. 'To the woods! Or at least to David's room . . . no, better still, to *my* room, then I won't have to hump your not inconsiderable weight up all those steep and narrow stairs.'

'What about your work? What about . . . heavens, Nibby, put me down, I've got a bus to catch. I mustn't be late for work!'

Nibby held her for a moment longer, then stood her down reluctantly. 'You're a tease, my girl . . . why pretend I could carry you off when you'd no intention of allowing me to do any such thing? And this evening the kids will be here and if I so much as hold your hand they'll start nudging and asking difficult questions.'

'The only answer's marriage,' Alice said pensively. 'Now if we really had gone to London to get married, the way Sassy thought we had, there wouldn't be a problem. We could march boldly into your bedroom when we got back from work and no one could say anything.'

'Couldn't they? You underestimate the young, my dear! However, I get the drift of your conversation; I am to marry you in order to get certain privileges; right?'

'Absolutely spot on, old bean,' Alice said cheerfully, borrowing from Michael's friend Topper's vocabulary. 'You've hit the nail on the jolly old head.'

'Shut up, you sound like a last year's copy of *The Gem*.' Nibby took a quick look at the clock, then put his arms round Alice and drew her close. 'How about a tiny sample, eh? We'll say you were sick and ill.'

'Oh, Nibby, we shouldn't! It's not right, you know very well . . .' He quieted her with his mouth and after a long and totally unsatisfying kiss he picked her up again and made determinedly for his bedroom. Alice sighed, wriggled out of his embrace, and then allowed herself to be led through the white-painted door and into his room, which still smelled of new plaster, new curtains and new wood.

'We shouldn't,' she said almost automatically, as Nibby pushed her on to the bed and rolled on after her. 'We really shouldn't. What would David say?'

'Don't give a hoot,' Nibby muttered against her neck. He began to kiss, to caress, to cajole. Alice, responding like billyo, kissing back, muttering under her breath, arching her body delightfully when he touched it, seemed quite ready and willing to part with far more than the tiny sample Nibby had asked for; until he actually started to try to get down to brass tacks, as he phrased it to himself, pushing his hands up the

361

back of her jumper and trying to turn her so he could undo her bra. Then she resisted, though her face wore a wistful, excited expression which meant, Nibby was sure, that she was enjoying it every bit as much as he.

'Oh come on, darling, you'll love it,' he murmured presently, when he realised that in spite of apparent willingness and eagerness Alice was still rather more untampered with than he wished her to remain. 'I'm not asking much . . . just let me undo this thing . . . you'll be beautifully comfy, I promise . . . I won't do anything you don't want me to.'

He was, naturally, of the opinion that once he started Alice would want all the things he wanted, but he had not allowed for her sturdy independence. With a sigh – admittedly a sorrowful sigh – Alice pushed him away, sat up, and pulled her jumper up and her skirt down.

'There! Wasn't that lovely? I'm tingling all over,' she said brightly. 'Now I really must go to work.'

Nibby sat up as well. He, too, was tingling, though rather more in some places than in others. He scowled at his beloved.

'It was lovely, but so's one sip of water when you're thirsty – provided you know you're going to be allowed to drink the rest of the glass,' he growled resentfully. 'Do you know what it does to a fellow, to let him go so far and then stop him dead?'

'No, I can't say I do. But I dare say you can tell me what happens to a girl if she lets him go as far as he wants?'

'I don't know what you . . . oh!' Nibby felt his face begin to burn. 'Oh, that! Well, naturally I wouldn't have . . . I mean you aren't the type of girl who'd take . . . well, if you think I'm the sort of fellow to get you into trouble then I don't know why you bother with me!'

'Because I love you.' Alice kissed his cheek, then his nose and then, very gently, his mouth. 'And I'm going to walk up the aisle as nice little Alice Thomas, even if ten minutes later I'm hurling moral rectitude – and my white satin knickers – out of the nearest window. You don't mind, do you, Nibby? We can get married as soon as the banns have been read – I'm over twenty-one and so are you.'

Nibby put his arm round her and returned the kisses, also with gentle care. Then he rubbed his face against hers.

'Dearest, darlingest Allie, yes I do mind, but you're right and I'm wrong and I'll just have to put up with permanently aroused and permanently unsatisfied feelings until you've done that walk up the aisle. More cuddlings? I won't overstep the mark, I swear it.'

'Sweetheart, we can't, I must go to work!' Alice slid her shoes on and danced across to the door, blowing a kiss over her shoulder as she opened it. 'Have a good day, see you this evening!'

'I've done as you asked, comrade, and continued with the surveillance,' Yakov told his superior officer, back at OGPU headquarters. 'And in a way, you could say you were justified. He *does* slip out now and then, when everyone thinks he's at work.'

The older man behind the desk leaned forward, his eyes gleaming. 'Yes? I thought so! Where does he go and who does he meet?'

'He goes to one of those poor refreshment booths, built out of the sides of old packing cases under a railway arch. Cheap, warm if they have sufficient customers, but not the best place to meet a fellow dissident. Too open for secrecy, and in the middle of the afternoon too empty of other customers.'

'Yes? Come on, man, who does he meet?'

'No one. Sits at one of the side counters, scarcely says a word to the proprietor, even. First time he was there I followed him, watched, followed him home. He didn't speak to a soul and went straight back to the office. Next time I let him go, but followed the only other person in there.'

The elderly man tutted impatiently as the other paused.

'Well? Where did she go?'

'She? It was a young boy, not a woman. He sauntered around looking in shop windows and kicking at the snow, then went over to the east side of the city and went into a big apartment block.' Yakov produced a grubby notebook. 'He went up to the fifth floor; he's the third son of eight boys, his mother's a street cleaner, father's a navvy.'

'Name?'

Yakov peered harder at his notebook, bending his head to hide his smirk. He had heard the way the chief's voice suddenly went flat, recognised both his disappointment and acceptance that the name no longer mattered. A boy of lower-class working parents would not interest the OGPU, and although one could pick on most people and cry false evidence, it would not be wise to do so with the type of low-grade mentality that such a family would produce.

'No name, comrade. It isn't too easy to get these people to talk if you ask a question that might be thought official. But the boy is called Nicholai.'

'Hmm. So's half Moscow.' There was a longish pause whilst the boss considered. Yakov used it to wonder why he was so often forced into falsifying evidence. Usually against someone the State wanted to convict, of course, but on this occasion simply to get himself off a painful and pointless exercise. He had very soon realised that Yuri Obreimov was far too intelligent to be caught in wrongdoing, and if they wanted letters forged the Party had people far better at it than he. No, his job in this case had been surveillance and he had done his best until the afternoon when he had followed Yuri to the railway arch place. It had been the end! The fellow had sat in that wretched place for an hour, sipping weak tea, then he had left, so rapidly and unexpectedly that Yakov had lost him. On the second occasion, Yakov had decided to follow anyone even vaguely near Yuri in the café, but there had been little choice, for the place had been deserted apart from a young boy with patched boots and his suspect. Even as he chose to follow the boy, though, the idea had been forming in his mind. How to get away from this thankless task without dishonour. How to prove to his masters that they had got the wrong sow by the ear.

Now, standing apparently poring over his notebook, he waited for his chief's decision. After all, in the normal course of his duties he followed young men, young women, government officials, even Party people from time to time. Sometimes it was described as for their own protection, at other times for the good of the State, but whatever the reason at least he was usually given subjects to follow who had more to their lives than the constant, soul-destroying slog from a government office to a second-rate flat and back again. Eleven weeks of that! Eleven weeks of waiting in the same dark doorway for the same man to shamble into view; eleven weeks of lurking in another dark doorway for hours and hours at a stretch, just to do the same walk back again. It was too much to ask of any man, especially now, when the whole of Russia was spending its time trying to fill its belly!

'Very well. I'll put you on another assignment, I think, Yakov. This fellow's either lost interest in the traitor or gone to ground for a bit. We'll pick him up later, I'm sure of it. Come back in three days and I'll give you your new instructions.'

Yakov thanked his chief with just the right air of deference; no hint now of whining . . . had he not got his own way?

He left the offices briskly. Nice to reach the end of a case and to know that for three days he would be able to stay in his room with his fat little wife and their small, sturdy son. When he returned to work the frustrations of his eleven wasted weeks would be gone and he would be eager to start on the new assignment.

He did not look behind him as he pushed his way through the bad-tempered home-going crowds.

# CHAPTER SIXTEEN

David had learned to shamble; now he shambled across the thick snow on the pavement and made for the crude shelter of an old-fashioned refreshment room. It was unattractive, but he was only a bird of passage, so could not try his luck at a communal dining-room, and anyway from what he had seen so far you stood a better chance of a meal in one of the privately owned cafés than in the State-run dining-rooms.

It was warm inside, but even one sniff at the air could tell you what food was on offer; potato and leek soup and weak tea, with the possibility of a slice of black bread if you were lucky.

David went to the counter and paid in advance for his meal, then sat at a table near the window, despite the cold. He had got past the stage of constant fear, in which every man, woman or child who so much as glanced at him in passing was an OGPU agent, but he was still wary. His Russian had not been queried; in the Caucasus they thought him a plainsman, here in the Ukraine they assumed he came from the mountains. But danger, if it came, would come from outside; he wanted to be facing it.

The soup was thick and quite tasty, the bread filling. This was a small town, deep in the heart of good farming country, so food was not as hard to come by as it had been in the city he had stopped off at a few days ago. Something must have gone badly wrong with all their famed planning, David told himself, eating his soup as slowly as he dared. They ruled with a rod of iron, they told the peasants what to plant and when to harvest, what to charge and how much they must produce. At a guess, the problem was probably the forced collectivisation; the farmers had been dispossessed as Fedor had, the peasants who took over had not been capable of using the resources now at their disposal with any skill or even with moderate efficiency, and the farmers of course, seeing what was coming, had not bothered to plant what they could never reap, had sold off their beasts and their grain and their tools and equipment so that they would have a nest-egg when they were taken away, or that their children might eat well until that dread day.

And now, under mismanagement, the country was slowly starving, slowly realising that there was no food. The peasants on their collectives or still scraping a living from their acres would suffer hardship, but it would not be they who starved and died – it would be the city dwellers, even the townsfolk. They had to buy to eat, and when food was short even the most avaricious peasant would not sell. The government had found that out years ago, when they had first started their Five Year Plan system; without the co-operation of the farmers and peasants no plan could work, and the folk who tilled the soil could not be forced to produce food just to pass it on to the government, no matter how vigorously they were exhorted to do so.

David thought of Pavel, outlawed, somewhere in Moscow, and he began to eat his soup a little more quickly. How would she eat, once hardship bit? Where would she hide? He had faith in Yuri, who would do his best, but he knew from personal experience and from what Nibby had told him that in Moscow the OGPU were more active than in any other part of Russia. Suppose they found her? She would be entrained for Siberia and slavery at the drop of a Party card, and if they did not find her, then she might easily simply die of hunger. She would have no ration card, no documentation such as any Russian needed to get work. Stateless, homeless, alone, she would not be able to get out of the country no matter how she longed to do so.

It galvanised him, the thought of his Pavel in such a state. He finished up his soup, shoved the rest of the bread into his pocket, and set off back to the railway station. There was no waiting-room, but he was as capable of curling up on the platform with his quilt over him and his knapsack for a pillow as any Russian peasant, and at least when the train did deign to arrive he would be one of the first aboard!

Pavel and Baru were crammed into a wooden truck through

the slats of which the wind whistled constantly. When it snowed, which it did frequently, snow came in as well. And of course they were not alone; the truck was crammed with people eager to get a train away from Moscow and the shortages which were already making life difficult even for the righteous, who had ration books. For the unrighteous, of course, life was meant to be difficult, but even they were beginning to realise that there were compensations in conforming if it meant food.

The truck was full, Pavel thought, of non-conformists. She had not realised that her state of unrighteousness was shared by so many, but there was scarcely a person present who had a full set of documents. One had lost a job and fled, another had wanted another woman and fallen foul of a person in authority, yet another had been cast on the world by the death of a husband and had decided to go home, only realising aboard the train that she had no means of identifying herself should the militia come aboard.

'Not that they will,' someone in a long fur coat, worn to a shine of leather at elbow and rump, complained. 'They've got more sense than to push in here. There isn't room for a spy's eyebrow, let alone a body – even the *bez prizorney* ride on the roofs from choice when the train's as crammed as this one.'

It was a slow train, but everyone was friendly – a far cry from Moscow, where no one was, Pavel thought – and in such circumstances hardships shrank and seemed less terrible. Food, such as it was, was shared as far as one could make it go round, and Baru ate boiled turnip and scraps of bread and disappeared every time they had an overnight stop. She caught rats, Pavel knew, and she quite envied the dog her ability to live on the country, so to speak, for she herself would have to get a job when they reached the Caucasus. Her money was almost non-existent; only by working and earning would she be able to get over the mountains.

The train would take her a good part of the way that she wanted to go, but then she would have to work until she could hire some means of crossing over the Caucasus. That was, if she took Yuri's advice and headed for the Krestovy Pass, with the Military Road to guide her. Ah, but if she took the other, wilder road . . . and the nearer road, too, if you could honour it by such a term . . . then she could be her own guide! She had a feeling which she could not explain that her luck would lie in crossing the Klukhor Pass, but Yuri was right when he said that the eastern road over the mountains was the easier, and possibly the only way at this time of year, with the snow so thick and the weather worse, even, than usual.

David would come by the Klukhor, if he came. Not even to herself did she acknowledge the hope that she would find him searching for her before too long. She did not dread the journey ahead of her because now that she had made up her mind to go she wanted to get it over with, but she did worry about what would happen when she tried to bribe a fisherman to take her along the coast and into Turkey. And also what would happen to her there. She spoke Russian, not Turkish, and had no knowledge of any strange nationality other than David.

'Train's stopping.' A friendly man in his mid-thirties dug Pavel in the ribs as he said the words. 'Good thing too; I'm dying for a pee.'

The foolhardy slid the door back a little and relieved themselves on to the track, the cowardly and the elderly used the corners of the truck. The smell, when you came back in after an hour or so in the fresh, iced air, was indescribable, but when you'd been shut in the truck for a couple of days you simply did not notice. You were as much a part of it as everyone else.

'I wonder where we are?' Pavel applied her eye to the nearest crack in the wood, but the wind made it water so much that it was a pointless exercise. 'Is it a station, do you suppose, or has the driver run out of water again?'

'We could supply him with enough to do a good few miles,' someone joked, for no one relished the thought of removing clothing and one's bladder was usually bursting before one took steps to ease it. There was a general laugh and a shifting of bodies; stops were welcomed, too, because on country stations even in these hard times you found peasants selling food. Pavel, counting her kopeks, could not afford to splash out even when she saw milk going cheap or withered, red-cheeked apples for sale, but she bought bread whenever she saw it and she and Baru, though they were both thin as laths, were healthy enough.

'It's a station!' someone shouted, and the door creaked

open. A rush of icy air and a handful of lazy snowflakes sought out every unprotected patch of skin and Pavel shivered and tucked her chin deeper into the scarf which had been Natasha's goodbye gift to her.

'Take it and wear it in health,' her friend had said, a sob thickening her voice. 'Come back one day, dushka, in happier times. Ah, what fun we could have had, if you had been here in summer.'

'And with papers,' Pavel had said, laughing through her tears. 'What a wretched nuisance I have been to you, dear Natasha, and how wonderfully kind you have been to me! One day I'll come back . . . or perhaps I'll send you a big huge parcel of goodies instead. How would that be?'

'I'd rather you came back,' Natasha snuffled; 'I wish you'd stay . . . I wish you'd leave me darling Baru. She doesn't want to go, do you, precious?'

'Precious' sniffed at Natasha's wet cheeks and slowly moved her plume of a tail, then turned, as she always did, to Pavel. Their relationship had changed in the city; Pavel had become the protector and Baru the protected, for the dog was worried and confused by the traffic, the people, and the buildings which hemmed her in on all sides. But once they got back into the country again she would take her rightful place beside Pavel, pacing tall, knowing that she could tackle anything – wolf, bear, man – which might threaten her young mistress.

'Come on, lad, don't stand there dreaming!' A friendly hand propelled Pavel roughly out through the now wide open doorway. 'I can see food – what is it, can you tell?'

'Oh, wonderful, it's vegetable stew,' Pavel said breathlessly as she dropped on to the platform. 'I wonder if I can afford a bowlful each?' She would share a bowl with Baru if she had to, but she knew the big dog needed more nourishment than she had provided so far. Once back in the mountains she could catch herself a hare or a rabbit and feed fat for a few days, but here, in civilisation, rats and a bit of bread and boiled turnip were all Pavel had seen her eat.

The food was not expensive, but it took the last of Pavel's kopeks. Never mind, she consoled herself as she and the dog gorged on their first good meal for days, this won't have to last us much longer. In a few hours we shall be near enough to the mountains to leave the train. Probably by dawn next day they would be able to see the peaks against the sky.

'How long shall we be here?' Pavel asked the driver, having walked the length of the train to do so, but he only shrugged.

'Depends how long they take fuelling and watering,' he explained as he climbed back into his cab. 'We'll be late arriving . . . but then we always are.'

But despite the driver's gloom Pavel had not been settled back in the straw of the truck very long before the train began making steam. Baru came loping in, pushing between the people and then cramming herself as small as she could behind Pavel's legs, and, as always, she had timed it just right. With a snort and a hiss of steam the train began to move, the platform became crowded with round-eyed peasants waving to friends or perhaps just waving to the train, and then they were in open country once more.

The door had been left partially open for latecomers, but now the last one clambered aboard and two of the stronger men applied themselves to the task of shutting it again. It creaked and groaned, then began to close, and the light gradually dimmed until they could only see each other's faces with difficulty.

'Well, I'm for a nap.' The man next to Pavel crouched down in the straw, then sat, bundled small, and gestured to her to follow suit. His wife was already down, their child in her lap. Pavel and her neighbour leaned against each other like a couple of book-ends; Baru leaned against Pavel. Warmth enfolded them all, despite the cutting draughts and the constant movement and rattlings of the truck.

Just before she slept, Pavel reflected how lucky she was; with every rattle, every creak, the nasty, smelly, draughty truck was taking her nearer David.

'What was the commotion about, then?' David looked inquisitively at the man on the narrow wooden bench beside him, who had been able to look out through the top of the narrow, filthy and steam-obscured window of yet another slow train. They had heard screams and shouts, curses, and shots, but could see nothing until someone had forced the tiny top pane open a short way.

'Nothing much – just the *bez prizorney* at it again. I imagine they'd robbed someone, a foreigner probably or a high Party official, and the authorities started a chase.' He chuckled, sitting down heavily and making the bench creak beneath his weight. 'They won't get caught, of course . . . this is a slow train.'

'What difference does that make?' a woman sitting further along the seat said curiously. 'There isn't another stop for miles!'

'The *prizorney* don't care about stops. They'll take to the train roof at first – they ride the roofs like the cowboys you see in Western films riding their bucking broncos – but if the pursuit gets too hot or if anyone's fool enough to climb up after them they'll simply jump.'

'Oh? And the railway people won't follow them? After all, if a lad can do it without hurting himself, why not a grown man?'

'Who wants to be stranded in the middle of the steppes, when someone's waiting for you at home? The *prizorney* don't mind because they have no homes, they just travel to squat somewhere different, but a railway official doesn't want to lose track of his life for days whilst he walks to the nearest station and finds another train going in the direction he wants. And he'd have left his job in the middle, too, which the State wouldn't approve of, even if he did catch a ragamuffin or two – not that he would, of course; they'd disappear down rabbit holes or melt into the landscape somehow. They don't live long if they aren't cunning and tough, you know.'

'They're a disgrace,' the woman said in a grumbling voice. 'In the old days . . .' She looked round the carriage, caught David's eye, and turned a dark, uncomfortable red. 'Well, I don't approve of theft.'

'Nor I,' David said mildly. 'But I don't approve of the *bez prizorney* being treated the way they are, either. They haven't chosen to be outlawed; they were mostly left with little alternative.'

Someone muttered about children's homes and was silenced when the woman, who seemed a practical person, gave it as her opinion that they were less like homes than dirty holes children should be kept away from.

'Windows smashed, no furniture save for iron bedsteads,' she told them. 'And the children told to find their own bedding and them with not a kopek to call their own. How are they supposed to find bedding? Under gooseberry bushes?'

'Off linen lines,' someone else contributed. 'My woman feeds the *prizorney* as you'd feed a wild bird that would starve, else. Or she did. Now it's all she can do to feed our own young 'uns.'

'Aye, they're a problem, sure enough,' an elderly peasant contributed. 'But they'll be less of a problem by the spring, if this hard winter goes on and there's no more food made available.'

No one pretended not to know what he meant; it was clear to all that homeless children could not live under present conditions, that they would die unless the State did something to help them, and did it quickly.

'You look to be a man who's travelled a bit,' someone said to David presently, as the conversation looked like flagging. He was a timid-looking fellow, thin and pale with wispy fair hair and eyes which blinked constantly behind his round, metal-framed spectacles. 'Is it like this everywhere in Russia? The food shortages and no fuel and the cold at its worst?'

'Not in Georgia, of course,' David said, 'and I'm hoping Moscow won't be as short of food, being the capital, you know, but . . . yes, it's bad everywhere, I believe.'

'I expect the whole world's suffering; the government says it was a bad harvest,' the woman said timidly. David thought wistfully for a moment of train-travelling when he had first come to Russia; then, everyone on a train seemed to take on a new lease of life, a new right to criticise. But that, of course, was before Soviet officials became so aware of their power. Then, every traveller would not only tell his life history to all and sundry without fear of reprisals, he would cheerfully condemn every official, would defy anyone who tried to smother him in red tape and would trumpet his wrongs, his opinions, his innermost feelings, at the very top of his loud, strong voice.

How different things were now! From even the swiftest glance round the carriage it was possible to see that his seven fellow passengers were all strong-willed and opinionated people, with the possible exception of the fair-haired man in pince-nez, and he looked as though he was a teacher or a minor official himself. Yet no one would dare to voice outright criticism of the State, not even during the course of a long journey like this, where they would all get to know one

373

another before reaching their destination. At the most they would have a sideways swipe at it . . . *But comrade, I wasn't criticising the State, indeed, not, it was the bez prizorney, comrade!*

'I don't think it's universal,' David said cautiously; he was in an even worse position to criticise the State than his fellow travellers, 'but this is a land of change.'

'Very true,' the peasant said rather bitterly. 'I am on a collective, though I am travelling to Moscow to see my niece married. The manager is not a man of the land.' He looked round at their faces. 'But he will doubtless learn, in time,' he concluded gruffly.

'As we all shall.' It was the man with the pince-nez. 'It doesn't do to criticise, comrades. One never knows . . .' his voice faded away, as indeterminate as his appearance.

'To a wedding, eh? Well, I hope the bride and her man will be very happy,' another passenger put in. 'Is she young? Beautiful?'

'Foolish, she's foolish. She's marrying a city fellow, and her as pretty and good a girl with a dairy herd as ever I knew.' The peasant shook his head and sighed so gustily that his yellow-streaked moustache blew up and down like a curtain. 'But there you are, modern ways, modern ways! When I ventured a word of reproof to my sister she said girls had minds of their own these days and that in any case, if the lass wanted a change, she could always divorce him.'

There was more tutting at this and David leaned back in his hard seat, closed his eyes, and let his thoughts wander.

They always wandered the same way, though; to Yuri's flat in Moscow, where he would learn Pavel's whereabouts. And after that he let himself think about home, the cottage, the workshed on the edge of the salt marshes, his family and his friend.

Just before leaving home, Nibby had announced himself in love with Alice. Was it real love, David wondered now, or was it simply that Nibby, as he well knew, was susceptible, over-sexed, and unused to going without? Alice was a darling; once she had been full of vivacity and charming naughtiness and had undoubtedly appealed to his friend, but now? Now she was such a sober creature, with her mind fully occupied by her job, her housework and her mothering of the younger ones, to say nothing of feeding and clothing them all. He had noticed, of course, that Nibby wanted Alice's attention, that he hovered round her, defending her with zest when the younger ones took advantage of her good nature. But it was one thing for Nibby to admire Alice, particularly when she was the only female available, and quite another if he began to pay her special attention. David did not want Alice hurt and he knew very well that she liked his friend and would probably love him given the opportunity. They would get on like a house on fire for a bit – to do Alice justice, it never occurred to him that she would fall for Nibby's blandishments and become his mistress – and then Nibby would tire, turn away, and Alice would be heartbroken.

It was hard to imagine Nibby being sufficiently serious about Alice to start an affair, but then David supposed it was possible that Nibby might enjoy having a girl who really wasn't his type at all. If so, could he trust Nibby not to overstep the mark? He sighed and opened his eyes, to gaze out over the rolling, snow-covered scene outside. He was a long way from home and could do absolutely nothing about the situation there, so why worry about it? Alice was a marvellous sister but she was rather a prude, old-fashioned and by no means pretty. She had a beak of a nose and a pale little face. Nibby was probably suffering from a fit of gallantry, because it was true that Alice did get put upon.

David closed his eyes again and saw Pavel behind his lids. She was kneeling in their makeshift tent, taking off his blue shirt. He watched with increasing pleasure as her beautiful bare back came into view, as she turned to smile at him, holding out a hand for her own shirt so that a pink-tipped breast was visible for a moment.

In reality, of course, she had then put on her shirt, but this was not reality. Pavel came towards him . . . he put his arms round her, their lips met . . .

David dreamed to his own invention and longed for the train's arrival.

Alice usually got home from work first, by dint of scurrying round, but today she had been lucky. Her employer, a very go-ahead young man in his mid-thirties with a wife who had been more or less thrust upon him by his family and a couple of very small and very spoilt children, informed his perfect secretary that he was going to see an old friend from his bachelor days and could drop her off at her door in mid-afternoon, so that she would get a few hours off to see to her own family's dinner. Alice, very grateful to nice Mr Rex, who treated her as a human being whilst his father, Mr George, scarcely noticed her at all save as a typist who made fewer errors than most, got on with her work at record speed. When Mr Rex came and jerked his head at her round the edge of her office door, therefore, she was able to jump to her feet and fetch her cardigan and handbag at once, for all the letters were signed, sealed in their envelopes and ready to post. Mr George was out seeing a client, Mr Frederick was immersed in a long legal wrangle with the local authority, and the clerks did not dictate letters to anyone as precious as the partners' secretary, so Alice was free to leave.

'We've got to get a move on,' Mr Rex said, taking her arm as they emerged from the dusty solicitors' office into the street, 'because I don't want Sadie to go ringing up for me. I've told her I shan't be back until late, but you know what women are.'

Alice did not reply; criticism of a wife she had only met twice was out of the question, but since on both occasions when she had met Mrs Rex the older woman had been complaining to her husband in an audible whine, she did not feel like defending this particular member of her sex.

'Hop in, Miss Thomas.'

Alice hopped. It was a lovely car, a sports model with a fabric roof which rolled back in warm weather. It was not rolled back today, but as he opened the door for her Mr Rex handed Alice a silk scarf.

'Put that round your hair, my dear,' he advised her. 'I'll just put the roof back; I like the sun on my head, don't you?'

Alice took the scarf and murmured that she did like the sun on her head, and as she tied the scarf on could not but notice that it smelt sweetly of some expensive perfume. She cast a speculative glance at her employer; Mrs Rex always smelt of baby powder and violet cachous, but of course it was perfectly possible that she used expensive perfume when they were invited to some smart function. Possible, but somehow not terribly likely, Alice concluded uncharitably. Mrs Rex did not look as though she would splash expensive perfume around.

'Comfortable? Right then, here we go. Hold on!'

Mr Rex was a dashing driver; the car positively zoomed out of town and up into the hills. In less time than it takes to tell they were outside the gate of the cottage and Mr Rex was getting out and coming round to let Alice alight.

'Thank you so much,' Alice said rather breathlessly, climbing out of the car and smiling at her employer as she pulled his scarf from her head. 'You've saved me a tedious bus journey.' She hesitated, but good manners won. 'Would you like to have a cup of tea with me, or are you in a hurry?'

She knew, of course, that he was in a hurry, and was totally taken aback when he consulted the heavy gold wristwatch which he wore on one hirsute wrist and announced that he would be delighted to accept and could spare ten minutes or so.

Cursing her upbringing, Alice went ahead of him up the short path and in through the front door. The hall was small, square and, now that she thought about it, shamingly empty of furniture. All there was to be seen was the hallstand and the table with the telephone on it. Alice took off her cardigan and hung it on the hallstand, then turned to Mr Rex, but he was only wearing a sports jacket, a gleaming white shirt and grey flannels since he was off on a trip out, so she could scarcely urge him hospitably to take his coat off. Instead, she led him into the kitchen, realised with a mortified flush that one did not take guests in there, and turned abruptly in the doorway, cannoning violently into Mr Rex who was rather closer on her heels than she had expected.

'Oh! I'm awfully sorry, I didn't mean . . . you must sit down in the front room . . .'

Alice started well, but was dismayed to find that Mr Rex did not attempt to retreat, nor indeed to fall back as she almost plastered herself across his chest in her attempts to change direction. He put both arms round her, clasped them just below the level of her waist, and smiled down at her, his eyes dancing.

'Oh, Miss Thomas, what *are* you doing? You nearly knocked me over!'

Alice should have been tart, even rude. Instead, scarlet with embarrassment, she could only stare up at him, her mouth a little open, her lip trembling, her eyes wide and surprised.

She was still gawping when Mr Rex bent his dark and handsome head and kissed her, and Alice, who had never even thought of him as a human being, let alone a man, found herself kissing him back ... not because she wanted to, or thought it a good idea, but simply because she was too surprised to take any sensible action and her mouth, which had grown greedy for Nibby's kisses, seemed quite unable to differentiate between one man and the next.

So it was her fault, in a way, that Mr Rex's hands closed firmly round her bottom and dragged her so close that you couldn't have got a conveyancing sheet between them, and that presently, when the kiss had gone on and on for an impossibly long time, he should slide his hands up her back, beneath her neat white blouse, and unfasten her bra with such speed and efficiency that Alice had no time to protest before her blouse was up round her neck and Mr Rex's hands, having dealt so masterfully with her bra, were diving down the waistband of her grey skirt, tackling a variety of undergarments such as knickers, suspender belt and waist slip with complete confidence, and then gripping her buttocks so hard that she was forced to scream.

Mr Rex's mouth muffled the sound so that it was less a scream than a shocked gurgle, and then Mr Rex picked her up, carried her quickly across the kitchen, and wedged her uncomfortably but efficiently in the corner of the room, with the maidsaver against her right hip, so that he could continue with his unwanted attentions – for Alice's body, coming out of its identity crisis, had no doubt that Mr Rex was the wrong fellow – and could, in fact, carry them far beyond what Alice's body had grown to enjoy and expect from Nibby Hawke.

Fortunately, Mr Rex took his mouth from Alice's at that point, probably believing that she was now all in favour of his behaviour. He tugged hard at her blouse, buttons popped and material tore, and just as he lowered his head, for what vile purpose Alice could only imagine, she did three forceful things. She stamped on his foot and lifted her knee sharply, feeling it sink into unidentifiable flesh, she tore her arms free of his grasp and swung a satisfyingly clenched fist at his ear, and she screamed.

Mr Rex drew back, clasping first his lower abdomen and then his ear. He was rather red in the face and his hair was disarranged and suddenly Alice felt very sorry for him. Poor man, he only knew meek little Miss Thomas the perfect secretary, he did not know Alice Thomas who had run wild with her brother David and his friend Nibby and learned to fight and swear and run with the best. He had entered the house behind Miss Thomas, but it was Alice who had injured him and now intended to chuck him out!

Whilst he clutched, Alice adjusted her skirt, tried to ignore her buckling stockings sliding down her buckling knees, and pulled the edges of her blouse together over her gaping and empty bra.

'Wait here,' she ordered him unnecessarily, since he still appeared to be struggling for breath. She was only gone a minute, but in that minute she fastened his unfastenings and buttoned his unbuttonings – those that were not still settling in nooks and crannies between the kitchen floor tiles – and pulled her cardigan on over the wrecked blouse.

When she returned Mr Rex had taken a seat, unasked, and was pulling up a trouser leg the better to examine a bruised shin. Alice smiled primly when he looked up.

'Would you like that cup of tea? It won't take a moment, the kettle's on the hob.'

He hesitated, but he was an intelligent man and must have recognised the only way out of his difficult position. He nodded shakily.

'Thank you, Miss Thomas, a cup of tea would be very nice.'

Alice made the tea, allowed it to brew for thirty seconds, and then poured two cups. She handed one to her employer.

'Sugar, Mr Rex?'

For the first time since their brief but bloody encounter Mr Rex smiled.

'As if you didn't know, Miss Thomas – two lumps, please!'

'After that, everything was fine,' Alice said, putting Nibby's plateful of stewed beef, onion and carrot down on the table in front of him. 'He drank his tea, complimented me on my biscuits – he ate two shortbread ones and a melting moment . . . don't laugh, silly, that's what they're *called* . . . and then he got into his car and drove off. He waved, too, and said *See you in the morning, Miss Thomas* as nice as you please.'

She had told Nibby a watered-down version of Mr Rex's

strangeness, but even so he did not attempt to eat his stew but stared up at her, his mouth grim and his eyes stormy.

'The swine! How dare that stiff-collared little runt come here and try to mess around with my girl! I'll go down to that office tomorrow and I'll . . .'

'You can't, and he isn't little, he's about your size,' Alice said calmly, pouring their tea. 'We need my job, Nibby, it's the only regular money we've got coming in. I'm sure it was just a momentary madness and he won't do such a thing again. I can't think what made him do it at all, actually.'

Nibby's brows began to assume their normal position and his mouth smiled a little.

'Can't you? I can! A woman in love has an aura . . . doesn't matter if he thinks of you as prim Miss Thomas, you can't suppress the fact that you're happy and loved. I expect he noticed without even knowing he'd noticed, and acted on that. And on the fact that you'd invited him into an empty house without realising how very unwise it was.'

'Yes, I see.' Alice had not mentioned that she had kissed him back and did not intend to do so, but she quite saw that she had been unfair, even though it had not been deliberate. 'Well then, shall we forget it?'

'By no means.' Nibby's brow was darkening again so Alice leaned over and kissed him. Magically, Nibby began to smile, then started to eat his stew. 'Do you know what I'm going to do first thing tomorrow morning, young woman?'

'Not go into town and try to hit Mr Rex on the nose?' Alice said anxiously. 'Because it wouldn't help a bit.'

'No. I'm going to take a day off and go into Chester. And I'm going to buy a special licence.'

'Oh? For the new boat?'

'No, idiot, for you . . . us! A marriage licence! I want you under lock and key, safely married to me with no excuse for bringing Mr Rex or anyone else into the house for any reason other than to meet your husband.'

'A marriage licence! But won't it be awfully expensive? Wouldn't it be better to go and see the vicar and get him to arrange a date and read the banns? That only means three weeks . . . a month at the outside. I thought you said we'd wait until David gets home.'

'Ha! With you going around looking as if you've heard

380

marvellous news, your eyes glowing and your hair shining and your cheeks pink instead of pale . . . how long would it be before some other interfering male thought it was him who lit you up like that?'

'Oh, is that what happened?' Alice cried, much enlightened. 'You mean poor Mr Rex thought I had a crush on him? Well, what a fool the man is – as if I'd go and get a crush on a married man!'

'I don't suppose men feel all that different when they're married,' Nibby said apologetically. 'I expect he still feels a bachelor at heart, and if he's quite good-looking – you did say he was, didn't you? – then he won't see himself as different just because he's married.'

'He is quite good-looking – well, very good-looking,' Alice conceded, knowing that she had said no such thing. 'So it's all right for a married man to cheat on his wife? And go after secretaries who happen to look prettier than usual for one reason or another?'

'No, of course not. It's very wrong. But not so wrong as a wife doing it would be. If you follow me.'

'I understand perfectly. And if you think, John Hawke, that it will be wrong for you to go after other women when we're married, but not as terribly wrong as it would be if I did the same . . . with other men . . . then I don't think I want to marry you.'

'Oh come on, Alice, you know you're dying to marry me! And I'm dying to marry you. I won't cheat, I promise. Tell you what, we'll have a bargain, shall we? If you want to play around just tell me, and if I want to play around I'll tell you. That way, we'll both toe the line.'

Alice laughed and surrendered, knowing very well that she wanted Nibby on any terms but quite determined not to tell him so.

'Right. Get on with your stew. The kids will be in soon and I want to have the table cleared before then so they can get on with their prep.'

'All right, all right. Anyone would think we'd been married a year already, the way you nag. Where are the kids, anyway?'

'Having tea with Topper . . . Michael is, I mean. Sassy's gone to the art exhibition with Liza and Liza's mother is giving them both tea afterwards and running her home in the car. What do you think of it?'

'Of what? Liza's mother's car?'

'No, idiot, of the stew! It was made under duress, you know, after Mr Rex's visit.'

'It's prime,' Nibby muttered through a mouthful of dumpling. 'I'm marrying you for your cooking, nothing else.' He swallowed, took a sip of tea and then beamed at Alice. 'Now let's wash up and clear away and then, if the kids aren't back . . .'

'If the kids aren't back we'll walk down to the boatshed and you can show me what you've done today. I'm a young woman about to be married, so I won't stay in a lonely cottage with unreliable young men. Now when you're married, it'll be quite different!'


'David! Come in! Come along . . . d'you know I never thought I'd see you again after all that business, and here you are, large as life and looking, thank God, very unlike yourself, except that I'd know you anywhere!' Yuri had shut the door after ushering David inside the flat, and now he took him through to the small living-room. 'Tanya's in the kitchen. She'll bring us tea, she always does when I have a visitor.'

'I'm hoping the beard and the haircut and the Russian clothing will keep me Sergei Morosovski in everyone's eyes, and that no one will even think about David Thomas. So if you don't mind, Yuri, stick to Sergei, even when you're talking to Tanya. Where is she?'

'Tanya? I just told you she's . . .'

'Pavel, you idiot! Where is she? When can we meet?'

Yuri stared. 'Pavel? My God, of course . . . I don't know why but the moment I set eyes on you I thought she must have sent you . . . she's almost certainly gone, then.'

'Gone? Where? They've not . . .'

'Of course not. She'll have started to make her way to meet you in Turkey. I wrote, you see, saying she was staying here, but it wasn't safe, there was a fellow following me, the janitor here keeps a beady eye on us all, even Tanya, and the food situation's pretty desperate . . . plus Baru . . .'

'Baru? You mean to say she had that great hound with her?'

'Too true. She found somewhere to stay, a woman who was

glad to have the dog for protection and Pavel for company, but remember she only came to find Eva and she searched for weeks with no success. She had no papers, she ate in a communal dining-room, the one the friend who put her up used, but because of the food situation again it was only a matter of time before someone asked a question she couldn't answer. It was terribly dangerous, Davidski, so I told her to go, lent her money, and then wrote to you saying she was on her way. I'm sorry, I had no idea that you might miss both letters.'

'I didn't. I got the first, and decided to come in and fetch her when I got the message that the second had arrived, the one saying that Pavel was in Moscow looking for Eva. It was the third I must have missed.'

'Yes, of course, I was forgetting the very first letter, the one telling you she was leaving the farm. Did you come that way? See anything of the new people? It distressed Pavel very much that she was leaving Fedor's farm in such hands.'

'No, I didn't go near it. It isn't really on any route, and to see anything of the farm itself you have to go right into the valley. In fact I kept well clear of the whole area, because by then I knew she was in Moscow, and my beard hadn't grown too well. I knew people had seen me with Pavel a couple of years ago, people in the market, old men herding cattle in the mountains, and I didn't want to risk being recognised before my chin-fungus had grown sufficiently.' The two men had been standing in the centre of the small room, talking, but now David sat down heavily on the nearest chair and put his head in his hands. 'Christ, it never occurred to me that she might have left! What in heaven's name do I do now?'

Yuri sat down in the chair opposite. It struck David for the first time that his friend was looking a good deal thinner and older than the mere two years which had elapsed since they had last met justified. There were new lines on Yuri's face, and his cheekbones were so prominent that they cast shadows beneath them.

'Yuri . . . are you all right?'

'Sure I'm all right. Oh, the weight loss, you mean. We're all thinner in Moscow this year – it's the new Soviet speciality, slender citizens. But I don't know how best to advise you. You see, she was undecided which way to cross the Caucasus, whether to try to use the old military road which crosses the eastern mountains via the Krestovy Pass, or to go by the Klukhor, which she knows well. If she goes by the Krestovy at least she has a road to follow which does not lead her into any glaciers and which is used by a good many others. And she'll go to Tbilisi, rather than Ochemchiri; in Tbilisi she'll merge, but in a little place like Ochemchiri she might stand out rather more.'

'So you think she'll try the Krestovy?'

'I advised it, but . . . ah, Tanya!'

Both men waited for Tanya to bring in the tray, David smiling but saying nothing. He knew how the beard changed him, but Tanya had known him for a good few months – would she be fooled? She put the tray down and turned to him, stared, looked down at the floor . . . and then glanced back at him, a slow smile spreading across her face.

'Davidski – it is you! What joy to see you in our home once more!'

'Hello, Tanya, it's a joy to be here,' David said, getting to his feet and kissing her cheek. 'How did you recognise me?'

'By your voice, through the door,' Tanya admitted frankly. 'When I came in and saw you sitting there, with all that beard, I couldn't understand how I had made such a stupid mistake, but then I looked closer, and it was our dear Davidski!'

'I'm glad it wasn't on my appearance alone,' David admitted as she began to pour out three glasses of pale tea. 'I'm absolutely banking on the beard to keep me out of trouble with the OGPU.'

'It's a good disguise,' Yuri admitted. 'I was expecting you, but even so I wouldn't have recognised you without the voice . . . plus the fact that I've been thinking about you so much.' He turned to his partner. 'Tanya, did Pavelinka ever give you a clue as to which road over the mountains she would take? The Klukhor or the Krestovy?'

'No. She listened well, that one, when we talked, but said very little.' Tanya handed a glass of tea to David, another to Yuri, and then sat down and addressed them once more. 'Did you know, David, that Pavel could not come here? The caretaker, you see, keeps an eye on the flats to see who comes and goes and at that time we had a man who watched us . . . oh, nearly all the time. OGPU, of course. So usually Yuri met her at some convenient place, but once or twice, when it was impossible for him to do so, I went instead. She is brave and good and would not put us in jeopardy by coming here.'

'No, she wouldn't hurt anyone if she could help it,' David agreed, remembering how she had behaved over Fedor's refusal to allow her to leave the farm with himself. 'Then what must I do? Should I make my way back to Turkey as quickly as I can, or risk Tbilisi, or try Ochemchiri? She went by rail, you said?'

'Ah . . . one other thing,' Tanya put in. 'Wasn't she going to work before she crossed the mountains? Her money was very low.'

'Yes, she was.' Yuri looked upset. 'I tried to lend her more, but it was difficult . . . look at Tanya!'

'She's the new Moscow model as well,' David said grimly, realising for the first time that Tanya's slimness was not of her choosing. 'I'm glad Pavel didn't take your money and leave you short, Yuri . . . but what would she work at? What does she know?'

'Farming. How to herd cattle. She'll do farm work. She's still a lad, by the way.' Yuri sipped his tea, then stood the glass down. 'If I had to bet on it, you know, I'd bet she'll go by the Klukhor, even after all my good advice. Certainly she'll try for work in the country she knows rather than going on to where she won't know a soul.'

'I wonder . . . you don't think she'll return to the farm in the valley where she was brought up? You say she was distressed by the peasants' lack of knowledge or interest in Fedor's place? Then she might, mightn't she?'

'I don't know about that . . . it seems a bit foolish, if she does. The local people will have been told to keep their eyes peeled for her, no doubt, and of course they know she dressed as a boy when she herded the cattle and sheep.'

'You're probably right; it was just an idea.' David drank more tea, then stood up. 'I'd better be going; can I get out without being spotted? I don't think your janitor saw me as I came up – I used the stairs, not the lift – but it wouldn't do, would it, for the Party to find out that you'd had a strange and bearded visitor?'

'No, it wouldn't. But by a bit of good luck you came in at around the time a good many workers return from their jobs, so he won't have had time to check on everyone. It's only those that ask directions or use the lift who get watched. We'll go down the stairs, and Tanya will get a neighbour to go and chat to the caretaker and see that he's occupied as we cross the foyer.'

All went smoothly, so smoothly indeed that David remarked on it.

'It's an old game we all play,' Yuri said, accompanying him into the street for a moment. 'Where are you staying? If we can help in any way . . .'

'Just forget the whole thing; I'll write if . . . when . . . we get back home.' David pressed his hand and then walked away, pushing through the fresh snowfall. He looked over his shoulder once, but Yuri had disappeared back into the warmth of the block once more.

David was only in Moscow for five days, but they were five very nasty days. He saw *bez prizorney* everywhere, skinny, hopeless and thievish, and realised that the Muscovites were frightened of the ragamuffins, the homeless ones. They were a blot on the nation's escutcheon and they were desperate . . . they had nothing to lose so when they hit they hit with all their force, when they lied they did so with total conviction, when they stole they grabbed and ran. They were at the bottom of the pit and could sink no lower; nothing could degrade them further.

Food was shorter, possibly, in this great city than in other places. David had no doubt that the higher echelons of the Party ate well enough, and they saved face, if you could call it that, by feeding foreigners with a sort of desperate generosity, but the people themselves starved. Here, rations were almost all that was available – David could well see why Pavel had left, and he only hoped that Eva was not amongst the *prizorney* he saw, flickering, ragged shadows slithering ahead of him through the crowds, as he waited for the train which would take him back over the ground he had so recently covered, to Pavel's mountains.

He had only been in the city five days, yet when he finally got on to a train heading for the mountains he noticed a subtle change in the travellers surrounding him. They were going, not to visit or to return home, but to try to find somewhere where food was still grown, or stored, or even hoarded. If you had a cousin on a collective, now was the time to visit him. If you had come from a village renowned for its good potato crop, now was the time for a reunion. One particular family was simply travelling to get away from the slum they inhabited and the misery they had left behind, for two of their children had already starved to death and, when the last of the wood was burned and the last of the paraffin used up, it was a choice between buying a train ticket and praying for a better chance elsewhere or remaining in Moscow and dying when the money ran out.

The misery in the carriage was almost palpable, and it both depressed and frightened David. Pavel was so alone! She had Baru but almost no money. How would she manage? What would she do if she could not find work? He must hurry . . . hurry! Yet the train was as slow as if it, too, were starving. It clattered and clanked and groaned across the great flat stretches of the steppes, the grass hidden by the unending fall of the snow, the air biting cold so that when the train stopped and hunger might be appeased, the passengers did not fight each other to be first down on to the platform but lingered on board, dreading the bitter chill on their starving and weary bodies.

On that journey, nothing seemed to go right. Food was sold on the platforms, but it was meagre food of poor quality. Bread simply never came their way, though frosted potatoes and carrots were stewed up in big cauldrons and a small bowl was offered for an exorbitant sum, or a sum that seemed exorbitant to most of the train's many passengers.

Soldiers travelled with them, further up the train. Raw-boned, passive young men, they suffered the cold, the screams and shouts of their officers, the lack of food, the slowness of the train, with seeming indifference. David supposed they had joined up in the hope of a decent meal at least once a day — if so, they were disappointed, since they joined the scrum on every platform where food was available — but they were somehow menacing, as though hunger had turned them into wolves to prey on the people instead of sturdy watchdogs to protect them.

But even the militia were suffering from the cold and the lack of food. Occasionally one saw policemen, but they were not engaged in persecuting wrongdoers or chasing the *prizorney*, they were mainly walking up and down the streets, trying to keep warm and probably hoping for a hand-out from a tradesman, if anyone in their town still had food stored away.

It was strange, but the further from Moscow they got the deeper grew David's depression. He told himself that he was probably only a week or two behind Pavel, that presently he would see her, hold her, and they would escape together, but in his low state even this held no real attraction. For weeks he had walked a tightrope, acted a part, strong in the certainty that he would soon hold his girl once more. Now he simply slogged grimly on, hoping but no longer certain of anything save the cold, his own hunger and the misery with which he was surrounded.

The knight in shining armour who had ridden in on his white horse was long gone, and David Thomas had nightmares in which he saw Pavel lying dead on a station platform as the train thundered through, or hanging by her neck from a lamp-post whilst a crowd of OGPU men danced with pleasure beneath her swinging feet. When the train finally gave up the ghost in a town out on the plain and the passengers were told it was three days until the next one was due through, he scarcely cared. He walked wearily into town, found himself a lodging, and settled down to wait. He had bargained for a meal each evening – potatoes – and two glasses of tea, though it would not actually be tea, since this was in very short supply, but a herbal concoction of his landlady's. Further than this he could not go, or be expected to go. In his heart he did not believe he would ever see Pavel again and he was resigned to it; his one thought was to get this nightmare journey over and get back to his own place, to Deeside, where he belonged.

*'With my body I thee worship . . .'*

Nibby said the words reverently, his voice a little shaky. Alice, not in white but in a pretty sapphire blue wool skirt and jacket, with a candy pink blouse under it and a candy pink hat perched on her smooth brown hair, held his fingers lightly in hers and knew that this was the most important thing that had ever happened to her and wished desperately that David could have been there. It was hard to be married with no mother and no father present, but to marry without your brother to give you away merely because he happened to be thousands of miles away in a foreign land was harder yet.

Of course she had Ned. He had said, magnanimously, that he would do the giving away bit even before she'd asked, and he had not complained when she had refused to allow his elder daughter to be a bridesmaid.

'I'm not wearing white, as we can't afford to splash out, but Sassy will take my bouquet when I hand it to her,' she said lightly, trying not to let Ned see that she minded. 'Afterwards, we're all going back to the Hall. The Rafts have offered to let us have the wedding breakfast there. It won't be much – I'm making most of it – and it's family and very close friends only, but it'll be better than trying to cram people into the cottage.'

Maria had been awfully good. She had insisted that Alice did the cooking in the big, modernised kitchen at Carmel Hall and had helped her not only with the cooking but also by providing ingredients which 'just happened' to be handy. Alice knew that Maria was doing it for all the wrong reasons, but nevertheless she appreciated that there was genuine kindness under it all and allowed herself to be persuaded.

Ned had not approved of using Carmel Hall for the wedding breakfast, but upon reflecting what an upheaval it would cause in his own solid house had agreed at least that it was 'good of Maria'.

And now, at last, it was all happening. Behind her the church was full, for she was popular and most of the men from the yard as it had been in her father's day had turned up to see the young 'un wed. The Rafts were there, of course, the old boy grinning as if Alice were his, fat Mrs Raft snuffling a surreptitious tear into a large handkerchief because weddings always made her cry, and Maria doubtless imagining that it was herself at the altar, with David by her side.

'. . . and may they ever live in perfect love and peace together, and live according to thy laws; through Jesus Christ our Lord. Amen.'

The congregation murmured reverently and there was that sound of feet surreptitiously scraping, of skirts shushing and whispering, of gloves being collected, handbags lifted, children hissed out of their preoccupations, which heralds the end of a church service.

Alice waited and increased the pressure of her fingers on Nibby's and felt him squeeze back, heartened by the fact that it was nearly over, no doubt. Poor Nibby, who had not been to

389

church since he had left school, had been horrified at the thought of going through the ordeal without David beside him and had wanted a register office ceremony, but fortunately his father had stood buff, so he had gone through with it, though with a good deal of trepidation as the day approached.

From the organ, the music that she had waited for blared out. Dum dum de dum dum dum dum . . .

It is surely only possible to float down the aisle in a long white dress, with a veil which obligingly floats out behind one. Yet Alice managed to float. So great her happiness, so ecstatic the face that she turned to the waiting congregation, that not one person commented on or even thought about her plain attire and the murmur went round that should always go round . . . doesn't she make a lovely bride?

Nibby's arm, which had quavered and wavered, was rock-solid now as he saw daylight ahead of him. He marched, Alice floated and behind them Sassy was dimmed by their glow, turned into a pretty but ordinary girl in a low-necked, mid-night blue velvet dress and matching slippers.

In the vestry realisation struck when the vicar addressed Alice as Mrs Hawke and she signed with her brand new name: Alice Horatia Hawke. Nibby looked despite her efforts to stop him and dug her in the ribs and laughed at her because she had a silly middle name, and then he signed too . . . John Archibald Hawke . . . and she laughed openly, and called him Archie, and then someone told him to kiss the bride and he did and all the fears, the tears, the worries and frustrations of the past few days fell into ashes and there was only Alice and Nibby, and being married, and longing to get back to the cottage to be by themselves at last!

'The food's prime, you must admit.'

Michael dug Sara with his elbow, speaking with his mouth delectably full of salmon mousse, a creation of the Rafts' cook. Sara, balancing a plate piled indecently high, sighed, nodded, and then whispered in his ear.

'Yes, I know . . . but fancy staying here for a whole week, whilst those two have our cottage all to themselves! It really is *not* fair!'

'Alice says to take notice, because once it was ours and perhaps one day, when Dave and Nibby are rich, it will be again. She says we should love it, even if we can't actually remember living here very well.'

The Rafts had thrown open the big drawing-room and the dining-room to their young friends' guests, but in truth only the drawing-room was necessary, because it was a huge room and the guests, as it turned out, few. The family were all there, sure enough – Ned and his wife and their two daughters, Lydia and Norman, Julia and Harmer – but they had not liked to ask too many friends so it was mainly the principal people from the old shipyard, colleagues from Alice's office and Nibby's school friends, and relatives who lived near enough and who had remained on good terms with the young Thomases even after their change of abode.

'I'm glad David isn't here,' Alice muttered to Nibby as the two of them finished greeting their guests and began to pick nervously at the food on the big central buffet table. 'He'd hate it . . . not being here by right, as it were.'

'Oh, I don't know, it seems big and echoing after the cottage,' Nibby said loyally. 'The gardens are lovely in summer, I know, but not at this time of year.'

'The snowdrops under the copper beech will be out,' Alice reminded him. 'Oh, Nibby, remember the games we used to play in the stables, and the way the groom used to bawl at us if we mucked the hay about, because he said we took the goodness out of it?'

'Don't I just! I'm afraid I'll never be able to give you a home like this, darling, but one day we'll have our very own cottage . . . I'll make a garden as good as this, only it'll be smaller, and . . . Allikins, when can we slip off?'

'When it's over, I suppose,' Alice said. Suddenly, Nibby seemed different; larger and stronger and a force to be reckoned with. She took his hand and he turned hers in it so that his finger could trace letters and patterns in her palm. She giggled and tried to pull away, but he held on hard and took her wrist in three fingers and a thumb, using his forefinger to draw with, holding so that she could not escape. It was odd; exhilarating and frightening and suddenly she was as keen to get back to the cottage as he, though her eagerness was touched with very real apprehension. Both her married sisters had made remarks to the effect that she should feel free to ask them anything she wanted to know about marriage, but she had scorned to do so.

She remembered, however, that Lydia's mother-in-law had had several talks with Lydia prior to the wedding, and that Lydia had gone giggling off with Julia prior to Julia's own marriage. But it's different for me, she assured herself, because I'm marrying Nibby, and we've known each other for ever. There's nothing that Nibby and I can't talk about, nothing I don't know about him.

'Eat up, then,' Nibby recommended. 'They won't let us go until we've eaten something. I heard Mrs Raft telling Maria to be sure you made a good meal.' He snorted scornfully. 'As if you had some ghastly ordeal ahead of you which would take away your appetite for weeks and weeks. Absurd!'

Alice's heart plummeted into her little black court shoes. She remembered once, in the stables, she had watched the big old labrador, Gunner, having his wicked way with a young labrador bitch brought from away to mate with Gunner because he was a first-rate retriever and his puppies would be valuable.

The little bitch, whose name was Rustle, had been very coy and very eager until Gunner came down to what David had called brass tacks, and then she had made an awful fuss, biting at Gunner and yelping and finally, when David and the groom between them had got her to stand, shaking and shivering and whining from beginning to end of the performance.

'Just like a woman,' David had remarked, dragging Alice back to nursery tea when she would much have preferred to stay with him. 'First they want something and when they get it they whine and yelp and say it was all a trick and it hurts and they hate it.' And, Alice now recalled, he had looked remarkably smug . . . he had been fifteen then, she twelve.

But she was being silly. Nibby was Nibby and Gunner was just a dog, and she was no simpering little Rustle to yip and snap and whine. She and Nibby loved each other, she enjoyed his lovemaking very much; no doubt now they were married and he wanted to do other, more interesting things, she would enjoy those too.

'Come on, love, eat up.'

'I'm not very hungry,' Alice whispered, eyeing the food on her plate. How huge the vol-au-vent with the salmon mousse bulging out of the top, how sinister the sausage roll!

'I expect you ate heaps at breakfast,' Nibby said understandingly. Only she had been unable to eat any breakfast at all, because of the excitement. 'Never mind, just nibble at it, alter the shape a bit, and then we'll stroll over to my father and you can stuff it into the earth round that palm in a pot . . . see it?'

Alice nibbled, feeling sick. She wished she had let Lydia tell her just what *did* happen when one got married. She trailed after Nibby and shoved her food into the plant-pot, not even bothering to cover it up properly. Nibby's stepmother hugged her large stepson and then put her arm round Alice's waist.

'You look very lovely, my dear. Now I expect you'll want to get into your going-away things; can I come up with you?'

'I've only got a thick coat, and that's in the car,' Alice explained. One glance at Mrs Hawke's sweet, gentle face had convinced her that here was the right person to ask a few pertinent questions of, but even this, it seemed, was to be denied her, for Nibby took her arm in a very proprietorial fashion and said abruptly that they would really have to be on their way, otherwise it would be dark before they reached the cottage.

After that there was nothing to do but put a good face on it, and indeed, Alice told herself, it was downright ridiculous to fear the unknown when the unknown was her own darling Nibby Hawke!

So she sat behind the uniformed chauffeur who came with the hired car, and waved and blew kisses and threw her bouquet out of the car window and saw Sara grab it and bring it down smartly on Michael's head. And then she waved a bit more and sank back in her seat and let Nibby hold her hand and stroke her knee out of the chauffeur's view, she hoped.

It was not far to the cottage; the light was lit in the kitchen, but it was not yet dark although the sun had disappeared and grey twilight was creeping over the mountains.

Nibby thanked the chauffeur and they watched the car make its way carefully down the hill, then they turned and went into the cottage. When Alice was in, she saw that Nibby was locking the front door carefully behind them.

For one minute common sense fled and sheer panic took over. What was he doing? How dared he lock them in? She said as much in a voice suddenly a little higher than usual and he turned from the door and crossed the hall in a couple of strides to take her in his arms. She was still wearing her thick coat, but he slid his arms underneath it and hugged her tightly.

'What's the matter, darling? Why do you think I'm locking you in? I'm locking other people out!'

'Oh,' Alice said in a very small voice. 'Why? We never lock the front door.'

'Tonight we do.' His voice was firm, tender, and a tiny bit amused. Alice frowned, affronted. Was he laughing at her? But it appeared he was not. He took her coat off with great gentleness, hung it on the hallstand, and then led her through into the kitchen, but they did not stop there. They continued into the little short passage and through the door of Nibby's room. Their room.

When they were inside, Nibby shut the door, but not cruelly or finally or anything like that, just softly. He stood there for a moment with his arm round her waist, and they looked at the room.

Alice had seen the new bed Nibby had ordered, but not in position, for he had not allowed it. Now she gazed at it, and it looked very big and very soft and luxurious. Sinful, too, with a blue silk counterpane and pale blue blankets. There was a little stove burning blue, which made the room warm and pleasant, and a carpet on the floor. A blue and white carpet, to match the blue and white curtains. There was also a lamp, unlit as yet, though the dusk outside was softening and deepening. Soon it would be quite dark and they would be able to lie in that big bed and watch the stars come out.

'Alice? Shall we . . .?' Nibby jerked a thumb at the bed. Alice looked hopefully round for a diversion, and discovered one. A washstand. 'I'd like to wash, first,' she said timidly. 'Will that be all right?'

'Sure. Or you can have a bath, if you'd rather; we both will. The water's hot and Mrs Evans made up the fire to last all night. How about it?'

Alice thought a bath would be nice, but she recognised a further attempt on her part to put off the married bit, so she shook her head, cleared her throat, and poured a little water into the handbasin. It was cold, but she was so hot herself that the water would warm as it fell on her.

'No, I won't bother with a bath right now; perhaps later. Now I'll make do with a quick wash.'

She dabbled her hands, splashed her face, dried both carefully on the nice clean blue and white towel which hung on the rail beside the washstand and then squared her shoulders and turned to her newly acquired husband.

'Well? What do I do next? I'm as ready as I'll ever be,' she said as boldly as she could. 'Only . . . it's awfully early to go to bed!'

# CHAPTER SEVENTEEN

Alice woke early next morning and knew at once that she was married, that she was in their beautiful new bed in their beautiful new room, and that a whole new way of life was opening up in front of her.

Last night had been all right. No, not all right, more like wonderful, she thought half-guiltily. All her fears had been groundless, or at least greatly exaggerated. And afterwards they had lain and watched the stars appear in the dark sky through the bare branches of an apple tree which grew near their window, and she had known such happiness that she had wanted to whoop for joy. She had told Nibby, lazily, curled up in his embrace with her head resting on his chest, and he had laughed, squeezed her and told her to whoop away since they were alone in the house.

There was a little brass alarm clock on the window sill; its face showed that it was not so early after all – seven thirty was getting-up time for weekends, or at least it was for her and Nibby, with their various tasks to tackle. She turned her head and looked at Nibby's sleeping face and felt her heart turn over. His mouth always looked as if something was amusing him when he was awake but asleep it was relaxed, gentle. She slid softly out of bed and crept across the room, glad of the carpet instead of the polished boards which predominated upstairs. She opened the door softly and went out, down the short corridor and into the kitchen. The fire was low but the room was still pleasantly warm.

Alice's honeymoon nightie was a sensible garment, just white cotton with frills. She padded contentedly round the kitchen making up the fire and then boiling the kettle for tea. She would take Nibby a cup and wake him with a kiss . . . her stomach turned over . . . and then they would both decide what to do with the whole blank beautiful day at their disposal.

She made a tea-tray complete with biscuits and carried it through to the bedroom. Disappointingly, Nibby was awake. He grinned at her and sat up expectantly.

'Tea! I'm sorry you had to get it, I should have woken first, but I was jolly tired . . . I worked hard last night, and I hope you appreciated it the way you ought!'

Alice felt her cheeks grow hot but she laughed with him.

'If you have any doubts, dear John, I'll get back into bed and we'll forget all about the tea and our responsibilities. Now what should we do today?'

Nibby put the cup he was holding down on the tray again and held out his arms.

'Come here and I'll show you!'

'But what about . . .'

'Alice! Didn't you promise to love, honour and obey? Come here!'

Pavel had agonised over what she should do when the train reached the town nearest to her old home, but in the event she need not have worried, since she really had no choice. She had not a kopek left in the world and she and Baru were both extremely hungry. So she left the train and walked into the town she had once known, if not well, at least slightly.

Since the State had decreed that days of the week were no longer relevant, since one's day off, in a shop or factory, varied from week to week and from month to month, she could not say that today was a Monday, a Thursday or a Friday, but it was definitely not market day.

Today, the streets seemed dead, and what life there was centred round the railway station. In the streets the piled-up snow was grey below and white above, the pavements thick with frozen slush. The houses wore that closed, uninhabited look which Pavel had associated, in Moscow, with a block of workers' flats when everyone was out at their jobs, but here, as she knew very well, few women worked except on market days and in their own homes. She also noticed that few fires burned, and that was unusual; there was wood to be gathered, surely? Paraffin, which was used a lot in the cities, was in short supply, but here they must have all the wood they needed.

Further up the road a boy in rags sat on the pavement's edge, scratching something in the ice with a sharply pointed stick. Pavel approached him.

'Hello! Where *is* everyone? I'm looking for work and for somewhere to stay; can you tell me where to try?'

The boy looked up. He had a round, flattish face and slanting eyes. He looked vaguely familiar, yet Pavel could not put a name to him and he obviously did not know her.

'Work? It's the wrong day; market day's tomorrow.'

'So I see, but surely people don't only work on market day? Who works on the farms?'

'The collectives, you mean. There isn't much work at this time of the year, though they say when spring comes they'll build up the herds again.'

'Build them up? But how . . . I don't understand.' Pavel sighed and put a restraining hand on Baru's collar. 'Where are your parents?'

The boy jerked a thumb at the house behind him.

'My mother's in there. Father's out.'

Pavel stared from the house to the boy and back again; he did not look as though he belonged there, somehow. The people of the town had been not rich, but they had been comfortably off, well-to-do. Their children were dressed plainly perhaps, but in thick, warm clothing. They had a school and a town council which worked to keep the town in good heart, and the market kept them, if not in plenty, at least comfortably. But the boy was unlikely to lie to her; she crossed the piled-up snow and knocked sharply on the wooden front door.

It was several moments before the door opened inward and a face looked round the edge. The woman was not old but she was all wrong for the house – the wife of such a house would have been younger, brisker, with a child the age of the one sitting on the pavement's edge. And this woman was a peasant, with straggly hair, big, gnarled hands like a man's and ragged clothing. A servant? Townspeople did employ servants, but a servant would be neat and tidy, not like this uncouth, brutish-looking woman.

'Er . . . do you live here?' Pavel said with unaccustomed bluntness. 'The lad said . . . I'm trying to find work and a place to lay my head and I wondered if you could advise me.'

'We live here. Why? Did you know the Zhdanovs? They went in the purge.'

'The purge? Whatever do you mean?'

'There aren't many live here now as lived here six months ago,' the woman said with a certain relish. 'They took from the poor and downtrodden, see? So now they've gone to the timber camps to learn what work's all about and we've been moved in. We run the shops and the men'll work on the land when the weather's right.'

'And the farms? The collectives? Your son said something about building up the herds when spring comes.'

'That's right. They killed off the sheep and cattle, most of 'em, at the backend. Now they've few beasts, but the herds will be built up when the snow goes and there's grazing for all.'

Pavel sighed and walked slowly away from the woman's indifferent gaze. Was this why the town had fallen into such a state? If the herds were run down then no one was going to have butter or milk to sell, let alone other things . . . but what of the harvest? Barns should have been bulging with grain and root crops with no stock to feed. Then she remembered someone telling her that good farmers, who knew they were about to be dispossessed, had not sown their acres, had sold off their stock – as Fedor had, she remembered belatedly. She had been living on Fedor's hard cash ever since leaving the farm weeks and weeks earlier.

And the peasants had not understood hill farming, so they had either killed off the cattle or allowed them to be killed by wolves, and so they had no food to take to market, no grain to sell. The people who could have saved the country with skill and knowledge gained the hard way were stuck away in timber camps in the cold north, slaving through a Siberian winter which probably made this one look quite mild.

The waste! Of lives, of knowledge, of good farming land and beasts! But where did it leave her? With diminished herds and nothing to sell, how could she expect to get employment? No one would want her, or be able to pay her if they did need her, she supposed.

For the first time, Pavel felt near to despair. She would never reach Georgia, never cross into Turkey, never see David again! She slid her hand into Baru's collar again and turned her face to the hills; if she was going to die she could at least make an effort, first, to live. She would go back to Fedor's farm and see whether they could offer her either work or at least shelter until she could work. If not, if they denied it, she would climb high up, to the shepherd's hut, and she and Baru would do their best to last out the winter there.

It was a pity that there was no food available and that she had no money to buy it with anyway, but you never knew, Baru was always resourceful and a good hunter, perhaps she would be able to catch game for them. Pavel could gather wood, light a fire, roast meat . . .

Her natural optimism asserted itself as she strode out along the track that would lead eventually into the high hills. Where there's life there's hope, she told herself. One way and another she and Baru would survive because they wanted to do so.

The train had come at last and David and his fellow sufferers had climbed aboard. It was slow, it was old and it was cold, but at least they were moving once more. David dug deep into his pocket and bought wisely when the opportunity occurred, and it began to seem possible that this journey would end one day and that he would see his home again. Sometimes, when it was not actually snowing or when a glimpse of a pale, watery sun could be seen through the shifting clouds, he actually felt that he was close to Pavel and not chasing some ghostly will-o'-the-wisp which, if he caught up, would just slide mockingly through his clutching fingers.

The decision to get off the train at the town nearest the mountains came almost without a conscious thought – he just woke one morning knowing that it was what he was going to do. So when they drew in at the small station, unfamiliar beneath its blanketing snow, David climbed stiffly down and set off on foot for the hills. There was no public transport as such out here, but he managed to get a lift in a pony-drawn sledge which took him many miles, and he slept in a rough tumbledown house full to the brim of peasants who were, they told him proudly, making a collective. They fed him well enough, but they warned him never to speak of it since they were supposed to send all their food to market.

'All?' David said disbelievingly, but they assured him that it was so and showed him a letter telling them what they must sell to the State.

'It is all, you see, because we are not yet used to farming,' an elderly man told him. 'I swept the streets in Pyatigorsk until the State decided I could be better employed here. When we grow accustomed perhaps we shall be able to grow more food and have better beasts, so we shall have something left for ourselves, but at the moment' – he shrugged expressively – 'at the moment we lie to them, what else can we do? If we told them there was anything they would take it all, so we tell them there's nothing, that the man who owned the farm stripped it bare, and they believe.'

'I don't blame you,' David said, eating maize cakes with butter on them. 'How many cattle do you have?'

'Not many. Six cows and a bull. We shall put the cows in calf soon, someone said it was right. And when the snow clears we'll plough . . . we have a horse. But until then we keep the cows inside in the sheds and feed them what we can, and the bull roams free during the day but comes back to the cows at night. We hope he'll survive, but the wolves are hungry; they come right up to the house in the night, you know.'

'So I believe,' David said. 'I wish you success.'

But he did not think they would do as well as their predecessors; after all, they were starting with enormous disadvantages. They believed the State would do as it declared, for one thing, and did not have enough intelligence to work out why they were in the position they were in, for another. If the State meant it when it declared all the collectives would be given free grain for the spring planting, where was that free grain coming from, when they did not have enough to feed their people? They resented the State's arbitrary seizing of their hard-won meat, grain and dairy products, but did not realise that this meant their collectives would never rise above subsistence level for the people who worked them. Or not whilst things remained as they were now, at any rate.

David left that particular collective when he had rested and had bought enough food to see him satisfied for a few days, and struck up into the high mountains. The regime could scarcely expect to collectivise the *aouls* and the tiny *koshes* perched high on the rocks, where people were so poor that no one could accuse them of anything save the sin of poverty. He would make for the high mountains, therefore, stay in the *koshes* with the Caucasian herdsmen, and ask for news of a young lad with a big dog who talked about getting a job here.

He felt strong and hopeful once more when he left the collective, but at noon a storm blew up and a great lanky dog attacked him when he headed towards a lonely *kosh*; only his shouts and his vicious parrying blows from a stout stick he had equipped himself with saved him. He crawled into the *kosh* feeling utterly worn out and hopeless . . . and found himself transported.

The *kosh* was exactly the same as all the ones he had visited with Yuri a lifetime ago. The welcome, the tall men with their big dogs and their *burkas* slung round their broad shoulders, the warmth of the fuggy air, the lovely, delicate women, the smoke-blackened sods which formed the roof, it was all the same. Even the food was the same – roasted pieces of sheep, flat maize cakes, sour cream and cheese. Perhaps it was simply that a great ponderous machine like the State could not reach everywhere, perhaps it was that people so poor could not be further reduced and no one envied them their wild and precarious existence, but whatever the reason there was a sturdy sameness about the *kosh* and its inhabitants that made David feel there was still hope for humanity.

When they had eaten and he had explained his quest, fruitlessly because they had seen no strangers here save himself for many months, he curled up on a sheepskin near the fire and slept almost at once. If he kept to places like this and husbanded his resources, he would get safely into Georgia without too much hardship. Once there, he intended to find work before crossing the border again.

The shepherd's hut was deserted when Pavel reached it. The storm which had come up seemed to have blown itself out, but she was very tired and did not think she would have reached its sanctuary without Baru's help. She had hung on to the dog's collar and been more or less dragged for about a mile up the steepest part of the path.

The door was pulled to but she pushed it open and the pair' of them staggered in, too exhausted to fear that they might not be alone, and as it happened they were. The hut had not been used for some time; Pavel could see that at a glance. A pile of straw in one corner and some pine boughs were the only things in the small, square room.

'Do we make a fire?' Pavel knew she was too tired to do anything but sleep, so she did not attempt to answer her own question. Instead, she pushed the straw into a pile and she and Baru crept into it. Then she spread her *burka* out over them both and within two minutes they were fast asleep. Just before she actually lost all touch with reality and plunged into dreams, she told herself that tomorrow they would go down into the valley and see what Fedor's successors were doing. It was clear they were not using this hut or herding sheep . . . but that was for tomorrow; for now she must sleep and recuperate her strength.

She saw the farm first from the top of the valley, then descended by the long, winding path through the pine trees. She was weak and very hungry but hope kept her going. Surely they had not let the farm go too badly? From the mountain top it had looked very much as usual, though she could see no beasts in the corrals; perhaps they had already taken them out to try to scrape a way through the snow to the grass that lay underneath. If they had it was foolish, because there was feed in the big barns and cattle and sheep lost condition if they were walked miles and were still unable to find grazing, but the peasants she had spoken to months previously would not know that, they would simply do their best to see that the cattle and sheep were kept fed.

After that first glimpse, of course, the farm was out of sight for a long time, but as she rounded the last bend in the track and it came into view a pang shook her. Home! If only it was home still! If only she could go to the door, knock . . . and find Eva there, smiling at her, telling her it had all been a horrid mistake, that Fedor was in the stables helping a calf to be born, and Nyusha in the store-room fetching flour for a cake. But she knew that things were very different when she got only a little closer. No dogs rushed out to greet or growl, and the corrals were not only empty, they had known no beasts for a long time. The snow on them was smooth and unmarked, great cushions of white dimpling low where the fencing was but without a sign that any animal had trodden on the clear expanse.

The snow in the yard was trampled, but it should have been cleared; even in the worst weather Fedor had kept it swept so that they could go to and from the house without getting all clagged up with the stuff. And though smoke rose from the chimney there was no other sign of life. No people bustled around the milking shed, no cows lowed, no horse turned its head to its owner and whickered a welcome.

She and Baru made for the door, Baru with her tail up at first and then gradually drooping until it was all but between her legs. Her friends, the other dogs – did she remember, miss them? Pavel could not tell, but could see that the dog was puzzled and unhappy. Certainly she would not have forgotten the farm where she had spent so many happy years, but she walked with her mistress, slow and proud, and then stood back as Pavel raised her fist and knocked on the door.

A woman opened it. Pavel knew her at once; it was the same woman who had been present when she had left the farm for the last time. She had been a big woman and now she was bigger, her low-slung breasts bulging behind the cheap stuff of her dress and her face rounder, the chin doubled. She looked blankly at Pavel.

'Yes?'

'I need work. I was here once, to buy stock from the farmer. I dare say you won't remember if you have many visitors.'

The woman's attention was caught; her gaze raked Pavel up and down and then she nodded.

'I remember there was a boy . . . d'you want work?'

To Pavel's delight the voice was eager now, almost lively.

'That's what I said. Do you need a lad?'

The woman started to nod, then seemed to remember something. 'Come in, you and the brute of a dog – we could do with a dog . . . the wolves . . . I remember Stefan saying that you'd talked of wolves . . . he wished he'd listened. But before I say any more I'd better get the men. Stefan's still in bed but Lipi's out in the barn. I'll fetch him.'

'Shall I fetch him, whilst you wake Stefan?' Pavel said tactfully. 'Did they send others . . . you said the Party had promised you more workers once you'd settled in.'

'Did I? No, in the event they decided to wait till spring. Things are good in one way, though . . . we've enough food.' The woman paused, for she had turned towards the door leading through to the bedrooms. 'There's a system . . . a quota system it's called . . . but Lipi said it was impossible this first year so we told the men who came that we had nothing, we hid the remaining sheep and cattle and Lipi took the horses up to the high pastures and kept them there all day . . . so we're safe for this year and next year can take care of itself.'

'I see. Right, I'll go to the barn,' Pavel said, trying hard not to laugh. The Party's quota system was being treated with the contempt it deserved all over the country, by the sound of it. But it would not happen after this first, chaotic year – next year the Soviet would have got its act together and woe betide any collective not handing over the greater percentage of its yield to the State!

Lipi was the little old man she remembered from her last visit; white-haired, white-bearded and bent, but with a firmness about his mouth that was missing in the other two. He was feeding the stock and the boy she had seen in the yard was helping him, laughing, lugging the heavy buckets round as though he had been doing it all his life. He stopped short when she and Baru entered, and nudged the old man.

'Dedushka, it's a fellow . . . it's the fellow that came before, the day we first came here, remember? And he's got the biggest dog . . . here, girl!'

Pavel thought the little boy a repulsive object, with his shaven head and unfamiliar Mongoloid features, but Baru did not appear to share her feelings. She was not a forthcoming dog, but she moved slowly towards the lad, neck outstretched, and then, slowly, her plumy tail began to move from side to side and she actually nudged the boy's cheek with a cold, wet nose.

'The woman of the house asks that you come indoors for a moment,' Pavel said to the old man. 'She's waking Stefan.'

'About time,' the old man said shortly. 'Sasha, finish the feeding.'

'Of course, Dedushka.' The boy held out his hand to Baru. 'May she stay out here, with me?'

'If she will,' Pavel said, but was not surprised to find that Baru was still by her side when she returned to the kitchen. What did surprise her was that her old friend looked back, twice, towards the stable; that nasty little boy had hidden charms, obviously!

In the kitchen the woman was pouring tea into glasses and the tall man with tufty dark hair was sitting at the kitchen table, eating oatmeal with a wooden spoon at a considerable rate. He glanced up as they entered, grunted, and then returned to his meal. Lipi, however, would have none of this.

'Stefan, where are your manners?' he shouted crossly. 'We have a guest, do you not see?'

In some confusion, Stefan set down his wooden spoon and goggled at Pavel; his blue eyes were curious, his cheeks pink with embarrassment. Pavel felt rather sorry for him, and she smiled at him with grave politeness.

'I'm sorry to disturb both your sleep and your meal, but I have come to see whether you need an extra worker. I know the farm quite well – I've been herding beasts in these mountains all my life . . . I wouldn't ask much money, just my keep and a few kopeks . . . so if I could be of use . . .'

'Your keep! Where's your family, then?'

Pavel almost answered that he knew as well as she, then remembered that she was supposed to be a neighbour.

'Gone,' she said briefly. 'There are strangers at my father's farm and no place for me. But this place is much larger . . . I don't want to join a collective on the plains, I'm mountain born and bred.'

'I don't think we need outsiders . . .' the man Stefan began, but was abruptly put in his place by Lipi once more. The old man pulled out a chair and sat down, then banged on the table.

'Yes, we need you; we can't manage with a woman, a halfwit, a child and an old man past his prime,' he said crossly. 'Bring me my oatmeal, woman, and some for the boy. What's your name, lad?'

'Pavel Ismaelovich,' Pavel said quickly. If local people recognised her they might call her by her name before they realised that she was still wanted by the authorities. It was safer to stick as closely to the truth as possible.

'I am not a halfwit,' Stefan said sullenly. 'Shame on you, Father, to call your own son such things! Where's Sasha?'

'Finishing the feeding; he'll come in for his oatmeal when he's finished his work and not before, unlike some.' The oatmeal came and everyone began to eat, Pavel with undisguised eagerness. But halfway through her generous portion she put her spoon down, feeling faint, and turned to her hostess.

'May I give the rest of my share to Baru? She's very hungry,

406

but she doesn't eat much and she's very useful, she kills rats and sometimes catches rabbits.'

'Aye, feed the animal,' Lipi said carelessly. 'My woman will look out some scraps for her, won't you, Luyeva?'

Surprise suspended Pavel's hand in mid-motion as she handed the plate down to Baru, but she did her best not to show it, and presently, when Luyeva came to the table and gathered up the plates, she saw that the older woman was pregnant, her stomach bulging against the calico apron she wore over her dress. Lipi's child? He looked a bit old to be fathering brats, yet she supposed it must be his child since he had referred to Luyeva as his woman and not as his daughter or daughter-in-law. Was Sasha his son then, as well as Stefan?

She had guessed partly right, she realised, as the family gave each other contradictory orders, shouted, mumbled and generally prepared for the day ahead. Lipi did not refer to Luyeva as his wife, but he did let drop the information that she was his second woman and not his first, and that Sasha was her son, though he was more of a son – contemptuously – to Lipi than his real son, Stefan.

'You can sleep with Stefan,' old Lipi said presently, when the meal was over and Luyeva was tackling the mound of dirty bowls and the pan and their tea-glasses. 'We have two bedrooms here, one for my woman and me and one for the rest of the family.'

Stefan muttered that his room was quite crowded enough with the boy sharing already, and Pavel said hastily that she would sleep out in the stables, snug in the straw with Baru.

'It's more fitting,' she said tactfully, when Lipi seemed inclined to force the issue. 'I'll be happier – I am never parted from my dog.'

Stefan gave her a grateful look, sowing a germ of suspicion in Pavel's mind that time reinforced rather than alleviated. The old man might domineer and rant at them all, and he undoubtedly knew more about farming than any of them save for Pavel herself, but could it be that he was being happily cuckolded by his own son whenever Stefan saw an opportunity present itself?

The question of her accommodation settled, Pavel, after the first satisfying breakfast to pass her lips for weeks, set to to learn the routine that the Berisavo family had worked out for themselves.

It was not a bad routine, save that they never lit the wolf-fires, which meant that they had to cram as many of the animals as possible into the stables. They had sold off most of the herds, which Pavel thought dreadfully shortsighted, but she could scarcely criticise on her first day.

Instead, she decided to work on Stefan, who obviously resented his father's dominance but showed it by being un-cooperative and lazy instead of proving himself the man his father denied he was. That first day she worked hard beside him, pointing out various ways in which he could improve methods, suggesting things which Fedor had made the general practice years ago but which had simply never occurred to the Berisavos.

By night-time, she was in everyone's good books; Lipi guessed that the ideas which his son was putting forward with such confidence were Pavel's, but he did not resent this, and praised Stefan twice in such a way that the younger man's shoulders noticeably squared. Stefan gave her a grateful glance, and Luyeva, pleased to have another man to mother, pressed food on her. When Pavel showed her how to stack the stove so that it would not go out during the night, she produced a damp and faded piece of blanket and insisted that her guest should sleep on it in front of the warm stove, at least while the nights were so cold.

'When spring comes, you can help us build up the herd,' Stefan said, as the family sat round the stove that evening. 'You were buying stock when you first visited us here, weren't you? We don't know much about stock; we had two sheep, a goat and some rabbits down on the plain.'

'That's quite a lot of livestock for a small place,' Pavel said consolingly. 'But I do know a lot about building up a herd, so perhaps I'll be useful.' She felt a pang, oddly enough, at the recollection that she would certainly not be here when spring came – and another pang, a sharper one, when she realised it was quite possible that she would not be able to get over the Pass before the spring for lack of money, and that once spring arrived she would be unable to cross anyway because of the risk of avalanches and glacier movements.

When the family had taken themselves off to their beds,

Pavel curled up on the blanket in front of the stove, with Baru curled round her, and looked at the room through half-closed eyes. Nyusha's rugs were still in place but filthy dirty; the table was still the same one, but it was chipped and battered and well grimed, too, with food particles and dust from the fire. Luyeva was no housewife, not by Nyusha's standards at any rate.

Once, in this very room, I came to David when he was lying in his sleeping bag, and we kissed and cuddled and I wept because I could not go back to England with him, Pavel reminded herself. Now, though, I am not so foolish. Now I shall work hard here and save my money and hoard food and other little necessaries, and as soon as I'm ready I'll take myself and Baru through the Klukhor and go down into Georgia and across into Turkey and be with David before I know it!

Just before she slept she remembered that representatives of the State would be around in the spring, to check up on all the collectives and to hand out free seed, and possibly to help with the stock build-up. She would have to make sure she was well out of the way when that happened!

David was in a *kosh* when the sickness hit him, and it was just as well, for had he been between dwellings, in the great outdoors all alone, he would certainly have died before he could have reached help.

It struck suddenly, the sickness. One moment he had been chatting to his host and looking forward to the meat which was roasting over the fire, the next he was feeling sick and strange. Then he had decided he must get outside, the warmth in here was not mere warmth but unhealthy heat, unbearable steamy sweaty heat which made him want to vomit.

He did not even reach the doorway before he felt himself go giddy and weak at the knees, felt himself sway and clutch. And then the hut tilted around him, the faces all went black instead of white, like the negative of a photograph, and he pitched forward on to his face. For seconds, probably, he just lay there, terrified by what had happened to him, seeing with frightening clarity the dirt floor in front of his eyes and hearing the buzz of startled conversation which ran from man to man when he did not move. And then darkness crept up across his vision, even more frighteningly, for it came slowly, from below, as though he were watching a glass being filled with ink.

When everything was black the worst heat he had ever dreamed of enveloped him and he spiralled away with it into nightmare.

He woke, days or weeks later, he could not tell which, to find himself still in the *kosh* but tucked away in a corner, on a pile of sheepskins, with the babushka watching him.

He was very weak. She addressed him, not unnaturally, in Russian, and he could not understand a word she said. He spoke to her in English and she was terrified and ran from the *kosh*, calling for her sons to come quick, the sick man had gone mad, he had a devil lodging in him which spoke in a strange tongue and looked at her evilly through the man's blank eyes.

It was a good many days later that he found himself beginning to understand their speech, though he never again made the mistake of addressing them in English. Instead, he kept to sign language and the simpler words, until one morning the man of the *kosh* came in with a grumble about grazing rights, and David found that he had understood every word.

He was not yet out of the wood, however. He now knew he was in Russia, he even knew that he was not supposed to be here and that he was in mortal peril if it was discovered that he was English and David Thomas, but of the rest he remembered nothing.

Am I a spy? he asked himself, lying in the sunshine which streamed in through the open doorway and sipping fresh goat's milk from a rough wooden cup. Have I come here to do something definite? It worried him that he could remember so little, but common sense told him that he had already learned one thing: memory returned at its own speed, but it did return. He had been very ill and obviously his mind was affected, but if he just let himself be lazy the memories would come. In the meantime he felt guilty about accepting hospitality which he could neither return nor pay for, so he began to carry out small tasks for the family. He milked the goat, he helped to grind maize for bread, he began to teach the youngest child his letters.

The weather was growing warmer; green grass covered the ground, the sun shone, a sweet breeze brought all the scents of spring to his eager nostrils. He began to take walks and to help with the lambing, and when he was invited to do so he rode one of the sturdy and agile Caucasian ponies behind the herd and helped to take them up to the high pastures, gilded now with the wonderful spring alpine flowers and richly covered in the green, green grass.

More memories came now, every day. Alice, Nibby, Sara and Michael came to remind him that he had a home far from here where he was daily awaited. He thought about the boatyard which he and Nibby were trying to build up, and hoped desperately that he had not ruined everything by his long absence. One day he remembered Yuri and his trip to Moscow, and then, when he honestly believed he had total recall, he knew, blindingly, why he was in Russia at all. He was not a spy, he had not come to pass messages on to Yuri nor to carry messages back. He had come for Pavel and she had not been there, she had returned to the mountains before him!

Once he knew that, of course, he was in a fever to be off, for until that moment he had felt no real urge to return. It was because his subconscious had been waiting for him to remember the real reason for his presence in this alien country, he supposed, but now that he did know he could not wait to get back to Turkey. She would be waiting for him, believing him faithless, or she would have tried to get on to Britain without him . . . if she had managed to contact Selim – or he her, rather – then at least she would have been given money and advice to get her safely to his home.

His hosts were polite and no one could have been kinder, but when he told them he had remembered everything and that he was trying to cross the Caucasus so that he and his affianced wife could marry in Georgia they were kind but firm. He could not possibly cross the Pass now, it would be deadly dangerous, now was the time of the avalanches, the moment when the glacier would start to melt in the hot sunshine of early May – it would be madness to go now. He must either wait until August, or he would have to travel east to the Krestovy Pass, where he could go by the military road down into Tbilisi.

If he had been stronger, David told himself, he would have gone through the Pass alone, or undertaken the long journey to the Krestovy Pass, but as it was he could only agree that he must wait until August. He was reluctant to admit it, but it was clear as a bell that he could not go anywhere alone. Poor little Pavel would have to wait in Trabzon or go back to Britain without him, for there was absolutely nothing he could do to help her.

But he could write a letter. It would be dangerous, but the wild mountain men were not easily frightened. He begged Djhon, who was a man of about his own age, to take his letter down into the nearest town with a post office and see that it got posted. He had a little money left and gave it to Djhon for the necessary stamp, and then fished paper out of his pack, and a pencil, and wrote to Yuri.

When he had told Yuri what had happened and asked him to pass a message on to several interested people explaining his long absence, he folded the page into a rough envelope, addressed it, still in pencil, in a shaky hand and gave it to Djhon for posting. And then, feeling that he really had done all that could possibly be expected of him, he went back into the sunshine and began to crush maize in a stone pestle with a stone mortar. He felt very happy.

'It's another ewe; you're in luck, Stefan.' Pavel delivered the lamb with a neat twist of her wrist and grinned at Stefan. His shyness had long since evaporated and he trusted her now with his secrets, though he had never been able to explain why he had taken his father's second wife for his mistress — for Pavel's flash of suspicion that very first night had proved to be correct. Lack of a suitable substitute, she supposed, for even when they had farmed — if you could call it that — on the plain, they had lived in a remote community which mainly met at market or when they attended a wedding or some other festivity, when presumably Stefan's extraordinary shyness had prevented him from paying court to a girl in the normal fashion.

Strangely enough, Luyeva seemed to have a genuine fondness both for Lipi and for his son; she was blossoming, with all the good food she was getting now that the snows had melted away, into a reasonably good-looking woman. Her stringy hair had thickened and softened and was now a nice, glowing brown, her skin had improved, and her figure, once the baby had been delivered, proved to be shapely as well. Even her hands were not as rough as they had been when Pavel had first met her, though they would always be large, square hands.

The baby was a boy; he was large and healthy and remarkably like Stefan, but no one commented on the likeness and indeed there was no cause since the two were supposedly brothers. Pavel believed them to be father and son, but no one ever actually admitted that this was so. She was no longer in doubt over Luyeva's relationship to Stefan, though. A hasty entry into the big barn in search of a turnip to use as a bribe for the mare whilst she and Lipi tried to deliver her foal, which was a breech birth, had resulted in her nearly treading on the entwined bodies of her hostess and her employer's son. Pavel had seen enough animals mating to know very well what was going on and had beaten a hasty retreat, though she had told Stefan, afterwards, that only a fool would take a chance like that.

'But I knew my father wouldn't leave the mare,' Stefan said, mildly surprised. 'Anyway, Sasha was supposed to be watching out for us, only he ran off, the little devil.'

'You didn't *know* your father wouldn't leave the mare, you just hoped he wouldn't,' Pavel reminded him. 'And the baby's only a few weeks old; what do you think your father will say if Luyeva has to tell him she's pregnant again?'

'He'll be proud as a peacock, specially if it's a boy.'

Pavel presumed from this that Lipi, despite his years, was still active; she pitied Luyeva, caught between two male animals and being heartily serviced by both, but then realised that she was being presumptuous; Luyeva had only to send Stefan to the rightabout or tell Lipi she was tired and her problem would be over. And what was more, she suspected that Lipi was well aware of the state of affairs and quite content. After all, he was old, and left to him alone Luyeva would probably not have conceived at all. What was more, Luyeva obviously enjoyed making babies, and if Stefan had not satisfied her she might have been more demanding than Lipi would like. So all in all the strange, triangular relationship did seem not such a bad idea.

But now, in the lambing-pen, Pavel and Stefan were just two stockmen, each one delighted with the lambing. The ewes had dropped twins more often than usual, and the preponderance of ewes meant that the herd would probably treble in a year. Pavel, cleaning up in the kitchen after the last birth, found herself almost regretting that she would not be here to see it . . . but only almost, for still her feeling for David was an unquenchable fire.

Summer was upon them now; the days were long and light and the work was easier because of the small herd, but even so Pavel and Stefan worked long hours ploughing, planting, putting vegetables in the garden, weeding, and trekking up into the mountains with the cattle and sheep so that they did not graze the meadows directly around the farm until they were bare but used the higher reaches whilst the weather allowed.

When Sasha ran in one day, white-faced, to say that a man had come to the town about the quota and the planting of various grain crops, Pavel was taken by surprise, but Lipi was in no doubt what they must do.

'Pavel, take all but the bull and a cow and calf up into the hills,' he ordered crisply. 'We don't want them poking their noses in here and shoving our quota sky-high. Sasha, you herd the sheep up as well. The pair of you had better go tonight – get as far away as you can and stay away. When it's safe, either Stefan or Luyeva will come and fetch you home.'

Pavel and Sasha set forth that very night, with Baru running alongside their mounts. Pavel saw the sense of it and had packed her saddlebag with food, for she was determined that they would not return too soon and be caught. She knew the Berisavos wouldn't mention her and supposed that it would not matter if they did, but even so she was best out of the way. She still had no papers, no ration cards, and though it no longer seemed to matter much, with so many others in the same boat, she did not want to get hauled back to civilisation for any reason. They might not connect her with a girl named Pavelinka who was wanted for treasonable activities so that they could condemn her to a timber camp, but they would be bound to find some fault with her false identity. Better to keep out of the way.

It was forty hours before she saw Stefan toiling up the sloping meadow towards the tiny shepherd's hut made out of furze and pine branches. She ran down the slope towards him, eager to confirm that it was now safe to return. He was smiling broadly as he approached, and picked Sasha up and swung him round before setting him down on the grass again.

'It's all right, he's gone,' he greeted her. 'It was easy, really, though of course he asked scores of difficult questions. But we told him what a hard winter it was and how the man before us had killed off most of the stock and about the wolves taking the rest . . . we told him that the soldiers had killed the dogs and the man was very annoyed, his face went quite black with temper and he said the soldiers were fools, the country was being run by fools, for a mountain farmer relies on his dogs to warn him of danger and keep predators off his stock.'

'What about the quota? And are they sending others to help run the place as a proper collective?' Pavel asked, as they turned round and began to walk up towards the shepherd's hut once more so that she and Sasha could collect their things. 'I just hope they're too busy with the farms on the plain to worry about us for a bit.'

'You're probably right – the chap didn't mention any others arriving, at any rate. But he was very interested in the *kulak* who had it before us, wanted to know where the fellow had gone and whether he'd taken his family with him. Remember that soldier asking about the girl who'd gone missing? She had a name similar to yours . . . I can't recall quite what it was. Well, anyway, he asked about her, whether we'd seen her, said the authorities hadn't given up, they still wanted to know about her if she showed her face here. So naturally I said I'd do my best to see she was held if she came back and said I'd send someone into town with a message if it happened. I don't know whether he believed me, but at any rate he stopped asking questions soon after that and went prodding and prying round the house and the barns and the stables . . . made some quite nasty remarks about us not having enough horses to manage a place the size of ours . . . and then Luyeva gave him a glass of tea and a hot maize cake and he went.'

'Well, thank heaven for that! Did he mention when he might call next?'

'Just before harvest, he said, which gives us two or three months. Usually, they say in the village, we get more warning because the inspectors call on the farms nearest the towns first, so us people in the outlying places hear when we go in to market. But we've been too busy to go to market and we haven't had a lot to sell, so our only advance warning was Sasha.'

'Well, at least we're safe for a bit,' Pavel said thankfully, loading up her horse. 'And the quota? You didn't say.'

'Oh, didn't I? Actually I forgot to mention it and when he

said nothing I kept mum. But Lipi thinks they won't set a new quota until they see what sort of harvest we have, so we probably won't get away with selling the government short a second year.'

Chatting happily, with Sasha running ahead and throwing stones at everything that moved, the little group made its way slowly down the mountainside and back to the farm.

It had taken David the best part of a day and a half to get to the farm, and a good deal of courage to march boldly down the narrow path into the valley. He had been haunted by a sense of déjà vu, and had very nearly turned tail and fled when the door had been opened by a very fat, frightened-looking peasant woman with an equally fat but cheerful baby in her arms.

Right up to that moment, though, he had half-hoped, half-believed, in a miracle. He had thought Pavel would be there.

Of course he told himself that she would not answer the door, but he did think she might have been in the kitchen, either getting a meal or doing some task. Then of course he realised that the barn was the place to find her . . . the stables . . . the corrals. Finally, he had decided to come right out with it and question the ancient, bent old man who was grooming a neat little bay mare and the gawky son who had shown him round, sullen with suspicion or shyness, for it had speedily transpired that the Berisavo family were expecting the collective inspector and thought David was he.

But there was no sign of Pavel and they had denied employing anyone save their own family.

'Why would we need employees?' the old man had said bitterly, indicating the empty corrals with a wave of his arm. 'The *kulaks* slaughtered some beasts and sold others, they did not want to leave with empty purses and cared nothing for those who came after. And then there were the wolves . . . no one told us, comrade, that we should light wolf-fires against the beasts stealing our stock, so what cows and sheep were left we lost in the first severe winter nights. And by the time we realised and herded them into the shelter of the stable and barns it was too late for most of them. They were wolf-meat.'

Remembering his role, David had been stiff with him; no use grumbling over your own inefficiency, comrade, that sort of approach. But he had left no stone unturned. He had reminded the peasants that the girl was wanted by the State and had impressed upon them the sin of harbouring such a one . . . they were sure they had seen no one like her? Nor any stranger who might have been the girl disguised, perhaps as a youth? For he had remembered that Pavel had travelled to and from Moscow as a boy and would probably remain a boy until she was safely out of the country.

Both men, however, were firm in their denial. They had seen no one, knew nothing, and had no reason, comrade, to lie.

He had been about to leave when he remembered Baru. Where, he asked them, are your dogs? And had been furious and sickened to hear of the soldiers' behaviour, so sickened that he had been unable to hide it, but they had taken his sudden diatribe against the soldiers and the State as further proof of his keenness to see the Soviet get its just deserts and had placated his rage with tea and maize cakes, promising to do better next year, to keep the wolf-fires burning brightly and to have a good-sized herd by the following spring.

As he left the farm, David looked up at the eternal snows of the great mountains and wondered whether to have a go at the Pass right here and now, because he was sure, now, that Pavel had gone before him. He had lost so much time during his illness that she would be in Turkey by now, waiting for him, or, even better, journeying to Britain.

He had been uncertain, before, what to do for the best, but now he realised just how much hope he had been pinning on the farm; he had really thought that Pavel would seek shelter there and remain there, furthermore, until she could safely use the Klukhor Pass. He had indulged in delightful fantasies of the two of them meeting there and tackling the Pass together, but now he dismissed such dreaming. He would stop shilly-shallying and hoping for some sort of sign from somewhere; he would set out as soon as he was able for the Krestovy Pass and the free world.

Eva and Kevi lay on their backs in the sweet hay, with their faces to the sun, and ate strawberries stolen from a garden and crisp young lettuce leaves. They were happy, partly because they were in the country and on their own, having left their group making a shelter in the woods about a mile away, but mostly because they were alive.

The winter had claimed three lives out of their nine souls. Ania had slipped away, dying of nothing in particular except for hunger and cold. Little Josef had followed her in a matter of days. And lastly they had lost Igor, who was strong and brave and sure of himself. Yet he had died, though not of cold or hunger. He had died in the police station and had been thrown out of it on to a rubbish heap, as though he mattered no more than the filth and rags there already.

The rest of them mourned their dead comrades, but life had to go on and Josef and Ania had been passengers, once the severe cold and the real hunger gripped. They were both too frail to withstand it, and Eva thought that Ania had been quite glad to let go, quite glad to slip away. She hoped, piously, that Ania was warm in heaven. And then forgot them both, because Kevi was talking.

'. . . not leave it so long this year,' he was saying. 'Last year we found the church all right in the autumn, but we didn't discover the vault until much later and then we hadn't hoarded food. Next winter it must be different, or we shan't just lose three, we'll lose the lot. I've been hungry before, but last winter was the worst.' He shuddered and rolled over on to his stomach, rubbing his face against Eva's as if the touch of skin against skin gave him reassurance. 'You're a tough kid, Eva. You're looking good again, too.'

'I'm getting fat,' Eva said happily. The dreadful hollow suffering had left their faces and they were beginning to look almost like children again. 'I'm getting brown, too. I do like brown arms, don't you?'

'Mm hmm.' Kevi's concurring hum was lazy, absent-minded. He was staring straight ahead unseeingly, and a frown line had appeared between his light brown brows. Eva could see that he was deep in thought. 'If only I knew what to do for the best! I can write and read and so can you, but school seems a lifetime away.'

'True. Does it matter?'

'I don't know. Sometimes I think it does and sometimes I don't. When we're grown up we may need schooling. What'll we do for jobs?'

'I'll marry someone rich,' Eva said at once, seeing a way out. 'Then he'll do the working and I'll just lie around and eat all day and be beautiful. Why don't you marry a rich woman? Then you wouldn't have to work.'

'Don't be stupid. For a start you're going to marry *me*, and I'm not rich; not yet. And for another start, I'm going to marry *you*, and you aren't rich either.'

Eva felt her cheeks begin to burn with a gratified blush; marry Kevi? It would be wonderful to marry Kevi and have a little cottage somewhere and know that you were quite safe and would be with him always. But it did mean that they really should consider how they would earn money when that marvellous day came and they were two adults.

'I'd like that,' she confessed. 'Will it be long before we can earn money? Girls not a lot bigger than me work in shops and things.'

'I know, but they're not *bez prizorney*,' Kevi said regretfully. He plucked a long strand of hay and then threw it down and pulled her towards him, towing her on her tummy over the ground until they were both hard up against the hedge, sheltered and shaded by it, with its long, scratchy branches hiding them from the outside world. 'Tell you what, why should we wait to get married? Why don't we do it now?'

'Get *married*? In a *hayfield*? That isn't getting married,' Eva protested. 'You go to the town hall and the chief man, whatever he's called, marries you. The girl wears a white dress and the fellow wears his best suit and there are presents, and a cake, and lots and lots of food and drink.'

'Oh, pooh, that's for *Them*,' Kevi scoffed. 'We'll do that one day, I suppose, but for now it'll have to be a *prizorney* wedding. We do it like this.'

He pulled her roughly into his arms and began to tug at her clothes.

Eva laughed and shoved him.

'Dear Kevi, don't be so daft! Why are you trying to tear my nice new shirt? Don't hurt it, it's quite my favourite thing and as long as a dress on me. Look, if you like . . .'

She stopped because he gave a sort of frustrated growl and shook her, none too lightly. Then he put both his arms round her really tightly and tumbled her flat on to her back. He was on top of her, tugging at her new shirt, and she heard the material give and began to whimper, no longer amused by his behaviour but almost frightened by it.

419

'Kevi, what *are* you doing? Look, if you want it to come off I'll take it off, but don't rip it, please. You know how difficult it is to look respectable these days.'

He rolled off her, crossly, and stared at her.

'Get on with it, then,' he said flatly.

'Well, I will if you like, but I don't see . . .'

'You don't have to; just get it off when I say.'

Eva removed her shirt, folded it and laid it down on the grass. She had a ragged vest underneath it, and a pair of very ancient patched trousers. She intended to steal a skirt when she could but for now the trousers would have to do and she could run faster in trousers.

'And the vest.'

'Why? Oh, is there a stream?' She pulled off the vest with cheerful abandon, suddenly believing that Kevi wanted to bathe, and that was all right by her. She loved to swim, adored the feel of water cleansing her body. She pulled her trousers off and squatted by Kevi as he began to follow her example. He stripped to his disgraceful raggedy shorts, and then turned and looked at her. But he did not look at her face; his eyes went lower.

Eva, interested, looked down too. She saw that her body had changed in the past few weeks; she was now the possessor of two nice little breasts with very tiny pink nipples. She looked at them with some surprise, because after the winter of starvation she had never expected that her fatness would take on such a pretty shape. Last time she had taken all her clothes off, in the autumn, she had been flat as a boy in front.

'Well, look at that!' she said. She touched them experimentally but they were tender and new and she took her fingers away quickly. Now that she came to think about it, she was not at all sure that they were not a sign of some ailment, because they felt very odd, they tingled, and because Kevi was staring so the little tiny pink nipples suddenly hardened and hurt worse.

'You're growing up,' Kevi said. His voice was husky. He had been kneeling opposite her, intent on removing his own clothing, but now he came closer and put his naked arms around her naked back, drawing her near to him. The tingling in her new acquisitions got worse. She tried to pull away but Kevi would not let her. He held her tightly and then, with one swift movement, crushed her against him.

It hurt abominably! Just for one moment she could not think straight for the pain, and that must have been why she bit. Her teeth sank into Kevi's shoulder and he grunted, then held her with one arm and used the other hand to smack. It was a very hard smack, but though she cried out softly he still did not release her. Her breasts throbbed now, as well as tingling and hurting, so she tried the gentle approach.

'Please, Kevi, let me go; they hurt, you're crushing me.'

'Eva, I have to hurt you, just a little bit. It's . . . it's what I have to do.' But he let her go for a moment and then, so suddenly that she was not prepared for it, he took her little new breasts in his hands and began to squeeze, not hard, and as he squeezed he used his thumbs to rub her tiny little pink nipples.

Eva was frightened by the intensity of sensation which followed this strange caress. Her whole body began to throb and she heard herself whimpering, but not with fear this time; it was the natural reaction to the feelings he was rousing in her.

'Lie down.'

It was a harsh command, yet he made it sound more like an entreaty. She was still wondering what he meant when he picked her up, with one arm round her and the other hand still busy on her breasts, and laid her on her back. He was rubbing her breast, murmuring to her that she must not cry out, that she was growing up, she was fifteen which was a woman more or less and he was seventeen which was most definitely a man, and as he talked he was tearing off his shorts and then he lay down on her, only he wasn't heavy, he was leaning on his elbows, and then he slid his arms under her shoulder blades, lifting her up a little, and began to kiss her mouth.

For a little while she simply enjoyed the kissing, but then he began to push his tongue into her mouth and she grew apprehensive once more. She had heard tell of *prizorney* trials of strength and feats of daring; was this one of them? She did not feel either strong or brave, trapped by Kevi's body like this, and she could not understand why he was doing it, which was worse. He had never hurt her in all their time together, he had been the gentlest of masters.

When he began to pull her about again and push his knees firmly between her legs she started to cry and ask him what he was doing, but he told her she must be sensible, that he would not hurt her very much and that it was all for her own good anyway. He pulled and manoeuvred and got terribly hot and bothered after that, and Eva tried to be patient and put up with it, and then he suddenly thrust forward, and she screamed, she couldn't help it because he really had hurt her, she knew he did not know what he was doing but something was really jabbing into her. She drew up her legs and tried to wriggle away from him, but he had her by the shoulders and he forced her down on to whatever it was that had jabbed, forced her and forced her, and then all of a sudden, when she thought she might quite possibly die, she felt that tingling and throbbing all over her, and Kevi moved easily in her and she moved too, and clutched his shoulders and told him that she loved him, that she wanted him, that he must . . . he must . . . he must . . .

There was a rush of pleasure so intense that she had to muffle her cries against his shoulder and a moment later he flopped down on top of her, panting as though he had run ten miles, and he kissed her face all over, little kisses, and touched her gently and with loving hands and told her that she was now his wife according to the *bez prizorney* law, that she was a good girl and he would treat her well.

'Is it all over, now?' Eva said. 'That was a strange thing, Kevi. It hurt at first, but afterwards . . .'

'Yes? Afterwards?' He was smiling at her and suddenly she knew what he had meant when he had called himself a man; he was a man and she had been a stupid, giggly little girl until ten minutes ago. Now she was a woman. She looked down at her own body, for he had rolled off her and was lying quietly by her side, and her breasts seemed to have got bigger and her nipples were scarlet now, not pink, and they had a smiling look.

'Afterwards was wonderful,' she said. She tugged at a lock of hair which was hanging over his forehead. 'When you are a wife . . .'

'Yes? What?'

'Well . . . does a wife only have to do . . . that . . . once?' He was laughing at her now, his mouth teasing.

'Why? Is once enough?'

Eva sat up, throwing pretence to the winds.

'Oh, no! Once is *not* enough!'

# CHAPTER SEVENTEEN

Summer was advancing and the Berisavos were learning fast how best to run the farm. Pavel had grown fond of the family; she adored Pippi, the baby, and she saw that the others were not lazy, not really. They had been afraid of the unaccustomed work and so had pushed it away from them, not doing things which should have been done because they did not know how to do them. Once she was there to guide they could not have worked harder or more enthusiastically if they had been born and bred to mountain farming.

As warm, sun-filled day followed warm sun-filled day, interspersed with the great rain-sweeps which enriched the crops and kept the grass a brilliant green, Pavel kept a weather-eye on the Pass. Give it a couple more weeks and I'll get through easily, she told herself, and tried not to feel guilty over leaving the family. The trouble was, she could not make up her mind how much – or how little – to tell them. She could not just disappear, because if they were worried they would set a search going, and she knew them well enough by now to know that even a quiet reminder that she would not be here for ever would panic them. They had no self-confidence, did not believe they could manage without her, though Pavel thought that they would do very well.

In the end, she decided to leave a note, which seemed heartless since none of them could read except for Sasha, and his ability was not much trusted by his seniors. But if she told them she was deadly afraid they would not only try to stop her but succeed in doing so. They were fond of her, but they thought she was essential to their welfare; if necessary they would lock her in the stable, or try to find out more about her to blackmail her into remaining with them. They were simple people and the fear she had lifted from their minds by her mere presence could not be borne a second time, or so they would think. She must get away without their knowledge.

The day came when the Pass was clear and Pavel drove the cattle down from the high pasture that evening, determined to make her move the very next day. She had been hiding food away for some time and the shepherd's hut on the mountain top contained an odd assortment of stuff. She had bought tinned bully-beef when they went into town and had secreted a large cheese, well wrapped in paper, and a sack of flour with a little wooden tub of lard.

She had a sacking bag into which she had put a few essentials, and she thought that she would simply leave the farm around midday and walk up into the hills saying that she wanted to check on the sheep in the top pasture. Once up there she would put her note in the hut where no one could miss it and then when they went searching for her they would find it and take it back to the farm for Sasha to interpret. It was a bit risky, perhaps, but she intended to drop some hints today which, later, they would remember. And she dared not leave a note in the farmhouse; they would find it before she wanted them to do so and follow before she had a big enough start. The note, already written and hidden away in her bag, simply said that she had to get to Georgia on urgent business connected with her family, but that she would get in touch with them as soon as she could. Sentiment had dictated the ending.

*You have been very good to me and I shall never forget you,* she had written. *You know I wouldn't leave unless I had to . . . forgive me and think of me often, as I shall think of you.* She had signed it Pavel, because she had taught them all her name one evening round the fire, and had written theirs down for them so that they, too, could write a signature and not just a cross when the time came for them to sign documents on behalf of the collective.

'I'm going up to the top pasture, to make sure the shepherd's hut is still in good repair,' Pavel said casually at breakfast that morning. 'You have to keep an eye on it or it won't be weatherproof when the autumn storms come and you need to use it overnight.'

'Right; you know best, Pavel,' Stefan said, rasping his chin with one big hand. 'Do you want Sasha with you, in case you need some help to repair it?'

'No, I don't think so. I dare say you can find plenty for him to do round here,' Pavel said, having pretended to give the matter some thought. 'I'll take Baru though – did I tell you I saw a bear in the next valley the other day? They don't do much harm at this time of year, apart from grubbing up vegetables from time to time, but I'd feel safer with the dog.'

'Of course. Sasha, see how the sick cow is; I don't want her mixing with the rest of the herd until she's fit. I'm off to fetch the cattle whilst Father feeds the stock.' The two men left the room whilst Sasha hastily finished his oatmeal.

Pavel had isolated the cow two days ago and now it was going to be useful, since it meant that Sasha would be going off in the opposite direction from herself. The cow was improving rapidly and would probably be able to join the herd again today, which was good news too, especially as it meant that Sasha would be occupied with the animal probably until the midday meal.

She watched the boy leave the kitchen, then turned to Luyeva; if only she could say goodbye properly, but there was no chance of that. However, she would drop a few hints before going.

'It's a long time since I've heard from my family,' she said casually, as Luyeva began to chop vegetables into a pot. 'I wonder whether I might see my cousin if I go on a few miles further, after I've checked the hut and done any repairs that are necessary. It wouldn't take me long, and I might get news of my parents.'

'I'm making lamb stew for tonight,' Luyeva remarked. 'Don't be too late, will you, Pavel. Sasha dug some new potatoes as well, and I'll make a fruit pie.'

'I might eat with them,' Pavel said, still casual. 'I hate to miss a lamb stew, but . . .'

The door burst open. Sasha stood there, his chest heaving.

'Men, coming up the track; soldiers!'

Oddly enough, instead of fear a feeling of strangeness gripped Pavel, the feeling that this was not real at all but a dream or a replay of a dream. She stared blankly at Sasha whilst behind her Luyeva, with the peasant's normal fear of

425

authority, began to cluck and to run about the kitchen as though she would lose her head if a thing was out of place.

'Where's Baru? Don't let them . . . oh, Pavel, don't let them hurt Baru!'

Abruptly Pavel realised that this was real, as was Sasha's fear. He had seen soldiers shoot dogs . . . she ran across to where Baru lay and caught at her collar.

The soldiers were closer than she thought; she was still kneeling on the floor holding the dog when the door, which Sasha had left slightly ajar, was pushed wide and four men entered, two in the faded uniform of the great Soviet Army.

Pavel, with her arms round Baru who was growling and muttering like a thunderstorm, realised that she was properly caught; no papers, no true identity and no way out. But for the time being at least, the soldiers were paying no attention to her. The officer, or at least she took him to be an officer since he was so plainly in command, looked slowly round the room, assimilating the fact that it contained a woman, a youth and a little boy.

'Lipi Berisavo?'

'He's feeding the stock,' Pavel said, when Luyeva and Sasha simply stared at the man. 'Shall I fetch him?'

The soldier shook his head. 'No, let the boy go.' He gestured to Sasha, who disappeared promptly in the direction of the stable. 'Is that dog safe?'

'No,' Pavel said frankly. 'I'd best tie her up.'

She tried to get to her feet but the officer shook his head at her, frowning.

'No, wait a moment. You Stefan?'

'He's . . .'

'Yes, that's right.'

Luyeva's voice was drowned by Pavel's quick-thinking reply. After all, why not? All they knew was that Stefan was Lipi's son, and Stefan was with the cattle and wouldn't be back until late. These men were probably just passing through; after all, the government inspector had been and gone weeks ago – unless the soldiers had come to settle more peasants on the collective which was not yet a collective? But even if they meant to stay, Pavel told herself, she could still simply go, and she would get Sasha to one side, or go up to Stefan, and tell him

426

to say she was just a neighbour . . . there was sure to be a way out.

'Well, Stefan, these men are government inspectors, come to see how you're managing. I see you've taken over from the previous family, the Lazarovs – have they all left? The girls too?'

'Oh yes, comrade, they were taken away a good seven or eight months ago. But we have done our best. We did not know, at first . . .' Baru was trying to pull free of Pavel's hold on her. Pavel grabbed more firmly at the soft, loose skin and long fur round her neck. 'Baru, sit!'

'Baru! You kept the dog, then?'

By God, these people were thorough, Pavel thought, muttering that of course they had kept the dog and trying to prevent Baru from leaping up and tearing out the man's throat. She had a way – a sharp way – with uninvited guests. And yet . . . she was no longer growling. If Pavel had not known better she would have thought Baru wanted to welcome the men!

The door was pushed open from the outside; Pavel geared herself up to convey a message to Lipi not to call her by name, to say that these were government inspectors, though she knew that the old man would say almost nothing, left to himself. The peasants' deep-rooted suspicion of anyone in authority would ensure that he scarcely said a word. But it was not Lipi, nor was it Sasha. Bold as brass, Stefan strode into the room, words already on his lips.

'Luyeva, put me up some bread and cheese. I'll take the cattle . . .' He stopped short, the colour draining from his face. He looked both guilty and terrified.

'Ah, Lipi Berisavo,' the officer said easily, obviously used to people's initial reaction to himself and his men. 'These men are government inspectors, they've come . . .'

'I'm not Lipi, I'm his son, Stefan,' Stefan said. 'I'll fetch my father.'

Helplessly, Pavel continued to crouch by Baru, her arm about the dog's neck, but she was no longer restraining her, she was staring, like a bird fascinated by a snake, at the officer.

He was staring at her. She was sure she had never seen him in her life before, but . . . was it recognition which warmed his eyes? She scrambled to her feet just as one of the men began to say, in a puzzled voice, that the lad was Stefan Berisavo . . . and

Baru launched herself straight at the officer's chest.

The soldier shouted and raised his gun, but the officer was quicker. He put his arms round Baru, bending a little in order to do so, and said in a quiet but penetrating voice: 'Enough of that! Baru and I are old friends. Pavel, you were insulted because you thought I'd not recognised you, but you were only a child when we last met. You'd better get up off the floor, though, and restrain your animal before she decides she's welcomed me enough and tries to chase my companions out of her kitchen.'

A vivid blush bathed Pavel's face and her heart, which had been beating too fast anyway for comfort, promptly doubled its rate. She could not imagine how the officer knew her, nor when he had met Baru, but at least it seemed she was not about to be arrested for impersonating Stefan! However, one of the men in civilian clothes had been staring rather hard at her.

'Pavel? I seem to recall a missing youth . . . about six, eight months ago the State sent for a youth of that name . . . Where are your papers, boy? What's your last name?'

'Ismaelovich,' Pavel said after a second's pause whilst her mind scrabbled frantically for the name she had given Stefan months before. 'I have no papers; when my parents were taken away from their farm further in the mountains I was out with the sheep. I came back to find strangers in my home.'

'I wonder?' The man was looking at her spitefully. 'You're too old to have been simply ignored . . . it's my belief you're a runaway.'

'From what? And why should I lie to you?'

'Because I believe you're the boy who committed some crime . . . murder, I believe . . . on the train which carried you and your parents to the timber camp. Yes, it's coming back to me now, the child killed two soldiers, no less, with the long knife all the Caucasian men used to carry. This lad is a murderer!'

'I'm Pavel Ismaelovich,' Pavel said, her voice trembling. 'I don't know what you're talking about!'

The officer broke in.

'I think the boy's speaking the truth, comrade,' he said easily. 'As you saw, the dog recognised me, and although I haven't seen him since he was a child . . .'

The soldier with his gun still on his arm cleared his throat and spoke politely.

'Comrade, you said you'd known the woman of the house many years ago; is this her boy? If so, then he must at least stand trial . . . he's murdered men!'

'He's murdered no one,' the officer said brusquely. 'However, that is not for us to decide. When we return to the nearest town we'll make enquiries . . .'

For a moment Pavel thought it had worked; the man in civilian clothes looked baffled, then half-satisfied, as though the mere mention of making enquiries was enough, but then the suspicion came back into his face.

He lied to us; why should he lie unless he's guilty? I insist he's arrested and sent to Moscow for trial.'

It was a nightmare; Pavel put her hand on Baru's head, half-hoping that she would be unable to feel the thick fur and would know she dreamed, but Baru moved beneath her fingers, turning to give her a trusting, adoring glance. The men were grouped between Pavel and the door, the peasants, only half-comprehending, stood uneasily, watching the small drama unfold.

'Very well, comrade, if you feel so strongly.' The officer stepped forward and took Pavel's wrist. 'I arrest you, young Ismaelovich, for a crime you did not commit under a name you do not own.' He glanced derisively towards the man in plain clothes. 'Is that right, comrade? Serious enough for you?'

The man muttered something but his companion said, uneasily, 'We've a job to do here, Igor. Let's get on with it.' He turned to Stefan. 'You are in charge here?'

'Yes . . . no, it's more my father. He's feeding the stock; shall I fetch him?'

'No. We'll come out with you.' The second civilian gave the first a sharp look. 'Come along, Igor; the officer will deal with the boy.' He turned to the younger man. 'Why not take the boy, under guard, to the farm he speaks of? There will be records there, no doubt. You can then prove he is who he says he is.'

'And who I say he is,' the officer said easily. 'Very well, I'll do that.'

But the first man shook his head obstinately. He was clearly far from satisfied with the officer's attitude.

'No. If he's the murderer he's a slippery one and I want him taken straight into custody – find him a prison cell in the nearest town, man, don't go off into the mountains with him or it'll be another soldier we're reporting dead. Go now, right away, and you can be back before nightfall.'

But being ordered about by a mere civilian, it seemed, stuck in the officer's craw. He shook his head.

'I'm in charge here, and my duty forbids me to go off on a wild goose chase. Don't worry, I'll see the boy's kept under guard.' He took hold of both Pavel's wrists. 'Get me a piece of rope,' he said to the nearest soldier. 'A bit for his wrists and a length to hold on to him with, then he won't run far.'

When the soldier returned with a length of rope he tied Pavel's wrists to one another and then, under the suspicious civilian's eyes, put a loop round her neck.

'There. Now get on with this inspection. Is this the only collective you're visiting today?'

'No, of course not. We shall do this one in the morning and another three miles further on this afternoon. I've got a list . . .' He delved into his pocket but did not consult his paper; instead he stared very hard at Pavel. 'Ismaelovich . . . Ismaelovich . . . there's no one of that name to be visited.'

'They aren't there any more,' Pavel said quickly. 'I *told* you.'

'But they weren't there . . . at least, I doubt it very much.' He looked sourly at the officer. 'We'll see, shan't we? What do you intend to do with him?'

'Keep him by me. Tonight, when you've inspected these two farms, we'll make our way to the town and if I'm satisfied that there is a case for this one to answer, then I and one of my men will entrain for Moscow with him. Does that satisfy you?'

'And what will you do whilst I examine this place? And the next?'

'I shall examine my prisoner. I'll go into the barn and ask him some questions.'

The civilian heaved a deep, exasperated sigh.

'Very well, Lemensk. Don't forget, I shall be watching you!'

The officer did not deign to reply; he swung on his heel and, pulling Pavel behind him, made for the barn.

Once in its shelter he took her up to the hay-loft and they sat down, side by side, on two trusses of hay. Baru prowled uneasily at the foot of the ladder but could not manage its steep ascent.

For a moment the officer said nothing, but then he untied Pavel's hands and raised a brow at her.

'Well? Aren't you going to ask me how I know you – how I know you're a girl, what's more?'

Pavel jumped; no one knew she was a girl, she scarcely dared to acknowledge even to herself that she was a female. How could this man know? She looked hard at him in the dim light. He was tall, with dark brown hair and eyes, and his calm, high-cheekboned face was younger than she had assumed at first; possibly he was no more than in his late twenties. His skin was tanned nut-brown from the outdoor life he led and his hands, loosely clasped over the end of the rope he held, were square and reliable-looking. But she was sure she did not know him, had never met him before today.

'Well? Can't you remember me? Of course, you were only a kid, but I'd have thought you'd have had some recollection of such a handsome fellow as me!'

He was teasing her! A member of the armed forces was actually smiling at her, treating her like a human being – no, more than that, a friend!

'Was it . . . was it before I came here? When I was with my . . . my real family?'

'It was . . . I brought you here. After what happened there was no one to take care of a couple of girls, so I brought you to Fedor and Nyusha. Do you remember me now?'

She was frowning at him, striving to remember. There had been a man, she knew that, and they had ridden many miles on a great, tall horse. But she could not remember a thing about him, save that he had seemed very old and a little stern. That had been eleven, twelve years ago, so could it really have been *this* man?'

'Were you the one who carried us on his horse?' A memory suddenly took her by the throat. 'Did I nip a horsefly off your hand?'

His face was split by a broad, white grin.

'Well done, dushka! You did, indeed you did! It was the only sign that you'd given for days and days that you were even alive. I was so pleased; I'd been afraid that you'd lost your mind over . . . well, over what happened. I've often wondered

431

about the pair of you — where's the little one? Eva, wasn't it? Or was it Konkordia?'

Pavel frowned; the second name seemed to echo round in her head in a very unpleasant manner, as though he had not spoken it so much as cried it aloud. She could hear it echoing round a chasm . . . she shook herself. She was being absurdly fanciful, particularly as Konkordia, though a pretty name, was not one she had come across or even heard before.

'Eva's my little sister. That other name . . . I've not heard it before, but when you said it, it seemed to echo, sort of.'

The man shuddered, an involuntary movement which shook the truss of hay Pavel was sitting on.

'Then you really don't remember? Not anything from . . . before?'

'No, nothing. I never have been able to and Fedor and Nyusha didn't know anything, except that everyone in the family except us was dead. I suppose that must have meant my mother and father, and perhaps an uncle or an aunt. But Nyusha just said our parents were gone and no one else wanted us.'

'Well, that's more or less what happened. Now, young lady, what am I going to do with you? One thing's for sure, I'm not taking you to Moscow to stand trial for a crime I'm sure you didn't commit, so you'd better tell me exactly what's been happening and just what you have done.'

'I don't know that we've got time,' Pavel said ruefully. 'It's an awfully long story! The only crime I've committed is that I was to have married an Englishman and the only crime he committed was being an engineer at the time of the trouble.'

'Phew! And he left you?'

'No! Well, not in the way you mean. His mother was dying so he had to go home, and whilst he was away the engineers were put on trial and he wasn't allowed back into the country. Fedor had agreed that we might marry, but not until my seventeenth summer, but of course by then David wasn't able to get back into Russia.'

'I see. So where was your crime? In *not* marrying him?'

'Nothing so simple. Like a fool I wrote to him and he wrote to me and one of his letters was opened and by the most awful bad luck it was the one where he suggested I should go over the mountains into Georgia and escape through into Turkey to meet him. So the authorities knew I was planning to leave Russia illegally, and we knew collectivisation was spreading into the Caucasus, so we decided to go at once – all of us. We made our preparations and packed our things, only I was sent to town to sell dairy produce and post a letter to David telling him what we were going to do, and while I was away the soldiers came.' She shivered a little at the memory and the young officer patted her shoulder. 'When I arrived home Fedor and Nyusha and Eva were about to be taken away and of course the soldiers were waiting for a girl, and I was in my boy's clothes, so they suspected nothing.'

'And you've stayed here, with the people who took over the farm? But there's been no news of your sister? The little one?'

'No. I didn't stay here at first, I went to Moscow to try to find Eva. Everyone said she wouldn't be sent to a timber camp, not at her age. Only I couldn't find her, so I came back to try to find work, and I settled here. They're very nice, the Berisavos, really they are.'

'And it never occurred to you to go across the mountains yourself, and cross into Turkey? No, of course not, that was a stupid question, a bit of a girl like you! So what did you intend to do?'

Pavel shrugged. She had no intention of telling this soldier what her plans were, even though he seemed friendly.

'Stay here, I suppose, and work hard.'

'And stay a boy? Come, come!'

'I hadn't thought that far ahead,' Pavel said honestly. 'I suppose I'd have come clean some time.'

'Hmm. And now I've got to rescue you for the second time. There's even a chance I might be able to find out what's happened to Kon . . . to Eva, I mean. You're sure Fedor and Nyusha are in the timber camps?'

'Pretty sure. Could you find that out as well, do you think?'

'Perhaps. But first we're going to have to get you out of the muddle you're in, and that means leaving this place and turning the clock back, in one way at least.'

'I don't understand, comrade,' Pavel said, having watched his face hopefully for a few minutes. 'What good will that do?'

'Comrade! My name's Rudi Lemensk; Rudi to you. What I'm trying to get at is a change of identity, but a real change, if you understand me. You're known as Pavel Fedorovna Lazar-ov; right?'

'That's my name.'

'Wrong! Your name, little one, is Pavel Petchorenovna.'

'*Is* it? Well, what a mouthful! But who can prove it?'

'Who can disprove it? You come from an *aoul* high up in the Caucasus and you are the niece of Kevi Ryazan and the daughter of Petchoren Ryazan, two brothers who were both, at one time, in the Red Army. I shall set off on the train with my prisoner, Pavel Fedorovna, but when I arrive in Moscow it will be with the child of my old friend, Pavelinka Petchorenovna.'

'It sounds easy; but won't they want to know what became of your prisoner?'

'He will escape, I think. Or die in the attempt. Anyway, we'll get rid of him.'

'It sounds too good to be true,' Pavel breathed. 'One thing though . . . are you sure you're the man who brought me here? That man seemed quite old, yet you seem young to me now.'

'I was twenty when I carried you off; to a child of five or six twenty is quite long in the tooth; I'm thirty-three now.' He grinned at her expression. 'How old did you think I was?'

'I'm not very good on ages, but I suppose . . . about twenty-six or seven.'

'Thanks! Look, I'd like to get going before that fellow gets back; I don't want him to see too much of you.'

He got up. Pavel got up too. Fate, it seemed, was now taking a hand in her affairs and giving her very little choice in the matter. This soldier would take her away from the farm and stop her from joining David, but he had promised to try to find Eva, and anyway if she ran away from him now she might be caught by someone less sympathetic and find herself imprisoned for daring to write to a foreigner, with absolutely no hope of reaching David.

'Come along, prisoner.' He tied her wrists again, not very tightly, and led her towards the farm.

'Are you sure you won't get into trouble?' Pavel, with her hair curling a little over her ears and a skirt and blouse on, felt very different from the boy prisoner who had sat sulkily on the hard wooden bench of the train beside her captor. Now, wearing the full blue cotton skirt and white blouse which Rudi had bought for her, she looked in the window-glass and saw a fashionable young lady, a cardigan slung round her shoulders, sandals on her feet and her hair perhaps a little shorter than was fashionable . . . she did not know much about fashion, though . . . but with a neat and very feminine figure.

'If I do it'll be worth it to see the little girl grown up,' Rudi said. 'Take my arm and we'll have a meal in the best restaurant this town can provide. And after that, we'd better get on another train bound for Moscow. I've got a story for my colonel which is so wild he's bound to believe it.'

'Oh? Tell me.' Pavel hung on his arm and felt like any young girl out with an attractive man. She had seen the glances shot at Rudi by other women, and knew he was attractive.

'I'm going to say that you're my childhood sweetheart, that you'd come down from the mountains and masqueraded as a young man to get work without being molested by rough peasants, and that you and I had planned to meet and marry. I came to the farm, saw you and recognised you at once, of course, but could not give you away in front of the people who'd employed you. So I seized on the chance misidentification to get you out of there and back to Moscow. See?'

'It does sound wild,' Pavel admitted. 'But suppose they insist on us marrying?'

'You're too young,' Rudi said at once. 'Let me tell you, Pavelinka, that you don't look nineteen.'

'I know; it's being slight, I suppose,' Pavel admitted. 'That was how I got away with being a boy for so long, of course . . . that and having a small, fairly straight nose and a boyish face.'

'Hmm. Seeing you in that blouse and skirt I can't imagine how I was ever fooled for a moment. But anyway, let's find that restaurant.'

'Right.' Pavel wriggled her wrists and smiled at her companion. 'It feels good to be free.'

It occurred to her then that he could just let her go, just go back to his colonel and say the boy had jumped the train and been killed. Boys were always jumping trains and being killed and Russia was too busy with the ones who lived to bother to make trouble for the dead. Of course she had never told him that she still loved David, still wanted to get out of the country. But if she just went . . . if she really did slip away . . . who

435

would now be hurt by it? Rudi could not start a search going for a girl, if he wanted to get her back.

On the other hand, though, there was his reputation as a soldier; he would not want to say his prisoner had escaped, and even if he could produce a body, which was not impossible, she supposed, there might be someone willing to identify the body, not as hers but as someone else's, someone with a real identity. It was too risky for him, it could ruin his career.

Then there was Eva. If she let him down, ducked and ran, she would be throwing away the best chance yet of finding her sister and she would be going knowing that she had, by running away, put two people in the cart. He would probably be severely punished . . . they might reduce him to the ranks, or he might even be sent to a timber camp himself, in Siberia.

She watched his face as they squatted on the station platform. Rudi Lemensk, who had saved her from abandonment and poverty once and, it seemed, was prepared to do so again. The only person alive, she supposed, who knew about *before*, that strange faceless period which haunted her dreams but refused to allow her conscious mind so much as a hint of its existence.

She wanted to know about that time, yet she was also afraid of it. Rudi was a soldier, and so, apparently, were her father and uncle. The only permanent and solid part of her past to remain with her had been Baru, and now she, too, had gone, for she had remained at the farm with the Berisavos when she and Rudi had left.

The train, making a great deal of noise and fuss, drew in and Rudi stood up and held out his hand to pull her to her feet Together, they went towards the train. The people let the uniform through, perhaps a trifle grudgingly, and Rudi put his arm round Pavel's shoulders so that she would not get pushed away from him.

It was a nice novel sensation, to feel protected. Pavel's half-hearted thoughts of leaving the train at the next stop, or possibly simply jumping when it slowed, retreated. She had a lot to gain by staying with Rudi. If she could only trace Eva . . .

'What are you thinking?' Rudi had squeezed a place for them both on yet another hard wooden bench and now, as the train wheezed and heaved itself into motion, he turned to look at her and spoke low, for they were surrounded by other travellers. 'Or dare I guess? You're wondering whether to ditch me and let me make my own excuses to my colonel, aren't you? Well, Pavelinka, you won't do it. The girl who nipped the horsefly off my hand wouldn't put me in a spot like that.'

'And if I did? If I proved you wrong?'

'Then I'd simply have to catch you and hand you over; law of survival,' Rudi said calmly. 'And don't think I wouldn't do it – I'd catch you if I had to follow you to England and drag you from your David's arms.'

It was said lightly, but Pavel could hear the steel beneath the easy tone. She shivered.

'Nevertheless, I stay because I want to, not because I'm afraid to run. And when we find Eva . . .'

'If, Pavelinka. There's no guarantee that she's alive, even, and the *bez prizorney* don't bury their dead with nameboards.'

'The *prizorney*? Oh, but surely she'll be in a children's home? If she's with the *prizorney* we'll only find her by chance!'

'True. But she must have been assigned to a children's home, so it will be easier to search for her in that area. Now, let's forget such things. Tell me, very softly if you please, the story for my colonel, only in a lot more detail. We must both be word perfect.'

Afterwards, looking back on the rail journey, Pavel realised that though Rudi said he trusted her he had not really let her out of his sight once, and by and large it was a good thing, since their story grew more and more convincing as they rehearsed it over and over, with a good deal of laughter at times.

Despite being a soldier – for Pavel disliked authority in any form and soldiers most of all – he was good company. Indeed, after four days on various trains, Pavel thought he was a good man. Sometimes, as they grew easier with one another, she asked him timid questions about her past, but he would never answer. Later, when they had brushed through the interviews ahead, he would tell her everything, he assured her.

When they arrived in Moscow, Pavel had intended to either slip away and see Yuri or ask outright whether she might visit a friend. But she did not want Rudi to go with her; they were both safer if Yuri never met her soldier, she was sure. Rudi might never knowingly betray her, but if he believed she visited Yuri because Yuri was a traitor, then he might, one day, mention Yuri's name to someone in authority . . . it was not worth the risk. She had got the feeling that he did not much like foreigners and his voice always went cool, detached, when he mentioned David.

But these hopeful plans were set at nought by the fact that Rudi's detachment had been moved on from Moscow. When they had discovered that the colonel was a day's train journey in another direction, off they set once more, this time as standing or crouching passengers in a truck crammed with people, to run the detachment to earth.

They were, it seemed, stationed at an aerodrome; they were guarding the new aircraft and keeping runways clear and peasants out of harm's way and generally acting as security.

'A far cry from the mountains,' Rudi said. He put his arm round Pavel and gave her a quick squeeze. 'This is it! Story ready?'

'Yes . . . but you'll do all talking, won't you? I know it by heart, but I don't want to be the one to say it!'

'I'll do the talking first; then the colonel will ask you to come in, I expect, to corroborate what I've told him. Once we've got things clear . . .'

'Once we've got things clear we'll start trying to find Eva,' Pavel said quickly. She never let herself consider the difficulties ahead. What would she do? Once she was no longer Rudi's prisoner she would have no official status at all. At first she had just assumed she would take a room somewhere in Moscow, near enough to keep in touch with Rudi whilst at the same time using Yuri to find out what had happened to David and what he wanted her to do next. But now, on an aerodrome miles from civilization, how would she manage?

They reached their stop; Rudi had telephoned ahead and a broken-down army lorry awaited them. The man driving it gave Pavel a funny sort of look and a half-smile. She did not understand it; why should he smile at a prisoner? As Rudi clambered up into the lorry's cab the man muttered something which sounded like 'So you found her!' but of course it couldn't be.

She sat down between the two men and felt the tension

mount as they drove across the broad, summer sweep of the great grasslands.

Rudi left her with a soldier to watch over her in a small waiting-room and went in to see his colonel. He was gone quite a long time and Pavel grew so terrified that everything went out of her head except her fear. When at last another soldier looked round the door, muttered to her guard and then beckoned to her, she was so afraid that when she stood up her knees buckled and she nearly fell down again.

But it was all right! Amazingly the colonel, a big, bluff man in his fifties with a broad plainsman's face and close-cropped grey hair, got to his feet, leaned across the desk, and shook her hand.

'So he found you, and in such a pickle, my dear,' he greeted her. 'He's a good chap, he'll make you a good husband.'

It was only Rudi's grip, tightening on her fingers until she nearly cried out, that stopped her repeating his last two words with such incredulity that he would have guessed her surprise.

'Y-yes,' she stammered. 'He found me.'

'When he asked to go with the detachment guarding the collectivisation inspectors I was astonished – he's above that sort of thing now, I told him – but then he said he was looking for a girl, his childhood sweetheart, and I understood. He could have gone in his furlough, but he wouldn't have had the authority to ask questions . . . and he found you masquerading as a boy, eh?'

Pavel blushed and nodded and this was plainly expected, for the colonel leaned across his desk and pinched her cheek.

'Well, well! And the inspector thought you a young man who'd committed a murder, I gather? Lucky for you that Rudi recognised you . . . though I don't think you could ever look much like a young man.'

'She was wearing the *tcherkasska* and the *burka*,' Rudi put in quietly. 'But I'd have known her anywhere, of course.'

'Of course. Then we'll have a civil ceremony in . . . how long can you wait? . . . let's say in two days. Then you can have married quarters, which will help.'

In a daze, Pavel echoed Rudi's thanks, and then the two of them escaped. They walked back to a long, low-built wooden building where Rudi had a room. He did not, of course, know which one it was, but a soldier on duty took them to it, grinned knowingly at them and left.

Rudi put a reassuring hand on Pavel's shoulder and they went through the doorway into the bare little room. Then he shut the door behind them.

It was strange, now that it had happened and they were alone at long last. He had thought about her, off and on, for a dozen years and more, wondered how she was getting on, whether he would ever see her again. Is it possible for a grown man to fall in love with a little girl? No, of course not; but it's possible for a grown man to fantasise about a little girl growing up, and that, Rudi supposed, was what he had done.

He had loved her uncle; he had loved the little girl, but only as an uncle might have done. He had felt responsible for her, and when he had heard that soldiers were going to be sent into the Caucasus to guard the collectivisation inspectors he had volunteered at once.

What had he expected to find? Everything as before? The small Pavel a little bigger but certainly not mature? He was not quite sure, but he had not expected to find the whole situation changed. He had guessed that the farm would be collectivised, but not that the Lazarovs would have been taken away. The army obeyed, but that did not mean it did not also think; he had been horrified by the way the good peasant farmers had been treated, but for some reason he had thought the State would have more sense than to evict mountain farmers and put ignorant peasants from the plains in their place. And to blame a young girl for falling in love . . . to pursue her and her family . . . it was the worst sort of stupidity.

But then he had found her and had known what it was like to run mad himself, for he had taken one look at the lad crouching on the floor with an arm round the neck of the big white dog, and he had known it was she. And with the knowledge, he had simply fallen, heavily and irrevocably, in love with the girl. She was not beautiful; she did not have the sort of figure he had looked for in the past when searching for a mistress or even for a one-night stand, yet she had, for him, an irresistible attraction and he did not think it would ever wane. Just the sight of her, the way her eyes slanted to look up at him, the curve of her lashes on her cheek, the cool feel of her fingers in his . . . it was as though the two of them were tied by an invisible cord and when she moved away from him even a little it tugged painfully at his heart.

His colonel had not even thought about marriage, that had been Rudi's own idea entirely; he could have taken her, he supposed, at any stage of their journey here, but more and more he had been convinced that she was the only person who would ever matter to him, that he must have her irrevocably; it was no use saving her from the State and then letting her go off into the wide blue yonder. She was a part of him, she whom he had not set eyes on for so many years . . . it was absurd, ridiculous, he should be ashamed of himself, yet he felt her rightfully his in a way he had never felt about any other human being in his life. Kevi had touched his heart once, and the lad Kevi had killed, but that had been nothing compared with the force of his feeling for Pavel.

He had been almost unbearably tempted one night, when they had got off the train at a small station because the engine needed urgent repairs. The place had been full of peasants and small-town officials, arguing, shouting, generally creating pandemonium. An official perhaps a little higher up the scale than the others had seen an officer in the Red Army with a prisoner at his side and had come over and offered a very small private room; there was only a straw palliasse, but if the officer felt he and his prisoner would be more comfortable there . . .

Rudi had hesitated, because even then he had known what would happen when they were alone. He would untie her wrists, feed her, let her settle down on the straw mattress, and then . . . and then . . .

'No. My prisoner and I will remain on the platform so that we can board the train as soon as the engine is ready,' he had said brusquely, with a decisiveness he was far from feeling. One night of pleasure, one night when the doubt and loneliness would be eased, would in no way recompense him for the lonely years ahead if she took fright and ran away.

But now they were alone. The small block of officers' rooms would be deserted at this time of day and he knew very well what the colonel would assume he and his long-lost love would be doing there, so they would certainly not be disturbed.

But his long-lost love was standing staring round the room,

taking in all the details, and then she turned to him, her grey-green eyes shining, and started to speak, faltered, and stopped. He could not stop his feelings from showing on his face any longer . . . he *knew* she did not love him, but she was not indifferent, he knew that as well. She trusted him.

He took her, very gently, in his arms. She leaned against his chest and said, 'Poor Rudi, what a muddle I've got you in!' and he realised suddenly that she thought him embarrassed by the situation and was sorry for him. If he was only careful, and moved very slowly, then he might yet hold this small, nervous bird in the palm of his hand.

'It's fine by me, but what about you? Will you mind marrying me?'

'What, just for the sake of your story, do you mean? Of course I don't mind . . . but you don't want a wife tagging around, particularly when I'm gone, because you might meet someone else. Will he really insist that we marry?'

'I'm afraid there's nothing else for it. But divorce is easy to get and very common, so if . . . when you want to go . . .'

'Well, if you're sure, we'd better go through with it, I suppose.' She pulled back a little, the better to see his face. 'Afterwards, when we're married and I'm living with you, will you be able to tell me about when I was little? And can we start looking for Eva?'

He was so delighted that he had to hug her again, and it was so marvellously satisfying to hold her in his arms, to feel the small, strong bones of her beneath the firmness of her flesh, that it was as good as any physical act he had ever performed. At thirty-three he was an experienced lover, with a good many girl friends, mistresses and whores scattered across his past. He had had his first woman when he was only fourteen and he had not been long without one since. Here, on the aerodrome, there would be women available if he wanted one . . . but all he wanted, right now, was to have Pavel near him, trusting him. Saying that she would marry him.

'Once we're married, I'll get some furlough . . . I'm due for some . . . and we'll have plenty of time to talk.'

Talk was, of course, the last thing he had in mind, but talk was good too, he reminded himself. Even now, on fire for the touch of her, he liked to hear her voice with its sweet mountain accent as she pointed out the various advantages of his small room . . . the cleanness, the airy view of the steppes, the hanging wardrobe for his clothes and the washbasin so that he need not go to the latrines with his men.

'How shall we go about looking for Eva?'

My Pavel is very single-minded, Rudi thought gloomily, taking her hand in his because he simply had to touch her and pulling her down to sit on the bed. No messing about, he told himself severely, for in the past when he sat on a bed with a woman it was always a prelude to getting in it.

'We'll have to make it semi-official, I'm afraid. I'll see what I can find out, first, and if I can't discover anything definite then I'll have a search done on some pretext. Don't worry, if she's alive we'll find her in the end.'

But he was prepared to spend years searching.

They married at the town hall and went at once to the railway station, where they boarded a train for a secret destination. Pavel thought it was all a bit silly, until they arrived, and then she was glad they had come. It was so beautiful! A lake surrounded by forest, a little cottage tucked away by the shore and Rudi proud as a peacock both of her – which seemed silly when you remembered she was only a chance-met child of a friend – and of the cottage.

'Some friends and I decided years ago that we wanted a *dacha* where we could spend our furloughs fishing, swimming, or just wandering in the countryside,' he explained as he unlocked the front door. 'It belongs to us all, but several of the others have wives and families now, so don't get up here much. It's mainly myself and Nicholai, and he's in Siberia for a year, doing guard duty.'

In the cottage, she bustled about being housewifely, for though Rudi had a local woman who looked after it and a man who kept the garden tidy, no one had prepared them a meal. Instead, Pavel and Rudi had shopped, and now Rudi was lighting the fire and Pavel was cooking. It was fun. She sliced and chopped and sprinkled flour and by the time she was halfway through preparing the meal he had come in to say the fire was lit, the oven hot, and why didn't she let him help?

'It's almost ready.' Vegetables and cubes of meat were tipped into a dish, rice was poured into a pan, and Pavel staggered through with the food to the kitchen, the main room

443

of the house. 'I'll stand this here, put the meat in the oven, and before you know it we shall be able to eat.'

'Marvellous.' He put his arm round her and led her firmly out of the house and down to the lake. 'Isn't that beautiful? Doesn't it make you want to bathe?'

'Yes, it does. Shall we?'

He nodded. He let her go and peeled off his shirt, then began to unbutton his trousers. Pavel took off her blouse and skirt, leaving herself respectable enough in vest and knickers, and hoped that this would be sufficient. When she and Eva had bathed at home, it had been naked, but she knew very well that men and women did not behave so. They either went into the water in separate places, or, if they bathed together, they wore costumes of some description.

Rudi looked across at her; he was smiling.

'No further? You've never been to the seaside, of course, but in Georgia, where the water is warm, one bathes naked.'

'Oh?' Pavel said faintly. 'Men and women? Together?'

'That's right. Shall I . . .' His hands went to the top of his underpants. Pavel gave a nervous shriek and he stopped, grinning more broadly. 'What a little prude you are, Pavel-inka! Very well, race you to the water!'

She was a good swimmer and knew it; she beat him to the little island in the middle of the lake, then let him haul her out on to the tiny strip of sand round it and lay beside him, letting the sun warm her, steaming gently in its rays.

'That vest is a hideous garment,' Rudi remarked presently. 'And it's clinging like a second skin anyway so why don't you take it off?'

'I'm not so rude,' Pavel said sleepily. 'AAAH!'

She sat up like a jack-in-the-box and Rudi sat up too, his eyes round. 'What is it? What's the matter? Have you been bitten?'

'The rice!' She dived back into the water and beat him back to land but too late; the rice was burning, smoke filled the *dacha* and billowed out of the back door as Pavel tore it open.

It took half an hour to rescue their meal and another hour to eat it, to drink the good wine he had been given by friends in his regiment and to wash up, wipe up and clear away. Only then could they head for the bedroom.

'Where do I sleep?' Pavel said, darting into the bedroom and eyeing the big bed approvingly. There were two small beds as well, all in the one room because of the men who had married and produced children yet who still had a share in the *dacha*.

'In the big bed.'

'That's nice. And we'll change tomorrow and you can have it.'

'No. I have it now, as well. We both sleep in the big bed.'

Pavel had been wondering what the arrangement would be ever since the moment she had agreed to marry Rudi. Would he or wouldn't he want a real marriage? But she had more or less persuaded herself that someone so kind and understanding would not expect her to sleep with him because of babies. If she had babies she would not be able to divorce him and go off to find David. She did not want babies, not at all, not one little bit. She looked up at Rudi, who was standing very close but not yet touching.

'Rudi . . . I don't want to hurt you, but I don't want to have babies.'

He had been looking at her with an expression in his eyes which she could not interpret, but at her words he threw back his head and laughed, and she could hear relief more than mirth in his laughter.

'Babies? My little darling, my dushka, my own sweetheart, you shan't have babies, I promise! Oh, Pavelinka, you don't know . . . you can't know . . . how I've wanted you, how I've dreamed of this moment.'

He was only wearing his trousers, for it was a warm night and he had not dressed himself again after their bathe. Now he picked her up and sat down on the bed with her on his lap. He began to undress her slowly and clumsily. Pavel held his wrists, meaning to stop him whilst she spoke, but she could not. He continued as though she had not touched him and when she tried to pull his wrists away it was as though he was completely unaware of her tugging.

Such strength was frightening, but Pavel did not let herself be frightened. She let go his wrists and put her arms round his neck. At once he stopped undressing her and hugged her. She spoke against the warm skin at the base of his throat, her mouth touching the pulse that beat there gently, between words.

'How – does – one – stop – babies?'

He hugged her harder and made her gasp.

'Stoopidchka! There is a thing . . . I have one here . . . but just forget all about it and let me show you how sweet it is to be loved by a man.'

Pavel woke in the dawn light, when the birds began to make their first tentative stirrings and to chirp and rustle in the branches of the trees that arched above the little *dacha*. She felt a sweet, tremulous happiness flood through her, closely followed by a terrible sense of guilt. She never should have behaved as she had – with such abandon, such breathless, helpless pleasure! Telling oneself that it was best to give in and let him do what he wanted so that she might find Eva was one thing; crying out and encouraging him and wanting more quite another!

She had tried to think of David, even once to pretend that it was David who lay above her, but it had not worked, for Rudi's lovemaking did not resemble David's exciting but tentative fumblings in the slightest. She remembered David's kisses very well . . . yet he had not held her as Rudi did, so that she felt both helpless and powerful, the gracious giver of such pleasure that Rudi, strong, brave and dominant, could be reduced to speechless trembling touches when they lay quiet at last.

Now, however, even thinking about the previous night made her want Rudi awake again. She nudged him briskly with an elbow and he grunted, turned towards her and then sighed and let his breathing deepen in sleep once more.

This would never do! Pavel began to stroke him and felt him wake. She continued as his arms crept round her. Soon, he was very wide awake indeed. He kissed her and rolled her on to her back and Pavel began to try to tell him that there were questions which she wanted answered.

But Rudi was smiling down at her in the grey light, and it was clear that he did not intend to answer questions. He put a finger lightly across her mouth, then bent his head. The questions ceased to matter.

'Now you must tell me about what happened when I was young, and why you think I've forgotten it,' Pavel demanded later, lying on her back with her arms above the quilt and with

Rudi's heavy head resting on her shoulder. 'Why did you come to our *aoul*, or did you live there as well? Were you a soldier then, or just a boy? Tell me as much as you can remember.'

'All right. I came to your *aoul* to find your Uncle Kevi, who had been in the army with me. We had been great friends.'

'Good. What was he like, this Kevi?'

Rudi laughed comfortably. He had already made up his mind just how much truth and how much fiction he would tell his little Pavelinka, and he had loved Kevi so much once that it was no effort to remember him only as a dear friend.

'He was older than I but younger than I am now, of course, and very handsome, very intelligent. Women adored him – he had enough of them, God knows . . . there was one in particular, who bore him a son, she worshipped Kevi. His mother – your babushka – used to say he was strong as a stallion, clever as ten schoolteachers and beautiful as a woman, and it wasn't a bad description. He was a good soldier too, though he was a Caucasian first; I don't know that he ever reconciled himself to the rifle, the long dagger was his weapon.' He stopped abruptly, remembering what use Kevi had made of that weapon, then continued quickly, but on a slightly different theme. 'Your father, Petchoren, was his elder brother. He was also handsome and clever, but when he married your mother he decided the army was no life for him and he went home, to his own place in the mountains.'

'And my mother?'

'I never met her, but she must have been very lovely. Her daughters were lovely, and all different. One had lovely hair the colour of amber, the next had hair the pale, milky golden brown of a young deer, and the next . . .'

'Three? Were there three? But I only have one sister – Eva.'

'Yes. Eva's hair was yellow as butter in sunlight.' Rudi looked sideways at her, at the line of her mouth and the small, straight nose, the eyelids now drooping lazily over her eyes as she contemplated something outside the window at the foot of their bed. 'You had another sister, but she died.'

'Oh. Did you know her? Was she older than me?'

'Yes, I knew her. She was older than you. Her name was . . .'

'Konkordia?'

He was surprised but merely said, 'Yes, that's right,' and waited for the next question.

447

It did not come. She continued to stare ahead of her but there was a slight frown line between her brows. He wondered if he was stirring memories which were better hidden, then shrugged and continued.

'As I said, I went to the *aoul* to visit Kevi and to meet these nieces he was always bragging about, and I did. Well, several of us did. But whilst we were there a dreadful thing happened which I don't really want to talk about. And your family died, all but you and Eva.'

'All? Surely not all? I thought they must have died one or two at a time, not all at once.'

'No, I'm afraid it was all. Dushka, I'd rather not talk about it, it was very sad, a dreadful time. When we had done all that we could do we left the place and took you and Eva and Baru down to the Lazarovs, because we knew they wanted children but had none of their own.'

'I see. But . . . Rudi, how did they die?'

He heaved a deep sigh and sat up. 'Tragically. Unnecessarily. I won't say more, my love, because it wouldn't help, it would only bring it all back, perhaps. Let's talk about what we shall do today.'

Pavel frowned, her soft, fawn brows drawing together over that small, straight little nose.

'I want to know, Rudi — I need to know. Please?'

He shook his head at her, not wanting to have to lie but determined to keep the truth from her. How could she lie with me, let me make love, touch her in her most secret and intimate places, if she knew that it was either at my hand or by my instigation that her uncle and father died, and through my carelessness that her grandmother and sister killed themselves, he thought desperately. She must never know.

'If you don't tell me . . .' Her voice trailed off, forlorn.

'Pavelinka, how they died isn't important, don't you see that? It's how they lived! Ask me anything you like about how they lived and I'll answer you truthfully. Don't ask me what must hurt you to hear and hurt me to tell.'

'But . . . it worries me, that I can't remember anything,' she explained, turning to face him. 'It's like a blackness, a nightmare . . . as though I was born at the age of six, to foster parents.'

'Perhaps it's better.' He turned and took her in his arms. 'All right, all right, if you must know. We were up in the mountains to see Kevi and your father, yes, but also in search of a murderer who had run away from our regiment. We spent the night in your *kosh*, well hidden, knowing that the murderer would probably come to see Petchoren to find out what the soldiers wanted. He did not come but during the night your uncle left the *kosh* to check on the sheep. He came back in abruptly, a young soldier who was afraid of the murderer woke . . . he shot your uncle, another soldier shot wildly because your uncle grabbed for the first man's gun . . . the bullet struck Petchoren. They both died.'

'I . . . see. And Babushka? Konkordia?'

'Everyone panicked; it was dark, you see, and there were people everywhere, one of them, we thought, the murderer. Bullets whistled through the air, there were cries . . . they died.'

'I . . . see. And the little, dark place in my nightmares?'

'Oh, my dearest, if only I could have spared you this! You ran away with the baby in your arms and hid from us in a little cave nearby. We coaxed you out, hungry and exhausted, and I put you on my horse and the rest you know.'

She was silent, cuddled trustingly in his embrace, and for a moment Rudi's self-revulsion was so strong that he nearly thrust her away from him. To lie – and on such a subject! But it was near enough the truth, and he could not bring himself to tell her of that terrible, useless double suicide which had weighed heavy on him for a dozen years. How could he have prevented it? He had lain awake many a night struggling with the answer to that one. To have followed faster? Not to have followed at all? Never to have fired the first shot? Ah, Kevi would not have hurt me, he had told himself a thousand times, he would never have hurt me. But there had been others, soldiers less experienced . . . and there was the lad Kevi had killed. He had to be revenged!

'Now tell me, dear one, about our lives in our *kosh*.'

He told her as he would have told a fairy story to a child. About their herds, their strong, courageous dogs, the river at the bottom of the ravine and the water which had to be lugged up the steep path two or three times a day in the leaky wooden buckets.

'If you'd stayed there you'd never have gone to school or learned much, other than how to make maize bread and sew,' he said, kissing her smooth hair. 'But it wouldn't have mattered to me; I'd have come back for you, and lifted you up and carried you away and made love to you, just the way I've done now, and just the way I'll do again tonight.'

She shivered, butting his chest with her head, then turning and licking the side of his face, biting him gently on the chin before pulling herself free and sitting up.

'I must write a letter.'

He did not pretend to misunderstand her but pulled her down again, to lie close.

'So you shall, in a moment. Who are you going to write to?'

'Well, to David, of course. I shall send it to a friend of his, who will pass it on.'

He knew, then, that this was the real moment of surrender; that last night had simply been compliance with his male strength combined with a certain amount of female desire. He caught her up and squeezed her and then kissed her mouth with all the passion at his command. When he let her go she was pink-cheeked, bright-eyed, and near to tears.

'You must understand that I loved David, Rudi, and did not intend to love you but just to please you. Now, however, I see that there are different kinds of love, and I love you in a different way. Not more, it wouldn't be right to say I love you more, because David and I didn't . . . David never could . . . I mean you're my husband and David never was.'

'And you'll stay with me? You won't repine?'

He did not know the effort it cost her to say that she would.

# CHAPTER NINETEEN

'David's not been the same since he came back. And then that letter, the one from Yuri . . . it really upset him.'

Alice, sitting on the end of her bed putting pin-curls into the front of her hair, watched Nibby in the mirror as he undressed. She was sure that if anyone knew what was in the letter Nibby did, but despite having been married for absolutely ages she was not at all sure that he would confide in her.

'Which letter? Oh, that one.' Nibby heaved a huge sigh and came over to stand behind his wife, a hand on each of her shoulders. 'My dear dope, David would tell you what was in it like a shot, only he thinks it will upset you and get you . . . thinking.'

'Thinking what? So you *do* know what it said! Tell me, John Hawke, or I'll burn your breakfast tomorrow morning.'

The letter had arrived that morning, a flimsy blue airmail envelope. David had pounced on it, read it through, and then crushed it in his fist, shoved his fist into his pocket, and marched out of the room.

'All right, all right, no need to get in a state. Pavel's married. To a soldier.'

'No!' Alice stared at Nibby's reflection, her face showing all too clearly the shock and consternation she felt. 'Oh, my poor Davie! How *could* she?'

'From what David told me, I don't think she had much choice. The authorities picked her up on some trumped-up charge – she was still dressed as a young man – and took her into custody. This soldier rescued her, but had to say she was his girl and the colonel of his regiment more or less forced them to marry. People do worse things than that in Russia, old girl; they are forced to lie and spy and die, if you'll forgive the rhyme, in order to save their loved ones from a beastly unfair fate.'

'Yes, I suppose so. Can't David see it like that, then?'

'He can, that's the trouble. He tried so hard, you see, but didn't manage to find her, and he feels he didn't try hard enough. But I gather she said she's as happy as she can be . . . he must learn to live with it, poor old boy.'

'We'll find him someone else,' Alice said brightly at once. 'It won't be difficult, he's such a dear.'

'Yes, that's what he said . . . Alice will try to get me married off once she knows. Those were his very words, and it won't do, darling. Really, you must let him know best. He isn't over Pavel by a long chalk.'

In his own room, David lay and stared at the ceiling and tried not to be bitter or think cruel and unrewarding thoughts. He had tried so hard to find Pavel, he had trekked through Russia at great personal risk, he had suffered from that ghastly illness and not known his name for weeks, he had visited the farm masquerading as a collectives inspector, yet it had got him nowhere. And some wretched soldier picks her up and black-mails her and she marries him! He groaned and shifted uneasily at the thought of his own little Amazon in another's embrace; it wasn't fair, it was not fair! What else could he have done? Why had she not simply run away from the soldier and come to him? Why could she not do so even now?

But he knew that she would not; the letter had made it clear that she felt herself committed. So, knowing that, he would have to thrust her right out of his mind and stop thinking about her or dreaming about her or fantasising that one day she would turn up on his doorstep, looking like a lost little boy-girl, wanting him.

If I can't have Pavel I don't want anyone, he told himself presently, turning over and trying to compose himself for sleep. All the stupid, giggling girls on Deeside could line up and beg me on bended knees to marry them and I wouldn't oblige. On the other hand, though, the life of a celibate was not at all appealing. So what would it be? An affair? A prostitute? What about a marriage of convenience? His, naturally.

The thought amused him. Whom could he conveniently marry? Whom would it benefit him to marry? In the old days, shipowners married their daughters to other shipowners' sons without a second thought – you kept the money in the family.

But he was no shipowner, only a boat builder, and so far as he could recall there was not one boat builder in the neighbourhood with a daughter that he'd take on as a one-night stand, let alone for life!

He was almost asleep when it occurred to him that just because he built boats there was no need to marry into the trade. Pavel had once told him he should dive down to the wreck of the *Royal Gold* and take the treasure of money and passengers' jewels to finance him and try to find proof that she had sunk through some cause other than her design or her building. If he had money, he could go down to the wreck. If he was the owner of Carmel Hall again he could do more than that – he could buy a bigger shipyard than anything he and Nibby could afford, or he could do something entirely different.

Maria Raft adored him. It was common knowledge that she did; her worship, indeed, had embarrassed him horribly before he went to Russia. Suppose, just suppose, that he could bring himself to make love to her? He laughed at himself, but nevertheless it was something to think about. If he could not have Pavel then he might as well settle for money and position.

But gentlemen did not do things like that; a gentleman would not marry a woman in order to get possession of her wealth. Not that there was any other reason for marrying Maria that he could envisage – God knew, the poor girl had been on the shelf long enough – how old was she? Twenty-seven? Twenty-eight? Mature, anyway.

But of course he would never do it; it would be too cold-blooded, too obvious. And think what little monsters the resulting brats would be with his thick black brows and Maria's combined! They would be hairy as young apes, he told himself, grinning into the pillow. No, it was absurd, he couldn't do it, not even for Carmel Hall.

Maria felt light, dancing. She had on a pale grey dress with a fluffy white jacket, white court shoes and light silk stockings. She crossed the sweep of the gravelled drive and got carefully into her new car, a sports model with the roof down, though it was late October.

She was going, ostensibly, to see Alice. Alice had not been in touch for several weeks because David was home and there was a lot of work on hand, but a couple of days ago she had telephoned and had asked Maria to come up on Saturday for tea.

'I don't work Saturdays, so we can have a chat,' she had explained rather self-consciously. 'The fellows will be working, but they said if we went down to the yard around teatime they'd show you round and then they'd come back for tea with us.'

'That would be lovely,' Maria had told her. 'Don't worry, I'll be on time.'

She revved the engine, selected the gear and slid down the drive towards the road, her excitement so hot in her throat that she felt she must sing to let some of it out. She was going to see David! It had been nearly a year since she had seen him last, but his memory shone ... by a great piece of luck she had managed to get hold of some of Julia's wedding photographs, ones with David on them, and she had had the best one framed. It stood beside her bed, though of course it was not officially there; really the photograph by her bed was a picture of herself with her first pony, but the one of David came out every evening when she was safely tucked up, and was put back each morning before she came down to breakfast.

Unfortunately, mistakes do occur, and she had left David's photo by her bed one morning when her mother had nipped into her room for some reason. At first Mrs Raft had been very cross with her, telling her that she was a fool and had no right to have such a photograph in her room, and then she had suddenly started to cry and had clasped Maria to her bosom and told her that she must forget wretches like the young Thomas boy and begin to think again about going up to London for a season.

'You're a lovely girl, you deserve better than to be stuck down here whilst all your school friends marry,' she had sobbed. 'I really thought that Mr Philip Openshaw was going to pop the question, during the summer.'

It would not have helped matters had Maria admitted that Mr Openshaw had indeed popped the question and had been refused. She had been tempted to accept for the selfsame reasons that her mother was now propounding – her school friends were all married now, many of them with families – but she had told Mr Openshaw that she was not thinking of marriage, not yet. She had hoped to keep him in reserve, in case nothing better came up, but with typical male thoughtlessness he had gone off and married someone else. Not that it mattered; she was well aware why Mr Openshaw had proposed marriage.

He needed a wife and it had to be a wife with money. His small business could not support two people and expand; one of them had to have private means. Once, she would have been sickened by such a reason for marriage, but now she was getting used to it. Mr Openshaw was not the first to ask her to marry him and she knew very well that not one of her previous suitors would have even given her the time of day had they not wanted a rich wife.

But now, driving down the quiet road and then turning off up to the right, towards the cottage, she told herself that although David would never marry her he was a good friend, and if he *did* ever realise her worth, it would be because she had worth, not because of her father's money.

It was a lovely afternoon and the cottage drowsed in the late autumn sunshine. It was almost impossible to believe that in a few days it would be November and one would wear suits and coats and galoshes as of right and put away all the light and summery clothing and the jackets and the swimsuits until next year. Far away to her right as she approached the cottage door the estuary shone, blue and gold, and farther still, a line on the horizon, shone the sea. From here it was immobile, without a ripple, not even a line of surf visible.

'Hello, Maria! Come in!'

Maria jumped six inches; she had not knocked, and she had certainly not heard the door open.

'Oh, Alice, you did give me a start! Isn't it a perfect afternoon? How are you? It's been ages . . . far too long, but you're a married lady now and you still work; it didn't seem fair to come calling.'

Alice looked very pretty; her dark hair curled softly across her forehead and she was wearing a lavender blue dress. She looked Maria up and down and then leaned forward and gave her a kiss.

'Maria Raft, you've lost weight! It suits you, indeed it does! What a pretty dress, too.'

Maria knew she had lost weight, though it had not been

intentional. She thought she had simply started to eat less when David had gone off to Russia, for she had worried about him, and it had been impossible not to take long, striding walks to try to get her mind off him and one thing had led to another until one day she had noticed, in her mirror, a new shape emerging. What with that and a new hairdresser, who had told her to leave her hair unpermed but to go in each week for a nice soft wash and set, she did feel she looked, if not better, at least different.

'Thank you very much. You always were pretty, but being married has made you prettier,' she responded. 'How are the children? And your husband? And David, of course.'

'They're all well, thank you. Michael's down at the boatyard with the men but Sassy's off on some junket with her friends, as usual. How that child expects to get into Cambridge next year if she doesn't work, I don't know.'

As she spoke she was leading Maria into the kitchen. She pulled a chair out and nodded to it.

'Do sit down! I'm sorry to bring you in here, but you know how small this place is and I'm still getting the tea. You're being treated like one of the family, I'm afraid, so it's tea in here, with lots of bread and butter, shrimps and cockles, fresh boiled crab, then a salad and some cress, honey or jam . . . not both, you notice! . . . and afterwards a choice of three cakes: my honey and walnut, Sassy's rich fruit loaf, and a lemon sponge we made between us. Oh, and there's delicious apple pie and cream, from the apples in the garden, if you like that.'

'It sounds a feast,' Maria said, her mouth watering quite briskly at the good baking smells coming from Alice's oven. 'I can cook a bit, but not like you; I couldn't feed five people – six today, because I'm here!'

'You could,' Alice assured her. 'It's easy. What's difficult sometimes is marketing, when you've got a limited budget. But it'll get easier as the fellows sell more boats. With David away for so long it was hard, but now he's back they expect to make a boat every two months – and they're charging more, too.'

'Can I help?' Maria asked presently, as Alice began to clean lettuce, radishes and cress. 'I could slice tomatoes and cucumber well enough, I'm sure.'

'Well, that would be lovely,' Alice said. 'Ah, I hear someone

. . . I thought they said we were to go down to the yard, but perhaps I was wrong.'

Michael burst through the back door, obviously the bearer of important tidings. He was tall now, fair-haired and cheerful, and at a quick glance seemed very grown up to Maria. 'Afternoon, Miss Raft, hey, Allie,' he said breathlessly. 'Nibby says could Miss Raft go down now, whilst there's still plenty of light. Then they can show her everything before it gets dusky.'

'Oh. Well, can you take her down, Mikey? I haven't finished, you see,' Alice said apologetically. 'Will you be all right, Maria? Nibby and David are so proud of their work.'

'Yes, if Michael shows me where to go,' Maria said eagerly. 'Do I need wellingtons, Alice? I've got none with me, I'm afraid.'

Alice laughed. 'You noticed the ranks of boots in the porch, no doubt! Yes, you'll need some – borrow a pair! We've got most sizes, I think.'

Maria went out and shuffled doubtfully through the boots, but eventually found a pair which seemed to fit. She put them on, abandoning, not without regret, her own smart white court shoes, and set off with Michael as her guide.

It was a good way down to the yard; they followed the bed of a small river, diving under a bridge over which the railway ran and crossing a goodly stretch of abandoned ground wild with long grass and rubbish. But then the shore itself began to blend with the grasses until they were on the verge of the sea marsh, and it was here that the Thomas & Hawke yard was flourishing.

It was quite a surprise. For a start, there were more buildings than Maria had imagined – three long, low buildings, two of them whole and one only a roof with four stout pillars supporting it. She had also expected to see Nibby and David alone, but two other men worked with them, or perhaps it would be more accurate to say a youth and a man, for the boy standing attentively beside Nibby was scarcely more than fifteen. All four turned round as Maria and Michael approached.

'Hello there, Maria,' David called. 'I see you brought your gumboots; I was afraid Alice would forget to remind you.' He turned to the man and the boy. 'I think that's all we'll get done now before the light goes. See you first thing Monday.'

The boy smiled at Maria, the man tugged at his greasy cap; then they made off the way she had just come. Nibby began to pile planks up, one on the other, and David headed for the large shed nearest him.

'Come on, Maria, come and see my engine – built under Nibby's stern supervision, mind.'

'I thought you did the hulls and so on and Nibby did the engines,' Maria said rather timidly, following him into the big, dark shed. 'That's what Alice said.'

'We did. The thing is, though, we're both trained engineers, though I've done more on construction than the engine side of things lately. But Nibby was the expert. Only now that there are more of us, we find we can get the men . . . old Tom and young Tony . . . to do most of the hull and the carpentry work, which leaves the pair of us free to do the more intricate engineering stuff.' He pointed to a mass of tiny parts, gleaming oilily in the last of the light. 'There it is; what do you think?'

'I can't say much because I don't understand engines at *all*,' Maria admitted ruefully. 'I wish I could, I'd love to sound intelligent, but I only know how to drive a car, I don't know anything about boats, and to tell the truth the engine of a car's a closed book to me. Daddy's taken on a chauffeur to mend the insides, not to drive the outsides, as he sometimes says.'

David looked at her thoughtfully across the bench. 'You've changed,' he said at last. 'Not your hair, I don't mean, though that's different. It's you. You didn't used to say things so straight out.'

'You've changed as well,' Maria admitted. 'You're thinner and you look . . . well, a bit older and quite a lot grimmer. But probably it's only the light,' she added hastily, terrified of offending him.

'No, it's not. I've been . . . very unhappy.' David looked at her again. 'What's your excuse?'

'Similar,' Maria muttered, examining the engine parts scattered all over the bench with false interest. 'Why were you unhappy, David?'

'I failed in what I went to Russia for. You?'

'You could say I just failed, I suppose,' Maria said. 'It's difficult for girls. David . . .'

'Yes?'

'What happened in Russia?'

'Nothing. I was ill, which didn't help, but I missed her, somehow. My Pavel. I came back here and a few days ago I heard from her. She's married someone else.'

'The fool!' Maria's words could not be held back. 'She could have had you, and she chose someone else? Oh, David, I'm sorry!'

'It wasn't quite that simple. Russia's a strange place, and I don't think she had much choice. But it meant I wasted months, all for nothing.'

'Well, if she's out of the picture, I suppose you'll start having more of a social life again? Going up to London and so on.'

'I don't think so.' David sounded rather amused, Maria thought, her heart lifting. 'Why on earth should I go to London because Pavel's married someone else?'

'Well, you aren't thinking of staying a bachelor, are you? I just thought . . .'

'I'm not searching for a wife, if that's what you *just thought*,' David said, his voice sharp. 'I leave partner-hunting to women; it's what they seem to excel at.'

'Oh? If you think I'm searching for a husband you can think again!' Maria heard with horror her own voice grow sharp, but there was no holding it, it seemed. 'I wanted to get married once, but now I've gone off the whole idea! I don't even *like* men much!'

'Then we should be ideally suited, because I don't like women at all, not Englishwomen,' David said hatefully. 'The only woman for me's married to someone else, so that solves my problem.'

'Good! Right. And now that I've seen your old sheds, I'm going back to have tea with Alice,' Maria said. She turned her back on him and snatched at the handle of the shed door. She gripped it and pulled – and it came off in her hand. For a moment she stood there, just holding it, and then, from behind her, David laughed. It was the last straw. Maria hurled the door handle across the shed, where it ricocheted off the bits of machinery and bounced behind the bench, and then she grabbed at the door.

It would not open. Behind her, David said bitingly, 'You spoilt little fool!' and brushed past her, reaching for the door.

It would not open for him either. Maria, in her turn, sniggered. David swore. He also kicked the bottom panel of the door, at which Maria giggled again.

David said another word, a slightly nastier one, and dropped to his knees.

'We'll have to find the door knob,' he said in a carefully neutral voice. 'Can you see it?'

'Not from here; I think it went over the other side.' Maria also got down on all fours and crawled under the bench.

Five minutes later she found the knob and handed it to David. He thanked her stiltedly, got to his feet, pulled her to hers, and then went over to the door. He fitted the knob into the appropriate hole and turned it. It went on turning.

'Did it work before?' Maria said.

'Of course!'

'Couldn't you climb out through one of the windows?'

'No. They're fixed, they don't open.'

David still sounded annoyed, but Maria felt pretty cross herself. Admittedly it had been she who had wrenched the door knob off in the first place but it had only come off because it was so old and loose, and that was *his* fault.

'Then what do you suggest we do? Settle down for the night?'

'Don't be silly.' David's voice was still iced vinegar and it ill became him, in Maria's opinion. 'Alice will come down presently, to find out why we're not up at the cottage, having tea. Then she or Nibby can let us out.'

'Why didn't they wait for us?' Maria asked after another silence. 'Michael went back too, I suppose?'

'Yes. I said I'd show you round so that they could get back and clean up. It's only a small house; Michael will wash in the kitchen sink and Nibby will use the bathroom. That means that I'll have to hang around waiting until someone's finished; or I would have, in the ordinary way.'

'I see.'

Impatiently, seething, they waited. And waited. It began to get dusk and it was also rather chilly. David shifted from foot to foot, then charged the door with his shoulder. It creaked but did not give. He lifted a foot and kicked with all his might and though the door did not give the wall beside it did. Maria could not help herself – a smothered giggle escaped, but it seemed that David was similarly stricken for she heard a snort, and then he turned to her, a hand held out.

'Here, I bet it's the first time you've ever left a building through the wall instead of the door! Shockingly badly put together, these old sheds! Give me your hand – we don't want you breaking a leg on the frame.'

They got out in good order. David offered her his arm and she tucked a hand in his elbow. They did not say much on the uphill walk back to the cottage, but once inside they both spoke at once to the group standing round the tea-table.

'Where have you been?' 'Why didn't you come down and rescue us?'

'What on *earth* . . .?' Alice's eyes were round. 'I say, Davie, you do take your time. I bet poor Maria was bored to tears! Nibby said you'd go on and on about your old engine until she was desperate, but I didn't think you'd be that long!' Alice turned courteously to her guest. 'Are you fascinated by engines, Maria? I'm afraid I simply don't understand them.'

'Nor does Maria,' said David, since his companion seemed temporarily bereft of speech. 'I'm afraid we've been cursing you three – the door knob came off the engine room door and we've been trapped for ages. If I hadn't kicked the door in we'd be there still.'

'The wall, you mean,' Maria corrected him. She smiled at Alice. 'Such a temper we both got in! I think we were quite rude to each other!'

'It was my fault,' David said handsomely. 'Poor Maria behaved beautifully whilst I cursed and swore and flung myself at the door. Anyway, I'll just wash and then we can have tea.'

Perhaps because of the long wait, the tea seemed even better than Maria had imagined. She had a plateful of everything and then second helpings. She drank what seemed like a gallon of tea and for once forgot her awe of the Thomas family. She laughed when David teased her and joined in all the idle gossip and chit-chat, and when the meal was over and she and Alice had washed and wiped up whilst the men put the china and cutlery away, she sat on the hearth-rug before the newly lit fire and played Monopoly and Newmarket and I Spy.

When it was time to go home she thanked Alice wholeheartedly for a lovely afternoon and then David walked her down to the gate and her car.

'I'm sorry about the door knob and all the things I said,' he told her as he opened the car door for her to get in. 'Tell you what, tomorrow's Sunday, we don't work on Sundays. Suppose we go for a ramble, just you and I? Would you like that?'

The long weeks of misery whilst David was away had taught Maria a lot; she did not jump at the bait with beaming eyes and wildly wagging tail.

'Thanks, but . . . where were you thinking of going?'

'Where would you like to go? Want to go up through the Loggerheads and climb Moel Fammau? Or would you rather go along the shore? We could go into Snowdonia, only that would mean we'd have to use your car. We could get a bus to Loggerheads, and we could walk along the shore. What do you think?'

'I think I'd enjoy it if the weather holds, but not if it's wet or cold,' Maria said, having given the matter her careful attention. 'You're on the phone, aren't you?'

'Sure. Shall I ring you first thing tomorrow, then, and we'll talk it over?'

'That would be nice. Goodnight, David.'

Halfway down the hill, though, Maria could feel the old bubbling excitement rising in her chest. It was impossible to believe, but it really seemed as if he were taking her seriously, treating her like a woman instead of like an embarrassing and unwanted elderly relation.

But even so, she must not rush at him, knocking him sideways in her eagerness to win his regard. Men were not like women, they did not have the same urgent need for approval. David would like her better if she did not throw herself at him, but it would be awfully difficult!

David came back indoors from seeing Maria off and threw himself down in the first easy chair he reached, then he eyed his sister approvingly.

'Well done, old thing; she was almost human today. What did you tell her, exactly?'

'You are horrid, David. I didn't tell her anything, except to come to tea. Oh, I mentioned you'd be here, of course, but nothing else. Why?'

'She was so much easier, much better company . . . and you should have heard her raking me down when I lost my temper with her! I can't bear it when she's humble.'

'There you are, you see; she really isn't a bad old stick.'

'Not a bad old stick? What a way to refer to the future Mrs Thomas!'

Alice stared, then shrugged. He was clearly in a strange mood; better humour him, she supposed.

'Well, if you're searching for a rich wife I suppose she's the obvious choice. You aren't serious, are you, Davie?'

'Never more so. Any of that honey and walnut cake left?'

'I've taken an administrative post, in Kharkov. We'll have a flat, probably quite a small one, and you'll be able to work if you want to. At least you'll have papers and be a perfectly legal person.' Rudi laughed as Pavel shot across the room and straight into his arms, to cling round his neck with throttle-some force. 'No need to strangle me, I did it as much for myself as for you. It's no life once you're married, the army.'

'It's been nice, though, in a way. I've enjoyed seeing the aircraft and getting to know your friends.'

But it had not been nice, not really, and they both knew it. Pavel had never felt so restricted in her life. The aerodrome was supposed to be top security, which meant that guards tended to be trigger-happy and that, in turn, meant that wives were not encouraged on the base. In fact she was the only military wife there, for it turned out that when the colonel had talked about married quarters he meant that Pavel should go back to their base outside Moscow and live there until Rudi could join her. This she had absolutely refused to consider.

'If they make me, I'll run away and never come back,' she muttered against Rudi's uniform jacket, when he broke the news to her. 'I don't mind doing that, but I don't want to hurt you.'

He could not know and must never be allowed to guess how horribly torn she was by her loves. She adored her husband, gloried in their lovemaking, yet there was a still, secret part of herself which simply continued to love David despite every-thing – and, alas, to want him. He was quite different from Rudi. He was not nearly as protective or as serious. Being nearer to her in age and experience meant, she supposed, that they would have had a more even and shared relationship, instead of as at present, with Rudi so much the dominant partner, the one who would take all the responsibility and who bore most of the worries of their situation.

So of course when she had told Rudi how she felt, he had swept her into his arms, hugged her tight, and said she should stay, no matter what. And she had. For several long weeks she had been more or less confined to his small room, the common room at the end of the hut and a quick trip to the latrines whenever they were free from shouting, hurrying officers. Now and then, when he was able to do so, he took her out and they drove in the old lorry to a nearby township and watched a film at the cinema or bought bits and pieces in the shops or just drank tea and talked. Sometimes they went deep into the tall grass country and lay down in the pale sunshine of autumn and watched the wildlife and made love far from the creaking straw mattresses and metal-framed beds of the army compound.

'You're a good lass; I couldn't ask for a better.' He patted her bottom and turned her round so that they both faced the window. 'How about not looking out at that for the next year or so, eh? And I should say that I haven't made the final sacrifice, I've not left the army, not really. I'll still be working for them, but instead of the uniform and the gun I'll carry a pen and an abacus. There's a university at Kharkov, and a huge tractor factory and a scientific institute . . . plenty of things to guard.'

'If you're not uniformed and gunned . . . armed, I mean . . . then why will you be guarding things?' Pavel asked, leaning back against his broad chest.

'I'll be dealing with the administrative problems of guarding; paying wages, seeing that shifts are worked out right, that sort of thing.'

'Oh! But you'll be a clerk; Rudi, you'll hate it! You've always gone on about small minds and small jobs . . . oh, Rudi, you'll end up hating me because I've taken away the job you love.'

'You're wrong. You haven't taken away the job, no one has. I just put it to the colonel that I'd never seen the other side of army life and that now, with a new wife, seemed like a good time to have a go, and he agreed. So next time they need someone to train recruits or to take a raiding party up into some remote part of Russia to sort out trouble, they'll probably look round and say 'Lemensk hasn't seen any action for a while; let's send him!' and I'll be back in the thick of it whether I like it or not.'

'That sounds better, but will they let me stay in the flat if you have to go off somewhere I'm not allowed?'

'I think so, but we'll face each jump as we come to it, hey?' He plonked a kiss on her cheek, then let his lips move caressingly to the corner of her mouth and spoke against it. 'We'll be leaving in a week; can you start packing?'

She had so few possessions that it was funny; she laughed and kissed him back, then pushed him towards the door.

'I know, you're doing a perimeter check or something. Go and do it, I'll get things ready for packing.'

'What did I do before I found you?' Rudi pinched her cheek and opened the door. 'Not long now, sweetheart!'

The flat was marvellous to Pavel and to Rudi as well; to have their own little home with a separate bedroom and living-room was wonderful enough, but add to that a kitchen with running water and a gas stove, a gas fire in the living-room and, miracle of miracles, a combined bathroom and lavatory – it was beyond Pavel's wildest dreams.

They were hard up, though, despite Rudi's good clerical job, and when Pavel was told she could work if she wished her joy knew no bounds. Kharkov was on the plain, which was pretty boring, but at least there were plenty of jobs. She could work at the Institute in some menial capacity, she could work in the factory making tractors, or she could work part-time on a collective.

She knew she would choose the collective, of course, and Rudi took it for granted as well, though he did try to persuade her to at least try factory work first.

'You'll get much more money,' he urged. 'We're not poor, but with things so expensive . . .'

But it was no use. She knew she would go mad shut up in a factory all day with the noise constantly battering at her, and anyway the girls on the collectives wore nice blue dungarees and she felt easier working in trousers than skirts.

So within a week of moving to Kharkov Pavel had found herself a rusty old bicycle and a job on a collective five miles away. There were no horses, but perhaps because she was young and amusing or perhaps because her husband was an official, she was allowed, now and then, to drive the older of the two tractors.

'When winter comes they'll not need me,' she told Rudi regretfully, after her first few days of work. 'But there's bound to be something . . . do you know the scientists' wives have nannies for their children! I could be a nanny.'

'You could stay at home and cook me good meals,' Rudi said, laughing at her, because like all apartment blocks theirs had a communal dining-room where poor food was sloppily served three times a day. 'Did you ever taste anything like those potatoes?'

'I never did. Shall we forgo the temptations tonight and have our meal up here?'

'Did you bring anything home?' Working on a collective had its advantages in that it was possible to take food home quite legitimately, as part of your pay.

'Yes. A string of onions, a bag of potatoes, a few apples and some quite good quality flour. I'll whisk up some *blinis* and we can have them with the last of that honey and some cooked apple, but that's pudding, after all. How would you like some bits of fat pork and fried potatoes?'

'After what they give us in the dining room it sounds heavenly. And there's a concert tonight, at the Park. Would you like to go?'

'I'd love it,' Pavel said happily. 'Isn't Kharkov *gay*?'

'After that aerodrome, anywhere would be gay. But you're right, we can have a good life here. And I'm setting the wheels in motion, now that we're settled, to see if I can discover where Eva's got to.'

'Soon, winter will come.'

'That's right.'

'What shall we do then? We can't stay here!' Eva looked disparagingly round her, at the dell which had been home to them all summer. Kevi had woven boughs of willow into a shelter, and coated it with mud and moss. Their little *dacha* was hidden from the casual passer-by, deep in the thicket of an old, overgrown wood, but close enough to farmland for them to take as much fruit and as many vegetables as they needed.

Other things came their way, too. Eggs, the odd chicken, a

466

pigeon caught in one of Kevi's traps, fish from the river. They had fed well, this summer.

The gang had scattered because now that she and Kevi were married they did not want the others with them all the time. They found great pleasure in one another's company, talking incessantly, touching, finding out about each other. But with the coming of winter they would have to re-gather, Eva knew, even if Kevi was reluctant to admit it. By themselves what chance would they have in the markets when food was scarce? And they must find a good place to keep out the cold and live all winter through.

'Well, Kevi? Where shall we go, then? To a city, of course, but which one? How do we find the others? Shall we return to the church and the vault?'

Kevi shrugged and yawned and despite her annoyance Eva's heart softened towards him. He looked so beautiful, half naked, bronzed and fit, his hair streaked with gold from the sun and a lazy, teasing smile tilting his mouth.

'What does it matter? It isn't winter yet!'

'Oh, Kevi, how could you say such a thing? Do you realise it's about four months since you made me your woman, and before you took me you were saying that we must not be caught out by winter again. That we must find a good place and start hoarding food early.'

'Did I? Yes, I suppose I did. But that was for eight or nine of us. With just us two, it'll be easier. Besides . . .' He hesitated, watching her through his lashes, his eyes no more than gleaming slits. 'Besides, I thought we might turn respectable now, you and I.'

'Us? Turn respectable? I thought we were *bez prizorney* for ever, or at least until we were quite grown up.'

Kevi sat up, but only for long enough to pull her down on top of him. He held her face in his hands and looked deep into her eyes; she could tell by his mouth that he was trying to be serious, but that he was laughing at her really.

'How grown up can you get, foolish one? We are living as man and wife; it is even possible that you might have a child . . . our child. It's time we became respectable . . . and besides, there's an armistice for the *prizorney*, I told you that a week ago, when I was helping the harvesters. The little ones can apply to go to school and the older ones can start trying for work, if they can read and write, which I can. The State has actually admitted we exist!'

'How could I have a child?' Eva demanded, staring down into Kevi's smoky dark eyes and discovering that she did not much want to be respectable, not if it meant having a baby. 'You may be grown up, but I don't think I am.'

'You could have a child – I *told* you – because we're living as man and wife – that's how one gets children. Look, you're right, winter's coming on, and this time I think we ought to apply to one of these children's homes.'

'But we aren't children! Oh, Kevi, lovely Kevi, don't tease me!'

'We can live in the homes until we're nineteen . . . later, even, if we haven't managed to find a place of our own by then. Really, Eva, we ought to at least give it a try.'

'But . . . will they let us be together, just as we are now?'

'Of course! I wouldn't like to be the person who tried to stop us! Look, we'll jump a train tomorrow, before the weather turns, and find a sizeable town with a good children's home in it. Some are very bad, you see; we don't want one of them.'

'Well, all right, if you're sure. But suppose we hate it?'

'Then we'll move on, of course.'

Rudi found out about Eva more by chance than intent, despite his resolutions. It was just luck, really . . . or bad luck, depending how you looked at it. There were masses of old files in a cellar attached to his new offices, files which had been brought from all over the region, and he happened to find one dealing with the collectivisation of the Caucasian valley farms so naturally he started to read.

An hour later, very slowly, he closed the file. There could be no doubt about it; Eva Fedorovna Lazarov had been in serious trouble . . . no wonder she had never turned up at the children's home which awaited her! She had jumped the train at some stage, or perhaps there had been *bez prizorney* already aboard who had seen her dilemma and helped her. Whatever the reason, she had become a fugitive, and though the authorities had put the word about and searched, she had not been found.

Perhaps she was dead; impossible to say for sure, and Russia

468

was a vast country. It might be a good deal kinder and more sensible to tell Pavel that her sister had died as she jumped off that train, rather than let his wife continue to hope.

And yet . . . and yet . . . there was no absolute proof that Eva was not alive and well, somewhere. And although he had no doubt that Pavel loved him truly, there were times in the darkness of the night, as he lay wakeful and she slumbered, when he remembered the other bloke, the one she had meant to go to, and thought about losing her. Then he told himself that whilst Eva was somewhere in Russia she would stay with him. So why lie? Why not admit she was with the *prizorney* and therefore untraceable, but that one day, if they were lucky, they might come across her?

And in the end, that was what he did; he told Pavel that Eva had jumped the train rather than go to a children's home in the north and that so far as he knew she was still at large somewhere in Russia. Pavel nodded and sighed and said she only hoped the poor child was happy, and added, as a rider, that she was quite sure Eva had not died. There they left it. Pavel never let any of the *prizorney* pass through Kharkov without questioning them about her sister and once or twice thought she had a lead, but it always came to nothing. Eva was not that unusual a name, and when the *prizorney* admitted they knew a girl called Eva further questioning usually revealed dark hair, a different patronymic or too many or too few years. One boy did seem to have all the answers . . . yes, he knew Eva Fedorovna, though she was not known by the second name any more but only by the first. Yes, she had gold hair and was pretty by any standards and she had often told them tales of the Caucasus and her life there. Where was she now? Ah, if only they knew! She had split up – well, they all had – when the summer came; heaven alone knew if they'd ever meet up once more.

But now, with winter on the horizon, Pavel started to worry again. Everyone knew that the *prizorney* died like flies in winter; how could she find Eva and save her from the extreme cold? Rudi reassured her; the children were a stain on the State's conscience and they were being charmed and wooed and gathered together so that they could become good citizens once more. Eva would doubtless be brought in, along with the rest, and when that happened he would somehow manage to acquaint himself with her whereabouts and they would go, together, and rescue her.

He did not intend to hunt, but had he somehow found out where Eva was he had already decided what to do, and it was the kindest and best thing for Pavel. He would keep his knowledge to himself. Pavel, whether she knew it or not, was very unlikely ever to set eyes on her sister again.

When Kevi finally decided that they had found themselves a good town with a good children's home in it, they walked up to the door and introduced themselves, with some trepidation, as Kevi and Eva, and explained that they wanted to get jobs and live in the home for the winter.

The superintendent was a handsome, silver-haired man in his mid to late fifties. He did not press them for details of their full names, which he probably realised he would be unable to obtain from them anyway, but accepted the fact that they had come. Kevi announced that he was Kevi the Wolf, and his woman was therefore Eva the Wolf. The superintendent opened his eyes rather wide at this and looked shrewdly at Eva, but then sent them off upstairs to be given some clothing and beds.

Eva was ushered into a long room filled with beds, and turned, to see Kevi being led off further along the corridor. It was an extremely cold day, and somehow the dormitory seemed even colder than outside, though in fact it was not. Each little iron bedstead had a straw mattress and a couple of white blankets . . . luxury indeed to one who had lived rough for as long as Eva and Kevi. But Eva did not intend to sleep alone; she preferred curling up in Kevi's warm arms.

She followed him up the corridor, saying as much as she went, but he turned to her, admonishing.

'Go to your room, Eva. We'll talk later. There are rules here which apparently must be obeyed. Don't worry, I'll see to things.'

Eva trailed sulkily off to her own dormitory and presently was joined by a very mixed group of girls indeed. Some were far older than she, some very much younger, there were even a few of her own age. They grinned at her, quick, shy grins, and then began to tell her about the home, and school, and their lives.

Most of them had lived rough all summer but had capitulated and come in for the winter. Most were attending school, even the big girls of eighteen or more. Several had married under *prizorney* law but none of them seemed to have their men with them.

'The *bez prizorney* mate for months, not years,' a skinny, lively red-haired girl with sharp green eyes and even sharper elbows remarked to Eva. 'I've had four men . . . *prizorney*, naturally . . . in the past eight months. Last winter I sold myself for bread, once to a policeman, which was heroic, everyone said so. This winter, though, I'm not going to go through it again, I'm prepared to go to school and say yes ma'am, no ma'am rather than go hungry and freezing cold.'

'Kevi the Wolf wouldn't want anyone but me,' Eva said slowly, staring at the girl. 'What's your name?'

'Lise; I'm sixteen and a bit. Who's Kevi the Wolf? Do I know him?'

'No, you don't. And you'd better not try to know him.' Eva knew her rosy little face and sun-bleached hair did not present a particularly ferocious picture but she scowled as nastily as she could at Lise. 'Leave Kevi alone; he's mine and I'm his, and no one else can have him!'

'Here we don't have rules like that; if I want to make a play for him I can, and if I get him that's your hard luck. But you can make a play for someone else, of course.'

'I don't want anyone else; I told you, we just want each other.'

Lise smiled mockingly. 'Ah, but that was before Kevi the Wolf met *me*; once he's seen me he may well feel different.'

'We'll see,' Eva said stiffly. 'I won't feel different, though. Never, never, never!'

Presently, when the children were all called downstairs to the communal dining-room, her feelings were justified; there was not a man or boy there as handsome as Kevi, nor as charming. Unfortunately, she was not the only one to notice this. The red-haired Lise took one look at Kevi and tried to change her place at the table to sit near him, and she was by no means the only one. Eva had noticed other girls looking at him but it had never bothered her because no one had ever told her, as Lise had, that a *prizorney* marriage was not for ever. But she sat close to Kevi and, when the meal had been handed round, told him that she did not like this place, not at all, and wanted to move on.

'I want to be with you all the time,' she said forlornly. 'They won't let us be together here.'

'Yes they will; can't stop us,' Kevi said with his mouth full. 'But even family people go to work! When a family girl and boy fall in love and marry, they aren't with one another all day long.'

'Aren't they? Then I'm glad we're *bez prizorney*,' Eva retorted. 'I like to be together all the time. And anyway, farmers are.'

'Farmers are what?'

'Together; with their wives, I mean. Nyusha and Fedor only had to call, except when he was at market.'

'Or out herding cattle.'

'Well, yes, or out herding cattle. But the rest of the time . . .'

'Or at a neighbouring farm.'

'Yes, I suppose. But the *rest* . . .'

'Or guiding people through that pass you told me about.'

'Oh, shut up!' Eva snapped, flinging down her spoon and turning a black look on Kevi. 'Why are you suddenly being hateful?'

Someone leaned across the table and put a pale, freckled hand on Kevi's arm. Someone was showing a good deal of bosom as she leaned forward; Kevi's eyes rested on the dark hollow between her breasts.

'Kevi, is your woman being a nuisance? I'm never a nuisance, I always do just what I'm told. Why not try me?'

'Do you want me to remove a few dozen freckles with my nails?' Eva snarled, pushing Lise's hateful hand off Kevi's arm. 'Leave my Kevi alone, you horrible creature.'

'Don't touch *me*, little Miss Fancy Pants, or I'll pull every dyed hair from your empty little head!'

'Try it!'

But though Kevi was grinning, he was not prepared to let anyone touch his Eva. He put his arm round her shoulders and pulled her to him.

'Leave her alone, Red; she's my woman and I won't have her bullied.' He looked fondly down at Eva, who looked adoringly up at him. 'Eaten enough?'

'Yes, thank you,' Eva breathed. 'Can we leave here now?'

'No. We're staying here. You'll go into school tomorrow,

just for a few days to see how you get on, and I'm going to try to get work. But now we'll go to bed.'

'Whose?'

'Mine, I think. I don't fancy having a jealous woman tearing my blanket off just when I least expect it. Come on.'

But a surprise awaited Kevi. He stripped off in the empty dormitory, got into his bed and pulled Eva in after him. Fortunately, they were still at the crooning and cuddling stage when the superintendent appeared in the doorway. He looked at Eva's silvery fair head tucked into the curve of Kevi's shoulder and spoke peremptorily.

'Out of there, young woman! This is the male dormitory. You belong in the female one.'

'She belongs here,' Kevi said drowsily, giving the superintendent a wicked grin. 'By me.'

'No, lad. Girls sleep in the female dormitory, so if you'll just get out of that bed, young lady . . .'

Eva pushed the blanket down half-heartedly, but Kevi shook his head at her and pulled the blanket up again.

'No, I said! Either she stays or we go back on the streets.'

'Then you'd better get out! Remember, I want that girl back in the female dormitory before the rest of the lads come up to bed!'

He left them, and Eva tickled Kevi's chin with her curls and said resignedly, 'I suppose I'd better go, had I? It's awfully cold for sleeping on the streets.'

'Stay where you are!' ordered the martinet in the bed sternly. 'I meant what I said. If I'm old enough to start looking for work then I'm old enough to sleep with my woman. Just let them try and stop me!'

Another boy, entering the room at that point, heard Kevi's last words and gave them some advice whilst climbing into his own cot.

'That's right, feller – it goes on all the time. They try to bend us to their ways for no good reason. But for the sake of peace and quiet get the gal to keep her head under the blanket until the super's done his rounds, or tell her not to come in until it's going dark. Otherwise you'll spoil it for everyone.'

'Are they all married then, the *prizorney* way?' Eva enquired of her lord and master, once the other boy had apparently fallen asleep. 'I didn't know!'

'They aren't; don't worry about it. They're just going with girls, not like you and me,' Kevi said rather obscurely. 'I'm glad you're here, I don't think I could sleep, else.'

'Nor me. I'll get up first in the morning, though, shall I, so that I can be back in that girls' place before they come round again?'

'Might be safest,' Kevi murmured sleepily. 'Night, Evalinka!'

'Goodnight, Kevi.'

Once again the State had not prepared sufficiently well for the harsh winter and food ran short, but this time, with the home and Kevi's salary, things were not so bad. School, Eva decided, was bearable. She was a clever girl and soon caught up with the rest of her class, even making some friends amongst the family girls, though when one of them showed her admiration for Kevi by actually daring to ask him to come to the cinema with her, she soon put a stop to that.

'I'll tell your mother you're running with a crook from the *bez prizorney*,' she threatened. 'And if she doesn't stop you making eyes at him I'll make you sorry.'

The family girl, blushing scarlet, told Eva stiffly that she could not help it if Kevi admired her, and went redder than ever at the sound of Eva's derisive laughter.

Lise was a thorn in Eva's flesh, because she so obviously admired Kevi and would not be scared off, as other girls were, by Eva's bristling and proprietorial attitude. One day, Eva decided, Lise would have to be taught a lesson. But not yet.

So she had to put up with Lise's constant, irritating presence, even when Lise took to sleeping with the boy in the next bed purely, Eva was sure, so that she could keep an eye on Kevi – and he on her.

The winter was passing, and Eva began to get more of a waist, and her hips curved and her legs grew longer and more lissom. Kevi was not the only youth in the home to admire her, but she did not care a jot for any of the others. She wished Kevi could imitate her single-minded attitude, but sometimes she caught him looking at other girls, particularly the loathsome Lise, with more interest than he should have, and it made her terribly unhappy – and uncertain, too. If Kevi was not her lover, then what was her life worth? Not much, she felt sure.

Sometimes she had bad dreams, and when the worst dream

of all came she would cry out and clutch Kevi and he would wake her with kisses and caresses and dry her body with a rough piece of towel, for she would come out of the dream soaked in sweat. And then they would make love, quietly and tenderly, under his blanket, until she was soothed and calm once more. And then they would sleep and Eva would know that all was well.

She longed for the spring to come, with its promise of summer. Kevi did not much like his job, which was in a factory and was thus both boring and repetitive, and Eva was sure that once the good weather came he would be as eager to shake the dust of the children's home off his feet as she was. Next year, she planned, lying curled up in his arms, next year we'll find a place of our own and I won't go to school, we'll both work so that we can manage without anyone else, and we'll not have to put up with any of this. To be fair, she disliked as much as anything the young men who eyed her hopefully, who grabbed her arm in passing, who tried to put themselves where her gaze would fall upon them. All she wanted was Kevi; she rarely thought of Pavel now and almost never of Nyusha and Fedor. They belonged to a past which she had all but forgotten, and Kevi alone was her future.

# CHAPTER TWENTY

Spring had been slow in coming to North Wales, but when it did come it was all the sweeter for the harsh winter it followed. David and Nibby had worked hard all winter long and had, as a result, sold three sturdy fishing boats as soon as the weather allowed them to launch and show off the results of their labours. Now, as a celebration, they were taking the girls to Llandudno for the day.

'Won't it be exciting – a whole day out!' Alice's eyes shone with the thrill of it. 'What will you wear, Sassy?'

Sara was a dressy little thing and favoured high-heeled pumps, sheer silk stockings, and figure hugging garments of some description. What was more she had a young man – Philip Lowther – and he had to be impressed. She considered her sister's question, standing in the centre of the kitchen with the ironing board up and the iron – an electric one – poised over a white cotton shift.

'Oh, I don't know. I thought my sailor suit – the skirt and jacket, you know, and that dear little hat that goes with it. High-heeled shoes, of course, and a navy and white striped bag for my things. Only . . . will the boys mind if I ask Phil?'

'Well, you'd better ask them when they come in for tea, only I rather thought it was to be just the four of us – Michael's going down to Topper's for the day – and if you bring Phil it will make it uneven.'

'David could ask a friend,' Sara objected, slowly lowering the iron on to the cotton. 'I'll ask one for him if you like; there are heaps of pretty girls in my class who think he's awfully handsome, the mad fools.'

'He's a dear,' Alice said absently. She had finished the family ironing and was watching her sister with considerable anxiety; though Sara was fond of clothes she was awfully careless and if she made a great singe on her shift she would expect Alice to replace it and money was, as usual, short.

'Oh, a *dear* ... perhaps, but that isn't why they all make eyes at him and hope he'll glance in their direction, it's because they think he's a rake, and because he's got that sad, disappointed lover look ... and also because he's got It.'

'It? Don't talk in riddles, Sassy, there's a love.'

'Oh, Alice, how can you be so old-fashioned? He's got Sex Appeal — haven't you heard it called It before?'

'No, I can't say I have. Do get on with that garment, dear, before the iron gets too hot and burns something. Tell me about one of these hopeful girls, then.'

'Well, there's Sandra Fox, she's got the most gorgeous hair, waist-length and a sort of chestnut red colour, she thinks he's ever so lovely! And there's Elsie George, she's that cheeky little girl with the black shiny bob and the pink cheeks; David said she looked like a Dutch doll when I brought her home to tea here. And then there's Victoria Johnson, who's ...'

'All right, all right. Which one of them would be most delighted at the prospect of a trip to Llandudno with a married couple, you and love-bird Phil and Davie?'

'All,' Sara said promptly. 'I tell you, his black curls and dark eyes have wreaked havoc in my class. Shall I put the word about?'

'No, you'd better leave it for a few days. In the meantime, I'll have a word with the boys, see what they say.'

'You can have a word with David right now,' Sara said, finishing off her shift and standing the iron on end to cool. 'He's just come across the side of the house, heading for the back door. He'll be here by the time I count to ten. One, two, three ...'

The back door opened and David strolled in, talking over his shoulder as he came.

'... and then I tried a different tack; I thought we might go for the lower, leaner line, so I showed the drawings to Ben and he liked them, said we'd do well to make more, though of course that was only ...' He broke off and looked round at the two girls. 'Well I'm damned, Nibby was with me two seconds ago; where's he gone?'

'He's getting the washing off the line,' Alice said in a voice heavy with apprehension. 'It's not that I'm not pleased, but if he's anything like you his hands will be filthy and it took me most of the morning to get that lot washed and pegged out. Here he comes.'

Nibby breezed in, his arms full of washing.

'Here we are, love, all nice and dry,' he greeted Alice, leaning over to plonk a kiss on her forehead. 'I've brought it in because I'd like the shirts ironed as soon as you can get round to it; Ben was down just now and he wants us to take drawings up to London to see some bloke . . . there's a boat show which he thinks could bring us a lot of business.'

'You two! David, Sassy and I were just discussing our day out in Llandudno. She'd like to bring Philip and suggested she might bring a friend to make up the numbers.'

David turned round from the sink; his fists were lathered in grey, oozy bubbles.

'Make up numbers? Oh, I see what you mean. Well, if we're asking anyone else I'll ask Maria. Might as well. You all like her OK, don't you?'

'She's all right,' Sara said, obviously disappointed, 'but I thought you'd want someone who's a bit of fun; you can't call Maria fun, can you?'

'You can, actually,' David said. 'She's getting better, I don't know why; much easier, wouldn't you say, Alice?'

'Yes, she is. I don't really know why, but she's not so stiff and awkward with us; I suppose she's beginning to feel natural in our company,' Alice said. 'All right, David; will you ask her or shall I?'

'You can . . . no, I will,' David said. He rinsed his hands under the tap and turned to dry them on the roller towel behind the door. 'What day did we plan to go?'

'Next Wednesday, if it's fine.'

'Right. I'll borrow Mike's bicycle and go down this evening and fix it all up.'

There was a pregnant silence. David had not once visited Carmel Hall since they had moved out so many years ago. Nibby spoke first.

'Going to take a look, Dave? You could 'phone, of course.'

'I could, but I'd rather go down there.' David turned and grinned at their interested and slightly startled faces. 'It's no use being an idiot and refusing to admit that there are strangers . . . well, the Rafts, then . . . living at the Hall, so I'm going to take my courage in both hands and do as you suggest, Nibs, and take a look. Whilst I'm there I'll ask Maria to come to Llandudno.'

It was odd, and more than a little painful, to cycle down the familiar drive after so many years. The painful part, David supposed, came from the strong, almost unbearable belief that when he reached the house his mother would run out to meet him and his father would emerge from the study, grinning from ear to ear, delighted with this stocky, ugly son of his who was actually following in a long line of Thomas footsteps by building boats.

I've done a lot of losing lately, David told himself wryly, as he cocked a leg over his bicycle seat and coasted to a halt outside the front door. Am I going to continue to lose, or shall I turn things round a bit? He knew in his heart that to marry without strong affection was a fool's trick, and, worse, that owning Carmel by cheating on Maria would end perhaps not just in tears but in the tragedy of two lives wasted. But love . . . he did not even want to fall in love again, not after Pavel. If only he had not gone to Russia! He believed, now, that if he had not gone he would not have brought her memory flooding back so strongly. Once on the Caucasian soil he and she both loved, it had been almost as if she were with him, though always just ahead and out of sight.

He had come home heartsick and weary but still sure that she would come, and he had left help for her, and plenty of money. Selim had been very supportive, as well, and had promised to do his best to get word to David within hours of her crossing the border.

It had all been in vain. The letter, in her own familiar scrawl, had put paid to all that. She was married, her husband was a good man, David must forget her. And one way to forget her was to throw himself wholeheartedly into the business and make money – only there were Alice and Nibby, fathoms in love, touching lightly, glancing warmly, whenever he looked at them, and it made him feel not only horribly lonely but uncomfortable into the bargain. They should have their own place . . . but he did not fancy trying to keep order with Sara and Michael, far less paying all the bills at the cottage without the considerable help Alice gave with her steady salary. They needed each other and would do so possibly for years to come. If *only* the white knight had ridden home with Pavel sitting on the saddle before him! With all of them working together they would have made a go of it, he was certain. Even now, it looked as though once this boat show idea got under way they might find themselves suddenly making money.

He looked up at the house whilst propping his bicycle against the old stone mounting block. If the Rafts had changed it, the years between had mellowed it so that change was no longer the first thing one noticed. The curtains were different, perhaps, but the beds underneath the front windows were bright with spring flowers and by the dining-room window, sheltered by the forward jut of the larger reception room beside it, the jasmine bloomed, the soft scent of it stealing into David's nostrils, a poignant reminder of those other, earlier days, when he had watched the jasmine for a sign that spring was on its way.

He was doing no good standing here, though, so he walked up the two shallow steps, curved with age and a thousand feet, and lifted the big brass knocker, bringing it gently down with a dull thud. There was a bell, but it had never worked in his day and he did not now intend to put it to the test.

The door opened without fuss and a girl he recognised but to whose face he could not put a name smiled at him.

'Hello, Mr David! Come in, Miss Raft's expecting you. She's in the study.'

His favourite room! The room which spoke more of his father than any other room in the house! But he followed the maid, frowning, trying to remember who she was, or whose daughter, whose girlfriend.

She opened the study door and he got it. 'Thanks very much, Gill; how are you keeping?'

'Fine, thanks, Mr David.' She gestured him inside and shut the door behind him.

David turned to face the room.

It was so different that it could not possibly have reminded him of anything but that this was no longer his house as he had once known it. The walls were papered in a pretty floral pattern, white background with pale petals well scattered. The paintwork was white too, and the carpet was dark red with a black and gold pattern. There were some easy chairs, chintz

480

covered, and a little day-bed, an antique with gold satin upholstery and curled arms and back blackened with age. A small, feminine desk stood in the window bay, facing towards the view. There was a fire in the grate, china ornaments on the mantel, a beautiful copper bowl full of logs and another, shallower bowl full of fruit standing on a half-moon table against the wall.

Maria was there, sitting on the day-bed, but she had risen to her feet, was holding out her hand, only David was still absorbing the room. There were flowers on the window sill, beautifully arranged, and more flowers in a tall vase to the right of the fireplace . . . no, not flowers, branches of jasmine and some willow. Being in the warm had brought the leaves out a good month before their time – pale yellowy-green leaves, a colour as lovely in its way as the clear acid yellow of the jasmine flowers.

'David? I'm sorry, I didn't think it would hurt you – it's my room now and very . . . very different, wouldn't you say?'

He took her hand but instead of shaking it he patted it with his other hand. It trembled in his and her eyes were uncertain. Had she planned this moment, planned to be brisk and businesslike, forgetting that he would possibly remember the room with love or pain because it had been his father's study for so long?

'You've made it very nice, Maria, really, much nicer than it was when we lived here . . . well, to be honest, completely different.' He put her hand down and walked over to the window. 'It was a working room then, all dark practical paintwork and hard-wearing carpet and of course Dad had a drawing board set up in the window and his desk was bigger and faced the door so that he could sit behind it whilst his men sat on the other side and they could both see the drawings they were discussing.'

'Yes, of course. It isn't very sensible, my desk facing the view, but I work better being able to glance up every now and then and see what's happening outside. And my work isn't important, not like Mr Thomas's work was; I do the figures for the estate and so on. Would you like to have a look round, now you're here? Only . . . well, it has to be different, you know . . . it would have been different if your family still had it because carpets wear out and fashions change. If you'd rather not . . .'

'No, I'd enjoy it.' He turned to face her again and smiled easily down at her. For the first time he realised that her eyes were such a dark blue that one could easily have believed them to be brown or black . . . they were beautiful eyes and though her short, stubby black lashes could not be thought lovely they made a striking frame for the eyes, particularly now that she had lost some of her high colour and fined down a bit. She was not, he told himself firmly, a bad-looking girl at all.

'All right. Shall we go round first or would you prefer tea or coffee first – or a drink?'

'Coffee would be very nice, but shall we take a look round now? Then they can be making the coffee whilst we're out. Your parents won't mind?'

'They won't mind at all.' She was leading the way out into the hall as she spoke and now she stopped, looking doubtfully first at David and then at the many doors, all painted cream and gold and all shut, which surrounded them. 'Where shall we go first?'

'Let's start with the door on the right – it used to be the dining-room – and work our way back to your study. I don't expect the kitchens and staff rooms have changed at all.'

'No, they haven't, and the dining-room hasn't much, either.' She threw open the door and went through it, with David following. 'See?'

David stared. It was exactly the same! Even the furniture . . .

'We bought the whole room, more or less, because we knew we couldn't better it,' Maria said almost apologetically. 'The big drawing-room was the same, though we had to replace the curtains and the carpet's getting awfully faded.'

It was the same through much of the rest of the house. The Rafts had either copied quite faithfully what the Thomases had had, or they had actually bought furniture and fittings at the sale. But when they went upstairs the changes were more apparent.

Bedrooms which David remembered as being scruffy, lived-in places with cheap carpeting and built-in wardrobes were now exquisitely furnished and decorated. It did not worry him that his old room now had rosebuds on the walls and pink silk curtains, nor that the carpet was obviously brand new with its dark cream background garlanded with more roses.

But when he hesitated by the stairs which had led to the

nursery apartments, Maria did not encourage him to mount them.

'It's . . . it's just empty up there, except for packing-cases and so on,' she said. 'Let's go and have our coffee now, shall we?'

He had to agree, but he was a little disappointed. So much of his life in this house had been spent in the nursery rooms, and he had wondered often whether the old rocking horse, the big dolls' house and the brass fender as high as a paddock rail were still up there or whether they, too, had been sold.

Presently, however, sitting in the study drinking coffee and eating almond biscuits, he brought the conversation round to the subject of his visit.

'As I said on the telephone, we've got plans for Wednesday; we're going to Llandudno for the day, just Alice and Nibby, Philip and Sara, and myself. I didn't much fancy playing gooseberry, so I wondered if you'd be kind enough to come along and keep me company?'

Maria stared doubtfully at him. She opened her mouth to speak, closed it, then opened it again.

'Oh, David! I would love to go with you, but it's really family, isn't it? I mean wouldn't you rather . . . someone closer . . .'

He interrupted her without compunction, knowing that in all probability she would stutter herself into saying something she would later bitterly regret.

'Enough of that, Miss Raft! When I ask a girl to come out with me for a day I don't take kindly to being told I really ought to be taking someone else! Now, let's lay it on the line for you. If you refuse my invitation I shan't rush out and ask someone else, some cousin or other, I shall simply go by myself, mooch around all day in Llandudno feeling a complete spare part, and get home tired out and cross.'

She laughed. She looked almost pretty when she laughed.

'Oh, David, what a liar you are! You'd probably pick up some pretty little thing within ten minutes of arriving and take her round with you all day and have a wonderful time. But . . . if you're sure you mean it, of course I'd love to come.'

'That's good. Well, the charabanc leaves from outside the town hall at nine, which is awfully early, but it gives us more time in Llandudno. I'll come for you at half past eight and we can walk down together.'

483

'Walk? Isn't there a bus?'

'Probably, but the walk will do us good; don't you want to be done good to?' The too-ready colour suffused her face and David was sorry he had teased her. He stood up, put his coffee cup carefully down on the half-moon table, and walked over to her. She had finished her coffee so he took both her hands and pulled her to her feet.

'It's all arranged, then. See you on Wednesday, early.'

She went with him to the door and watched him mount his bicycle and ride off, bent over the handlebars, positively whizzing over the gravel, then she turned and went indoors. David, glancing back, saw the door close but knew that she would have gone straight to the hall window.

Women are odd creatures, he mused as he pedalled. That girl's been keen on me for years, she's put herself in my path, she's tried to get in with my family, in short she's been a bit of a bloody nusiance. But the first time he had asked her out, merely for a ramble, she had not gone with him, first because of the weather and then, when he chose a milder day, because she had had a previous engagement. He had been quite piqued, and had decided not to bother with her any more, only . . . he really did not fancy playing gooseberry all day with his brother-in-law and sisters, and though she had tried to refuse at first she had accepted graciously enough in the end.

He was pleased she had not offered the use of her car; if she had done so he would have been really annoyed, though of course he would not have let it show, and he would have turned the offer down with a finality which might, at a later date, have been regretted. Half the fun for the girls, he thought paternally, would be the charabanc ride, the gobbling of unsuitable food on the back seat – if they were fortunate enough to get the back seat – the shared laughter, the rowdy singing, the sense of holiday which would start as soon as the charabanc began to move.

Maria watched through the hall window until David and his bicycle had sped round the bend and out of sight, then she rushed through into the kitchen. Mrs Raft, sitting at the kitchen table and watching Cook icing a cake, greeted her with a big smile.

'Eh, luv, you look excited! What did he want, then?'

'Oh, Ma, he wanted to take me out! So thrilling . . . to Llandudno, on a charabanc outing! They're all going, Alice and John Hawke, David's sister Sara and her boyfriend Philip, and David himself. Only he said he'd feel a fool playing gooseberry and he asked if I'd go along as well.'

'Did you tell 'im there was no way, Miss, like what we telled you to say?' demanded Mrs Grimm, the cook. It would be no exaggeration to say that the entire female staff at Carmel Hall were advising Maria on how to land Mr David, though probably no one would have put it quite so frankly. 'Don't bite 'is 'and off next time, Gill said, I 'eard 'er clear as clear.'

'I remembered, and I did just what she said, I said it was very nice of him but wouldn't he like to take someone closer, as it was a family outing. And he said if I turned him down he wouldn't ask anyone else, he'd just spend a miserable day by himself. So I said yes, and he seemed pleased, really he did.'

'That's lovely, Mea,' her mother said happily. 'Ever since David came home from Russia you've looked your best, though I was sorry, at first, when you lost all that weight and stopped using rouge . . . you looked a poor, pale thing I thought. Only, I don't know, I've got used to it and I'm bound to say it suits you.'

'If David likes it, that's all that matters,' Maria said, but she spoke with her old intensity and Mrs Grimm shook a reproving finger.

'Now that's enough of that, Miss! Gill's told you often enough that Mr David never did want what was handed to him on a plate, he always wanted what he couldn't have, so just you bear it in mind and keep that little bit of distance between you and before you know it he'll be popping the question.'

'Sorry, I forgot. It's just that he's important to me – always has been. I've never believed in love at first sight but I saw him and my insides turned over and they've been turning over the moment I clap eyes on him ever since, so it must mean something!'

'Sounds as if you've eaten something you shouldn't,' Mrs Grimm observed. 'Now what do young ladies wear for a day at the seaside? Just you give Miss Alice a ring on that tellyphone upstairs and drop a hint or two, see? If she's wearing her best then you can follow suit, but I dessay, for the seaside, it'll be cottons and a cardy.'

Maria, her cheeks as pink by nature as she had once made them by artifice, shot out into the hall and snatched up the receiver. She gave the operator Alice's number and presently was speaking direct to her friend.

'David's asked me to come with you to Llandudno on Wednesday,' she said, after their initial greetings. 'We won't be too smart, I dare say, for a day at the seaside; what'll you wear?'

'I've got a blue gingham dress and a white jacket and sandals,' Alice told her. 'And I'll wear my cream straw hat if it's sunny and a rainhood if it's wet. Oh, and I'm taking an umbrella anyway, in case.'

'What's Sara wearing?'

'Oh, you know Sassy, she'll have every garment she owns out of her wardrobe half a dozen times between now and Wednesday, but she'll probably settle for what I'm wearing – a cotton dress and sandals. She won't wear a hat, though; she says her hair's so curly that hats rise up and look ridiculous.'

'I've got a nice simple cotton frock,' Maria said untruthfully. 'I'll wear that. And I've got some sandals, of course. Do we have to take food or anything?'

'Oh no, we'll lunch at a restaurant somewhere. But I'm taking a flask of coffee and some sandwiches – it's quite a long drive down. I bet Nibby and David will bring bottled beer, but I can't take to it.'

'All right, then, if you're bringing sandwiches I'll bring some fruit and some of Mrs Grimm's chorley cakes. David's calling for me at half past eight. Are you coming with him?'

'No fear, you're welcome to the walk, the rest of us are catching the early bus. See you on Wednesday then, Maria.'

Maria replaced her receiver and hurried back to the kitchen. She smiled excitedly at the two women whilst snatching up her handbag and checking that her purse was safely within.

'I'm going to drive into town first thing on Monday; you were right, Mrs Grimm, I need a simple little cotton frock!'

It was a really glorious day, the sort of day when the mountains stand out against a sky so clear and blue that it hurts the eye. Sitting on the coveted back seat of the charabanc, which she had not even known was coveted, squeezed between Alice and David, Maria knew total happiness. David's thigh was hard up against hers, the blue of her dress complemented, if it did not match, her eyes, and already at least three girls had cast envious glances at David and almost approving ones at herself.

The atmosphere aboard the charabanc was a holiday one, the mood giggly and light. Sara and Philip had their arms round each other, Alice was snuggled into the curve of Nibby's shoulder and David – wonder of wonders – had his arm stretched out along the top of the seat so that when she put her head back Maria could feel her hair brush the sleeve of his dark navy blazer.

The rest of the passengers, if you could call such a light-hearted crew passengers, were on works outings. A number of small shops in town had clubbed together to hire the charabanc and, when they realised they could not fill all the seats, had offered the tiny firm of Thomas & Hawke the remaining places.

So now, speeding through Snowdonia, Maria could relax in the certainty that they had sunshine, they had good cheer, they were in the right sort of mood, and it was going to be a gloriously successful day.

'Look at the lake!'

'Oh my; beautiful, isn't it?'

'Still cold, though . . . what price a bathe, eh?'

'I di'nt bring me swimsuit!'

'I knew it were me lucky day . . . I'd luv to see you without your swimsuit, chuggin' across Llandudno bay!'

Isn't it called sparking, when boys tease girls and girls tease right back? Maria asked herself dreamily. Sara and Philip were giggling and nudging, amused by the chatter from the rest of the bus, but Alice and Nibby stared dreamily out through the windows and David, with his arm very nearly round Maria, seemed in a world of his own. But not the grim, worrying world he had inhabited lately, if one went by appearances. Today he looked content enough, and when she said something about the scenery he answered at once, so obviously he was not in a dream.

All too soon, though, the ride was at an end and the charabanc drew up on the front. Maria, tumbling out of the bus with the rest, saw the sparkling blue sea, calm as a mill-pond today so that the houses and hotels along the side of the Great Orme were reflected in the sea as plain as plain, and was doubly glad she had come. The tide was out and Sara, a baby still for all her grown-up ways, was sitting on the prom pulling off her sandals and stockings and Alice, sensible, motherly Alice, was following suit. Maria did likewise and hated her white legs until she noticed that everyone was in the same boat; no one had had the chance to get their legs even remotely coloured, but anyway it did not matter because the men were taking their shoes and socks off and rolling up their trouser legs and soon everyone was heading for the sea.

The water was cold! Maria gasped and clutched David, who providentially happened to be nearest, and he put an arm round her waist and forced her out further, until her dress got splashed – not that she cared a jot – and she screamed and protested, though not very loudly or very wholeheartedly. She only did it at all, in fact, because it seemed to be *de rigueur*.

Presently they came out of the water and went over to the big rocks right under the Orme and searched the pools for little crabs, tiny fish and anything else that moved. Maria, flushed with the chase, had time to reflect on her own trips to the seaside as a child; the walk along the prom, the ice-cream cornet if you were good, the brief skirmish on the sand with bucket and spade, next a paddle – holding Father's hand – and then the hasty drying of the toes in case of catching cold and the too-rapid walk up the beach and along the prom, with the small Maria, hand to side, trying to fight a stitch, back to the car and the driver and tea in china cups and scones and butter and cake, eaten with great propriety at one of the better hotels. Where had her parents gone wrong? Had they not realised that a child wants and needs to get thoroughly dirty and wet from time to time? Why had they never allowed her to dabble in pools, to chase shrimps through the tide race, to scream and skim stones and stand in the wet quicksand until her feet disappeared and only her ankles remained? She supposed that it was all in an effort to make a lady of her . . . if only they had known! Alice was a real lady, her parents were always saying so, but she paddled and screamed and chased about with the rest . . . and she had eaten sandwiches and cake and drunk coffee from a flask in the coach, and no one had minded or thought less of her.

At half past twelve Nibby proposed lunch and everyone stared blankly at their watches and each other and declared that never had the time gone so fast. Then they ran up the beach, put their shoes and stockings on again – in the girls' case shielding each other modestly with their skirts when they began to fasten their suspenders – and set off for the town centre, for they were all ravenous.

They found a delightful restaurant in Somerset Street and ate a huge meal, finishing up with an iced pudding which, Maria assured them, Mrs Grimm herself could not have bettered. And then, lethargic and sated, they made their way to a seat under the trees on the prom. Slumping down on the silvery grey wood, Alice announced that she wanted a nap. Nibby put his arm round her, cocked his panama over his eyes, and said that he would keep her company. Sara, dragging Philip, set off for an amusement arcade. David, eyeing his sister and her husband ruefully, asked Maria if she would like to join them.

'I'll sit here if you like,' Maria said, wondering desperately what she was expected to say. 'But I'm not really tired, not sleepy-tired, anyway.'

'Good! Then how about walking up to the top of the Great Orme with me? There's a café up there where we can get a cup of tea.'

'It's not real climbing, is it?' Maria asked rather anxiously, eyeing the great grey humped shoulders of the Orme. 'My shoes aren't terribly practical.'

'No, it's all right – it's possible to go up it in a car, I believe, and we'll take it slowly.' He held out his hand; Maria took it unbelievingly. 'Come on, the view's worth it once you get there.'

Halfway up, Maria realised that she and David were alone together for the first time since they had been shut in his shed with no door knob.

Until that moment she had been indulging in a perfectly ordinary, if rather breathless, conversation, but with the realisation her mouth dried and her voice followed suit. She was Alone with David! She felt she should make use of this opportunity, but she could not think of one sensible thing to say. And what was worse, when she glanced sideways at David he was looking at her with gentle amusement. She was sure he had guessed what she was thinking. Horrified, she burst into speech.

489

'I've been meaning to ask you, what happened to that Russian girl of yours to make her marry someone else? I thought it was going a bit far . . . I mean you were engaged, weren't you?'

It was the worst thing she could have said; David's face changed before her eyes. The humour drained away, leaving his eyes bleak, his mouth tight. Yet when he spoke his voice sounded ordinary enough.

'We weren't engaged and she married someone else, that's all. Her husband's kind and good; I'm neither. Sit down, you're exhausted.'

She opened her mouth to say she was nothing of the kind and he took her by the shoulders and pushed; she collapsed in an untidy heap on the grass, opening her mouth to voice a protest.

She never said a word; his mouth came down on hers, hard, vicious, with such force that she found herself on her back with a rock digging into her shoulder blades and really hurting whilst David's weight pinned her down and his mouth bruised her, his teeth cracked against hers, his hands dug into her shoulders so violently that she would have cried out had she been able.

It was full afternoon, though the sun was low in the sky, and they were lying in close proximity to a much-used path. It did not occur to Maria immediately that this was a piece of rare good fortune, but it did later, for David's hard hands came up from her shoulders and one grabbed her throat, terrifying her, whilst the other seized her breast and began squeezing until she had to scream, even against his mouth, a muffled, gurgling moan of pain which brought him out of whatever madness he had been in. He squatted back on his heels and she took great, burning lungsful of air whilst tears of pain and shock ran down her cheeks.

'See what I mean?'

She cringed, afraid he meant to do the same thing again, but just then some people came down the path from the summit and David calmly took out his handkerchief and wiped her tears away with it, then pulled her to her feet. She stood, swaying, for a moment and saw his face soften.

'I'm sorry, but you did rather ask for it! Don't mention Pavel again, please, as you can imagine it's rather a sore subject.'

490

'Apparently so,' Maria said thickly. She touched her throat. 'You hurt me.'

'The eternal female cry!' David said sarcastically. 'Look, I've said I'm sorry; let's forget it, shall we?'

She should have turned on her heel and gone down the mountain path and joined the others. She should have told him just what she thought of him and warned him never to lay a finger on her again. She should have done anything except what she did do, which was to follow him meekly as he strode off towards the crest above them, letting the tears run down her cheeks because she had spoiled it all and now he would never look at her again.

They reached the summit, or rather David did, and he stopped and waited for her. She was breathless again, and looked a sight. He sighed, took her shoulders in his hands, but gently this time, and scrutinised her face. Then he shook his head and fished his handkerchief out once more.

'You do look a poor thing – Maria, I'm a swine to take my temper out on you like that – I don't know why I did it. Let me tidy you up a bit and then we'll have some tea and go over to the look-out and then we'll go back down to the others.' He cleaned up her face, touching her bruised mouth tenderly, muttered again that she never should have said it, and then combed her hair with his own pocket comb and took her hand.

'Come on, where's that tea?'

All through tea, *bara brith* thickly buttered and cakes, Maria was too subdued to do more than murmur thanks when he passed her something. She was upset with him, naturally, but most of all she was furious with herself. Fancy hurting him like that, getting his feelings for that girl out and staring at them, criticising even, daring to question! He had hurt and frightened her, but he had been sorry at once. No, the fault was hers. The more she thought about it the guiltier she felt, and when at last, as the sun slipped into a bed of rose and gold cloudlets, leaving the sky streaked with colour and fading, above, to a glorious turquoise blue, they stood up to go she was sure he would never speak to her again and knew it served her right.

'Want to go up and see this sunset? It's a glorious sight . . . you'll see the Isle of Man very likely, on an evening like this.'

She went, of course, and gasped with pleasure at the great stretch of sea, the shadows on the sands below, the miniaturising of the town and countryside. And this time, speaking without thinking, she said the right thing.

'Oh, David, it's lovely, the most beautiful view I've ever seen! That other business was all my fault and I've forgotten it, but this . . . I'll remember this for ever!'

She was genuinely moved, and turned to him, her mouth trembling with the force of her feelings, to find him genuinely moved also.

'I'm a fool; whether you know it or not when you think of today you'll think of . . . of that.' He put his arms round her and pulled her close, and now his mouth was curved, his eyes gentle, full of remorse. 'Think of this, instead.'

It was the most marvellous experience of Maria's life, that kiss. Gentle, loving, then suddenly passionate so that she allowed her bruised lips to part almost without realising what was happening to her. His mouth left hers then for a moment and he kissed across her face to her ear and then back again to her mouth which, this time, opened eagerly for him.

He broke the kiss, a little breathless, and held her away from him.

'All right? Better?'

She ducked her head, self-doubts galloping back. Was one supposed to enjoy kisses or was that too much of a giveaway? Had her mouth told him what she strove to keep secret – that she adored him, wanted him, was prepared to put up with anything if it meant she might be near him?

But apparently he had not expected a reply, for he put his arm round her waist and tugged her close to him. She was tall but he was taller, so they set off like a badly matched three-legged race until she lengthened her stride a bit and he shortened his, and then they were a matched pair, and came down the mountain path at a good rate, presently breaking into a trot and laughing at their own antics.

They saw the others from on high and waved and shouted and Nibby and Sara ran up to meet them, exclaiming at their lateness, the hunger which everyone was suffering and the speed with which they would have to eat their high-tea.

'Don't say a word,' David hissed, tugging Maria closer yet and giving her waist a loving nip. 'We don't want them to

492

know we've already eaten or they'll wonder what we've been up to when we eat again . . . fighting's hungry work, don't you find?'

'We didn't exactly fight,' Maria murmured. 'Anyway, it's forgotten, don't you remember?'

They reached the prom and joined the others.

Alice looked shrewdly at Maria and David as they came down from the Orme, and knew something had happened. Maria's mouth was looking very well kissed indeed and her hair was all over the place, to say nothing of a certain shine to her eyes and the way she kept looking over at David. I hope he didn't overstep the mark, Alice found herself thinking apprehensively, for you did not have to be particularly intelligent to realise that Maria thought a great deal of David and would be prepared to do a lot to please him. She also knew that Maria was not David's type and that he had turned to her more as a companion than a lover. So why the kiss? Unless they'd quarrelled and then kissed and made up?

But guessing did not help much, so Alice enjoyed her tea and then, with the others, wandered through the lamplit streets to the meeting place.

The charabanc was there already, half full, and there was a lot of noise and a good many crates of bottled beer. The driver welcomed them in and David and Nibby turfed some usurpers off the back seat, then the six of them settled themselves.

Alice noticed that the order of seating had changed, though, and wondered whether it was just coincidence that Maria was now in the extreme right-hand corner with David next to her, Sara next to him and Philip next, with herself and Nibby last. If she had not known better she would have thought that they wanted to canoodle, but it seemed unlikely – Maria would not have the nerve to suggest such a thing and David, she was sure, would not have the desire.

But the bus was beginning to move off, and the lights, which had been on, were going dimmer and dimmer. Alice knew very well that on the return journey there would be a good deal of kissing and cuddling and swapping of seat-partners going on amongst the younger generation, and she hoped Maria would not be shocked, especially when the beer began to circulate and the boys got rather more daring. Many a girl, Alice knew from the talk in the office, had found it necessary to use force to keep pure on a return coach journey!

However, she presently found that Nibby wanted to cuddle and murmur, and married woman though she was she found it very sweet. It took her mind off other people, and anyway, trapped in the other corner of the coach seat it was impossible for her to know even if David had his arm round Maria. So she settled down with her husband, and watched through the window as the dusky town slipped by.

By the time the coach deposited Maria at her own gate, and David walked her up the drive and kissed her goodnight, Maria was in seventh heaven. For two solid hours David had kissed, cuddled and stroked, patted and pinched . . . all in the nicest possible way! By the time they climbed down from the charabanc, indeed, Maria was on fire all over, and very much wished that she could have invited David indoors, to continue at his leisure and in private all the lovely things which his hands and mouth had hinted at in the coach but had been unable to carry out.

However, such thoughts must never be said aloud. They reached the front door, she asked him if he would like to come indoors for a nightcap, David declined politely on the grounds that he had a long day's work in front of him the next day and went, whistling, down the drive. Maria used her key to let herself in, trotted past her parents' room with no more than a tap on the door and a mutter that she was safe home and would see them in the morning, and dropped down on the little square stool before her mirror.

She was not, she admitted, a particularly pretty sight. Mouths which have been kissed, on and off, for two hours tend to spread and blend with the surrounding face, particularly when the man doing the kissing has a strong and pricklesome beard which, by seven in the evening, is as harsh as the very best emery paper.

Her eyes, however, were looking both large and shiny, perhaps because tiredness and excitement had smudged deep shadows around them or possibly because they had nearly started from her head, once or twice, over David's delightful but unconventional behaviour.

Her hair was like a bird's nest, too, but then everyone had

looked rather rumpled; even Alice, a married woman, had spent the five minutes after the lights were switched up again in smoothing her hair and tugging her clothing into place.

Maria leaned forward and spoke solemnly to her reflection.

'Well, Mea, did you have a nice day?'

'Lovely, thanks.'

'And are you seeing David again?'

'Oh, yes, yes, yes!'

'Why? He was rather horrid to you on the way up the Orme.'

'Oh, but so nice, later!'

'Hmm. Do you think he's serious?'

But this was a question which her reflection, it seemed, felt unqualified to answer. It just giggled and looked away . . . and Maria jumped up and ran through into her bathroom and turned on both taps. It was not too late for a nice hot bath and David had said 'See you again – I'll give you a ring' as he turned away. She would lie in the water and daydream about . . . about things.

In his own home, David tore off his clothes, decided not to bother with washing, and got into bed. Settling down, he tried to talk himself out of some rather severe guilt-feelings, because there was no doubt about it, he had led Maria on. All that petting in the coach had no doubt done her ego lots of good, but it had also undoubtedly woken in her appetites which she had not previously known she possessed; equally certainly, it had woken in him the same appetites, which he knew all about but was frantically trying to ignore and deny.

So would he really get in touch with her again, ask her out again, take her to a dance or to the pictures or even out walking by the shore? He knew he would and he also knew why; because after today she would be as keen as he to let him go a bit further and a bit further.

But you aren't seriously interested in Maria Raft, he reminded himself crossly, so you mustn't lead her on. She's not your type, not pretty, not fashionable, not graceful or elegant. Nothing but harm will come of it; leave her alone and go find yourself the sort of woman who understands what you want and can give it without losing her heart or her head. Or start seriously courting someone – there was that little blonde thing on the bus, giving him the eye whenever he looked in her direction on the journey down to the coast. He knew where she worked – he could pop in there any evening and take her to the flicks or dancing. Girls who looked at a fellow like that, in David's opinion, knew very well what the fellow wanted and were quite willing to provide it in exchange for a few nights' fun and some money spent.

What's special about Maria? he asked himself, and knew that it was not specialness in this case which attracted him but the fact that the business of courtship, of spending time and money softening the girl up, would be totally unnecessary. She was willing, nay eager, and she was sufficiently innocent not to bother about consequences. Not that he would ignore consequences, he would take all the usual precautions, but it would be nice not to have to keep making reassuring noises, nice not to have to pretend a deep devotion. It would be like the carefree days of living with Galya, who had no intention of spoiling her neat, muscular little ballerina's body by bearing unwanted children and so had taken to using her own means of birth-control.

Presently, he let his mind wander away from his body's needs to other things. Like why his love for Pavel had been sufficient to keep him from chasing other women for so long. Inexplicably, it seemed that as soon as he knew she was unattainable, he wanted someone to take her place. Yet her place had been only in his mind; he had never possessed her.

But it only did harm to think about Pavel, because even if he had never made love to her she had been his in a way that no one else ever had, not even Galya. He sighed and shrugged the covers up to his ears; let's count sheep, he instructed himself, or planks of wood or design-drawings. Let's do anything other than think thoughts which only disturb and distress.

And presently, puzzling over how to lighten a hull without spoiling the line, he fell asleep.

'I really thought he liked me quite a lot, but he hasn't been near me for two whole weeks, he hasn't phoned, he hasn't so much as walked by the door.'

Maria wailed the words with tears trickling down her cheeks, but she continued to clip away at the ivy round the stables even in her distress and she did not look round to where

Gill was standing just behind her.

'Two weeks is nothing, Miss. They're awful busy down at the yard, you know. They're getting a boat ready for this here show that's up in London, and Mr David's had a feller wanting an original design for something bigger, so he's been working on that, too.'

'Yes, but . . .' Maria sniffed, wiped her nose on the sleeve of her dark grey cardigan, and turned to face the maid. 'You see, Gill, I made a bit of an idiot of myself. I let him kiss me in the charabanc coming home, that day we went to Llandudno. I suppose he thinks I'm cheap and doesn't want any more to do with me.'

'Rubbish, Miss! Mr David's not like that, not a bit! Anyway, you're quite a friend of the family now. Why don't you go round there? Not to the cottage, perhaps, when Miss Alice and her John and the kids are all home, but down to the sheds, of a morning, maybe.'

'The men will be there,' Maria said, sniffing again and turning back to wield the clippers crossly on the innocent ivy. 'And Nibby . . . he'll guess why I've gone down.'

'Wrong. What you want to do is go down one Sunday morning, when you know the coast's clear. Mind you, whilst they're so busy they're working all hours so it's not much use, and when the work eases off they'll likely be up here to see you, or phone or something. Look, since they took on my Nigel to give them a hand I hear quite a bit, and Mr David's that miserable . . .'

'Miserable? Oh, Gill, I'd do anything to make him happy! Shall I go down this Sunday?'

Gill sighed to herself. She had been fond of David for years, first as a sturdy, independent little boy, then as a sturdy independent youth with a wicked smile and a way with the girls, and now as a young man whom life had treated harshly — at least in Gill's opinion. Losing first the father he adored, then the family business, then his ancestral home, then his mother, and now a girl who meant a lot, judging from his haggard appearance directly after he had heard.

She liked Maria too. Ill at ease, either too gushing or too shy, first pushed into one thing by her mother and then dragged out of it and shovelled into another, she thought Maria had done remarkably well to remain practical, to have a sense of humour, and to continue to like both her parents and other people. Gill had no time for Mr Raft and not a lot for his wife. They had great ambitions for their only daughter and they loved her in their own way, but they lacked understanding and subtlety. Mr Raft would have bought David for her if it had been possible, but failing that they simply expected her to put the lad out of her mind and concentrate on finding someone else. Good advice, possibly, but not much help to one as head-over-heels in love as Maria. Now Gill, who had a soft spot for David still, could see that it might be to both Maria's advantage and David's to make a match of it. David had lost his love, so was fancy-free, and he wanted Carmel Hall and he needed its assets – the landing stage, the stretch of shore leading down to deep water; and Maria, to put it bluntly, needed a man. The fact that she appeared to have decided that only David would do was just good luck for them both.

On the other hand, Gill knew very well that it would not do for Maria to throw herself at the lad's head. So she had plotted and planned and done her best to train the other girl out of the bad habits her parents had inculcated in her: over-dress over-make up, over-gush . . . then grab. It wouldn't work, not with a gentleman like Mr David.

So now she shook a reproving head at the painful, heartfelt words.

'*Anything* to make him happy, Miss? Don't forget you're a young lady, not some back-street trollop. You won't do yourself any good, talking like that.' Maria sniffed and rubbed her sleeve across her eyes in a gesture so spontaneously that of a hurt child that Gill's heart melted. 'Oh, I know you meant it kindly, but I've told you before and I'll tell you again, Mr David never did want what lay at his feet. You just hold back a bit.'

'All right, Gill, if you say so. When can I go down to the shed?'

'Wait till I give you the word; all right?'

'All right. I – I do love him, Gill.'

It was Gill's turn to sniff. 'That's as maybe. Just you wait until I say.'

David had made himself a hammock, and when he finished work, now that the lighter evenings had come, he was apt to cast himself into it and swing gently and gaze out over the estuary and dream.

The truth was, life in the cottage was too homely and full of warmth and affection for someone who saw his life as blighted. After the day in Llandudno he had thought things out and spoken harshly to himself. He was dam' nearly pursuing Maria, and for one thing only, and it was fair neither to himself nor the girl. If Pavel had been free he would have brought her back to the cottage and she would have mucked in because the life he would have offered her would have been miles better than anything she might have had in Russia, but for any ordinary girl life in the cottage would be both squalid and unfair.

Alice was expecting a baby. She and Nibby had not planned the child, nor had they intended it, but now that it had happened they were both going round with ear-to-ear grins, and even Sara seemed vaguely pleased. But David knew that he should either get out of the cottage himself and take the two younger ones with him, or let Alice and Nibby go, yet he could not bring himself to do it. He would never manage the young ones without Alice, and though they were managing, albeit precariously, without Alice's salary, life without her sensible, practical presence would be downright dreadful.

So the only answer seemed to be to keep out of their way as much as possible, and that meant either going into the village pub for a drink which had to last all evening, or staying late at work and then spending time in his hammock.

On this particular evening there had been a beautiful sunset, a slow gathering together of the unearthly and glorious colours which sometimes come when the wind is high and wild. The hammock, straining at its ropes, was a good place to lie in weather like this if you could enjoy the violence of the elements, and David was learning to relish a gale or a quiet sunny evening or even one of the treacherous sea-mists which rolled up the estuary, providing that it could be watched and wondered over from his hammock and did not include a generous soaking of rain in its wake.

It was strange, really. The sun had sunk at last and he had closed his eyes for a moment against the after-glow and was indulging in one of those silly, bittersweet fantasies in which he was lying in the hammock just as he was lying at this very moment and a pair of cool little hands crept over his eyes and a well-remembered, much-loved voice said *Guess who?* and of course it would be Pavel, come thousands of miles to him, when he sensed someone beside the hammock. He turned his head, about to open his eyes, when two hands hesitatingly covered his eyes and a voice said, 'Guess who's come visiting, David!' in a tone so nervously coy that he nearly hit out.

Politely, however, he removed the hands and looked. Maria stood there as he had known she would. Because of the wind she had a scarlet scarf tied cornerwise round her head and she was wearing a full scarlet skirt with blue embroidery round the hem and a white blouse with a high neck and long, full sleeves.

'Oh, hello.' David made to get out of the hammock, but she smiled rather sweetly and shook her head.

'It's all right, there's no need to move. I just came down because it's ages since I've seen you and I wondered if you were all right. I went to the cottage first and Alice gave me a Cornish pasty she'd made for your tea, only you didn't come in, and a letter. Here.' She fished the letter out of the pocket of her scarlet skirt and it was a thin, foreign-looking envelope with Yuri's well-remembered writing on it.

David almost snatched it, but not quite. He sat up, swung his legs over the side of the hammock and slit the letter open, unfolded the pages and began to read.

The letter was just a letter; it did not contain one word about Pavel or her husband, it never referred to her in any way. It simply told David, in a typical joky way, that much to his dismay his old friend Yuri was about to become a father.

David went to fold the pages and put them down in his lap; he looked up at Maria and started to say something conventional about the letter and his friend Yuri and found he could say nothing. The disappointment lay on his heart like a lead weight, and it seemed to have stolen his voice, too, for though he opened his mouth no words came. He looked away and felt the tears of disappointment rise to his eyes, though he would not let them fall, and a great lump came into his throat.

He stood up; he would make some excuse, walk away from her, save her the embarrassment of seeing a grown man weeping over a letter – and not even a sad or pitiful letter, merely a note from a friend. But before he could move Maria's hands were clasping his tightly and she was gazing up at him devotedly out of her very beautiful, violet-blue eyes, made larger and more lustrous by the tears which stood out in them.

'Oh, David, I've been so unhappy, and I can see you're unhappy too,' she said. 'I'd do anything to make you happy, anything at all!'

David found his voice.

'It's all right, it doesn't matter, it's just that a letter from Russia brings it all back. Are you going to walk back to the cottage with me?'

She blinked back her tears and nodded.

'Oh yes, if that's all right. Have you finished here?'

'Almost. I've just got some stuff to tidy away in my office. I shan't be more than a few moments.'

The two of them made their way to the larger of the wooden sheds and into David's office with its worn rag of carpet, its big leather swivel chairs and the old leather-topped desk which he had rescued from Carmel Hall years ago and had only just brought back into use.

'Take a seat,' David said, collecting his papers and putting them into the safe. 'I shan't be long, I'll just . . .'

He turned round and stopped speaking. The papers dropped from his hands and he crossed the room in a couple of strides. He and Maria were in each other's arms for a few seconds only, then they stumbled to the nearest chair and collapsed in it. Maria's scarlet headscarf fell off and lay on the floor like a pool of blood.

'I don't care what happened, I'm just so relieved that he's obviously happier,' Alice announced, taking her last garment off and casting it on the chair. She looked critically at her naked body in the mirror, then turned sideways and looked again. Nibby, already in bed, applauded and she turned and threw her hairbrush at him, then had to go and rescue it in order to brush her locks. 'Shut your face, boyo! You can see I'm fatter from the side, can't you? What was I saying? Oh, and where's my nightie?'

'You were saying that David seemed happier,' Nibby said, throwing the nightdress across the room to his naked, hair-brushing wife. 'It's since that letter from Yuri came, you know; I wonder what it said? Dave said it was simply a crow of triumph because Tanya's expecting, but I'll take a bet it's more than that.'

'Hmm, probably. You don't think it's got anything to do with Maria, do you? She took the letter down to him and they've been seeing quite a bit of each other since then. I suppose it could be that.'

'Possibly; if so, then good for them.' Nibby moved over as Alice climbed into bed, then he put his arms round her and hugged her. 'Who knows, perhaps there'll be another announcement soon.'

'What? You don't think David will ask her to marry him, do you? Oh, but he used to dislike her so – and there was something after that day in Llandudno . . . he looked guilty, to me, as though they'd had an almighty row and then made it up after.'

'What's wrong with having rows and making it up? It's my favourite part of having rows, the making up.' Nibby ran an experimental hand over his wife's stomach. 'Are you *sure* there's a baby in there? If so it's a very tiny one!'

'Of course it's tiny, it isn't going to get itself born for ages yet, and don't change the subject, I was talking about David and Maria. Do you really think they're in love?'

Nibby pretended to consider whilst letting his mind go over the events of the last few days. Maria was in love all right, they could scarcely get her out of the workshop, but he didn't think David's heart was touched at all. On the other hand, he was jolly sure that the two of them were having an affair. You'd only got to look at Maria when she was looking at David, and you could see . . . it was something in her expression, a sort of eager submissiveness . . . but he did not intend to tell Alice any such thing.

'No, they aren't in love – or at least Dave isn't, but he seems quite fond of her, and he isn't going to fall deeply in love with anyone after Pavel. It hurt him too much and he's still too involved.'

'Then he shouldn't marry anyone,' Alice said sleepily. 'Oh Nibs, darling, ought you to do that? With the baby and everything?'

'Certainly I should. How cuddly you are with that nice, bulgy little tum in front! Come here!'

*

David waited until the house was quiet and everyone was asleep, then he slipped downstairs, a shadow amongst the shadows, and went to the back door. He kept it well oiled and now it opened easily, the bolts sliding back without a sound. He made a tiny noise, a night mouse's squeak, and a figure detached itself from the shadows of the front hedge and stole across to the house. He pulled her inside without a word, and still without a word the two of them climbed the stairs and slipped into David's bedroom.

David got into bed and watched whilst Maria dropped her coat on to the floor and then took off the dark blue dress and slippers she wore for her stolen excursions. In the moonlight flooding through the window she looked oddly pure and very beautiful, with all the colour drained from her body and the shadows on her skin boldly black, dramatic. She took off the last garment and came over to the bed. His skin prickled with excitement – he had half-doubted that she would come to him here – and he pulled back the covers and caught her round the hips. He pulled her forward, kissing the satiny skin of her stomach, then tumbled her into bed.

For a moment they just lay there, hearts beating so loudly that it seemed impossible that someone would not shout to them to be quiet, then David slid his hand beneath her, between the sheet and her warm body, and pulled her closer. He moved slowly, without haste, enjoying every moment, and remembered the frenzied, frantic mating which had taken place when she had first become his mistress. That had been awesome and violent, but it had also been what they both needed and wanted, for they both, in their separate ways, had been starved of physical affection for too long. It still made David smile to remember how they had hurtled round his office, one minute in the chair, the next on the carpet, the next somehow transported to the desk. And she had been as eager as he, not holding back even at the moment of ultimate surrender, when he had expected cries and resistance. She was quite a girl, Maria.

So now they made love in slow motion, taking their time, every movement careful, almost studied, until slowness and care were cast aside for that brief, frantic moment when neither could hold back any longer.

They lay still for a long time after that and then she slid out from between the sheets and stood for a moment, looking down at him and smiling. He smiled back, lazily, and then sat up and watched as she put her clothes on. As soon as she was dressed they went through the whole procedure in reverse – they stole down the stairs, across the tiny hall, through the kitchen and out of the back door.

Some way down the road, David knew, her car would be parked. He stayed in the doorway, motionless, watching until she disappeared. And shortly afterwards, heard her car start up and waited again until the engine noise slowly diminished with distance.

The brief interlude over, David returned to his room and got back into bed. He let his thoughts dwell briefly on her return home . . . the quiet car purring into its garage, Maria tiptoeing across to let herself in by the side door, the quick glide up the stairs and into her own room and thus to bed. It did not occur to him until he was very nearly asleep that not once from the moment of letting her into the house until he closed the door behind her had either of them said a word.

# CHAPTER TWENTY-ONE

'*Bez prizorney* don't take jobs!'

The boy who spoke was thin and active, about Eva's own age, and she had caught him stealing turnips and had hailed him before Kevi – one glance at Kevi though and huge grins had broken out on both faces. They had been in the same gang five years earlier and had recognised each other at once. The only sour note was that the boy, Pieter, had been stunned and horrified to hear Kevi actually admitting that he and Eva were working for this particular collective.

'If they've got any sense they do.' Kevi jerked his thumb at the pile of stolen turnips. Small, white and succulent, they lay in the sunlight, each one representing a meal for a *prizorney*. 'We can have all we want, and the work's not too hard. I tell you, it's a good way to spend the summer.'

'I can have all I want too; and not just from this collective, from anywhere I happen to be,' Pieter assured his friend. He pointed at Eva. 'Who's she?'

'My woman. By winter we'll have saved enough to get a place for ourselves. Then we shan't have to go back into a home for the bad months.'

Pieter nodded reluctant agreement with this statement.

'Yes, I was in a home last winter but the food was filth. They made me go back to school – I hated it, I was shamed by little kids three or four years younger than me. My reading seemed all right, but that was street signs and public notices; with books I didn't have the knack.'

'I was in school as well,' Eva said smugly. 'I got on all right. But Kevi says I needn't go back next winter; we'll both get jobs in a town somewhere.'

'Take the turnips then,' Kevi said abruptly. He piled the vegetables into Pieter's thin arms. 'But don't rob this collective again because you'll get caught; set a thief to catch a thief isn't a bad proverb, and Eva and I know how the *prizorney* go about things. We've caught several already and seen them beaten for their behaviour.'

'Hmm; it's all this government interference which is going to finish us,' Pieter said gloomily, standing there with his arms full of the small, greenish white globes. 'Once you wouldn't get a peasant daring to beat a *prizorney*, but now they'll lay about them without a qualm.'

Seeing him off the premises, Kevi reflected that the boy was right. Now that the *prizorney* were being re-educated, fed and taken back into society, people no longer feared reprisals from the few that were left. He and Eva had been lucky in that they had decided to go straight and had chosen their own way back, but others had been taken off into protective custody whilst they were taught how to be good Communists and made members of their local *Komsomol*, who made sure that they continued on the path of Party righteousness.

Walking back to the farmhouse now, with Eva's hand in his, he reminded himself ruefully that this good life, which he had praised so highly to Pieter, would not have been his had he not been a fool, back in the children's home. On the other hand, though, he would have been stuck in that factory, probably, until the end of time, bored and frustrated, even if he had saved his money and rented a little flat for the two of them.

The truth was that Lise had offered herself once too often and once too blatantly. Eva had been in school and it had been Kevi's day off, so they had thought they were safe; they had been in the girls' dormitory, in a highly compromising position, when Eva had walked through the door.

Kevi thought that he would never forget her face, not if he lived to be a hundred. Shock had drained it completely of every vestige of colour, and pain had made her mouth look pinched and grey, her eyes suddenly old.

He had pushed Lise away viciously, wishing with all his heart that he had never succumbed to her overt and practised blandishments, and hurried after Eva, but it had taken him thirty minutes to run her to earth and two hours to convince her that what he had done had not been a sign that his feeling for her was wearing thin or that she no longer attracted him, but merely that he was young and virile and Lise had offered herself and he had accepted the offer.

'If you're speaking the truth, then let's leave,' she had pleaded, after her tears had all been sobbed out and she had let herself be convinced of his continuing passion for her. 'I hate this place, hate it, and I hate that Lise. Please, dear Kevi, let's go into the country as we said we would! I don't want to stay under the same roof with someone you've had in your arms.'

He understood, or thought he did. That night and all the next day they behaved very correctly, Eva staying in her dormitory and Kevi in his. He went to his factory and told them that he would be leaving at the end of the week, told Eva that she must pack up her books and all her personal possessions and he would pack his. He had not spoken a word to Lise all this time and scarcely dared look at her in the dining-room or hallways, because Eva was all he had and he knew he loved her more than he had ever expected to love anyone in his life.

Nevertheless, on the day they left, he looked for Lise; just to say he was sorry how things had turned out, just to say goodbye. He had, after all, taken from her.

He had sent Eva ahead of him, to wheedle a peasant returning from a good day in the market into giving them a lift, so he was safe enough. He searched the home, then thought of the dormitory; Lise was a lazy little cat, and if nothing more exciting offered itself she was often to be found sprawled at her bed, either sleeping or eating or occasionally flicking at the pages of a book or newspaper.

She was there, lying on her stomach, her face turned away from him. He spoke her name, softly, then louder. She ignored him. She could, he knew, be sulky and she certainly had cause, he supposed. He spoke again, louder still.

'Lise? It's Kevi. Come on, girl, I only want to say goodbye, we're off, Eva and I. And to tell you I'm sorry for the other afternoon.'

She did not move, but Kevi dared wait no longer. If Eva persuaded a peasant to give them a ride out into the country in his cart then she would not be best pleased to find that Kevi and their luggage were missing. He shrugged and turned away.

'All right, be like that. See you one day, Lise.'

Later, when they had found themselves a collective where they needed more labour, he was sorry he had left Lise the way he had, and a picture of her lying on her bed kept returning, to worry and vaguely distress him, though he had no idea why he should have felt like that.

But now, walking back to their quarters, Eva's mind was plainly on far pleasanter things than children's homes and her old rival. She skipped along, singing under her breath, obviously happy, and presently she spoke, confirming it.

'Aren't we lucky, Kevi, not to be *bez prizorney* any more? I was always afraid when we rode the trains, though I never told you, of course. I always thought I'd fall. I do hate heights and when you're high on the roof of a train with the countryside whizzing past it seems even higher than it really is.'

'Aren't we *bez prizorney* any more?' Stupidly, until she put it into words, it had never occurred to him that their situation had changed so radically. After all, they had not changed, they were still Kevi and Eva, and he knew that because of his past he would always defend and help the *prizorney* when he could. Damn it, he still felt one of them, respectability or no! Long ago he had decided to deny his parentage and had chosen a name for himself, Kevi the Wolf, and Eva had never told him her patronymic either, had simply accepted that she was his woman and took his name. But if she was right, and he supposed she must be, then respectability had advantages and he might as well make use of them. They were workers now, they could apply for ration cards, identity papers, all sorts. They needed nothing on the collective, of course, save their own hard work, but later, when they moved into a city for the winter, they would need papers and a past of some sort.

He said as much to Eva, who slanted him a wicked, twinkling glance out of her round blue eyes and said that it sounded pretty dull stuff, and couldn't they leave it until winter. And, on reflection, he agreed that they need not seriously consider total respectability yet.


'David? Is that you? Can you come round?'

David, picking up the telephone in the cottage hallway as he passed, was surprised to hear Maria's voice, since their relationship, which was an extremely close one, had gone almost totally underground, but he answered her readily enough.

'Where are you, Maria? What on earth made you telephone now?' He lowered his voice. 'Aren't you coming to see me later?'

He had been amused and quite touched by the fact that she

came willingly to the cottage after dark most nights, unless he told her not to, or she was unable to get away. It was easy enough for him, of course; now that they had fallen into a routine he simply remained up and working until he heard her car down the lane. Then he pretended to do various things like making himself a hot drink and so on and his last act before climbing the stairs was to shoot across the bolts, noisily, on the front door. Only he shot them across after he had first opened the door stealthily and pulled Maria inside.

He had gained the reputation of being a light and restless sleeper and he knew Alice worried and said that he was still upset over losing Pavel and had not slept properly since that last letter from Yuri; he had to grin to himself at this since Maria had become his mistress within minutes of his reading that letter and one thing had obviously covered up quite another.

But now the voice over the telephone sounded different from Maria's usual breathless, excited tones; it sounded petulant and rather worried.

'I can't come to see you tonight but we simply must talk. We hardly ever talk at nights, do we?'

He grinned; nights were for action!

'No, that's true. And anyway, we can't carry on much longer, it's too dangerous with Alice's condition.'

It was a very real fear with him now that he might be in bed with Maria and suddenly find Alice at his side telling him to telephone for an ambulance because the baby had started. He had warned Maria a week ago that their meeting place, if not their activities, would have to change.

'Oh David, I can't think straight; how soon can you be here?'

David glanced at his watch; he had come in to make himself some tea since Alice and Nibby were both out and the kids were staying in town for some school event, but he supposed he could go down to the Hall right away, except that it would look rather odd. After all, no one really knew he even saw Maria any more — let alone how much of her he did see!

'Look, we've got a sail-boat ready for testing. Can you walk down to the landing stage? I'll meet you there in thirty minutes if that's all right.'

He half expected her to make some comment on his being

ashamed to meet her in public, but she said nothing of the kind so perhaps she enjoyed their clandestine relationship as much as he. Though whether I enjoy the secrecy of it or the fact that it means I don't have to acknowledge that there is a relationship I'm none too certain, David told himself guiltily as he turned round and left the cottage again. It was pretty mean of him, but he knew he had no desire to let everyone know he was carrying on with the rich Miss Raft. People would say he was after her money and position and it simply wasn't true – all he wanted, right now, was her body!

In the lane which led, by twists and turns, down to the boat sheds, he considered his position. It was rather nice – unmarried, unattached, with no husbandly duties save one, and that the one that most men stuck their heads in a noose in order to get, he told himself smugly. Ah, David Thomas hadn't been too bright in the past, he had let himself become an almost professional loser, but this time he had done all right!

It was a grey evening, but the wind was mild on his cheek and swelled the sail nicely but not vigorously, so that he enjoyed an easy sail down to the landing stage which he remembered so well. He drifted in, his sail flapping loose, and jumped ashore to tie up to a post. Then he looked round for Maria.

She was there, standing in the shelter of the trees. She was wearing a dark brown dress which did not suit her. She moved forward as he went towards her, then stepped back again, into the trees' shade. When he got within six feet of her he could see she had been crying.

'What's up?' It sounded unnecessarily brusque, but her reply was equally brief.

'I'm pregnant.'

David's heart did a nose-dive into his boots. It was not fair! Damn it, she couldn't be . . . couldn't know already! Look at Alice, married for a year before there was a sign of a child. And anyway, he had taken precautions every time she had come to him. It couldn't be his baby; she must have been playing fast and loose with someone else, someone less careful.

'You can't be!'

'David, I am! I've missed my period twice and this morning, when I was dressing, I couldn't get my blue skirt to fasten. I wish I was wrong, but I don't think so. What shall I do?'

He was panic-stricken. He looked at her face, tear-streaked, and then let his eyes drop to her waistline. She did not look any fatter to him, but Alice had gone round looking perfectly normal and ordinary until, overnight it seemed, she had suddenly stuck out in front like the prow of a ship and had taken to concealing smocks and dresses with lots of pleats and silly little bows and white collars.

'I don't know what you should do – dammit, woman, I took every care, I always used a sheath ... it's supposed to be impossible for a woman to conceive through one of them! Look, you're mistaken, you've got your dates wrong or something, you're not thinking straight.'

He looked up at her face again and, absurdly, she was smiling though tears still formed in her eyes. She held out both hands and took his, gripping so tightly that her knuckles whitened. He looked down at her big, bony hands and it made him think of the pains of childbirth, of the bearing down part he'd read in Alice's books, and the way a woman suffered. But she was speaking, and her voice had a wobble in it as well as a laugh.

'Oh, David, you can't have forgotten the first time? In your boat shed? We neither of us knew what was going to happen ... we acted like a couple of fools, I'm not denying it, but it was just skin to skin, wasn't it?'

'Oh, then! But that was the first time, Maria; no one conceives the first time, I'm sure I've read that in Alice's books. Look how hard some people have to try for children ... the first time's different, it isn't for making babies, it's for ... well, experience, I suppose.'

She laughed; it was a watery little sound but it took some of the strain out of the situation.

'David, it must have been then, otherwise I wouldn't be able to tell yet. What do you want me to do?'

He dropped her hands. He wanted her to get rid of it, that was what he wanted her to do, but she was not a knowing girl, like some, she was incapable of making the necessary arrangements. His mind flew feverishly from one avenue of escape to another; he could find someone willing to do an abortion on her in London or Liverpool – probably even in Chester, except that it was a bit near home. But how could he smuggle her away from the Hall for long enough to do the deed? He had no idea how such things were done but he imagined she would be in hospital for a day or two, possibly more. It would place her in a damnably awkward position, because she wasn't a girl with friends away or anything like that, she was always at home – or if she did go away, she went with her parents.

He looked at her, in her ugly brown frock, her face all tear-blubbered and her mouth trembling. Poor girl! She had been good to him – generous. She had never refused to come creeping through the night to him, never suggested that it might be pleasant for a change if he was the one who had to trek home in the dark afterwards instead of lying, heavy and sated, in a nice warm bed. She had never demanded public recognition of her status, either, accepting that he wanted her only for what she could give him. He had never bought her so much as one single chocolate, let alone a box, he thought confusedly. Was he going to continue to take, take, take? Would he take not only her body but the child within it, with never a word of thanks or a gift in return? It was not as if he was in love with anyone else, or had any hopes of marriage, for he had neither the time nor the energy for courtship now that Pavel's love could never be his. He drew Maria into his arms and kissed her wet cheeks and then her trembling mouth. Obedient still to what she considered his rightful desires, she let her lips part beneath his and he knew, despite what he had done, what she thought he would now demand of her, that she would let him take her if he indicated that he wanted to do so.

He broke the kiss and held her a little away from him. No use beating about the bush. If you give, give generously, with both hands, with your whole heart.

'Maria, I don't deserve you and I won't blame you a bit if you turn me down . . . but . . . will you marry me?'

A slim hope was raised when she simply stared and then burst into tears, but it was soon drowned. He had never seen a woman cry so much. Tears seemed to spurt from the unlikeliest spots: he was convinced, at one time, that they flowed from her ears as well as her eyes, so soaked did they both become. But even through the flood, she managed to say that she would marry him, she would indeed!

Alice guessed as soon as he told her that he and Maria were to be married, which was a blow to his pride, but she seemed to be the only one. Everyone else congratulated him heartily, told him he was a lucky blighter, and asked for an invitation to what would undoubtedly be the wedding of the year.

Alice said that even if he had turned to Maria in the depths of his unhappiness and behaved like a complete cad, at least he was doing the gentlemanly thing by her now.

'What will her parents say, though?' he asked unhappily. He was quite prepared to be castigated and possibly turned from their door when the inevitable moment came. Alice, however, was worldlier than he.

'Premature birth,' she said briefly. 'Parents have been claiming bouncing babies were seven-month children since the dawn of time; why shouldn't the Rafts follow suit?'

'Then you don't think they'll tell poor Maria never to darken their doors again?'

Alice laughed.

'Bless you for an idiot, David Thomas,' she said kindly. 'Mr and Mrs Raft have schemed and plotted and *yearned* for this moment; if they'd known it was possible to entrap a man by getting in the family way they'd have advised Maria to try it! Don't worry, they're proud as peacocks and pleased as punch!'

'She didn't entrap me, though,' David said honestly. 'She'd have got rid of it – or tried to – if I'd asked her. The truth is, I rather like her; she's got guts. And though I shouldn't say it to you, she's awfully good at the old you-know-what.'

'David! What a thing to say to a delicately reared girl!' Alice then rather spoilt the effect by adding: 'Anyway, how can you tell she's any better than the next person? Surely you haven't been going round doing it with other people as well?'

'Gosh, Allie, I'm only human, you know,' David said, disgusted at such a narrow view. 'Of course I know what other women can do, and some are better than others.'

'How? After all, they're all doing the same thing, essentially.'

'Ask Nibby,' David said rather rashly. 'He'll tell you.'

'Nibby only knows about me.' There was a pause. 'Doesn't he?'

'Yes, undoubtedly,' David said wearily. 'I wish I'd never said anything about it; I should have known a woman would only make silly remarks.'

'I shall ask Nibby, and I'll tell him why!'

'Go ahead; don't blame *me* if he shouts at you.'

Alice had been pottering about the kitchen as they talked. Now she got out a bag of peas, settled down at the table, and began to shell them. She was working so furiously, and with such concentrated venom, that the peas rattled into the saucepan like machine gun fire. Poor Nibby, I'd better drop a word of warning, David thought, horrified at what he had so nearly said. But trust an innocent woman to assume that the man she loved was innocent too!

'David,' Alice said presently, ceasing fire for a moment. 'Why is it wrong for a girl to be experienced and right for a man?'

'Because men don't get pregnant, love. Men are made different in their minds from women, you know, as well as in their bodies. They have to take the lead and know how to act; women tend to follow, wouldn't you agree?'

'Ye-es, perhaps. But does that mean they make love with women they don't even like much, just so that when they do meet the right one, they'll know what they're doing?'

'It's not quite as straightforward as that, but you've got the rough idea. I'm not saying anything about Nibby, mind, but quite a lot of girls want to sleep with a chap but don't want to marry him. See?'

'No, but I'll take your word for it. David?'

'What is it *now*?'

'Had I better not ask Nibby?'

'Much better not. You see, if he told you he was experienced you'd resent it and if he isn't he might be ashamed to admit it.'

'Gosh! Men are very strange.'

'And so, dear Alice, are women!'

Despite David's many and various fears the wedding was arranged in record time and no one said anything — to him, at least — about being in a hurry. Mr and Mrs Raft were in their element, faces beamed at David whenever he entered Carmel Hall and Maria's beam was the widest and most loving of all.

'Come up and see our room,' she said a few days after they had first decided to marry. 'Dad wanted to redecorate it but I said no, you'd not want that, we'd do it at our leisure.'

'*Our* room?' David frowned. 'Did you say our room?'

'Well, naturally. Where did you think we'd sleep, once we were married?'

It seemed absurd but he simply had not considered the matter. Did I really believe they would let me continue as I am now, with Maria tiptoeing up the stairs every night and then making her way home, he wondered, aghast at his own simplicity. The Rafts knew he could not provide Maria with a home of her own, they must know that the cottage was uncomfortably crowded already, without adding another grown woman to the rich mix. So where else should they sleep but at Carmel Hall? And did that mean he would live there, too? With her mother and her father and the servants, many of whom had known him as a boy?

He followed her up the stairs and into the room. It was one of the master bedrooms, as big as all the bedrooms at the cottage put together. There was the big double bed, brass-knobbed, silk-canopied, two day-beds like the one in Maria's study downstairs and a couple of easy chairs. Next door it had its own bathroom and lavatory so that they could, if they wished, be completely private.

'It's very nice. But I have to be at the cottage weekdays. I can't get to work otherwise, and anyway I need to be near the phone and so on.'

'What's that, silly?' Maria pointed to a white telephone on the table under the window. 'You can phone in if you want, or give customers this number.'

'It will take too long to arrange. Look, couldn't we stay here at weekends and spend weekdays at the cottage?' He put an arm round her and tugged her close. 'We've been managing in my bed for long enough!'

She sighed blissfully and rubbed her head shyly against his cheek. Her hair was very coarse, but now that she no longer crimped it it looked good even if it felt a bit like wire wool.

'Oh, David, you're so naughty! But it wouldn't work, living at the cottage. I'd have nothing to do all day and as I got bigger the bed would get less possible. No, we'll have to make arrangements for you to get to work and back . . . can you drive?'

'Cheek! Yes, I can, but I haven't . . .'

'Use mine. No, don't be silly, once we're married all my things will be yours anyway. If I need a car when you're

515

working I'll borrow Dad's. Is that fair?'

'It's more than fair, it's generous.' David repressed a sigh. He did not enjoy being the constant object of Maria's generosity, but he had brought it on himself. 'But look, love, we can't live with your parents for ever! It wouldn't work, there would be quarrels, we'd begin to get on each other's nerves . . . take it from me.'

'Oh, but hadn't I mentioned it? Dad's already bought a piece of land. It's right next door to the Hall, it abuts, or whatever the expression is, and they're going to build a little place there.'

'For us? Oh, my God, they . . .'

'No, David, *not* for us; for them! They've enjoyed living at the Hall but it's always been miles too big for us, and though Dad did mean to start something up he never got round to it. So they're going to move into the house when it's built and leave us here . . .' She paused coyly. 'Us and the baby, of course. And all the other babies. I want a big family, don't you?'

David, who had never given the matter a thought, said dutifully that of course he did and preceded her down the stairs in a pensive mood. He really should have talked to his prospective father-in-law about a number of things, but a guilty dread of letting Mr Raft know that he had seduced his daughter had kept him at a careful distance from the older man. If the old couple were really leaving the Hall, though, then it was time that some discussing was done. The boatbuilding business was thriving, but it could do very much better if it was moved right up the coast to the Carmel Hall grounds, to say nothing of the fact that David knew very well the old boy still owned the crumbling slipway and derelict sheds that were all that was left of the once mighty Thomas yard. They were further up the estuary still, but if one had the money to dredge out the channel . . . it would actually be possible to build, if not ships, at least very large yachts there!

After this interlude, David did find the courage to have a word or two with Mr Raft about their future, but the older man proved evasive.

'Just let's get one thing done at a time, David, me lad,' he roared, clapping David's shoulders so hard that David feared dislocation. 'Just let's get you and my girl married and then we'll talk business.'

Since it lacked only a day to the moment when Maria would walk down the aisle towards him, David could hardly object to this. And next day found him, nervous, scrubbed, standing in the aisle with Nibby at his side, whilst Maria, in a long white bridal gown with a veil yards long and a bouquet big enough to hide any bulges at her waist, glided up to him and put her trembling fingers into his.

She looked mysterious with the veil down and surprisingly pretty with it back; someone had dissuaded her from make-up, which was a good thing, but excitement had given her eyes a shine and morning sickness had provided an interesting pallor; she looked very bridal with those amazingly dark blue eyes shining in her pale face and her black and heavy hair gleaming like a horse's coat from brushing. David pushed the wedding ring on to one large-knuckled hand and gave her fingers a squeeze and saw the blood fly to her cheeks; it was a miracle to him how she could still find a hand-squeeze exciting. With me, it has to be a considerably more intimate squeeze, he thought ruefully; was it love that coloured his every move for her, making a mere touch or a brush of the lips into a Happening? He supposed it must be – it certainly did not happen in reverse!

They were having a honeymoon because Maria had flatly refused to walk into their room for the first time with her parents hovering. However, for various reasons it would only be a two night and one day honeymoon, at a big hotel in the centre of Chester. They would leave in the bride's car, driven by the groom, and would dine in the hotel before making their way to their room. David, driving off with the usual accompaniment of tin cans clattering from the back bumper and confetti all over his hair, shoulders and knees, wondered again how many people would guess that this wedding night would be a repeat performance and nothing for anyone to write home about.

He had reckoned without Maria. First of all, they had not slept together for a month, so he was surprised to see how much she had altered. When she undressed, which she did with unmaidenly alacrity, he saw that her breasts, never exactly small, were larger than he remembered, the nipples very full and swollen. Oddly enough her waist seemed satisfyingly slim still, though as she pointed out, her stomach was more rounded. Together they admired the changes, and then, anticipation

517

having been thoroughly aroused, he tumbled her into bed and fell in after her.

Thirty minutes later, sated and exhausted, David flopped over on to his back and contemplated his brand-new wife with mild astonishment. How on earth did she manage to be inventive and exciting in bed and perfectly ordinary, even slightly boring, out of it? But since he erroneously supposed that marriage would prove to consist of more bed than bored, he believed himself to have made a good choice. He pulled Maria, who was smiling sleepily, into his arms, planted a smacking kiss on her mouth and told her she was wonderful.

'So are you,' Maria assured him, just before they both fell suddenly asleep.

'Another winter, and still not a trace of Eva.'

Pavel and Rudi, arm in arm, were leaving the theatre where they had watched, with great appreciation, a performance by the Bolshoi, when the first snowflakes drifted down from the dark sky. They were nothing much, over in a moment, but as Pavel said, a sign of winter.

'No, but remember, dushka, neither you nor your sister are children any more. Eva must be . . . well, about seventeen or so, I suppose. And you're of age . . . twenty-one at last, eh?'

'Seventeen isn't a very great age,' Pavel said ruefully. 'But you're right, of course. She's probably married and hoping for a family.'

'Quite probably.' Rudi hesitated, the arm that was linked with hers giving a little jerk. 'Darling one, have you ever thought about seeing a doctor . . . I know it's only a year, but we've tried very hard and had absolutely no luck.'

Rudi had given her long enough to settle down and then he had told her that he longed for children. She was much younger than he, of course he realised that, but a young mother had more time and energy for babies and she seemed fond enough of little ones . . .

She had agreed at once that they would try for a child, but despite their efforts she had not become pregnant. Rudi brought books home, they read them from cover to cover, Pavel stopped work, took things easy, ate plenty of all the right food . . . and still did not conceive.

'It's not that I haven't thought of getting advice,' Pavel said now, 'but I can't imagine what else they can do! We seem to have covered everything ourselves and still no babies come.'

'No, dushka, but a doctor who knows about such things might recommend something we've not thought about. Would you go to the Institute, just for me? Someone was saying that they've got a new method . . . they say it works . . . it might be worth a try.'

Agreeing, Pavel trotted beside him, her high heels click-clicketing on the hard pavement, and wondered why her dear Rudi, who was such a strong, broad-shouldered, narrow-hipped specimen of humanity, should be unable to father children. Or it was possible that she herself was the person at fault. Until they went for tests they could have no idea, and she and Rudi had not much liked the idea of being mucked about, even for the sake of the babies they both wanted.

Pavel had not wanted them at first, of course. But as time passed and she began to fit into the life in Kharkov, she realised that a baby would probably stop all her stupid uncertainties and the longing, which it seemed not even time would erase, for David. If she had a child she could sublimate her love for David in loving the baby, and that would make her a better wife for Rudi, for she knew that she was not as good a wife as she might be.

It was nothing you could put your finger on, most of the time. Just a certain slowness, a lack of response in her. If he noticed it he was silent on the subject but perhaps, Pavel thought hopefully, he simply did not notice. When the need to cry and cry and bite wildly at the bedclothes came to her, she made sure she only indulged it when he was out of the building. Often she could be serene for weeks at a time and then it would come over her in waves, the need for David which she knew to be absurd and fanciful yet could not deny.

'So will you go to the Institute, dearest? Tomorrow? Just to satisfy me that we've left no stone unturned?'

Pavel was still assuring Rudi that she would go and gladly when they reached the foyer of their block of flats.

'There's more trouble in Germany,' Rudi remarked, as they got into the lift and pressed the button for their floor. 'The powers that be want me back in uniform.'

Pavel considered, her head on one side.

'Do they? Would you like it? You've been marvellous,

sticking to your dull old figures all this time. Why don't you have a go? What's it to be? Training recruits?'

'Perhaps. It's all a bit vague at the moment. But you'd not object? If I went back into uniform, I mean.'

'Silly, of course I wouldn't. But if it meant you going away for a while then I'd like to work again. I feel a fraud often, making the days go by whilst you work.'

The lift hummed to an unsteady stop and Pavel opened the doors but Rudi caught her arm.

'Hey, wait a minute! Making the days go by? Do you miss your job?'

She missed it hellishly, not only the work but the companionship and the animals. Now she nodded, mute, her heart in her eyes. Oh, if only he would see that it was not her work which had prevented her conceiving, if only he would let her go back again, so that she was not so bored and lonely! Rudi loved being the provider for them both, taking all the decisions, paying the bills, doing the worrying. If I had married David we were going to search for that wreck, she reminded herself. He and I, not just he. Perhaps I'd have been a better wife in a shared marriage; sometimes she felt that this was Rudi's marriage and she merely happened to have become a part of it.

'You should have told me before,' he said severely. He pushed her ahead of him out of the lift and then, outside their front door and before so much as putting his key in the lock, he gave her a satisfyingly hard kiss, straining her to him in a very unmarried sort of way. 'Stoopidchka, how can I please you if you don't tell me when I'm wrong? When you've tried the new treatment at the Institute you can go back to work . . . unless you're making a new little Lemensk by then, of course.'

'Of course,' Pavel echoed dutifully, preceding him into the flat. So the baby, if she did start one, would help her to forget David and help Rudi to keep her happily domesticated. Poor little thing, it had quite a busy future before it. She took off her thick coat and hung it on the hallstand, then went into the kitchen to make a drink before bed.

She did not think of Eva again until she and Rudi were in bed and Rhudi made his first tentative approach – not that there was anything tentative about his lovemaking once he got going, she reminded herself ruefully, turning into his arms. It was so peculiar to think of Eva married, of her nice little sister doing . . . this!

Despite all their resolves to save money and become respectable, Eva and Kevi still rode the train back into the city, choosing Moscow this time because neither of them had been there.

'We need all our money for an apartment, we can't spare any for train journeys,' Kevi told Eva severely, but she thought that it was not the money he lacked, he hated to think that he really was such a part of the establishment now that they rode in trains instead of on them. Besides, there wasn't much thrill in sitting for hours and hours on a hard wooden bench with a lot of smelly peasants.

Fortunately, they set off this time before winter was upon them, squatting on the roof in the nutty autumn air with the wind not really strong enough to be a hazard. There were other *bez prizorney* on the train too, mostly boys who had gone into homes and tried to become ordinary people again but who had reneged during the hot summer which had just passed. Like wild animals, though, they knew that they must find themselves somewhere to shelter during the winter months or they would die, so they were off to find either a good children's home or work, or possibly just someone to scrounge from.

Arriving in Moscow was awesome, but she and Kevi managed to find their way to a reasonably respectable area and with money and papers Kevi soon persuaded the manager of a block of tenement flats to let him rent one, provided he started work on the following day.

The flat had only one room and there was a shared lavatory and a big shared kitchen, but the landlord pointed out that it was perfectly possible to cook everything you wanted on the stove, and Eva thought it was better than squabbling over a kitchen, no matter how big, with every other woman in the block, so they took it.

'Tomorrow we'll go out and buy a few things but for now this'll do us,' Kevi said. 'Get some water, Eva, there's a good girl. There's a tap on the bottom landing – I saw it as we came up.'

'What shall I carry it in?' Eva said, looking round. 'There isn't anything suitable.'

521

'Use this basin.' It was shallow and not ideal for carrying water but there was nothing else, so she set off down the stairs, the basin under one arm.

The stairs were very steep and rather dark and halfway down them she met someone coming up. It was another girl, like herself, carrying a jug of water, moving carefully from step to step so that she did not jerk any of her precious burden out on to the stairs. She glanced quickly up as she heard Eva coming towards her and Eva caught just a glimpse of her before she reached a landing, crossed it, and disappeared through a door. She was an ordinary looking girl really, with red hair and a pale, freckled face. Eva stared at the doorway through which the girl had disappeared and her heart started doing nasty little tickety-tackety dances. That girl had looked just like another girl, a long time ago, in a children's home. That girl . . . whatever was her name? . . . had spelt trouble and Eva did not like girls who made trouble. She stared for a moment longer at the door, then continued on her way down the stairs. Reaching the tap, she half-filled her basin and then went up the stairs again. But outside the doorway of the flat which belonged to the red-haired girl she stopped for several moments and she forgot she was carrying water and let the basin droop so that when she got back to Kevi again she had less than a cupful in her basin.

'Eva, where the hell's the water?' She held her basin out and he looked, cast his eyes up to the ceiling, sighed, and then took the basin from her, stood it down and smacked her as hard as he could across her bare legs. Eva jumped and scowled at him, then her lip began to tremble; he had never hit her deliberately, to cause her pain, in their lives together before that moment.

'Why did you hit me? I'll fetch more water, I must have spilt it coming upstairs.'

'All right, all right, it doesn't matter, this will do.' He picked up the water and drank it in one long, thirsty swoop. 'As for hitting you, it was . . . it was to teach you not to dream when I send you on an errand.'

Eva said, gruffly, that she was sorry and began to sort out their meagre possessions, but she told herself that it was that girl's fault; she had made trouble already and she'd not even set eyes on Kevi!

*

522

Alice's baby was a boy; they called him Richard, because Alice liked the name and Nibby did not mind what it was called, so long as Alice was all right.

David, awaiting his own happy event without much enthusiasm, was quite surprised at the way Nibby behaved; he kept parading round and round the shed saying, 'Hawke & Son... Thomas & Hawke & Son...' until David bade him, rather crossly, to shut up.

'The kid's not much bigger than a propeller, and you're turning him into a shipbuilder,' he said. 'If this is what having a son does to a fellow I hope we have a daughter.'

'Ha! Sons are something to boast about, sons are useful,' Nibby shouted, above the noise in the shed. 'Daughters may be decorative, but that's about all they are!'

'Oh? I'll tell Alice you say so – she was someone's daughter.'

'Hmm. Coming for a celebratory drink, chaps? My treat, of course.'

The cottage hummed with activity too, whenever David went in for some reason or other. Nappies seemed to grow on trees – they were certainly on every available surface on wet days – and Michael, whose voice had broken, complained on three different notes – basso profundo, tenor and alto – that a fellow couldn't sit down without being dripped on. Alice, looking prettier than ever, presided over her mixed bunch with as much humour and good sense as always, and Sara came home from Cambridge and went to stay with Philip's people because 'there isn't room for another flea in that cottage'.

There was more drama when Michael announced that little Ricky and his parents were squeezing out their own flesh and blood – he missed Sassy's evil ways, David could see that – and Alice wept and Nibby roared, but it was all settled amicably in the end. Two days under Philip's parents' roof was enough to send Sara scurrying home ... they had a maid and you couldn't make yourself so much as a round of toast without asking permish., and Philip's father had tried to kiss her behind the kitchen door ... so that gave Alice her confidence back. And then Sassy fell in love with the young man who came twice a week to help Michael with his maths, and Philip and his parents were cast thoroughly in the shade.

David loved visiting the cottage but always felt a little guilty over being there, for they did have very limited room and must

523

have breathed a sigh of relief every time he left. It was, however, very different from home.

Carmel Hall was home, now. His parents-in-law had moved out and he and Maria had spread themselves, though not yet to a bedroom each, because when he suggested it might be a good idea – we can still visit, he said, when she began to cry – Maria refused to consider it.

They kept the same staff on and Maria hired a nanny for when the baby arrived, but somehow the house seemed cold and empty after the crammed, happy, nappy-festooned cottage.

David had been up to the nurseries, though, and had taken Maria to task for telling him, ages ago, that they were empty and abandoned. Maria had laughed at him, self-confident over this matter at least.

'I had no idea, then, that we'd ever marry, but I was sure you would,' she confessed. 'I thought when you did and your wife had a child, I'd send you the things as a present.'

When she said things like that David knew she was a good girl really and hugged her and made much of her. The dear old rocking horse had been cleaned and polished and repainted, all ready for the new generation of Thomases to try his gallop, and the dolls' house had been refurbished too, Sara and Michael coming up specially and vastly enjoying all the fiddly work of getting it into tip-top condition.

Yet though all the plans for moving the shipyard back to its original base were under way, David still found Maria easier at night than during the day. Even now, hugely cumbersome and liable to fits of tears and depression, it seemed she could throw off all her woes in bed with him; but let him make one perfectly ordinary remark during the day . . . such as remembering that the first time he'd met Nibby had been when an unseen hand had felled him with a snowball in the stableyard . . . and she would start to cry and flounce out of the room.

'It's just nerves because she's expecting, lad,' Mrs Raft said comfortably. 'She'll steady up once the babe arrives, never you fear.' But David sometimes had his doubts.

He did not know for sure, but sometimes he thought she quite simply knew he did not love her, and that it coloured her attitude towards him to such an extent that she could rarely be natural. At other times, though, he accepted that she was nervous of the coming event and would settle down when it was over.

He was doing his best, what was more, to be everything she wanted; he was supportive, understanding, sympathetic, so it seemed hard when he plainly failed to please.

David was out on the estuary, trying out a boat, when the baby started. He glanced towards the landing stage, for he had sailed upriver, and saw a small figure waving frantically. He sailed closer, and it was Gill, using her apron as a flag.

'What is it?' he hallooed, tacking towards her, and Gill bellowed into the wind, 'Baby's starting, Mr David,' and had him scurrying down on the landing stage at full speed, very nearly ramming a brand-new yacht which would have cost the firm of Thomas & Hawke a pretty penny. However, he managed to tie up without even scraping the paint and he and Gill ran all the way up to the house.

'Mrs Thomas started an hour ago, sir,' Gill panted as they ran. 'She's in ever such a taking . . . kept saying she'd be all right and she wouldn't do nothing until you got here. Mr Raft drove round to the cottage and then sent a message to the yard but you'd left, of course. So they told me to run down to the landing stage and see if I could catch your attention.'

'Good girl,' David said briefly. 'Where is she? In bed?'

'In her room.' Gill ran in through the side door and shouted, 'He's here, Mr Thomas is back!' and then collapsed on to the nearest chair, fanning her hot face with one flapping hand. 'Best to go up, sir,' she advised, but David was already heading for the stairs.

He burst into their bedroom to find Maria pacing the floor, her mother in tears and the nurse, Fortescue, turning down the bed. As soon as he appeared Maria ran across the room to him and her mother stopped crying like a tap being turned off.

'David – it's started! Do you want to be here, or would you rather I went into the nursing home right away?'

David hesitated. Plainly the nurse thought Maria had some time to go before anything happened or she would scarcely have suggested his wife climb into bed! Equally plainly, his mother-in-law wanted Maria safely in the nursing home, where they could deal with the coming event. But Maria herself? She was flushed, but he could tell she was neither afraid nor apprehensive.

'My love, I want what's best for you. Do you want to go now? If so, I'll take you. But if you'd rather wait a bit, that's fine by me.'

'Well it isn't fine by me,' Mrs Raft broke in, her little eyes glinting dangerously. 'This is my first grandchild and I want it born in a nursing home, not in the car on the way. Now be sensible, the pair of you, and get going!'

'Maria?'

'I'll be lonely there, I'd rather wait until it's a bit nearer. The doctor said the pains get closer and closer. They're quite a long way apart at the moment. Can't I wait?'

'Yes, of course . . .'

'No, certainly not . . .'

The words burst from two throats simultaneously; Maria set her lip and the nurse looked amused, but David had had enough.

'I'm sorry, Mother, but this is between Maria and me. You're very welcome to stay here, but you must let us know best on this occasion. Maria, love, lie down on the bed and I'll chat to you for a bit.'

'I'm not lying down, I want to keep moving.' Maria turned and glared first at David and then at her mother. 'Go *away*, Mum . . . that's what David meant, wasn't it, David?'

'I wouldn't be so discourteous . . .'

'Indeed, Mea, if you let your husband speak to your mother in such a manner there's . . .'

'You take her to the nursing home, Mr David,' the nurse advised, under cover of the violent disagreement now animating mother and daughter. 'Don't go leaving her, stay with her, then at least there'll just be the pair of you. This way, she'll be so set on getting her own way the child'll be born on the floor!'

David saw the justice of this. He looked around and picked up Maria's case, neatly packed in readiness for a week, then took his wife's hand and began to tow her towards the door.

'No argument, my love,' he said as Maria began to object to his caveman-like treatment. 'Nurse suggests that we go and get you booked into the nursing home and that the two of us settle down there, in your nice private room, and have a game of cards or a listen to the wireless, or we could just sit and hold hands, if the fancy took us. And then, when baby does decide to arrive, you're in the right place; see?'

'Oh, you'll stay?' Maria stopped resisting and began to smile. 'That would be so nice, David! Fox got the car round, all ready.'

They reached the nursing home in good order and were greeted by a capped and aproned matron who led them straight to Mrs Thomas's nice little room and showed Maria where the bell was, and how to operate it. She told David that there was a waiting room just up the corridor with plenty of magazines, so if he would like to take himself off for a few minutes she would send a nurse along to help Mrs Thomas into that pretty nightie . . . my, how beautifully things were made these days, weren't they? . . . and thus into bed.

'It's all right,' David said coolly, 'I'll help my wife to change,' and was rewarded by a look of burning adoration from Maria and a slightly chillier one from the matron.

The nightie really was rather pretty; white cotton, full and airy, with a richly embroidered yoke and flounce. David was just admiring it and telling Maria how nice she looked when she sat down, hard and abruptly, on the edge of the bed.

'David, I . . . oh, David, whatever have I done? Oh dear, oh gosh, oh David!'

'Heavens!' David leaped for the bell, pressed it so furiously that it sounded off like a fire alarm, and then picked up Maria's feet and, with scant ceremony, tipped her into bed and on to her back. Then he heaved at her shoulders until she was at least level and resting, more or less, on the bank of embroidered pillows.

'All right? Where the hell are the staff in this place?'

The door opened slowly and a large woman in a pale blue dress with a white apron and cap said, 'Did you ring, sir?' in an odiously reproachful tone.

'Yes I did! Look!'

The nurse looked, gasped, and shot into the room, moving with remarkable rapidity for one of her size.

'Gracious, I thought the lady was a new admission . . . ring the bell again, sir, for mercy's sake!'

David rang the bell again desperately and to no avail and tried to avert his eyes from all the groaning, grunting and frantic activity taking place on the bed.

'Go and fetch someone, sir,' the nurse said. David risked a quick glance. Maria's knees were straddled in a workmanlike pose and the nurse was pushing with all her might on those knees, as though by doing so she would prevent Maria from escaping via the end of the bed. At the same time, she adjured Maria to grab the rail at the top of the bed and 'push, push down hard, my dear girl!'

David escaped into the corridor and shouted. A figure appeared and scuttled past him. Not wanting to leave Maria to the tender mercies of what appeared to be extremely inefficient females, he then returned to her private room just as Maria gave an extra loud cry, both nurses echoed it, and David actually saw the pointed mound that was Maria's distended stomach suddenly seem to shrink and shrivel down on itself.

'It's a boy,' a voice remarked conversationally somewhere near his right ear. 'A dear little boy. Here, Mother, you may hold him for a moment whilst I deal with the cord.'

David peered, blenched at what was going on at the nurse's end of Maria, and smiled hopefully at the other. White, glistening, panting, Maria's face suddenly smiled back.

'It's a boy,' she said proudly. 'Did you see him? Wasn't he *quick*? It wasn't so bad really, David, though the last bit hurt rather. Oh, look at his dear little hands!'

David looked. The hands were all right, if you liked hands like cockle rakes, but the rest of their son looked pretty rum; he was very red for a start, his face looked like a boiled lobster and his nose looked recently punched, as did his swollen, lashless, gummy eyes.

'Isn't he hideous?' he said. He touched the red and angry cheek and it was soft as a rose petal. 'He's got some hair, though; it's curly!'

'Yes. He really is rather beautiful, isn't he?'

Obviously his remark about the creature's hideousness had not been heard and David was glad. Poor little blighter, its lot would be hard enough with a face like that without having an unappreciative father as well.

The nurse took the baby back and tipped it upside down. It wailed – who could blame it – and she righted it and wrapped it in a towel. Maria was being dealt with, the other nurse was still swabbing her down with some clean-smelling liquid and David didn't know how to refuse when the baby was placed firmly in his hands.

'There you are, Father; not many men have seen their sons

born, not these days. What will you call him?'

But David was too busy staring into the tiny face to heed her words. Someone had once told him that, at the moment of birth, a child will for an hour or two exactly resemble its father. This one was the image of his own father, Alyn Thomas. Of course he had never seen his father as a child, but the baby *was* Alyn; the squashy, unformed nose, the mouth that had never yet smiled, the way the hair grew, even . . . and when he looked closely, as he was looking now, it was red hair!

'Hello, Alyn,' he muttered. 'Well, you old devil, wouldn't you be pleased if you could see this one?'

'Alyn; that's a good Welsh name,' one of the nurses remarked. David, looking up, was about to say that it was his father's name when Maria spoke from her clustered pillows.

'Let's call him Alyn, for your father, David,' she whispered. 'He'd like that, I bet!'

'He'd like it more than anything,' David said, still looking down at the tiny little face with its pouting lips now moving irritably as though it was muttering bad words beneath its breath. 'How do you do, Alyn Thomas the second? I'm your dad.'

The nurses laughed and Maria did too, but the look that went with the laugh was tender.

# CHAPTER TWENTY-TWO

Eva was dreaming again; Kevi always knew when it was a bad dream because she gave such a performance – whimpers, squeaks and a good deal of thrashing about before the climax of a muted scream so terrible that he always tried to wake her before she reached that point.

He was very cross with her, though; so cross that he was tempted to be really cruel, and let her stay in the dream to its bitter end. He lay there in the dawn light, watching her face, more childish than ever in sleep, the mouth soft and pouting a little, the long, light lashes soft as moths on her flushed cheeks. But because he loved her he could not bear her distress and as her breathing quickened and her hands clutched and clenched he put a hand on her neck, and moved her head, then shook her a little, breaking the dream, bringing her eyes open, still full of fear, sleep-mazed, but recovering, clearing as she looked at him.

'All right? Better now?'

She shuddered strongly, wiped her face with a piece of the blanket which covered them and sat up. She looked round and a little frown creased her smooth, fair brow.

'Where are we?'

'We're in a disused barn, miles from anywhere, thanks to you.' He sighed. 'There we were, comfortably settled in Moscow, both of us with good jobs, and you go and get yourself into trouble. Why on earth couldn't you have simply kept your feelings to yourself, instead of shouting about corruption? I don't understand it – it was as if you *wanted* us to be forced to leave.'

Eva smiled complacently.

'I did. I told you at least a week ago that I didn't want to stay in the flats but you wouldn't listen to me, so I watched in the

530

factory and I noticed what that foreman was up to, and I told! Do you blame me?'

'Yes, I do,' Kevi said roundly. 'It was stupid, and I can't bear stupidity, and the foreman simply said you were lying, so all that happened was you lost your good reputation and we had to leave.'

'Oh, Kevi!' Eva threw herself into his arms and kissed the tanned v of skin at the neck of his shirt. 'What does it matter? It's summer, I wanted it to be just us again, same's it was last year! We didn't save as much money as we thought we would, so why not make for the fields and woods again? No one should have to work all year through!'

'I think you made the fuss because of that girl on the landing below ours,' Kevi said shrewdly, and saw by Eva's expression that his guess had been a good one. 'Why on earth be so jealous of a girl like her? She was a decent kid, not beautiful or anything but intelligent and honest. She lent me books – you were jealous of that, too, weren't you? –.and started to teach me English! But it was plain as a pikestaff that you resented it and couldn't bear me to so much as speak to her. Why, for God's sake? She was not likely to take *your* place!'

He had expected her to pour scorn on even the suggestion, but instead she hung her head.

'Oh, you say that, but how could I be sure, when you kept going into her room and sitting over her books?'

Kevi was so exasperated that he shook her – hard this time, so that her teeth cracked together and her face went red. Then he let her go and she slumped back on the hay, tears forming in her eyes.

'Look, woman, am I never to speak to another female, or look at one, or get into the lift with one, without your jealousy making life impossible? If you're going to behave like that, I'll take a mistress just to teach you a lesson, I swear it!'

He expected fury, defiance, a hurling in his face of his promises to her when he had first made love to her, but instead the face she lifted to his was white and stricken, the mouth trembling.

'Oh, Kevi . . . don't! You are all I've got and all I want; if you went with another woman I'd kill myself. And her. And you, if I had to!'

'If you do it in that order then I'm not worried,' Kevi said.

He put his arm round her. 'Don't you see that you'll drive me to behave badly by your possessiveness? It isn't as if I've ever looked at another woman save in friendship, but you see evil where none lurks!'

Eva started to cry. 'I won't be jealous again, now that the girl on the lower landing can't bother us, really I won't! But . . . couldn't you help me a bit, Kevi? If you wouldn't laugh with them, or put your arm round them when you're together, it wouldn't be so painful for me. It's when it really starts to hurt me, in here . . .' she put a hand to her breast '. . . that I decide to take action.'

'It's natural to me to put a hand on a shoulder when I'm talking, whether it's a fellow or a girl,' Kevi said, rather untruthfully. He liked girls and possibly, left to himself, might have gone a good deal further than a friendly touch or a kiss when Eva's back was turned — but Eva's back, alas, was so rarely towards him! She kept an eagle eye on his most innocent activities and sometimes she made him feel a fool, a real mummy's boy tied to his woman's apron strings, with her sudden appearances and the way she hustled him out of the company of anyone she suspected of being attracted to him.

'You wouldn't like it if I did it,' Eva said mournfully. 'When that man pushed me into a corner in the loading bay and started to kiss me you punched him on the nose and told him to find his own woman and not try to steal other people's!'

'Well, yes, but you hated it — you were trying very hard to get him off by yourself. Now if you saw me struggling in the grip of some woman who was trying to make me kiss her, that 'ud be different. I'd welcome your interference!'

'Would you heck!' Eva scrambled to her feet, tears forgotten, and punched Kevi playfully on the shoulder. 'You're awful, Kevi the Wolf, and I love you! What shall we do now?'

'Try for work . . . no, I've a better idea. Why not travel, give ourselves a bit of a holiday? I've never seen the sea and I don't suppose you have either, so why don't we make for the coast and get work when we reach it? We've plenty of money to see us over the next few weeks — we could even ride in the train instead of on it if you like.'

'Really? You really would take me to the seaside? Oh, Kevi!'

Kevi spread out their blanket and began to put their few possessions in it. Perhaps now was a good time to try to bribe

Eva not to behave quite so badly in future.

'Look, Eva, we'll go to the seaside, but I'm warning you, I want no displays of owning me whilst we're there or I'll do something you really won't like, and that's a promise.'

'Oh Kevi, you wouldn't beat me?'

'No, indeed; you'd quite enjoy that,' Kevi said cruelly, enjoying Eva's startled purr of laughter. 'The seaside's bound to be full of girls, so if you start nagging I'll get a real little cracker and go off with her for two or three days. See?'

'You wouldn't!'

'Eva, I would! I'm a man and you don't own me!'

'I do . . . we own each other.' Eva saw his expression and shrugged sulkily. 'All right, all right, it's a deal!'

Rudi Lemensk was back in uniform and his wife was back at work. Pavel, cycling along the road, waved to the truck with its burden of soldiers and several of them waved cheerfully back because they knew that Sergeant Lemensk was the name of the man sitting up by the driver and the young girl wobbling along on the bicycle was his pretty little wife.

They did not know that she had endured every form of cure known to scientists for inability to conceive and had just emerged, still childless, from almost a year of mudbaths. If I started the course shy I'm certainly not shy any more, Pavel thought rather resentfully. Being dunked in thick, clinging warm mud by a young, intense doctor was still embarrassing after a year of it. Specimens, samples, different ideas, strange tablets . . . nothing had made the slightest difference. She had not even begun to conceive and she supposed she should be grateful that she was not pulled down by miscarriages, for she had seen other women at the Institute who seemed able to carry a child for only three or four months and thought their lot infinitely worse than her own.

It had been suggested, not unnaturally, that it might be Rudi who was at fault, but the tests which had been carried out did not find anything wrong with Rudi either. Her favourite scientist at the Institute had suggested that it might merely be that they were both too eager for babies, but since Pavel did not particularly want children, save to please Rudi, she thought this solution unlikely. Another sufferer, when they were closeted side by side in their mudbaths, had announced that she was sick of going through the mill for what she was sure was her husband's fault and was going to find herself another man.

'Only for a child, mind . . . and I shan't tell Gregor,' she assured Pavel. 'If I don't conceive after going with some young bull from the factory then I'll give up!'

But Pavel was not interested in going to such lengths; all she wanted now was to emerge from the treatment with a certificate announcing that she had done her best, and could now go back to work.

And at last, they had admitted they could help no more and had interviewed both her and Rudi to come straight out and say so.

'There's nothing wrong with either of you,' the doctor said cheerfully. 'Perhaps too much anxiety, too much eagerness for a child. What I suggest is that you both make up your minds that there will be no little ones for you and take up your normal lives again. Comrade Lemenskova should go back to work and you, Comrade Lemensk, should give up the desk job and get into uniform. I can't give you any guarantees, but let's say I wouldn't faint from surprise if, in a couple of years, you came back with a bouncing baby in your arms.'

So they had done just that. Rudi would be training recruits for a month now, leaving Pavel to cope alone, which she was perfectly capable of doing. She envied Rudi in one way, since he would be taking a party of hopeful lads, officer material he called them, into the Caucasus for a couple of weeks of intensive physical training, but other than that she was prepared to be content with her lot.

Before leaving, Rudi had bought her a puppy. Sentimentally, she had wanted to call him Baru, but had settled in the end for Techot which, freely translated, meant 'leaking'. It was unhappily appropriate at the moment, but Pavel hoped for great things by the time Rudi returned. Techot, being only very small, was in the rucksack which Pavel had slung round her shoulders; his small, fluffy head with its coal black nose was stuck out of the top, his round, dark eyes gazed eagerly at the road speeding by beneath their wheels, the people at the roadside, the occasional car and the lumbering farmers' carts. Now and then he stretched up and either chewed at his mistress's hair or nudged her neck and gave a little yap.

'He'll keep you company now, little more, but one day he'll be as good a guard dog as Baru,' Rudi had promised, putting the pup into her eager arms. Looking at its pin-like teeth, Pavel could not help thinking that someone had taken her husband for a sucker, but it was the thought that counted, and the fact that Techot looked like being both nice-natured and obedient.

But of course a puppy so young could not be left shut up in the flat all day. Rudi had probably thought of that; it was even possible that he hoped if Pavel had the pup she would not feel the need to return to work, but if so, he was disappointed. Pavel and her puppy had found work easily enough on a very big collective just outside town and they were making their way there on this bright spring morning.

'First, we will see to the pigs,' Pavel told her companion over one shoulder, and nearly wobbled off the bike. She righted herself, re-balanced, and continued both on her way and with her chatter. 'Then we will go in for breakfast . . . doubtless they will feed you as well, Techot. After that we will clean byres and stables and things for hours and hours . . . very good for our muscular development . . . and then it will be time for lunch, and we must hope it isn't bortsch, because bortsch isn't awfully good for little white puppies, it's so easy for them to grow greedy and turn into little pink puppies!'

Presently, she was joined by another cyclist, a country girl like herself who had married and moved into the city but came out each day to work. They exchanged greetings and news and their speed increased as the day brightened until at last the collective appeared and they rode down the long path between the rows and rows of crops and into the farmyard itself, there to lean their bikes against a haystack, remove their rucksacks – and, in Pavel's case, the puppy – and make their way into the big barn to be sent about their various tasks.

Alyn was not quite twelve months when Maria announced she was pregnant again. David, coming in late after an exhausting day, said, 'Grand, old girl, couldn't be better,' and Maria burst into tears.

That brought David at least partially out of his daze of

tiredness. He and Nibby were erecting a new shed on some of the land which they had paid to have cleared in the old shipyard. Having spent money on the clearance, though, they had decided that the new building, for the moment at least, would have to be a task for them, and had set about it lightheartedly a couple of months ago.

Sales, however, had been brisk and they really needed the new shed and the deeper draught which would be possible here, so now they were slogging all out to get the shed finished and then, they hoped, they would move up here, just he and Nibby, and let the men continue to work on the smaller stuff down in the old sheds.

So now, with a weeping wife on his hands, David had to pull himself together, forget his aching muscles and blistered hands, and start finding out just what was wrong. Maria did not cry without good reason.

'What's the matter, love? I thought you'd be thrilled over a second baby; you've always said you wanted a big family.'

'Yes, but not this soon; Alyn won't even be two by the time this one's born and I'm finding him a handful already.'

It was true that Alyn was a naughty baby. With his tight red curls and his wicked, laughing face, he could get into all sorts of mischief already; David could well imagine that by the time he was two he would be more than one woman's work, to say nothing of a younger child. But Maria did have help.

'Yes, but Nanny Fortescue's awfully good with him,' David said now. 'He minds her, you say. She'll help with the new baby too, I'm sure.'

'She can't give birth to it, though, can she?' Maria snatched his coat, which he'd been holding in one hand, and slung it on to the hallstand. 'You don't understand how hard it is for a woman. You're selfish, David – you never think of anyone but yourself.'

This was so unfair and so unlike Maria that David could only stare; she was obviously distraught, but why should she turn on him like this? At her own suggestion, she was the one who took precautions against unwanted pregnancies, so if anyone was to blame it must be her, not himself.

'Look, you've sprung it on me rather suddenly,' he said now, putting an arm round her waist and giving her a squeeze. 'Come into the living-room and sit on my knee and we'll talk it out sensibly.'

Sniffing, Maria agreed, but when she sank on to his lap David had hard work not to wince. She had put on a good deal of weight, and though she adored showing physical affection she had never learned to sit easily on someone's lap, but always dug her knees and elbows in where it hurt most.

'Now we're comfy tell me all about it.'

'I saw the doctor because I thought I might be ... you know ... and he says my blood pressure's too high and the baby's either big or twins and in any case I've got to lose weight. I find I've got plenty to do with one, I don't feel I can cope with another just yet, especially not with a huge big baby.' She knuckled her eyes and sniffed, her cheeks red and tearstreaked. David tried not to notice how unattractive she looked when she wept, with little success. But, he reminded himself valiantly, appearances did not matter, her happiness did. He kissed the side of her face and attempted some sweet reason.

'Look, love, losing weight won't be too bad and you'll feel better for it. What's more, if you do lose weight and keep your intake down the chances are the baby won't be any bigger than Alyn was, and look how quick and easy that birth was.'

'It may have been quick but it certainly wasn't easy,' Maria said, affronted. 'It was terribly painful, you've no idea. Quite often the quickest births are the most painful, I've heard my mother say so many a time.'

'I've heard people saying second births are much easier than first ones,' David observed, but this, it appeared, was the wrong thing too.

'Don't patronise me. It's all very well for you, demanding your marital rights, having all the fun ...'

'I never do! We make love, sure we do, but I don't demand anything, you're as keen as me!'

'I am not! I hate the whole business, if you want to know!' She heaved herself off his knee and stormed out.

David eased his aching legs, sighed and stood up. What on earth was the matter with Maria? She had been odd and rather weepy for a couple of weeks or so, but he was sure she enjoyed married life, not just bed but all of it. But he knew pregnancy made some women hard to live with at first; doubtless in a few weeks she would go back to normal again.

A month later, things were so bad that David decided to confide in Alice. Maria's tempers, tears and tantrums had got steadily worse, culminating, last night, in an evening of stony silence and then, when he had tried to make love to her, instant rejection accompanied by a diatribe about his greedy masculine desires so virulent that he had felt the iron enter his soul and had turned his back on her, determined never to touch her again without an express request that he do so.

Bewildered, hurt and also furious, because he could see no reason for her sudden rejection, David had agreed sulkily to take her to Chester for a few days to stay with her parents and see the doctor at the nursing home where she had given birth to Alyn, though he would not stay with her, of course. The Rafts had not stayed in their small house on the estate for long, but had moved into a large and handsome house in Chester with a garden which sloped down to the river.

During the drive, she had started on how she did not want this baby, and David, already upset, had reminded her, rashly, about her birth control method.

'If you didn't want another, why didn't you use your cap?' he enquired.

It was a red rag to a bull. Did he not realise how hellishly uncomfortable it was? Had he any idea of the contortions to which Maria must stoop to get it into an effective position? And anyway, if she had not used it, it was because she had not expected him to make such sudden and unmannerly demands, so it all came down to his attitude, in the end.

Next evening, straight after work he went back to the cottage.

He had chosen a good time. Alice was in the garden, setting plants in the front beds; Nibby and Michael were up at the sheds still and Sara, of course, was in college. Richard, having had his tea, a bath and a bottle, was in bed and asleep, so David was able to confide in his sister without fear of interruption.

'Alice, old girl,' he started, squatting down on the garden path beside her. 'I'm in trouble. Have you any idea what's wrong with Maria?'

Alice sat back on her heels and dusted her hands together.

'Wrong with her? Well, I wondered if she was expecting again . . . is she?'

'You mean she hasn't told you? That beats cockfighting. I'd have sworn you'd have been the first to know. Yes, she's expecting again, and she's been absolutely awful, to put it mildly. I can't do a thing right, she blames me for the whole thing though she's got a Dutch cap she's supposed to use — unless, of course, she wanted more children. And now she's made it plain she doesn't want to make love any more.'

'Some women think it wrong to do it when they're pregnant,' Alice observed. 'Maria's quite old-fashioned in some ways; does she think it will do harm?'

'No, of course not! Alyn's all right, and we . . . well, she didn't object then. Quite the opposite, in fact.'

'Is she being poorly, do you suppose? Morning sickness and so on?'

'She was, but she's over it. It's almost as if she's suddenly realised she doesn't like me much, after all. I can tell you, life's hell down at the Hall right now.'

'Well . . . once or twice lately, when I've heard her snap at you, I've wondered if she's suffering from a guilt thing.'

'Guilt? What on earth do you mean?'

Alice laughed and got to her feet.

'Let's have a cup of tea and finish our chat indoors. There are people who think Maria entrapped you, you know. They think she caught you by getting pregnant with Alyn so that the only thing you could do was marry her.'

'What nonsense! She let me choose, take the decision; if I'd asked her to have an abortion she'd have gone ahead with it. No, I put my own head in the noose, if you understand me.'

'Oh, Davie!' Alice's eyes were full of sympathy. 'You're a good old boy; you deserve better than she's handing out at present. Do you want me to have a word with her?'

But this David could not allow. He would speak to her, come to some sort of agreement. He left Alice that evening sure that things would soon improve. After all, despite the fact that he knew he was not in love with Maria, they had had a good marriage by many standards until she found herself pregnant once more. When the new baby was born the would be her old self again, he was sure of it.

A week later, Maria came home. She made sharp remarks about the amount of time he had spent in the nursery with Alyn and Nanny Fortescue, though heaven knew Nanny was a respectable enough companion, engaged to the blacksmith in the village and with a flat chest and large feet. Other than that she was just as before; sharp and critical. She would not say a word about her little break and when David asked her what the doctor at the nursing home had said she turned a bright scarlet and told him to mind his own business. When he pressed her, really worried now, she told him quite cold-bloodedly that they were not, after all, going to have a second child.

'I decided I wouldn't go through with it,' she said, undressing for bed and then sitting down in front of the dressing-table to brush out her hair. 'That's why I went; they admitted me to the nursing home and it was all over in a couple of days.'

David stared. 'You had an abortion? Without telling me?'

'That's right. I don't want any more children, though I'm fond of Alyn. Now that the decision's made I'm going to ask Alice to bring Ricky here more often; the little boys are lovely together, it's nice for both of them to have another child to play with.'

David was bewildered and hurt that she should choose to have an abortion when the child was legitimate and would have been dearly loved, but he felt that it was her business because he knew that he did not love her and probably never would. He would never leave her, but though he would do his best to be a good husband he would never try to flog his flagging spirit into loving her. She had chosen to take her own decision over their unborn child and he could not deny her the right. But all his love, in future, would go to their son.

'Have some more chicken, Father.'

David was always polite to his in-laws and this was the first time they had been round to dinner since Maria's abortion, so though David would not have dreamed of mentioning the matter he could not help a certain curiosity. After all, Maria had been staying with them when she went into the nursing home . . . did they approve? It seemed unlikely – no one could have been prouder or fonder of a grandson than they were of Alyn – but on the other hand they had always been indulgent parents. Would their indulgence stretch to the aborting of an unwanted second grandchild?

Mr Raft refused more chicken with a genteel shake of the head, then had three helpings of the cook's raspberry cheese-cake. But later, when David took him down to show him how work was progressing on the new boat shed, he grasped David's arm and squeezed it affectionately.

'It were a dreadful thing,' he said obscurely, nodding away, 'But you're a brave lad, same as our lass. A brave couple.'

Clearly, David thought angrily, Maria had told them she had lost the child and not that she had got rid of it. But again, that was Maria's business, not his. He had been forced to admit to Alice that the baby would not, now be born, but even with her he had not even hinted at the truth and Alice, too, assumed Maria had lost the child due to junketings whilst on holiday with her parents.

When the Rafts were leaving, having gone up to the nursery to kiss the cheek of little Alyn, still for once as his grandmother indulgently remarked, Mrs Raft, in her turn, took the opportunity of a quiet word with David whilst Maria and her father discussed the petrol consumption of his new Rolls. She drew David aside, a fat little paw on his forearm.

'Be good to her, David, and patient. It's a hard thing for a woman, to lose a little one.'

David, gritting his teeth, assured her that he would continue to be good to Maria, and when they got into their own room he asked her rather tartly why she had ever told her parents that there was a baby, rather than simply keeping them in ignorance of the whole thing.

'Of course I had to tell them; how else could I have afforded the nursing home?' she said brusquely. 'Oh, I didn't tell them it was for an abortion, if that's what's worrying you, I told them an investigation because I'd been so sick. And then I said I'd lost the baby, so it was all right, they neither of them suspected.'

'I see. Well, I dare say it's all for the best. Will you read for a bit tonight, or do you want to go straight to sleep?'

'I'll go straight to sleep, thanks. I'm very tired.'

But David thought she did not sleep for some while; she lay beside him to be sure in the darkness, very straight and still, but he heard her light breathing for a long while and once, when it seemed to falter and she gave a little gulp, he thought she was crying and moved to touch her hand.

'Maria? Are you . . .'

'Leave me alone, David!' She snatched her hand away at once and her voice was strident, irritable. 'I'm going to get a bed put up in the dressing-room. I think it would be better for both of us.'

He said nothing, but withdrew to his own side of the bed immediately and very quickly fell asleep.

'Maria doesn't look well,' Alice remarked in August, when the entire family had decided on a trip to the seaside and Maria had agreed to accompany them. They were all sitting on the sands at Llandudno, in the shelter of one of the breakwaters, whilst Maria, a little distance off, introduced an excited Alyn to the delights of paddling. She held him under the arms and swung him back and forth so that his toes dashed up a spray, making him squeak with excitement. Nearby, Nibby and Richard were building a sandcastle solely in order that Richard could trample it flat again with bare pink feet, so Alice and David could talk uninterrupted. 'She's lost quite a bit of weight.'

'Yes, the doctor said she must ages ago,' David affirmed. 'She's not thin, though.'

'No, not thin, but a bit strained. Come to that, old boy, you don't exactly look in the pink yourself.'

'Oh, I'm all right.' David lowered his voice. 'We're getting on better since she moved out of our bedroom. But she's terribly touchy and easily annoyed – she howls for no reason that I can see and then when I try to comfort her she hits out at me, physically and orally, and I slink away feeling a beast.'

'That's awful, Davie! But I had a word with the doctor last time he came in to see Rick, and he said high blood pressure can make women very difficult to live with. They can appear almost insane at times, when the weather's warm and they're anxious anyway.'

'Yes, perhaps that's it,' David said without much conviction. 'Never mind, at least you never hear her shout at or even get annoyed with Alyn.'

And that, he reflected, getting to his feet and strolling down the beach towards his wife and child, was the weirdest thing of all, that she, who claimed not to like children, not to want more babies, could have endless patience with their naughty little son – and not only with him but with Richard too, when Alice brought him visiting.

He reached the pool just as Maria, arms obviously tiring, sat their child down plonk on the sand beside the water. David bent over and tickled Alyn's toes, getting a gleeful gurgle and a handful of wet sand at the same moment.

'You little devil! Just you wait, Daddy will throw you . . .' he picked the baby up and swung him back and forth, 'right into the sea!'

'He'd probably love it,' Maria observed. 'One of these days, young man, your daddy will teach you to swim, and how will you like *that*, eh?'

'Why can't you teach him? Why is it always Daddy who had to do the nasty things, like sloshing around in freezing cold water?' David said plaintively.

'I can't swim,' Maria said briefly. 'Come on, Al, Mummy will show you how to build a sandcastle!'

'Mr David!' Gill came flying down the sloping lawn as David hurried down to the water. It was Sunday, and since Maria seemed to have no desire whatsoever for his company he thought he would take himself off sailing for the day.

'What is it? What's the matter?' His first thought was for Alyn, eating his breakfast egg when he had last set eyes on him, yolk up to the eyebrows. 'Is the lad all right?'

'Yes, he's fine. But . . . you're sailing today?'

'Yes, I thought I would.'

'Oh. It – it's awfully windy and wild. And Mrs Thomas gets upset when you're out in bad weather. I – I wondered if you might stay at home with her today.'

David stared. This was unprecedented! For the past week all Maria had done every time she set eyes on him was nag, and he was frankly fed up. He thought he had the sympathy of all the staff, for he often saw surreptitious glances cast first at Maria and then in his direction which seemed to indicate wry understanding.

'Gill, are you *sure*? Mrs Thomas almost ordered me out of the house just now – didn't you hear her?'

'Well, Mr David, I did, and I tell you straight I don't know what's got into her but I do know she's up there now, lying on the big bed, crying as if her heart was breaking.'

He made it up to the house in twenty seconds flat, even running uphill, and then crept up the stairs and into their bedroom.

Maria was lying on the big bed where he now slept, through no fault of his own, in solitary splendour. She was clutching his pillow, with her head buried in it, and crying, as Gill had said, as if her heart would break.

David sat down on the bed very gently and put his arms round her shoulders. She jumped as if she had been shot, and then sat up, her face tear-blubbered, and tried to wrench herself free of him. Normally David would have allowed her to escape, but this time, in the face of such distress, he held on tight.

'No, don't struggle, my love, just let me cuddle you until you feel better,' he crooned, pulling her into his arms. 'Come on, Mea, tell me why you're crying, don't hate me, don't hate me . . .'

'H-hate you? Oh, David, I don't hate you!' The words were torn from her despite herself and she made another futile effort to escape, but she was weak from her long bout of tears and he had little difficulty in holding her still in his arms.

'Come on, go on crying if it helps, and then tell me what's the matter,' he coaxed, heaving her right up and on to his lap. This time she did not resist but simply lay, sobbing, against his chest.

He did not know when or indeed why the comfort suddenly turned into something stronger and more positive, he only knew that it did and that Maria seemed to have cast off the shell of rage and dislike which she had worn for so long. She let him love her, she was sweet to him, and when he lay quiet on the bed at last, his arms still round her, she heaved a great, deep sigh and said softly, 'Oh, David, I'll never forget how nice you were to me just now!'

David chuckled. 'You were pretty nice yourself. Now isn't that a lot better than being cross and horrible and bottling things up? Going to tell me what was the matter, why you were crying?'

She sat up and picked up a brush off the bedside table. It was one of his but she began brushing her long, thick hair. It crackled with electricity and he smiled lazily up at her, lounging on his back, enjoying this moment of quiet together – the first for months and months.

'There's nothing the matter – not now. I'd kept it up for too long, being . . . oh, never mind, I'm so happy now, David!'

'Good; you sound like the Maria I married instead of the one who's been snapping and snarling at me lately. You've not been well, but you're obviously feeling better.'

'Yes. Much.' She continued to brush, gazing out through the window at the wind-lashed branches of the cedar tree. 'Well, off you go, then, have a nice sail – but don't go out too far, will you? I get terribly nervous when you go out a long way – I don't trust the sea one bit.'

'That's because you can't swim. You must let me teach you.'

She looked across at him, the brush suspended, her eyes very bright. 'Maybe I will. Do go now, Davie. Be home in good time for tea, won't you? I've asked Alice and Nibby over.'

'Oh, charming . . . still, you did tell me in the end! But I won't bother to go sailing; I'd rather stay here with you and the boy.'

She looked crestfallen; her smile faltered.

'David, trust you . . . please go off, just as you'd planned. Be very careful and come back in nice time for tea, but do go! I've got a lot to do before you come home and Alice and Nibby arrive.'

He let himself be persuaded because it was obviously what she wanted, but on his way down he popped into the kitchen and there was Gill, sitting on the table swinging her legs and watching the cook making pastry. She slid off the table when she saw David and came over to him so that they could talk without the entire staff overhearing.

'Well, Mr David? Was she all right?'

'No, you were absolutely right to fetch me, and thanks very much, my dear . . . but she's all right now. We reached a better understanding than we've had for months and months, thanks to you. You don't know what she's planning for this afternoon, do you?'

'No, sir. Why?'

'Oh, because I suggested staying behind, not going out with the yacht, and she was horrified, said she'd got something planned. A surprise, no doubt. Alice and her husband are coming to tea though, so it may have something to do with that.'

'Cook's making a very sustaining tea, so probably Master Michael's coming too,' Gill remarked, chuckling. 'I'll keep an eye on her for you, sir, but I'm sure everything will be all right now.'

It was a good day for a sail in the right boat, David reflected, as he struggled to turn his little craft head to wind. He had had a magnificent day, one of the best, sailing way out almost as far as Point of Ayr, going round Hilbury island where he had once spent such an eventful night, and coming up the estuary again at a spanking pace, in what he hoped would be good time for tea.

The tide was with him too, which helped pile the knots on. Above, the sky lowered, dark, ragged grey clouds hurling themselves across the heavens as though they, too, were racing with the tide.

It was always weird, sailing with the ingoing water, feeling godlike in the power that surged and hissed and swept you inshore. David stood at the tiller, watching the cloudrace and the sail and shouting aloud in his delight as he and his craft whipped past the buoys, a solitary bobbing seagull, the earth-bound trees and reeds straining to the wind's command. 'Faster than a horse can gallop!' he shouted as they bore down upon the old sheds where once he and Nibby had started their small business. As the speed increased David began to declaim, hurling the words of the old poem up into the heedless wind: *The western wind was wild and dank with foam, and all alone went she!* It was true, the boat was the only craft on the estuary, and now, as they flew, foam did indeed fly off the bows and cling for a moment to the taut sail.

The exhilaration was so great that he nearly missed the landing stage but he spotted it in time and grabbed a rope to pull his mainsail loose and turned the tiller. She slowed, slowed, slowed . . . and then, right ahead of him, he saw something turning, bobbing and turning, as the tide raced onward.

No one could have spent as much time as David had on the Dee estuary without recognising it, albeit with a sinking of the heart. A body. Some poor sailor, perhaps, lost overboard a hundred miles away and brought here to rest by the racing tide. Or a cocklewoman, leaving it to the last minute to take her bucket ashore. Or a fisherman, torn from the rocks by the spiteful seventh wave and sucked into oblivion. He knew the procedure, of course. He lowered the sail and got out the oars and rowing strongly, manoeuvring neatly, he trapped the thing ... for it could not possibly have lived, not in that racing, eager flood of water ... with an oar against a sand-bank and then hauled it aboard and tumbled it into the bottom of the boat.

It was Maria.

He rowed ashore dumb with shock, and the rain began and soaked him until he was as wet as the corpse in the bottom of the boat. He tied up despite hands numb with cold and climbed out of the boat, the body in his arms. She was sodden, yet lighter than he would have expected.

Three yards up the bank and she had grown heavy, too heavy to be held in the arms like a child. He put her over his shoulder gently, carefully, saved from the horror of what he held by the deep inner conviction that it could not possibly be she.

It took him a long time to reach the house and when he did, and let himself in through the side door, he could not bring himself to slither the body down on to the floor, the tiles already puddling with mud from his feet. He carried her through into the hall ... and saw that the maid had just opened the front door to Alice and Nibby, with the little boy in Nibby's arms and everyone smiling and exclaiming.

David stood very still; water dripped off him, he could see the rain shining on his lashes, each one carried its tiny diamond chip of liquid. The water dripped faster off his burden, though, pattering down on to the big marbled tiles, falling like rain, like salt rain, like a flood.

Alice said: 'Hello, David, what have you got there?' and she was smiling, pretty, her hair curling briskly, just touched

with rain, the surface of her curls just misted with it. Not like
. . . not like the hair which hung down by his knees, thick and
black and sewn with sand and weed . . . mermaid's hair.
Dead hair. The corpse's hair.

Nibby said: 'Hush . . . better get out of here, Allie, love,
and take the boy, it's . . .' and Alice cried out low and sorry
and came towards him and David backed away, and slid on
the marble, and felt dizzy and cold . . . cold as the thing
which dripped and dripped over his shoulder . . . cold as his
hands and his face. Cold as his heart.

When she was laid out and washed and cleaned from the
sand and the sea, he imagined she had come down after him,
come down to persuade him not to go after all, and had
somehow tripped, fainted, fallen into the flooding tide. That
was what they all thought, at first. But then, after the brandy
and a hot bath, he went into his bedroom – her body was in
the blue room – and found the note.

It told him everything, it solved all the puzzles. It made him
feel at once the biggest cad in the universe and a fool and . . .
thank God . . . a man who had done his best.

She had gone to the doctor after Alyn's birth and he had
been worried by certain symptoms and had treated her for
them . . . a growth, he had said, but curable, he was sure. She
had said nothing, believing that to worry her husband or her
parents was foolish and unnecessary. Then she found she was
pregnant and, delighted, returned to the doctor. He told her
that the growth was far advanced and that she was unlikely
to live to bear the child which, in any case, would only be a
burden to the father, left to cope alone. He advised her to
have an abortion, during the course of which they would
remove as much of the growth as was practicable, to perhaps
prolong her life a little.

She was sorry she had been so horrible to him, she said, in
her rather uneducated handwriting. She had not meant it, but
oh, it had hurt her to destroy their child, she could not face
doing it again . . . for to conceive again when the pregnancy
could not possibly go to full term would be a deliberate sin.

Knowing that she was going to leave him she had not
wanted him to get more and more fond of her, and besides,
demonstrations of affection only made her cry and that upset

him; so she had kept him at arm's length until that very morning.

*It was very sweet, and you were wonderful,* she wrote, and surely at that point her handwriting was firmer, the words more decisively chosen? *But it didn't matter by then, you see, because I'd made up my mind to finish this afternoon, and I'm going to do so. The pain's worse and that means my temper's more difficult to hold, and I've never been horrid to Alyn and I won't start now; I want him to think of me kindly. Thank you, David, for my happiest years, and don't worry that you didn't love me – I knew it right from the start and it didn't matter; what mattered was that I loved you.* She had signed off with no flourish, no bravado. Just with *Love from Maria,* like a little girl.

David stayed in his room a long time, looking at the letter. He thought about burning it, but then decided not to do so but to keep it well hidden away. If people believed it to be an accident, then an accident it would remain. But if there was ever any query, he wanted the letter to exist and not to be lost for ever. Having made up his mind, he went down to where Alice and Nibby waited.

Alice had wept and wept; she and Maria had grown first friendly and then fond. Their children were about the same age, they had many similar interests. Nibby was practical and sensible as ever. He would arrange the funeral, he had already sent for an undertaker . . . would David like him to drive over to Maria's parents and break the news to them?

David went himself, and brought his in-laws back with him to help keep an eye on the little lad as his mother-in-law phrased it and to see their daughter's body and to arrange the funeral.

Alyn was too young to know what was going on, which was a good thing. Alice came every day and of course Nanny Fortescue was marvellous, keeping the baby amused and pushing him out each morning in his big black pram with the blanket with lambs and ducklings embroidered on it and letting him toddle round the nursery all day, wiping away a tear when he called Alice 'Mumma' and telling everyone what a wonderful woman Mrs Thomas had been.

David stumbled through the days, not knowing where he stood or what he should do next; leave the house? It was not his, it was his father-in-law's. After the funeral, when the family gathered, he mentioned the fact to Mr Raft and was advised, gruffly, that the house was his as long as he wanted it and young Alyn's after.

'Nay, we've no use for it, lad,' Mr Raft said, his old eyes red-rimmed from much secret weeping. 'What good would it do us, wi' the Chester house an' all? We never gave it to Maria in so many words, perhaps, but it were hers and now it's yours. Boatyard an' all.'

He thanked the old man, of course, and then went round amongst his guests and received their condolences and tried very hard not to wonder what they were thinking. And later, when they had all gone and the cook had brought him a good hot dinner because he looked poorly still, he got up and walked round the great house, ownership of which he had coveted for so long, and found he hated it.

After a whisky and then another he went up to his room and fell, exhausted, into bed. He tried to remember the house as it had been before Maria but it was gone into the mists of the past. Carmel Hall now held only the ghost of his married life here, though the old life would come back once he had become reconciled to his loss.

He had not loved her, yet he knew he would miss her. She had done her best to drive him away for his own sake but she had never quite succeeded, and now he would keep only gentle memories of her.

There was a fire in the grate because Gill said he would need a warm room whilst the weather remained so chilly. He could hear the logs creaking and settling as it burned down and down and finally went out. He lay for a long time listening to the fire and regretting every harsh thought he had ever allowed into his mind towards his wife, and just before he slept he remembered how, on the day she died, she had lain across this bed hugging his pillow and weeping.

It brought his tears then, and he wept for her.

# CHAPTER TWENTY-THREE

'Isn't it odd, he longed for Carmel all those years ... I suppose we all did ... yet now that it really belongs to us Thomases again he doesn't want it. He says it's too big and lonely and old-fashioned and it reminds him of Maria, and he wants to move out.'

Alice, bathing Richard with difficulty, because of her expanding waistline, for she was expecting a second child in less than a month, spoke to Nibby between splashing bouts. Now she lured her son's attention away from vigorous attempts to rid his bath of water and got him to try drowning a plastic duck, whose vigorous resurfacing after each attempt earned it roars of laughter.

'He's lonely,' Nibby said unnecessarily, since Alice was all too aware of her brother's condition. 'What he wants is a woman.'

'He's got the cook, and Gill, and Nanny Fortescue and all the rest, what does he want with another one?' Alice smirked at her deliberate obtuseness and Nibby bent over the bath and splashed a bit more water on to her rubber-aproned lap.

'Cheeky brat, you know very well what I mean. He should remarry.'

'Oh, that! Actually, I disagree. He married Maria on the rebound from that little Pavel he talked so much about and look what happened. The last thing he wants is to try again. No, what he really wants is a companion, someone to share the house.'

'That's right, another wife.'

'No, Nibby! Can't you understand that he doesn't want his emotions all churned up again, not so soon? He simply wants companionship.'

Nibby leaned over and gave her a quick kiss on the cheek,

then reached into the bath and abstracted Richard, who immediately began to shout his dismay at being forced to leave the bath and then, on being plonked on to his mother's lap, squiggled off it and ran, wet and naked and steaming, out of the bathroom and could be heard giggling richly as he descended the stairs.

'Oh, Nibs, do fetch him, he'll slip . . .'

Nibby was back in a moment with the miscreant soaking his shirt and demanding to go back in the water, but as soon as Alice began to dry him he stopped shouting and lolled comfortably in her arms, muttering away to himself about the supper he intended to eat presently and ignoring the adult conversation taking place above his head.

'Where were we? Oh yes, I was leading up to making a suggestion.'

'I can guess it,' Nibby said rather gloomily. 'Darling, I know the cottage isn't much and I know you feel Alyn needs a mother as well as Nanny Fortescue and David, but I really don't want to surrender my independence, such as it is.'

'Do you think I want to? Oh, Carmel Hall was my home and I love it still, but even so I wouldn't want to leave here. No, what I was going to suggest is that we let Michael and Sara move in. Sara's such a lively girl and despite having a hundred boyfriends she hasn't shown the slightest wish to marry any of them and with her lovely degree in modern languages she shouldn't have any trouble in getting a job locally. People want languages, especially in shipbuilding, when they're dealing with foreign buyers and so on.'

'It's a great idea,' Nibby said, showing too much enthusiasm; Alice stood up, Richard, towel-wrapped, in her arms, and gave him a slit-eyed look. 'Are you trying to tell me something, dearest?' she asked sweetly.

'Well, it would be nice just to be us three . . . or us four, pretty soon,' Nibby admitted. 'And it would give the kids more scope; Michael gets pretty frustrated not being able to ask friends home without endless planning because of space and Ricky's bedtime.'

'All right, we're agreed then. Will you put it to David or shall I?'

'Me. I'll go down there later and we'll talk it all out. I've been meaning to have a chat about the new sheds for ages, only somehow the moment I get into them it's all go until leaving-off time, and then we're both too tired to care.'

'Go down after dinner,' Alice suggested as they went through to their bedroom. During termtime Richard slept in Michael's room but because of its size she always got him ready for bed in their own quarters.

'Yes, all right. What's cooking?'

'Beef and onion pie. And a rice pud for afters. If you can get down to the Hall full of that little lot you'll be doing well – or are you going to drive?'

Their car was elderly and jealously used, for though building small boats was making them a living, it was not making them rich.

'No, I'll use Mike's bicycle.' Richard, gowned and ready for bed, slid off Alice's knee and headed for his own room, remarking over his shoulder as he went that he wanted his teddy from downstairs before the story.

'I'll get it,' Nibby said amiably. 'What a demanding child we've reared, Mrs Hawke! You start on the story, then perhaps I'll get my food a bit sooner.'

David had his own meal in solitary splendour, brought to the table by the latest girl that Mrs Grimm was 'training up', as she put it. They did not stay long, the girls, partly because there was no good bus route into town for the cinema and partly, David believed, because Mrs Grimm bossed them about and they felt the lack of a mistress to whom they might otherwise have complained.

It was a good meal but he was not terribly hungry; he moved roast lamb and roast potatoes into and out of the gravy and mint sauce and turned the peas from a neat pyramid into a scattered skein, then sat back and waited for the pudding to arrive. He thought about his sudden ownership of the Hall.

Mr Raft had made it over to David, by deed of gift, in trust for Alyn. And he had done the same with the old shipyard. He had also made over Maria's personal money, which meant that it was possible to keep the house staffed and so on, though it still meant David would have to begin making big money soon, or the house would simply be an albatross hung round his neck, costing him more than he could ever afford.

Sometimes he felt grateful for the gift and sometimes not; where on earth would he get the money to dredge out the channel and get the shipyard into production again when there was a world-wide depression on? War and rumours of war did not ease matters, though he supposed that if there was a war at least ships would be in greater demand than they were at the moment. But could he build them? Trawlers were a possibility and biggish yachts, but nothing larger, or not yet, at any rate. The long-ago scheme to take a look at the wreck of the *Royal Gold* and then use the old designs to recreate her seemed like the ravings of an unsound mind. He had been very young then, very hopeful, seeing the world as his oyster, waiting to be used.

If he had Pavel to spur him on ... would it make a difference? He knew it would. He could still, after so long, see her as clearly as though she stood before him; the short, softly waving boyish hair, the big, greeny-grey eyes, the humour in her tilted smile. It was no use telling himself that by now she had been married three years and would have a string of children and hips like a barn door, because he simply did not believe it. She was *his*, confound it, and that Pavel, his Pavel, was still there somewhere. Unattainable perhaps but existing.

In the middle of the pudding course Nibby bounded in and at once his heart lifted. He waved a spoon at Nibby to bring up a second chair and told the girl to fetch another helping of summer pudding. Nibby made a token protest, of course, but he had a legendary appetite; he waded in and was replacing his spoon on a spotlessly clean dish long before David had done more than eat about half his fruit. When he explained his errand, however, David had to tell him how things stood.

'It isn't just the size and the loneliness, it's money,' he told Nibby, over coffee in the conservatory. 'Mr Raft doesn't understand, but a place like this needs constant work unless you can figure out a way to make it pay for itself. Once, the shipyard ran the house as well, without effort, then of course when the Rafts bought it they had all the revenue from their shoe shops and clothing factories. But now, even with Maria's money, I'll be at my wit's end in two years to know how to keep going. I can't sell it, that's written into the trust fair enough, but the time will come when I can't live in it, either. So I've been very tempted by the idea of moving out now, before it's used up all the little money I do have, and taking a flat or even a cottage somewhere near at hand. With no staff to pay and no everyday running costs, I might keep it in reasonable repair for the next few years.'

'I can't advise you,' Nibby admitted. 'You'd think that with the size of the grounds and the size of the house you could do something with it, but I suppose you aren't allowed?'

'Yes I am, I can do anything I like with it provided I don't raze the house to the ground or muck up Alyn's inheritance in any way,' David assured him.

'Then there has to be a way.' Nibby scowled into his coffee. 'Look, have Mike and Sassy for the summer vac., and we'll all think hard. We're bound to come up with something.'

Kevi moved round their room like a shadow. He had a bag in one hand and he was selecting items and dropping them into it, choosing perhaps a little haphazardly, a little carelessly, but at least doing it at last.

He was leaving Eva. He had threatened, talked about it, even thought about it, but now he was doing it. Whenever he looked towards the bed his resolution wavered, so then he looked at the piece of torn newspaper on the corner of the dressing-table and it gave him the impetus to continue packing.

He had just put his newly washed and ironed shirt into the bag when Eva stirred and he froze, unable to resist glancing across at her as her movement brought her face free of the covers and one childish arm came up and lay across the pillow, the fingers slightly curved, the skin a smooth, light brown.

Looking at her, it was impossible to believe that she was anything but a lovely child and a peaceful, innocent one at that. In fact, Kevi was still by no means sure — but he did know that the jealousy which she did not seem able to control was souring their relationship. He had to take a stand some time, and here seemed a good place to leave her.

They were in a decent room for once, at a seaside resort in Georgia. He had enquired about the outlook for the winter and was told that winter was cooler, certainly, but not like winters in the rest of Russia. Here, they ate well all year round and did not suffer from cold. And because it was a resort much favoured by eminent Party members money flowed quite freely, so there would be work for her after he'd gone. He hoped she would find another man, though it stabbed him like a dagger in the heart, the thought of his Eva in someone else's bed. But, he reminded himself fiercely, one must be practical; leaving her might well be the saving of her. Without him to be jealous of, perhaps the jealousy would dissipate.

The last item went into the bag. Kevi glanced round, went towards the piece of newspaper to take it with him and then changed his mind. It might be better to leave it; she might read it or she might not – it might mean something to her or it might not – but he would let her work it out for herself.

He moved to the door. As his hand touched the door knob she stirred again and muttered something. He hesitated and heard the dream begin. He put the bag down as she began to whimper; should he push the bag out of sight, get back into bed, and comfort her out of the nightmare? If she woke too soon she might follow him, trail him across country, refuse to let him out of her sight.

He hesitated, irresolute, then, taking courage from the fact that she had temporarily ceased to mutter and move, he slipped outside the door and shut and locked it behind him. Then he put the key down on the floor. That would prevent her following him until she could wake someone up to let her out.

He began to steal down the stairs. As he reached the foyer and pushed his way out into the still dark street, though there was a paler line to the east, he heard the scream start, wobbling up from a moan to a shriek, in the room he had just left.

He hurried, then, running on his rubber-soled shoes as hard as he could in the direction of the railway station. It was only her nightmare – poor brat – but he dared not stay. Eva must learn to come to terms with her dreams alone, as he must.

Eva's own scream woke her; she lay, panting and sweat-soaked, too terrified even to move until she was sure she was safe in bed and not still in the dream, falling, falling.

She had suffered the dream for a long time, but Kevi usually woke her before it reached the worst stage, the part where the woman seized her in her arms and leapt from the cliff. This time, though, he had not been in bed so he had been unable to rescue her. No wonder she felt so dreadful, no wonder her heart and head pounded the way they did! Poor Kevi, he must have slipped out of bed to go to the lavatory on the half-landing – he had drunk a lot of wine at the party they had attended the previous evening – and was presumably still there, possibly suffering from a hangover.

When the terror receded a little and her heart slowed to normal, she sat up and looked towards the door. It was closed, which was odd but not unknown; Kevi did not much like leaving her in the room, sleeping, with the door open. There were always strange people in cheap apartment blocks, you could not be too careful.

She waited a bit, then slid out of bed and padded over to the basin on the table by the window. There was a thin sliver of soap and a good, thick towel. She was naked so it would be easy to wash herself down, dry herself and then wander back to bed. She did not want to greet Kevi when he staggered back into the room, probably with a fierce headache, smelling of fear and of a long night in bed. Better to be sweet and welcoming – there had been too many reproaches lately, too many tears and tempers. She knew it, but with so many girls lying about the beach, so many in the dance halls and on the streets, it had been impossible to ignore the way his eyes slid over every passing female.

When she was nice again she went and lay on the bed and waited. She waited and waited, but he did not come.

She went over to the door; perhaps he had been taken ill, perhaps he needed her!

The door was locked.

Puzzled, Eva went to the window and looked out. It was only just beginning to get light – where on earth was he? She walked back to the door, tried it again, then stood back and examined it as though a good, long scrutiny might reveal the secret of its being locked against her.

Presently, just to make certain, she gave it a tentative rattle; then she lay on the floor and peered underneath it. Odd! She

557

could see the key lying on the boards outside, glinting in some stray ray of light. Had Kevi gone off early, locked her in by mistake, and then knocked the key out somehow? It seemed unlikely but what other explanation could there be?

Outside, the light was strengthening. Eva brushed her hair and went to clean her teeth, then noticed Kevi's toothbrush wasn't there. Her heart gave a most peculiar little hop. She ran across to the chest of drawers where they kept their clothes and checked, her breathing coming very fast. His shirts had gone and his grey wool jumper. She tried their hanging cupboard; his trousers had gone. She looked under the bed; no shoes, or at least only her light sandals.

He must be teasing her, of course, pretending to do what he had so often threatened; he would not really leave her, he could not do such a thing, she was his, if he had packed a bag he would have packed her in it, he would never leave her, not really.

But perhaps, in her heart, she believed it, when she saw that he had taken his long knife. A thin dagger, it never left him when they were on the move. It was his sole defence, but it cut through ropes that might have hindered them, it hacked firewood out of a thicket, it gutted rabbits and jointed them, it was used as a spit to hold the meat over their fire. He did not carry it at work or when he was just strolling around a town or city; he left it at home where it came in useful to peel potatoes or to slice old, iron-hard swedes into cubes for the pot.

Once she knew the knife had gone she knew Kevi had gone too. Leaving her. Deliberately.

For a moment she panicked; she ran at the door, rattling it desperately, calling out in a loud voice that she was locked in . . . she was in No. 3, on the second floor, and would some-one please come at once. No one did, of course, because it was very early in the morning, but she did hear a groan from the flat next to theirs and someone swore, quite loudly.

After that she calmed down, because panicking was use-less. She got an ordinary kitchen knife and went to the door, then lay on her tummy and slid the blade under it. It took time, but at last she had the key on the right side of the door once more and was able to unlock it.

Able, yes. But she did not do it, for suddenly there was a

dangerous world out there, waiting to get in, and she did not want to let it near her, not until she had worked out what she was going to do.

She went over the room with a fine-tooth comb then, and of course the first thing she noticed, almost, was the torn piece of newspaper. She glanced at it without much interest, it was only newspaper, but when she had searched the rest of the room and discovered nothing but that Kevi had taken their money, though he had left her a fat little bag of roubles, she turned once more to the newspaper. Perhaps there would be a sign there, a clue of some sort.

The first side she read had a story, very brief and bare, about a girl being found, knifed to death, in a room in a town somewhere, at some time. It was only a torn piece, she could not tell whether it was a very old paper or quite a recent edition. So no help there. She turned over to the back . . . and it was an account of an expedition into the Caucasus, to tell the Soviet citizens how wonderfully well the collectives were doing now that they had been established for a few years.

Eva sat and stared at the article for a long time, wondering. Then she got up and began to throw her own things into one of the blankets from the bed. It was clear as clear – he had gone to the Caucasus, perhaps even to the farm she had called home for so long! Why he had gone there she had no idea, save that he wanted to punish her for her bad behaviour – she acknowledged that it had been bad – but it never would be so again, she was a reformed character!

She had all her things, or all the ones she needed, packed neatly in the blanket, when she remembered that she was leaving quite unprotected, thanks to Kevi taking their knife. She searched through their poor collection of cutlery and found the old bread-knife, which was long and fairly strong and would, she supposed, do in an emergency. Then she started off downstairs.

On the second landing a door opened and a head poked round it. It was Mitzi, and she had caused trouble with Kevi by enticing him to go swimming with her when Eva wanted him to remain by her, lying on the nice warm sand. Mitzi was vile, a really wicked, nasty girl. She pulled a face at Eva, then popped back into her room. Mitzi was a bad sort of girl in other ways, too – she took men to her room. Kevi might easily have gone there, only Eva had been too careful, had never let him out of her sight.

This morning he had been out of her sight. He had locked her in. Suppose he had gone to Mitzi? Suppose he had left the paper as a false sign of his whereabouts, hoping that Eva would go rushing off to the Caucasus in hot pursuit, leaving Kevi lying quiet in Mitzi's sordid little room?

Only one way to find out. Eva went to Mitzi's door and tried the handle. It opened easily. She slipped inside, pulling her blanket-wrapped bundle after her and dropping it against the door. Mitzi was lounging on the bed, naked, painting her toenails with goldy stuff out of a little bottle. She did not stop when she saw Eva but merely said baldly, 'What in hell are you doing here? Get out of my room!'

'Where's Kevi?'

'I don't know; you don't mean to say he's not with you?' She laughed, then held one foot high in the air, admiring the glistening half circles of gold. 'Well, Eva, you are slipping!'

'Has he been here?'

'Mind your own business!'

Eva was about to leave the room when she thought she heard someone or something move in the curtained off part where they all kept their clothing. Was it Kevi? She turned back into the room, staring at the curtain. If he was here she would make Mitzi suffer for her lies . . . if he was here!

Rudi was the only one who never started Techot barking, so as soon as the key grated in the lock and the door opened and Techot gave a little squeak of excitement, Pavel knew Rudi's leave had started. She had been cooking in the kitchen, tired after a full day on the collective – they were branding cattle – and was contemplating a quick meal of stewed vegetables followed by a hot bath when the key had turned in the lock.

She flew across the kitchen and into the hall and had her arms round Rudi's neck before he was more than two paces inside, laughing up at him as he laughed down at her. Despite their hopes she had never quickened with a child, but Rudi never made her feel inadequate, though of course they saw far less of each other now that he was on active service.

They kissed . . . they had not seen one another for four months, so it was quite a long kiss . . . and then Pavel led him into the kitchen, chattering about the meal she was preparing and the fact that she had a basket of soft fruit – his favourite, raspberries – all ready for cleaning, down under the sink in the cool and dark.

'A whole month,' Rudi said presently, as they sat down to supper, hastily made into enough for two by the addition of a tin of corned beef and half a loaf of Pavel's coarse wholemeal bread. 'Think of it, dushka, a whole month off, before I have to go off again. It'll be border patrol, too, which is horrible, so the month will be all the better for what comes after.'

'Which border?' Pavel shovelled food into her mouth briskly, to chew whilst he answered her. She worked hard on the farm and ate well; mealtimes were always something to look forward to.

'Finnish, of course. There'll be trouble there; the Soviet'll make a push and get back some of the land that's been tricked out of our possession.'

'Oh, come on, don't go all Party politics on me,' Pavel said through her mouthful. 'The Finns aren't a huge, aggressive country – that's us.'

'Oh, well, we toe the Party line; soldiers must.' Rudi helped himself to another slice of bread and buttered it. 'Now, old girl, how about a bit of a holiday?'

'A holiday? Oh, how lovely it would be. Where?'

'Seaside?'

'I'd like that so much. Just for a day, do you mean?'

Rudi laughed. It would take them a good deal more than a day just to reach the coast.

'No, this will be a *real* holiday; a couple of weeks at least. What do you say? I'm entitled to it, so we'll have free accommodation and vouchers and things.'

'Oh, Rudi, it would be so nice. Will they give me time off from work, though?'

'I'd like to see them deny it, after the way you slave for them! No, don't worry, you're as entitled as I; you're a Soviet worker just as much as me.'

It was great fun, packing for their holiday and telling all their friends where they were going and why. They were loudly envied and Techot, who had grown into a fine-looking dog, had no lack of offers to keep him until the Lemensks returned. Train tickets were booked, a place was reserved for them at an hotel – a double room with a sea view, Pavel told her fellow workers ecstatically – and at last the day dawned when they were to leave.

And then the messenger came.

Rudi tore open the little grey envelope and read the contents, then grinned briefly at Pavel and squeezed her hand.

'Don't worry . . . change of plans but only a bit and only because we're going in the right direction, to start with. I've got to go to HQ, but I won't be gone long. Go to the station, there's a good girl, but don't go getting on the train until I get there.'

So Pavel watched him leave and then did all her little, last-minute things and took Techot down to the flat of her friend Tireana with a list of instructions . . . how to feed him, when to walk him, where to put his basket with the bit of blanket in at nights.

'Anyone would think he was your first-born,' Tireana teased and Pavel laughed and tried not to mind that he was the only child she seemed likely to have. He was a nice dog, she loved him, but he had not the character to take Baru's place in her heart – though Baru, she knew, would be long gone . . . big dogs like her do not normally live much over ten years and Baru had more than had her fair share of life even before Pavel left her with Sasha, at the farm.

She went to the station, wondering idly what they had found for poor Rudi this time. Perhaps a short tour in the coastal area after their holiday? It would be a nuisance since it would mean her travelling home alone – for the collective would not want her to be away for more than a fortnight – but as long as they got their holiday she must not grumble. Rudi was a serving soldier, after all.

Pavel sat on her bench with her luggage piled round her and watched the passing faces and waited for Rudi.

'This time the girl was lucky, so we've a name and a description. They've sent for you to go because you made enquiries about the girl before we knew rightly who she was, and because someone in Moscow said you'd seen her once, years ago.'

'I've not seen her since she was two,' Rudi said baldly. 'If it *is* her, which seems doubtful. Why are you so sure this time?'

'Because the girl identified an old photograph; it was taken when Fedorovna was no more than twelve, the parents had both the girls done, what they used to call studio portraits. They were a rich family – *kulaks* – and when a travelling photographer came to the nearest town he photographed them and had the photos hand-coloured and they were put away in a drawer. The older girl moved (thank God, thought Rudi fervently) and she's an ordinary-looking girl, plain even when blurred, but the younger's a real beauty, striking, and the girl Mitzi had no doubt. She said "Why, it's Eva!" as soon as the OGPU man produced the picture.'

'And you're sure it was she who attacked this . . . this Mitzi? Why? Was it a girl's quarrel over some young man? Or something more?'

'It was over nothing, Mitzi said, but she's damned lucky to be alive! She was left to die in her own blood, but it wasn't the knife the attacker used in other cases, it was a bent old bread-knife and Mitzi's rib-cage deflected the blow. It slid along and down, but not deep enough to do mortal damage fortunately, or we might never have got a line on her. She's a clever one, never strikes until she's sure they're moving on.'

'They?'

'That's right. She's got a fellow, name of Kevi the Wolf; they called her Eva the Wolf too. Odd, that they should have named her so aptly before anyone knew about this business.' He sighed, suddenly looking older, for he was a youngish man of no more than forty. 'In a way you can't blame the kids – they were *bez prizorney* for years, roaming the streets, with every man's hand against them.'

'But the boy . . . Kevi, did you say?'

'That's right; know him? A lad no more than a couple of years older than she, I believe. They ran together for years, but apparently this last attempted murder was too much and the boy left her.'

'No. Just a coincidence. They've not found him – suppose it was he who killed the women? It seems more of a man's crime than a woman's.'

'What about the soldiers in the train going to the children's home? Stuck a dagger into them calm as you please the kid

563

did, and she no more than twelve or thirteen at the time. Then jumped the train . . . the father, Fedor, tried to take the blame, wanted to die for it, but fortunately for him he was roped and too far gone, anyway, so they knew it was the child.'

'Fortunately? Why, what happened to him?'

The man shrugged; he was impatient to hear Lemensk say he would lead the hunt for the girl, but the soldier must know the full facts.

'A poor choice of words, perhaps. He went to a timber camp and died two years later. A bad way to go.'

'Yes.' Rudi did not wrap it up. 'He was a good man. Doubtless the State had its reasons.'

'Doubtless.' Neither man meant what he said but it would have been most unwise for either to show it. 'Now, Lemensk, the situation is this. She's a killer, this pretty little girl, and she's hunting, we think, for the boy. He's not a bad boy, he's had a hard time of it, and we don't want to find him with a knife through the heart as well, let alone the girls she'll finish off if any of them so much as look at him. We found a torn piece of newspaper in the room they'd shared and it mentioned the Caucasus. We don't know if the boy headed that way but it's possible. Somewhere along the line a peasant who remembered the boy's mother told us that the father had been a Caucasian. But we know the girl's going there, because she told Mitzi before she attacked her.'

'The Caucasus is a big area,' Rudi said mildly. 'There'll be no hope of catching her unless you're prepared to send an army in.'

'We can't do that, not for one lass, even if she is a dangerous killer. But we've a shrewd idea that she'll come via the Klukhor Pass, because her money fell out of the bundle when she was searching for the bread-knife, so she'll not have a lot to spare. And besides, it's the nearest way from where Mitzi was found.'

'Well, she's chosen a good month for it; it's passable at this time of year but not before or after,' Rudi commented. 'She's the Georgian side, then?'

'That's right. And like you, she knows the Caucasus is a big place and she doesn't know where her quarry will head. But the article on the Caucasus I mentioned dealt with the collectivisation of the valley farms, and that just about describes her father's place. So I think you ought to make for it.'

'I see.' Rudi hesitated. 'I can refuse, I take it? You see, my wife and I were about to set off on our first holiday since we got married . . . we've got places at a Soviet workers' hotel on the Black Sea coast . . . I'd hate to have to tell her we couldn't go through with it after her collective have given her time off and everything.'

But even as he spoke he knew he must go, for Pavel's sake as well as for Eva's. He had known about the soldiers on the train for quite a while, and had felt uneasy about the child. She was, in a mad sort of way, his responsibility, because he had not taken one child to the Lazarov farm, he had taken two. So now he knew he would go through with it and do his best for Eva if he caught her. *Bez prizorney* were often treated far more leniently than others, because they had been forced into all sorts of actions just to keep themselves alive. But . . . murder? He could not say. Killing the soldiers could just about be classed as self-defence, but the others? He had heard about the girl in the children's home who had been knifed as she lay on her bed . . . they had suspected a girl called Eva then, or the boy with her, but it had only been a suspicion; no one had seen anything to make an accusation stick.

'Yes, you can refuse. But there's no need to interfere with your wife's holiday. It won't take you long; either you'll catch the girl as she comes through the Pass or you won't. We've got men posted at all the other passes, with copies of the photograph, but she may slip through the net even so. I'll arrange to have your holiday — and your wife's, of course — extended, and if you've seen nothing after say, five days, then we'll take it that the bird has either flown or gone a different way, and you can go straight over the Pass and join your wife in Georgia. We'll lay on a truck, naturally.'

He had sighed and accepted, then hurried back to the railway station and told Pavel that he was wanted, but only for a few days.

'I'll come with you as far as I can,' he said. 'Then you can go on alone. Explain at the hotel that I shan't be far behind you.' He gave her a squeeze. 'Poor dushka, our very first holiday! But never mind, I wouldn't enjoy it if I knew I was letting anyone down.'

On the train, settled in 'soft' seats, Pavel wanted to know all about his mission. He was tempted to tell her, but suppose things went wrong? Suppose Eva was shot before his eyes by some trigger-happy soldier? Almost worst of all, though, was the fear that Eva would have to stand trial for a series of brutal murders ... if that happened, Pavel would be bound to find out and her shock and distress, her deep unhappiness, could only be imagined.

Nevertheless, whatever happened she should go to her hotel and start her holiday. She was an easy-going, natural sort of girl who got on well with everyone; she would not miss him just for a few days.

When the train reached his destination he gave her a long kiss and a hard hug, promised to take care of himself, and jumped off on to the platform. His truck was there and a group of young, ill-at-ease men in uniform waited beside it. He sighed; his detachment looked as though it had only been born yesterday. But they should not find their task too taxing. One of them was intelligent and well set up – he might come in handy in an emergency, though pray heaven there would be no emergency. If he could only speak to the girl, explain, then they might still brush through it with neither scandal nor tragedy to further blacken things.

Pavel waited until he was well clear of the station and then she, too, climbed down from the train. She had labelled her luggage clearly, it could go on without her. All she brought was a bag slung across one shoulder and that was all she would need. She intended to head for the nearest house where she could find lodgings and then keep her distance so that Rudi did not know she had disobeyed him until he was actually heading for the station once again. She had no intention of spying on him or making his life difficult, but neither did she intend to face the horrid business of walking into a hotel, alone, and explaining her husband's absence to a sneering hotel desk clerk. No, it was better this way, she was here now and comfortably within reach of Rudi. He had said nothing but she had seen the recruits in their stiff, ugly uniforms; no doubt this was yet another training exercise.

She found a room for a few kopeks and moved into it. How pleased Rudi would be to find her here when he came down from the hills! And in the meantime this was the little market town and up in the hills was the farm, the Berisavos and possibly even Baru. She would definitely find time to go up and visit them; they would be so pleased to know that she was all right, happily married and fit and well. She would go first thing in the morning.

Eva had to ask about the Pass, which was a nuisance, but she was filled with an exultant certainty that Kevi was near and that the Pass was her quickest way to him. It was strange that she should feel like this, so alive and light and happy, because she had eaten very little since getting away from that nasty apartment block, where that nasty girl lay on her bed with her little gold toes in the air . . . bloodstained little toes, Eva thought viciously, heading for the hills . . . having tempted Kevi from the path of righteousness for the last time.

She had eaten, of course, or she could not go like this, her legs making good time, her arms swinging briskly. Some apples from a laden tree, a piece of bread flung out for a dog but pounced upon by a hungry runaway, a melon, big and juicy, lying in a field like a vast sow relieved of its litter. It was not, perhaps, terribly satisfying food, for she had been running away now for days and days – she did not know how many having quite lost count – but it was enough to walk on.

It was a pity that, as she climbed higher, she should have suddenly started seeing girls. Lots and lots of girls. Not that they could hurt her, because they were all dead; she had killed them herself so she should know. Lise, Ania, Katerina, Ilsa, right down to the latest and deadest, Mitzi. She had hated them all, each and every one, so it was a pity that they should suddenly turn up here, dodging in and out of the rocks, pulling faces at her, shaking their red or yellow hair over their eyes and mocking her because they were faster than she.

It had not occurred to her before, perhaps because she had never seen them all together, but it was very strange that they were all either red-haired or blondes. Poor Kevi, there were a great many red-heads in life, and possibly even more blondes. Never mind, once she caught up with him she would reassure him that he was safe with her; she would get rid of all the red-heads and blondes for him, they should never get him.

Night came before she reached the Pass, but it was all right with her, she was on her way now and nothing would stop her. She *knew* Kevi was not far away, she could feel his presence on her cheek in the night wind. She would rest until morning, she decided, there must be a little cave or a hole in the rocks where she would be safe until it was light.

She found a little cave, high, high up, when night was almost upon her. She crawled inside it and curled up, as a badger or a fox would curl up, and fell asleep almost at once.

From their bivouac amidst the rocks to the side of a steep gorge, Rudi watched the sun come up. He had not slept, though he did not know why, for he enjoyed being in the mountains. He had dozed, though, and felt fit and well this morning, capable of tackling whatever came.

The boys . . . he could not think of them as soldiers . . . slept still. On reflection he was glad they were only lads, and raw recruits at that. He intended to grab Eva and then take her aside and talk to her, try to make her see that she was in deadly danger and must plead her life as a *bez prizorney* — provided, of course, that it was she who had attacked the girl Mitzi and not the lad she lived with . . . Kevi.

That was an odd coincidence, that his name should be Kevi. He remembered his old friend still, though he would have preferred to forget him. He pushed it away, the knowledge that Kevi's blood was on his head, and that of Petchoren, Pavel's father. He had given himself an unconditional discharge over the whole matter, because he had been told Kevi was a murderer and because he still remembered with affection the boy who had been his victim, but since then he had seen a lot more and knew how different things frequently were from how they could be made to appear. Had Kevi killed that boy? It was not like Kevi to do a thing like that.

He thought of what Pavel might say if someone told her Rudi Lemensk was a murderer not just of one man but of a whole family. Rudi killed your father, your uncle, your babushka and your elder sister. Two he shot and two he caused to commit suicide, to jump from a high place. Would Pavel believe them? She would say but Rudi's not like that, Rudi is gentle; he loves children and is kind to old people. My Uncle Kevi was his friend, my father never harmed him.

The light grew stronger and over the mountain peak, the sun's rays shone red.

Pavel woke with the sun and jumped out of bed, sticking her head immediately out of the window of her small room. The mountain air was so good, so clean and fresh! She was excited at the thought of going back to the farm, of meeting the Berisavos again, so that dressing was a quick matter, washing was skimped, and she was downstairs in the family's kitchen, eating porridge, before the sun had done more than tilt its rays on to the roof tops.

'Do you know the collective run by the Berisavo family?' she asked her hostess as she ate the porridge and drank a glass of very good tea. 'They farm up in the mountains – a big farm it is.'

'The old Lazarov place? Yes, we know 'em. Why? Want to go up there, do you? You could hire a horse.'

'I used to work there,' Pavel explained. 'Yes, I'll hire a horse if you know someone who'll lend one for a day.'

They lent her one of theirs, naturally, an elderly nag but quite capable of taking her up into the mountains. Pavel wished she had brought her *burka* and her worn *tcherkasska*, but she had a pair of trousers which she used for work and a trim blue shirt so she wore them instead. Looking critically at herself in the mirror she knew she would not pass for a boy – the shirt was narrow and showed her shape – so she would have to come clean to the Berisavos, but it did not really matter. They would laugh and be astonished and that would be fine by her.

She rode off into the blue morning, singing to herself, wishing that Baru loped at her horse's heels and then for some reason remembering David. In fact the memory of him was so strong as she rode along the trails he and she had once traversed together that she began to plan another expedition before she returned to the village in the foothills. She would like to go up to the Klukhor Pass, to the place where she and David had spent that eventful night, and sit up there in the sunshine and dream.

At the top of the valley she hesitated; should she go down? Down into her recent past? And find it all changed? Even from here she could see that they had done away with the corrals and that the pastures were ploughed and sown with crops. They were arable farming now, then, and no longer herding beasts. It seemed a shame and a terrible waste – crop farming was for the plains, not the hills and valleys – but it would be interesting to hear how they were getting on and whether they approved of the new-style farming.

She turned her horse's head into the valley.

Eva dreamed. This time it was a gentle dream, though she was in the mountains and gorges of the Caucasus, wandering along with her hand in someone else's hand. She was quiet and content, happy to feel the sun on the back of her neck and the grass cool beneath bare feet. It was strange to be so content, she had not felt so calm and happy for many years.

When at last the person spoke, she looked at her companion for the first time and it was her sister. Her sister was talking, comforting Eva, telling her that the bad time was nearly over and the good time about to start. Eva wanted to know if Kevi would be a part of the good time and her sister smiled and said of course, Kevi had been here, with her, for years and years – had Eva not realised?

Well, of course Eva wanted to know where Kevi was and her sister said she would take Eva to him, so they walked on, hand in hand, and again Eva felt the sun warm on her neck and the grass cool beneath her bare feet, and the dream was good, filling her with quiet thoughts, and it occurred to her that whilst she was in this mountain country with her sister's hand in hers, she would never see the red-headed girls or the blonde girls, and she would never feel jealous again.

'Here's Kevi,' her sister said, and Eva looked and saw a man, tall and handsome, with dark hair falling across his brows and into his laughing eyes. She screwed up her own eyes against the sun; was it Kevi? Kevi grown into a man, whilst she wandered amongst the mountains, searching for him? She looked up at her sister, who smiled down at her.

'Do you remember Kevi, little sister? He's strong as a stallion, clever as ten schoolteachers, and beautiful as a woman, so Babushka used to say.'

'Yes, I remember him.' She smiled back at her sister, at her sweet, remembered face and the bell of amber hair which swung forward as she bent down to Eva's little height. 'And I remember you, Konkordia.'

As she said the name it sounded echoingly, like a bell, like a knell, sounding and resounding, until she woke.

She was still in the cave and she rubbed her eyes and went at once to the entrance, hoping that some vestige of her dream would have remained, that the wonderful elder sister would be out there waiting for her, wanting to guide her across the mountains.

But outside the cave there was only early, slanting sunshine, and pure mountain air and the sound of a river roaring through a distant canyon and a lark rising up and up into the blue above.

And yet . . . that was not all. Peace was there and contentment, much as it had been in her dream. Her feverish need to cross the mountains and find Kevi seemed to have left her; she wanted him still, but she would find him and she need not worry about anything because she was being led, in spirit if not in actuality, by that girl in her dream, that . . . what was her name? It seemed to have fled with the night, but she could still remember her face and the way her amber hair fell forward as she leaned over Eva.

She began to climb the path; it was stony and steep but it was no effort to mount it. Presently she found some whinberries, ripe and sweet, and they quenched her thirst and made it easier to go on. When she came to a little, tumbling waterfall she drank again, and soaked her hands and face and slicked back her hair, though it soon dried as the sun climbed. She continued upwards and onwards. She had not felt so utterly peaceful since she was young, at home here in the mountains.


The Berisavos were working when she reached the farm, but Pavel went out into the fields nearest the house and found Luyeva and they had a little weep on each other's shoulders when Luyeva told Pavel that Lipi had died the previous year and she and Stefan, though married, were no longer in charge of the collective. Sasha had gone away to be educated, and Baru had died, a stiff, proud old dog, a bare twelve months before.

'We used to say she was waiting for you,' Luyeva said. 'Of

course, we didn't know you were a woman . . . my, wait till I tell Stefan!'

But Pavel could not wait, and anyway, it was clear that Luyeva was in a difficult position on the collective; once she had been married to the chief man, now she was not. It behoved her to work hard and speak small or she might find herself reported for some imaginary fault and herded off to a labour camp. It would not do for someone to report that an attractive young woman had spent hours chatting to the Berisavos. So Pavel left the valley and climbed into the saddle at the top – her nag was too elderly and stiff to have enjoyed the climb up the narrow path – and remounted on the edge of the cliff and turned the horse's head towards the Pass. It was a lovely day. She might not get very far, but she would go in that direction – and besides, she wanted to visit Baru's grave and Lipi's. They had been buried side by side – the Berisavos thought it fitting that a brave old dog and a brave old man should lie side by side – in a meadow with a stream and a waterfall, just as one entered the Klukhor Pass.

As soon as she reached it, Pavel knew that it was her meadow, hers and David's. They had lain on the grass and eaten their picnic before tackling the Pass. She knelt on the grass by the double grave and wept a little, for Lipi and Baru, but she was not sad for them because they were both old and had led good and useful lives.

Then she got up, hobbled her old nag because she would not need him for a while, and began to climb up and into the Pass. She did not know why she wanted to go – probably there was more of David in the meadow than in the Pass, for she doubted if she could find and make a memory-shrine of the cleft in the rocks where she and David had first made love to one another. Yet she wanted to go forward; something was pulling her on.

Rudi saw her first; a slip of a thing, he thought wonderingly, with the binoculars held up to his eyes, toiling along the steep mountain track, head held high, step light. He had been told she had no money, he could see for himself that she had no baggage or luggage of any sort, yet she came on strongly, looking like any other child out for a stroll in mountain country on a sunny day.

Through the binoculars he could see her face quite clearly; she was sun-kissed, her bare arms brown, her cheeks flushed, her small nose freckled. Her hair was really beautiful, no wonder that boy Kevi had taken her everywhere with him, it curled all over her head in little, soft, silvery curls and made her look cherubically young and innocent. Was this a murderer, or just a confused little girl?

He had warned his men to keep still if they could, not to step forward. He had explained as little as possible but felt he must say that they were here to arrest a young person as much for her own good as for the good of the community at large and he did not want the young person warned or frightened by suddenly seeing soldiers – even such a scratch lot as yourselves, he had added, making them grin sheepishly, but they promised to keep still and in the shadows from the towering side of the cliff.

The ambush, if you could call it that, was in a good place, better than most. Rudi had chosen it carefully because the girl must come this way, assuming she would stick to the path, and there was a short strip of grass with a tiny, crooked silver birch growing on it between the path and the edge of the precipice, at the foot of which the river ran and plunged on its rocky bed. Additionally, because the ledge of the path was at its widest just here, there were tall rocks, man-sized, behind which his backup troops could lurk. An ideal ambush, because he would stay behind his rock until she was within grabbing distance and then step out, grab, and have his say with her.

He continued to watch her through the glasses and then turned abruptly, because one of the young soldiers had hissed something in a startled whisper. The sound bounced and reverberated off the rocks and made him conscious that the girl was getting nearer and that the young men should be in hiding, not watching with him.

He hustled them, with gestures, back into hiding and was stepping back on to the path with his glasses raised to his eyes when she came round the corner, catching him totally off guard. She was wearing a blue cotton dress and she had very blue eyes. She stopped dead as she saw him and it was all wrong! She was a dozen feet away from him and on the outside edge of the path ... if she ran round the edge he would have the devil's own job to cut her off and he did not want a chase, with those boys and their confounded guns behind him. For a moment they stood there, stone figures, not a muscle twitching, and then the girl moved.

Eva had been humming beneath her breath as she came round the corner; to find a soldier in uniform right in her path was heart-stopping. She jolted to a halt, fear seeming to stop even her blood's flow so that she felt paralysingly cold even in the full sun.

The soldier did not move, either. He seemed as surprised, and was probably as frightened, as she. Then she saw his eyes glint and knew he was going to move, knew, even, that he would move to his right and her left, towards the soft green grass between the lip of the precipice and the path. Even as his eyes moved, before any other part of him had relaxed from its frozen stillness, her senses, sharpened to animal intensity by fear, saw another movement. Someone was standing in the deep shadow of the rocks over to her right and his left . . . another soldier. If she moved that way she would be caught between soldier and soldier, trapped!

She ran towards the precipice.

Pavel, panting from the climb, came round the corner from the opposite side of the mountain and saw the whole thing like an overdramatic stage set; the soldier on the path, the child darting towards the cliff edge, the young recruits charging out from behind their rocks. One of them, a bright-faced, intelligent youngster, screamed a name . . . a syllable . . . and the girl turned, at bay, her feet right on the crumbling edge. The soldier had almost reached her; he slowed, spoke, began to inch forward faster and faster . . .

Eva had meant to hurl herself over the edge, she was so terrified of capture, but then someone shouted her name and she knew that it was Kevi come to rescue her. She stopped, right on the edge, and turned a face pale with fear but already flushing with hope towards her rescuer; only it was not *her* Kevi, it was the other Kevi, the man she had dreamed of.

He had been kind and good in the dream, he would help her, he would take her to her sister . . . what was her sister's name? Pavel was her sister, why had she thought that it was anything different . . . the man, Kevi the man, was saying her sister's name over and over, telling her something, holding out his arms to her. And she knew that he was telling her it was no good, that there was only one way to keep the peace and contentment she had found in her dream last night.

He reached her and grabbed her, just as she swayed backwards, over the edge. They fell together, arms clasping, mouths opening to the rush of air, and Eva felt safe, beloved, and joined her voice with his as he cried a name aloud to the echoing rocks, and their cry was snatched from their mouths by the splendid speed and the savage wind, and crashed into silence by the cruel crags.

Pavel saw that it was Rudi, and that he held Eva in his arms, just as they fell. She rushed to the edge, screaming his name and Eva's, and heard, for the second time in her life, a death-cry diminishing as the dying plunged to their end. She fell to her knees on the grass, but she fell because someone had grabbed her from behind and pulled her down, back and out of danger. Someone who had been sobbing, 'Eva, Eva,' whilst the tragedy on the cliff-edge was acted out to its terrible finish. Pavel looked and it was only one of the raw recruits, but he was crying, his mouth was pulling itself into hurt baby-shapes, and she took him in her arms and cried too, for her dear Rudi, who had been doing his best for Eva, and for Eva, who was only a child, and even for this young soldier, who trembled and shook in her arms and took great, sobbing gulps at the air and wept on.

And she cried for the others, whom she had not remembered until this moment. For Uncle Kevi and Petchoren, killed by the soldiers and lying on the floor of the kosh in the shape of a cross. For Babushka, old and mad, taking that flying leap to her death. And for Konkordia, who had gone because Babushka called, and who had begged Pavel to take care of baby Eva.

# CHAPTER TWENTY-FOUR

It took them all the rest of the day to get down from that ledge in the Klukhor Pass. The recruits were all children and Pavel suddenly felt far less than her twenty-three years. But though they were children they had courage, for the young man who had wept with her – he told her his name was Kevi, and that he was Eva's boyfriend – made them climb down the precipice, by another narrow little goat-track he had noticed, to see to the bodies.

'We can't leave them here,' he said, his eyes fuzzy and unfocused with grief, 'the vultures will have them, and the wild beasts. We must bury them before we leave . . . after all, there are plenty of witnesses to what happened.'

The recruits all had rifles and bayonets and they used them to dig a shallow grave. It was no use digging deep, for they supposed that men would come from the military or from the government to see the bodies, but even so they did their best. It took most of the day, but they got the grave dug and then they buried the bodies . . . Pavel and the youngest of the recruits were allowed, by the boy Kevi, to go and sit by the river where the noise of the water would drown the noise of the earth being shovelled back on top of the crushed and splintered remains . . . and then they went back and helped to roll big boulders across the grave. Kevi agreed, when Pavel suggested it, that they should roll the boulders in the shape of a cross so that they might tell the authorities how they would find the bodies, if they wished to do so.

It was exhausting and sickening work and when it was done they made their weary way out of the Pass and back to the meadow where Pavel's raw-boned nag still grazed. The recruits had tents and it was late; they pitched camp and gave Pavel her husband's tent and they shared their iron rations with her and they put her tent a little way from the others, so that they should not hear her weep.

But Pavel could cry no more, she could only lie in Rudi's tent and send him her thanks across the million twinkling miles to the stars, wherever he was, because he had done his best to save Eva. The boy Kevi seemed to know why the authorities had wanted Eva, but he had not wanted to talk about it, apart from saying that she had killed soldiers on the train going to the labour camp, and had more lately killed a girl when she was, he thought, a little mad.

Lying in Rudi's tent, which still smelt of his hair and body and of the tobacco he smoked, she thought that she and Eva were both lucky in that they had been loved by good men; Kevi was only a boy, but he would be a good man, one day. And Rudi, though he had shot either Uncle Kevi or Petchoren or possibly both, had been a good man too.

And there was David. He was a good man. He had tried to come to her, he had waited and waited for her, and written and sent money, but in the end they had lost each other through no fault, really, of either one.

And then it occurred to her that they were no longer lost; she had found Eva and lost her for ever and she had lost Rudi too. But she no longer owed anyone anything – she could leave Russia tomorrow and no one would regret her going, no one would probably even notice.

She had a train ticket to Georgia of course, but if she went down to the town tomorrow and got on that train she would be Pavel Lemenskova again, a grieving widow, and she would not find it easy to slip away unnoticed.

There had been a tragedy in the Klukhor Pass; two people had died – or had it been three? Who knew she had been there? Only these lads, and she was sure that none of them would tell if they were asked very nicely not to do so.

Despite the darkness, she sat up, bolt upright, and in the faint starlight her eyes were shining.

Oh, Rudi, would you deny me this? Would you want me to go on denying myself? Never admitting my love for David, because I owed you so much? Yes, alive I owed you much and never would have left you, but now the debt is paid.

I can go home!

*

Next morning, she and Kevi walked apart and talked for a long time. Pavel learned tragic things about Eva, but she told Kevi that the little sister she loved had still been there, underneath the jealousy that had become, at times, very like madness, and Kevi had agreed.

'She was brave and loving and generous,' he told Pavel. 'Perhaps the jealousy was my fault – I don't know. And the killing frightened me so badly that instead of letting her know what I knew I tried to deny it, even to myself. And when it got so bad that I could no longer deny it I ran away. I told myself that she killed to keep me to herself and I was doing the right thing but it wasn't true; I loved her and I was afraid for her, so I ran away.'

'The strange thing is that you ran right into her,' Pavel pointed out. 'How did it happen? Did my husband choose you?'

'No! I joined up because I wanted to go far away from her, and I was drafted to the collectivisation scheme which everyone said was a bit of all right, you just had to keep an eye on the peasants and make sure the right food quotas went to the government and so on, and then before I'd had more than a day here an urgent message came through that there was a fugitive coming across the Klukhor and a detachment of recruits was wanted to accompany an experienced officer, who would apprehend the wanted person.'

'And you had no inkling that it was Eva?'

'No – the army tells you nothing you don't actually need to know; I didn't know it was Eva until she walked round that corner in her little blue cotton dress . . .' His voice wobbled and he stopped for a moment, cleared his throat and continued 'I knew it was a woman before because I caught a glimpse of the dress, but I didn't know . . . it didn't occur to me for a moment, until she came round that corner . . .'

'I wonder if Rudi knew? Sometimes I think he must've and other times I think he couldn't have. It's a strange and terrible thing, but Rudi first met me years ago, when he was mixed up in another tragedy . . .' she gave a shaky laugh, 'poor Rudi, we seem to have been bad luck for him, we Ryazans.' She had forgotten she knew the name until she spoke it, and Kevi turned to her, his brows rising.

'Ryazans? How very odd! I once knew someone with a

name very like that, only I can't clearly remember . . . it's a long time ago. I was with the *bez prizorney* for many years, from the time I was six or seven.'

'I've only known the name myself for a few years,' Pavel admitted. 'I was very young when my father was killed and we – Eva and I – were taken to the Lazarovs, and for some reason my mind simply wiped out all my early life so that I seemed to have been born at the age of about six on the Lazarov farm in the valley where I was brought up.'

'It's an odd thing, memory,' Kevi agreed. 'What'll you do next, Pavel? Will you go back to Kharkov and your apartment and the collective?'

'No. With your help, Kevi, I shall go right away from here, over into Georgia and then, with luck, out of Russia altogether. You see, I was engaged to a foreigner until the foreigners were turned out of the Soviet Union. Rudi saved my life when I was apprehended by an official for a crime I had never committed . . . my God!'

'What?'

'The crime – it was for murdering two soldiers on a train. Oh, my God!'

'Yes. Eva's crime. So you'll leave the country and go to your lover; I don't blame you. Do you want us to keep our mouths shut, me and the lads?'

'Would you? I've done nothing, truly, and you won't get into trouble because of me, the Soviet isn't interested in me, I'm nobody to them. But they don't like even nobodies escaping the net, do they?'

'No, they don't. Very well, we'll say we never saw you. How will that do?'

'It would be wonderful. What about you, though, Kevi? What will you do now? Stay in the army? Find another woman? Go chasing some other star?'

He laughed down at her, handsome, devil-may-care, a lock of dark hair flopping over his bright, heavy-lidded eyes.

'Oh, me? I'll be all right. I'm like my father – my mother used to say he was strong as a stallion, clever as ten school-teachers and beautiful as a woman! I'll never forget Eva, of course, but . . . Pavel? What are you staring at?'

Pavel started and looked away.

'Nothing . . . only you . . . it's just that my babushka used to say exactly that about her son. He was another Kevi. He was . . .' She hesitated, looking up at her companion again. 'He was very like you.'

'A devil, eh? Well, odd though it may seem, especially in the circumstances, I like the army, I want to make it my career. If there's a war – and it seems pretty certain there will be, the way Germany's carrying on – then at least I'll be trained to fight and not just eager. And God forgive me I love pretty women, so I don't suppose my poor baby has turned me into a celibate . . . there couldn't be another Eva, but there'll be another woman, don't you fret.'

'I shan't.' Pavel held out her hand. 'I'm going now, Kevi, over the Klukhor and out into Georgia before anyone thinks about me. Shall I send you a letter when I get there?'

He considered it, then smiled but shook his head. He turned to the other recruits; in their officer's absence he had assumed command of them without any fuss and they obeyed him without fuss also; a good start, Pavel concluded. 'Ready, men? Then we'll make for the foothills.' They had their rucksacks packed, and now they began to scramble them on to their backs. Kevi shouldered his own pack and then, surprisingly, stood to attention and snapped a salute to Pavel.

She half-waved, half-saluted, then set out across the clearing towards the Pass, turning as she reached the rocky ledge up which she must presently scramble. The boys were making their way across the meadow, leading her nag, heading for the foothills, but Kevi looked back and waved again.

'Goodbye – cousin!' he shouted. 'Think of me!'

Pavel's heart lifted. He was, she was sure he was!

'Goodbye, Kevi – may God go with you!'

She watched until the little group had disappeared from view and then turned her face once more towards the high peaks.

In the end, all the thinking came to one conclusion: that Alice and Nibby should move down into Carmel Hall and sell the cottage and that they would have a separate establishment there from the Thomases. It made sense, it gave them a little cash to play with, and it enabled them, in the end, to start the project that Nibby and David intended to try.

The stable block would be converted into living accommodation and they planned to take paying guests who would come for the express purpose of learning to sail. It had not seemed particularly possible until David had mentioned their dilemma to Roy Masters on a trip to London, in the course of which he had popped in to see Roy, partly from friendship but also to see whether Selim had ever heard any news of the Lazarovs. Roy, taking him out to lunch, had agreed completely with David that it was a shame to let the place fall into disrepair but had also agreed that their one solution – to turn it into an hotel – was unlikely to succeed in a place where the clatter of industry from the river was louder than the trill of birdsong.

'But if you set up a place where we could send young people for training and toughening up,' he had suggested with apparent idleness, 'then that really could work. You're within easy reach of Snowdonia, so they could go there for climbing, map reading, et cetera, yet you're right on the estuary which would mean navigation, learning about boats . . . and you say the grounds are extensive – they could, presumably, learn to shoot there?'

'Well, yes, but I can't see the army . . .'

'Nor I. This would be . . . different. Somewhere reputable companies and government departments could send people to be trained without the whole world knowing about it. You and Nibby both speak Russian, don't you?'

'Yes, of course. I speak it well enough to be mistaken for a Caucasian on the plains and a plainsman in the Caucasus! Nibby's not done it to the same extent, but . . . look, old man, you aren't thinking of turning us into a sort of school for spies, are you?'

'My dear fellow, perish the thought! You could give language lessons, though . . . not many people speak Russian really well. There's a crash course which you could handle easily . . . it would mean a chap staying with you for three months perhaps, with all the other training . . . you'd get to know them pretty well, and they could come back there for de-briefing.'

David was staring, mouth open.

'De-briefing? What are you talking about? Look, before you get carried away remember I'm bringing up my boy there, and my sister Alice and Nibs have two kids, a boy and a girl. There'll be no end of coming and going once they reach school age, they'll want friends to stay and so on. I admit I'm terribly tempted, it sounds just the sort of place I'd love to run, but you'd want to keep it quiet and it would be plain impossible.'

'No, no, you're quite wrong; we don't want somewhere like that, places like that are tucked away in the wilds of . . . well, in the wilds. What we want is somewhere just as you've described Carmel Hall – plenty of traffic in the estuary, plenty going on, the chance to slip over to Liverpool and take a look at the big stuff – to leave from the port if necessary. Nothing undercover, nothing secret . . . except possibly the language business.'

'We-ell, look, why don't you come up for a couple of days and take a look round and discuss it with the family? If it's to be a family business the decision has to come from us all.'

'I'd like to.' He grinned at David. 'Your sister Alice is a poppet; I made a play for her you know, when Nibby brought her up to London that time.' He chuckled. 'Served the chap right; I could see it annoyed him, but he should have spoiled her a bit himself. Pretty girl.'

'She's a respectable young mother now,' David assured him. 'If you want to be gallant to anyone, save it for Sassy; she's a holy terror!'

He had not meant it seriously but Roy Masters came up for a long weekend – and had to be prised away from Sara just to take a look at the stable block and to go down to the yard and see the boat sheds where David proposed putting the fast sailing boats they would build to teach on.

'He's fascinated by someone who isn't smooth and cap-able,' David said, but Alice thought otherwise and was proved right. Sara went off to London for long weekends and came back full of the places she had seen in Masters's company. Roy made ludicrously weak excuses to turn up on their doorstep with roses for Alice and chocolates for the children, took a perfunctory look at whatever work was being done, approved it, revved up his sports car and took off for a day at Chester races or a quick flip over to Dublin on the ferry . . . Sara went along to keep him company.

Three months after their first meeting, he and Sara announced their engagement and nobody was particularly surprised, though Michael made it plain that he did not much relish having a brother-in-law who was obviously off his head.

'No one in their right minds would want to marry Sassy,' he said loud and often. 'She's as crazy as a coot and as mad as a hatter and she'll make some poor blighter a rotten wife.'

'She's learning Russian,' Nibby remarked caustically. 'A girl with a degree in modern languages, a girl who speaks French and German like a native, learns Russian as well. That's love for you!'

The house was always full now, with the family, the men working on the construction of the living quarters, people down from London advising. David spent time with all of them and when he wasn't working he spent time with Alyn and Richard, reading to them, playing with them, taking them out on a visit to Chester Zoo, a day at the seaside, even sedate boat-trips or visits to the yard.

Yet he was lonely with a fierce, sharp aloneness which sent him off by himself in good weather and bad, to sail right out to the mouth of the estuary, or to walk alone in Snowdonia, or simply to mooch out along the sea marshes, watching the vigorous bird-life which thrived there.

On a wild and windy day in autumn, with the leaves being torn from the trees and hurled down on the ground or whirled through the air, he had one of his sudden urges to be away from all the noise and the fuss of family life in which he felt that he had no real part. He told Alice he was going sailing, shook his head and grinned at her worries over his safety in such a wind, and reminded her that he was a big boy now, quite capable of staying ashore if the gale worsened.

He kissed Alyn before he left, told him to be good and said he'd read to him when he got back; Alyn, squatting in a blanket-tent erected in the nursery and bossing Richard about, nodded briefly and returned to his game. It was Sunday, when the house abounded with people to play with; one father less was no particular hardship.

Carting his picnic, which had turned into a small feast, out of the side door, David ran into Nibby, entering at a canter having visited the stables for some purpose. After they picked up the picnic and sorted out the armful of ropes which Nibby had been carrying, Nibby said, 'Where are you going?'

'Oh, nowhere, just out. I thought I'd go for a sail.'

'But you'll be back in time for lunch? Elizabeth's coming.'

'In that case, no, I shan't.' David laughed at Nibby's crest-fallen expression. 'I'm sorry, old boy, she's a nice girl, but she really isn't my type. Do tell Alice and Sassy to stop traipsing all their unmarried girlfriends up here, in the hopes! I'm not the marrying kind.'

'Don't leap to conclusions, David, old fruit; they just want you to have a friend.'

'Huh! See you for dinner . . . only if you change Elizabeth's invitation from lunch to dinner I'm warning you, I shan't turn up this evening, either.'

'Don't be so silly, as if we could! See you later, then.'

David made his way down to the boat shed and began to get his favourite yacht ready for a day at sea. The tide would be at the full at around three in the afternoon, which gave him a good day's sailing before he need bring her back. On a decent day, of course, he could have brought her home at low tide and anchored offshore, but at this time of year it would not have been wise. Better go by the tide and have her safe in the boat shed. When the centre opened, of course, they would have completed work on their own channel, so that the boats would be able to go out and come back whatever the state of the tide, but for the time being that was impossible.

David warped the boat out of the sheltering shed and met the wind full in the face. Exhilarating and fierce, it tugged at his clothing and fretted at the mains'l, still furled to the boom. He began to prepare for departure.

Pavel came down the gangway in a crush of people and did not even know she was on British soil at last for several steps . . . not that it was British soil, of course; it was cement or tarmac or some such thing. But then she felt the steadiness of it, and let the people carry her along to the customs sheds.

She was an old hand at customs sheds by now, or their equivalent, for it had taken her months and months to reach this point. Sliding surreptitiously round railway sidings, on and off trains, in and out of abandoned warehouses, old, overgrown woods, shepherds' huts, she had made her way slowly nearer.

Lack of money had not helped, because though it had been

straightforward enough getting through the Klukhor Pass — the most straightforward part of her journey now that she looked back on it — she had been forced to invent an identity for herself and get work on a collective before she could even consider her next move.

Winter came, but winter in Georgia was not like winter in the mountains or even on the Russian plains; she weathered it, saved hard, and left by fishing boat just as she and David had once discussed.

She arrived in the end not in Trabzon but in Istanbul, because the fishing boat she had boarded in the beginning did not put her ashore but transferred her to another fishing boat, and it too put her aboard another craft and thus she came to Istanbul because it was easier and safer for her helpers.

She spoke no Turkish, of course, but she managed to get a job as a waitress in a café, and that kept her going until she could find some means of moving on. She was not proud, she was prepared to take any chance that offered. She had been unable to afford to go direct to almost anywhere, it had always been a short voyage to such-and-such or so-and-so, then a period of work, then another voyage . . . or overland trip . . . or once or twice a hitch-hike.

She had very little luggage and her passport was probably forged and certainly not her own, but the photograph was, and no one had queried it. And anyway, none of it mattered. She was here, in Britain, and somewhere, David was here too! She had his address and though she could speak no English save for a few catch-phrases he had taught her, she had enough common sense to hold out the piece of paper with his name and address on it, enough experience to catch trains or buses or farm carts, until she reached her destination at last.

Alice happened to be crossing the front hall when the door-bell rang, so naturally she went to the door. She swung it open and smiled at the scraggy little person in the worn coat and skirt who stood there, all eyes, and said, 'Yes? Can I help you?'

'David Thomas?'

The girl held out an extremely worn piece of paper; it had

the name David Thomas written on it and the old address. Alice nodded her comprehension.

'Oh, you want David . . . Mr Thomas. I'm afraid he's out at the moment though; can I help you?'

The girl said something in a foreign language; it lilted up at the end so it was presumably a question. Alice shook her head.

'I'm afraid I don't understand; don't you speak English?'

The girl obviously understood the drift of Alice's question because she said, 'Niet,' sadly . . . and with the small word, lights exploded in Alice's brain. Had a miracle happened? Could this possibly be the girl there had been all the fuss about years ago? Once, her name had been on everyone's lips, but then she had married someone else, and David had married Maria and they had stopped talking about her. Alice looked desperately at the girl's small, anxious face. What was she called? She had never heard anyone use the Russian for 'What is your name?' let alone 'Were you my brother's girl-friend?', but there was always sign-language. She touched her own chest lightly. 'I am Alice.'

The girl responded at once. 'Pavel . . . Pavel Fedorovna.'

Alice smiled. 'Alice . . . Alice Thomas.'

'Aah.'

'David,' Alice said loudly – the Englishwoman's answer to the foreigner's lack of understanding – 'David will be back quite soon. He has gone sailing.' As she spoke there was a commotion in the hall behind her and Alyn and Richard emerged from the study, rather furtively. Alice called them over and introduced them.

'Our babies, David's and mine. This is David's son Alyn and this is my son, Richard.'

The girl nodded but there was uncertainty in her smile now. Alice wished Nibby would appear, but he had gone to fetch Elizabeth for lunch, and Sara, who could have helped, was off somewhere with Roy. However, she must not keep the girl standing on the doorstep all morning.

'Come in, Pavel. Come through into the study, take your coat off . . .' Gestures made that part obvious; Pavel's droopy brown skirt was topped with a faded blue blouse and for the first time Alice realised she carried a bag, old and cracked; presumably it held all her worldly possessions – and she had come from half a world away, all by herself, with nothing save that bag and what she stood up in.

They went into the study and Alice kissed Pavel on the cheek and hugged her quickly, then led her over to the window. Out on the estuary there was only one boat, its sail straining in the breeze. It was unlikely to be David since it was heading upriver and David had announced his intention of steering clear of the house whilst poor Elizabeth was lunching with them, but nevertheless Pavel would understand what David was doing if Alice pointed out the yacht. She did so, and as she did so, she heard their car drawing up outside the front door. She touched Pavel's arm but Pavel was staring out at the yacht and gave only a jerk of her head in acknowledgement of Alice's information that 'Nibby's home, he can tell you everything, he speaks Russian quite well!'

She hurried out of the study and ran out of the doorway, her eyes bright with excitement.

'Nibby . . . it's that girl . . . Pavel! She's come to see David!'

Understandably, it took Nibby a moment or two to get her drift, and then there was Elizabeth . . . she was a tall and stately blonde with a nice figure and a ready wit, but it took her all her time to understand that a friend of David's from Russia, a girl who spoke no English at all, had simply turned up on their doorstep.

However, in five minutes or so they had it all sorted out and Alice led Nibby back to the study. They threw open the door and gazed . . . at the empty room. Pavel had fled.

Pavel saw the sail and guessed that the girl was saying it was David out there, sailing that boat. There had been some confusion in her mind at first over whether the girl was his wife or his sister, but then she remembered that his sister was called Alice, so that was all right. There were babies, one of them seemed to be David's . . . did he have a wife, then, somewhere in this huge house? But once she had seen the boat and knew David was on board nothing else seemed to matter. She stared and stared, and then turned to the girl, and the girl had gone! The door was shut, and she was alone.

It was an old sash window, but it slid up quite easily. Conscientiously, because of the wind, she pulled it shut behind her, then set off at a fast trot down the long sloping lawn. She reached the shelter of some woods, and the wind which had buffeted her seemed calmer here, or perhaps it was only because it buffeted the trees instead. Through the strip of wood she ran, and saw, on her left, a lake. Not a very big lake, but it was dappled with leaves, little brown and yellow and red boats, being blown across it all in one direction as the wind ruffled the water.

She ran on, burst through the last of the trees and was in a meadow. Down across the meadow and she was crossing rough grass, tufted, reedy, with cushions of soft moss to ease the aching feet.

She reached the bank of the great estuary; there were miles and miles of smooth sandy mud or muddy sand – it was impossible to guess which without setting foot on it. Channels of water criss-crossed it and the sea was coming in, coming in fast, fairly roaring over the dark sand, the little waves creamy-tipped as they foamed and splashed and filled the channels and covered the land. She sat down, cross-legged, on a little wooden landing stage and watched, fascinated, as the Dee came home.

David had had a good sail, but he had not eaten his picnic and he was hungry. He turned the boat's head away from the sea and decided to behave himself for once and to think of Alice, who was only doing her best to make him happy. He would head for home now and go and do the polite to Elizabeth and eat a huge lunch and then, because he had got rid of his restlessness and the need to be alone, he would take Alyn and Ricky out somewhere and give them tea, spoil them a bit. It would mean that Alice and Nibby could have an afternoon to themselves for once.

The wind was still perilously close to gale force, but David was used to the conditions and knew the estuary like the back of his hand. He brought the boat round at just the right moment, when the racing tide was sufficiently full for him to reach the landing stage without running aground, and headed for the shore, loosed the mains'l and brought her head to wind, and just at that moment he saw the small cross-legged figure sitting on the jetty.

He was staring so hard that for a moment he lost concentration; the boat, taking advantage of his momentary lapse, drove at full speed for the jetty, taking it nose on with such force that David, the experienced sailor, found himself flying through the air, to land face down in the shallow water and thick mud. He struggled to his feet, trying to wipe the muddy sand out of his streaming eyes, and grabbed for the edge of the landing stage, temporarily forgetting the person who had been sitting there moments earlier until she knelt on the edge and held out her hands to him.

He touched them, and an electric shock arrowed through him; unconsciously he pulled, then let go, to clear his eyes so that he would be able to see if his instincts were right . . . and the figure before him landed squarely on his chest just as he managed to get his eyes open sufficiently to see for himself that small, much-loved face, only inches from his own.

It was the tiniest glimpse before her weight knocked him off balance once more and the pair of them, clinging like limpets, landed in the muddy water and were totally submerged for a few vital seconds.

It did not matter, nothing mattered but that she was here, in his arms. They lurched to their feet, kissing, murmuring love-words, clinging, two soaked and muddy figures, unrecognisable save to each other.

When Nibby and Alice reached the landing stage they were treated to the extraordinary sight of David and their visitor standing waist-deep in the Dee, kissing and hugging with hungry indifference to their situation. The yacht which he had just left was apparently abandoned, moving backwards away from the landing stage and appearing to be about to accompany the tide.

'I'll get the boat,' Nibby roared to his wife. 'Tell that idiot to come ashore before he begins making love to his wench. It's not decent.'

Alice stood back as David scrambled up on to the landing stage with Pavel in his arms. He stood her down, ignoring Alice because he was completely unaware of her; Pavel filled his vision.

'So you've come!' He put his muddy arm about her shoulders. 'Do I take it you aren't married any more?'

'Not any more.'

'Me neither; but I've a son. Did you and your chap have kids?'

'No. I had mudbaths, but even then I didn't have babies,' Pavel admitted. They set off towards the house she had just left so hurriedly, with Alice, unnoticed, following.

'*Mud*-baths?'

'Yes. They say mudbaths help you to conceive and Rudi wanted a child so I went to the Scientific Institute at Kharkov and they bathed me in mud for a whole year. But it didn't work.'

David looked down at her. Her hair hung lank, water dripped off her pointed chin and she was as well covered in Dee mud as anyone can be. He squeezed her waist and then kissed the side of her face; he loved her so much that it was a slow burn in his stomach just to touch her, but he could not help laughing as she looked up at him, so serious, so indifferent to her sodden state.

'What's funny, Davidski dushka?'

'Well, nothing really. I was just wondering what sort of mud they used in the Scientific Institute and whether Dee mud will prove more efficacious!'

It did. Ten months to the day after she landed in England, Pavel Thomas gave birth to a daughter. They thought about calling her Eva, but in the end they settled for Constance. It was the nearest they could get to calling the baby after that other child, the sister who had been forgotten for so long, but who was forgotten no longer.

# EPILOGUE

'I can't see anything! Darling David, I'm a good swimmer, why won't you let me slip overboard and have a look?'

David had taken Pavel, at her request, out of the estuary today, in his latest boat, a sturdy fishing craft quite capable of far longer and more dangerous voyages than this one. Now, anchored off the sandbank on which the *Royal Gold* had sunk years before, Pavel was peering down into the rocking waves, trying to catch a glimpse of the wreck.

'You may be a very strong swimmer indeed, my love, but you aren't used to the sea, and you've never dived, and besides, it's devilish deep. Even if you did get down there, all you'd see would be thick swirling sand and perhaps a dim outline of her hull and that's only if you were very lucky indeed. No one knows precisely where she went down, you see; it would take a team of professional divers weeks, possibly, to locate her.'

'Well, I think you're mean. All those dreams, Davidski, of diving down to the wreck and finding treasure, or discovering how she was sunk, and you won't let me have the adventure of even trying!' Pavel sat on the side of the boat, the wind ruffling her short, curly hair, looking just like his little Amazon from the Caucasus and not a bit like the mother of his two children. 'Oh, go on, let me have a teeny go!'

'No. Come here.'

David was lying in the stern, and she went to him at once and curled up against him, kissing the side of his face, fluttering her lashes in butterfly kisses against his cheek, doing her best to charm him into giving her her own way.

'Oh, David . . . dushka mine, why can't I have a go?'

'Because it's terribly dangerous without the proper equipment and so on, and because of currents and undertows and

591

other horrid things. Sweetheart, we've got a good life, everything's going our way, the centre's doing better than we ever dared hope; don't expect me to risk anything, let alone you who are so precious, over a ship that caused so much pain.'

Pavel heard the seriousness in his voice and sighed, then moved away from him, stretched and went to bring up the anchor.

'All right, I was only fooling around, really, I'm not terribly interested. Shall we sail home?'

She was a good crew; neat, quick, efficient. As they tacked up the estuary and into their deep-water channel, Pavel told herself that the *Royal Gold* was not for her. But maybe her children, or possibly even their children, would go down to her and make the discoveries of which she had once dreamed.

She was first out when they reached the jetty, tying up with the air of one who has performed the same task a thousand times. David came ashore more leisurely, checked that all was well, and then they strolled up to the house together, arms round each other's waists.

'Happy, dushka?' David's voice was a little anxious; he would have given her anything that was in his power to give provided it contained no danger.

'Very happy. Don't worry, stoopidchka, we can't have everything; we'll let Alyn and Con have the adventure of the *Royal Gold*, shall we? We've had so much.'

'Very well, if you insist.' They laughed at each other, then strolled, hand in hand, towards the house.

# A Selection of Arrow Bestsellers

| | | | |
|---|---|---|---|
| ☐ | The Lilac Bus | Maeve Binchy | £2.50 |
| ☐ | 500 Mile Walkies | Mark Wallington | £2.50 |
| ☐ | Staying Off the Beaten Track | Elizabeth Gundrey | £5.95 |
| ☐ | A Better World Than This | Marie Joseph | £2.95 |
| ☐ | No Enemy But Time | Evelyn Anthony | £2.95 |
| ☐ | Rates of Exchange | Malcolm Bradbury | £3.50 |
| ☐ | Colours Aloft | Alexander Kent | £2.95 |
| ☐ | Speaker for the Dead | Orson Scott Card | £2.95 |
| ☐ | Eon | Greg Bear | £4.95 |
| ☐ | Talking to Strange Men | Ruth Rendell | £5.95 |
| ☐ | Heartstones | Ruth Rendell | £2.50 |
| ☐ | Rosemary Conley's Hip and Thigh Diet | Rosemary Conley | £2.50 |
| ☐ | Communion | Whitley Strieber | £3.50 |
| ☐ | The Ladies of Missalonghi | Colleen McCullough | £2.50 |
| ☐ | Erin's Child | Sheelagh Kelly | £3.99 |
| ☐ | Sarum | Edward Rutherfurd | £4.50 |

Prices and other details are liable to change

---

ARROW BOOKS, BOOKSERVICE BY POST, PO BOX 29, DOUGLAS, ISLE
OF MAN, BRITISH ISLES

NAME ..............................................................................

ADDRESS ..........................................................................

.......................................................................................

.......................................................................................

Please enclose a cheque or postal order made out to Arrow Books Ltd. for the amount
due and allow the following for postage and packing.

U.K. CUSTOMERS: Please allow 22p per book to a maximum of £3.00.

B.F.P.O. & EIRE: Please allow 22p per book to a maximum of £3.00

OVERSEAS CUSTOMERS: Please allow 22p per book.

Whilst every effort is made to keep prices low it is sometimes necessary to increase cover
prices at short notice. Arrow Books reserve the right to show new retail prices on covers
which may differ from those previously advertised in the text or elsewhere.

# Bestselling Fiction

| | | | |
|---|---|---|---|
| ☐ | Hiroshmia Joe | Martin Booth | £2.95 |
| ☐ | The Pianoplayers | Anthony Burgess | £2.50 |
| ☐ | Queen's Play | Dorothy Dunnett | £3.95 |
| ☐ | Colours Aloft | Alexander Kent | £2.95 |
| ☐ | Contact | Carl Sagan | £3.50 |
| ☐ | Talking to Strange Men | Ruth Rendell | £5.95 |
| ☐ | Heartstones | Ruth Rendell | £2.50 |
| ☐ | The Ladies of Missalonghi | Colleen McCullough | £2.50 |
| ☐ | No Enemy But Time | Evelyn Anthony | £2.95 |
| ☐ | The Heart of the Country | Fay Weldon | £2.50 |
| ☐ | The Stationmaster's Daughter | Pamela Oldfield | £2.95 |
| ☐ | Erin's Child | Sheelagh Kelly | £3.99 |
| ☐ | The Lilac Bus | Maeve Binchy | £2.50 |

Prices and other details are liable to change

---

ARROW BOOKS, BOOKSERVICE BY POST, PO BOX 29, DOUGLAS, ISLE OF MAN, BRITISH ISLES

NAME. . . . . . . . . . . . . . . . . . . . . . . . . . . . . . . . . . . . . . . . . . . . . . . . . . . . . . . . . . . . . .

ADDRESS . . . . . . . . . . . . . . . . . . . . . . . . . . . . . . . . . . . . . . . . . . . . . . . . . . . . . . . . . .

. . . . . . . . . . . . . . . . . . . . . . . . . . . . . . . . . . . . . . . . . . . . . . . . . . . . . . . . . . . . . . . . . .

. . . . . . . . . . . . . . . . . . . . . . . . . . . . . . . . . . . . . . . . . . . . . . . . . . . . . . . . . . . . . . . . . .

Please enclose a cheque or postal order made out to Arrow Books Ltd. for the amount due and allow the following for postage and packing.

U.K. CUSTOMERS: Please allow 22p per book to a maximum of £3.00.

B.F.P.O. & EIRE: Please allow 22p per book to a maximum of £3.00

OVERSEAS CUSTOMERS: Please allow 22p per book.

Whilst every effort is made to keep prices low it is sometimes necessary to increase cover prices at short notice. Arrow Books reserve the right to show new retail prices on covers which may differ from those previously advertised in the text or elsewhere.

# Bestselling Fiction

| | | | |
|---|---|---|---|
| ☐ | Saudi | Laurie Devine | £2.95 |
| ☐ | Lisa Logan | Marie Joseph | £2.50 |
| ☐ | The Stationmaster's Daughter | Pamela Oldfield | £2.95 |
| ☐ | Duncton Wood | William Horwood | £3.50 |
| ☐ | Aztec | Gary Jennings | £3.95 |
| ☐ | The Pride | Judith Saxton | £2.99 |
| ☐ | Fire in Heaven | Malcolm Bosse | £3.50 |
| ☐ | Communion | Whitley Strieber | £3.50 |
| ☐ | The Ladies of Missalonghi | Colleen McCullough | £2.50 |
| ☐ | Skydancer | Geoffrey Archer | £2.50 |
| ☐ | The Sisters | Pat Booth | £3.50 |
| ☐ | No Enemy But Time | Evelyn Anthony | £2.95 |

Prices and other details are liable to change

---

ARROW BOOKS, BOOKSERVICE BY POST, PO BOX 29, DOUGLAS, ISLE OF MAN, BRITISH ISLES

NAME......................................................................

ADDRESS...................................................................

..........................................................................

..........................................................................

Please enclose a cheque or postal order made out to Arrow Books Ltd. for the amount due and allow the following for postage and packing.

U.K. CUSTOMERS: Please allow 22p per book to a maximum of £3.00.

B.F.P.O. & EIRE: Please allow 22p per book to a maximum of £3.00

OVERSEAS CUSTOMERS: Please allow 22p per book.

Whilst every effort is made to keep prices low it is sometimes necessary to increase cover prices at short notice. Arrow Books reserve the right to show new retail prices on covers which may differ from those previously advertised in the text or elsewhere.

# Bestselling Women's Fiction

| | | | |
|---|---|---|---|
| ☐ | A Better World Than This | Marie Joseph | £2.95 |
| ☐ | The Stationmaster's Daughter | Pamela Oldfield | £2.95 |
| ☐ | The Lilac Bus | Maeve Binchy | £2.50 |
| ☐ | The Golden Urchin | Madeleine Brent | £2.95 |
| ☐ | The Temptress | Jude Deveraux | £2.95 |
| ☐ | The Sisters | Pat Booth | £3.50 |
| ☐ | Erin's Child | Sheelagh Kelly | £3.99 |
| ☐ | The Ladies of Missalonghi | Colleen McCullough | £2.50 |
| ☐ | Seven Dials | Claire Rayner | £2.50 |
| ☐ | The Indiscretion | Diana Stainforth | £3.50 |
| ☐ | Satisfaction | Rae Lawrence | £3.50 |

Prices and other details are liable to change

---

ARROW BOOKS, BOOKSERVICE BY POST, PO BOX 29, DOUGLAS, ISLE OF MAN, BRITISH ISLES

NAME.................................................................

ADDRESS..............................................................

.....................................................................

.....................................................................

Please enclose a cheque or postal order made out to Arrow Books Ltd. for the amount due and allow the following for postage and packing.

U.K. CUSTOMERS: Please allow 22p per book to a maximum of £3.00.

B.F.P.O. & EIRE: Please allow 22p per book to a maximum of £3.00

OVERSEAS CUSTOMERS: Please allow 22p per book.

Whilst every effort is made to keep prices low it is sometimes necessary to increase cover prices at short notice. Arrow Books reserve the right to show new retail prices on covers which may differ from those previously advertised in the text or elsewhere.